O F

L O V E

A N D

L I F E

OF
LOVE
AND
LIFE

Three novels selected and condensed
by Reader's Digest

The Reader's Digest Association Limited, London

The Reader's Digest Association Limited
11 Westferry Circus, Canary Wharf, London E14 4HE

www.readersdigest.co.uk

ISBN 0-276-42874-9

CONTENTS

By Bread Alone

Sarah-Kate Lynch

At nineteen years old, Esme knew what it was like to be lifeless and dull, lightly freckled and chastely English. It took a holiday in France and a moonlight meeting with the man of her dreams to change all that. Louis taught her how to love, how to bake perfect sourdough bread—then he broke her heart. Fifteen years later, Esme's heart is in danger of breaking again and she dreams of her nights in France: a time when she was truly happy.

 Prologue

THE MOMENT Esme's espadrilles hit the smooth stone floor deep down in the heart of the tiny *boulangerie*, she knew that up until then, she herself had only been half-baked.

The sweet, sharp scent of sourdough bread cooking in an oak-fired oven whirled around her unsuspecting senses and unleashed a hunger inside her she had not known existed.

The air was hot and thick with the promise of life's simple and not-so-simple pleasures. She could feel that. She could smell it. She could taste it on the tip of her tongue.

Bread. Yes, bread. *Pain au levain*, to be precise, the speciality of the house. Never mind the baguettes, the croissants, the chocolate or custard pastries after which she had so recently hankered. Compared to just one crumb from the sourdough *boules* baked not ten feet away from where she stood they were nothing. No other paltry pretender could ever hope to measure up to the beauty of those fat round loaves with their thick crunchy crusts and shining, soft flesh.

Esme licked her glistening lips, her mouth watering. She had been eating the bread up there in the outside world for a week now, but had only dreamed, literally, of getting this close to the heart of it all. The atmosphere was overwhelming. The air cloaked her in its moist, sweet arms, and soothed the fluttering in her chest. She wanted to lie on that warm, worn floor and stay there for ever, sleeping. It felt like home, only better. Like heaven, only closer.

Here, in this ancient overbaked room carved out of golden stone and hidden underground above a lazy kink in the Dordogne River, was where it all began. And the beginning was the key, as she was soon to learn, because the secret to sourdough was its starter, the *levain*, the living, breathing, bubbling mixture of the past and the present that was added to every batch of flour and water to turn it into the future. For nearly two hundred years the starter in that hot, heavy room had been breathing life into sourdough *boules* and no other bread in the south-west, the whole of France, the rest of Europe, anywhere in the world, tasted anything like it.

Certainly, the bulk of each loaf was made with flour grown in the surrounding fields and freshly stone ground not a mile away, mixed with water from the river that wound below, and there was nothing very special about that, anybody could get that. But its soul, its essence, the spirit of its utter delectability was nowhere near so easily captured. That came from the faintly foaming *levain* and it drew its flavour from the past, from the crusty ancient walls themselves, from the sun that warmed the *boulangerie*'s yellow-striped awnings, from the faint scent of lavender that meandered down the stairs from the window boxes in the street, from the golden haystacks that sat squat and solid in the surrounding pastures, from the generations of bakers who had borne it, fed it, nurtured it, shared it, loved it.

Later, when Esme knew more, much more, and her hunger was being sated, repeatedly and not entirely by bread, she found herself drawn to the starter where it lay, breathing and vital, in the bottom of an antiquated wooden bin waiting to give life to the next family of *boules*.

Now she knew what magic it worked, she was spellbound.

For without the starter, *pain au levain* was not *pain au levain* at all, just a lifeless, dull and rather mucky mixture. But add that potent starter to that same limp combination, gently mix in salt from the marshes of Guérande, then give it time, a little warmth, the firm heel of a baker's hand, more time and, finally, some heat, some real heat, and *voilà*!

Esme knew what it was to be lifeless and dull, never more so than when she stepped into that hot, salty, sweaty little room. At nineteen years old, lightly freckled and chastely English, she was more keenly aware of her missing ingredient than ever. She was ready to rise. All that was missing was the baker's magic touch.

Near the end, she lifted a cool jar of the precious *levain* close to her face and breathed in its tangy, intoxicating tones.

'To think,' the baker murmured in his deep, low, chocolate-covered voice, 'there will be some of you and me in the bread you bake, Esme.'

Sheer joy and sourdough, from that moment on, would be forever tangled in her mind.

10

Chapter One

Fifteen years later, seventy feet up in the Suffolk seaside air, Esme was juggling quinces. She'd been carrying an armful of the oversized yellow fruit from the garden trug to her kitchen sink when she'd tripped over the dog and the whole lot had gone flying.

She lunged forward, grappling with the air, and caught a couple, but kicked one that had fallen to the ground so hard that it hurtled down the stairs. In a house that was six storeys high, with the kitchen at the top, this was far from ideal.

'Bugger,' she said as the remaining quinces wibbled and wobbled around her ankles, as Esme danced her way over to the stairwell. The quince, she could hear, had made it down the first eight steps, hit the landing wall, then bounced down the next eight. It was large and not quite ripe, and caused something of a hullabaloo.

'For God's sake, Brown,' she complained as the dog scrambled behind her on the polished floorboards, spreading the quinces further. She headed down the stairs, the stomp of her no longer fashionable Dirk Bikkenberg shoes adding to the din.

Slowing on Rory's level to take the next flight of stairs, she felt the unexpected sensation of Brown's nose slamming into her rear end and all but knocking her down them.

'Do you mind,' she admonished. 'You annoying bloody creature!'

'I beg your pardon?' the voice of her father-in-law harrumphed from below. For a man with two artificial hips and a wonky walking stick, he could move surprisingly quietly, Esme thought.

'Henry!' she replied, her features fighting a grimace. Henry occupied the first floor of the House in the Clouds and rarely ventured up this far. He had his own bathroom and kitchenette down below and shared a sitting room on the next floor up with the rest of the family, although the younger Stacks hardly ever used it.

'Sorry about the racket,' she apologised, descending towards his voice, 'but I tripped over Brown and dropped a quince, then the silly creature rear-ended me. You don't have it down there, do you? The quince, I mean?'

11

She rounded the corner and saw that the bruised and battered fruit was indeed lying at Henry's feet, leaking slightly.

'You wouldn't think they would travel so far, would you?' she chirruped, stopping a few steps above him. 'Perhaps we got it all wrong about the wheel. Perhaps it should have been quince-shaped.'

Henry looked at her as though she were speaking a foreign language. It was a look she quite often noticed on him, but before she could even wish that she had shut up earlier and saved him the bother of being annoyed, Brown pushed right past her, scuttled down to the quince, sniffed it, turned, lifted his leg and peed on it. Esme gaped wordlessly as splatters ricocheted onto Henry's brogues.

Henry, understandably surprised, temporarily lost control of his walking stick and staggered slightly, stumbling into the wall and knocking a portrait of his late wife off its moorings.

'For goodness' sake,' he rasped, puce with irritation. 'Don't just stand there, *do something*.'

Brown backed slowly towards the next flight of stairs, his eyes on Esme as he waited to see what the something might be.

'Well?' Henry asked again, flicking dog urine off his foot with as much vigour as any seventy-four-year-old with barely a real bone left in his pelvic region could. '*Well?*'

In the blink of an eye the House in the Clouds was alive with the clatter of six legs crashing down many wooden stairs as Esme lunged past her teetering father-in-law and gave chase. Downwards she lurched, Brown's fat shiny rump always just out of reach as she skidded through her and Pog's storey, slid past the sitting room, leapt down to Henry's level, then took the last flight to the ground floor two steps at a time.

For an animal that could spend an entire day slumped in front of the fire, he could move pretty damn quickly when he had to. Cornering, however, was not his strong point and in the tiny entrance hall his chubby brown body skidded and smashed into the occasional table, sending it and a vase of glorious red roses crashing to the ground. Still steaming ahead, he aimed his bulk squarely at the cat door and dived through it, the tip of his tail disappearing as Esme reached out to grab it.

The cat door rattled shut and the house was once again silent. Then Henry's stick tap-tapped across the floor above.

'Well done,' he called stiffly. 'I'll get a mop.'

'Oh, will you ever lighten *up*.' Esme froze as she was certain she heard Granny Mac call caustically from behind her closed bedroom door in her fifty-a-day Glaswegian docker lilt. 'You'll give yourself a heart attack with all your moaning, you silly old *goat*.'

Esme looked at the door of her grandmother's room, then up at the ceiling. She had heard, clear as day, she was sure she had, but had Henry? Esme blew out a lungful of air and decided to ignore what she had just heard. She could not afford to lose it this morning. She had quinces (two dozen) to paste, windows (twenty-eight) to wash, stairs (seventy-eight) to vacuum and a feverish son (four and a half) who was a worry at the best of times. He was passed out now on a beanbag in front of a *Bob the Builder* video, but that would not last for ever.

Turning to confront the destruction, Esme caught sight of herself in the hall mirror. Clear green eyes stared back at her with a fraught expression. She had done an awful job of taking off her make-up the night before and so had black blobby lashes with smudges below her eyes. The chic chignon she had imagined she had constructed atop her head earlier that morning was neither chic nor a chignon. In fact, her mad copper-coloured ringlets looked like a large ball of ginger wool that had been ravaged by angry kittens.

Her shoulders sagged as she took in her reflection. Was every life as chaotic as hers? she wondered. Did she invite more disorder than the next person? More catastrophe? The slapstick comedy of the peed-on quince rolled away to expose the dangerous slick that lurked just below Esme's surface. At this, her mind snapped shut, her eyes slid off their mirror image.

Today was not the day to contemplate the heartache that would swallow every second if she let it. Now was not the hour to confront the tragedy that had ripped her family to shreds.

Instead she would just take that relentless pain, that torturous memory and squash it down, suppress it the way she had every day for the past two years until it no longer consumed her but just hid inside her, deep and dark, small and hard. That way she could continue to put one foot in front of the other, to breathe in and out, to cook and clean and laugh and smile as though her worst nightmare had stayed just that instead of coming true and chasing her to a new life in a different place, a place where every nook and cranny was not haunted by the consequences of that dreadful day.

And by and large it had worked, that squashing. She had survived. Pog, her husband, had survived. Rory, their son, had survived. Separately, they had all survived.

But this past month had been hard. Even she could see it in those clear green eyes. And it was getting harder.

Sitting at his desk, three leafy, curly streets away, her husband Pog was thinking exactly the same thing.

It was now thirty-three days since Esme had baked a loaf of bread and he didn't know how to get her started again. His stomach churned as he contemplated the store-bought sandwich sitting bleakly in front of him. He poked it with a freshly sharpened pencil. It was yesterday's bread. No question. It had no bounce. No allure. No *joie de vivre*. It was not begging to be eaten.

Of course he had tried to talk to Esme about the baking, it worried him beyond comprehension. He knew what sourdough meant to her. But the day Dr Gribblehurst came out of Granny Mac's room saying he had done all he could, Esme had stopped. How, he asked himself, could he talk to her about bread, about Granny Mac, when there was so much more that needed talking about? Over the past two years, the unspoken words between them had been covered up and buried and a thick comfortable quilt had grown across the top of their lives, concealing the chasm that grew deeper and deeper.

Everybody thought she was so carefree, so happy, so strong, so resilient, but Pog knew otherwise. And he wanted to help her, God knew he wanted nothing more, but he did not want to push her, to break her, to open the fine, delicate cracks he knew had invaded her hardened outer shell ever since that terrible, terrible day. He could not, would not, do anything to risk losing her, his gorgeous, garrulous, glutinous wife. She was all that had kept him going since then. She was all that kept any of them going.

His stomach gurgled hungrily, but the preservative-laden offering in front of him held all the allure of a Wellington boot. He needed Esme to bake. Esme's bread not only begged to be eaten, it demanded it.

Pog tried to remember the precise smell. But thirty-three days without it and already it was a fading memory. The saltiness he could get, the sharp, apple-and-vinegar tang he could recapture. But that sweet, warm, indescribably delicious mouth-watering element that stamped it as made every step of the way by Esme's soft and supple hands? Gone. Unbelievably gone. Just like the delectable, crusty loaves themselves.

Esme's soft and supple hands at that very moment were back in the House in the Clouds, picking up the shattered pieces of crockery. The vase had been a wedding present from her brother-in-law Milo, the son who'd chosen a proper wife and then cleverly vacated to New York City. Breaking it would no doubt be another black mark against her as far as Henry was concerned. She knew he thought her flighty and unsuitable and it must stick in his craw something wicked, she thought, that he had ended up under her roof through no fault of his own, other than badly investing his life's savings and ending up near penniless, to all intents homeless and without hips in good working order.

She reminded herself that he had every right to be in a permanently angry mood, and felt a twinge of guilt for owning a dog that would urinate on clean brogues.

'Hello-o!' she heard her grandmother's musical burr tring, as clear as a bell, from behind the closed bedroom door. 'I said, hello-o-o!'

Esme stood up, pushed the remaining jumble on the floor towards the wall and cocked her head to one side. Her grandmother's favourite singer, Rod Stewart, was softly rasping that he could be loved tonight, but not in the morning.

Gingerly, Esme opened the door and slipped into the room. It was dark, just the way Granny Mac had always liked it. She shook her head to rid herself of Rod and shuffled in the dim light towards the window, reaching out as she approached it to pull back the curtains.

'Hey, hot legs!' The voice of her grandmother suddenly filled the room. Esme spun round and found the old woman's eyes twinkling at her beadily from the end of her bed. The room smelt strongly of cigarettes. Cheap ones. Embassy Regals. Granny Mac's favourites.

The hair stood up on the back of Esme's neck. 'Granny Mac!' she breathed with disbelief as she sought out the face that she knew so well.

'Aye,' answered Granny Mac, 'amazing, isn't it, at my stage in life?'

Esme blinked. Feelings tumbled inside her, searching for a slot. Disbelief, fear, anger, delight: all clamoured for space. 'Granny Mac,' she said again, on the spur of that moment deciding to suspend her disbelief in favour of embracing her delight. 'You've been smoking!'

Her grandmother, her wrinkles in the drab light dissolving and blurring on her crinkled cheeks, simply cackled.

'I don't understand,' Esme said. 'I thought that . . . Well, how could you? I mean, for goodness' sake. You really ought not to . . . It's just that, well . . . Oh, shit,' she said suddenly. 'I am having such a strange day.'

'Well, turns out there is a quick way to give up smoking,' her grandmother said, 'but I don't know that I can entirely recommend it.'

Esme stood and contemplated the bed. She should not allow this, she knew that, of course she knew that, but how she adored her Granny Mac. And how she needed her! How she had always needed her. Without Granny Mac all the squashing in the world would not have kept one foot in front of the other since their move from London to the House in the Clouds. She was Esme's saviour. She always had been. And perhaps she always would be. Who was Esme to argue with that?

She threw her hands in the air and plonked herself down on the end of the bed. She looked in her grandmother's direction and willed the blackness to stop smudging that much-loved face, to snap it into focus. 'You know, I was just thinking about where I wanted to live,' she said, ignoring nearly everything, 'and I wonder if perhaps it is in here with you. I could smoke cigarettes and read *Hello!* magazines and spy on Gaga and Jam-jar next door. It would be just like the old days.'

Gaga and Jam-jar were the ancient neighbours who, despite rather oddly living in a windmill, were perhaps the straightest two people in Christendom, and loathed Esme and her eccentric tower of relatives with a passion.

'You'd have to go out and get the *Hello!* magazines for a start,' Granny Mac said. 'I'm dying for want of fresh dirt on poor Fergie.'

Esme felt a hot flush of devotion sweep through her. How she adored her Granny Mac. 'I thought you could never forgive her,' she said, 'for wearing that shocking hat to the Queen Mother's funeral.'

'Och, did you have to remind me about the Queen Mother? It upsets me greatly these days to hear about dead people, Esme. Spare a thought for them, will you?'

Esme sighed. 'This past month, Granny Mac, you know, since,' she struggled for words that would not upset her grandmother, 'since Dr Gribblehurst . . . Nothing feels right any more. I feel like I'm starting to unravel and I don't know why and it's bloody terrifying.'

'You do know why, you soft lass,' her grandmother said. 'You just don't want to face it.'

Esme felt fear clutch at her heart. Was this what she needed to hear? 'It's not that I don't *want* to,' she said. 'It's just that I can't. It's too soon.'

'But if you wait much longer,' her grandmother argued softly, 'it will be too late. And maybe not just for you.'

'Don't,' Esme pleaded. 'Just don't.'

The room, apart from the barely audible lamenting of Rod, fell silent.

'And what about that miserable old stoat upstairs, then, eh?' Granny Mac changed the subject to one of her favourites: Henry. 'Is he still getting on your wick?'

'No more than I deserve, I'm sure,' answered Esme. 'I mean I don't seem to be able to do anything right, but that's nothing new.'

'Have you considered a London telephone directory to the back of the head?' offered Granny Mac. 'Or a frozen leg of lamb, which you then proceed to serve up for dinner, or a bottle of wine?'

'I've thought about the wine,' Esme admitted, 'but only drinking it. I hadn't really considered the murder-weapon potential.'

'Och,' her grandmother said, disgusted. 'You're just not trying hard enough, Esme.'

Esme poked an errant curl back into her topknot. She was trying as hard as she could.

'Esme!' The sound of Rory's anxious cry filtered through from the top floor of the house to the bottom. Waking up was not Rory's best time. He suffered terrible nightmares, poor lamb, and the thought of what he dreamt about, to wake up so lost and lonely, chilled her to the bone.

'*Esme-e-e-e,*' he called again, his voice sifting through the layers of the house to find her. No matter how hard she had tried to get him to call her Mummy, he only ever referred to her by her name.

'Is the wee boy OK?' Granny Mac asked gently.

'He's fine,' Esme said, heaving herself off the bed, loath to leave the cosiness of Granny Mac's company. And, in truth, he was doing pretty well. The psychologist he saw every couple of months in London seemed pleased with his progress, and his speech was truly astonishing. For a boy who had not spoken a single word until the day after his fourth birthday, at which point he debuted with, 'I'd rather have a chocolate biscuit, if it's all the same to you,' his command of the English language would have put most grown-ups to shame. 'Truly, Gran,' she said. 'He's just tired, that's all. Honestly, he's fine. You don't need to worry about him.'

'So, it's just you then,' Granny Mac said. 'That I need to worry about.'

'Oh, I don't know,' Esme said softly. 'I'm feeling better already.'

'Is that so? Well, may I be so bold as to ask if that was a quince making its way down the stairs with such enthusiasm just before?'

'How could you possibly know that?' Esme was stunned.

'A quince, Esme? At this hour of the morning when you would normally, I am sure, be putting a loaf of your delicious bread in the oven?'

'I just can't,' Esme said sadly. 'Since you . . . since that day . . . Oh, Granny Mac, I'm just too . . . empty.'

'But now is not the time to let go of what is dear to you. Now more than ever you should be clinging to it.'

'I just haven't had it in me,' Esme said despairingly. 'It just went.'

'Well, just get it back, lassie. Just get it back.'

And with that Rory roared so loudly that Esme could bear it no longer and, to the retreating strains of Rod Stewart, she slipped out of the room and headed up the stairs.

As she clumped past Henry's room she saw that all signs of the recent quince-flavoured disaster had disappeared. He would be cleaning his brogues again, no doubt, his schedule thrown out most inconveniently. She clenched her buttocks, not because she was thinking of her father-in-law, but because her friend Alice, who was addicted to personal trainers, had told her that, combined with climbing the stairs ten times a day, it constituted proper exercise.

By the time she had clattered up the last set of steps to where Rory lay under his favourite blanket in a corner of the kitchen, she was puffing like an old steam engine. And her bum hurt. These were the ramifications of living in a house with seventy-eight internal stairs, but every time Esme looked out of the window of the top floor in her nutty tower she remembered why it was all worth while.

She scooped up her small, sticky, sobbing son and held him tight against her chest as she looked out across the rooftops of Seabury village, over the tips of the leafy green oaks, across the lake, or the Meare as the locals knew it, to the cool North Sea lapping at the pebbly shore.

She rocked Rory, quietly shushing him back from despair, and recalled the dreary, grey, London afternoon when she had happily abandoned her thriving publishing empire to drag Pog away from his office and up to the Suffolk coast to look at the house of her dreams.

'But it's not even a real house,' Pog had moaned, aghast.

'Leave it out,' Esme had teased, 'you're an architect—you're the last person who would know what a real house looks like.'

He did have a point, she'd agreed at the time, in that it was a highly unusual dwelling, but that was what appealed to her. They wanted to escape their city lives, didn't they? They wanted to start anew?

'But couldn't we just get a cute little cottage by the sea?' Pog had asked. 'Like normal people?' But they were no longer normal people, recent unimaginable events had changed that, and Esme wanted the House in the Clouds not in spite of its oddness, but because of it.

'But the whole village is not quite right,' Pog had complained, his face crumpled with worry.

Esme agreed that the village was from the Not Quite Right Shop—as Granny Mac would say—but that only endeared it to her further. The whole settlement of Seabury had been dreamed up a hundred years earlier by a wealthy landowner who wanted to custom-make a fairy-tale holiday resort for 'nice' people like himself.

He'd gone a bit overboard, it had to be said, on reviving the spirit of the Tudor Age, long since past, and so the town sported more than its fair share of inappropriate wooden cladding, heavy beams, curved roads and quaint if entirely unnecessary corners.

And over this eccentric collection of homes loomed the House in the Clouds, a giant dovecote, its tall, slender stalk painted black and peppered with tiny white windows and the big square room on top a deep, delicious red with pitched roofs and views of almost everywhere.

That theatrical landowner of yore had originally devised the house to add, rather dramatically, to the landscape, but more importantly to disguise the town's water supply, 30,000 gallons of which were once kept in what was now the kitchen and family room.

The House in the Clouds had been the antidote Esme thought she needed to the life she knew she could no longer live, her escape from the torment of tragedy, and Pog, because all he ever wanted was for her to be happy, had soon relented and the entire Stack clan had decamped.

'Where's Mrs Brown?' Rory whined into her neck as his hot little body clung to her. 'I want Mrs Brown.'

Esme kissed her son's thick, curly, bright orange hair and resisted the urge to tell him that Mrs Brown, as he had originally christened the dog, had been savaged by angry cave bears and would never be coming back. Not as a dog anyway. Possibly as a pot plant but definitely not as anything with a bladder.

'Where's Mrs Brown?' Rory continued to sob dramatically. 'Where's my friend, my only friend?' Esme shushed and rocked her son.

She caught a whiff of Rory's sweet, cranky little boy breath and kissed his nose, but at this he twisted away from her. At that moment, a gentle sea breeze blew in through an open window and nudged open the pantry door so the sun, like a torch beam on an inky black night, sought out the stone jar that sat smugly on the floor, its contents quietly bubbling and roiling. You may have given up on me, it whispered into the morning air. But I have not given up on you.

Chapter Two

GRANNY MAC HAD ALWAYS loved Rod Stewart. Rather bizarrely for a thrice-widowed matron in her sixties, she'd once even had her hair cut in a blonde 'shaggy' just like his. Each of those late husbands had had their own Rod signature tune and the merest hint of 'You're In My Heart' could always be relied on to conjure up her last, Jerry O'Brien. She had loved Jerry O'Brien deeply. Her first two husbands she had hardly missed at all, but by the time she lost Jerry O'Brien she could not keep melancholy at bay, because by then she was also minus a daughter, Beth,

Esme's mother and a perfect example of why misery and MacDougall women made such bad company.

Beth, never a sturdy creature, had found marriage, motherhood, adultery, divorce, life in general far too heartbreaking a business to continue contemplating and so had slipped away one wet London lunchtime, sung softly to sleep by a pharmaceutical lullaby. And so, as per clearly written instructions, her estranged mother was sent for, all the way from the windswept shores of Gairloch to the hustle and bustle of St John's Wood, where she was introduced, for the first time, to her five-year-old granddaughter.

Esme, sitting in a neighbour's flat, her flame-red hair impossibly jolly, had looked at her and smiled. And so began their life together.

Very quickly Granny Mac and her charge, who adopted the family name, became as thick as thieves, Esme, for the most part, delighting in having a guardian who thought homework a sick joke and After Dinner mints the perfect sandwich filling. Their lives were full and happy and they were both better off than they had been before.

And then Esme, aged ten, had come bursting through the door bearing Jerry O'Brien, sheepish and shy, saying she had found him at the bus-stop having watched him narrowly miss the alleged 11.07 to Camden, and he seemed in dire need of a cup of tea. Granny Mac thought all her Christmases had come at once.

How she loved that silly old man, with his badly dyed hair, ridiculous foibles and utter devotion to the two of them. He was her reward, she had assumed, for having a mother *and* a daughter who had chosen to desert her. Oh, yes, misery was a curse, all right.

Granny Mac herself had been abandoned as a child by a mother unable to keep waking up to a world she judged too harsh for her own gentle soul. Granny Mac carried with her this fear of such sorrow but never came close to feeling it herself until she lost Jerry O'Brien. After just one short year of happiness, it had seemed too cruel to bear. And, for the first time in her life, Granny Mac had let down her guard and watched from outside herself as the family hex crept in and filled her pockets of happiness with black, sticky ooze.

It did not last long. Esme rescued her.

Even at the age of twelve she had known that with a bottle of whisky, a lot of dark chocolate and all the Rod Stewart hits of the late 1970s, they would pull through. And they had.

So now Granny Mac's sole purpose on earth was to concoct a mixture that could similarly rescue Esme. And she would.

'You had better be bloody kidding me,' Esme breathed down the phone later that evening, quinces pasted, windows washed, stairs gleaming, son in bed, large glass of Chardonnay in one hand, phone in the other. 'Jemima Jones is getting her own column?' she asked Alice. 'In the *Sunday Times*? *The* Jemima Jones? *Our* Jemima Jones?'

'Oh, Es,' moaned Alice, nestled pink-faced and plump in her threadbare armchair in her run-down Shepherd's Bush flat. 'I knew you'd be upset but I've been dying to call you all day.'

'They gave her a column!' Esme squawked again. 'In the *Sunday Times*! But why?'

'Because she has reinvented herself as a society superwoman, that's why,' Alice answered. 'I have the paper right here. Can you bear to hear it? It is appalling, Es, honestly, you'd better get a bucket because you will be sick, I promise you.'

'Read it to me,' Esme commanded.

'*Married with three young children,*' Alice started, '*Jemima works tirelessly as a volunteer for Princess Diana's land-mine charity and is a permanent fixture on guest lists at London's most salubrious society events.*'

'A permanent fixture? Carpet is a permanent fixture. She's just a cocktail-guzzling leech,' cried Esme. 'She's probably screwing all the husbands!'

'And sons, by now, I should imagine,' Alice added, 'but that's not all. *Jemima devotes what little spare time she has to promoting a revolutionary Harley Street clinic specialising in removing disfiguring scars from children injured in war-torn hot spots. She is heralded among the fashionistas as the Woman Most Wanted To Wear Their Clothes, which is why all eyes are on her new column, which starts this weekend in our Style section.*'

Esme was flabbergasted. 'I just don't know where to start,' she said. 'That woman! Removing disfiguring scars from children in war-torn hot spots? Only if she gave them the scars in the first place, the horrible witch. Is it definitely her?'

'It's Jemima all right. There are photos to prove it. She's dressed up like there's no tomorrow, Es, Botoxed for Africa and so thin you can almost see right through her. It's disgusting.'

'Oh, I can't bear it. It's so unfair,' Esme erupted. 'Just when my life turns to complete and utter horse shit, up pops Jemima sodding Jones being extra sodding fabulous. It's intolerable!'

Once upon a time, Jemima Jones had worked for her. Years before, in her career days, Esme had plucked her from nearly a hundred interviewees, all in various degrees of desperation, to be her assistant on *TV Now!* magazine. Jemima had been totally inexperienced and lacked even the slightest academic achievement, but had been bright and funny and clearly willing to learn. Esme, her editor, had mentored the young and seemingly naive newcomer until she happened upon her one night at a champagne bar in Soho, smiling coquettishly and whispering into the ear of the witless group publisher.

A week later, Esme had been notified that Jemima was being promoted to group publishing assistant, effectively becoming her boss.

Alice had been the *TV Now!* receptionist at the time. It was where they had met.

'Can you believe the little snake-hipped slattern?' Esme had hissed over a sneaky chocolate bar in the photocopying room. 'What a bitch!'

'Now, now,' Alice had counselled. 'Be nice, Esme. She's just getting on like the rest of us. Good luck to her, I say.'

She was not to say it for much longer. Alice had been thrilled with the *TV Now!* job, her first since leaving school after falling pregnant to an Afro-Caribbean DJ, who had neglected to mention the perfectly nice wife and two children he kept just at the end of her street.

She'd been sidelined by her middle-class parents and had struggled alone to bring up her son, Ridgeley, but her fortunes had changed, in more ways than one, when she found work. Suddenly, she not only had money to spend but she'd broken a fairly substantial sex drought with a bicycle courier called Fred. He was six foot tall and made of muscle, didn't mind that she had a son, that she couldn't afford baby sitters. In other words, he was perfect. Or so she thought, until one morning not long after Jemima's promotion, when she opened the stationery store in search of staples and instead found Fred's bare buttocks jiggling furiously as he shafted the new group publishing assistant, legs akimbo, atop a stack of pink A4.

'That snake-hipped little slattern,' she blubbed to Esme, spraying half-chewed KitKat over the copier.

An enemy was born, but her star had continued to rise and its brilliance had outshone the both of them. She had gone on to launch a string of women's magazines, some with moderate success, others less so. Whatever she did was done with a lot of media coverage, but the industry was full of lesser mortals who bitterly bore the imprint of Jemima's stiletto heels on their backs and shoulders, and Alice and Esme were two such pincushions. Within six months of Jemima's promotion, *TV Now!* had folded, leaving the two of them jobless. For Esme it was a blow, but her CV still stacked up well enough. For Alice, however, the market proved flooded already with single mothers short on skills and the ability to do overtime.

She'd been in the same dreary job—answering phones for an overbearing tax consultant—ever since. Her son was now a recalcitrant teenager, her Visa card permanently blown out, her diets always a disaster and her search for the perfect man constantly turning up ones someone else had thrown away earlier, and for good reason.

They had been through a lot together, Esme and Alice, and while ninety miles of choked highway and tangled country lanes now separated them, they talked nearly every day for at least half an hour and continued to be each other's lifeline.

'I should be over Jemima by now,' Esme worried.

'You are over her,' Alice replied. 'She's still on the same old merry-go-round that you stepped off, after all. Don't go getting cold feet about where you are and what you are doing just because it's hard. Everywhere is hard. Everything is hard. You know that.'

'Dashing out a society column once a week doesn't sound hard,' Esme pointed out ruefully.

'Oh, Esme,' sighed Alice. 'Do you really think you want Jemima's life? Just getting your hair that straight would kill you. Life in the city is hell and full of bitches just like her. You should be happy with what you've got—a madhouse in the middle of nowhere, teeming with people and complemented, I think you'll find, by a dysfunctional goat, a rum bunch of chickens and some very angry bees.'

Esme grimaced. She hadn't the heart to tell Alice that the chickens were no longer rum. The chickens were no longer, period. One had been eaten by a neighbouring something or other and the other four had seemed to die of natural causes shortly afterwards—and she wasn't ruling out fatal bee stings. Her animal husbandry was already the topic of much mirth as far as Alice was concerned.

'You'll come right, Esme,' Alice was saying. 'Just give it time. Anyway, why did the dog pee on the quince, you never got round to telling me?'

Esme moved towards the refrigerator, tucked the phone under her chin and poured herself another glass of wine. She took a deep gulp and felt the wine's buttery warmth slide all the way down to the pit of her stomach and nestle there, happy.

'I don't know,' she answered, thinking about Brown's bad behaviour. 'It's been tricky lately, what with one thing and the other. Rory's, well, just Rory. You know. Poor darling boy. It's not been easy for him and Henry's as crotchety as hell. Oh, hello, darling!'

She smiled as Pog's footsteps finally turned into Pog himself. 'Hello, beautiful,' he mouthed as he collapsed into a kitchen chair.

'So quince paste then,' Alice was saying down the phone. 'That's great, Es. And so soon after that innnnteresting zucchini relish.' She paused, uncertain how to proceed. 'How's the baking, then, girl? *Où est le pain?*'

Pog had not been the only one confused and unsettled by Esme's failure to turn out her famous sourdough *boules*. There had never been anything magical about sourdough, as far as Alice was concerned. But when Esme stopped baking them, it worried her.

'What do you care?' Esme asked with a rehearsed lightness. 'And if you must know, Mrs Gladstone from down the lane liked my courgette relish so much she wants me to donate my entire stock to the village fair.'

'They're probably going to use jars of it for targets on the coconut shy,' Alice teased, relieved at having got thus far without upsetting the apple-cart. She decided to venture further. 'You know you could always, oh, I don't know, bake bread for the fair, Es.'

Esme baulked. She had been unequivocally unapproachable on the subject of her breadlessness, but Granny Mac's advice had been ringing loudly in her ears all day. She thought of the jar of starter, winking at her. She closed her eyes and willed herself to speak. 'Well, it's just for me, Alice,' she said. 'For us. I mean, it's not for everyone. I couldn't mass-produce it. It's personal.'

There was a small silence.

'It *is* just for you?' Alice risked.

'As a matter of fact, yes. Or it's about to be. Again.' Esme glanced at Pog.

'Oh, Esme,' Alice spluttered. 'I'm so pleased. That's great news.'

'Excuuuuse me,' Esme protested. 'Is this not the woman who usually says, "It's only bread! Get over it! It's the staff of bleeding life. People put butter and jam on it and eat it"?'

'I'll never say that again,' Alice vowed, 'I promise. My mocking days are over. I won't even mention, for as long as I live,' she adopted a phoney French accent, 'your deescovery of, 'ow shall I say, the *joy of bread* with Louis, international man of mystery, deflowerer of young Engleesh girls and possessor of the world's most enormous—'

Esme laughed loudly down the phone in a drowning-out sort of a fashion. 'You are a horrible, dried-up old harridan and I hate you,' she said. 'And you really shouldn't say things like that about my lovely husband Pog when you know he holds you in such high regard.'

Pog sat at the kitchen table and watched his wife prattle, aching with relief to see her acting more like her old self. And if his ears had not deceived him, she had been joking about bread. Could this mean . . . ? He dared not believe that something as simple as a few words from Alice could bump her out of this recent frightening new level of unhappiness. He would say nothing and simply hope that one day soon the house would smell the way it was supposed to, of crust and comfort.

Once Esme had said her goodbyes, always a ptoracted affair, and put down the phone, Pog abandoned his chair and came up behind her, kissing the back of her neck.

'You smell good enough to eat,' he said, nuzzling her.

'It's not me, silly,' she laughed, pulling gently away from his embrace and reaching into the oven for a fragrantly bubbling *coq au vin*. 'It's your lordship's favourite supper.'

'Jolly good,' Pog enthused, rubbing his hands together and sitting at the table again. 'So, how was your day?'

'Well, if you have a chance later tonight,' his wife replied, spooning wine-y gravy onto his plate, 'you might like to talk to your father about how your charming dog demonstrated his pent-up emotions on his shoes this morning.'

'Oh,' he said, sliding down in his chair. 'It's been one of *those* days.'

Esme put the steaming plate of aromatic chicken down in front of him and ran her fingers through his messy brown hair. It was lusciously thick and grew in a hundred crazy directions which she loved, especially when it was collar length as it was now. He had the loveliest face of any man she had ever known. Not rugged or classically handsome, necessarily. Just lovely. He had big brown eyes and smooth long cheeks, and the sort of teddy-bear good looks and gentle soul that made all women want to be married to him.

'Hugo Stack,' she said, using his given name, not the nickname no one could remember how he came by, 'every day is one of *those* days. But if peed-on quince is as bad it gets, then I suppose I should think myself lucky.'

'Peed-on quince?' Pog asked her, bewildered. 'Is that French?'

Esme laughed and her husband let the sound he loved chase the tension of a long day's work and worry out of his bones. She poured him some wine and they clinked glasses, each thinking their separate thoughts but both smiling at the shared triumph of making it through another day.

I can do it, Pog thought, as he watched her lick a fat drop of rich, red juice from the corner of her mouth. I can do it, as long as I have her. So what if he had to spend the rest of his life designing Tuscan loggias for pernickety pensioners instead of award-winning skyscrapers for international conglomerates? In fact, he liked it more than he thought he would, and the phone had rung off the hook ever since the day Mrs Murphy had hung the 'Architect' sign up outside the office in Seabury's main street. It was different but he could do it. As long as he had her.

When the alarm went off at six the next morning, Esme's eyes sprang open. Her heart was beating too quickly and her squashed and dangerous nugget was expanding inside her, crushing the breath from her lungs. Bread, she forced herself to think, bread. She thought about that jar of starter, panting in her pantry. How could she have denied herself its comfort these past weeks? What had she been thinking? She took a deep breath and slipped out of bed, shivering.

Pog rolled over into the warm place she had left and smiled to himself. In the bathroom Esme slipped on the purple fluffy slippers that everyone but her hated, and swapped her white linen nightie for a tank top and faded pink cotton cardigan and her old faithful jeans with the ripped knee and the soft denim that curved in all her favourite places.

She stuck her hair up in a skewwhiff arrangement—the chic chignon would have to wait yet another day—and scuffed quietly up to the kitchen, eschewing the light switches and instead rummaging for the matches and lighting her strategically placed collection of candles.

She pulled open the pantry door and dragged out her bin of bread flour, stone ground at the water mill in Pakenham, then reached for her scales and favourite jug, all sitting, ready and waiting, as though she had never abandoned them. She measured the flour, breathing in that wheaty smell of almost nothing, almost everything, then poured it into a big caramel-coloured bowl and added good old Suffolk tap water.

Then, she picked up her jar of starter and slowly lifted its lid, unleashing, bit by bit, its sharp, tangy perfume. Granny Mac was right. Now was not the time to let go of what was dear to her. Now was the time to cling to it. She drank in the smell, oh, how she had missed it!

She weighed out what she needed of the foamy elixir, added it to her bowl of flour and water, and plunged her hands into the mixture. It was cold and her hands reddened as they worked their way through the separate ingredients, rubbing them between her fingers.

Finally, when the mixture had stopped being separate ingredients and become a solid, silky mass, moving around the inside of the bowl in one single smooth ball, she lifted it out onto her wooden counter and let it sit while she fed the jar of starter. Equal parts flour and water she added, to replace what she had taken from it and to nourish it for the next day. Clearly, Pog had been doing this in her absence, for the starter was alive and kicking despite her having abandoned it. How had he known she would come back to it when she herself had not been sure?

And then Granny Mac from out of her Embassy Regal ether had barked her instructions and here she was back where she belonged, elbow-deep in sourdough and thanking God that she had so often bored Pog with sermons on her starter. Forget to feed it and it would shrink and discolour, she had often told him, meting out its punishment by baking nothing more than a flat, dull biscuit. But cherish and nurture it and it would grow and flourish, rewarding all and sundry with the resulting riches: fat, happy loaves, well risen and delectable.

She put the jar back in the pantry, almost sorry to lose sight of it, then threw a handful of sea-salt flakes into her mortar and ground it with a heavy pestle, releasing the scent of seashore violets from the marshes of Brittany as she did so.

It was not a quick process, making her own sourdough. Once she had mixed the dough to her satisfaction, she would leave it sitting for two hours to rise, then she would knock it back, shape it into a loaf, leave it a while, then coddle it into the linen-lined willow basket, where it would gently rise for another two hours before she baked it to eat for lunch.

In the meantime, there was work to be done. This second working of the dough was what made the difference between the ordinary and the sublime. It was Esme's favourite bit. She lost herself to the familiar rhythm of her breadmaking.

She added the salt to the plump ball sitting roundly in front of her and started rolling it slowly with one hand on the well-worn bench. Round and round she pushed it, gently but firmly, sweeping it round in the same wide circle each time. She felt the crunch of the salt tickling her palm and worked her hand hard down on the mixture, sweeping and circling, sweeping and circling, until it started to feel less moist, less sticky, less crunchy and more satiny and elastic to her touch. Her fingers tingled at being back in their natural habitat.

How it comforted her. How it calmed the turmoil within. How it rolled back the years, sliding over the hills and dales of time, flattening the pain and clearing the way to her sweet, seductive past.

Chapter Three

SHE HAD BEEN NINETEEN and ripe for the plucking when she and her best friend Charlie Edmonds had skipped the inevitable disappointment of a London summer for the tiny village of Venolat, perched above a horse-shoe loop in the Dordogne River in southwest France.

Actually, Charlie would have preferred to holiday in more popular Provence or, even better, on the glitzy Riviera where, he told Esme, they could both find ageing overtanned husbands with more money than sense and live the life of Riley for the next who-knew-how-long.

The only downside, Esme often thought, of having a gay best friend was that they were often in competition for the same boyfriends and she always, but always, came off second best. Charlie seemed completely irresistible while Esme considered herself more of an acquired taste.

'The overbronzed old-timers will just have to wait,' Charlie said gloomily as he and Esme sped through the narrow country lanes. 'Trust the Old Boy to have a house in the bit of France no red-blooded young man would be seen dead in.'

'You bloody well will be seen dead here if you don't stick to the right-hand side of the road,' Esme said, her knuckles clenched and white from clinging to the dashboard. 'And shut up anyway. You're lucky to have a father with spare houses.'

Charlie, a terrible driver at the best of times, was even worse owing to a hideous hangover courtesy of a very late night out in the West End. He was tired and cranky and Esme was frazzled too, being somewhat racked with guilt and anguish at leaving Granny Mac alone for so long.

'Hurrah!' trilled Charlie. 'We're nearly there.' A sign to Venolat pointed them upwards, away from the rolling green pastures and onto a narrow leafy lane that clung to the side of a substantial hill as it wound its way sneakily heavenwards.

'One more corner and I swear I am going to be sick,' he groaned five minutes later, looking pale, but Esme shushed him quiet as the car rounded a corner shaded by a canopy of ancient trees, and emerged into one of the most beautiful places she had ever seen.

'Charlie,' breathed Esme, 'it's gorgeous!'

To their left stood a church, pale yellow and majestic in the July after-noon sun, while on the other side of a square a bronze soldier stood in front of a stone memorial to men the village had lost. Further up, on either side of the narrow road, two-storeyed houses leaned over them, their sea-green shutters framing window boxes heaving with flowers.

Esme wound down her window and drank in the smell—lavender, definitely, and jasmine, she was sure, plus the smell of plain hot summer and maybe coffee too.

'Where did the Old Boy say it was?' Charlie asked, his bad mood dissolving.

'He said turn left at the fountain and ask at the *auberge*, whatever that is,' replied Esme, repeating what Mr Edmonds had told her.

'I think it's like an aubergine,' said Charlie, 'but bigger.'

At that point the road widened and they found themselves in a tiny square, with a fountain bathed in sunlight and serenely trickling water. To their right the lane led through an arch and obviously out of the village again. To the left was another lane with, perched on its corner, quite the prettiest bakery Esme had ever seen.

Its corner door faced out towards the fountain and was sheltered from the sun by a yellow-and-white-striped awning, above which appeared the simple word *Boulangerie*. The window boxes on either side of the building were painted the same shade of daffodil yellow, and bulged with red geraniums and miniature lavender bushes.

The shop was closed, yet Esme could swear she smelt the sweet yeasty aroma of baking bread still lingering in the air.

'Coming up, one *auberge*,' Charlie said, lurching to a halt just past the bakery at a small hotel covered in vines and discreetly signposted.

'An *auberge* is a hotel?' Esme asked, getting out of the car.

'One that sells aubergines, I think you will find,' Charlie said with authority, striding inside.

The two of them emerged five minutes later with the key to the apartment, which was apparently just round the corner, and a table for that night booked at the *auberge*.

They wedged the car in a twenty-three-point manoeuvre into the tiniest car park, pointed out to them by the *auberge* proprietor, and unloaded their excessive baggage from the boot.

'Follow me,' Charlie said, leading Esme back up the lane and turning through a stone archway that came out into the private courtyard of a three-storey building with dark, varnished shutters.

Stopping at double-shuttered doors, Charlie dumped his bags and unlocked the doors, then unlocked the French doors behind and entered a cool white hallway. To the left were old, worn stone stairs leading upwards, and straight ahead was a sort of living room with a cavernous double bedroom going off to one side.

'My room,' said Charlie. 'It will be getting most of the traffic so might as well be on the ground level.'

Esme slapped him on the arm. 'How do you know?' she said. 'I might turn out to be the biggest strumpet Venolat has ever seen, bringing home a swag of Frenchmen every night myself.'

'Es,' said Charlie patiently, 'if you brought home one it would be a bloody miracle.'

Charlie never tired of the subject of Esme's chasteness. He had done more than his bit, he felt, over the five years they had known each other, to help her in her efforts at being deflowered. At nineteen, she remained deeply embarrassed by her virginal status, yet too much of a romantic, in the absence of a knight in shining armour, to do anything about it.

'I'm waiting for the right one,' Esme reminded him grumpily. 'I'm special, remember?'

'Special all right,' Charlie said, heading up the stairs. 'You're an endangered species.'

They arrived on the first floor, which housed a long, dark, oak table and eight chairs and overlooked at one end the little lane through which they had just driven. At the other end was a kitchen, and to one side shuttered doors to a terrace. From there Esme looked back down to the glorious green valley below and the lazy loop of the river that meandered through it.

'We're in heaven,' she said happily. 'We can just swan around and eat cheese and drink wine for the whole lovely summer.'

Charlie shrugged and picked up her bags, then continued up more stone stairs to the top floor, which led them to an attic bedroom complete with enormous armoire, en suite bathroom, and a four-poster bed swathed in mosquito netting.

'Well, if you can't pull with a room like this,' he said, 'there's no hope for you.'

He dropped her bags on the floor and they both flopped on the enormous bed, staring in silence at the fan rattling gently above them.

'Charlie,' Esme said, turning to him. 'I've got a feeling that this is going to be the best holiday ever.'

'I thought I had that feeling too,' said Charlie, 'but it turned out to be gas. Bloody champagne cocktails, I tell you.'

'Honestly. Is that all you ever think about? I'm talking about, you know, the big deal. I'm just so ready for it.'

'Gagging for it is the expression, I believe,' said Charlie.

'I want him to be sulky and moody and dark,' Esme answered. 'Like James Dean in *Rebel Without a Cause* or Marlon Brando in *On the Waterfront*. Or a young Paul Newman,' she sighed. 'Wouldn't that be nice?'

'Too right,' he agreed enthusiastically. 'If a young Paul Newman turns up, I may just have to fight you for him.'

'Not fair,' said Esme firmly. 'You know perfectly well that a young Paul Newman, hetty or not, wouldn't choose me if you were an option.'

'That's not true, Es,' Charlie argued. 'It's not people choosing you that is the problem. It is you choosing them. You're too fussy by far. You're waiting for the fireworks and it's not like that, really it isn't.'

'It's not like that for *you*,' Esme corrected him, 'but I am different. I am going to wait for the real thing.'

Many, many hours later, Esme was slipping home through the empty streets of early-morning Venolat, breathing in the warm, still air and trying to get Bob Marley's 'No Woman, No Cry' out of her head.

She and Charlie had started the night with a mouth-wateringly delicious three-course meal and a bottle of *vin de pays* at the *auberge*, before discovering a tiny bar hidden in the backstreets.

There they had happened upon a rowdy bunch of Canadians, who had then hooked up with an even rowdier bunch of Dutch tourists. The night had ended at around four with Esme deciding that the very tall accountant from Toronto with thick spectacles and teeth that could eat an apple through the bars of a chair, as Granny Mac would say, was not her knight in shining armour.

By then she felt like she had drunk all the *vin* in the *pays* and was ready for her bed. Charlie, though, had other plans and so Esme bade them all farewell and headed home.

The outside air cleared her head and once she had shaken her curls free of the stench of everyone else's cigarettes, she felt exhilarated to be out on her own.

The sound of her black plastic-soled designer-lookalike sandals slapping the cobbles beat a solitary tattoo that bounced off the walls on either side of the lane. On her own. It would have been nice, Esme allowed herself to think, to go home and make love until the sun came up with some adoring man who would feed her chocolate Häagen-Dazs in the morning, in between stealing kisses on the mole she had and hated just below her left collarbone.

The toothy Toronto bean counter was not that man, of that she was pretty sure. Perhaps she was wrong about being ready. Venolat was quite small, she had come to realise, and it was possible she had already met every single person who lived there. She slipped into the square and walked quietly over to the fountain, perching on the side of it and trailing one hand in its cool, clear water.

All of a sudden the most delicious smell wafted gently round her curls and invaded her senses. Esme lifted her face to the moon and breathed in deep and long. Of course, the *boulangerie*! Bread was being baked as she sat there and smelt it, and for some reason it seemed like a gift, just for her.

The squeak of a rusty hinge and the slap of timber on timber tugged Esme out of her reverie. She leaned forward slightly, peering round the fountain but still hidden by its shadow. At first she thought she was dreaming or that it was the wine, or the moonlight, or that sweet, sour smell tricking her somehow, but what she saw took her breath clean away.

Leaning against the door, lit from behind by the light sneaking through from the back of the *boulangerie*, and from the front by the glow of the moon, flour greying his black curly head, dark eyes concentrating on rolling a cigarette, was the man of Esme's dreams.

How she knew this, she could not say. She had known she was ready, but even in fairy tales the princess didn't just happen on her prince in the village square. She had to fight for him, or he for her. Yet Esme knew, just *knew*, by the trembling in her knees and the butterflies in her stomach, that this was the man she had been waiting for.

Sitting there in the shadows, staring, she felt a shivery tingle start in her groin and swarm up to her heart, which greeted it with big, pounding pulses as though it had never properly beaten before. It ached. Truly ached. And then it sent the shivery tingle on its way through every ventricle, every vein, every tiny capillary to Esme's cheeks, branding her with the mark of someone in the first stage of a very dangerous desire.

The man (or was he a boy?) languidly lifted the rolled cigarette to his lips, the tendons in the arm she could see rippling under his smooth brown skin. Then he slowly ran his tongue along the line of glue on the top edge of the cigarette paper and when he got to the end, he lifted his gaze and shifted it to Esme.

Surely he could not see her? And if he could, what was she supposed to do? Suddenly move and act like she wasn't spying on him, or stay stock-still in case it was the fountain he was looking at and not her? Why, oh why, did she not know what to do?

He shifted his gaze back to his cigarette, pulled a lighter out of his pocket, brought the roll-your-own to his lips and lit it, her heart missing a beat as she watched his whole beautiful face bathed momentarily in the light from the flame.

He inhaled deeply, enjoying every moment, then slowly removed the cigarette from his lips and dropped it to his side. Slowly, slowly, slowly he smiled a smile so deep and dazzling that for a moment Esme felt dizzy and thought she was going to swoon. And up until that point she had been quite sceptical about the whole business of swooning, believing that it was an imaginary condition applying only to faint-hearted Barbara Cartland characters with their corsets done up too tightly.

But sitting there on that still-warm smooth stone lip of that trickling fountain outside that beautiful bakery, with the rich, dark eyes of this completely delicious stranger burning a hole clear through her, Esme felt like she had been emptied of every feeling she had ever had to make room for something entirely wonderful and new. Something very powerful. Something *passionate*.

It was the moment she had been waiting for all her life. This is not a dream, she thought. This is really happening.

Quietly, she stood up and stepped out of the shadows. The man of her dreams looked up again, and his eyes feasted on her and then his mouth slowly gave way to that dazzling, dizzying smile. He lifted one hand in what could have been a casual hello, could have been beckoning her to him. And Esme, who suddenly recognised within herself the most excruciating longing, took one small step in his direction, the moonlight dancing off her ringlets as she did so.

The moment was so magical she thought for a moment that she, who like her grandmother rarely shed a tear, was going to dissolve into them.

But then the moment was shattered.

'Bloody hell,' Charlie's voice rang out from behind her. 'The Dutch are a forward bunch, aren't they? Three in a bed I can handle, but five? I'm English for God's sake. Bloody disgusting. Es? What are you doing?'

Esme had swung round just for an instant at the sound of Charlie's voice, only to find that when she turned back to the *boulangerie*, her vision was gone, the sound of timber on timber ringing sadly in the still night air. The dream had melted in front of her, like a watercolour lying in the rain: one moment a landscape of staggering beauty, the next a gaudy puddle fast disappearing down a black, bleak drain.

Charlie staggered up to his friend, standing palely riveted to the ground, her green eyes huge in her lightly freckled face as she turned to stare at him with barely disguised horror. Even in his drunken stupor he could tell that all was not well.

'I say, Es,' he said. 'Are you OK? Whatever's the matter?'

'Bread,' she said feebly, willing the vision to come back. 'Look.' She pointed gormlessly towards the *boulangerie*.

Charlie, unsteady on his feet, sniffed the air. 'God, don't talk to me about food, I feel sick as a dog,' he said. 'What's pastis, anyway? Revolting. Come on, Essie, let's go home.'

Esme wanted to stay where she was and wait for the boy in the bakery to come back out again. But it all seemed so quiet. So still. Maybe she had been dreaming. It all felt very strange and she realised that perhaps home was the best direction in which to go, after all.

Lying in her bed some time later, though, her head still buzzing with red wine and blue cheese and the events of the night just passed, Esme could not get the baker boy out of her mind. It was silly, she knew, to lie in one's bed and warm oneself up with the memory of one look and a couple of smiles from a total stranger, if he had even been smiling at her.

But what a guilty pleasure it was to assume he had been.

Chapter Four

SIX BOYFRIENDS, one husband and ten pounds, mostly round her middle, later, Esme sat at her kitchen table high in the clouds, quivering with repugnance as she ogled Jemima Jones's inaugural Diary.

Pog, witnessing this and weighing up what it meant, had quickly departed to the garden shed, leaving Esme seated at the table, glaring at the Style section. Finally, she snatched it up and shook it open only to see Jemima smiling enigmatically out at her, looking blonde, wrinkle-free, girlish and gorgeous. She had never felt more like punching anyone in her entire life.

'As I kissed my darling boy Cosmo good night on Friday,' she read, 'he looked up at me and said, adorably: "Are all the other mummies as beautiful as you?"'

Esme tossed the paper down on the table again. Her hands itched to do something. She checked the kitchen clock—she had knocked back her bread nearly an hour before. She could start the second rising now.

Pog, although not saying anything, had clearly been delighted at the appearance of a freshly baked *boule* at lunch the previous day. He had eaten it as though he had never eaten anything before, and Esme herself had woken that morning with a flutter of something that wasn't, as had become the norm, dread. It was good to be back at the kitchen bench.

She poked her tongue out at Jemima and moved to where her dough was sitting plumply in its bowl, glistening with the olive oil she used to keep it from sticking to the sides.

She picked the warm smooth ball up and laid it on the counter, then, using both hands, lightly massaged it into the right shape and let it sit while she sprinkled a handful of flour on the surface next to it.

With one deft movement she turned the dough over, dipped it in flour and dropped it into the waiting linen-lined willow basket. It was not the real thing, not French and not made of willow, but the dough sat smugly in its mould. It would rise in its own good time. Esme tidied the kitchen, then went back to the table and picked up the paper again.

'I was dressed in gold Calvin Klein with Jimmy Choo heels,' she read, 'ready to go to the Dorchester for one of my charity do's, but at that moment I *felt like curling up beside my son and simply lying there in his bed all night, soaking up his adoration. How my heart ached for him as I handed the au pair a storybook* (Kitchen Confidential *by Anthony Bourdain—Cosmo is an aspiring cook!*) *and slipped out of the door.'*

Esme slapped the paper back down and got up to make herself a cup of tea. Cosmo? As in the magazine? She tried to quell her irritation. *Kitchen Confidential*? How old was this child?

'All right there, darling?' she asked Rory, who was watching *Shrek* for possibly the hundredth time. Like most mothers, she had sworn no child of hers would ever sit plopped in front of the television for hour after hour, but her son had woken up in an impossible mood and she could not face the consequences of battling over the remote control.

Rory didn't answer her. Did adorable little Cosmo watch videos and ignore his mother? she wondered. She sipped her tea, sighed, and flopped back into her chair.

'*It's not easy being a superwoman, as I am sure many of you appreciate,*' Jemima chittered. '*A working mother can be torn in so many different directions that the days just seem to pass in a blur. I am lucky that my husband Gregory, who's in banking, helps out a lot at home by engaging the services of two nannies, a cook, a driver and a gardener. It makes it easy to slip away and meet our social commitments without denying our three delightful children— George Quentin, who we call GQ, Marie Claire and sweet lovely little Cosmo—any of the attention they so richly deserve.*'

'Three delightful children, all named after magazines!' Esme dropped the paper again. 'Bitch!'

'You're not supposed to say bitch unless you're talking about dogs,' Rory said from his beanbag. 'Granddad says so.'

Esme felt shame add itself to the cocktail of feelings churning inside her. 'Sorry, sweetheart,' she said, 'but sometimes it really is the only word that does the job.'

Rory turned off the television and sat at the table, reaching for the packet of cereal Esme had ready for him. 'Who's a bitch?' he asked.

'Just a woman I used to work for who was once very mean and horrible to Mummy and who is probably going to be the next Prime Minister,' Esme replied sweetly.

'What happened to Tony Blair?' Rory asked, through a mouthful of cereal. 'The prat.'

Esme looked at him pouring sugar on his breakfast, his carrot-coloured hair luminescent against the muted creams and whites and pale blond wood of the top floor.

'Rory,' she said, moving round the table and sitting down next to him, 'you do know that grown-ups can do and say things that little children can't, don't you?'

'Yes,' said Rory. He kept eating, unfazed.

'So you must also know that you can't repeat things we say about people, especially if they are mean or horrible things.'

Rory shot her a withering look. 'Mrs Monk says people who are mean are usually sad inside and you should feel sorry for them,' he said. Mrs Monk was Rory's nursery teacher and a self-righteous old battle-axe if ever there was one, but Rory liked her.

'Is Mrs Monk wearing her brown wig this week,' she asked her son, 'or the red one?'

Rory thought about it for a moment. 'It's a new one,' he said. 'It's sort of silver. It's nice.'

He really could be very sweet, thought Esme, smiling indulgently and catching Jemima's eyes where they lay on the table.

'Rory,' she said, 'do you think Mummy is beautiful?'

Rory lifted up his bowl, drank the milk out of the bottom of it and shrugged his shoulders, saying nothing.

'More beautiful than Mrs Monk, maybe?' Esme wheedled.

'Mrs Monk has a moustache,' Rory answered. 'Everyone is more beautiful than her. She just has nice wigs.'

'Well,' continued Esme, 'compared to the other mummies then. Am I as beautiful? More beautiful?'

Rory looked at her as he pushed his chair back. 'The other mothers have got shinier hair,' was all he said. He picked up the honey jar and spoon Esme had ready on the bench and held them up at her. She toyed with refusing to move until he gave her the right answer to the question, but decided that would be churlish, as would pointing out that curly hair never shone like straight hair. It was a reflection thing.

'Come on,' Rory said, and they made their way downstairs and out onto the lawn where, joined by Brown, they trekked over to the wicker gate behind the house and stood looking mistrustfully and from a safe distance at the beehive.

The bees swarmed in an angry cloud around the blue-and-white-striped hive that Pog had paid a fortune for, and spent an entire weekend painting so it would match Esme's garden which grew rich in blue irises, lavender, roses and hydrangeas. The bees were all part of her dream of serving up a country breakfast with fresh-baked bread, farm-laid eggs and lazy spoonfuls of thick brown honey, fresh from their very own back yard.

So far, she had only managed the bread. The chickens had refused to lay and then died and in the six months that they had had the bees, only

Pog had got closer than ten yards away from them. On that spectacular occasion he had been stung sixteen times before retreating almost in tears, as Esme had looked on in hysterics from the garden gate.

'Bees, Dad!' Rory shouted this Sunday morning across the lawn in the direction of Pog's shed. The door opened and Pog's head poked out.

'Be careful, you two,' he called, then shut the door again. Esme considered the shed. They had six storeys of house, yet Pog, she knew, preferred this draughty little shack. She'd only been in there a handful of times: it was dark and cold and full of boxes and tools and jars of dirty fluid sprouting paintbrushes. Pog had a sort of nest at one end with a chair draped in an old oilskin and a filing cabinet piled high with ancient paperwork. An old apple crate provided a surface for his electric kettle and tea supplies. The whole place smelt funny, decades of garden fertiliser fused into the walls, she supposed, and on each occasion she had gone in there Pog had acted peculiarly, as though she was trespassing.

'A man needs a shed,' he said, whenever she moaned about the amount of time he spent there. And to be honest, she couldn't begrudge him his own little space. In most regards he was the perfect husband: handsome, kind, loving, understanding, generous, gentle. She thought fleetingly, as she stood there considering the dark, lonely shed, of the way she rolled away from him under the covers of their bed these days, and guilt scratched at her. There really was something very wrong with her. Here she was with all the ingredients of a perfect life sitting separately on the counter top of her future, yet now, more than ever, she seemed incapable of combining them. Was the past destined to always poison whatever was to come?

'What makes them so cross?' Rory asked her, and she turned her attention again to the bees buzzing furiously around their home. Brown, too, still on his best behaviour since the quince-peeing incident, turned to Esme for the answer.

'I'm buggered if I know, actually,' Esme answered them both, forgetting that buggered was another word she didn't want Rory using in front of Mrs Monk.

'Perhaps they don't want to live in a hive that looks like a house,' suggested Rory thoughtfully.

'What makes you say that?' Esme asked.

'Perhaps they want to live in a hive like in Pooh Bear,' he said. 'You know, sort of shaped like a pine cone but with ridges going around.' He looked balefully up at her. 'They might not know that that's their home. They might think they're lost.' He looked again at the angry bees.

Esme looked at his little pale freckled face with its screwed-up frown.

Would she ever know what was going on in that little head of his? Would she ever stop fearing for him? The love she felt for him, and the flicker of anguish that always accompanied it, vibrated right through her.

'I don't think bees have very big brains, darling,' she said warmly, resisting the urge to squeeze him, knowing he hated it. 'But you could be right about the hive. Perhaps we should try to find a pine-cone-shaped one. What do you think?'

Rory handed her back the jar and spoon.

'Don't care,' he said. 'Don't like honey anyway.' This was true. He never had liked honey. He only came with her because he didn't want to miss another major attack. Please, Esme silently begged the bees, please just calm down and let us come close. Please let something go right for me today. But somehow the buzzy little bodies sensed that most of the family preferred marmalade, and so stayed irate.

Rory turned and started towards the house, going, she knew, to seek out Henry, who might be permanently grumpy with her but was the picture of patience and devotion with Rory, who in turn adored him. She supposed she should feel grateful and she did, mostly.

She traipsed up the stairs to make sure her son and father-in-law found each other, then snatched the *Sunday Times* from the kitchen floor and tripped back down to Granny Mac's room.

The stench of Embassy Regal hit her the moment she opened the door into the gloom. Rod was waking up Maggie May because he thought he had something to say to her.

'I haven't got long,' she said, taking up her position on the end of the bed. 'You would not believe what a disgusting mess Rory's room is, and I haven't done any laundry for days. As for the garden, well, the veggie patch needs napalming and I am long overdue for goat-pooh patrol.'

'Well, if you can't squeeze me into your busy schedule . . .' Granny Mac huffed.

'Don't be silly,' protested Esme. 'I'll always make time for you, goose. Look,' she rustled the newspaper. 'Jemima Jones's first column. She's got a boy called Cosmo who's asked her if all the other mothers are as beautiful as she is.'

'Gay,' Granny Mac said matter-of-factly. 'What else does she say?'

'*Juggling family and career is an issue with which many British families struggle,*' Esme read in a simpering voice, '*and we are certainly no exception. The only difference for us, really, is that our children are quite mature and of above average intelligence in their demograph so we can explain to them, without tears or tantrums, why Daddy never comes home before bedtime and often still isn't there in the morning.* Oh, that sounds healthy.'

'*But back to our precious little four-year-old—he's only four?—and his adorable question. When we got home from the Dorchester, I snuck into his room and looked at him curled up in his tiny replica of Michael Schumacher's Ferrari.* Oh, couldn't afford the real thing, then?

'*I had met so many women that night,*' Esme read on, '*from all walks of life, rich and poor, short and tall, and it had struck me at one point, as my mind wandered while talking to Cherie (yes, that one!), that despite our differences, we are really all the same. We're all trying to hold together the fabric that makes up our lives, be they grand or oh so simple.*

'"*Yes, Cosmo,*" *I whispered to my precious sleeping son.* "*Yes. All the other mummies are as beautiful as me. In their own special ways.*"'

Esme dropped the paper into her lap, her head thumping against the wall as she stared at the ceiling. She could read no further.

'Esme!' Granny Mac said sharply. 'What is the matter?'

'I don't know,' Esme answered unhappily. 'I just don't know. But I feel wretched, Granny Mac. Wretched.' Her voice caught and she fought to control it. 'I've been so good up until now. So strong.' She stopped. 'And I've been baking again just like you told me to, which has been glorious. It's made a difference. It really has. I mean the blackness has gone.'

'But?' Granny Mac prompted.

'But still I have this terrible feeling. Oh, I don't know,' Esme sought the right words. 'It's like I've got a great big itch somewhere inside me but I can't tell where so I can't scratch it, but I can't concentrate on anything else while it's itchy. Have you ever felt like that, Gran?'

'Well, I had fleabites once,' Granny Mac retorted, 'from a particularly unpleasant cat called Pam that came with your Granddad Mac. Calamine lotion was the thing back then, I believe.'

'I'm trying to tell you my deepest darkest thoughts and calamine lotion is the best you can do?'

'And you think your deepest darkest thoughts are so fascinating? I've not a clue what you're on about with your scratching and your itching, Esme. If you want me to help you, you have got to help yourself, and spouting nonsense about bloody eczema is getting us nowhere.'

It was no wonder Rory liked *Shrek*, Esme thought. The caustic green ogre probably reminded the poor child of his great-grandmother. She abandoned any attempt at argument.

'I just want to be the old me,' she said, simply, instead. 'I want to go to charity do's at the Dorchester and drink frou-frou cocktails with Cherie Blair and have good uncomplicated fun.' She sighed. 'But everything is just so tainted with what's happened to us that I can't imagine ever being that old uncomplicated Esme ever again.'

'Och, Esme,' her grandmother was not entirely sympathetic. 'She wasn't so hot, that girl.'

'Granny Mac!'

'Well, it's time you started facing facts, lassie. You can't be her again. She's gone. It's true, what's happened to you has made you a different person, we none of us can go back and undo what's been done, Esme. We just have to live with the consequences and find a way to move forward despite them.'

'Well, don't you think I have been doing that?' Esme was stunned. 'I have moved forward, I have kept moving forward.'

'And this past month?'

'This past month is your fault,' Esme cried. 'You know it is. I can't do it on my own. It's too hard. It's too lonely.'

'Oh, not doing enough for you, am I? Well, I'll get up and dance a Highland fling, then, how about that? Never mind two strokes and the recent devastation of pneumonia.'

Esme ignored this, rustling the *Sunday Times* furiously instead. 'Well, Jemima Jones isn't helping, I can tell you that for nothing. Turning up with three delightful children, a brand-new career and not a single bloody crow's-foot in sight.'

'You're going to blame this hysteria on Jemima Jones?' Granny Mac asked incredulously. 'Oh, yes, that works. That works really well. Good job. Brilliant.' A deep sigh permeated the room. 'You know, you can point your finger any which way you like, Esme, but I think you know that if your bread isn't rising, you need to look at your ingredients.'

Esme was silent.

'There are weevils in your flour, lassie.'

'There's nothing in my flour, Granny Mac.'

'I'm telling you, there are weevils.'

'This has nothing to do with weevils!'

'It's all about weevils.'

'Well, I don't want to talk about weevils.'

'Well, you shouldn't expect to start feeling better until you *do* talk about weevils, Esme, and in the meantime don't come in here wasting my time with your incessant moaning.'

The telephone ringing upstairs shattered the ensuing quiet and Esme pushed herself shakily off the bed. She snatched the *Sunday Times* and fled the room without a backward glance.

'I'll get it, Henry,' she called, taking the stairs two at a time.

She slid into the sitting room on the second floor and grabbed the receiver on the eighth ring, gasping into it, 'Esme Stack!'

40

'I will never get used to that ridiculous name,' a voice crackled down the line. 'Really, Es. There was nothing wrong with MacDougall.'

'Charlie!' Esme cried, delighted. 'I can't believe it. Where are you?'

'Still in Honkers, darling, but not for much bloody longer. I'm on my way home. I never did get the hang of chopsticks, confounded things, although I've developed quite a taste for snake meat. And skin for that matter. I'm practically all reptile these days, inside and out.'

Esme laughed as Charlie's nonsense washed over her. 'Oh, Charlie, it's so good to hear from you, I can't tell you,' she said. 'I really can't.'

'Well, seeing me in the flesh ought to give you even more of a thrill,' he said modestly. 'I'm flying in on Tuesday and I thought I might come out to the deepest, darkest countryside for the weekend and stay. Check out the Good Life, Felicity Kendall and all that. Eat some organic wasabi or whatever it is you have there and maybe grab a glass or six of dandelion wine.'

Esme assured him she could provide alcohol from a totally synthetic source and food that had definitely been genetically modified, and put the phone down, tingling with anticipation at the thought of his visit. Something had gone right! Charlie did not have a sensitive bone in his body but had been blessed with the gift of good timing. If one needed a shoulder to cry on, he was no help at all, but if one needed someone to make them laugh and forget for a moment that they needed a shoulder to cry on, he was perfect.

She heard voices on the floor below her, followed by Henry's tapping and shuffling. 'We're going outside,' he called in his gruff voice.

'Righto,' Esme called back. She flopped back in her overstuffed armchair and contemplated the Style section, yet again. Could she stomach more Jemima? Could she keep away?

She turned to page two. What was little Cosmo doing now? she wondered. Bringing peace to the Middle East and curing cancer?

'Oh, fuck you, you silly cow!' she said savagely, throwing the paper on the floor and kicking it away.

'I beg your pardon?' a voice said from the doorway. It was, of course, Henry, with Rory standing beside him.

'She said "bitch" before, too,' Rory informed his grandfather.

'That's entrapment,' protested Esme. 'I thought you were outside! A person can swear to themselves, can't they?'

Henry and Rory looked at each other but said nothing.

Esme rolled her eyes. 'I'm sorry, I'm sorry. What's up?'

'Hugo has suggested a walk on the beach before lunch,' Henry said in his tight, clipped voice.

'What a good idea,' Esme said, going over and ruffling Rory's orange curls, and throwing a smile at her father-in-law in the hope of defrosting him. 'I'll have the bread baked and the soup heated and sitting downstairs in the garden by the time you come back.'

Rory shot her a strange look, then picked up his grandfather's hand and led him downstairs. 'She likes bread more than the beach,' he said as they crossed the lawn to Pog's shed. 'But that's OK.'

Henry said nothing.

Pog emerged, his face falling when he saw Esme was not with them.

'She's getting lunch,' Henry said, and the three male Stacks, along with Brown, headed out of the gate and down the leafy lane towards the unnecessarily winding road that led past the Meare to the beach.

Seabury was a village made, literally, for sunny Sundays such as this one. The Meare was peppered with brightly coloured boats being rowed, with varying degrees of skill, as the local swan population did its best to stay aloof and avoid collisions. The sky was as clear and blue as it could possibly be, the sun warming the giant oaks round the lake and sending Chinese whispers rippling through their leaves.

When they reached the warm pebbles of Seabury beach, the Stack males took off their shoes and socks. Rory, thrilled by the temperate breeze, the sparkling blue ocean, the earsplitting barks of his overexcited labrador, ran up and down splashing in the shallow waters of the shoreline, waving his arms and shouting to himself.

Henry and Pog sat on a wooden bench at the foot of the sand dunes and watched him.

'Your mother never cared for the beach,' Henry said, out of the blue, totally astonishing his son. 'Made her fret. The waves, you know, coming and going, never stopping or some such nonsense.'

She'd been gone nearly twenty years, yet still it hurt Henry so much to think of Grace that usually he simply couldn't. Usually, he kept his memories of her locked in a vault in his mind, where he managed to contain all the painful emotion he preferred not to confront.

His sons, he knew, had suffered as a result of his inability to share his grief. They had lost a mother, after all, and the two of them only in their early twenties. But he had lost his wife, the love of his life, his reason for getting up in the morning. How could he console his sons when all he wanted to do was howl with rage at the injustice of it all? He'd left his boys to sink or swim.

Milo, his first-born, had swum, finding strength in his career and his marriage to, rather sensibly Henry felt, a fellow broker with good child-bearing hips and a no-nonsense hairdo. They were settled in America now, doing everything according to plan and no trouble to anyone.

Hugo was a different creature, always had been. Dreamy, soft, more like Grace, he supposed. He'd swum too, but perhaps he had floundered a little, was floundering still.

Henry thought of Esme and his jaw clenched. His first impression of his daughter-in-law-to-be had not been a good one. She was right to think he considered her flighty and unsuitable. It had been a cold winter night at his old house in Kent and Hugo had turned up all bright-eyed and pink-cheeked with this jittery, bubbly, brassy redhead dressed ridiculously in fake fur and men's shoes. She'd been nervous and had drunk too much champagne.

He'd had trouble warming to her. They chafed at each other like mismatched cogs, always missing the connection. She talked too much and Henry, especially in the absence of Grace, was not a talker. He felt trampled by Esme's enthusiasm. All it served to remind him was how his own small well of ebullience had long run dry.

It had not helped when poor health collided with reduced circumstances and Henry, thanks to a run of bad investments handled by his neighbour's son-in-law, a trust fund manager with a well-disguised gambling problem, had had no alternative but to sell his Kent cottage and settle his debts.

Esme, he knew, had been distressed beyond measure at his obvious loss and embarrassment, insisting he move in with them as she was dying for want of a decent house-sitter. Hugo had been more fretful than her, and he had even overheard his daughter-in-law sternly reminding his son that this was what families were for and if they could look after Granny Mac, who was rude and insolent, they could certainly look after a gentleman like Henry.

But his pride was hurt, his dignity mulched, and he had not had it in him to accept her kindness. Through all they had suffered, he had held himself at bay and he did not like himself for it. But there was no going back. He was trapped in his own grief and remorse and could not claw his way to freedom. He did not know how to rebuild the bridge between himself and the next generation.

'I didn't know that,' Pog said, eyes on the horizon, confused and awkward in such uncharted territory. 'About Mum. And the beach.'

Henry said nothing. He wanted to reach out further, but it was simply beyond him. He looked across the pebbles at Rory, his bright red hair pinging off the blue sea behind him as he ran through the surf, white foamy chunks flying in the air in front of him.

And his heart, which nursed such pain and bitterness, swelled with love for the boy. Rory he would not disappoint.

Chapter Five

'BLOODY HELL, OLD GIRL,' Charlie cried, sitting in the driver's seat of a black Audi convertible, gawping up at the House in the Clouds. 'It's positively phallic. Did Hugo choose it or did you?' He pushed his designer sunglasses up on his head and flicked his eyes over her as she ran towards him.

'You look fantastic as always,' he said, jumping out of the car and squeezing her in a fierce hug. 'God, it's good to see you, Esme.'

Esme pulled back. 'You're looking pretty bloody gorgeous yourself,' she said. His hair was long and blond-tipped and fell boyishly across his forehead, the neatly tanned skin around his eyes only just beginning to pucker and crinkle. He looked, it struck her, like a younger, taller, more handsome version of Hugh Grant. 'Is that Prada?' she gasped. 'Head to toe? My God, you are a loss to the heterosexual world, Charlie.'

'But, darling,' Charlie said with a wicked grin. 'I am a gift to the other side. Try thinking of it that way.'

'Still beating them off with a big stick, eh?' teased Esme. 'Is there a great chunky gold medallion under that shirt?'

Charlie laughed and put one long arm round her shoulders so that she could nestle into his armpit, where they both knew she fitted. 'Now, are you going to ask me in or up or whatever it is you do to get into this monstrous abode—or not? What on earth compelled you to move to this creepy little town, Es, it's like something the Brothers Grimm might have dreamed up, all twisty and windy and things not the right size.'

Esma laughed. What was it with men and Seabury? The great lumps seemed so threatened by anything slightly imaginative. She ignored Charlie's question and gave him a grand tour of the property, starting with the dysfunctional pets and unconventional vegetable garden. To her amazement, he seemed quite excited by the prospect of Pog's shed.

'You mean it's just for him and no one else?' he asked, impressed. 'Sounds smashing. And does he spend much time in there?'

'He's usually in there all weekend,' Esme told him. 'But he's got some big project on the boil at the moment so he's at work today.' She realised she had been so distracted by her own anxiousness that she had not asked Pog exactly what his project was.

She bypassed Granny Mac's room with a swift, dismissive wave, took Charlie in to say hello to Henry, who treated him with polite deference, then gave him lunch in her kitchen—sourdough and homemade minestrone—which he wolfed down while claiming to feel queasy at the view from the top of the House in the Clouds.

After that, she forced him to walk with her to the Ashtons', where Rory had gone to play and where he had done four paintings, all of them solid masses of very dark brown. He had not spoken a word, according to Peggy Ashton, since he arrived, but had eaten a hearty lunch and stood there placidly as bubbly, blond, blue-eyed Annabelle threw her arms around him and kissed him goodbye.

Charlie seemed at a loss as to what to say to the little boy as they strolled in the sunshine back down the lane to the house. They had not met before, Charlie claiming at the news of Esme's pregnancy to be allergic to small children, and backing this up soon after by decamping to the other side of the world. He and Esme had met occasionally over the years for cocktails, usually vanilla daiquiris, during his visits home, and had kept sporadically in touch by phone and by mail, but he had never before seen her domestically *in situ*.

'So, is Annabelle your girlfriend then?' Charlie finally asked Rory as they meandered towards home.

Rory squinted up at him. 'No,' he said.

'Never too young to start though, eh?' Charlie joked.

'Start what?' Rory asked.

'Start having girlfriends, silly,' Charlie answered.

Rory looked at his mother.

'It's small talk,' she explained. 'It doesn't really matter. You just sort of go along with it to be polite.'

'Thank you very much,' Charlie cried indignantly.

'Well, there is no point asking a four-year-old about his *sex* life, Charlie,' Esme hissed.

'If it doesn't really matter, why would you want to talk about it?' Rory asked.

Esme laughed and Charlie turned to her. 'It's the body of a small boy,' he said, 'but the words of an old Scottish woman.' He broke off, suddenly embarrassed. 'I'm so sorry, Es—'

'So sorry nothing,' Esme said, breaking into a trot, and grabbing Rory's hand. 'Come on, darling. I think I saw gaudily wrapped gifts in the back of Uncle Charlie's sports car.'

The gaudily wrapped gifts were something of an icebreaker in the Rory–Charlie relationship department, as three of them turned out to be toy guns. The House in the Clouds had up until then been a weapon-free environment—all the books said that was the right thing to do—but Esme was relieved to see that her son reacted the way any other small boy might react: by instantly shooting everything including her, the sheep, the bees, Brown and even Henry.

The gift-giving did not stop there, either. There was a Paul Smith shirt for Pog, which Esme knew her husband would never wear even though it would look fantastic on him, and for her Charlie had bought a bottle of Must de Cartier parfum, which she no longer bothered to buy herself. On top of that, he produced two bottles of Cristal champagne.

'Sorry, Es, but I'm only here for the night,' Charlie informed her as he cracked open the first bottle as soon as the presents were unwrapped. 'The Old Boy's made plans for me and I can't really wriggle out of them. You know how it is.'

'Oh, Charlie,' Esme cried, disappointed. 'There's so much catching up to do. Can't you stay at least another night?'

Charlie put on his strict, older-brotherly look and handed her a glass. 'Come on, Es,' he cajoled. 'Don't make a fuss. Can't be helped and all that. I'll come back again. Next week if you want me to. I'm based in London now, you know, for the rest of my working days if I can manage it. Don't make me feel guilty, Es, you know I'm no good at it.'

Esme thawed slightly. 'I'm making you feel guilty?' she asked, impressed, taking a firmer grasp on the champagne flute. 'You're losing it, you big jessie!'

Charlie smiled his movie-star smile and charged his glass. 'That's more like it,' he said. 'Now, have a drink for God's sake, a man could die of thirst out here in the country.'

Pog got home just before eight, exhausted after spending the day in a series of very dull informal meetings with different members of the local council, which had, much to his surprise, awarded him the contract to beautify Seabury's wobbly main street. It had taken them nearly six months to decide he was the right man for the job, and now they wanted plans and costings within three weeks. By the time he trod home, Charlie and Esme had drunk both bottles of champagne.

They were lying on their backs on the sitting-room floor, laughing hysterically although they couldn't remember why. Pog quelled the whisper of loneliness that licked at him. He wished it was him that had her rolling on the floor in hysterics, but if it was Charlie or nothing, he'd take Charlie.

'Where's Dad?' he asked, after shaking hands with the man and accepting, rather bewildered, the Paul Smith shirt with which he had just been presented.

'I think he went to the pub,' said Esme, sitting up and wiping the tears of laughter from her eyes. 'There was a small amount of irritation at having a noisy guest in the house,' she continued as Charlie started to laugh again, 'followed by a flow of condescension with a smattering of contempt forecast for tomorrow.' Charlie was howling. Pog smiled and Esme felt instantly sober and guilty and mean. It wasn't Pog's fault Henry was cranky. And her husband looked tired and awkward. It was not her intention to exclude him.

'Rory's in bed asleep,' she said, suddenly more sensible. 'I think he has a new best friend.'

She looked at Charlie, who smiled winningly up at Pog from his position on the floor.

'Well, I think I'll join him,' Pog said. 'Dad, at the pub, I mean. Help him get home. Let you two catch up.' He smiled at her again, and Esme felt almost overwhelmed by an urge to fold herself into his arms and say all the things she knew he needed to hear from her.

'Charlie's only here for one night,' she blurted out instead.

Charlie started laughing uproariously again at this, clutching his stomach as he rolled around on the floor.

'He has to be admitted to a psychiatric ward tomorrow morning for immediate testing,' Esme continued. 'As you can see he's not quite right in the head.'

'As long as it's not catching,' Pog said pleasantly. 'I'll see you later.'

As his footsteps on the stairs faded away and the front door clicked distantly shut, Charlie sat up and attempted to compose himself. 'What appalling behaviour,' he said, drying his eyes with the sleeve of his shirt. 'No wonder the poor chap thinks I am a complete imbecile.'

'Don't be silly,' Esme said, standing up unsteadily and holding out her hand to her friend. Charlie groaned and let her help him to his feet.

'Come on, Charlie.' Esme said, heading up the stairs. 'The kitchen is a bombsite. I'd better go and tidy it up before Pog comes back.' They clattered together up the stairs and into the kitchen, where Charlie flopped onto a chair and Esme surveyed the devastation she had created making Rory a chocolate cake for his tea.

'Blimey, what a hovel,' she said as she started clearing the bench. 'Did I do this?' The dishwasher gaped meanly at her, its freshly cleaned innards glinting and reminding her what a slovenly housewife she was for not emptying it earlier. Slowly and carefully, so as not to break anything in her partially inebriated state, she removed its contents, before filling it up again with the messy utensils from her earlier baking.

After wiping the counter clean, she started excavating in the freezer for something to feed her family the following night.

'Hurrah!' she crowed, finally finding a leg of lamb underneath a spilt open bag of frozen peas and a box of half-melted ice lollies.

'There's homemade mint sauce in here somewhere too,' she muttered, diving into the freezer again. 'You should have seen my mint, Charlie, how it grew! I think NASA astronauts could see it from space.' Shuffling old margarine containers around she eventually found the right one, plucking it out with a triumphant look and holding it up for Charlie to see.

He was staring at her with an unreadable expression.

'What is it?' she asked, wiping imaginary fluff off her nose and checking her hair with her hand to make sure nothing jellied or minced or past its use-by date was stuck there. 'Don't look at me like that!'

Charlie shook himself out of his thoughts. 'I wasn't looking at you like anything,' he protested.

'Yes, you were,' argued Esme, suddenly remembering she hadn't fed her sourdough starter its evening meal of flour and water, and reaching into the pantry for the jar. 'You were looking at me as though you'd never seen me before.'

Charlie laughed. 'No, I was just thinking, that's all.'

'Thinking what?' Esme insisted.

'Thinking how amazing you are,' Charlie said softly, 'that's what.'

'Amazing?' Esme repeated. 'Me?' It was not what she had been expecting him to say. She started to slowly twist the lid off the starter.

'Yes, you silly girl, you,' Charlie said. 'After everything you've been through, you still seem so, I don't know, happy.'

'Happy?' The top of the jar popped off at just that moment and the pungent sweet and sour tartness of the ancient mixture hit Esme square in the face. Happy? In that instant, the mists of the past fifteen years fell away and she saw herself standing in that little French bakery, wrapped in a soft sheet of cocoa-coloured linen, cherishing every drop of the baker's sweat as it mingled with hers, and quivering with the joy of being loved.

That was happy.

She dropped the jar on the kitchen counter and the memory vanished, leaving her breathless and terrified.

'Esme?' Charlie said, alarmed. 'What's the matter? Are you all right?'

'Happy?' she gasped at him. 'You think I'm happy?'

Charlie was confused. 'Well, yes, in a Nigella sort of way, out here in your country birdhouse defrosting dead animals and growing the world's largest vegetables despite everything that's happened.'

An ache so deep she could not tell where it came from rose through Esme's chest and erupted in the form of a violent sob. She threw herself down on the kitchen counter, and, to her own and Charlie's horror, started to weep.

'Oh Lord.' Charlie leapt from his chair. 'Esme, what's the matter? Should I get someone? Esme, please. Are you all right? Shit, shit, shit. Should I get Pog? Oh, Esme.'

'I'm a bad mother,' sobbed Esme, 'and an awful wife and a horrible daughter-in-law. And then there's Granny Mac, oooh, Granny Mac . . .' She wept loud, sorry tears, heartbroken, into her arms, only vaguely aware of Charlie's awkward attempts to comfort her.

'I'm so sorry,' Charlie said as soothingly as he knew how. 'I should never have said anything. You're not at all amazing. Of course you're not. I'm so sorry, Esme, it's the booze. You're not happy, I can see that now. How could you be? Bloody stupid of me to suggest it. God, what an oaf. What a pig. An insensitive pig. I could just kick myself, really I could. Lord! What's the matter with me? Could be jet lag, I suppose, although I have been back five days, or is it four, and I did have a cold last month that took a bit of getting over—'

Esme lifted her tear-stained face and turned to look at him. 'Are you quite finished?' she asked, her tears drying.

'Oh hell, yes,' Charlie jumped back and wrung his hands uselessly. 'Yes. Totally finished. Completely. Utterly. Oh, Esme. What can I do?'

'You can give me a hanky,' Esme sniffed. 'And stop fluffing.' Charlie pulled a silk handkerchief from his pocket with lightning speed and thrust it at her.

'Here,' he said. 'And consider all fluffing as of this moment one hundred per cent stopped. Finito. Kaput.'

Esme laughed and blew her nose.

'I'm sorry, Charlie,' she said, so sadly that Charlie stepped closer again and took her in his arms, holding her tightly, wishing he knew what he could do to make her feel better and swearing to himself that if he knew what that was, he would do it.

'You're a good mother,' he said, her ringlets tickling his chin. 'And a good wife. You really are. You and Pog are the perfect couple.'

'I'm not,' Esme said, pulling away and handing Charlie back his handkerchief. 'We're not. I mean, we were, and I do love him, I love him with all my heart, I really, really do, but I just don't know if we can

49

bounce back to where we were, Charlie. There's just so much water gone under the bridge.'

'But of all the people I know, Esme, you deserve the most happiness.'

'Yes, well,' she said, as tears threatened to fall again, 'I'm starting to think that maybe I had my chance at happiness, Charlie. And maybe I'm not going to get another one.'

'Of course you will, Es. You must see that.'

'I don't know what I see these days,' she said, as a fat, lonely tear slid down her cheek. 'The only things I'm sure of seem locked in the past where I can't get to them. I mean, what say my big chance at happiness is back there somewhere? You know, in Venolat.'

'Oh, Esme. Not Louis. Not *still* Louis? After all these years?'

'Yes, Charlie. Still Louis. After all these years.'

Chapter Six

WHEN MORNING CAME to Venolat and sent a shaft of burning light through the shutters to hit Esme square in the right eye, she woke with a start and thought instantly of breakfast.

She took a shower and went downstairs, trying to ignore her throbbing headache. Charlie was sitting outside on the terrace, sunning himself and drinking orange juice out of a plastic bottle..

'Good morning,' he said chirpily. 'Caught up on your beauty sleep, then?'

Esme smiled and ran her fingers through her hair, as if there was even the remotest possibility that anything other than the strongest, most foul-smelling chemicals could ever straighten out its wayward kinks.

'I thought I might go to the bakery,' she said, 'and get us some breakfast. What do you fancy?'

Charlie sat up excitedly in his wrought-iron seat. 'Oh, yes, please, mistress,' he said in his best public-schoolboy voice. 'Something with custard and something with icing, if you'd be ever so kind.'

'Charlie, we are in France, not a Merchant Ivory film,' she said, grabbing the juice from the table and drinking out of the container herself. 'And unless I am mistaken I don't think France is especially known for its icing and custard. I think it is better known for its French bread and croissants. And brioche and—'

'Fine, fine, fine, yes, of course,' Charlie interrupted. 'Anything you like as long as it's food. I'm starving.'

Esme picked up her purse and trotted down the stairs, stopping to inspect herself, without admitting that was what she was doing, in the hall mirror by the front doors.

She had on an antique white slip dress she had bought at Portobello Market especially for the holiday. Its thin lacy straps sat daintily on her shoulders, showing off her long neck and passable collarbones (mole included) and containing beneath its fine, filmy cotton her bra-less nineteen-year-old bosoms, which sat pertly but not brazenly and were really only obvious if you were particularly looking for them.

The gentle film of freckles across her pale shoulders suited the dress, as did her loud, long mass of spiralling hair. Being ginger and freckly had not always been considered a winning combination, but Esme had to admit that the older she got the less she minded it.

She slipped outside into the burning morning sunshine and headed towards the *boulangerie*, her stomach quivering with something she thought must have been the result of last night's overindulgence— although a voice inside her head kept whispering to her that it could be something far more serious than that.

As the whisper got louder and the bread shop got nearer, however, her footsteps slowed. What was hope doing filling her head on an inno- cent trip to the bakery anyway, she thought. It was ridiculous. Childish. And this was only a routine visit to the local *boulangerie*, wasn't it? She was hungry, for God's sake. But for what? 'Oh, get a grip,' she said loudly to herself. This is real life, not a fairy tale. She was going to the bakery to buy some bread. End of story.

She pushed open the door of the *boulangerie* and almost swooned again at the smell. It was so, she couldn't put her finger on it—inviting, maybe? Comforting? Satisfying? No. Enticing? Maybe. She closed her eyes and sniffed. There was yeast and warmth, a soupçon of cinnamon, perhaps, a sweetness she couldn't place and the underlying tartness of salt.

Behind the counter, which was currently unmanned, row upon row of big brown round loaves sat side by side on wooden racks, staring out at her like smiling faces. There was no other bread in sight, not a baguette to be seen, just the fat round loaves, a basket of croissants and a bell. Esme felt herself shiver as she picked it up and gingerly rang it, the small sound seeming deafening to her.

She heard a door slamming back in the bowels of the bakery and the sound of feet fast approaching. Her heart raced as she felt her cheeks burning, and she tried to will them back to their normal colour.

A figure appeared in a flurry through the mesh-screen door behind the counter (that slap of timber on timber again!) and Esme felt herself gasp. Could it be?

It was the same dark hair, similar black eyes, a smile that had threads of the one she had seen the night before but was nowhere near as dazzling. And all this on a face that was considerably older and a body whose circumference was perhaps double that of the one by which she had previously been transfixed.

'Bonjour, mademoiselle,' the older, wider man said cheerfully. 'Qu'est-ce que vous voudrez?'

'Oh,' said Esme, suddenly unable to combine her fragments of schoolgirl French into anything remotely resembling a sentence. 'Croissants, please,' she said in her soft, confused British Isles accent. 'I mean, s'il vous plaît. Four.' She held up three fingers. 'Quatre.'

The man laughed. 'English?' he asked as he scooped four fat pastries into a paper bag.

Esme nodded.

'You are staying here in Venolat?'

She nodded again. 'Yes,' she said, 'it's lovely. C'est bon.'

He held the bag out to her. 'Anything else you would like?'

I would like to know where the younger, slimmer, sexier version of you is, Esme said to herself. To him she said nothing, as she looked round the shop in a drawn-out, overly contemplative fashion.

'What is your speciality?' she asked. 'Qu'est-ce que la spécialité de la maison, de la boulangerie?' She grimaced as she tortured the wide man's language, but his eyes stayed warm and friendly.

'It is plain,' he said, 'our speciality, but it is good. And it is certainly special.' He picked up one of the round brown loaves from the rack behind him and passed it over to Esme. She looked at it, uncertainly.

'Smell,' the wide man said, shoving it under her nose. 'Smell!'

Esme closed her eyes and breathed deeply. There was the warm yeasty smell that had enveloped her when she first came in. And the salt. And something else, too.

'Apple?' she opened her eyes and asked the baker. 'Pomme?'

'Yes, yes!' he nodded, pleased with her. 'Not many guess that. We make this bread, pain au levain, from apple, very old apple. It's in the starter, the chef. A long time since. Not bad for Anglaise. Good. Good.' He happily wrapped the bread in a sheet of bakery paper and passed it to Esme. 'For you,' he said. 'For nothing. I mean, for no cost.'

'Oh, I couldn't,' she said. 'You must let me pay.'

'You can pay for the croissants,' said the baker. 'Twelve francs, thank you, mademoiselle—but the *pain au levain* is a gift from me. You can repay me by coming back again, yes?'

Esme fumbled in her purse for the change. What about the boy? she wanted desperately to ask. What about the boy? But the question stayed stuck inside her as she shyly gathered up her bread and pastries, and, smiling at the wider, older baker, left the shop.

Every morning Esme repeated the journey. Every morning she convinced herself it had nothing to do with the boy. Every morning the question—Where is he?—threatened to burst out of her like a fork of lightning, but instead stayed broodily inside her head.

After a week, the vision by the fountain started to quiver and become unclear in her mind. Details got lost. The glisten of his sharp pink tongue as he licked his cigarette paper—had that not been in a movie she'd gone to in London? Perhaps, she thought gloomily, the moonlight had played a cruel trick on her and nastily presented the chubby middle-aged *boulanger* as the man of her dreams.

Two mornings later, though, something happened. When Esme woke up, it was not the man of her dreams who claimed her first thought. It was the *pain au levain*. She woke up tasting it, feeling its springy crumb bouncing around her mouth, its chewy crust battling her teeth.

She jumped out of bed, threw on an old pair of low-slung men's cricket trousers and a white tank top, and bounded down the stairs. Charlie was conked out in his ground-floor pit, but she knew he would be pathetically grateful to find the fresh bread ready and waiting for him when he awoke. They had given up the croissants after the first morning and concentrated instead on just the sourdough bread, which they ate with fresh homemade plum preserve Gérard at the *auberge* had given them. For lunch, they bought a slab of Brie from the Venolat corner store and smeared that on the *pain*, washing it down with a bottle of Bordeaux before planning the afternoon's sightseeing.

They fought over the crust. The crust made Esme's taste buds tingle. It was chewy and hard and had a powerful, almost cheesy flavour. It was in the crust that the sour nature of the dough left its calling card. The crumb was spongy and almost sweet to the taste, but the crust positively sang with the sharp, tart notes of apple vinegar and yeast.

The thought of it spurred Esme on as she practically skipped to the *boulangerie*, her mouth watering in anticipation. She flew round the corner and in through the *boulangerie* door, her eyes going straight to the happy smiling faces in their ancient wooden racks.

She opened her mouth to speak, but the *boulanger* got there first.

'Aha,' he said in a voice so smooth just listening to it felt like being wrapped in warm satin. 'The girl with the long red hair.'

Esme's mouth stayed open, but nothing came out of it.

It was not the old, fat baker with whom she had been sharing staccato chitchat for the past week. It was his younger, thinner shadow, the object of her moonlit vision, here in front of her.

Up closer, in the light of day, he was even more beautiful than she had imagined, and she had been imagining a lot. He was not tall, almost exactly her height, in fact, maybe an inch more, and she was fairly sure his hips were not as wide as hers, but he was wiry and strong.

His eyes were dark and shiny, like pools of something oily that fashionable shoes might slip on in a driveway. His skin was walnut brown and smooth on his arms, his neck, even his face, which looked as though it barely needed shaving.

'I'm Louis,' he said. 'Louis Lapoine.'

Esme closed her mouth and gulped, but couldn't think what the next normal step might be, so just stood there.

Louis smiled, as though this happened all the time, and reached for a loaf of bread, pulling out a sheet of wrap and placing it inside.

'My uncle tells me you are the only English person this summer who has not asked for a baguette,' he said, putting the bread on the counter in front of him and patting it.

Esme looked at the bread, then back at him. The words she had imagined saying were piled up in her throat, gridlocked.

'You are lucky to find us if it is *pain au levain* that you like,' Louis said softly. 'Nobody makes it much any more.'

Esme licked her dry lips and tried hard to breathe. She had not washed her face or done anything with her hair.

'The recipe has been in my family for two hundred years,' Louis continued, as though there were actually a two-way conversation going on. 'It has not changed in all that time. That's pretty good, hm?'

Esme, appalled at her own hopeless mawkishness, nodded woodenly, gulped and forced herself to say something.

'It's beautiful,' she finally managed in a creepy awestruck sort of a whisper, looking at the bread on the counter and thinking, as the words slid off her tongue, that they were totally the wrong ones to use.

Louis said nothing, just looked at her, the corner of his mouth and one eye uniting in an expression that could have been amusement, could have been alarm. Esme couldn't bear to humiliate herself any further and so jerkily forced her frozen body into a forward lurch, grabbed the bread from the counter, let the coins she had ready in her hand bounce and clatter out of her grasp, then willed her awkward limbs to turn her round and walk out of the shop.

'If you come back at midnight tonight,' Louis said coolly, astonishing her to a standstill at the doorway, 'I will show you everything.'

She turned and looked at him again, aware that she was having to try very hard not to drool. He nodded his head questioningly. Slowly, she nodded back. Then he smiled and disappeared through the screen door.

Esme stayed there staring for what seemed like an eternity. Her eyes remained focused on the spot where he had been, waiting for a sign that what she thought had happened had happened. And while no action replay ever came, Louis's velvet words still bounced around in her head telling her it was true, that he had asked her to meet him at midnight and he was going to show her everything.

It was too delicious for words.

'He's going to show you *everything*?' Charlie squawked when Esme jumped on his bed, woke him from his slumber, and repeated every word of the conversation in the *boulangerie*, leaving out only the bit where she stayed tongue-tied and lumpish and deeply unsexy.

'You said, "It's beautiful" and he said "Come back and I will show you everything"? I wonder what sort of everything he means.' Charlie sat up and rubbed the sleep out of his eyes.

'I just can't believe it,' Esme said with a shudder. 'It's like a dream, Charlie. You should see him. He is just so incredibly . . .' she searched for the right word, '*horny.*'

Charlie looked at her with renewed respect.

'Spoken like a real slut,' he said proudly. 'Details, please, mistress.'

'Oh, he's just gorgeous, Charlie. I can't tell you! I've never felt like this about anyone before. It just feels so fantastically—aaarrgggh.' Words failed her and she flopped onto the bed, her smile stretching as far across her face as it could manage.

Charlie gave her a funny look. 'Don't get too carried away, old girl,' he said. 'It's just your hormones waking up after spending your whole entire life in hibernation, after all. You've only just met the bloke, for goodness' sake. I mean, what say, for argument's sake, Louis just wants to show you how to bake bread?'

'I can't think of anything I would rather see more,' Esme said and she meant it. Nearly. She picked the loaf up from the end of the bed.

'OK,' said Charlie. 'OK. I believe you. It's just that I don't want you being hurt, Es, or disappointed.'

By ten to midnight, Esme's certainty that everything about Louis was fantastically 'aaarrgggh' had given way to the deep conviction that she had imagined the entire scenario and should probably, in the interests of bakers everywhere, go on a gluten-free tour of Siberia.

Charlie had gone out in search of more wayward Dutch boys, leaving Esme at home with her hammering heart, her topsy-turvy thoughts and half a bottle of Chablis, which she had taken in quick gulps between eight and nine thirty, for medicinal purposes only, she told herself, of course.

At two minutes to midnight she bolted out of the apartment feeling ridiculously Cinderella-ish and not at all sure that it wasn't the older, wider baker she was going to find whistling happily to himself behind the tantalising bakery counter.

Rounding the corner, she saw the faint glow of the bakery inner workings reflecting off the side of the fountain. Her mouth started to dry up and her knees to tremble, but she urged herself on, determined not to repeat her humiliating behaviour of earlier in the day.

As she approached the yellow-and-white-striped awning, a black figure stepped out of the shadows, the red glow of a cigarette the only bit of it she could clearly make out. She stopped and the figure moved into the moonlight. It was Louis.

Esme dumbfounded herself by laughing. The joyful sound, so light and happy, ricocheted round the little square, coming to rest neatly at Louis's feet.

'I was hoping you would come,' he said in his glossy voice with its seductive lilt.

'I was hoping I hadn't dreamt the whole thing up,' Esme answered, relief that she hadn't loosening her tongue. She reddened, which she hoped Louis couldn't see, and looked at his feet, where her laugh had finished. He was wearing white canvas espadrilles and she could see the bones of his ankles. She suddenly felt sick with the hopelessness of never having kissed that part of him, of any man.

Louis threw his cigarette butt on the ground and crushed it with a mesmerising twist of his hip.

'I have been trying to guess your name,' he said. 'You did not tell me.'

'Esme,' said Esme. Louis looked surprised.

'Esme,' he repeated. 'That's French, no?'

Esme was not equipped to lie convincingly at this point. 'No, it's Scottish actually,' she said. 'It was the name of a Highland terrier that belonged to my mother's next-door neighbour.'

Louis looked at her curiously and laughed. 'Well, as good a way to get a name as any, I suppose. Come,' he said, 'I will show you inside.'

He held out his hand and Esme, with almost indecent haste, reached for it. At the touch of his skin against her palm she could have sworn she felt a shock, and when he tightened his fingers round her hand she feared she was going to lose it completely. The feel of him, her first feel of him, just this tiny little bit of him, left her drooling, praying for more.

Inside, the front of the bakery was in darkness and the dim light shone out through the screen door. Louis pushed it aside and led her through into a narrow hallway lit with wall-mounted lanterns and smelling fragrantly of loaves past and present.

At the end of the hallway they passed a closed doorway and just beyond it turned down a set of ancient golden stone steps, trodden on so often over the years that smooth dips had been worn in the middle.

The stairs hugged two walls, turning a corner halfway and delivering Esme and Louis into the heart of the bakery.

For a moment, Esme just stood and soaked it all in: the smell, the feel, the taste, the promise of what was to come. She licked her glistening lips, her mouth watering.

The ceiling of the basement room was curved, as if built in a giant archway, and the bricks were burnt from golden brown at the bottom to chocolate brown in the middle to pitch black at the top. The smell was tantalising, so thick she could almost feel it, and the air was heavy and hot. She was glad she had worn just a thin white camisole and a vintage waist petticoat with her own espadrilles. The three hours spent choosing the outfit seemed now not to have been such a scurrilous waste of time after all.

The heart of the bakery was smaller than Esme had imagined. Along one wall sat a big mechanical stainless-steel mixing machine, next to it a long wooden bench, empty apart from a dusting of flour and an old-fashioned set of scales.

The opposite wall was filled with wooden racks, and at the end of the room through another small arch Esme could see the wood-stoked fire, not unlike the wood-fired pizza ovens that she had seen in Italian eateries at home.

'Someone has been baking bread down here for nearly six hundred years,' Louis said, his eyes following hers as she took everything in. 'First it was the monks who lived in Venolat—it was once a monastery, did you know?—and for a hundred and eighty-nine years it has been the Lapoine family.'

Esme traced a squiggle into the flour on the wooden bench, then inspected her floury fingertips. She wanted to know more about the bakery, the bread. But mostly she wanted to know more about him.

'You speak such good English,' she said.

'My best friend is English,' Louis said. 'The family moved here when we were both thirteen—that is seven years ago now—and we do a trade. I teach French. I learn English. It is good to share, no?'

He eyed Esme's top with a look she was sure was going to bring her out in blisters.

'It is good you wear white,' he said. 'You will not go home dirty.'

Oh, but I want to go home dirty, Esme silently trilled. Very, very dirty.

Louis watched her watching him, then looked up at a dusty anti-quated clock and clicked his tongue.

'It is time for me to start,' he said. 'If you sit on the stairs I can see you and tell you what I am doing. OK?'

Louis took off his T-shirt, revealing the corrugation of his ribs on his brown smooth chest and the silky black hair of his underarms. An army of goose bumps stood at attention from one end of Esme's body to the other.

He turned his back on her and she counted the muscles and sinews shifting and changing as he reached up and opened a chute coming down from the ceiling. A rush of flour hurtled into the steel mixing bowl. He closed the chute, turned on a tap sticking out of the wall and filled a tin bucket with water, which he also tipped into the bowl.

He switched the machine on and its gently rhythmic chugging filled up part of the room.

'In here,' Louis said, 'we keep our starter or our *levain*. You know what this is, no?'

Esme shook her head, her shiny, clean, twice-conditioned curls still bouncing way after her head had stopped moving. Louis turned to catch this and smiled.

'Sourdough, or *pain au levain*, as you know we call it, does not use yeast the way a baguette does, the way other bread does. We make our own yeast, our own rising agent, the *levain*, from the bacteria in the air, in this air. We made it for the first time a hundred and eighty-nine years ago with the juice of three apples from my great-great-great-great-great-grandfather's only tree.'

Louis laughed, a sound so sweet to Esme, despite the underlay of the mixer, that it seemed like singing.

'Great-great-great-great-great?' he said. 'Do I get that right? Yes, I think so.' Esme watched his shoulder blades stick out and recede again as he dipped his hand into the swirling dough. 'Anyway,' he continued, 'we make the *levain*, or *chef*, as some people call it, my uncle for one, way back then and every day we use it to make bread, then leave a bit behind for the next day, and the natural yeast in the *chef* becomes stronger and stronger and after all this time, you can see, well, you know, that it makes very good bread.'

Esme imagined running her fingers up his spine. 'How did apple juice ever make bread in the first place?' she asked.

'The apple juice ferments, fermented with the natural yeast in the Venolat air,' Louis said, turning the mixer off, pulling out the dough hook, and continuing to mix with his hands. 'After a couple of weeks, maybe, the many greats grandfather added flour and water, and every day after that he added more flour and more water, and then the *chef* got a life of its own. Finally, it had enough strength so that when he added it to more flour and water, it provided the gas to make the bread rise.'

His ear lobes looked edible. Esme was entranced. 'How did he know when it was strong enough?'

'He just knew,' answered Louis. 'Plus it would have been not a good colour and maybe it didn't smell so good. Sharp, like vinegar.'

His elbows were exquisite. 'And it never got so stinky you had to throw it away and start again?'

Louis turned round to face her, a light film of sweat shimmering on his forehead, one black curl plastered down above his eye.

'No, no, no,' he said. 'Stinky is not a bad thing. We would never throw the *chef* away. It is what makes Lapoine bread Lapoine bread. It is our special ingredient. The heart of the *pain au levain*. It makes us what we are.'

Esme stopped lusting and felt mortified. Here he was trying to share his passion with her and all she could do was ask idiotic questions. Her face must have registered her dismay because Louis's eyes softened.

'I mean that it is what we have. And if we had something different, we would not be making our bread, we would be making someone else's. *Tu comprends?*' He smiled at her and Esme noticed a little vein throbbing in his temple, the sight of which made her lips ache.

'Now I leave that dough in the mixer for two hours,' said Louis, turning towards the counter and pulling from beneath it a huge wooden box on wheels, 'and I work with this dough in the *pâtissier*.'

Louis pulled out a handful of the dough and half threw, half plopped it on the scales, which had they been given time to settle would have proved dead even. After doing this half a dozen times and getting it exactly right, Esme laughed out loud.

'How do you know?' she said.

Louis shrugged his shoulders, an enticing gesture from behind, and kept going. 'Practice makes perfect, don't you say?' he said. 'I have been working down here since I was seven years old. A *boulanger* can tell these things.'

When the counter was full of the right-sized dough lumps, Louis pulled out from underneath the far side of it a stack of willow baskets lined with linen, and one by one coddled each blob into a loaf-sized shape and slipped it into the basket. Then he pulled a low wheeled tray over from the other side of the room and stacked the baskets, four in each layer, one on top of each other, then filled the counter with baskets and repeated the process until the dough was all gone and the stack was taller than he was.

The rhythm of it was hypnotic. No movement was wasted. He weaved and wafted his way around the baskets like a wisp of smoke. His concentration was captivating. Esme was spellbound.

They had not spoken for nearly an hour, when Louis carefully wrapped the stack of baskets with a large linen sheet and turned to Esme. 'Draught is no friend of *pain au levain*,' he said. 'But me, I need fresh air.'

He stood on the stair next to Esme and held out his hand again. She took it, panicked that this meant he was dismissing her, that perhaps he had only meant to show her how to bake bread, that that was it. Yet what she needed he had not even started on. She followed him up the stairs, trying not to show her reluctance.

'What's in here?' she said, in a stalling manoeuvre, when they got to the top of the stairs by the closed door.

Louis looked at her with those deep, dark eyes, then opened the door, flicking on a switch that bathed the room in watery light. It was full of flour. Big white sacks of the dusty white powder were stacked against all four walls and the room had the most incredible smell, almost of nothing, but definitely of something. Esme was trembling, although the room was pleasantly warm. The heat of the bakery downstairs had left her sweating and the beads of sweat now stood to attention on her skin.

She turned to ask Louis where the smell came from, but he was standing so close she could think of nothing but what flavour his lips were. She looked straight into his eyes and when he put his hand on her arm, it was all she could do to keep from crying out.

Very gently, his fingers caressed the same spot on her arm until it felt like they were burning a hole in it and she thought she was going to have to pull away. Instead, she moved infinitesimally closer until just the slenderest gap separated them. Gradually, he fingered his way smoothly and seductively up to her shoulder, all the while their eyes meeting, their chests rising and falling in perfect time.

He wants me, Esme thought. She had never before wanted someone who wanted her back. It was a moment to savour and cradle.

It was also a moment to explore. And, seduced by her faith in what she was feeling, it was she who leaned in towards his exquisite face and sought out his lips with her own.

He tasted of bread. Sweet and sour at the same time and wonderfully, wickedly, wantonly warm. She drank him in. Could not stop.

Louis groaned beneath her lips and pulled her closer to him, his tongue exploring her neat white teeth and his hand sneaking up underneath her camisole and pressing against the small of her sticky, sweaty back. She pushed herself closer. She thrust her hips into his. She wanted to disappear into him. Her yearning overwhelmed her.

His other hand moved up behind her neck and snaked under her sodden hair as he pulled her into him. She ran her fingers over the wetness on his back, frantically tugging him to her despite them already being as close as two human beings ever could be.

Louis shuffled his thighs against hers, forcing her slowly backwards, and Esme let him, would have let him do anything, anything but leave. When the back of her calves hit something solid, she drew away from his lips momentarily as he lowered her onto a stack of flour sacks.

Esme wriggled back and pulled up her legs so Louis could climb in between them. Then she reached for him again and pulled his warm, delicious mouth close to hers. How had she lived without his kiss all these years, when now even a moment without it and she was lost? She pushed his wet hair back from his face, and licked the throbbing vein in his temple. He groaned again and lowered himself onto her as he buried his face in her neck. She felt the weight of his body on hers and treasured every pound, every ounce.

He lifted his head and she licked his ear, his neck, worked her way back to his lips again. Her kiss was drenched in a desire that went further, much further. But oh, to be kissed by this man! Esme didn't want it to stop. She wanted more. She felt his firm practised fingers run up and down her abdomen, then creep underneath her camisole. Louis's hand ran up her rib cage and found the nipple that had been waiting for him.

For a moment she disappeared. Just went. Somewhere she had never been before and could not describe in words. Somewhere heavenly. She was dough in his hands, his breadmaker's hands. She rose beneath his touch. And while he kissed her and kneaded her she soared out of her body, the bakery, the village, the world, until she swam drunkenly around in the starry ether, feeling things she had never, ever felt before.

Chapter Seven

WHEN THE ALARM went off at six on the third floor of the House in the Clouds the morning after Esme's champagne spree, her daily panic seemed to be sitting higher in her chest than it normally was, but she tried not to think about that, pushing it back down inside herself. Bread, she thought, bread.

She slipped out of bed, wincing slightly at the throbbing in her head, promising herself that she would never drink again, nor encourage Charlie to come and stay. He was lethal. She'd forgotten that about him. And she was not up for lethal these days.

Scraping around in her chest of drawers for something suitably hangover-ish to wear, she pulled out a cream cotton turtleneck that had lost its shape but gained a softness which she knew would be comforting next to her skin, which felt fragile and overstretched.

As she sat lightly on the bed and pushed her feet into her slippers a sharp snort from the other side heralded the waking of Pog. He rolled over, snuffling, opened his eyes and attempted a smile, despite his bleariness. His face was creased with marks from his pillow and his thick, difficult hair was all bunched up high on one side of his head. He looked so much like a little boy, so much like Rory, just like Rory, exactly like Rory, that for a moment Esme's entire body filled up with something hot and suffocating and she wondered if she could bear it.

'Are you all right?' Pog asked her, croakily, in a grown-up man's voice.

'Ssshh,' she whispered, aching with the hopelessness of her love for him. 'It's just morning. It's just bread time. Go back to sleep.'

Pog's eyelashes fluttered back down to his cheeks and his smile relaxed and slowly disappeared. Esme blew him a silent kiss and headed for the stairs.

In the kitchen, she pulled her jar of starter out of the pantry and remembered, with a shudder, what had gone on the night before. What had been said. What had been meant. She forced the matter out of her mind with a tuneless whistle as she dragged out the bin of flour, trying hard not to let its wheaty-ness seep into her consciousness and poke about where her memories were hidden.

Holding the starter as far away from her nose as she could, she mixed all her ingredients into the big caramel bowl, then pushed and pummelled the dough round the warm ceramic sides in an easy, steady rhythm until it formed the beginnings of a loaf. She tipped it onto the counter and left it sitting, pert and plump, while she fed the starter again, wiped up any spilt flour and returned the bin and the jar to their places in the pantry. She added the salt, then pushed up her sleeves to prepare for kneading the dough a second time.

The feel of her hands on her own arms as she did this, of skin upon skin, rang an ancient bell, but she stilled it. This was ridiculous! She had been making sourdough for fifteen years and it was not about Louis. It was not. It never had been. Well, perhaps a little, in the beginning, but not now. There could be nothing of his Venolat starter left in her own, now, or at least so little as to barely count. That was a whole lifetime ago and so much had happened since then. So much that had nothing to do with him. Since him she'd managed a career, marriage, motherhood and a heartbreak that made the one he caused feel like nothing more than an insect bite. So what was he doing now occupying so much of her mind?

She pressed her palm down into the dough and rolled it around, feeling it growing silky and smooth beneath her fingers. She flinched as she thought of herself wailing the night before about Louis and happiness. What on earth had possessed her?

Get a grip, she told herself, oiling the bowl and carefully placing her dough inside it to rise. Get a grip.

She felt a light film of sweat on her forehead, and as she lifted her hand to her head to wipe it away she caught sight under her armpit of Charlie. He was leaning against the handrail at the top of the stairs, wearing running shorts and clutching, if she wasn't mistaken, a newspaper. He looked unreasonably healthy.

'Work. I could stand here and watch it all day,' he drawled.

'And good morning to you,' Esme answered, hoping he could not tell what she had been thinking. 'What have you got there?'

'Went for a run to clear the head,' Charlie said, walking across the kitchen. '"Appropriated" the *Sunday Times* from outside the tea shop.'

'Get it away from me!' shrieked Esme, waving a tea towel at him. 'Throw it in the bin! Get it out of my sight!'

'Steady on, old girl,' Charlie said, dropping gracefully into a chair and opening the newspaper. 'It's the *Sunday Times*, not the *Sport*.'

From halfway across the room Esme could see Jemima's flawless face peering at her from the masthead, trumpeting the triumph of her column. Her headache returned. She felt sick.

'Remember Jemima Jones?' she asked Charlie, dully. 'That conniving little madam who shafted me at *TV Now!*?'

Charlie nodded. 'The pretty blonde with the legs up to her neck? Yes, I remember her.'

Esme flicked her tea towel in the direction of the glamorous photo on the front page. 'Still pretty, still blonde, still legs up to her neck, now spitting out perfect children and going to every bloody la-di-da function in the land and writing about it.'

'For the *Sunday Times*? Really?' Charlie was impressed. 'Sounds like just the sort of thing you might have done once upon a time.'

If that was true, it was no wonder Esme felt so enraged. She slumped into a chair and pulled out the Style section.

'Anybody else and I wouldn't mind, truly I wouldn't,' she insisted as she opened it up. 'But some people just get all the breaks and it's not fair. You shouldn't be allowed to be gorgeous-looking and lucky.'

Jemima smiled out at her, wearing a gold bikini, her hipbones razor sharp, a sparkling blue swimming pool in some fancy new resort in the Maldives twinkling behind her.

'*The sun and a wrinkle-free visage good friends do not make,*' Esme read, '*but when one is invited to fly First Class to Toss Kroker's newest luxury hotel to party with four hundred beautiful people, and dine on lobster cooked fifty different ways by Gordon Ramsay, Alain Ducasse and an entire village of minions, one simply ups the dosage of Ambre Solaire and throws a thong or five in the Birkin bag!*'

'Oh, for Christ's sake!' protested Esme, but Charlie was lost to the finance pages.

'*Toss has done a wonderful job of throwing up this modest little three-hundred-and-fifty-room palace with nine restaurants, three bars, two night-clubs and enough Philippe Starck to render the rest of the world sadly bereft of egg-shaped baths. Plus he's had the good sense to poach Christien, the foot god from the spa at Claridge's, so no tiny toenail goes unclipped or unpolished. And for just a hundred pounds you can even get your urine checked at the Matt Roberts gym to find out if you should be on the treadmill or the yoga mat. Don't ask me how that works—I was concentrating solely on ingesting fluids.*'

'Who says "ingesting"?' Esme demanded. 'Nobody, that's who.'

'*And speaking of fluids,*' Jemima continued, '*I would just like to point out that a martini is a martini and there is not and never will be a substitute. If you make it with sake, it is not a saketini, it is mouthwash. If you have the imagination to invent a new drink, for goodness' sake invent a new name as well.*'

'What's wrong with calling a martini made with sake a saketini?' Esme wanted to know, jiggling Charlie's paper to get his attention.

'Well, if it's made with sake it's not a martini,' Charlie said. 'It's another drink altogether and probably not a very nice one.'

'Oh, shut up, then,' Esme muttered crossly. 'If you are going to agree with everything she says you can just go back to your stocks and bonds.'

'All right then, read me out a bit and I promise not to agree with it.'

'*Mysteriously non-ageing Lothario Jeffrey Timms,*' Esme read out loud, '*threw an extremely high-energy fortieth at a friend's villa in Little Venice during the week. "It's amazing, really," a crinkled blonde slurred to me in the hallway, "we went all the way through school together yet I've just turned forty-six."*' Charlie let out a hoot of laughter which Esme quashed with a look. '*Mr Timms greeted guests at the door with a display of cartwheels and handstands, made all the more exciting by the fact that he was wearing a kilt, sans undergarments. Still, he was the belle of the ball until the caterers set fire to a side of beef and the local fire brigade turned up, fully dressed and oozing truthfully youthful charm. Next to them, Mr Timms's offering seemed some-what dry and withered, to say the least.*'

Charlie could not contain his mirth.

'But it's not funny!' Esme said.

'It is so!' he spluttered. 'An old wrinkly Jeffrey Timms cartwheeling down the hallway with a dry and withered offering? Normally, you'd think that's hilarious.'

'I would not.'

'You would so!'

'I would not.'

At that moment, Rory saved them from drawing out their childish spat by appearing at the top of the stairs in his karate suit, his hair, Esme noticed, brushed neatly back and, if she was not mistaken, slicked down with some of the hair gel she was constantly buying Pog. 'Hello,' the little boy said with feigned nonchalance to Charlie.

'You're up early,' Esme said, entranced by Charlie's effect even on a small boy. Was that normal? God! What if Rory was gay? She contemplated this possibility as she abandoned the newspaper and absently got her son's breakfast things together. Actually, come to think of it, she would probably prefer he *was* gay. Little Cosmo Jones was clearly gay, after all, and that didn't seem to bother anyone. Rory could go into business with Pog as an interior designer.

The sound of her possibly gay son fishing around in the pantry brought her back to earth. Rory emerged with a blue-and-white-striped Cornishware jug. 'Very nice,' Esme said, looking at it. 'Fashionably modern yet authentically retro. What made you choose that one?'

'It's the only one I could reach,' answered Rory plainly. 'Come on.'

'You know what,' said his mother, 'I've got a fantastic idea. Why don't you take Charlie out and he can show you how to milk The Goat.'

Before Charlie could finish his snort of derision, Rory had grabbed him by the hand and was tugging him towards the stairs. Charlie turned back to Esme with a disturbed look on his face. 'What's a goat again? Is it the one with the twisty horn on the front of its head?'

'That's a unicorn, silly,' said Rory. 'They don't exist.'

'Help, Esme,' Charlie whined pathetically.

'I'm sure your magic works just as well on the animal kingdom as it does on the human one,' Esme said with a sweet smile. 'There are plenty of wellies by the door—I strongly suggest you grab a pair.' She never had got round to pooh patrol.

She sliced herself a wedge of yesterday's bread, almost better than fresh with one day under its belt, smeared it with blue cheese and quince paste, poured herself a cup of tea and moved a kitchen stool to one of the tiny windows for a good view of what was about to happen in her garden.

From her position near the clouds, Esme could see The Goat tense up as she lifted her head from the newly planted nasturtiums on which she was feasting and clapped eyes on the boys coming towards her.

As Charlie and Rory were about to close in on The Goat, however, Esme was amazed that instead of leaping away at great speed, The Goat stood her ground. As the familiar little boy and the strange new man approached she simply looked at them with interest, her head cocked to one side in a contemplative and not particularly combative fashion.

'Don't tell me the bloody Charlie Edmonds charm *does* work on goats,' Esme said to herself as she pressed her face closer to the window.

In the garden, Charlie and Rory got within five yards of The Goat before Rory's confidence gave out and he handed the jug up to Charlie.

Rory pointed at The Goat's rear end and Charlie's gaze followed the little boy's finger. The Goat, whose face Esme could see, seemed to be looking almost coquettishly at him. Esme could swear the ruminating bloody mammal was batting her eyelids as Charlie came right up to her and slowly, apparently taking instruction from Rory, started to bend down and proffer the jug towards The Goat's nether regions.

At that moment, the delightful creature spun round, quick as a flash, lifted both hind legs and kicked Charlie so hard that he staggered backwards, the jug flying in the air, tripped over a spade lying in the grass behind him and fell on his bottom at Rory's feet, clutching his groin.

Esme, her smirk gone, leapt to her feet and ran to the stairs, sprinting down them and shouting in panic, 'Pog! Pog! The bloody Goat's got Charlie!' Brown skittered and scampered behind her as she bounded down the stairs two at once, still a time-consuming effort, grabbed a tennis racket from the hallway and dashed outside and round the side of the house. She could see that The Goat was now scratching at the ground with her front hoof, clearly getting ready to charge her wounded foe and his little friend.

'You evil bloody bitch!' Esme cried as she ran towards them, hurling the tennis racket in her fury as she did. Charlie was sitting up, looking pale and shaken but at least conscious, and Rory was crouched behind him, being brave but obviously frightened.

The tennis racket sailed nowhere near the offending animal but The Goat saw it all the same and did not appreciate the sentiment. Turning her attention away from the boys, she launched herself at the exposed and weaponless Esme. Esme gasped and spun round, only to see Henry coming out of the house towards her, red in the face and waving his stick. Despite her fear of being mauled by The Goat, her dread of leading the vicious animal to her father-in-law and having to live with the consequences of that forced her to half spin again and swerve round the other side of the house. If she could make it to the gate, she reasoned, trying not to hear the rat-a-tat-tat of The Goat's hoofs beating a frightening and fast-approaching tattoo behind her, she could probably jump it and leg it up the steps of the windmill to safety.

'Help!' she panted, as the hoof beats got closer. The Goat had very pointy horns, after all. 'Help!'

The fence lay straight ahead, hardly more than ten yards away, as Esme's legs burned with adrenalin and her breath tore at her lungs. She was so close! But not close enough. She felt something rip savagely at the denim of her jeans just behind her left knee and, hysterical and panicked, she stumbled and plunged forward with a desperate cry, hearing as she did a terrifying clanging followed by a spine-chilling shriek and a loud thump, none of it anything to do with herself hitting the ground.

Gasping for air and in a state of total confusion, Esme realised that she was still alive. She twisted round to see Charlie towering over The Goat's motionless carcass, which lay near her feet. The shovel he was holding appeared still to be vibrating slightly, which left Esme to assume that The Goat had worn it around her head with quite some force.

Before she could think or speak or move, Henry limped round the corner, equally breathless and agitated, with Rory bringing up the rear.

Esme watched Henry's face as he beheld The Goat lying there with her tongue hanging out of her mouth and blood dribbling out of her nose. At that moment, Pog's head, wet from the shower, appeared out of the window on the third floor above them.

'What on earth is going on?' he asked.

Henry had not yet regained his breath, Charlie was still stunned at the level of his own violence and Esme remained on an emotional roller coaster between bewilderment, horror and hysteria.

Only Rory had the wherewithal to answer his father.

'The Goat's dead, Daddy,' he said with much less emotion than one might have expected. 'She kicked Charlie in the nuts and he killed her.'

Esme grabbed at a lungful of air and looked up at Pog, who was frowning now in a strict fatherly way.

'Don't say nuts, Rory,' he said. 'It's not nice.'

She felt a small amount of astonishment that her husband would correct her son's language, mild really in the circumstances, when a family friend had just killed their goat. It didn't seem entirely appropriate.

'Well,' she said, ignoring Pog and getting carefully to her feet, examining herself for serious injury, 'you know what Granny Mac would say.'

She looked at Rory who looked straight back, his face remaining blank for a few seconds, until, like the sun breaking through the clouds on a bleak, grey day, it lit up, transforming the entire landscape of his personality. 'There's bin a murrrrrder,' he cried enthusiastically in a perfect Scottish burr as he beamed at his mother, then Henry, then Charlie.

There was a split second's silence before Charlie and Esme both started to laugh. Rory, thrilled with this impact, jumped up and down around the dead goat shouting, 'There's bin a murrrrrder! There's bin a murrrrrder!' while Pog retreated inside the window.

Henry, shaking his head with customary disgust, ignored everybody and moved stiffly closer to The Goat, prodding her corpse with his stick.

At this, the infernal creature scared the living daylights out of the lot of them by leaping to her feet in a show of being very much alive. Esme shrieked, Rory ran behind his grandfather and Charlie's hands flew to his aching private parts to protect them from further attack.

The Goat, however, had quite lost her vicious streak. She stood wobbling on all fours, then blinked and teetered unsteadily towards them, like a nervous young hostess trying to keep her composure after overdoing it on the vodka tonics. Esme and Charlie stood aside and watched as she proceeded to walk straight into the side of the house.

'Yes, well,' said Charlie. 'Not a murder after all, eh? Not even manslaughter by the looks of things.'

Henry pushed past him, leaning heavily on his stick. 'Much as you find this all terribly funny,' he said in a cold, pinched voice, 'it would probably be a good idea to take the poor creature to the vet in case she needs to be put out of her misery.'

'Of course, sir,' Charlie said, 'you are absolutely right. I shall take her myself. It's entirely my fault.' He patted The Goat's back, rather awkwardly, and indicated for Rory to come and help him.

A couple of hours later, after Charlie had taken the goat to the vet in his Audi convertible—causing quite a stir in the village by all accounts—and the animal had been proclaimed blind but in all other respects remarkably healthy, he and Esme sat in the kitchen drinking tea and reliving the event.

'Well, I can't see Nigella Lawson topping that, Es. You should really have your own column.'

'Don't talk to me about columns,' Esme shot back. 'You *friend* of Jemima Jones.'

'I don't think Jemima Jones is the problem,' he said.

'God, you and Granny Mac!'

Charlie looked confused, but ploughed on. 'About last night, Esme,' he said carefully. 'I'm worried about you, sweet.'

'It was all that champagne,' Esme said quickly. 'I didn't mean it. I don't know what I was talking about. It's not about Louis, Charlie. That was years ago. I probably wouldn't recognise him if I fell over him and he probably wouldn't even remember me. I was just Holiday Romance Number one hundred and seventeen.'

'No, you weren't,' Charlie said with such heartfelt tenderness that Esme found herself pressing on.

'It's just that sometimes,' she said, 'when things get on top of me, I wonder what it would be like if things had been different, back then, in Venolat, if it had turned out differently. If he and I had ended up together. It's silly, Charlie, really it is, but when things are tough I just remember that feeling of being in love with him and it was such a wonderful feeling. So strong and powerful and all-consuming. Delicious, really. And I wonder what it would be like to feel like that again.' She stopped, suddenly feeling naked and silly. 'Well, you know what I mean. You're the expert after all—falling in love every five minutes.'

Charlie looked blank. 'I'm not the one to talk to about love, Esme. I wouldn't recognise it if it came up and bit me in the backside. I'm more of a lust chap, really. Less complicated that way.'

'There must have been someone, Charlie, somewhere along the line, who made you feel sick and obsessed and despondent and ecstatic and crazy and all mixed up.'

Charlie laughed. 'Why would anyone want to feel like that? It sounds horrible. Why would you want to put yourself through it? I can't remember you putting yourself through it with Pog. Did you?'

'Pog was different,' Esme said. 'I love him with all my heart and soul, I really do, plus I know for a fact that he loves me more than he loves anyone else in all the world but,' and she hated the sound of that little word, 'it's just not like it was with Louis.'

Charlie looked at the old railway clock on the wall above Esme's head and pushed back his chair.

'Crikey, I'd better be going,' he said. 'Sorry not to be more help, Es, but you know I'm hopeless on the deep and meaningful stuff and much as I would like to stay and deafen your sheep or amputate your bees, I am actually pretty whacked after blinding the goat so I should head off.' He came round the table to kiss her goodbye, then caught sight of Jemima in her gold bikini, still lying brazenly on display.

'Bloody hell, is that her?' he breathed. 'Nice boobs, I must say. She's looking pretty fantastic, isn't she, Es? Well, I can see why you are miffed. God, look at those shoes—they must have cost her a fortune.'

When Esme realised he was not joking, but truly impressed, she snatched the page of the newspaper off the table and screwed it up.

'Thank you for your support, Charlie,' she said. 'This is the woman who is taunting me and all you can do is ogle her slingbacks and leer at her fake boobs, which are of no use to you whatsoever.'

'I don't know what you're so put out about,' Charlie said. 'Jemima Jones might be bitter and twisted about not living in a giant birdhouse in the country, for all you know. It's just a matter of choice, Essie. You made yours and she made hers. She just gets better shoes.'

Chapter Eight

'I'VE JUST CAUGHT Ridge shagging the next-door neighbour!' Alice cried down the phone a week later. 'In his room—at ten o'clock in the morning. Sunday morning! Mrs Bloody Miller, of all people. Oh, Es, what am I going to do?'

'Calm down, calm down,' Esme soothed. 'Which one is Mrs Miller? The blowzy mid-morning gin drinker or the mousy beige librarian?'

'Neither,' said Alice, 'she's the sexy, saucy newlywed, you know, from directly upstairs.'

'Blimey,' breathed Esme, 'the one that married the meaty, beefy, big and bouncy kick-boxer?'

'Yes,' moaned Alice. 'What am I going to do? If the meaty, beefy, big and bouncy kick-boxer finds out he will squash Ridge like the useless little worm he is.'

'Well, how's he going to find out? She's not going to tell him and neither is Ridge, I imagine. And you're not either, I hope. Alice, what are you thinking?'

'I'm thinking it's too hard to be the mother of a sixteen-year-old.' Alice's voice cracked. 'I don't feel grown-up enough. Nothing I do is right and nothing he does is right, either. It's horrible. I liked it when he was little and I was all he had and he loved me. I'm sorry, Esme. I know you don't need this but I just can't help it.'

'Oh, Alice,' Esme said, feeling dreadful on her friend's behalf, 'he still loves you, it's just hormones. It's normal to be shagging everything that moves when you're his age. You were.'

'You weren't,' cried Alice. 'You saved yourself. He idolises you, you know. I'm sure he wishes you were his mother. He looks at your lovely family with your house in the country and your doting husband and your labrador dog and he wonders why he couldn't have had all that.'

Esme was staggered. 'The house needs round-the-clock cleaning,' she said. 'The dog uses its bladder as a weapon and I did not save myself, I just never fancied anyone until, you know, Louis. It wasn't a good thing, really. I've never been able to quite get him out of my system.'

Alice's sniffling got quieter. 'You still have Louis in your system?'

'A little,' said Esme, wishing she hadn't said anything. What was Louis doing in her thoughts, in her conversations? She had been battling him all week. But like those invisible grains of Venolat flour still left in her jar of starter, bits of Louis remained ingrained and untraceable in Esme herself. 'Well, more than a little I suppose.' She caught her bottom lip between her teeth and willed herself to stop it there. 'I'm just thinking about him at the moment because Charlie's been here and sort of raked the whole thing up.'

'What do you mean, "raked the whole thing up"?'

'Oh, you know. Talking about Venolat and the boy I left behind sort of thing. Dredging up all those hideous old feelings. Oh, it's too silly to even talk about, Alice. It's nothing. Just some ridiculous middle-aged fantasy that helps me while away the seconds between cleaning the oven, ironing the clothes, scrubbing the toilets, that sort of malarkey.'

'You *fantasise* about him?' Alice stressed. 'Well, that sounds like more than thinking about him a little, if you ask me.'

'Can we stop talking about this now?' asked Esme. 'What are you going to do with Ridge?'

Alice cleared her throat. 'He is grounded for the rest of his natural life,' she said. 'And I am not going to let him watch Sky for a week.'

'Oh, that will really show him,' said Esme supportively. 'And what exactly do you expect him to do with his spare time when there is a saucy neighbour upstairs just waiting until she hears your footsteps in the hall so she can pop round for a cup of milk?'

Alice groaned. 'I never thought of that,' she said wetly. 'What's the opposite of grounding someone?'

Rory appeared at Esme's knee, a frown crinkling the flawless skin above his earnest brown eyes.

'Scuse me, Esme,' he interrupted politely.

'Just a minute,' Esme said to Alice, holding the phone away and pulling Rory's face towards her to give it a kiss.

'What is it, darling?' she asked him.

'We want to go fishing.'

Esme looked out of the window. The sea mist that had clung to the trees all morning had lifted, leaving it a spotlessly clear blue day.

'What a wonderful idea. I'll check on you with Daddy's binoculars, shall I? You could take your pirate flag and wave it at me.'

Rory looked uncertain. 'Aren't you coming?' he asked her.

'I'm just about to put the bread in, darling. It will be piping hot and crunchy just the way Daddy likes it by the time you get back. You run along and have fun.' She kissed his orange curls. 'Bring me back a whale,' she called after him, turning back to the phone.

'She's not coming,' Rory told Henry, who was waiting outside his room for his grandson.

'She's not coming,' Henry told Pog when they picked him up at his shed.

'She has to put the bread in,' Rory said, reaching for his father's hand.

The three of them walked to the Meare in silence.

Pog pulled a wooden dinghy into the shallow water and helped Henry climb stiffly into it, then hoisted Rory and his fishing rod inside and jumped in himself, picking up the oars. Like most locals, they paid Mrs Coyle fifty pounds a year for the right to use the hire boats whenever they wanted to as long as tourists weren't left queuing. About once a fortnight, weather permitting, they went out, but on their last few excursions Esme had been missing.

It was peaceful, the bark of a distant dog and the oars hitting the water the only sounds they could hear. Rory was facing his father, his grandfather behind him. The little boy's rod lay at his feet, his attention turned to the House in the Clouds, straddling the trees above them.

'Daddy?' He turned back to his father. 'Is there something wrong with Esme?'

Pog kept rowing, didn't falter, didn't meet his father's eye.

'No, Rory,' he answered. 'There's nothing wrong with Esme.'

Henry coughed, uncomfortably.

'She's been crying in Granny Mac's room,' Rory said.

'In Granny Mac's room?' Pog asked casually. 'Whatever do you mean?'

'I've heard her,' Rory answered. 'Sometimes there's laughing too. Isn't there, Granddad?'

Pog looked over Rory's head at his father. Henry gave a shrug.

Pog sighed. 'Your mother's just sad, Rory,' he said. 'But she'll be all right. You just have to let her be sad for a while.'

'How long?' Rory asked.

'I don't know,' Pog answered truthfully. 'But she's baking bread again and that's a good sign, don't you think?'

Henry felt panicked by the rawness of emotion on board the little boat. It was too close for his comfort.

'I think I just saw a carp, Rory,' he said. 'Do you have the bait?'

'Esme likes bread more than anything, doesn't she, Daddy?' Rory asked, pulling out a hardened heel of sourdough. His little fingers struggled to get the hook through the crust.

'Not more than anything, Rory. It's just very important to her. Dad, could you help him with that? He's going to hurt himself.' Pog dipped the oars in the water and gently rowed them back to where Henry had seen the carp.

'Why?'

'Why is it important to her? Well, you know that story, Rory. Mummy went to France when she was just a girl and a baker gave her the magic ingredient for her special bread and she's baked it every day since then.'

'Why?'

'Because it makes her feel good,' Pog told his son.

'Why?'

'Oh, Rory, do we have to play this game?'

'Yes, I thought we were here to catch fish,' Henry said grumpily. There was something in his tone that rankled with Pog, and with a start he realised that his father's uneasiness was replicated in his own churning stomach. Was Pog turning into a man who could fidget and bluster and ignore what was going on in front of him? He thought he had been doing the right thing, leaving time to heal Esme's wounds. But what if he was wrong? What if he had let Esme be sad for too long already? What if he was just being Henry all over again?

Pog looked up at the House in the Clouds and felt all the things he wanted to say to her float up towards the surface, stopping just short of it, like crocodiles submerged in a river, lethal but invisible. No, he *was* different. He knew his wife. She just needed time. He was sure of it.

'I'll tell you what, when we've caught our fish we'll go and buy Esme some of Mrs Coyle's homemade chocolates, shall we?' he suggested, spinning the little dinghy round. 'And the Sunday paper. That will cheer her up.'

Esme at that exact moment was being cheered up anyway, courtesy of Charlie Edmonds, who had just rung to invite her down to London for lunch the following day.

'Time to dust the cobwebs from your glad rags, missus,' he said. 'Meet me at the Orrery in Marylebone High Street. Their scallops will leave you drooling.'

Her good humour, however, did not last long. The chocolates only went halfway to assuaging her irritation at having Pog hand over the latest instalment from Jemima.

'Oh, I am going to *vomit*,' Esme dramatised later that afternoon as she sat on Granny Mac's bed, flapping her hand at invisible smoke and blanking out 'The Killing of Georgie'. 'It's just revolting, Granny Mac, it really is. The gall of this woman. Honestly. I can't believe they publish it. There should be a law.'

Granny Mac scorched her with her indifference. 'I don't know what all the fuss is about,' she said.

Esme threw the newspaper aside. 'I might have ended up having her career if I had played the game the way she did,' she railed. 'It could be me with a fancy column in the *Sunday Times*.'

'I didn't realise you wanted someone else's career,' Granny Mac said drily. 'Here was me assuming you were happy with the one you had.'

'Mine was hard work!' argued Esme. 'I had to work twelve hours a day to earn probably half what Jemima Jones gets for being a serial gate-crasher between seven and nine. It just seems to come so easily to her, Granny Mac. It always has.'

'And you wanted it to come more easily to you?'

Esme could barely understand her own chagrin, let alone explain it.

'Maybe if things had come easier,' she said, 'if I hadn't had to work the bloody hours, to try so hard . . .'

'What?' Granny Mac asked softly. 'What might have been different?'

Esme closed her eyes and tried not to think about the chaos, the turmoil, the devastation, the end of her life back in London.

She opened her eyes and concentrated instead on the photo of Jemima.

'Will you look at the size of that rock!' she exclaimed, suddenly noticing the diamond on Jemima's wedding finger. 'It must be four carats at least. It's bloody enormous.'

'Well, are you going to read me what the wretched woman has written or not?' Granny Mac boldly demanded. 'A person could die of boredom lying here listening to your wittering all day long.'

Esme shook the broadsheet newspaper for dramatic effect and started to read. *'What a week—why, my feet (thanks for the pedicure, Christien!) have barely touched the ground. It started on Monday night with an evening of thespian brilliance at the newly refurbished Court Theatre in N1. I didn't quite make it to the play itself—Marie Claire was getting her first bikini wax and needed my support—but the drinks afterwards were a riot. Gorgeous leading man Lin Forbes and I spent ages sipping courtinis (!) and discussing the pros and cons of being super-talented. In fact, we'd probably still be there now if pregnant single supermodel Minty Kloss hadn't caused such a sensation by turning up in a teeny-weeny Hawaiian skirt and a bra made of coconut shells. Apparently, she had got her invitations muddled and a luau in Brixton was sadly minus her presence. Anyway, as if her entrance wasn't quite enough of a spectacle, offering up one of the coconuts as an ashtray some time later certainly was. She's not even going to feel that little head shooting down the birth canal, it will be so small. Lucky her.'*

'That is so rude,' said Esme. 'I can't believe how rude she is. Can you believe how rude she is? It's just plain rude.'

'Get on with it, will you,' Granny Mac exhorted her.

'Sadly, I had to forgo attending the celebrity premiere of the new movie by that Finnish film director who wins so many awards, in favour of spending some quality time with GQ, our middle child who's very clever, especially at mathematics. I think he'll end up in banking like his father. Anyway, the poor child is being persecuted by his schoolmates for his dedication to his studies. I won't tell you what school, that would be unfair—but all nasty little boys in blue-and-grey-striped blazers should be very careful or they'll feel the grille of the Volvo station wagon on their backs. Just joking!'

Esme was so disgusted by that stage, she threw the paper down on the bed for the last time and left the room. There were dirty clothes to be washed, washed clothes to be ironed, ironed clothes to be hung in closets, an oven to be cleaned, floors to be mopped, an old man to be attended to, a small boy to be entertained and a husband to catch up with. She did not have any more time to waste on Jemima Jones.

Chapter Nine

ON THE TRAIN down to the city the next morning, Esme wondered why she had chosen to wear her La Perla bra, from the good old days. She was now at least a size bigger than she had been when she bought it, and the underwire was practically slicing her in two.

She hadn't mentioned to Pog, in the chaos of the morning, that she was going to be in London for the day. She had simply dropped Rory round the corner to Mrs McArthur, who looked after him sometimes on days he wasn't booked in with Mrs Monk, and then made her way directly to the station.

The morning had been a nightmare. Rory had woken up evil with grumpiness, Henry's hip was obviously giving him gyp, so he had a permanent black cloud above his head, and Pog had been completely preoccupied by an early-morning phone call from Ernie Albrecht, who was considering adding a pergola to his dumpy little house.

As a result, her nerves were so jangled that she had nearly burnt the sourdough, which never happened. After all these years she had developed a built-in timer in her head, and her nose could pick up the scent of her bread being almost ready to come out of the oven.

That morning, though, she had been so busy trying to wax her legs, get Rory out of his Spiderman pyjamas, clean cobwebs and bits of orange goop off Brown, who had been somewhere disgusting, listen to Pog talking about some coach lanterns, tidy the kitchen, pick some courgettes, that her nose had nearly let her down.

She'd been out in the garden when Henry, of all people, had opened a window and simply said in that clipped, controlled manner of his, 'Bread, Esme.' It was amazing how two such ripe and juicy words could shrivel and die on the wrong lips.

She'd only just caught the bread in time. The crust would be extra hard and sharp, but the crumb would still be delicious. She wrapped it in grease-proof paper and popped it in her tote bag to take to Charlie.

Anyway, in all of this she had not mentioned her plans for the day to Pog, and, sitting sweatily as the train clattered towards London, it occurred to her that she probably should have left a note. As the train drew into Liverpool Street Station, she surreptitiously patted her damp-ening armpits and pulled down the front of her top. High-necked but vaguely see-through, it gave her an excellent cleavage which, while wasted on Charlie, made Esme feel saucy again. And it was hard to feel saucy these days, given that she was usually covered in animal hair, up to her armpits in compost or covered in glue and sticky paper, while Rory sat in a corner saying in that calm, grown-up little voice of his, 'But you said you *knew* how to make a kite.'

Marylebone High Street had undergone a complete personality trans-plant since she'd last been there. Once a slightly dowdy, often forgotten poor relation of its fashionable neighbours Soho and Mayfair, it had become something of a spangly starlet in its own right.

There were smart bars and coffee shops wherever she looked, and trendy furniture and clothes shops too. She checked her watch and was slightly dismayed to find herself with twenty minutes to wait before meeting Charlie at the Orrery. She tried to start dawdling towards the restaurant, but Esme was not a dawdler by nature. She did everything at a hundred miles an hour, she was known for it. Even before pregnancy and old people and animals, loitering had not been an option. In the magazine world, everything was done at a rush to meet, or at least not miss by too much, ridiculous deadlines.

Motherhood had slowed her down, obviously, but not that much. Not enough, anyway, Esme thought, abandoning her lingering and deciding to go to the restaurant and have a posh cocktail, a something-tini no doubt, after all.

The Orrery did look beautiful, she could see why Charlie liked it. Exquisitely understated, not much colour, not much noise—the exact opposite of Charlie himself really, but the menu read so well she had to fight hard to keep herself from salivating.

'You must be Esme.' A waitperson of around twelve years of age, Esme gauged, approached her, surprising her by knowing her name. 'Mr Edmonds has called and sends his apologies but he's going to be half an hour late. Would you like to wait in the bar? My colleague Michael makes a mean French 75.'

'Is that the one with gin and champagne?' Esme asked. 'Because I had six of those once before and I never did find that camisole again.' With a jolt she realised what she was doing: flirting with a boy young enough, in some cultures, to be her grandson. She really did not get out enough.

'You know there's a Conran Shop next door,' the boy said, kindly ignoring her, 'if you're not keen on a cocktail.'

The Conran Shop was full of willowy wisps wafting around either shopping or working there, it was hard to tell which. Esme sucked in her stomach even though her nylon-mesh and Lycra-mix top was supposed to do that for her, and tried her best to waft too.

Rounding a corner on the second floor of the store, however, she happened upon a sitting receptacle of the utmost elegance, a Barcelona chair, and her stomach popped right out again as she admired it. Pog had often rattled magazines in her direction and pointed out the exact same chair, a big square combination of leather and chrome apparently designed for the King and Queen of Spain, and all Esme had done was pour scorn on the cost—£1,000 indeed. For a chair?

But in the flesh, the chairs were rather inviting. Deciding against the white one for fear of dirtying it, Esme sat herself down in the black one, wriggling her way to the back of it and stretching her legs out in front of her, luxuriating in the feel and comfort and price.

She closed her eyes and imagined being the queen of something, but almost immediately her stomach began to rumble and she was reminded that lunch was the reason she was in London. She opened her eyes and stood up, or tried to, but something kept her from rising.

This had happened to her before, on a seat covered in graffiti travelling at sixty miles per hour beneath the city. She thought about the tube and how she had lurched off it at Marylebone Station. A belch of panic worked its way up from her hungry stomach. She was 99 per cent sure she was stuck to the chair with someone else's gum.

Taking a deep breath, she wrenched herself sharply up and away. Unable to look at the chair, she instead swivelled her black skirt round so that its back was at her front and sure enough, a great gob, even worse, half a great gob of pink bubble gum was smeared across her rump. Slowly, she turned round to inspect the chair—the other half of the gum was there, sitting plumb in the middle of the black leather.

Why did these things have to happen to her? She bet nothing like this ever happened to Jemima Jones. She must have picked it up in the train. Was that why the sweet-seller at the station had eyed her rear end with such a grin? A grin she had mistaken for admiration?

Esme scrabbled in her bag looking for the Barbie manicure set Rory had given her for her birthday and insisted she took with her everywhere. The feel of her bread underneath its paper wrapping did nothing to calm her but she did find the pink zip-up purse, extracted the metal nail file, then slid to the floor on her knees.

After a furtive glance to check for staff she leaned in over the chair and started to scrape at the gum on the soft hide with the nail file. She was making good progress, when the whish and whoosh of the lift machinery distracted her. Someone was coming to the second floor! She picked as quickly as she could at the gum, relieved to see that it had not done too much damage to the leather beneath it. A small stain, perhaps, but nothing that some lucky soul with a spare £1,000 would spot.

The lift whizzed and burred behind her as it approached, making her hands tremble. She didn't want to rush the delicate surgery for fear of botching it, but she didn't want to be caught doing it either. The sticky mess was so close to being removed—so close, but not quite there.

The lift doors clanged open and Esme whispered, 'Please, please, please,' under her breath, as she tried desperately to get the last of the gum off the chair. Suddenly, the final obstinate piece miraculously came away and, suppressing a whoop of joy, she looked up just as an exceptionally well-dressed, dark-haired, dark-eyed, dark-skinned man walked round the corner from the lift shaft, saw her, looked away, then stopped still in his tracks and looked at her again.

The world, for a moment, seemed a strange and unfamiliar place.

For a while, nothing happened. They simply stared at each other in disbelief. But there could be no doubt. She knew at once that it could be no one else but him. It was Louis, long-lost Louis, rising from the ashes of her past and standing there staring at her.

'Esme,' Louis finally said in his voice made of melted dark Hershey bars. 'Esme, is that you?'

'Yes,' Esme answered in a voice she recognised not from screaming at Brown nor placating her son nor discouraging her vegetables, but from many, many years ago, 'of course it's me.'

They stared at each other again, unsure as to what to do next, until Louis took a hesitant step forward.

'You are on the floor,' he said gently, reminding Esme exactly where, indeed, she was. With a jerky movement, she stood up, then made the crucial mistake of running her hand through her hair as she often did when rattled. Her hand, at the time, was holding the Barbie nail file complete with recycled gum, which, once it made contact with Esme's collection of curls, glued itself to a hundred strands of her strong red hair. When Esme realised this, she wanted to die. She stood there, her hand in her hair, knowing she had only two choices, to leave her hand there, or bring it out without the nail file. Neither seemed fetching.

'Esme,' Louis said again. 'Are you all right?'

Esme looked at him, opened her mouth to speak and shut it again. Was she dreaming? Was it possible that just when her thoughts had been so cluttered with images of the French lover from her past, he should appear right in front of her?

That was when Louis smiled. It was a slow smile that started in the Cupid's bow in the middle of his mouth and spread outwards to the upturned corners, where it crept up his cheeks and crinkled his eyes. Inside, she crumpled.

Of all the fantasies in all the world she had simply not fathomed one as outlandish as this.

After all, here, standing in front of her, was the man whose very name to her defined longing, defined lust, defined true, true love. He occupied a space in her head that no one else in the world had ever or could ever share, could even come close to sharing.

And now, after all this time, after so many dreams and imaginings, here he was standing right in front of her and a slightly soiled Barcelona chair, while she had Hubba Bubba gummed in her hair.

Her hand dropped limply to her side and she shook her head slightly, feeling the nail file wiggle and wobble above her right ear. She had not been prepared for this. She did not know how to get the gum out of her hair. She did not know how to confront the man who had stolen her heart, then broken it. And if she didn't know how to do either of those things separately, she sure as God made little green apples did not know how to do them together.

Louis's eyes soaked all this up. And then he simply took another step towards her, reached out and took her hand.

'Come,' he said, and tugged gently at her. Esme felt the tingle of his flesh on hers and the years dropped away as though they had never existed. Every cell in her body vibrated with joy at being reunited with the forgotten sensation of Louis's touch. She floated on air, she neither knew nor cared where she was going, she simply let herself be pulled by him. Wherever Louis wanted to take her, Esme realised, she would go. Whatever he wanted her to do, she would do it. Never mind Pog. Never mind Rory. Never mind The Blind Goat and the father-in-law and the House in the Clouds. This was her destiny. Her escape. He was the one.

'Excuse me, mademoiselle,' the one said, the sound of his voice extracting Esme from her trance. The counter was where Louis had taken her and he was now using his mesmerising tone to address a languid assistant. 'Have you some scissors I may borrow for a moment? My friend is in need of them.'

He looked back at Esme and smiled again, giving her hand enough of a squeeze to nearly stop her heart. Then he took the scissors from the baleful girl at the desk, gently released Esme from his grip and moved closer, so close that she could feel his breath on her neck and it sent goosebumps up her spine.

Holding the scissors in one hand, with the other he lifted up the hair from the back of her neck and slowly, carefully ran his fingers up behind her ear through the tangle of her hair, inching his way gradually, his fingers firm and hard on her scalp, making tiny circular movements.

I am going to have to tell him to stop, Esme thought, fighting to keep from groaning with pleasure. I am a married woman about to behave badly in a very posh shop with the man who broke my heart fifteen years ago. I am going to have to scream at him to stop. But the feeling of his fingers on her head, the smell of him, the force of him, the ecstasy she was holding at bay: she was totally powerless to fight it.

Louis himself came to her rescue. His fingers located the stuck nail file and stopped their rapturous head rub. Deftly, he isolated the curl on which the gum was riveted and, in one seamless move, snipped at it with the scissors, then presented Esme with the nail file, its sticky little friend, and about six inches of one of her copper-coloured ringlets.

It was a disgusting sight, and Esme wished he would throw the whole sorry mess away. It occurred to her then, though, that she should probably say something. That she had said nothing since confirming that she was who he thought she was when she first saw him. But words escaped her. Words formed a picket line and refused to let her cross it.

Louis raised his astonishing eyebrows, leaned over the counter and gracefully dropped the file, gum and curl into the wastepaper basket. Then he stood up straight and looked at her again.

'Bloody hell,' said Esme at last and her heart thumped as Louis smiled his slow spreading smile again.

'My pleasure,' answered Louis, as though she had just thanked him, which, she realised with a clunk inside her head, was exactly what she should have done.

'Yes, yes, of course,' Esme said, taking hold of her senses and lining up words in an almost orderly queue to make an entire sentence. 'I'm meeting Charlie for lunch. Next door,' she said, as though one and a half decades had not elapsed since the three of them last saw each other. 'You remember Charlie, don't you? We were staying together in Venolat. Anyway, I'm meeting him there . . .' she looked at her watch, 'about now actually.' She was scared to stop speaking. She could not let Louis slip away. 'I don't suppose . . . well, you could always . . .' He looked at her, amused. 'Louis, would you care to join us?'

She couldn't believe what she had just done. Why? But why not? With Charlie around she felt sure she could trust herself to act normally and to go home to her family whom she loved and who loved her. It would be fine.

'I can think of nothing better,' Louis said, smiling and opening out his arm, inviting her to walk in front of him. 'After you, madame.' And Esme, knowing that one of the things Louis liked most about her was her bottom, walked as gracefully as she could out of the shop, thanking God and his ridiculous sense of humour for the fact that her skirt was still twisted on back to front, so he would not be looking at the remains of a juicy wodge of someone else's bubble gum.

A crisp maître d' was on the phone when Esme and Louis got to the top of the stairs at the Orrery, but upon seeing them his face registered welcome relief.

'Mr Edmonds,' he said into the receiver, 'she has just walked in. I will pass you over to her. Thank you, sir. See you soon.'

Esme took the proffered phone. 'Charlie?' she said. 'Where are you?'

'Oh, Es,' the raddled voice of her friend came back to her. 'I hate to do this to you but something has come up at work and I don't know if I'm going to be able to make it to our lunch. I know you came down to London especially and I wouldn't stand you up for all the world, you know that, but the client from Hell has demanded a two o'clock meeting and I really need to—'

'You must come, Charlie,' Esme butted in, trying to keep the panic out of her voice. 'Louis is here.'

Charlie was silent for a moment.

'I'm sorry?' he asked.

'Louis,' she repeated as calmly as she could. 'Louis, the baker from Venolat. You remember.'

'Jesus,' Charlie finally said. 'Bloody Michael and his French 75s. You're seeing things, Esme.'

Esme laughed, in what she hoped was a sophisticated and casual fashion, given that Louis was standing less than a yard away. 'No, silly,' she said. 'I mean it's actually Louis, the real thing. I just bumped into him in the Conran Shop. After all these years—can you believe it?'

'Frankly, no,' answered Charlie. 'Are you sure it's him?'

Esme sneaked a glance at Louis, standing at the desk next to her, looking perfectly in place the way he always had.

'I think I would know,' she said, 'don't you? It's given me something of a surprise, Charlie, and I've invited him to join us for lunch.'

'Well,' said Charlie, clearly flabbergasted. 'What a bugger I shan't be there to watch the whole lovely thing unfold.'

Esme stood on her toes and squeaked down the phone with the exertion of not unleashing a string of Granny Mac's most venomous invective on him.

82

'Look,' Charlie said calmly, obviously starting to enjoy her discomfort. 'I think the two of you should take the booking and I'll pay for the lunch. How's that for a deal? I have an account there and—'

'Oh, we couldn't possibly,' Esme interrupted loudly, aware the maître d' was tapping his pen on the desk and trying not to look agitated.

'You could possibly,' said Charlie. 'You will possibly. Listen, Es, I really have to dash, but say hello to Louis from me and I want details, darling, details, so ring me later and tell me everything. Oh, and have the salmon.' With that he hung up and the line went dead.

Esme handed the phone back to the maître d' and smiled wanly.

'Table for two as guests of Mr Edmonds?' he asked and she nodded, afraid to look at Louis but aware, somehow, that he was smiling at her again. She had never wanted to eat anything less in all her life.

Seated at their table overlooking a pretty, leafy park across the road and the hustle and bustle of Marylebone High Street, Esme wondered how long she could keep staring out of the window and saying nothing.

She sneaked a look at Louis, who had never felt the need to fill silent spaces with unnecessary words and so was sitting there cool as a cucumber, perfectly happy to be sneakily looked at.

His hair, Esme could not help but notice, was just as black as it had been when she last saw him, but perhaps it was receding a little at the front. This suited him though, she thought. How typical! He still wore it unfashionably long at the back but this too was right for him. Those black eyes must have held a thousand more secrets by now, but little about his face had really changed.

He was wearing a very dark grey Savile Row suit and a very pale grey business shirt and matching silk tie. He looked positively edible and it made her feel sick. How could she possibly be sitting here opposite him? It felt like a dream.

A suited waiter appeared at her elbow with all but a click of his heels.

'Bread?' he questioned, proffering her a basket.

She looked across the table at Louis, whose faint left dimple appeared.

'Have you any sourdough?' Louis asked.

'No, sir,' the waiter replied. 'Just the kibbled wheat slice and our chef's own fresh-made rolls.'

'We will both have one of each,' Louis said, and Esme's heart quickened for the hundredth time in the past half-hour. If she got through this lunch without a coronary, she promised herself, she would find a religion, join it, and go to church or temple or synagogue or wherever the hell she had to every day for the rest of her life.

Chapter Ten

AFTER NINETEEN YEARS of being flat and dull, once Louis added his starter to Esme in the hot salty flour store of the Venolat *boulangerie*, she rose. The bits of herself that she had never been sure of before suddenly all made sense. Her pieces fell into place.

'If you tell me he completes you I will seriously have to slap you,' Charlie told her, but Esme laughed aside his cynicism. She felt happy, truly, deliriously, deliciously happy, for the first time in her life, and nothing could change that.

She had been Louis-ed and she was never going back. Without him she might never have discovered the pure and glorious sensation of knowing, knowing deep down inside at the most intimate level, with absolute certainty that the man she loved loved her straight back.

It was different from knowing that Granny Mac loved her, or Charlie, or her distant father in his own peculiar way, or her dead mother, for that matter. They had to love her. That was how families, how best friends worked. But Louis . . . what Esme loved most about him was what he loved about her.

He loved her hair. He adored her freckles, was forever counting them and giving them names, in French, as he kissed them separately and succulently. Her bottom neatly fitted in his two hands, nestled expertly in his lap. He treated her breasts like crown jewels, lifting and holding them with reverence and kissing the nipples as though they were rings on a fat pope's finger. Just hearing him say her name made her tingle all over. He made her feel like the ridiculous fairy-tale princess she had always wanted to be. She couldn't get enough of him nor he of her.

After deflowering her in the dusty upstairs room that first fantastic night, Louis had taken her back down to the bakery and refloured her on the counter.

Then, momentarily sated, he had taken the linen sheet off the stack of bread baskets and wrapped it round her, and she had sat naked beneath it on the steps and watched him work.

First, he stoked up the fire, then, reaching above his head to a rack hanging from the ceiling, he pulled down a paddle with a handle long enough to reach the back of the oven. Swiftly but carefully, he upended the baskets of dough he had stacked earlier two at a time onto the paddle, then expertly sliced a flowery 'L' into the top of each one with a little razor-wheel contraption that he held between his teeth as he slid the loaves two at a time into the oven.

The dough, spongy and floury and so ready and willing to head into that fiery furnace, had reminded her of herself, only moments before. So full of promise! So teetering on the brink of becoming something much, much better, something it was made to be.

When every last *boule*-to-be had been safely tucked in the crackling oak-fired oven, the well-worn wooden paddle lifted back into its ceiling rack, the floor swept and the baskets stacked neatly under the bench, Louis slipped up and sat on the step behind Esme, wrapping himself around her.

They sat like that, his lips nuzzling her hair, her cheek, her ear, for a long, lovely time, until Louis lifted his head, sniffed the stifling air, and excused himself to bring the perfect loaves out, two at a time, and place them on the waiting empty racks.

'It's all in the rise, see?' he told Esme, wafting a pair of fat happy *boules* in front of her. 'Look, see the gloss on the crust? Perfect.'

How he loved his sourdough. And how Esme loved that about him. He emptied the oven, wiped the sweat off his brow with his discarded T-shirt, then pulled Esme to her feet and kissed her deep and lazily as the sweet smell of the cooling bread embraced them like a warm blanket.

Finally, Louis disengaged himself and whispered that his uncle would soon be arriving, that she should go home and he would see her again at midnight or later, if she preferred.

He led her naked and glowing upstairs to the flour room where he retrieved her clothes and dressed her, lingering over the tiny buttons on the ancient, delicate camisole. He kissed her hipbones as he knelt and gently pulled up her Marks & Spencer knickers, then ran his tongue lightly around her belly button, tickling her.

She slipped out of the door just as the sun poked its first pink and yellow fingers over the village ramparts. The world was a far more colourful place as Esme wafted home than it had been when she had slunk hesitantly out hours before. Everything looked different. But then, everything *was* different. At least, nothing would ever be the same.

That day, after she'd slept the sleep of the very recently enlightened and completely exhausted, bits of the night kept wafting in and out of her consciousness, making her feel dizzy with desire.

Charlie, of course, had insisted she regurgitate every second.

'He really said that?' Charlie asked, looking revolted as he lay next to Esme on her bed. 'He said he had been waiting for you all his life?'

Esme squirmed. 'Oh, it sounds so corny when you say it, but when Louis said it, Charlie, oh my God! It's just what every girl wants to hear.'

'You really are a strange bunch,' Charlie said, reaching for a juicy peach from the nightstand beside Esme's bed. 'I'm so glad I'm not relying on you lot for my jollies.' But he did agree that it was a perfectly romantic way for Esme to be relieved of her virginal status.

That night, though, Esme was strangely fearful as she sidled up to the *boulangerie*. What if he wasn't there? Or didn't want to see her? How could she survive another night, another minute, without him?

But Louis was there, the red glow of his cigarette dancing in the dark as he discarded it, ready to take her in his arms, which he did.

'I wait all day for this kiss,' he said, after drinking from Esme's lips for what felt like for ever. For the first time in many hours, she felt her heart relax. It was not going to come crashing down around her. It was really happening. They made long, languid love straight away on the counter of the shop. Afterwards, Louis heated croissants in the oven downstairs, which they ate hungrily with Belgian chocolate he had bought for her. Their appetites were insatiable.

'You're going to wear it out!' Charlie scolded her two weeks later, when Esme slipped into the apartment as the sun rose for the umpteenth morning in a row.

'Oh my God, Charlie,' Esme prattled, 'he is just such a gloriously divine specimen. He's just so completely, fantastically—' She flailed. Words simply did not do him justice.

'You have got it bad,' Charlie said with a strange tone in his voice.

'Why do you say it like that?' Esme wanted to know.

'I didn't say it like anything,' he said snippily.

'Oooooh,' teased Esme, 'don't tell me you are jealous because I have finally got a boyfriend.' Her worry disappeared, chased away by the hot flush that swept over her at the sound of that last word.

'Well, if you are sure that is what he is,' said Charlie. Esme's hot flush sank to her toes.

'Of course that's what he is,' she said quietly. 'I've seen him every night for a fortnight. He's told me he loves me. I'm going to see him every night for the next fortnight, maybe for every fortnight of my entire life. If he's not my boyfriend, Charlie, what else would he be?'

'So you're going to stay in Venolat for the rest of your life? Or is Louis going to come back to London and live with you and Granny Mac?'

'Well, thank you very much, Captain Bring Down,' Esme said.

'Actually, we haven't really talked about it.' Once she heard this out loud, she wished she'd kept her mouth shut. They hadn't talked about it. They hadn't talked about much. She had just assumed that because she was mad about Louis and he was mad about her, they would find a way of being together.

But of course she could not leave Granny Mac behind in London and was not sure if her grandmother would want to come and live permanently in Venolat. And anyway, it was too early to talk about the future. The present was too enticing. But she had never been more sure of anything than she was of the way Louis felt about her.

'Don't you think it's strange,' he asked, 'that Louis never invites you to his house, Esme? That all this torrid lovemaking takes place at his work?'

'He lives with his uncle and aunt,' Esme answered.

'Well, doesn't his uncle come to work during the day, Es? Couldn't you see Louis at his place then?'

Esme felt a niggle of something she couldn't be certain wasn't fear. 'Are you trying to get rid of me?' she asked. 'Are you up to something?'

Charlie's usually worry-free face looked at her with unaccustomed solemnity. 'No, Esme,' he said. '*I'm* not up to anything.' He was silent for a moment. 'I'm worried about you, that's all. It's just that . . .'

'It's just that what exactly?'

'It's just that as someone who shags a lot of men, Esme, and not all of them readily available, I have to say that if you are not being invited to Louis's house there is probably a very good reason.'

Esme thought briefly about swallowing her anger, but it erupted out of her too quickly. 'What is the matter with you?' she shouted at Charlie. 'Is it really so hard for you to believe that Louis might be madly in love with me?' She then turned and ran upstairs to collapse face down on her bed, fists clenched and eyes shut tight.

The truth was that while her body had been asking nothing of Louis other than his own flesh and bones over the past few heavenly weeks, her mind did have tiny vents of doubt.

Why didn't he ask her back to his house? she had wondered. It was on the other side of Venolat, he had told her already, halfway to the next town, too far to expect her to walk to and from. She had wanted to insist, to make more of a fuss about it, but something had stopped her.

That night, she stayed at home, had an early night for which her desperately tired body was truly thankful, and at daybreak slunk downstairs and across to the *boulangerie*, where Louis was just taking the *boules* out of the oven.

'Esme,' he said, instantly dropping the paddle on the ground and coming to meet her at the bottom of the stairs. 'What happened to you? I was so worried. I did not know . . .' He looked so unhappy and fretful that she cursed herself for having doubts and for depriving herself of him for all those extra hours.

'I fell asleep,' she lied sheepishly. 'I've only just woken up.'

He rubbed the dark rings under her eyes with his thumbs and looked at her quizzically. 'Esme,' he said. 'I missed you. I thought perhaps . . . perhaps you do not want me.' He pulled her close.

'I want you, Louis,' she answered him, her voice husky with longing.

'Thank you,' he whispered. 'Thank you.'

'Your uncle must be nearly here,' Esme said, feeling treacherous. 'Why don't you come to see me when you're finished? At my place.'

Louis pulled away from her, something, she couldn't be sure what, flickering in his eyes. 'You don't like the *boulangerie*?'

'I love the *boulangerie*,' she replied, 'but I have flour stuck in bits of me I didn't even know existed, and I have a very nice bed just a hundred yards away from here. So I will see you in an hour or so?' Esme prompted him. 'First door on the right through the brick archway next to the *auberge*? You'll have to knock loudly so I can hear you from my room.'

Louis smiled and her heart melted. 'Maybe two hours,' he said.

She skipped home, stopping at the end of Charlie's bed to inform him that Louis would be arriving sometime later, and went upstairs, where she promptly fell asleep, to be woken by a distant rapping on the front door. She collected a sheet round her shoulders and danced down the steps to receive the love of her life.

She drew him upstairs where they stayed in bed all day while Louis made sure all her crevices were completely flour-free. In the late afternoon, they both draped themselves in sheets and Esme watched Louis create the most delicious omelettes out of the rotting components of the refrigerator vegetable drawer. They drank cold white wine and toasted each other on the patio overlooking the Dordogne, and Esme wondered what she had done to deserve being so happy.

Charlie even joined them for a drink, as Esme had hoped he would. She wanted Charlie to see what sort of a person Louis was. How he loved her so obviously.

'Right, better dash,' her friend said after making stiff conversation and quaffing a glass of wine. 'Hot date over in old Lalinde tonight, you know. Better make myself presentable and all that.' He stood up as if to go. 'Esme tells me you live over that way, Louis,' he said.

'In that direction, yes,' Louis agreed.

'You must tell us where. Esme and I were thinking of hiking over that way at the weekend. We could drop by and say hello,' Charlie gushed.

Louis was nonplussed. 'I am not there at the weekend,' he said with a shrug. 'I deliver the bread to other villages at the weekend.'

'Maybe one evening before you go to work then?' Charlie suggested.

Louis shrugged again. 'Sure, if you want to,' he said. 'When do you think you will come? I must check with my uncle first.'

Esme felt sick. She was scared but she had to admit to herself— although never to Charlie—she also wanted to know how this was going to play out. She held her breath.

Charlie laughed, not cruelly, he wasn't cruel, but not nicely either.

'You have to ask your uncle if you can have visitors? Poor chap. And you look so grown-up!'

'No, no,' Louis agreed, 'it is not usual, you are right. But my family is not usual, not normal, if you like. I live with my uncle Louis, I am named for him, and my aunt. But she is very ill, she has been for many years. Arthritis,' he stumbled over the word. 'She is bedridden. That is why my uncle works during the day and I am the baker,' he explained. 'In most *boulangeries*, the baker's wife runs the shop. But Tante Marie has been unable to work since I was very young.'

'Oh, Louis, I am so sorry,' Esme said. Charlie had the good grace to look ashamed. But not for long.

'What about your own parents?' he asked.

A dark cloud passed over Louis's face. 'What about them?' he asked back, the first signs of aggression in his voice.

'Where are they?' Charlie persevered.

'They live in Paris,' Louis said tersely. 'But I am not in communication with them.'

'Louis,' Esme couldn't help saying. 'Why ever not?'

'My parents move there four years ago,' Louis said darkly, 'when I am just sixteen, but I do not wish to go with them so I stay here.'

'Oh, really?' Charlie sounded disbelieving. 'I imagine most lads your age would die to live in a big city like that. All those bars and nightclubs and pretty girls and bakeries.'

'Please,' spat Louis, 'you call them bakeries? Monkeys could make bread the way they do in Paris. All those baguettes with their flimsy little crumb and flaky crust? That is not bread. Those are not bakeries.'

'You're *angry* about baguettes?' Charlie teased and Esme loathed him for it. Could he not see that this was important to Louis, that this was what Louis was about?

'You have to admit,' Esme said to Charlie, 'that Louis's bread tastes better than any you have ever eaten in your whole entire life.'

Charlie shrugged but did not disagree. Louis smiled at Esme.

'That is because we make it the way it was meant to be made. With the ingredients from the air and the fields and the river and the touch of our hands, hands that have been making it this way for two centuries.'

'So what about your parents then? Why aren't they still here making your delicious bread with their hands?' Charlie was keen to return to the subject of Louis's family.

'My uncle and I agree exactly on the principles of the *boulangerie*,' Louis said, his face darkening again, 'but not so my father. Papa was keen to make changes, many changes. My uncle and I were not.'

'What sort of changes?' Charlie persisted.

'You probably do not understand,' Louis said rather dismissively to Charlie, 'but Esme does.' Esme glowed beneath his sentiment. 'To bake *pain au levain* the way we always have, the way we do, is—' he searched for the word, frustrated in his passion— 'it is honourable, if that is what I mean. The baker has always been at the centre of village life in France. He feeds people. And he puts his honour and his love and his skill into every single *boule*, separately, that is what makes him an artisan. That is what makes him different from a machine. That is what makes him want to go to work late at night and not leave until there is enough bread for everyone and he has left a little bit of himself in every loaf.'

Charlie looked confused, but Esme reached for Louis's hand and unclenched it, taking it in her own.

'Your father didn't want to do it that way?'

'My father wanted to borrow money for a machine to cut dough into the right size for baguettes, and for another machine that would roll the dough into the right shape, and for an electric oven that would cook ten times more baguettes than the oak-fired oven we have been using all this time. He wanted to stop making *boules* and just make baguettes and buy in frozen pastries from a big factory. He wanted to have nothing to do with the bread but the money.'

Charlie was obviously struggling with the concept that this was unacceptable. 'Isn't that why most people work?' he said. 'For the money?'

'Most people are not artisan bakers,' Louis said, and Esme squeezed his hand tighter.

'So your father is a baker in Paris?'

'My father is a businessman in Paris,' Louis corrected him sharply. 'He owns a factory that mixes and rises and refrigerates baguette dough and then delivers it through tubes from big tankers to *boulangeries* throughout Paris. I want nothing to do with it.'

How Esme loved him in that moment, his face fierce with passion for his work. Her heart swelled with pride.

'Yes, well, I had better get going,' said Charlie, clearly not as impressed. 'Lovely to finally meet you, Louis.'

'Your friend does not like me,' Louis said when he had gone.

'Oh, he does,' cried Esme. She could not bear the thought that the two most wonderful men in her life did not get on. 'That's just Charlie,' she added lamely. 'He's very, you know . . .'

'Suspicious?' Louis suggested.

'I was going to say English,' she said, and they both laughed.

That night in the bakery, as she watched him weigh out the dough, upend the baskets and carve his swirly signature into every single loaf, leaving a little bit of himself behind him in each one, she was desperate to have more of him.

'I want to make some myself,' she announced from her spot on the stairs. 'Sourdough. At home. For you. I want to know what it feels like.'

'Truly?' Louis asked, his body glistening with sweat.

'Truly,' nodded Esme. 'Please let me. I want to do it. For you.'

'You know, the *levain* has never left the *boulangerie* before,' Louis said as he kissed her goodbye at dawn, handing over a willow basket, a bag of flour, and a stone jar of his family's precious starter. 'I hope it brings you luck.'

'It already has,' Esme said, leaning into him again, his lips soft and supple against her own.

'To think,' he murmured, 'there will be some of you and me in the bread you bake, Esme.'

'Like a child,' she said without thinking, then blushed at her foolishness. Couples in the first flush of true love did not talk about babies, even she knew that. But Louis seemed unruffled. He brushed a curl away from her neck and smiled at her so kindly she wanted to cry.

'Yes,' he said, 'I suppose. Like a child. Made with love.' He kissed her again and went back inside.

Esme floated through the rest of the day, her faith in her lover fully restored. And she baked. For the first time, she baked. One beautiful, brown, slightly skewwhiff *boule* of sourdough bread just the way Louis had taught her. Next to the joy of sex, it was the most satisfying discovery she had ever made. She loved the feeling of flour and water under her fingers, and the way the texture changed as she mixed it. She slept deeply and untroubled on both two-hour occasions she left her mixture to rise. And despite the unreliable and unknown nature of the apartment's little oven, she watched through the glass door as her *boule* turned perfectly from dough into bread.

What possessed her to deliver her first offering in person to Louis's house that afternoon, she would never know. She must have realised, as she looked up his uncle's address in the phone book, that in the circumstances it was a foolish thing to do. She could have taken it to him at the bakery at midnight. There was no reason to go to his house. To surprise him. To catch him.

When she got to the modest house hidden in the cool shade of half a dozen leafy trees partway to Lalinde, she was hot and dusty and tired.

She knocked at the door and it was opened almost immediately by a pretty, tired-looking woman a little older than herself, carrying one child on her hip and another in her belly. The woman had straight, brown, slightly dishevelled hair and a peaches-and-cream complexion.

'Hello,' she said. She was English. 'Can I help you?'

Esme stared as a dark-eyed, dark-haired toddler ran up the hallway behind the woman and hurled itself at her legs.

'I'm sorry,' she said. 'I think I must have the wrong house.'

'Oh, yes?' the woman said. 'Who are you looking for?'

'I'm looking for Louis,' Esme said uncertainly, clutching onto the glimmer of hope that she was indeed at the wrong house.

'Oh, really?' The woman raised her eyebrows. 'What for?'

'I wanted to give him this,' Esme said, the horror of her situation claiming the pale skin of her cheeks as its own and brightening them radiantly. She held up the bread and the woman opened the tea towel and looked at Esme's *boule*, then closed it again.

'If there's one thing Louis doesn't need, trust me, it's more bread,' she said tiredly. 'Who are you?'

'I'm Esme,' said Esme, the saliva disappearing from inside her mouth as her happiness spiralled downwards. 'I've been helping,' the lie stuck in her throat, 'Louis at the *boulangerie*.' Any pretence of helpfulness slid off the woman's face. 'I'm learning to bake sourdough.'

The woman hitched the baby up on her hip and looked the dusty, silly young girl on the doorstep scornfully up and down.

'Who are you?' the dusty, silly young girl asked in a quavery voice.

'I'm Diana, his wife,' said Diana, his wife. 'Did he not mention me?' Her eyes had hardened to a frightening shade of icy ocean blue. She turned and yelled over her shoulder. 'Louis!' With all her might, Esme willed the man this woman was hailing not to be her Louis, the Louis who had told her he loved her a hundred times over the past few weeks. The Louis in whose arms she fitted so perfectly. But as he rounded the corner into the hallway, tucking a white T-shirt into the front of his faded blue jeans, there was no doubt at all that her Louis and this other woman's husband were one and the same.

He looked up and saw her, and seemingly, without even flinching, came to the door and stood behind the woman. His wife. His English wife. The best friend who had moved here when Louis was thirteen? *It is good to share, no?* How could Esme have been so stupid?

'Hello,' Louis said. 'So, you try the baking yourself?' The mild hiccup in his English was the only sign he was at all unnerved.

'Who is she?' his wife asked rudely, shifting the baby on her hip again and shushing the toddler behind her.

'I told you,' Louis answered, 'she is the English girl who wants to learn about *pain au levain*. Tante Marie needs help in her room, Diana. Can you go?'

'You told me no such thing,' his wife snapped back. 'I'm not completely stupid, Louis.'

Ignoring her, he leaned over towards Esme and lifted the tea towel, raising his eyebrow and shaking his head in a mildly approving fashion. 'Not too bad,' he said, looking at her and meeting her eyes as though he had not stared into them just hours before, professing his deep and undying devotion. 'I say you need to work a little on your mixing technique. Maybe leave the dough a little longer in the basket.'

Esme struggled to keep breathing. Louis's wife was looking at her with such contempt she was surprised her skin wasn't breaking into welts.

'Come back tomorrow,' Louis said casually, 'and we can work on your kneading.'

Esme tried to smile, but the muscles had frozen in panic. 'Thank you,' she found her voice saying politely, if a little shakily, 'but I am just about to leave. For England.' Louis gave a little lacklustre shrug and Esme wondered how she was expected to keep on living. 'I just wanted to say,' she fought on, even though tears had actually sprung from her eyes now and were trailing down her cheeks, 'thank you.' Then she turned and fled.

'You bastard!' she heard his wife spit behind her. 'You filthy bastard.'

Louis started to protest, but Esme was running as fast as she could away from him, his wife and his children and did not care to know what he was saying. His shrug of indifference at the news she was leaving had told her everything she needed to know. As if the fact he was married and the father of two, nearly three children was not enough on its own. She had been sleeping with a married man! Louis had given her something that was not rightfully his to give. The contemptuous look on his wife's face kept flashing in front of her as she ran all the way back to Venolat. Charlie had been right; she was a fool, a silly little fool.

Her tears formed streaks through the dust on her cheeks as she pushed open the door of the apartment and ran up to her room. She pulled her suitcase from under the bed and clumsily threw her clothes into it, her ribs aching with the sobs that racked her.

She dragged the case down to the kitchen and barely able to think, to breathe, started scratching out a note to Charlie.

You were right, was all she could manage in the end. *He's married. Gone home. Esme.*

The words 'He's married' pounded in her head as she searched the kitchen for her rucksack. How could she have been so wrong about him? It didn't seem possible.

Her eyes fell on the stone jar of *levain*, sitting on the kitchen counter, and she picked it up and pressed it, cool as the waters of the river below, against her burning cheek. Her eyes closed and her sobbing slowed. So, Louis had lied. So, he had tricked Esme into handing him her heart. So, nothing about him was real. Nothing except his bread. That was real. She had seen it, she had smelt it, she had tasted it. She had made it. She slid the stone jar into her rucksack and slipped out of the apartment. So, she would have something to show for it after all.

Chapter Eleven

A DECADE AND A HALF later, sitting across a crisp white linen tablecloth from each other on the opposite side of the Channel, Esme and Louis agreed, with fewer than a dozen words between them, that the bread was as good as you could get at any restaurant in London but not as good as Lapoine's.

After a glass of Bollinger, which she downed with indecent haste, Esme concentrated on trying to stop worrying about the implications of meeting in secret with her old lover, even though it had been a secret from herself.

She watched Louis's slim brown fingers gently crumble his olive roll onto his plate as he looked at her and smiled his comfortable smile.

'Esme,' he said with such kindness that she felt it in her toenails. 'It's all right. Relax.'

She was suddenly tired of being herself. She didn't want to get gum in her hair. She didn't want to stutter and stammer and keep the things she really wanted to feel, to know, at arm's length. She had been doing it for too long. Since Venolat, since Notting Hill, since that other awful black day just over a month ago. It was exhausting. It was pathetic. It was a habit so ingrained that she had begun to think it came naturally, but sitting here with Louis she realised how bloody hard it was.

'How could you do that to me, Louis?' she asked him. 'How could you tell me all those things—that you loved me, that you wanted to be with me for ever, that I was special—when you were married to Diana, when you had children with her? I didn't understand it, Louis, I still don't understand it. I thought I was the one. I was sure I was the one. You certainly made me feel as though I was.'

Louis turned seamlessly to the waiter who appeared just then for their order.

'I will have the foie gras and the beef and madame will have the soup and the salmon,' he said. The waiter nodded and retreated and Esme continued as though they had never been interrupted.

'Do you know what that did to me, Louis?' she asked, aware that she was opening the floodgates, yet feeling strangely detached from the flood. 'It took years to let anyone love me again. Years!'

'I meant everything I said to you, Esme. Everything,' Louis said with a passion disguised by the smooth low timbre of his voice. 'But the time was not right. I apologise for that but not for what I said to you. I meant every word.'

'But you had a wife, Louis, and little children. How could you possibly have meant every word?'

'Just because I did not act the way a gentleman should does not mean that I was not being honest with you, Esme.'

'Well, you were certainly not being honest with one of us, Louis.'

'Yes, but I am not the one who ran away in the night, Esme, never to come back,' he said.

'Louis, you had a wife, a beautiful wife. I met her. I was humiliated by her, and rightly so, too. You turned me into a slut, Louis! And you shrugged at me. After everything we had done together, you shrugged at me!' She knew the shrugging was the least of his wrongdoing, but, oh, how it had hurt.

'That was not the time to tell Diana, Esme. I would do that, I would have done that when the time was right but instead you turn up like that at our house and everything is ruined. If only you had waited.'

Esme's skin prickled at what she was hearing. If Louis was telling her that they could have had a future together, she did not want to hear it. He was telling her fifteen years too late.

'And then,' Louis said, gaining momentum in her silence, 'what was I to do? You knew how to find me, Esme, but how was I to find you?'

Their waiter slipped in between them and gently placed their food.

'You could have tried,' Esme continued, amazed that the things she had kept in her head for so long were sliding out so loudly and easily. 'You could have got it out of Charlie, for God's sake. All you'd need to do was tickle him. He was there for another two days.'

'Charlie?' Louis hissed. 'Did he not tell you, Esme, about the night I came to find you? About the night you went away?'

Esme's heart stood still as she shook her head.

'I came to find you and he tells me that you have gone and when I beg him, *beg* him to tell me where you are he beats the living *shit* out of me, Esme.' He leaned urgently in towards her. 'I needed five stitches under my nose,' and with that he stuck his neck forward and she could see the faint scarring from an old wound that had not been there when she had explored every inch of his body in her youth.

She wanted to reach out and touch it but instead tried her soup. It was delicious. Yet what he said made her feel ill and uneasy. What if he had tried to find her? What if Charlie had stopped him? What if the last fifteen years of her life had been the wrong ones?

'I waited for one month, six months, a year for you to reach me, Esme, but you did not,' he said, sitting back.

'But why would I, Louis? You had a wife and children. I wasn't the sort of person who would break up a family. I'm still not. *You* were the one in the wrong, Louis. If it is anybody's fault, it is yours.'

Louis sighed and his shoulders slumped in a gesture of total desolation. 'Is it about who was right and who was wrong, Esme?' he asked her quietly. 'Is that what you really think?'

'How is she?' Esme asked, holding his gaze and slurping back the last of her wine. 'Diana?'

Louis looked wretched. 'Do you think I could have gone back to Diana after you?' he breathed so quietly she wasn't sure if she heard him properly. 'For even a moment? Do you not know me at all, Esme?'

At that instant, something inside Esme unzipped itself and spilled violently out into the no-emotion zone where she required, for her sanity, nothing of the sort. With a clang of cutlery and glassware she stood up rapidly, excused herself and dashed to the Ladies, where she sat on a lavatory-seat lid and shook so violently she thought she was going to throw up. All this honesty was hard to handle. The answers she was getting were not necessarily the ones she wanted to hear. She concentrated on her breathing, trying to get air deep into her lungs.

After five minutes she started to feel calmer. She left the cubicle, splashed her face at length with cold water, reapplied her make-up, sponged the last of the gum off her skirt and turned it the right way round, then returned to the table.

Louis half rose out of his chair as she approached. 'I am so sorry,' he said as she sat to find her main course awaiting her and despite her inner turmoil, looking rather gorgeous. 'These are old wounds and I have no business opening them again.'

'Shall we eat?' Esme suggested with a calm she got from she didn't know where. She let the delicacy of her lightly spiced fish fill all the corners in her body that were otherwise buzzing with anger and regret and sadness and guilt. Food was good like that. And when she felt she had control of her emotions enough to speak properly, she did.

'So you are not with Diana, then?' she asked.

'No,' answered Louis emphatically. 'She lives in Venolat with Emily and little Marie and Jean, he is eighteen now, but I see them only maybe two or three times a year. I live in Paris,' he added.

'She was the best friend, wasn't she?' Esme asked. 'The best friend who moved to Venolat when you were both thirteen? Who taught you English? Who you taught French? It is good to share?'

Comprehension dawned on Louis's handsome face.

'Yes,' he said. 'Yes, she was once my best friend but we never should have married. When my father fought with my uncle and moved with my mother to Paris, well, I made my own way. Diana was my family just as much as Marie and Louis. And when she fell pregnant with Jean . . . I was just seventeen. We were too young.'

'So, did you marry again?' Esme asked casually.

He stopped, a forkful of food halfway to his mouth, and shook his head. 'No,' he said. 'I never married again. There have been others of course but nothing, nobody . . .'

'What do you do in Paris then?' she asked, amazed by how normal she was sounding. 'Don't tell me you went to work for your father?'

'But no, of course not,' Louis said, disgusted at the suggestion. 'I am still not in communication with him,' he said. 'I work for the federation of master bakers. I travel around the world teaching people how to bake *pain au levain*, you know, the old-fashioned way, just like I taught you, Esme. The tradition is almost completely lost in this world of *supermarchés* and fast food. Even in France I am teaching the art of baking sourdough bread. It seems silly, no?'

97

'It would seem silly to do anything else,' Esme answered with fervour. How she had always loved that passion of his. 'Your uncle must be so proud of you, Louis. How is he?'

Louis stopped eating and let his knife and fork collapse on his plate as his eyes dulled and dropped to a spot in the middle of the table between them. 'My uncle died,' he said quietly, 'just over a month ago.'

Esme felt a sharp pain. His sadness at losing his uncle would have coincided with her own black, breadless hole. The loss of his uncle with the slow shake of Dr Gribblehurst's jowls and all that followed.

A glimmer of possibility floated into Esme's future. Maybe it would not be poisoned by what had happened to her in Notting Hill. Maybe it would be saved by a past much sweeter. Despite what had happened back in Venolat, despite what had occurred in the intervening years, perhaps Louis really was her destiny. She realised, suddenly, that what she felt for him now, sitting across the table in a smart London restaurant, was exactly what she felt all those years ago on the unforgiving sacks of unbleached wheat flour from the pastures of the Dordogne.

And if Louis were to stand up now and reach for her, she knew that she would go. In fact, parts of her were tingling in anticipation of that very possibility. Parts that should know better. Parts that should be reserved for the attentions of her husband Pog.

His name clunked in her brain. Pog. His kind, dear, uncomplicated face hovered into her consciousness, despite the chasm the past two years had dug between them, and grinned at her. She closed her eyes for a second and cleared her head. What had happened in Notting Hill had not just happened to her. It had happened to him. It had happened to all of them. She could not escape it alone.

'I am so sorry,' she said to Louis, 'about your uncle. I really am. I know what it feels like and you must be devastated.' She pushed her plate away from her and moved her chair back, as if to stand and leave. 'The thing is that I really have to get going.'

Louis was looking at her, confused. 'But why?' he said. 'Esme, please.'

Esme was scrabbling around on the ground in search of her bag. 'I have to fly, Louis. I'm sorry. I can't tell you what it has been like to see you again—'

'Yes, you can,' Louis said, leaning forward in the same urgent fashion as he had before. 'You can stay here and tell me. We can have cheese. They have beautiful French cheese here, Esme. All your favourites.'

Esme shook her head and wondered for a moment if the rest of her body was shaking with it. 'The thing is,' she said, finding her bag and plonking it on her knee to form a comforting extra barrier between herself and him, 'I just feel extremely sort of thrown by bumping into you today. I mean, I've thought about it for years, of course, but I never thought it would be like this. I always imagined that I would yell at you and call you a bastard and tip crème brûlée on your head or something.'

Louis stared at her. 'Esme,' he said, 'I cannot believe you have changed so much you would waste a crème brulée.'

It was a joke, but not entirely funny.

'That's what I mean,' said Esme. 'I feel as though I haven't changed a bit. I feel like that same silly young girl who fell in love with the village baker and just assumed she was the woman of his dreams as much as she assumed he was the man of hers. And it's ridiculous because I am really not that person any more.'

Louis's smile had spread across his face again.

'You were the woman of my dreams, Esme,' he said. 'You still are.'

Esme cleared her throat and pushed thoughts of lying naked with him away. 'Louis,' she said, 'I am not. I am happily married. I am a mother. I live in the country and grow vegetables. I dye my hair. I am half a stone heavier.'

'I like you better with more roundness,' he said. 'It suits you.'

Esme was suddenly aware of every extra inch of her roundness (half a stone, indeed!) and felt supremely uncomfortable with it. Not for the first time, she silently resolved to join the Seabury yoga group even if they were twenty years older than her. The thought of Seabury brought a lump to her throat and she stood up.

'I am taking my roundness back home to the country now,' she said, fishing in her bag for her sunglasses and finding, well, how could she miss it, the loaf of bread she had brought for Charlie. Her heart skipped a beat and she pulled it out of the bag and handed it to Louis.

He took it, a look of delight claiming his whole face, raised it to his nose and sniffed it, then tapped the base with his finger, his eyebrows rising at the wonderful hollow sound.

'Perfect *pain au levain*,' he breathed. 'Well, a little overcooked, perhaps, but still, you bake bread!'

'Every day, nearly,' she said, 'since back then. With your great-great-great-great-great-grandfather's starter. I took it with me, you know.'

Louis raised the loaf again and closed his eyes, pressing it to his cheek, inhaling deeply. His smile appealed to her hormones in a way she could not fathom, and she tried as hard as she could not to wish herself in the *pain au levain*'s place. Louis opened his eyes again and must have read something like this on her face, because he put the *boule* on the table and stood up, moving in close to her.

99

'Esme,' he urged. 'This cannot be coincidence, you and me, the *pain au levain*, today after all this time.' He pulled back a bit. 'Someone,' he said, raising his eyes skywards, 'is trying to tell us something.'

Esme also drew back slightly. 'Yes,' she said, 'and that someone is me. I am trying to tell you that I have to go.' She turned towards the door.

'I will be here on Thursday next week at one o'clock,' Louis said. 'And I would like to see you here too, Esme.'

The way he said her name, lingered on it, savoured it, nearly brought her to her knees there and then, but instead Esme smiled what she hoped was a smile that said she would not be there the following week—although in truth she did not know that for a fact. She did not, at that particular point, know very much at all. She wafted out of the restaurant, smiling and thanking the Orrery staff, and in a cloud of bewilderment and bedazzlement, she turned to go down the stairs. She was halted in her tracks by a high-pitched tinkling laugh that came round the corner well before its owner, who by the click-clack that echoed in the stairwell was wearing a pair of exceptionally high heels.

Because of the sort of day it had been so far and because she recognised those two sounds, especially together, Esme knew she was about to come face to face with none other than Jemima Jones. But, of course! Why wouldn't she? Clearly, there had not been enough surprises in the day. With astonishing speed she veered into the Orrery's tiny bar, at the top of the stairs just opposite the entrance to the restaurant, and plonked herself into a big wing-backed chair.

Unfortunately for her, Jemima Jones came through the door not long after. She was dressed in white and surrounded by a collection of twentysomething men and women all in black and elbowing each other out of her wake.

Jemima did a theatrical double take when she saw Esme sitting in her throne-like seat, on her own, trying to pretend she hadn't been in the throes of shovelling down a handful of salted almonds.

'Esme MacDougall?' she trilled from across the small room.

'Stack,' said Esme, to her great embarrassment spitting out little bits of chewed-up nut as she did so. 'It's Stack.'

'Stack, of course,' Jemima said, laughing. 'I heard you got married and things.'

Esme said nothing. She wondered which 'things' Jemima had heard.

'You've moved to the country, haven't you?' Jemima continued, flicking her long, golden hair over her shoulder. 'So what brings you to a place like this, darling? It's media types and business boys from floor to ceiling as a rule.'

She turned and shone a dazzling smile at the barman. 'Champagne, darling,' she ordered him. 'All round.' She looked at Esme. 'You'll have some, of course,' she said.

'A French 75,' Esme said with an authority she was delighted to find roaming around free for the taking.

The tiny golden arch that was Jemima's eyebrow raised itself minimally, given the restraint it was under by virtue of being, as Alice had so correctly put it, Botoxed for Africa. She stood in front of Esme's chair, looking as long and silky as Esme felt short and fubsy.

'I'm writing a book,' lied Esme suddenly, 'about hair clips.' It had been such a strange day.

Jemima seemed barely to listen. 'I'm having a meeting,' she said, throwing her hair in the direction this time of the people in black, who were murmuring among themselves, 'about getting my own talk show on television. Can you believe it?'

Esme smiled encouragingly.

'Perhaps when your book is published,' Jemima said, her expressionless face leaving Esme no clue as to whether she was being facetious or not, 'you could come and talk about it.'

The waiter delivered Esme her French 75, which she snatched with a nervousness that could have looked like greed.

'That would be brilliant,' she said, smiling winningly and gulping back half of the lethal drink. 'I'll let you know closer to the time.'

The people in black started murmuring more loudly on the other side of the room and Jemima rolled her eyes.

'I'd better go,' she said. 'Work, work, work!' And she twirled to give Esme a perfect eyeful of her tiny Stairmastered-within-an-inch-of-its-life butt. Esme gulped down the rest of her cocktail in one second flat.

'Do keep in touch,' Jemima said, over her shoulder, before accepting a cigarette from one of her adoring crowd and getting down to business.

Esme stood slightly unsteadily, collected her bag and her thoughts and teetered forward.

'Thanks for the drink,' she said timidly and slid out of the door.

'We paid for her drink?' she heard one of the men in black say, and her embarrassment was so acute that she forgot until she was at the bottom of the steps that the scab of her unrequited love for Louis Lapoine had not two hours ago been ripped off and left bleeding.

She looked at her watch. She was just, as she stood there, missing the 2.30 to Ipswich, and would have to ring Henry to get Rory from Mrs McArthur, which he would count against her all week if not all month.

It was too hideous a prospect to contemplate.

Chapter Twelve

'WELL, I'LL BE JIGGERED,' Granny Mac breathed, impressed, the next morning, when Esme slid into her room smelling strongly of fresh bread. 'If there's not more than the merest hint of young Louis Lapoine in the air I'll eat my hat!'

Her hat sat on top of her wardrobe and looked extremely unappetising. She had bought it in 1949 when it looked like an enormous pink hydrangea, and age had not improved it.

Esme had not breathed a word to anybody about her lunch the day before, and as far as she was aware only Charlie and a handful of waiters knew anything about it.

'What do you know about Louis Lapoine?' she asked briskly, pulling the bedclothes straight and whistling unwittingly to the inevitable Scotsman crooning in the background.

'I know as much as you do,' her grandmother said. 'And I know that no matter how much you'll try to love again, Esme,' she stopped for dramatic emphasis, 'the first cut is the deepest.'

Esme thought about disagreeing, arguing, but it seemed pointless. 'I had lunch with him yesterday,' she said evenly instead, taking up her position on her grandmother's bed.

'I knew it!' roared Granny Mac. 'I bloody well knew it! And?'

'And he had hardly changed a bit except that now he wears a posh suit and travels the world spreading the good word about sourdough.'

'And?'

'And we had a very civilised and delicious meal and I missed the 2.30 train and Henry had to get Rory from Mrs McArthur so I am up there with Adolf Hitler in his books today and even though I've done nothing wrong I feel sick about Pog and—'

'Oh, please, enough,' Granny Mac demanded in her usual straightforward manner. 'Cut to the chase, why don't you? Tell me more about the Frenchman. Is there still something there?'

'What do you mean?' Esme asked in a small voice.

'Do you have to dance around everything that's even slightly tricky, Esme? Let alone the big stuff?'

Esme sat there, listening to her heart beat, wondering what was happening to her.

'You have to start somewhere, you know, lassie.' Granny Mac's voice seemed to soften. 'It's not going to get easier, do you realise that? It is never going to get easier. You have to start letting it go.'

The room fell silent and heavy with words unspoken from either end of the cosy single bed.

'I miss him,' Esme finally whispered into the darkness.

'I know you do,' her grandmother said. A tiny crevice of candour infiltrated the black air between them and Esme realised with something that could have been a gasp, could have been a sob, that she felt like a woman whose very tight corset had just been loosened the tiniest bit, letting her breathe easily for the first time in a long, long while.

At just that moment the doorbell rang and she instantly felt the black boot in the small of her back of someone tying her corset tighter again. She straightened up.

'The door,' she said. 'I'd better . . .'

Moments later she was staring aghast at Jam-jar standing on her doorstep and holding a scabby-looking donkey with what seemed to be a broken and badly splinted back leg.

'Well, I'm really not quite sure what to do with a donkey,' she said to her neighbour, whose enormous eyes goggled out at her, terrifyingly oversized, from behind his ancient Coke-bottle lenses.

'It's a he,' said Jam-jar and to back him up the donkey chose that moment to drop his organ, also terrifyingly oversized, from wherever he had been keeping it and, appearing to stand on tiptoes, if donkeys even had them, urinated gushingly on Esme's doorstep.

Jam-jar seemed not altogether surprised and stepped niftily aside, missing the worst of it, but Esme got such a fright she shrieked and jumped backwards. The poor donkey also took fright and reared clumsily sideways, managing to spray huge jets of donkey pee through the open door and directly into Henry's brand-new Wellington boots. He had gone to Stonyborough three days before, on the bus, to get them. He would not be happy.

'Oh, no! Not again,' she cried. Henry's footwear was a magnet for the stuff. Jam-jar grabbed at the donkey's halter and it retracted its enormous protuberance, steam still rising enthusiastically from the puddles on the ground and in her hallway.

The tap-tap-clomp that always preceded Henry heralded his imminent arrival. Esme, slightly panic-stricken, hovered dangerously, wringing her hands before grabbing up the Wellingtons and slinging them inside the door of Granny Mac's room just seconds before her father-in-law hove into view.

'What on earth is going on?' he demanded, taking in Esme's flushed face, the elderly neighbour and the lame donkey.

'For God's sake, don't give the poor thing to her,' Henry said over Esme's shoulder to Jam-jar.

Esme felt a little catch at the back of her throat which she recognised as hurt. 'Don't be silly, Henry,' she said, as kindly as she could, before turning to Jam-jar. 'The Goat was really not my fault. Apparently they go blind quite often without anything to do with spades.'

'I wasn't aware I was being silly,' Henry harrumphed. 'Have you seen my Wellingtons?'

Oh God, thought Esme. Does it really always have to be like this?

'She put them in the—' Jam-jar started to say before Esme leapt outside, shutting the door and Henry behind her.

'He's only just got over Brown peeing on his brogues,' she hissed. 'Please, I need time to explain the boots.'

Jam-jar glanced nervously back to the safety of his windmill.

'Gladys from the bookshop in Seabury brought us the donkey,' he said in his usual expressionless tone. 'It's been hit by a van and patched up by the vet but no one's claimed it and we can't keep it as we've no fencing.'

The donkey looked so gloomy Esme couldn't bear it. She didn't need another handicapped creature on her hands but then again, who else would take care of the poor thing? Besides, despite telling herself she didn't care what Henry thought, she did care what Henry thought and she wanted to show him that she could do more with animals than repeatedly diminish their capacities.

'I'll take him,' she said, and Jam-jar turned immediately and without a word started to shuffle away. 'Come on, Eeyore,' said Esme, using barely a sliver of imagination to christen the donkey. His big dark eyes looked at her glumly and she led him slowly past the house and through the willow gate into what had once been a tennis court, where she untethered him and watched him hobble towards a patch of dandelions.

God knew what donkeys ate, she thought. Or drank. And the poor thing was probably gasping for a drink after emptying his bladder so spectacularly. She headed back to the house, thinking she would get a bucket and fill it for Eeyore, but as she approached the front door, it flew open, and there stood Henry with a face like thunder, holding up his dripping gumboots.

'I suppose you find this amusing,' he challenged her.

'Of course not,' Esme tried to reason. 'I just put them in there because

I thought I could clean them up before you found them.'

Henry quivered with rage. 'I am perfectly capable of cleaning them myself.'

'Well, I'm sure you are but I just thought I could save you the bother since it was me who opened the door to the donkey.'

'Oh, so it should have been me opening the door then?' Henry fumed, catching the wrong cog yet again.

'For goodness' sake, Henry,' Esme sighed, exasperated. Her father-in-law was acting as if she'd peed on his boots herself.

'Your grandmother's room smells revolting,' he said. 'And you shouldn't be spending so much time in there.'

Esme blushed. 'That's none of your business,' she said quietly.

'My son is my business,' Henry said. 'And your son is my business. And they both need you out here.'

Esme gasped at the hardness in his eyes and Henry instantly tried to recant. 'Esme,' he said, his old, craggy face collapsed with regret. He had not meant it to sound cruel but saw that it had. He held out a pleading hand to her but she whirled round and disappeared into Granny Mac's room, slamming the door behind her, throwing herself on the bed and howling tears of rage and misery that had been pent up so long they barely knew what they were there for.

'Och,' Granny Mac said soothingly, 'there, there.'

'Henry hates me,' Esme sobbed. 'Things keep weeing on him. It's not my fault. Everything's too hard. And Jemima's got my life.'

'Oh, Esme,' her grandmother sighed. 'How can you be so blind?'

'I've had to be blind,' wept Esme. 'If I suddenly open my eyes and start seeing everything I will die.'

'Well, if you keep your eyes closed, you can hardly consider it living,' Granny Mac said. 'Say his name, Esme. Just say the wee boy's name.'

'I can't,' wept Esme. 'I just can't. I can't think about him or hear about him or talk about him. I just can't. Oh, Granny Mac, what shall I do? Everything's such a mess. Of all the times to meet Louis, now just seems so wrong. What's to become of me? And Pog? And Rory? What's to become of all of us?'

'Oh, now's not such a bad time,' Granny Mac said soothingly.

'How can you say that?'

'Well, has seeing the Frenchman again made you feel better or worse?' Granny Mac asked.

Esme closed her eyes and tried to take control of her sobs and think about the true answer to that question.

'It felt good yesterday,' she said honestly. 'But it feels bad today.'

'And why did it feel good, do you think?'

'Because,' answered Esme, 'he made me feel like the girl I used to be.'

'Well,' Granny Mac said softly. 'Maybe, finally, we're getting somewhere.'

Upstairs, the phone rang. Esme wiped her eyes and leapt up the stairs, grateful, in a way, to be safe from having the blatantly unhealed wounds of her distant and not-so-distant past poked at by the interfering spectre of her grandmother.

It was Charlie on the phone, wanting to do a bit of poking of his own.

'Was he still gorgeous?' he pestered her. 'Was he still sexy?'

'What is it with everyone?' Esme grumbled. 'Why do you all want to know about that?'

Charlie was surprised. 'Who else wants to know? Did you tell Pog?' he asked. 'I thought you might have kept your little tryst to yourself, Es.'

'No one,' she said. 'I didn't. It wasn't a tryst.'

'Well, whatever it was I bet it spiced up your life, eh?' Charlie ploughed on, hounding her for details.

'He told me he came to find me the night I left Venolat, Charlie,' Esme said. 'You never mentioned that.'

A small silence travelled uncomfortably down the phone line. 'Well, why would I have told you that, Es? And what difference would it have made, anyway? It didn't make him unmarried.'

'No, but it means that I wouldn't have spent the last fifteen years thinking he was a complete and utter shit who never gave a toss about me when it turns out that actually he did.'

'Really?' asked Charlie with a cough. 'Do you suppose that's true?'

'Why wouldn't it be true?' Esme asked incredulously.

'Well, I don't know,' Charlie said awkwardly. 'He wasn't exactly the most trustworthy fellow in the world, was he?'

'You are so bloody cynical, Charlie,' Esme said angrily. 'He's got stronger principles than you or I. He is still turning his back on his family fortune and teaching people how to bake sourdough. I mean you could hardly say the same about our careers, could you? You don't give a tinker's cuss about yours and I don't even have one.'

'Calm down, Esme.' Charlie was rattled now too. 'It was just a chance meeting. It's not like you are going to up and run off with him.'

The very suggestion gave her a tremor of excitement.

'Actually,' she said. 'I could just up and run off if I wanted to. He isn't married any more, he doesn't live with his kids, he travels the globe making the world's most delicious bread. It certainly seems a pleasant enough alternative to standing ankle-deep in donkey pee worrying about what a crappy mother you are.'

'Essie,' Charlie's concern was clear, 'are you all right? I would have thought lunch with Louis would have been a little surprise pick-me-up, not a cat among the pigeons.'

'Yes, well, lunch with you might have been a pick-me-up but with him it has unleashed a whole—'

The feel of someone's lips on the back of her neck sent a jolt of fear up her spine. She gasped.

'Unleashed a whole what?' Pog asked behind her, before moving over to the stove top to put the kettle on. 'Sounds exciting. Is that Alice?' He must have come home for lunch and she'd not heard his footsteps on the stairs.

'I'd better go,' Esme said into the receiver. She felt guilty and grubby. 'I'll talk to you later.'

Pog slumped down at the kitchen table and smiled at her, and Esme's heart swelled with love and confusion. What the hell was the matter with her? They may not have had the romance of the century, she and Pog, but she had never doubted for a moment how much he adored her. She could see it now in his eyes, despite the baggy black cushions beneath them and the thin veil of things he never told her lurking in front of them.

She sat down opposite him. 'Is everything OK?' she asked.

'It's fine,' he said with what she thought could have been a slightly forced smile, 'although my father seems to be doing something very strange outside with the garden hose and if I'm not mistaken a wounded wildebeest of some description.'

Esme rolled her eyes. 'Don't ask,' she advised, her heart racing as she examined her feelings for this man and wondered how there could be room left to entertain thoughts of Louis.

'I thought I might go into Stonyborough this afternoon,' Pog said, 'and see if I can drum up a bit more work. Apparently that falling-down old pub at the end of the High Street is up for sale, so whoever buys it might be looking for an architect of my supremely outstanding skill. What do you think?'

In their old London days the thought of Pog trolling the high streets for renovation work would have had them gurgling derisively into their Chardonnays. Was it worth it? Had they made the right move?

'What about doing up Seabury—when will you hear about that?' she asked helpfully.

Pog looked surprised and she realised that he already had heard. She felt instantly mortified at having been too preoccupied with herself to think about him and got up and went to his side, cuddling him and kissing his head, sniffing his Pog-smelling hair.

'Oh, darling,' she said. 'You got it? Congratulations. I'm so sorry. That's wonderful news. When did you find out?'

'Oh, not long ago,' he said brightly. 'Don't worry about it. It doesn't matter.' This was not true and they both knew it. But who between them would be the first to open the Pandora's box of what really mattered? Pog, though, thinking of Rory's sad little face and enquiring eyes out on the Meare and feeling suddenly reckless, decided on the spur of the moment to at least wriggle the lock.

'Esme,' he said. 'I've been thinking.'

'About what?'

'About counselling.'

'Oh, really?' Esme's voice was light but her shoulders had frozen. 'For whom?'

For us, Pog wanted to say. For you and me and our two darling boys. He eyed his wife and her square frightened shoulders across the canyon of grief between them.

'Esme,' he said quietly. 'We can't go on like this.'

'Like what?' she whispered.

'Like two normal people constantly tiptoeing around this great gaping puddle, terrified of stepping in it in case we bloody drown.'

'Don't,' she pleaded. 'Please, Pog, don't.'

'I miss him, Esme,' Pog said, and his voice caught. 'I want to talk about him.'

He expected her to flee, but she didn't. She stayed there still and square, looking straight at him.

'I'm not ready,' she finally said, barely audible.

'But I am,' Pog answered her, the strength almost back in his voice.

'Then *you* talk about him,' she said. '*You* get counselling.'

She looked so frightened then, so lonely and small and lost and hunted, that Pog's bravery abandoned him.

'I'm sorry,' he said, shaking his head. 'I don't mean to upset you. Please, forget I mentioned it.'

Her shoulders stayed tense, her face rigid with fear. Pog felt cruel. He knew she wasn't ready. But, like Rory, he wondered how long they would all have to wait.

'Any chance of a sarnie?' he asked, abandoning the dreadful subject and watching her shoulders slowly relax. He'd had a bag of crisps and two custard doughnuts since breakfast, but the kitchen was ringing with the sweet smell of freshly baked sourdough and if there was one thing that would give Esme back her equilibrium, it was slicing into a freshly baked loaf.

Her face collapsed with relief and she jumped up and pulled out a bread knife.

She wasn't ready, but she was closer. He knew that. Those weeks when she had stopped baking he'd been worried, but since her return to sourdough there had definitely been a change, a lift, in her spirits. Without that early-morning ritual life had been torturous in the House in the Clouds.

For once he felt he had done the right thing in his despair by feeding the starter, despite Esme's insistence that she would never need it again.

So it hadn't bubbled and burped the way it did when Esme mollycoddled it, but it had smelt vinegary and sharp and had not turned its nose up at the healthy meals of flour and water he fed it.

And when, for whatever reason—would she ever tell him? Would he ever know?—Esme returned to it as he had prayed she would, it had turned itself into a perfect *boule* and hurrah, they were back in business again. So, his wife's behaviour had been slightly odd since her return to bread-baking—it was her slightly odd behaviour that had attracted him to her in the first place.

He had spotted her across the room: a life raft of colour in a sea of black-clad architects. Her hair had been piled on top of her head so that her red curls were like an eccentric fountain cascading down over her shoulders and back. She was wearing a citrus green wraparound top that hugged her curves and a black full skirt with red platform boots and a tiny red-leather backpack and was picking at a tray of smoked salmon canapés. When he got closer, Pog saw that she was taking capers off some of the soggy pancake things and placing them on others, which she was then popping in her mouth.

'We're a perfect match,' he said to her from across the catering table as he reached for a de-capered snack. 'I don't care for the little green balls myself.' She looked up at him, her big emerald eyes slightly horrified at having been caught, and he fell in love with her there and then.

A blush that matched her backpack crept up her chest and onto her face and she opened her mouth to speak, but realising it was still full of food, shut it again. Pog felt an urge to snatch her into his arms, which, as it turned out, was pretty much what happened. The capers in Esme's mouth, confused by being interrupted in their journey to her stomach, went down the wrong way. Esme choked.

Pog then leapt, fast as lightning, round the table and encircling her from behind, her backpack buckle scratching his belly as he did so, crushed her with such force that a ball of munched-up blini and sour cream spotted with half-chewed caper shot out of her mouth. They gazed, aghast as the creamy-looking clump flew straight back onto the catering table where it landed in a plate of cheese and walnut balls.

Before either of them could move a muscle, a hand belonging to an extremely fat man reached, unseeing, and popped Esme's regurgitated snack into his mouth.

Pog was frozen in fascination, Esme in horror. Yet nobody else seemed to have seen. The fat man merely licked his fingers and reached for more canapés.

'I think we should get married,' Pog said, when his paralysis evaporated and he held out his hand to introduce himself. 'I'm Hugo Stack.'

'Esme MacDougall,' reciprocated Esme. 'I think we should have a sit-down meal at the wedding, don't you? Bite-sized snacks can be dangerous. I never knew that.'

The first night they stayed up talking and laughing and watching old Peter Sellers films. The next day they walked in Kew Gardens, ate at the River Café—how he loved to watch her eat!—listened to jazz until the wee small hours, and then the next day she took him home to Granny Mac and fed him her homemade sourdough. Sitting in her warm little flat eating cannellini bean and pesto soup with his first ever inch-thick slice of Esme's *pain au levain*, Pog realised that the missing piece of the jumbled jigsaw puzzle he had long felt like had been found.

He had loved Granny Mac from the word go, too. She was just the opposite of everyone in his family. Totally outspoken, insatiably curious, straightforward to the point of irascibility. He loved it and she loved him. She thought he was perfect for Esme and told him so within a minute of meeting him. Esme, who blushed at everything, simply smiled and laughed at this, unembarrassed. The bond between the two women was awe-inspiring—anyone either of them loved was let in without question.

Pog, who knew his parents loved him but had spent his lifetime wondering if they liked him, found being at the MacDougall flat in St John's Wood unbelievably comforting. Henry and Grace had been adept if aloof parents. Feelings were never discussed or displayed. Conversation revolved around Henry's work, Grace's garden, the boys' careers, the weather. At Granny Mac's place, though, emotion ran wild and free and the small, cosy rooms echoed with laughter and Rod Stewart. There, Pog never need wonder how anyone felt, he just knew.

He bit into the bread and felt it surrender to his tongue, the tartness of the apricot jam hitting the back of his throat just as the sour crust of the bread met resistance from his teeth. There was such joy in eating, thought Pog. He watched his wife watching him as he ate his lunch. He felt happiness and he felt despair. It was a combination he was used to. He wiped the crumbs from his face and kissed Esme goodbye, then went back to work.

Esme too felt happiness and despair, for the same and for very different reasons. She was consumed with what Pog had said, what Granny Mac had said, and with heart-thumping silent re-enactments of the day before's lunch. Had she really asked Louis why he broke her heart? Why had she done that? The damage had long been done and there was nothing to be gained by stirring up the past. The present was enough of a hornet's nest, after all.

Chapter Thirteen

'WHAT THE HELL have you been up to?' Alice barked down the phone on Sunday morning.

'Nothing,' Esme answered her friend. 'Except laundry, polishing the stairs, making the beds, stewing apples, polishing more stairs, ministering to the donkey, trying not to strangle my son, polishing more stairs. You get the picture.'

'It sounds far more exciting the way your friend Jemima puts it,' Alice said crisply, rustling the *Sunday Times* as loudly as she could manage while holding the telephone under her chin. 'I didn't realise she still had it in for you to quite such a degree. Is there something I should know?'

'Jemima?' Esme was bewildered. 'What does she have to do with anything?'

'You only feature in her column this morning, Esme.'

In the hurricane of thoughts that had whirled round her head in the aftermath of her lunch with Louis, Esme had quite forgotten she had seen Jemima.

'What on earth are you talking about?' she asked Alice, but as she did her bewilderment curdled and turned to dread.

'*Which slightly dishevelled-looking former Fag Mag editor,*' Alice read out, '*was spotted during the week sucking back champagne cocktails all on her lonesome in the bar of smart Marylebone High Street eatery the Orrery?*'

'Oh my God!' whispered Esme.

'That's nothing,' said Alice, reading on. '*The sad little Ginger No Friends has been hiding away deep in the Suffolk countryside for the past few years but obviously needs to pop her head up for air and a sip of Taittinger every now and then, and who could blame her?*

'*All those warm lagers and pork pies down at her local pub can obviously play merry hell with a girl's waistband. No wonder this once-rising star of the London publishing scene needs to escape back to the big city every now and then. And for the one or two of you who may have been wondering what project the rumpled little creature is working on now? It's a book about hair clips.* My God, where does she get this drivel from? *And I don't know where she's doing her research but it's certainly not on her own head. I guess the perm is obviously still alive and well and living in the countryside!* And in case you weren't sure about how sarcastic that is supposed to be, Es, there's an exclamation mark.'

Alice, finally, was silent. 'Are you still there, Es?'

Esme felt too anaesthetised with humiliation to speak. How could that unspeakable woman embarrass her this way?

'She called me a Ginger No Friends?'

'Well, were you sitting there all on your own swilling champagne or not?' Alice demanded. 'And if so, why wasn't I invited?'

'I was supposed to be having lunch with Charlie,' Esme said, her lips white with dismay. 'But he never turned up. Is she saying I looked fat? Is the bit about the pork pies meant to say I looked fat? Because if she's saying I looked fat I think I might seriously have to kill her.'

'You think that's worse than calling you a once-rising star?' Alice wanted to know. 'When after all it was she who shot your rising star down in the first place. She is evil and she must be destroyed. And I think she is saying you looked fat but you don't.'

Esme collapsed into a chair and tried to sort out in her mind what was the worst thing about appearing in Jemima's column. For a start, neither her husband nor her best friend had known she was out for lunch that day. She'd been unable to come up with a way to make her meeting with Louis seem innocent, even though it was, and so had fudged the details of what she'd done with her day. As for Alice, if she'd told her she had met Louis, she would have told her that he wanted to see her again and Alice would have insisted she stop being so bloody stupid. She supposed she had been avoiding that.

'Oh, Alice,' she said down the phone. 'What am I going to do? Pog doesn't know I went down to London for the day, nor does—oh my God—Henry! They will jump to all the wrong conclusions and how dare she call me sad and little. Did she really call me sad and little?

And rumpled? And a creature? Oh, it's too hideous for words.'

A slight frostiness chilled the phone line. 'You didn't tell Pog? What's going on? Is there a wrong conclusion to jump to?'

'No. Nothing. No,' Esme said hastily. 'There's absolutely nothing going on. I just stupidly, for no reason, didn't tell him. You know how he is about Charlie. He's probably the person Pog likes least in the world which is not really saying much because he still likes him and everything but, oh shit, I'm all over the place at the moment, Alice, you know that. It wasn't on purpose. I didn't mean it. And now to be ridiculed publicly by that long streak of, of, of—' She struggled to come up with an apt description.

'Weasel's piss?' suggested Alice.

'Yes, weasel's piss. It's just too much. It feels like just too much.'

'Nobody will know it's you,' Alice said assertively, deciding to be supportive. 'And anyway, Pog doesn't read the Sunday Times and Henry wouldn't bother with Jemima's column and to be honest, you should be thankful that she didn't come to your house. You should hear what she has to say about Primrose Beckwith-Stuyvesant's new place.'

'Really?' Esme asked without interest. Her own troubles seemed too many and varied to contemplate anyone else's.

'Get a load of this,' Alice started. 'It's right under the bit about you. *I had heard that poor dear Primrose had decided to do the decorating herself but nobody had quite prepared me for her spectacular lack of skill in this department. You'd imagine that someone with a name like Primrose would know the difference between caramel and brown, would you not? Anyway, I am sure that somewhere in Morocco lurks a second-rate seventies bordello owner who is wondering what happened to all his furnishings. Try Belgravia, Ahmed! That's my advice. All eyes were supposed to be on Juniper Smythe, the stepniece of the hostess, who has recently announced her engagement to PR king Lance Silverspoon but frankly it was hard to make the poor girl out among the kaleidoscope of garishness that is Primrose's drawing room.'*

Esme's own misery was left bobbing, temporarily, in a sea of sympathy for poor Primrose.

'She is a complete and utter cow,' she railed, astonished at the level of Jemima's bitchery. 'It's like a horrible nightmare.'

'I won't read you the bit about Marie Claire's first piano recital then,' suggested Alice, 'because it may give you a duodenal ulcer. And compared to poor Primrose, you didn't do so badly really.'

'No, I'm just a fat, lonely has-been who has ginger hair in need of clips that looks permed but isn't,' said Esme. 'I'm just swell.'

'God knows where she got the story about the hair clips. The woman is obviously completely deranged. Why fabricate something like that?'

'Yes, well,' coughed Esme, 'I did see her at the bar in the Orrery and we had a perfectly pleasant conversation. In fact she bought me the drink, or the teenage TV producers who were courting her did, much to their own horror. Oh God, what a mess!'

'Don't tell me she is getting her own TV show,' shrilled Alice. 'If she gets her own TV show you won't have to kill her because I will have done it for you. Did she look good?'

'Gorgeous,' Esme said dully. 'A little mask-like in the face obviously but very tall and slim and blonde and—'

'Ridge!' Alice pulled away from the phone and called to her son. 'Ridge! Wait a minute. Esme, I have to go. Ridge has just come in and it's been three days since I've seen him. Hold on,' she called to her son. 'I'll ring you back later,' she gabbled to Esme. And she was gone.

For the rest of Sunday, Esme felt so close to tears or a nervous breakdown or a full confession (even though she hadn't really done anything, she kept telling herself) that Pog put her to bed, like Peter Rabbit, with a cup of camomile tea at 7.30. Every time the phone rang, her heart dropped down to the pit of her stomach and churned.

The next day she stumbled through her chores convinced that her husband was going to storm into the house at any moment waving the newspaper and shouting, 'What is the meaning of this, you filthy hussy,' which, of course, he never did. Pog was not a stormer and anyway, the House in the Clouds was probably not an ideal place to storm. If you were still full of bluster and huff after six flights of stairs you were most likely not someone who preferred eating homemade bread with their wife to watching football with the lads down the local.

By the end of the next day Esme had started to relax and think that maybe Alice was right, that no one would ever know it was she that Jemima was talking about.

By the end of the day after that, however, her relief was verging on something that seemed to approach resentment. She had even gone so far as to get Alice to fax a copy of the hideous column up to her—she had definitely not bought the paper herself—so she could read it to Granny Mac once 'I Was Only Joking' faded away to a reasonable level.

'It's bloody hilarious,' her grandmother roared. 'Oh, she has spunk that one. I've not laughed so much in a long, long while.'

'It's not funny, it's horrible. She's humiliated me,' Esme answered.

'In front of whom?' Granny Mac asked her. 'As Alice says, no one would ever know it was you. I mean who would ever imagine that you would be sitting in a fancy bar in Marylebone swilling cocktails on your own in the middle of the day? Nobody, that's who. It's a ridiculous notion.'

Granny Mac had, as was her wont, hit the nail on Esme's head. Who *would* ever imagine that she would be sitting in a fancy bar in Marylebone drinking cocktails on her own in the middle of the day?

Nobody. That's who. It was a ridiculous notion. They, whoever they were, would be too busy imagining her running up and down a thousand stairs in her hideaway hole in the country with her head in the clouds like the rest of her house. They would be imagining her trying to tighten the splint on her donkey's broken leg, milking her blind goat, taming some mad bees, kowtowing to her difficult father-in-law, wrangling with her recalcitrant son, pouring all her leftover love and ancient desire into fat, brown, round loaves of bread, hiding from the tragedy about which others still spoke with words that stayed choked up and constipated in her own throat.

'It hasn't always been a ridiculous notion,' she told her grandmother. 'Once upon a time nobody would have been surprised to find me swilling French 75s in swanky surroundings in the middle of a weekday. Am I so much of a has-been bloody hausfrau these days that no one could be surprised by me? When did I get so pathetic? So predictable?'

'The problem is not that you are a has-been bloody hausfrau,' Granny Mac answered her eventually. 'And the problem is not Jemima Jones.'

The room was deathly silent. The temperature seemed to have plummeted. Esme felt cold with dread. She started to shiver.

'The problem is you, Esme. You and your loss.' The words came painfully slowly and cut right through her. 'The worst loss a woman, a mother can suffer.'

'It's not that,' Esme said, her teeth chattering.

'You can't keep pushing it away and not feeling it, Esme. It's not working. Especially not now with me the way I am '

'It's not about that,' whispered Esme. 'It's not about him.'

'Oh, Esme, aren't you tired of this?'

She was tired, unbelievably tired. Too tired to deal with what her grandmother wanted from her.

'It's about Louis,' she insisted, feeling cowardly but determined. 'It's all about Louis.'

Her grandmother's displeasure was palpable, the air in the dingy room clanged with it.

'Have it your way, then,' Granny Mac said finally. 'But if it is Louis stirring you up, for God's sake have the guts to let yourself be stirred.'

Esme sat stock-still on the end of her grandmother's bed.

'He wants to meet me for lunch again tomorrow,' she said.

'I know,' answered Granny Mac.

'I want to go,' said Esme.

'I know,' answered Granny Mac.

'Because even though it is vastly complicating matters, it feels—' she sought out the word from the carnival in her mind, 'good. Like the end of something. Or,' she was loath even to think such a thing, 'heaven forbid, the beginning.'

'I know,' said Granny Mac. 'Just not like you're stuck for ever in the bloody middle.'

'That's right,' agreed Esme. 'Is there anything you don't know?'

'I know everything you do,' said Granny Mac. 'It's just that sometimes I know it sooner. I'm good like that.'

'You don't think I am wicked?'

'Oh, don't flatter yourself! You truly think you're the first person to suffer a loss so enormous you can't confront it? You think no one else has ever tried to escape the reality of their life with the fantasy of another? It's nothing new. It's all been done before.'

'Is that supposed to make me feel better?'

'You tell me what it's supposed to make you feel.'

'Honestly, at times like this I don't know why I bother, Granny Mac,' Esme snapped, standing up to leave.

'Oh, aye,' Granny Mac said rudely. 'Silly me. Bottom smacked.'

Esme left the room and started the climb up to the kitchen. She had soup to make, a pair of Pog's trousers to mend and afternoon tea to prepare for Henry and Rory, plus the oven was horribly overdue for a clean and the windows in the sitting room were so filthy she could barely see out of them. She had a lot of housework to get through if she was going down to London the next day to meet the love of her life.

'The *first* love,' she corrected herself out loud.

'What was that?'

Unfortunately, she had corrected herself out loud while passing Henry on the first-floor landing.

'Oh, nothing,' she smiled. 'Just talking to myself.'

'Yes, well, there would seem to be an awful lot of that going on around here lately,' he said gruffly. 'And in my day that thing out there would have earned itself a bullet between the eyes, not a lot of fussy mollycoddling by a bunch of ignorant city people.'

'I thought you liked the donkey,' she said, surprised. 'And Rory certainly seems to. It's good for him to have another friend about the place.' She smiled brightly but Henry shot her a look of such inexplicable contempt that she simply turned and traipsed up the stairs.

116

She defrosted some chicken stock, chopped a pile of carrots and parsnips, hand-stitched the trousers Pog had split bending over at Enid Entwhistle's house to inspect a blocked drain, then rang Alice at work to see what was happening with the wayward Ridge.

'He's got a job in some restaurant in the West End,' Alice gabbled down the phone. 'And I think he is spending the nights with Mrs Miller. He barely speaks to me, just grunts as he comes and goes and I seem incapable of doing anything about it. It's such fun.'

'What about Mr Miller?'

'He's off on an oil rig for six weeks at a time, I do know that much but not from my hulking ingrate of an offspring. From Olive upstairs.'

'The blowsy mid-morning gin drinker?'

'No, the mild-mannered mousy librarian. Anyway, she says it's not the first time Mrs Miller has "entertained" during her husband's absence and that I should not be too worried and that, get this, Ridge is such a nice young man. He picks up her shopping from the supermarket and brings it home for her. Every week. Has done for nearly a year. You could have knocked me over with a feather. The things you find out!'

Esme heard the pride in Alice's voice and felt thrilled for her.

'We always knew he would turn out well in the end, didn't we? By the way, I thought I would come down to London tomorrow,' she said, 'and we could catch up with a drink in town after work. Do you fancy it?'

'Do I what!' said Alice.

When Esme woke up the next morning, she felt an excitement she could remember from the Christmas mornings of her childhood.

Pog, still asleep, snorted, rolled over in their bed and flung one arm across her middle. Esme looked down at his floppy rust-coloured hair and his sleep-squashed face, and wondered how she could love him so much but have a stomach full of butterflies fluttering in anticipation of a different man altogether.

When had she turned into this person who could lie and keep such dangerous secrets? She gently removed his arm, dressed and went up to the kitchen to get her bread started.

Even high up in the sky Esme could smell the rain that had fallen on the grass overnight. Her senses were on red alert, just as they had been all those years ago in Venolat.

Her tap water jumped excitedly into the jug before she poured it in with the flour, and her starter seemed more wildly exuberant than usual, she was sure. She could swear that it smelt of that little *boulangerie* by the fountain. Esme lifted the jar to her face and breathed it in. There was definitely something special in the air this morning.

She plunged her hand into the bowl and swirled the wet mixture between her fingers. Again and again she danced round the bowl until the floury, watery mixture turned into dough and started to feel like skin against her hand. She threw the salt into the bowl and kneaded it in, pressing and pushing and very gently pummelling until the crunchiness was gone and the dough was silky and skin-like again.

She rolled it out of the bowl and started working it on the counter. With the heel of her hand she pushed it away from herself and with the curve of her cupped fingers she pulled it back, again and again. With every pump of her arm she thought of Louis. Her teeth on his skin, her lips on his neck, his fingers in her—

'Bloody hell, Essie, you'll do yourself a mischief!'

The sound of her husband's voice gave her such a fright that for a moment she was completely lost. She felt so utterly, embarrassingly caught in flagrante delicto that she could barely believe it was only bread she was making.

Pog came up behind her and wriggled into her.

'You're going at it hammer and tongs, Esme,' he said. 'What's all this flour and water done to deserve that?'

He kissed her neck and she felt ill with artifice. She turned in his arms and kissed him, pushing all thoughts of Louis deep down inside.

'Delicious,' Pog said, pulling away and looking at her. 'It's not right that anyone should look as good as you at this ungodly hour.'

He scratched his stomach. 'Couldn't go back to sleep,' he added, yawning. 'Anything I can do to help?'

Esme shook her head and went back to her bread, listening to him scrabble around in the pantry for his breakfast cereal.

'I have to spend another twenty-six hours talking to Ernie about his "loggia" as it's now called,' he said as he mooched about the kitchen. 'And I think I have a meeting today with an Ipswich developer who might be keen on that Stonyborough pub. What about you? Anything exciting planned for today?'

Esme tried not to stop the rhythm of her kneading.

'Actually, I thought I might go down to London for a spot of shopping and to meet Alice for a drink,' she said lightly.

'Oh, that's right,' Pog said. 'Henry mentioned you'd asked him to look after Rory. Good on you, darling, say hello to Alice from me.'

All the way to London she thought about his adoring face and she kept thinking about it as she sat at the same table in the Orrery, fidgeting with her table napkin and waiting for Louis.

She had a wonderful husband, a healthy child, a lovely home. Why the hell was she risking all that for some duplicitous little French baker who had broken her heart a hundred years ago, and without whom she would happily have kept on living had not fate brought them together over a bubble-gum disaster next door?

But when Louis walked into the room and saw her, all her doubts disappeared, to be instantly replaced by nothing but the certainty of chemistry. His effect on her was pure and physical and no amount of debating the appropriateness of ther situation could change that.

He walked across the room, late but not rattled, and kissed her on each cheek. They burned. He looked into her eyes. They swam. He reached across the table and took her hand in his. She let him.

She could not remember, afterwards, what they talked about over the scallops and wild mushrooms and crispy-skinned duck. She could see nothing but the dark intense features of his face in front of her, the hustle and bustle of the busy restaurant moving behind him blurred and out of focus like a modern-day cooking show.

'I want you,' she longed to say to him. 'I want you now. Over there. On that banquette. The way it was.' But even as she opened her mouth to speak she knew she wouldn't. She shut her mouth again. Instead, it was Louis who spoke.

'Tell me about your children,' he said quietly.

'Child,' said Esme. 'Child. I have a son. Rory. He's four and a half.'

Louis looked at her, slightly quizzically, as though he somehow knew otherwise. He did not speak, just kept looking straight at her.

She felt suddenly icy cold and boiling hot at the same time and her chest started to rise and fall too quickly. The toxic fumes of her inner demons were dancing close to a naked flame, and she could feel it so dangerously it took her breath away.

Something deadly was trying to escape the constraints of her heart, and for less than a split second Esme pictured the relief of letting it go, and in that fraction of a second it bolted for freedom.

'I have one son,' she said again before she could taste the words on her lips, 'but he had a twin brother.'

It was out now, floating in the space between them.

'Ted,' she said. 'Teddy.' How strange the feel of his name was on her tongue. How lonely and lost. How long had it been since she had said it out loud?

Actually, she knew.

It had been two years, two months, thirteen days, twenty hours and forty-seven minutes.

Esme floated up to the ceiling of the restaurant and looked down. She saw herself about to tell this heart-stoppingly handsome perfect almost-stranger about the day, the hour, the minute, the second she stopped being herself and became a mother of one.

And the tears that she had found so difficult, so impossible, to shed for her poor little Rory—Pog clone suddenly presented themselves for the inspection of Louis Lapoine, her long-lost lover, and the waiting staff and patrons of the Orrery restaurant.

Oh, but they had been such a long time coming.

Chapter Fourteen

LIFE HAD BEEN GOING WELL for Esme and Pog until that cold, cruel spring day in Notting Hill.

Their respective careers, in which they had both managed to spend quite some time up until then floundering, had clicked into place and they were separately charging full steam ahead.

Pog, through an old college friend of his, had won a modest contract the previous year to refurbish a small investment brokerage in the City. He had done such a good job that when the company had been bought out by a big German firm, they engaged him to do a similar job, only ten times bigger, in another empty shell near St Paul's.

Esme's career too had finally stopped hitting potholes and seemed to be running along smoothly. When she had been deposed by Jemima and lost her job at *TV Now!*, the road back from ruin had been bumpy, to say the least.

Humiliated by her ousting, she'd accepted a job running an old men's smoking magazine published by a company that made pipes and cigarette papers. *Vogue*, it wasn't. But Sebastian Goodhart, the elderly publisher/pipemaker, adored Esme from the moment she whirled into his office with her ginger bob and slash of red lipstick, and under his gentle and bemused patronage, she and the funny little magazine flourished.

In fact, in less than a year, it doubled in circulation, partly due to Esme's hard work and sheer dedication and partly due to the newly fashionable trend towards cigar-smoking: a bandwagon on which she had been quick to jump.

Sebastian Goodhart was delighted and on the strength of her success with *Smoke*, picked up an industry title much ignored by the rag trade called *Apparel*, which Esme similarly turned around for the better.

Both magazines, however, were subscription only, and Esme's dream was to edit a successful newsstand magazine. The one she had her eye on was a little-read tome called *Baker* which languished at the back of the magazine racks behind the glossies, at all good bookshops.

Soon she was the editor of three magazines and her feet barely touched the ground as she flew between her home in Notting Hill and her expanding West End office off Oxford Street.

'Och, look out, here comes Rupert Murdoch,' Granny Mac would say rudely when Esme rushed in the door after work, usually just to change and bolt out again to some industry function or other.

Granny Mac lived with Esme and Pog in a crumbling Victorian terraced house in probably the least salubrious part of Notting Hill. All Souls Road. When Esme had moved in with Pog, Granny Mac had come too. It was inconceivable that she should do anything else, and Pog, bless his heart, had not only never said anything about it, he had barely thought about it.

Following Henry's investment 'hiccup', Pog convinced him to invest what little he had left in the top flat of the All Souls Road house, and eventually drew up plans to renovate its three poorly conceived separate dwellings back into one house with room for all the generations.

Granny Mac was very sceptical about this. 'It's not natural,' was all she would say. 'If I wanted to live with another cranky old bastard, I'd send Esme out to find me a husband.'

The house, like every other one in the street, had a long, leafy back garden into which you would, when the conversion was finished, step out from the kitchen or dining room. Pog had pretty much left it alone apart from mowing the lush green lawn occasionally, and its perimeter was clogged with mature trees and overgrown shrubs.

Esme had big plans for this luxurious outdoor space. But its pièce de résistance had come to her in a blinding flash as she worked her sourdough on the scratched stainless-steel worktop obscenely early one morning, obscenely early being the only time she could squeeze it in.

Her mind had drifted while working the dough, back to that village square above the kinky Dordogne, with its graceful little fountain trickling water into its bowl.

'You have got to be kidding me,' Granny Mac breathed when Esme showed her the plans she'd drawn up a month later for a tiled courtyard of her own, complete with boxed topiary olive trees and the crowning centrepiece of a six-foot fountain that wept extravagantly into an elaborate circular pond. It was as close as she could get to the one behind which she had hidden when she first saw Louis, given that so many years had passed in between.

'You don't like it?' Esme had asked her sour-faced grandmother.

'Oh, sure, I like it,' Granny Mac answered sarcastically. 'Me and the Count of Monte bloody Cristo. What in God's name are we going to do with a fountain?'

'You don't do anything with them. You look at them and admire them and they add ambiance and interest.'

They agreed to disagree. Well, that is to say, Esme agreed to disagree. Granny Mac agreed to no such thing and ridiculed the fountain at every possible opportunity.

'Perhaps we could have a bubbling brook,' she suggested politely to Pog on one occasion with an evil glint in her eye, 'or a waterfall. Had you thought about a waterfall?' Pog, as always, refused to take the bait, just smiling and shrugging his shoulders.

In the month before the renovations were to begin, however, life in the Notting Hill house was turned on its head.

Esme fell pregnant.

It was an accident. That is to say, they had always wanted children but had planned on waiting another couple of years. Mother Nature, of course, put babies before fountains and so gave Esme a dose of gastroenteritis, which upset the rhythm of her contraception long enough for the reproductive fairies to do their bit.

The house in All Souls Road fair hummed with happiness when they broke the news to their elders. Henry was actually seen to smile at Granny Mac and not be hissed at in return.

The plans for the house and the garden were shelved while talk turned to all things baby, and, after the twelve-week scan, all things babies.

At the news they were having twins, Esme had thought her husband was going to explode with pride and joy, and Granny Mac attempted the dance of the seven swords, such was her excitement.

Esme, despite having ankles swollen like fence posts with retention, worked like a Trojan to make sure no one could accuse her of abandoning her career in favour of motherhood, and stopped work just two weeks before the babies were due.

Granny Mac and Pog were at either end of her to bring the little boys into the world, and it was without doubt the happiest day of all of their lives. Ted emerged first at five pounds one ounce, and Rory twenty minutes later at five pounds two.

'Ginger Megses, the two of them,' Granny Mac cried delightedly, as Pog looked into his wife's tired eyes and loved her so much he thought he might burst.

And so began a new arrival of Stacks into the tumble-down house in All Souls Road. Even Henry forgot his bitterness and entered into the spirit of calming and soothing and, to Esme's surprise, playing with the babies, who grew fat and happy under such love and attention.

Pog and Esme were fascinated by the twin-ness of their sons. From their very arrival each baby seemed secretly, silently aware of the other. Take one away and the remaining one would go on alert, eyes wide and ears almost pricked for any sound that might help identify the other's whereabouts.

The boys may have looked identical but their different personalities emerged very early on and were a constant source of fascination. Teddy was impatient and loud, while Rory seemed more tolerant and self-contained. Teddy would suck greedily at Esme's nipple, always hungry for more, while Rory needed encouragement to feed. When they moved on to solids, Teddy only ate egg yolks and Rory only whites. Teddy liked crusts, Rory discarded them. They were matching halves of the same little entity.

And how those boys were loved!

Alice cherished them as well as, to their surprise, did twelve-year-old Ridgeley.

'He's always desperate to get here,' Alice smiled, as she sat on the sofa sipping coffee one Sunday afternoon while Ridge played with the boys on the floor 'It's the only thing he ever shows any enthusiasm for.'

Of course, it wasn't all plain sailing, far from it. In the first few months Esme, like many a new mother, suffered the worst excruciating doubt and terror of her entire life. There were moments when she felt so alone, so responsible, so scared, it was almost unbearable.

Eventually, though, her convoluted road map of stretch marks started to fade and so did her fear that motherhood was too hard, that she couldn't do it. She could. It was hard work but Esme was used to that and soon enough tiny pockets even started appearing where her mind strayed away from bottles and nappies and sleep patterns and back to the innermost workings of Goodhart Publishing.

When the boys were a little over nine months old, she went back to work, leaving them in the care of a sunny, outgoing Australian nanny called Tracey. She had thought she was ready for it, had looked forward to it even. But her first morning back she had felt physically sick with guilt, was crying in the loos by lunchtime and at two o'clock concocted a business meeting in Chelsea, lunged for her bag and ran out of the door to get home to her boys.

They were pleased to see her but had survived the day better than she had. As Pog said, their twin-ness was a huge help. They were never alone. They always had each other. And now they had the irrepressible Tracey and, lurking in the background, Granny Mac and Henry who watched like hawks for signs she was an alcoholic or a slave-trader.

She was neither and the boys loved her. Granny Mac was not convinced, saying she reminded her of a horse-rustler she once met in Gretna Green and Henry was similarly unimpressed.

Esme trusted her, though, and as the days passed into weeks and months, her enthusiasm for her work returned in spades until mixed with the duties of motherhood there was barely a second in her day left unspoken for. She felt pulled in a thousand different directions but somehow managed to hold it all together and even allowed herself to believe—in the rare moments she had to indulge in such thought—that perhaps she could be a career woman and a mother and be good at both.

Through it all, she baked. It was another tug at the restraints of time but no one, nothing could persuade Esme to give up her sourdough.

Tracey's sunny personality, however, was slowly receding behind a cloud. Nine months of being at home with Granny Mac and Henry Stack could do that to a sweet-natured young thing from the Colonies.

'They're just so mean,' she wailed to Esme, who came home one day to find her sitting outside on the front steps crying. 'They sent me to put the rubbish out and locked the door behind me. And that was at three o'clock. I've been trying to get in ever since.'

Esme loved working, but loved getting home to her family as well—except on nights like this.

'It's like having four children in the house,' she complained when she fell into bed that night. 'And the littlest ones are the least trouble of all. It's those old ones causing all the problems.'

Esme burrowed in as close as she could to her cuddly husband. Despite being exhausted, despite being worried, despite trying to split herself in too many directions, she had never felt happier. Everything she had ever wanted was in this house and as long as she had her boys and her granny, she was OK. More than OK.

But she had perhaps underestimated what an important part of the equation Tracey was. When the still-distraught girl rang the next morning at seven o'clock to say that she was not coming back it ripped something of a hole in the fabric of the happy household.

But before Esme could even look into nursery fees, Granny Mac and

Henry formed a seemingly united front and insisted that between them, they could look after the twins.

'Was this the evil old menaces' plan all along, do you think?' Esme asked Pog over the phone during the day.

Pog refused to see the dark side. 'Look at it this way, Es,' he enthused. 'Without paying the nanny, we can probably afford the renovations.'

'My fountain!' squealed Esme.

And so, at eighteen months of age, the twins were left at home with their grandfather and great-grandmother, who, while abhorring each other, managed to do an excellent job of adoring them.

Despite any doubts anyone had about this child-care arrangement, the twins thrived under the new regime. Teddy walked in the first week—they were late developers when it came to moving—with his not nearly so curious twin following in his footsteps a fortnight later.

Teddy remained cuddly and kissable while Rory squirmed and squiggled out of arm's reach from the moment he could crawl. Esme loved their differences. She was intrigued by the boys' connection with each other. They had almost never, even as tiny babies, cried at the same time, as though they had worked out that it was better to have all their mother's attention than half of it, even if it meant starving or putting up with a wet nappy for a bit longer.

They were slower than most toddlers to talk, which Esme, at first concerned, discovered was quite common with identical twins. One magical afternoon, when everybody else in the house was out or resting, she watched her babies share a secret, silent joke for the first time ever. It reminded her that they shared something she never could, and while it saddened her for selfish reasons, it also thrilled her that Rory and Ted would always have each other. That there would always be the two of them. The leader and the led. The loud and the quiet.

The day Rory became an only child had not begun like any other, and afterwards Esme could not believe she had not seen disaster hanging heavy and horrid in the air. For a start, she had slept in even though she had to be out of the house by 8.30 or her day went to pieces.

She had twice been up in the night to Rory who had a streaming cold, and she was grumpy even before she stubbed her toe on a large power tool left lying in the dusty hallway by one of the builders.

The house was in ruins. The floorboards had been sanded but not polished, skirting boards replaced but not painted, walls framed but not lined and bathrooms plumbed but not completely. The kitchen was finished and so were the living room and the boys' bedroom, thankfully, so that the children had somewhere to play when the builders were working, but it was far from ideal.

And, in an idiotic burst of wanting to get it all over and done with as quickly as possible, Esme had brought the landscapers in at the same time. As a result, the back garden was only partially tiled and spotted with large pyramids of earth, whether coming or going, she knew not.

In the midst of this sat her fountain, or the pieces that would eventually become her fountain. The bowl had been sited by the stonemason himself and bolted to a concrete pad, but the centrepiece lay on its side, providing a leaning post for two spades, a large sack of compost and the assorted unidentifiable detritus of half a dozen labourers.

On top of this, though, and far more worrying, Granny Mac was not her normal self. Pog had been the first to notice it, and had mentioned to Esme that her grandmother had twice failed to bite back when Henry was obnoxious. Esme had hardly given it a thought until she followed her grandmother up the stairs a few days later, and had to slow herself down to avoid overtaking her.

She could not remember a time when she had not had to run to keep up with the woman.

'Are you all right?' Esme had asked her.

'Och, what are you doing sneaking up on me,' Granny Mac had grumbled. 'Can an old woman not even be an old woman these days?'

But the morning that Esme slept in, she was astonished to find that Granny Mac, who'd been an early riser since Adam was a cowboy, was still in her bed, too.

'There's no need to look at me like that,' Granny Mac said croakily. 'You don't need to call MI5 just because I took an extra twenty winks. Now leave me alone to get dressed.'

The kitchen, to Esme's relief, was a relative oasis of calm, with Henry quietly feeding the boys their breakfast. He gave his daughter-in-law the barest of glances.

'You'll be out again this evening, I take it,' he said in his clipped way.

'Who, me? No,' Esme said, shoving a bit of bread in the toaster and attempting to run her fingers through the bird's nest that was her hair. She poured not quite boiling water onto a tea bag in a dirty cup, and, sipping it, peered at the calendar on the refrigerator.

'Oh, shit,' she said, then bit her lip because Henry hated her swearing in front of the boys and even if he didn't, she shouldn't do it anyway. 'I forgot. I said I would go to Ridge's parents' night with Alice tonight.' Ridge was not terribly academic nor sporty nor charming, and Alice hated going to meet the teachers on her own.

126

She didn't need to look at Henry to know he was glowering at her, and reached into her bag for her diary, flipping it open to the day's date. As well as the planning meeting, she had a lunch with the executives of a major hosiery manufacturer on the brink of placing an advertising contract with *Apparel*, page proofs to check for *Smoke*, her fortnightly catch-up with Sebastian and the official opening of the *Baker* test kitchen. It was going to be a difficult day.

Teddy smiled at her from his highchair and blew a snot bubble out of his nose, which gave Esme something she realised in retrospect was probably the last truly happy moment of her life. A snot bubble.

She got up, kissed both her sons on their curly ginger heads, and turned to Henry.

'Could you keep an eye on Granny Mac for me?' she said in as low a voice as she could manage, for fear her grandmother would hear her. 'She seems a bit off colour . . .'

Henry spooned porridge into Teddy's open rosebud mouth. 'There are homes for people like your grandmother,' he said.

'Yes,' she said, 'homes like this one.'

Henry harrumphed and Esme bristled, but then reminded herself that he was just a lonely old man who needed love and attention like anyone else.

'Please,' she said, appealing to the good nature she was sure he must have but kept so well hidden. 'I'll take tomorrow off and see if I can trick her into going to the doctor, but today I just need your help a bit more than usual.'

'You're taking me for granted,' Henry said.

'I'm sorry,' she smiled sweetly. 'It won't happen again. Tomorrow, I promise, I'll make up for it.' A crack of thunder ended the conversation and she swore quietly to herself as she looked at the new (unpainted, handleless) doors out into the courtyard, where fat raindrops were pinging hysterically off the tiles.

Pog tramped down the stairs, his floppy hair still wet and his cheeks flushed as he nodded and listened to someone on the other end of his mobile phone.

'See you tonight,' he mouthed, rolling his eyes, and then kissed Esme on the forehead and went into the kitchen.

'Bye, Granny Mac,' Esme called up the stairs, jumping from foot to foot as she waited for an answer.

'Granny Mac? Are you—'

'For God's sake!' her grandmother roared, appearing round the corner onto the landing. 'Will you get about your business and leave me be!'

And she marched robustly down the stairs, pushing Esme out of the way as she headed for the kitchen.

The day passed in a blur. Esme hadn't even had time, she realised as Shonel from the art department hurried her up about the test kitchen do, to go to the loo. It was five past four already and she was supposed to be making the key speech in ten minutes.

'Come on,' Shonel urged her, 'everybody else is already there.'

Esme took a quick glance at her phone before deciding that her bladder needed attention before she checked in at home. She had picked the damn phone up half a dozen times to ring and check on her grandmother, but had been interrupted on every occasion.

'I'll ring home in the taxi,' she said to Shonel. 'You go and grab one while I go to the loo.'

Sitting in the back of the cab, Esme rummaged around in her bag, eventually finding her phone only to discover its battery was flat.

'Oh, bollocks,' she said. 'Shonel, can I borrow yours?' Her art director looked sourly at her boss.

'They give you brain cancer,' Shonel said. 'They're far worse than cigarettes.'

Arriving at the test kitchen in Portland Street, Esme was immediately swamped by well-wishers, staff members and advertisers availing themselves of the free Pinot Gris, Irish cheese and freshly baked breads, sourdough not among them, she could tell, just by sniffing the air.

'Is there a phone here?' she asked Jenny, a truculent teenager with a wicked feel for pastry whom she had taken on to help in the kitchen.

'Not bleedin' likely,' Jenny answered her. 'You try telling British Telecom you're in a hurry and see how far you get.'

'Shit, shit, shit,' Esme muttered before turning on her energetic smile and calling for everyone's attention, the formalities about to begin.

Afterwards she grabbed a glass of wine from a passing waiter and as she gulped desperately at it, happened to notice a lanky man slipping a phone into his pocket.

'Excuse me,' she trilled. 'Could I borrow that?'

After eight rings it clicked onto the answerphone. Esme felt a clunk of worry in her stomach. She checked her watch. It was five thirty. The boys should be having their tea. Why was no one answering?

She dialled the home number again—still it rang and clicked onto answerphone. Then she tried Pog but his phone was turned off, no doubt during his meeting.

'Do you mind?' the lanky man asked her, reaching for his phone, which, at that moment, Esme realised was the same outdated model as her own. 'I'm sorry,' she said, clutching the phone as she slipped through the crowd and out of the door, ignoring his surprised whining behind her.

Having hailed a taxi, she jumped in and slipped his battery into her phone. For a full minute she stared at the tiny LCD screen as her own phone flickered into life, telling her it was on, then telling her it had a signal and then, with a series of loud terrifying beeps, informing her that she had one, two, three, four, five messages.

Shakily, Esme pressed the button to reveal the contents of the first message. 'Henry rang, please call home,' the first one read. 'Henry says call home,' read the second. 'Call home asap,' read the third, fourth and fifth.

Esme felt the glass of warm Pinot Gris rise up in her stomach and hit the back of her throat. She tried to tell herself that probably nothing major was wrong, but still she could not ignore the taste of fear.

'Please,' she said as loudly as she could, knocking on the cabby's window, 'Please, could you go faster?'

The house in All Souls Road was still standing, which at least allowed Esme to breathe again as she threw a twenty-pound note at the cabby and raced up the stairs to the front door.

'Hello!' she shouted in the hallway. 'Henry!' The kitchen was empty, as was the living room. 'Granny Mac!' she called again, panic rising.

'I'm up here,' Henry's irritated voice bounced down the stairwell. 'In the bathroom. Where the hell have you been?'

His crotchetiness assuaged her panic. She felt the blood rush through to all its rightful places again. She breathed deeply as she pushed the bathroom door open.

Henry was sitting on the edge of the bath, holding a naked Rory wrapped in a towel on his lap. Before she could get any closer, the little boy heaved and Henry gently rolled him towards the lavatory where he vomited a trickle of clear fluid into the bowl.

'Oh, my poor baby,' Esme cried, kneeling beside them. 'How long has he been like this?'

'He's been going at both ends since two o'clock,' growled Henry, and Esme looked at his wrinkled scowl but saw in his eyes that he was worried and scared, not cross.

Esme put her hand on Rory's head. It was hot, but not dangerously so. His body was limp, though, and he opened his eyes to look at her but did not raise his head.

'Where's Teddy?' she asked.

'With your grandmother,' Henry growled. 'In her room.'

'Should we take Rory to the doctor, do you think?' Esme asked her father-in-law. 'Or the hospital?'

'I rang the surgery,' Henry answered her. 'And they said it's just a virus. They've had a waiting room full of it for the past two days and it should pass in twelve hours. I expect Ted will get it too.'

A wave of guilt pulsed through Esme but she pushed it away. She should have been here. She should have rung the surgery. She should be worried that Teddy would get the bug too.

'Are you all right with him?' she asked, nodding at her poor sick son as she stood up.

Henry shot her a look which she knew meant: 'Haven't I been up until now?'

Esme's relief that all was well was short-lived. The moment she walked into Granny Mac's room it was clear that something was wrong. Her grandmother lay on the bed fully clothed but seemingly awake, and as Esme approached her did not move or even look her way.

'Granny Mac!' Esme chided. But there was no response. And as Esme leaned over her she realised with horror that one side of her grandmother's face had collapsed downwards.

'Granny Mac!' Esme cried again, taking her grandmother's thin shoulders in her hands and pulling her slight body towards her own.

Her grandmother gurgled and Esme held her tighter, too many terrifying thoughts crowding her mind. Why had she gone to work? Why had she ignored the warning signals? 'Don't leave me,' she whispered, rocking her grandmother awkwardly back and forward. 'Please, please, please don't leave me.'

Granny Mac gurgled again, louder this time, and Esme, suddenly aware that she should be doing something other than holding her and pleading with her, lowered her back onto her pillow.

'Eegggghhhh,' her grandmother moaned, saliva drooling from the dropped side of her mouth. 'Eeeegggghhhhyyyyyy.'

'I'm going to call an ambulance,' Esme said as soothingly as she could, yet she felt nothing but terror and turmoil. 'I'm going to get some help.'

'Eeeegggghhhhh,' her grandmother groaned again, seemingly more agitated this time. 'Eeeegggggghhhhhy.'

She fixed Esme with her bright black eyes and despite her incapacitated state held her granddaughter's distraught gaze.

'Egg,' she said almost clearly. 'Eggy.'

Ted, thought Esme. Teddy. She immediately started to pant and stood up off the bed. Where was Teddy? Her grandmother's eyes were still fixed on her and Esme knew in that moment she had something to fear.

Teddy was supposed to be in here with Granny Mac, Henry had said so. Idiotically, she looked under the bed.

'Is he in here somewhere?' she asked, even though she knew her grandmother could not answer her. She checked the wardrobe, knowing that he probably wasn't there either, then despite the dreadful feeling that she should not leave Granny Mac alone like this, stumbled into the hall.

'Henry!' she called. 'Have you seen Teddy?' She checked the twins' bedroom, not allowing herself to fly into a fully fledged panic, then slipped out into the hallway again. Henry was standing by the bathroom door, still holding a floppy Rory.

'Teddy is not with Granny Mac,' Esme said. 'I think she has had a stroke, Henry. When was the last time you saw her? What did she say?'

'He's not in her room?' Henry was confused. 'I sent him in there, not long ago. Just before you came home. Are you sure?'

Just before she got home. Esme breathed out. It hadn't been long. He would be fine.

'You check our room, I'll check downstairs,' she instructed. He might have slipped downstairs when she was in the bathroom with Henry or in with Granny Mac. Granny Mac!

She leapt downstairs, had a quick look around, then picked up the phone, punching in 999 and asking for the ambulance service.

'Thirty-nine All Souls Road,' she said, as she checked the cupboard under the stairs and the space behind the sofa where the boys often hid. 'Morag MacDougall. She's never been sick a day in her life but she seems sort of paralysed and one side of her face isn't working properly. Is that a stroke? I mean it sounds like a stroke. Do you think it's a stroke? Will she be all right?' She was gabbling, she knew, as she moved back into the kitchen and checked the pantry. How would this woman on a headphone know if Granny Mac would be all right?

'Thank you,' she said as the woman repeated the address. 'How long—' but the words dried on her lips as she suddenly saw what she had missed before—that one of the paintless, handleless doors from the kitchen into the courtyard was slightly open. She dropped the phone and raced outside. There were lethal tools and probably dangerous poisons lying willy-nilly all over the place. A little boy could come to terrible harm out there.

'Teddy!' she called, not noticing that the rain still fell. 'Ted!' There were few places to hide and she knew the seven-foot-high brick wall round the garden was impenetrable. Where was he?

She trod across the damaged lawn, mud sucking at her shoes, to check the shrubs and foliage round the perimeter. 'Teddo!' she called as she pushed sodden branches out of the way. 'Baby boy!'

There was no sign of him.

She turned and ran as quickly as the sticky ground would let her back inside, sliding as she passed the fountain bowl on a bit of black polythene that had been draped over it and spilt over the side and across the ground.

Henry was in the kitchen, still holding Rory who was crying now, his face twisted with pain and distress.

'Your room,' Esme said.

'I've checked it,' Henry told her over Rory's howling. 'I've checked everywhere upstairs.'

The doorbell rang, making him start.

'It'll be the ambulance,' Esme said, pushing past him. 'She's upstairs,' she told the two paramedics. 'I'll show you.'

But then she stopped and spun round. 'My son,' she said. 'We can't find him.' He wasn't upstairs and he wasn't downstairs. She turned again and started to lead the ambulancemen up the stairs. Well, he must be outside.

She stopped yet again. 'She's in the room at the end of the hall. On the left.' How could she leave Granny Mac alone with these men? Her grandmother would kill her.

'It's all right,' one of the ambulancemen said. 'We'll sort out your gran. You find the nipper.'

Esme bounded down the stairs again, bumping into Henry, completely grey in the face and still holding on to a roaring Rory as he emerged from the cupboard under the stairs.

'I've checked there,' Esme said. 'I've checked everywhere. I've looked in every nook and cranny and hiding place and hole I can think of. There's nowhere outside he could be. Nowhere that we can't see—'

As her words dried up, she and Henry turned at the same time and looked out through the kitchen door again. Out to the fountain bowl, with its sloppy black plastic covering.

'Who put that there?' Esme asked as she floated towards the door. Her wet feet slid on the slippery tiles as she scrabbled towards the fountain, falling over on her knees just short of her little bit of Venolat. Clawing blindly at the overhanging polythene, she pulled it away and dragged herself up to the lip of the fountain.

Teddy's chubby, toddler body lay there, face down, his arms outstretched, his ginger curls indelibly brilliant against the murky darkness of the bowl. Did she scream or not? Certainly her mouth was stretched open in a dark raw hole as she frantically clawed at the icy water, reaching for him, turning him over, but she knew by his touch that she was too late. She pulled him from the water then sank back onto the ground, clutching his limp, sodden, freezing-cold little-boy body to her chest, her mouth still stuck in a frozen howl, her eyes staring into a future she did not want to contemplate.

The rain fell on the two of them, plastering her hair to her head and darkening it to the exact shade of her son's, brilliant still against the blackness of everything else.

The bright yellow vest of an ambulanceman pushed past and was at Esme's side in a flash. He took the little body from her—forced her to give it up—and then placed him gently on the soaking tiles, rain pinging off them as he tipped back Teddy's head, held his nose and blew into his twenty-seven-month-old lungs.

It was into this tortured scene that Pog, having cancelled his meeting after clearing his phone of distraught messages from Henry, walked.

Esme looked over the body of the hopeful ambulanceman breathing into her lifeless son and met the eyes of her husband. His red anorak was blurred and out of focus, but not so the look on his face. The world stood still. She wanted it to end.

And, in a way, it did.

Chapter Fifteen

'YOU LOOK BLOODY GORGEOUS!' Alice squawked as Esme walked into Rockwell Cocktail Bar on Trafalgar Square, to find her friend already sucking on a watermelon and basil daiquiri.

Esme hid her blush by taking off her jacket and getting settled on the chaise next to Alice. The truth was, she felt different.

Being with Louis, talking to Louis, had changed her. She had left him, reluctantly, in Marylebone High Street after sharing the kiss she had dreamed of all these long Louis-less years. Her heart, so scrubbed raw by relieving herself of the buried memories of losing Teddy, her beautiful baby Teddy, had swelled up with hope and desire as Louis had reached for her and pulled her into him.

'My poor Esme,' he had said, kissing her ear, her eyebrow, her cheek, the remains of her tears. 'My poor, poor Esme.' And it had been such a small movement, tilting her head back and making her lips available.

She had had no doubt he would accept her offer of them.

It was all unfolding so naturally in front of them. It felt like Louis was sloughing off the heavy, rotten layers that had built up over the past two years, and the old fresh, shiny Esme was emerging from underneath.

She had groaned beneath his kiss, felt those hipbones once more against hers, tasted the salty sweetness of his mouth, felt his hand cupping her breast, thanked God her La Perla had stood the test of time.

Louis had drawn back, his eyes dark and wet, his lips glistening.

'I must go,' he said. 'But I feel wrong to leave you like this.'

'No, no,' she said quickly. 'I'm fine. Perfectly fine.' And it was true, she was. She felt light with the relief of unburdening the memories of her darling Teddy without the air being sucked from her lungs and a fog clouding her head. Louis had done that. Louis had set her free.

'I do not know what it has been like for you since Teddy—' Louis had dropped his gaze, yet Esme felt nothing but warmth now at the sound of that name. 'You are a brave and remarkable woman, Esme.'

'I'm nothing of the sort,' Esme murmured, but she basked in his praise nonetheless. She felt more tied to him now than ever, but he was behind schedule and she had to meet Alice.

Alice. How was she going to keep Louis to herself? she thought. How could she not spill the beans to her best friend, the one from whom she had never before kept anything? How would Alice not notice that everything about her was different now?

'So,' Alice prompted, interrupting her thoughts, 'is it something that comes in a bottle or is it something Pog does to you before slipping on his Y-fronts and going to get your breakfast cuppa?' Alice persisted.

Confusion turned to understanding, and at the mention of Pog slithered away to become shame and remorse. Of course she could not tell Alice about Louis. What was she thinking? She might feel shiny and new but she was sailing in murky waters.

'I've changed my moisturiser,' she said brightly, scaring herself at the smoothness with which she lied. 'Some natural thingie from Neal's Yard.'

'Stick with it, sweetheart,' Alice said, handing over the cocktail menu. 'You look positively glowing.' Another obvious possibility occurred to her. 'Hey, you're not—'

Esme shook her head, thinking her friend couldn't be more wrong if she tried.

Alice put down her drink and reached over to squeeze Esme's hand. 'I'm sorry, darling,' she said, and the sympathy in her voice made Esme feel sick with duplicity.

How could she have just shared the contents of her unmentionable loss with Louis, whom after all she hardly even knew, when she had never been able to, with Alice, her soul sister? The subject of Teddy had been out of bounds completely since his funeral, a day so bleak and painful and raw she still could not conjure up its memory. Esme had been unable to speak her lost son's name to anybody, even Pog, even Granny Mac, for goodness' sake, until today. Until Louis and his big black searching eyes and long brown breadmaker's fingers.

Louis had unleashed—yet again—something in her that nobody else had been able to tap, and Esme felt so light with happiness and relief and horror and fear that she could barely even think about the fact that she had agreed to meet him again the following week. At his hotel.

Despite the fireworks exploding in her head, she managed to trade the usual gossip and girl talk with Alice as they put away another cocktail.

Louis made her feel, she realised as Alice burbled about a failed singles dance, like the Esme she really was: the Esme he had discovered back in that salty little bakery so many years before. That was why she could talk to him about Teddy. Because she was nothing to him apart from that collection of skin and flesh that had so enraptured him despite the complication of his marriage. She was not his wife or his daughter-in-law or his granddaughter or his mother. She could not upset him nor blame him nor hurt him nor herself by digging up the events of that terrible day. She did not have to be the person that terrible day had turned her into in his presence. She was Esme, plain and simple.

'You are a million miles away today, missus,' Alice interrupted her thoughts. 'That moisturiser sure has sunk in. What's the name of it?'

'Do you know, I can't remember,' Esme lied, again easily. 'I'll ring you when I get home. Speaking of which . . .' She gathered up her bag and her coat. 'Do come and visit soon, will you?' The thought of being at home, in the House in the Clouds, suddenly scared her. Everything seemed different now.

'You know I'm allergic to the country,' said Alice, standing up to leave as well.

In the train on the way home Esme replayed Louis's kiss a thousand times in her mind, clawing at the memory of the way his lips felt on hers, of the way his hands felt on her ribs, his thumbs below the underwire of her bra. But her buzz of delight kept giving way to waves of dread and remorse. She thought of Pog and how much she loved him. But then she thought of Louis and the way he made her feel, and there was so little comparison between the two that it scared her half to death. Then she thought of the photo albums she had been unable to look at since Teddy's death. They had disappeared from the second-floor sitting room after his funeral, but with a hot flush Esme knew instantly where they were. She thought of Pog's guilty face when she first infiltrated his shed, of the stack of redundant paperwork camouflaging the folders of snapshots. Suddenly she could not get home quickly enough. She wanted to see those two little red heads lying on her breast at the hospital, sitting in their blowup paddling pool, walking with Granny Mac before the stroke rendered her bedridden. A lump rose in her throat at the picture of a healthy Granny Mac, and Esme shook her head. What a day it had been. She was not ready for anything more.

The next couple of days passed in such a whirl of domestic chaos that Esme barely had a chance to think about what had happened in London. Even when she wasn't cooking or cleaning, her head did not know whether to be full of her stolen kiss with Louis or of her mental home movies of Teddy, so long forbidden that now, if she let them, they played over and over and over again.

Deep down though, beneath the rubber gloves and cleaning fluids and flour, she felt a little burr of happiness that permeated everything. Pog sensed this immediately and put it down to going to London and meeting Alice.

'You should do that more, you know,' he said the next night in bed, in the few minutes he was still conscious before exhaustion claimed him.

'Do what?' Esme asked.

'Go for girlie drinks with Alice,' he said. 'It's done you good.'

Esme was awake long after Pog had drifted off. Her burr of happiness waned and left guilt in its wake. Her heart pounded with love as his snuffles echoed round the room, then it ached, then it pounded again. She would not go to London and see Louis, she decided, as she tossed and turned. He had given her a priceless gift that she was coming to see would clear the way to a real life, a real future, with her family here in the House in the Clouds. But she could not give him anything in return. One kiss would have to do. But by the time she got up to make her bread, she had changed her mind again, and again, and again, until she could not remember if she was going to see him or not, and was so tired that she didn't consider it would matter either way.

On Sunday, Esme refused to buy a copy of the *Sunday Times*—she had no time to spare for Jemima Jones—and the next few days slipped by with her lurching from woeful remorse and self-flagellation to a giddy light-headedness of long-gone proportions. She hugged the secret of Louis close to her chest and with it, stolen thoughts of her angel baby. It was heavenly and hellish, all at the same time.

Pog, who had been monitoring her every shoulder slump for the last long while, was aware that she was battling something. While the low moods worried him, the highs brought joy to his heart. She had started humming again in the happy, thoroughly tuneless way she had done before. Her bread was tasting so sharp and zingy it made his mouth water just thinking about it. At night though, in their bed, she still turned her back on him. He could wait. For ever, if he had to.

'I thought I might go down to London again today,' Esme said casually on Thursday morning over breakfast. Until she opened her mouth to suggest it, she had not been sure she would go, but Pog beamed at her over his porridge. She was so encouraged she forgot for a moment why she was going.

'Be sure and give Alice my love, won't you,' Pog said.

He kissed her goodbye and headed off down the six flights of stairs to consider Meg D'ath's plans to convert her pint-sized potting shed into a granny flat for her mother-in-law.

Esme then spent nearly two hours getting showered and dressed, and dressed again, and dressed a third time, before finally settling on a pale green agnès b suit with a seriously short skirt. She felt embarrassed about parading it in front of Henry, so put her trench coat on over it before she went to check it was OK for him to look after Rory.

'Actually,' Henry said, 'it's not.'

'I'm sorry?' she asked sweetly. Why hadn't she thought of this before?

'I am going to play bridge in Stonyborough with Dr Mason and his wife,' Henry said briskly. 'They've been asking me for some time and it felt impolite turning them down yet again.'

She looked out of the window to where Rory was in the garden, attempting to brush poor Eeyore down with a broom. The pathetic creature seemed to be enjoying it.

'Never mind,' Esme trilled. 'I'll ring Mrs McArthur.'

The House in the Clouds seemed to have grown extra stairs as she stomped up to the kitchen to retrieve her address book. She really should have organised this sooner, she knew that, but then she would have been forced to admit she was going. It was like the difference between manslaughter and murder.

Annoyingly Mrs McArthur proved to be engaged. Esme tried her number four times in a row, all the while trying not to look at her watch more than once every fifteen seconds. She had to catch the eleven o'clock train if she was going to meet Louis at his hotel at one, and it was already ten past ten. The thought that she might not be able to make it shattered her: perhaps there really had been no doubt as to her motives. Perhaps it was murder after all.

'Shit, shit, shit,' she said under her breath as she quickly made a sandwich for her son, using deliciously mature Cheddar and that morning's sourdough. She scoured the pantry, finding a bashed-up little bag of crisps and a squashed chocolate bar, and then stomped down the stairs again, grabbing his day pack out of his room and putting in a warm jumper, his raincoat, a hat and his hastily prepared lunch.

She marched down to the bottom of the house and out of the door, where she removed the broom from her small son's clammy hands and informed him they were off to the baby sitter's, grabbing his hand and pulling him straight down the lane to Mrs McArthur's. The door was open, which it almost always was, and Esme went in to find the woman in all her Sunday finery, fussing about a little lace-covered table laden with garishly coloured cakes.

'Oh!' she said, when she saw who it was, with what Esme felt was some disappointment.

'I'm in a terrible spot,' Esme gabbled. 'Could you take Rory for the day? I have to go down to London and Henry's playing bridge with the Masons so can't watch him.'

Mrs McArthur's lips pursed significantly. 'Well, I am actually hosting the inaugural meeting of the Seabury Mah-jong Club this morning, in fact I thought you were one of my girls, so I'm sorry but I can't help you.'

Esme looked at her watch. She had less than ten minutes to get to the station to catch her train.

'Righto,' she said in a jolly voice. 'We'll be off then.' She turned and walked, as quickly as her heels would let her, down the drive and across the road. She could make it, she could, if she took Rory with her. Her son scurried along at her side.

'What's happening, Esme?' he asked.

'You're coming to London with Mummy,' she answered.

It wasn't until they were seated, sweating and steaming, on the train as it pulled out of Seabury Station that it occurred to Esme that while she was now indeed going to be able to make her rendezvous with Louis, it would be with the added complication of Rory.

'Are we going to see Alice?' Rory asked, looking out of the window as the countryside whisked by.

Esme felt wretched and decided then and there that she would take him to Hamleys toyshop and to somewhere smart for lunch, and then perhaps they would meet up with Alice or even go to a movie, and she would forget the ridiculous prospect of rediscovering her lost love.

But over the course of the next ninety miles she changed her mind, and changed it again, and again, and again until once more she was completely confused about her intentions and could only decide as far as going to the general area of Louis's hotel, which after all was not far from Hamleys, and where she also knew many a fine lunch spot, having worked in the area and its surrounds for most of her adult life.

It was the sensible thing to do, she told herself.

An hour later, standing in the street, wind lashing at her ankles and a fine rain starting to fall as her son whimpered beside her, Esme wondered if she would ever see sense again.

She had found Louis's hotel and walked past it three times before dragging Rory to the corner and stopping there, flustered and frayed. Her thoughts were having trouble collecting themselves, as though the unseasonable city wind was gathering them up like fallen leaves and blowing them every which way.

She had always fantasised that she and Louis would meet again, but that it would be something windswept and wild and hopelessly romantic. Something blurred round the edges and misty, like an old black and white Katharine Hepburn movie. And in just the past few days she had seen herself so many times knocking on the door of Louis's room and having him open it, sweep her into his arms and carry her to a four-poster bed, where he would make love to her in a way that would put those ancient sacks of flour to shame.

Never had she seen herself standing in the rain in the middle of this bland part of town, with a small, sweet, slightly snotty four-year-old whinging desperately that he wanted to do wees.

The gods, she had to accept, were conspiring against her. No matter how much she wanted to feel Louis's smooth nut-brown skin pressed hotly against hers, it wasn't going to happen.

She looked at her son's damp ginger curls. Had she really thought she would take Rory with her to meet Louis? Or had she brought him to keep herself from doing just that? Was Rory ruining her chances, or saving her life? Her marriage? Her bruised and battered heart?

'Come on, Ror,' she said finally, blocking out her thoughts and making her decision. 'We'll find a loo and have a nice cup of tea somewhere.' She took his hand and started back down the street.

Rory perked up instantly. 'Can I have one of those little cakes that's half brown and half white?' he asked enthusiastically.

'Of course you can, darling.' Esme looked at her watch. She had kissed her chances with Louis goodbye. Her feelings, at that moment, as she pulled Rory along, were so complicated she could barely identify them. Did she want to be a woman who cheated on her husband, anyway? Was that who she was? A cheat? An adulteress? The part of her that hoped she was not felt relief as she left Louis behind.

But what if he truly was the love of her life? Would she ever find happiness by walking away from him? A second time? The part of her that lusted after whatever it was he awoke in her felt anguish and resentment.

'Esme,' Rory wailed, adding to her turmoil. 'You're going too fast. I want to do weeeeees.' His little face was red with exertion and he was clutching at his trousers in anguish. Esme felt dreadful. On top of everything, she was a bad mother. She was still a bad mother.

She stopped and looked around the street. It was just three blocks from where she had worked at Goodhart Publishing and she knew there was no public lavatory nearby, just offices and a few furniture shops and her old gym, Body Works, which was just across the road. Of course!

'It's OK, Rory,' she said. 'We'll go where Mummy used to do her exercises,' and she dragged him across the road and up the stairs to the front desk, where the same yappy receptionist who had been there when she still frequented the place, before their move to the country, was filing the same old nails and reading what looked like the same old magazine.

'Blimey, we haven't seen you in donkey's ages,' said the receptionist.

'Don't mention donkeys,' Esme smiled. 'But I have a little boy desperate to go to the loo. Could he . . .?'

'Course,' agreed the girl, 'but you'll have to send him into the Gents. We get complaints, you know.' She rolled her eyes and Esme nodded sympathetically, then escorted Rory towards the men's changing rooms, pushing him in the door and telling him to find the toilet as quickly as he could, use it and come straight back out.

Waiting outside the door she was distracted by the sound of children clapping their hands. As it dawned on her what the sound was, a plot hatched so virulently in her mind that she was powerless to stop it.

The gym had a crèche. For a fiver an hour, you could leave your children under expert supervision while you did your thing in the weights room or the aerobics studio.

The part of Esme that did not want to be a woman who had an affair told her not to give it another thought, to stay right there and wait for her son. The part that cried out for Louis told her that if she tried she could still make it to the hotel. He might still be there.

Esme shuffled on her heels. Everything up until this point had been conspiring against her, against Louis. Yet here she was with a child who needed minding and a facility to do just that. Was it fate?

'You wouldn't do me a favour,' she said, sidling up to the reception desk. 'I've a couple more hours' shopping to do and my son is already dead on his feet. I couldn't possibly . . .?'

The receptionist checked that no one else was close enough to hear them. Esme was obviously not the first person to make this request.

'Twenty quid,' she said. 'And you'd better be back in two hours or I will sell him to the Gypsies.'

Rory emerged from the toilet with a big smile on his face, and Esme tucked his shirt in and explained what was happening. He was more than happy with the arrangement. Like his father, he was not a shopper and while he sensed the change of plan meant his cake was no longer just round the corner, he was pleased to avoid an afternoon of shoes and handbags. Gluing coloured things onto other coloured things was a pretty good alternative, as far as he was concerned.

Esme ruffled Rory's hair and smiled at the smattering of other children in the playroom, but her hand shook as she wrote his name on a name badge and for a moment she considered throwing the lurid bit of cardboard in the bin, snatching her son and running for home.

'Stop thinking,' she said out loud. 'Just do it.'

And so she found herself, not five minutes later, staring up at the Excelsior Hotel sign, on the brink of entering into something she knew could change her life for ever.

In truth, the Excelsior was not what she expected. It was a slightly dilapidated Victorian building of the type often converted to private hotels or guest rooms. The paint was peeling off the façade and the reception area was dimly lit and had a nasty stale odour about it.

Esme rang the bell and a greasy little man with a terrible case of comb-across hair came out, licking his fingers and smelling strongly of vinegar.

'Is there a Louis Lapoine staying here?' Esme asked him.

'Oh, yes,' whined the greasy little man. 'Monsieur Lapoine. Room sixteen. Up the first flight of stairs, love, and third on your left.'

So, the Excelsior did not stretch to a lift. Why would Louis stay in a place like this? Esme wondered as she climbed up the narrow staircase.

The six of room sixteen had fallen sideways and made a whole new number. Esme knocked and waited. Could there be some mistake?

But it was Louis's face that looked into hers when the door flew open, and she knew from the expression on it that he had given up on her.

'Esme!' he said, catching her by surprise by throwing himself excitedly in her direction to kiss each cheek. 'I thought you were not coming,' he said, his eyes bright with renewed anticipation. 'I wait for an hour, which in London, you know, is usually enough and when you didn't come, I think . . .' He shrugged. 'But now, here you are!'

The room was tiny, with a double bed—not of the four-poster variety—one ratty chair and a tatty dresser. It fell sadly short of her imaginings.

'Do you stay in places like this wherever you go?' Esme asked, looking around, trying not to sound critical.

Louis pulled her down beside him on the bed, which creaked rudely.

'We do not waste money on fancy hotel rooms at *la fédération*,' Louis said dismissively. 'We have better things to think about. Take off your coat, Esme. You are wet.'

He watched her greedily as she struggled out of her trench coat, feeling shy and silly even though there were many layers to go and she could be proud of her matching knickers and bra.

She looked up and met Louis's eyes.

'Do not be afraid, Esme,' he said, in his hypnotic soft voice, understanding her doubt. 'You were right to come.'

And he leaned in and kissed her so gently it was like drinking champagne. The bits of her that weren't loyal to her husband raced with excitement, and she heard a groan escape from her throat.

Louis pressed her slowly back on the bed, and she felt his lips on her neck and his tongue on her collarbone.

She pushed thoughts of Pog out of her head. This was so much more treacherous than a stolen kiss in a restaurant doorway. This was it. There would be no going back. And, already, her body was showing signs of being unstoppably on the track to Louis Lapoine.

Louis moved, slowly, up her neck, along her jaw and across her cheek until his lips met hers and she nipped at him, desperate for the bliss he could unleash in her. They kissed for an age. Her eyes were closed and her mind was locked in the past, where if she breathed in deeply enough she could smell the wood-fired oven, feel those well-worn steps beneath her back, taste that first crumb of sourdough, the crumb that would introduce her to delights of which before she had only dreamed.

Her pleasure was indescribable. She writhed with it. And all from a kiss! Louis drew back and looked at her, drinking in her enjoyment. Then, still looking, his hand travelled too slowly (no, not slowly enough!) down her rib cage, forgiving the indent at her waistband and continuing to her hips.

She reached up and traced the line of his neck with one finger from the corner of his mouth, back to his ear, his edible ear, then down to the collar of his shirt. Over his exquisite Adam's apple her fingernail trailed, then she started to pull at his tie, already loosened, noticing for the first time that it was the same one he had worn when they last met. And when they first met, in Marylebone High Street. In fact, it was the same suit and perhaps the same shirt, which, now she looked closely, was slightly grubby round the neckline.

Sensing her hesitation, he ripped the tie off himself, then unbuttoned Esme's jacket and brought his mouth down to her silk shirt, biting at her nipples through her new bra and rendering her unsure whether to scream for more or for him to stop.

Her body was working on its own now. She tugged at Louis's shirt buttons, undoing them to his waist then pulling the shirt away from his delectable shoulders.

She rose up and bit into him, savouring his taste. He was salty and sour, like bread. He wriggled downwards and ran his hands up her rump underneath her skirt and he tugged at her knickers, flicking his finger inside them against that soft, doughy skin.

Esme groaned and wriggled further into the middle of the bed. Something beneath her was digging into her shoulder.

'Ouch,' she cried as Louis pressed down on her and whatever she was lying on bit into her shoulder.

'Esme,' Louis moaned. 'Oh, Esme.'

She twisted round and grabbed at what lay underneath her, wrenching it out from under herself. Whatever it was was in Louis's suit jacket pocket, and she would never know what made her dip into it, but dip into it she did. It was the dusty track up to his uncle's house all over again.

She pulled out a baby's dummy. Pink and slightly gooey. Aghast, she felt her pheromones spiral back into control.

'But, Louis,' she said, looking at him, and wondering how his black eyes could still sparkle like that. Louis's children were teenagers now. And he did not even live with them.

'It's not how you think,' Louis said breathlessly, his erection nonetheless withering. He leaned down onto one elbow and ran the other hand through his hair. The cut was wrong, Esme suddenly noticed. It was too long at the back. And he had missed a few spots on those smooth nut cheeks when he shaved.

She pushed him off her, then sat up and looked around the room. There was no suitcase. No briefcase, even. The bathroom door was open and there were no toiletries by the sink. Her heart was starting to thump in her ears, and not in the way it usually did when Louis was present.

Something was wrong. There was a hip-flask-sized bottle of brandy, open and only half full, and two plastic triangles of chain-store sandwiches sitting atop the Bible on the bedside table.

'Oh my God,' whispered Esme. Chain-store sandwiches? She pulled at her blouse, which was open and exposing most of one ripe breast and a morsel of soft white stomach. Her skirt had twisted round and come unzipped and her tights were halfway to her knees. She felt sick.

She looked at the dummy in her hand.

'Whose is this?' she asked, trying to keep her voice steady.

Louis, his shirt still off, his trousers unbelted and unbuttoned, reached for her. 'Esme,' he said in his bewitching voice. 'Does it matter?'

Esme closed her eyes to the sound of half a lifetime of dreaming being flushed gently down the toilet.

'How can I have been so stupid?' she asked herself as she slid to the side of the bed, slipped into her shoes and started to right her skirt. She was shaking.

'No, no, no,' groaned Louis. 'Please, Esme. We should do this. We are meant to do this. You and me. Come on.'

But her rose-coloured spectacles were off for good. Her fairy tale had disappeared. All she could see was a tatty little man in a tatty little room and a married woman, every bit as tragic, who was trying to go somewhere that no longer existed.

'So let me guess—you're not married to Diana any more but you are married to someone,' she said, more amazed than angry as her fingers fumbled over buttoning her shirt.

'It doesn't have to be like this,' Louis said.

'It already bloody is!' Esme said vehemently. 'How could you do this to me a second time? After everything? After we talked about how much you hurt me last time and how I couldn't love anyone for ages and how you meant every word but the time wasn't right? I told you about Teddy, for God's sake. I have not been able to talk about him with anyone. Ever! I trusted you. Again. I trusted you and you could have ruined my life.'

Louis looked sad. 'Your life sounds ruined already, Esme,' he said.

'That's not true.' Esme was horrified. 'I have a perfectly good life.'

'Oh, yes,' Louis hit back. 'Then what are you doing here?'

'I thought you could save me,' Esme replied, realising as she spoke the words that this was the truth. 'I thought you could make me feel the way I did when I met you. Like nothing in between had happened.'

Louis, sensing a gap in her resolve, leaned towards her. 'I can, Esme,' he said earnestly. 'I can.'

She looked at him in wonderment as she reached for her coat and struggled into it. 'You can't,' she said. Oh God, this was not what she wanted! He was not what she wanted. 'Nobody can save anybody else.'

'That's not what your friend Charlie thinks,' Louis said, standing up and pulling himself together. Esme froze.

'What do you mean? What does Charlie have to do with any of this?'

Louis shrugged. 'Maybe meeting you again was not such a coincidence, Esme. That is all.'

144

She thought about the lunch, the phone call from Charlie, meeting Louis while she waited. What was Louis saying?

'Charlie *arranged* this?' she asked, her voice barely a whisper.

A hardness stole into his eyes as he did up his trousers and threaded his belt through the loops.

'I met him in a bar one night not so long ago and he was sorry for the stitches in my nose and tells me you still think of me, that you think a lot of me, and he offers to buy the lunch. At the Orrery. He thinks it will cheer you up and make you happy. He is a good friend, no? He even sends me this suit. Not really my colour, but still.'

Esme collapsed slowly into the ratty chair as her head spun. The whole thing had been a set-up? Destiny had nothing to do with it.

Louis, she noticed, was slipping his feet into badly scuffed shoes. He wore brown socks. He drank during the day. He ate chain-store sandwiches and he had a baby young enough to need a dummy.

'Do you even work for the bakers' federation?' she asked tonelessly.

'Oh, Esme, you are such a romantic.'

Esme sucked back a sob.

'There is no such thing as the bakers' federation,' said Louis tiredly. 'No one cares about *pain au levain*. You would be lucky to find it in Paris, let alone in the country where it came from, where it belongs. There is nothing magical about sourdough, Esme. Once, maybe, I thought there was, but not any more.'

'You can't mean that, Louis. You of all people. What happened to the *boulangerie*? What happened to your starter, the starter your many greats grandfather began two hundred years ago?'

A hard look crossed Louis's face. 'My uncle was offered a lot of money and so he sold the bakery.' His voice was bitter. 'Now it is an Internet café.'

'And your uncle, is he . . . did he really die?'

Louis was shocked.

'But, of course! I could never lie about something like that.'

'Well, you can lie about everything else, Louis. Do you live in Paris? Are you still a baker?' She was desperate for something about Louis to be right.

She could tell from the look on his face that he was tossing up whether to lie again, in itself providing the painful answer.

'No,' he said. 'I live in Hounslow, Esme. I live with my girlfriend Katarina and our baby Eleanor. I am the manager of the high-street Pret A Manger.'

Esme was too stunned for tears. She felt like she was skittering on air above a bottomless canyon. She felt sick to her stomach.

'But how could you, Louis, how could you? After your family had been baking in that building for all those years. It was you who said that the secret to sourdough was sticking with it, but then you just let it go!'

Louis shrugged again. He looked pitiful.

'You are foolish if you think it is anything more than just bread,' he said, and in that moment Esme knew he was not the Louis he had once been, just as she was not the Esme she had once been, and that there was no going back for either of them.

He picked up the brandy and drank from the bottle. He wiped his mouth with the sleeve of his shirt and looked at her.

'I have paid for the room,' he said. He picked up his jacket and walked out of the door. But instead of closing it behind him, he turned to her. 'Your bread, your *pain au levain*, was good,' he said, and she detected a wistfulness she did not think he could manufacture. 'Different from Lapoine, of course, but good.' And with that, he was gone.

Esme sat on the bed, speechless, her head reeling until she realised that the feeling that was surfacing above all others was one of relief. 'Thank God,' she breathed. She might have teetered, but she had not fallen. She was not a cheat or an adulteress. Close. But not close enough.

How could she have fallen for him a second time? How could she have been so stupid? Thoughts still whirred in her head, but they made more sense than they had in a long time, and all, at least, pointed in the same direction. Home. She looked at her watch. It was nearly four. She would pick up Rory, maybe go to Hamleys and then go back to her family, where she now knew she belonged.

Louis, she would forget. Charlie she would deal with later. Charlie! Did he really think he had been doing her a favour? Was that his idea of helping? Pog she could not wait to wrap her arms around.

She hurried through the streets. It was still, of course, raining. She took the steps to the gym two at a time. Her receptionist friend merely raised her eyebrows as Esme headed for the crèche, trying to pick Rory's orange curls out in the kaleidoscope of colour.

'Forget something?' the crèche supervisor asked. Esme laughed. 'No, I'm back,' she said. 'For Rory.'

The girl's face paled. 'But he's gone,' she said. 'Your driver picked him up. He's been gone for more than an hour.'

Esme hit her head on a tiny little table as she fell to the floor. It wasn't a faint so much as a collapse. She had lost a child before. She knew what it felt like. And it felt like this. Like being lost yourself. With no chance, ever, of being found.

This time, though, she deserved it. And the pain was unbearable.

Chapter Sixteen

THE POLICEMAN WHO ARRIVED in the gym manager's office less than ten minutes later had trouble making sense out of what Esme was saying.

Hysteria had her firmly in its grip and showed no signs of letting go.

'We don't have a car,' she sobbed. 'My son Teddy died two years ago.'

'I'm terribly sorry,' the policeman said. 'But I'm going to have to ask you some questions.'

Panic gripped every ounce of Esme's body. Her son had been taken while she had been acting like some two-bit hooker in a D-grade porn film. He had been taken. He was gone. She had lost both her sons. And yet again there was no one to blame but herself. Her heartbreak had taught her nothing.

She trembled as she tried not to think of what else she was about to lose. It was about Rory, of course it was about Rory. But also, her own foolishness and treachery would be laid out on the table for all to see, and try as she might she could not ignore this.

'Oh God!' she cried, dissolving into more tears. 'What have I done?'

'Mrs Stack,' the policeman said gently. 'I know this is hard for you, but it's important that we think clearly. That we don't jump to any conclusions. Is it at all possible that your husband arranged to have your son picked up?'

Esme shook her head. 'He doesn't know,' she said. 'I'm not even a member.' Her hands, trembling in her lap, started clawing at each other. 'Who would do this?' she cried. 'Who *could* do this?'

'Well, that's what we have to try and think about,' the policeman said calmly. 'But we should find out from Mr Stack, just to make sure, that it was nothing to do with him. Most cases like this, Esme—can I call you Esme?—turn out to be little communication hiccups. You thought you were going to come back and pick Teddy up but your husband—'

'Rory,' Esme corrected him, bleakly but loudly. 'It's Rory.' She was stuck in a deep, dark hole and she was never going to get out.

'Of course,' the policeman said, feeling wretched. 'Rory.' Teddy was the other son. This poor woman. It might be a communication hiccup, but then it might be worse. It was a sick world, after all.

'So, if you would just like to ring him,' he said gently, 'your husband?'

Tears spilled down Esme's cheeks. 'I went to meet a friend,' she said, 'at a hotel.'

The policeman instantly understood.

'I see,' he said, some of his sympathy draining away.

'Rory was supposed to stay at home, but his grandfather was angry with me so I had to bring him,' blubbed Esme. 'I came in here and saw the crèche and, well, I thought there were rules,' she sobbed. 'I thought only I could pick him up.'

Even the policeman had to agree that should have been the case. That it had been a terrible mistake on the crèche supervisor's part. She too was distraught, and had been taken to a separate room for questioning and to try to give the police an Identikit picture of the kidnapper.

'Ms Marshall says your son seemed to know the man,' the policeman said, looking at his notebook. 'A black man in his twenties.'

Esme wept uncontrollably. What would this do to Pog? To lose his second son and his unfaithful wife in what would basically amount to a single phone call? It would kill him. And he was such a dear, sweet, gentle soul. She wanted him then, desperately, helplessly, stupidly. How cruel that the only person she wanted to reach for when she was in this kind of trouble was the person she had betrayed to get in it in the first place. But Pog was the rock she clung to, safe and secure.

Of course they suffered their own dysfunctions: what couple didn't? She should have talked to him about Teddy, had known that all along, but as time went by it had got harder to bring up that lost and lonely name, and he had never talked to her, either. They were just two little lost peas bobbing about in a giant ocean of misery, each keeping an eye on the other to make sure they stayed on course, yet stopping just short of throwing a line in case it sucked them both underneath the surface. There was the fresh pain, too, of Granny Mac to consider and avoid. She should have reached for her husband these past few weeks, not pushed him away and instead resurrected her past.

Sitting in the manager's office, her son lost, her lover a fraud, her life in tatters, all Esme wanted was Pog. But he would not want her. Not after this. Her sordid, sad little secret had cost them everything.

'We didn't even do anything,' Esme sobbed wildly at the policeman. 'I don't love him. I love Pog. I just wanted to come and get Rory and go home and live happily ever after. That's finally what I wanted! And now what chance do I have?'

'I am sure it's just a misunderstanding,' the policeman said. 'Could you have mentioned the crèche to someone else?'

'But I didn't even know we were coming here,' Esme said. 'We just came in to use the loo and then I saw the crèche—' Her heart stopped. 'Could someone have seen him in the changing rooms? I didn't go in. People complain. He went in on his own. Oh please, please, please . . .'

The policeman's heart sank, but he tried not to let her see it.

'Well, the front desk will have a record of everyone who was here at the time, so we shouldn't have too much trouble tracking him down if that is the case,' he said. 'Now, I know that in the circumstances it is a delicate matter and perhaps not the easiest thing for you to do, but I am going to have to insist that you ring Mr Stack.'

More than two hours had passed since Rory had been snatched, and still her perfectly blameless husband was blissfully unaware. Esme knew the policeman was right.

'I'll go and check on the Identikit picture,' he said, and placing a kindly hand on Esme's shoulder, he left her to it.

How could she ring Pog? How could she tell him what she had done? Time was ticking away, taking Rory further and further from her.

At this realisation, she knew she could not wait any longer.

She was in such trouble, they all were. And Pog needed to know.

She picked up the phone and, weeping, punched in his work number. Mrs Murphy answered almost straight away.

'Is Hugo there, please?' Esme asked, trying hard not to hyperventilate with fear.

'Chance would be a fine thing,' snapped his secretary. 'Gets a phone call from London and hightails it down there quick smart,' she said. 'Left me here to hold the fort entirely unaided, I might add.'

'London?' Esme echoed. 'Whatever for?'

'Don't ask me,' Mrs Murphy said. 'It's not like he tells me anything. I'm just chief cook and bottle-washer, me. Wouldn't tell me if the building were burning down, I expect. But come time to photocopy plans for the new one and you can be sure that it'll be muggins here who—'

Esme hung up. She felt like a cartoon character who had been hit on the head. Birds tweeted around her. Sense could not get in. The door behind her opened and a tap on her shoulder alerted her to the return of the police officer, behind him the Identikit artist.

'Ludkin here thinks he has a fairly good image,' the policeman said.

'The crèche supervisor reckons he's about six feet tall, just a bit taller than myself,' said Ludkin, who was five feet eight if he was lucky. 'Quite well spoken, plainly dressed in clean, sport-style street clothes, and, as you are aware, known to the victim.' He realised his gaffe immediately. 'That is, known to your *son*.'

149

But Esme was not listening to him. She was staring at the line drawing in front of her and it was staring back.

The soup in her head suddenly started to clear, as the straight lines and subtle shadings emerged from a stranger's blur into a frighteningly familiar face. All was not lost. It had been a hiccup of some description.

Esme's tears dried as she burped out something approaching a laugh. She looked at the policeman, her eyes shining, and pointed at the picture. The kidnapper was someone she knew. And he was not a kidnapper. Nor was he a black man in his twenties—rather, a coffee-coloured boy of sixteen.

It was Ridge. Ridge had taken Rory.

Relief flooded through Esme like intravenous Valium. Rory was fine. He was with Ridge. Why, she couldn't fathom, but she also knew that her little boy would be safe. There would be an explanation. The police could go home. So could she. So could Rory. So could Pog.

Moments before, her life had lain in ruins at her ankles. Now bits of it had risen up into the air, and although all were currently floating just out of her reach, she knew that if she could just grab them and join them all up together again, everything would be all right.

Esme allowed herself a further injection of guilt at the way her relief, while almost entirely over Rory, was yet tinged with traces of her Excelsior secret. Her marriage was not lost. Her secret was safe.

Esme snatched up the phone again and stabbed in Alice's home number. It barely rang before she heard her friend's anxious voice on the other end.

'It's Esme. Is Rory there?'

'Yes,' Alice cried. 'He's fine. He's absolutely fine. I mean I don't know what is going on but Rory is fine, Esme.'

'Thank God,' Esme cried. 'He's OK,' she said to the policeman, who, seeing the look of joy on her face, could not muster up a trace of annoyance. Sometimes, he thought, he bloody well liked his job.

'Who's that?' Alice asked. 'Where are you, Esme?'

'It's the police,' Esme told her. 'I'm at the gym with the police. We thought Rory had been kidnapped. I've been going out of my mind.'

'Oh, Esme! They won't press charges, will they?' Alice was panicking. 'It will ruin his life and he only did it because—well, because he loves Rory so much and he's just a bit screwed up and he would never, ever hurt a hair on his head, on anyone's head, and I know you probably need me to be your friend right now, but honestly, I could kill you, Esme. I could just throttle you. Ridge has told me about the Frenchman. How could you? Behind Pog's back. Behind all of our backs. I'm so angry, Esme. I know it's been hard for you with Granny Mac and everything, but it's hard for all of us, Esme. And even harder now. Why didn't you tell me? Oh, Esme, please don't let them press charges. Please!'

'Ridge knows about Louis?' she asked, lowering her voice.

'He saw you, Es. In Marylebone High Street last week, snogging. And then outside the hotel. He works right next door—didn't I tell you? At the bistro. He followed you to the gym. Oh, Esme, it's not his fault. He's just a confused kid. Please don't ruin his life. He knows he did the wrong thing. He rang me as soon as Rory started asking for you.'

With a downward beat of her heart, Esme realised that her own foolishness and treachery were not out of the picture just yet. Her little boy was safe, but she was not. And as for darling, damaged Ridge, of course she would protect him. From what, she didn't know, but there were enough ruined lives in the offing as it was.

'I won't,' she said quietly. 'I wouldn't, Alice.'

'Of course,' breathed her friend. 'Of course. I just had to make sure. He shouldn't have done it, Es. He knows that.'

'Does Pog know?' Esme asked, sure that her husband fleeing to London was unlikely to be a coincidence. Silence.

'He does,' Alice said eventually. 'Ridge rang him first. I think he told him everything and then Pog called me. He assumed I must know what you were up to with Louis. I mean, you've never not told me anything ever before, Esme.' Alice started to cry. 'I'm so sorry,' she wailed. 'You and Pog always seemed so perfect, despite everything.' Esme was feeling sicker as every minute passed. 'How could you do this?' her friend sobbed down the phone.

'Nothing happened,' Esme intoned. 'With Louis. I bumped into him in town, the day Jemima saw me at the Orrery. We had lunch, twice, and I talked about Teddy and then nothing happened. Absolutely nothing. It was all a mistake.'

'Pog is on his way here,' Alice said. 'You'd better come.'

Esme nodded wordlessly and slid the phone back into its cradle, the policeman watching her as relief and happiness slid off her face into a puddle on the floor.

'I'll give you a lift,' he said. 'Probably best you avoid the tube after a day like today.'

Esme stared at him blankly. 'How can I face them?' she asked him, as though he could truly help her. 'I've only gone and cocked up my whole life. I mean, I thought I had it all under control. I thought I had found a way just to goddamn carry on and for nearly two years, I bloody well did. You know? I really bloody well did. Then Granny Mac goes and has another stroke. And then she gets pneumonia. And everything goes to pot. I go to pot.'

A silence, surprisingly lacking in awkwardness, grew between them.

'It can't be easy,' the policeman eventually said, 'going on with your life when you've lost a little one.'

Esme nodded, miserably. Life after Teddy had barely been life at all. It was like pretending to live, really. Why hadn't she seen it at the time? She'd been so determined for everything to return to normal, for everyone to return to normal, to cover up the hole left by the loss of their little boy, that she had simply gone through the motions, keeping the outside world happy, yet all the while she'd been shrivelling up inside, relishing her numbness. The memory of her son had become a hard, dry, nasty little nugget inside her and, for some reason, Louis had been able to nourish it. Granny Mac had seen that. But then she would.

'Would mess up your head,' the policeman was saying, 'make you do mad things, I imagine. Grief does that to a person. I've seen it a thousand times.' He stopped and waited for Esme to look at him. 'I expect the same goes for Mr Stack,' he said, with an encouraging raise of his eyebrows.

'Why are you being so kind to me?' Esme asked him.

'Because you look like a woman who could do with a break,' the policeman answered, with a smile, and he stood and nodded at the door. 'Shall we go?'

Esme's future lay cold and harsh and flat in front of her. But could it be worse, she asked herself as she let the policeman lead her out of the gym, than the soft and slushy murk of her fairly recent past?

The policeman, whose name, he'd sheepishly told her on the way to Alice's flat, was also Ted, had done his best to calm her fears by reminding her that her son, after all, was safe and that was what really mattered.

'Thank you, Ted,' she said, when he dropped her at the kerb.

'I should come up and make sure the boy is all right,' he said. 'You go ahead and I'll park the car and be right up.'

He wanted to give her a moment on her own. She had been humiliated enough without turning up on a policeman's arm.

'It's me,' she said into the speaker and the door was buzzed open.

By the time she reached the third floor she was gasping for breath, her trench coat flapping round her body, her hair stuck to her neck as she pounded on Alice's door.

Her friend, her face pinched and unfamiliar, opened it wide and looked towards the front room. Her anger hung hot and heavy in the air, but Esme's guilt glands were already full and overflowing.

She walked into the room and there was Rory, sitting on the sofa.

Stifling a sob, Esme knelt on the floor, feeling, disgustedly, her tights tugging at her crotch where she had failed to pull them up properly. How could she have exposed her family, her son, to her sorry, sordid mistakes? She pulled Rory to her, hugging him close and smelling his innocent little-boy smell as she nuzzled his neck and kissed him.

'I'm so sorry, darling,' was all she could say. 'I'm so sorry.'

Rory put up with this for a few moments but then pushed her gently away. 'It's OK, Esme,' he said. 'I made a giant panda out of Play Doh and then Ridge came and got me. We went on the bus and the tube and he bought me some sweets and an orange drink.'

Ridge stood by the fireplace, fidgeting and looking dangerous in a way she would never have guessed he could. She started to say something, but the angry teenager interrupted her.

'You don't bloody deserve him,' he said. 'You've got everything right in front of you and you can't even see it. You make me sick!'

Esme was stunned. Ridge was shaking with rage.

'I'm so sorry,' she started to say, even though Ridge was just as much in the wrong as she was, even more, possibly, but his anger could not be contained.

'You have this husband who worships you,' he seethed, 'and this kid who thinks you're the cat's pyjamas and you'd throw it all away on a lying little French git who just wants to get into your pants. It's disgusting!'

'Ridge!' Alice spoke sharply from the door.

'It's true, Mum,' her son answered her, and he sounded so young and so hurt that Esme could not hold back her tears. That she could damage her own family was one thing, but to hurt Alice's was incomprehensible.

'Please,' Esme bawled at him from the floor, her face awash. 'Please forgive me, Ridge. I've been stupid, but I didn't mean to hurt you or Alice or anyone. I just—'

'You just never thought about anyone apart from yourself,' roared Ridge, his rage giving way to tears. 'You're nothing but a—'

Thankfully, for everyone in the room, the intercom rudely heralded the arrival of Pog.

'You don't deserve him,' Ridge hissed as Alice buzzed him in.

'You think I don't know that?' Esme said quietly, sitting up on the sofa next to Rory. How she was going to get through the next few minutes, let alone the rest of her life, she did not know.

Alice opened the door and Pog walked in, barely acknowledging her as he strode straight towards his wife and son.

'Oh, Esme,' he said with no trace of rancour, and Esme could not even look at him. She just looked at the floor and cried. Pog knelt down and hugged his son to his chest, but Rory was sick of being hugged and soon resisted.

Pog, then, put his hand on his wife's knee. 'Esme,' he said again, even more gently, which only made her cry harder.

'Why are you being so bloody nice to her?' Ridge shouted, his tears making his voice mean and throaty. 'She's only been shagging some slimy little frog behind your back.'

'That's enough!' commanded a new voice. Henry's voice. Esme looked up just long enough to see his miserable face attached to his miserable body, standing by the doorway next to a distraught Alice. Esme's hands flew up to her face to cover the tears she could not stop, and disguise her shame. Why had Henry come?

'But you're just—' Ridge started to say.

'*Enough!*' It was Pog this time. 'Stop it, Ridge. Esme has enough going on without you having a go at her, too.'

He turned to Esme and put his other hand on her other knee. Still she could not meet his gaze. Rory shifted closer to her on the sofa.

'But you shouldn't—' Ridge started again, tears and anger mixing on his face.

'You don't know everything there is to know, Ridge,' Pog said tiredly. 'You don't know what Esme has been through.'

'I do know,' insisted Ridgeley. 'I've known her since I was born, haven't I? I've known her for longer than you have.'

'Yes, but the past couple of years, the last couple of months, have been hell for her and you're not—'

'So her son died and her grandmother—'

'*That's enough!*' Pog roared again. It was such a rare sound, his voice angry and raised. 'Let's not forget the part you have played in all this today, Ridge.'

A silence thick with secrets and regret hung over the sad collection of friends and family so suffocatingly that Esme almost wished Ridge would start shouting again.

The buzzer rang once more, giving them all a fright, and they waited in painful silence until Alice opened the door to Ted, who took in Esme and the little boy, asked a simple, 'All right?' and excused himself at her unhappy nod.

'Alice, why don't you take Ridge to the pub?' Pog suggested in a bright, sensible voice after the policeman had gone. 'I hate to toss you out of your own home, but I think we need some time alone here.'

Alice nodded and looked relieved. Watching her favourite family disintegrate in front of her very eyes was hardly pleasant viewing.

'We'll take Rory,' she said, reaching her hand out for him, but Rory shook his head.

'I'm staying with Esme,' he said.

'He shouldn't hear all this, Pog,' Alice said gently.

'Oh, Alice,' Pog said and he sounded so sad that Alice's eyes filled with tears again, 'he has to hear it. We all do. Really, it's time.'

Alice grabbed her angry son and hustled him, protesting, out of the door of their flat.

After they left, nobody said anything and the room was filled with only the sound of Esme's sobbing. She had no idea how she was going to resurrect her life, and knew that it would probably never be the same again, but the damage she had caused others, she was prepared to repair, no matter how hard and no matter what the sacrifice.

When she could bear to, she raised her eyes to meet Henry's. He was sitting now on the chair by the window, turned slightly sideways to her.

'I'm so sorry, Henry,' she said before dissolving into great hiccupping sobs again. 'I know I've always been a disappointment to you, and that this only proves that you were right all along, but I really, truly am sorry.'

To her added distress, she felt a small clammy hand through the fabric of her coat and looked down to see that Rory was rubbing her leg, comforting her.

She watched the bone-coloured fabric grow fat dark dots as her tears fell on it. When the dots got smaller, she looked up at Henry, ready, with the help of her little boy and his gentle caress, to take her punishment.

To her horror, Henry, far from steaming at the nostrils, was also weeping, his hand, red and purple with his old man's veins, shaking as he brought it up to wipe a string of mucus from his nose.

'No,' he said, his voice thick with the glue of grief. 'It is I who should be sorry.' He sobbed with a shudder that racked his whole body. 'I have been cruel,' he said, 'and unreasonable. And I have been a coward.' His voice splintered, unable to string words together any further.

Confusion interrupted Esme's own unhappiness.

'Don't be silly, Henry,' she said. 'A coward? You haven't been a coward. What do you mean?'

After one more shuddering sob, Henry took a deep breath, drew himself up in his chair and looked at Esme with heartbroken eyes.

'It was me,' he said. 'It was me who pulled the plastic over the fountain.'

Esme sat completely still.

'Your grandmother told me to do it first thing in the morning,' Henry continued, wretchedly, 'when it started to rain, but I didn't. Just to be blessed contrary, I didn't. I did it at lunchtime, after she had asked me twice more, and by that stage the bowl was already full of water.' His shoulders shook as he fought to keep control. 'I should have emptied it out, but I thought covering it would keep the boys from harm. I never dreamed that anyone would . . . that Teddy would . . .' His lips trembled and his eyes blinked rapidly to ward off fresh tears.

'If it wasn't for me, Teddy would be alive,' he exploded. 'He would be alive and none of this would have happened.' Hearing Henry say his name shocked Esme completely tearless. The sound of it ricocheted round the room.

'Teddy,' she said out loud. Nothing happened. She took Rory's hand and rubbed it. 'Teddy,' she said again. Rory looked at her and smiled.

'Teddy,' he repeated. 'Rory and Teddy.'

Her heart bleeding, but her mind suddenly, strangely calmed, she looked at Pog, whose unfathomable brown eyes were there, ready and waiting, to return her gaze.

'Why couldn't I talk about him?' she asked her husband. 'Why was it so hard for me to say his name?'

'It wasn't just you,' said Pog. 'It was all of us.'

'But I'm his mother,' Esme said. 'I'm the one who was opening a test kitchen while he was'—her mouth was as dry as a bone—'at home, in need of me. I'm the one who took too long to find him. Who never thought to check the fountain. Whose idea the bloody wretched fountain was in the first place.'

'But I was there,' Henry said. 'I was there and in control and I could have stopped it happening from the very beginning. It's my fault and you've had every right to hate me for it.'

'Nobody hates you, Dad,' said Pog. 'Even though you often give us reason to and not because of Teddy, but because you can be rude to Esme and ungrateful when she is one of the sweetest people alive.'

'Esme hates me,' Henry said. 'She's blamed me all along and she's been right to. It was my fault.'

'I've done nothing of the sort, Henry,' Esme exclaimed. 'Do you think I had a moment spare from blaming myself? It was not your fault. I'm his mother and I should have been there looking after him and I should have found him before it was too late. It's not about the plastic. It was a good idea to cover the fountain. It was the right thing to do, the sensible thing to do. It was just—'

'It was just bad luck,' Pog said, getting up off the floor and squeezing in next to Esme on the sofa. He leaned forward and put his head in his hands. 'It was just one of those terrible things that happens: that you think will happen to someone else but in this case happened to us.'

Esme closed her eyes and saw Teddy's ginger curls floating in a shiny black slick.

'It's true, Esme,' Pog said quietly. 'I know you think it was bad management on your part, on my part, on our part, but other people work hard and have busy lives in the city and their children don't die.'

Behind her closed eyelids, Esme lifted Teddy out of the water and held him to her chest again.

'I think we did the right thing leaving London,' Pog continued, 'leaving that life behind, moving to the House in the Clouds and starting again up there. I really do. It's been good for Rory and it was good for Granny Mac, too.'

Henry sniffed in the silence that ensued, and although her eyes were closed and her head was resting back against the sofa cushions, Rory climbed into her lap and snuggled into her neck.

'Sometimes, Esme,' he said quite matter-of-factly, 'I talk to Teddy.'

Tears slid down Esme's cheeks as she wrapped her arms around him.

'I know he's not here,' Rory said, in case they thought he was young and silly, 'but I still talk to him.'

Pog cleared his throat, for the first time seeming to struggle with his emotions.

'Esme?' Rory tugged at her and she opened her eyes and looked into his, finding in them something she hadn't known she needed, but wondered now how she could ever have missed. She kissed her son and drew strength from him.

'Yes, darling,' she whispered. 'I know.'

'It can be our little secret, if you like, about Granny Mac,' Rory whispered back, snuggling up against her, and she treasured him more in that moment than she had treasured anything ever before.

'I've not been myself these past couple of months,' she finally said to the room. 'I've been struggling. Everything seemed wrong. Nothing fitted properly. I felt wretched on the inside. All messed up and horrid.'

She thought of the turmoil that clawed at her innards all the time and wondered, dimly, if perhaps now that everything was out in the open, she would be free of it.

'You're always so damnably cheerful,' Henry said. 'How are we supposed to know when there is something wrong?'

Esme almost laughed. 'Well, you're not,' she said. 'That's the whole point of me. You can always rely on me to make you laugh and feel better. It's actually one of the things I like most about myself.'

'But, Esme,' Pog said, the pain clear in his voice, 'you can't go through what you've been through and still bear that responsibility. It's too hard.'

This was true, Esme knew, but only to a point.

'But, Pog—if I climbed into bed with a vat of gin and cried myself to sleep for a year, what would you do?'

He knew the answer as well as she did. 'I would climb in too,' he said. 'To be with you.'

A faint whistling from Esme's lap told her that their son, after saying his bit, after sharing a little magical drop of himself with her, had nodded off to sleep. She smoothed his curls off his forehead.

'Well, I couldn't bear that,' Esme said softly, so as not to wake him. 'I don't want to think anyone else could feel the same deep, dark, horrible, awful bloody pain that I do. It would be the end of me.'

'He would never let that happen,' Henry said, with some of his old fierceness. 'He loves you too bloody much. For better or worse.'

'It's true,' said Pog. 'I love you so bloody much, Es.' And he exploded into tears so loaded with grief that Esme thought she simply could not bear it. Her aching heart rendered her silent.

Henry, at this, pulled himself out of his chair, took the sleeping Rory off her lap and wordlessly limped out of the room.

Then, out into the air between them, so full of unspoken thoughts and raw, ragged feeling, burst the declaration Pog had long been holding and hiding.

'I love you so much,' he exploded again. 'You'll never know how much, Esme.' Tears pinged off his cheeks and onto the carpet. 'I just—' His voice shook but he took a stuttering breath and ploughed on. 'Talking about it doesn't do it justice, Es. I don't know the right words, what to say to make you feel better. I just know that I have adored you since the moment I first saw you and that if you were to leave'— the thought brought with it fresh tears but he brushed them away—'if you were to leave it would be devastating . . . but that's not even the word. It would be . . . God . . . living hell, Esme. Absolute living hell.'

He tried to curb his emotion before he continued. 'But I've thought about it all afternoon, I mean I've thought about the possibility for years. And if you want to go off with Louis,' he said, 'and live in some bloody bakery in the middle of France, well, part of me wants to shake you till your head drops off, Esme. How could you do this? To me? To us? But part of me only wants you to be happy, because you bloody deserve it, you truly do, no matter what, so I will help you pack your bags, Esme. I will fold your clothes and brush your hair and rub lavender moisturiser into your legs before you go. I might die afterwards, or at least never live properly again, but if going with Louis is what will make you happy, then I will help you, Esme. I will. I swear I will.'

He had a lot to get off his chest. Esme sobbed silently next to him.

'But will he ever love you the way I do? Will he love the way your hair springs out one side of your head first thing in the morning, or the way you smile in your sleep, or the little fold of skin near your armpit? Does he know that you can't stand marmalade, but eat apricot jam out of the pot with your fingers? Will he understand that you need to take Panadol an hour before a bikini wax or it makes you cry?'

Esme had never heard anything so clearly in all her life.

'I know he's a baker. I know he bakes bread. I know that's what you love about him, Esme, but there's more to life than bloody bread, you know. Man cannot live by bread alone, Esme. Everybody thinks you're so strong, so capable, so funny, so amazing and you are, my God, you are. But I understand you like nobody else ever will. I understand that you needed to wait to talk about Teddy. I understand that you can't look at Rory without wondering how being half a twin for the rest of his life is going to affect him. I understand that Granny Mac was the real love of your life and everyone else came second and I love that about you, Esme, I really do. And if you go with Louis and I never see you again, I will still wake up every day and thank God because every day with you has been a marvellous bloody gift and I treasure each moment.'

What have I done to deserve this man? Esme thought, as she watched him pour his heart out into a puddle in the middle of Alice's swirly orange and brown carpet. How could she ever have doubted that where she belonged was with him?

Esme slid off the sofa, sank to her knees in front of Pog and took his hands from his bowed head. She placed his precious arms round her shoulders.

'Nothing happened with Louis,' she said softly. 'I had lunch with him twice, Pog, and I went to his hotel today but nothing happened, I swear to you.' She stopped. How could she hold anything back from Pog when he had just bared his own battered soul so bravely to her?

'I thought it might,' she said, sniffing as her tears dried, 'happen, I mean. With him, Pog. With Louis. I talked to him about our baby, our Teddy, and it just felt like such a huge bloody release that I thought it must mean something, that there was more to it. But once I got there and saw him for who he really is, I just . . .' She thought about the dummy and how it had saved her from making the worst mistake of her life. Without it, she might not have seen who Louis really was until she had already betrayed her husband. Maybe destiny had played a part after all. She cleared her throat. 'I don't love Louis,' she said, and the words tasted far from sour in her mouth. 'I've been lost and scared and I thought meeting him again was a sign that I could find the sort of happiness that I knew when I was young and uncomplicated and pure, not the screwed-up, heartbroken mother of a dead little boy.'

Pog clasped her tightly and wept into her curls.

'But I was wrong, Pog,' she continued. 'I don't think I can ever have that happiness back. I think it's a once-in-a-lifetime thing.' She felt her husband shudder with anguish as she realised she had not put it the way she meant it.

'Shhh,' she hushed him. 'I don't mean it like that. I mean that I don't want it again. I think I can have a new kind of happiness. I *have* had a new kind. A better kind. With you.'

She lifted Pog's face so his waterlogged eyes met hers.

'I've loved you from the moment I spat up the regurgitated cheese ball, Pog. You're my best friend in all the world, I trust you with my life. You're the kindest, sweetest, most patient, adoring husband any woman could ever hope for and you are the father of my son, my sons. There is no other man in the universe I will ever want for that job. You've loved me and taken care of me and I can't believe that I have even got close to messing that up, Pog, and if I could wind back the clock I would, but I can't, you know that, because you know just when I would wind it back to.'

Pog nodded as his eyes filled with tears again.

'We have to move on,' Esme continued, a path clearing in her mind, 'we have to look forwards not backwards. I haven't really understood that until now because the future seemed so grim, so Teddy-less, but we can do it, with each other, I know that now. Oh God, Hugo Stack, I love you! With all my heart. I truly, truly do. I know I don't deserve it, but do you think you can ever, will ever, be able to forgive me?'

Pog looked at her with his steady, unwavering gaze. 'It's not about forgiving you, Esme, it's about being sure you love me as much as I love you, because if you don't, I can't bear it.'

'But I do!' cried Esme. 'I do! That's what this whole horrible mess has taught me. Honestly, Pog, I've never been more sure about anything.'

He was silent for a moment and when he spoke, his voice did not need to be chocolate-coated.

'I know you think you're plain old flour and water, Es. And that Louis was your starter, but that's not true, it's never been true. We're the flour and water and you're our starter. You're the best thing that ever happened to any of us,' he said, and she leaned in and kissed him, tasting the salt of his tears and the promise of their future.

It was delicious.

Chapter Seventeen

ESME AND ALICE both sat on Granny Mac's bed but the *Hello!* magazine they had brought in to ogle was discarded between them.

'You have been *what*?' Alice was asking Esme, aghast.

'I have been talking to her,' Esme answered, her cheeks going pink. 'I know it sounds nutty, but I have. She told me to start baking bread again and she encouraged me to go and meet Louis.'

'But, Esme, sweetie, Granny Mac is dead,' Alice said. 'She died two months ago.'

'Well, I know that. That is why it sounds nutty that I have been talking to her,' Esme returned, as though Alice were the crazy one. 'But I found her in here, sort of sitting up large as life, the day that Brown peed on the quince, and she started talking to me and I started talking back.'

Alice was stunned. She stared at the ceiling and wriggled her jaw, uncertain what to do or say.

'Oh, don't go all thingie on me, Alice,' Esme pleaded. 'You wanted me to tell you everything from now on, so I'm telling you.'

'But, Esme,' Alice groaned. 'That's loony! People don't come back from the dead in real life. It only happens in films.'

'I know,' her friend sighed. She was silent for a moment. 'You know, when Teddy died, I thought that as long as I had Granny Mac everything would be all right. That was all that kept me going, Alice: the thought that she was there for me. Just for me. She was mine. She would never let me crawl into a hole and not come out again, and, as you know, MacDougall women have a habit of doing that. I just never let myself contemplate a life without her, so when she went, with so little warning, I think a switch flicked in my head that I couldn't unflick myself without a little bit of help.'

'Esme, you mustn't say things like that.'

'But it's true, Alice! There's no blueprint for surviving the death of your child, you know. You bloody well grasp onto whatever you can to stop yourself from drowning, and for me it was Granny Mac. She was my life raft, keeping me afloat. And I thought I would know when I had to let go and that I'd have the chance to prepare for it, but instead

Dr Gribblehurst just steps out of her door after his regular visit and tells us to make arrangements, that it's a matter of hours and it was.'

'And so,' Alice said, rather sceptically, 'she came back, from the other side, from beyond.'

'From wherever,' Esme said. 'Don't laugh at me! I know it's losing-your-marbles territory. My God, you think I don't know that? And now I sit in here like I did before and think perhaps I was just imagining her. Perhaps I was only telling myself things I already knew, suggesting things I really wanted to do. But the room felt different, Alice. It felt full of her. It smelt of her, too. You know, Embassy Regal. And Rod bloody Stewart was always playing. You know how she loved to sing along. He seeped from the walls, Alice.'

She looked around at the walls, now freshly painted a gentle spring yellow. The smell of smoke was gone. The hat was gone. Rod was gone. Sun streamed into the room in which she had shared such a strange time with her grandmother.

'I've told Pog everything *but* this,' Esme told Alice. 'And I will tell him. I just thought I would test it out on you first and see what happened, and I have to say I don't know that I would consider it a raging success.'

'Well,' conceded Alice, 'I don't think that you shagging Louis was the best idea Granny Mac ever had, but then you technically never actually did, and along the way the little slimeball did seem to clear your pipes on the, you know, Teddy front.' She bit her lip. She was so used to danc-ing around the subject that it still felt unnatural to broach it.

Esme smiled, sweetly, sadly. 'I miss him,' she said and Alice breathed again. 'But I can think about him now without hating myself. And I can remember more than the snot bubble he blew out of his nose that last morning.' Her voice faltered. Alice scooted closer and hugged her. 'But it feels better,' Esme whispered. 'Better than before when I could hardly bear to look at Rory without seeing that same little face, never growing up, just staying two and a bit for ever.'

'Oh, Esme, I'm so sorry.'

'It's all right,' wept Esme, 'I'm much happier now.' Her shoulders shook with grief, but instead of pushing it away, she let it embrace her, and with that, as she had gradually learned, came a warmth, a calmness.

'He was a gorgeous boy, wasn't he?' Alice said, gently rocking her friend.

'Yes,' sniffed Esme, her tears subsiding. 'He was. Remember the night you baby-sat and he ate the contents of his nappy?'

Alice laughed. 'How could I forget? I had to clean it out of his teeth, for goodness' sake. And what about the time Ridge swapped their clothes and the crumblies never noticed, and it wasn't until you gave them a bath that you realised what he'd done and swapped them back?'

'Don't!' Esme cried. 'That makes it sound like I was such a crap mother!'

'You are the best mother a boy could have,' Alice said robustly. 'And Teddy might not have had you for long, but he couldn't have had anyone better. Don't shrug me off, Esme, it's true. And I know you worry about Rory and who wouldn't, in the circumstances. But he is actually one pretty cool little bloke and he is going to be all right. He might have lost his brother but he's still got two wonderful parents, a doting grandfather, adoring friends and a donkey with the biggest dick I have ever seen in my whole entire life.'

Esme laughed, and the sound bounced round and round the sunny room, chasing away, once and for all, the spirit of the past.

Alice squeezed her again and they sat there, quietly staring at crumpled Elizabeth Hurley on the cover of *Hello!* magazine squashed between them, until Esme abruptly sat up.

'Time to put the bread in,' she said to her friend. 'Come on, clench those buttocks.'

'Unfurl the flag, sherpa,' Alice grumbled as she heaved herself off Granny Mac's bed and headed up the stairs.

Up in the kitchen Esme's dough sat proud and floury in its linen-lined basket. Esme loved this last raw look at it. She opened the oven door and pulled out the baking stone she used to even out the temperature and give her bread a crispier bottom and chewier crust.

Gently but quickly, she upturned the basket just millimetres above the heated stone and out plumped her *boule*, making an almost inaudible sizzle as it hit the heated ceramic surface.

Swiftly, she took the waiting razor and cut a few clever lines into the skin of the dough, then shut the door and flicked the steam jets on three times in quick succession.

Although she had done this a thousand times before, she could not help but crouch down and watch her bread through the glass door of the cooker. She still saw the magic in every single bake and she was sure she always would.

'Esme,' Alice said, from her position at the kitchen table, 'you never finished telling me about what happened with Charlie.'

Esme put the kettle on. Yes. Charlie.

Obviously, her first intention, once she got her family back to the House in the Clouds that awful, wonderful day two weeks before, had been to take out a contract on Charlie and get him killed, stone dead.

He had risked so much in his little turn at playing God that Esme doubted she could ever look at him again, let alone speak to him. But it had been Pog, kind, gentle, remarkable Pog, who had finally talked to him at length on the phone and then suggested that maybe Esme should go and meet him and listen to what he had to say.

So it was that the previous Friday Esme had found herself looking at Charlie over a very expensive glass of Riesling—his treat—and wondering how much of a fuss it would cause if she choked him then and there.

It was lunchtime and they were sitting upstairs at Assaggi in Notting Hill, as far away from the pitfalls of Marylebone High Street as Charlie could manage.

'Darling, I'm so glad you finally agreed to have lunch with me,' he was saying. 'It's been awful these past two weeks. If you'd hung up on me one more time I swear I was going to have to—I don't know—not top myself but do something pretty drastic. I've been quite distraught.'

'Yes,' Esme said demurely, not ready to let him off the hook, 'it must have been terrible for you.'

'Oh, Esme,' Charlie said. 'Please, please forgive me. I never meant to hurt you, of course I didn't. I would never do that. I would rather, what? Stick needles in my eyes? Wear synthetic boxers? Reveal my natural roots? Oh please don't freeze me out, Esme, I can't bear it.'

Esme swirled the rich straw-coloured wine in her glass. Of course she hadn't come all this way to ignore him, and she wanted him to know that before they were asked what they wanted, so she could order up large and not feel bad that he was paying.

There were things she had to say to him, though. Questions she had to ask.

'Why, Charlie?' This was the main one. 'Why did you do such an awful thing?'

He sighed and took a deep breath. 'It's the most terrible cockup. Really. I was in some Spanish bar off Tottenham Court Road one night,' he said, 'not long after I came to stay with you in the country and there the little turd was, propping up the bar and snivelling into his Rioja.'

'He was snivelling?'

'Well, no, but he was pretty bloody miserable. Anyway, I recognised him straight away. I suppose I had been thinking about him after what you said that night, you know, about him being your one big chance at happiness. And there the little shit was sitting right in front of my nose. Well, the idea just came to me. What if you could see him once again? Naturally, I assumed that just one look and you'd realise that the life you've been living has been the right one after all. I just wanted to give you a slice of your happiness back, Es. I thought you could have a lovely romantic lunch at my expense, perhaps a bit of a snog in the lavs and then go your separate ways. I thought it would cheer you up.'

'But you bought him a suit, Charlie. You turned him into someone he wasn't,' protested Esme.

'Esme, he was always someone he wasn't.' He took a gulp of his wine. 'OK, look, to be honest, the suit was a bit of a mistake, I agree. I'd actually bought it for someone else but, oh, never mind. Anyway, it was you who turned Louis into the handsome prince, not me. And I am incredibly sorry for what I did, and when I think of how much worse it could have been I cringe, darling, I honestly cringe. But I didn't do it to hurt you. I thought I was doing you a favour. Adding a bit of spice to your life. I was trying to be nice.'

'Well, why couldn't you tell me that he was working in a sarnie shop in Hounslow and let me go and find him the way he really is?'

'Yes,' Charlie sighed. 'I can see now that would have been better, but at the time I wanted you to have your little dream, Es. You love all that romantic stuff. You always have. And I thought how marvellous to meet this man looking all dashing and international and saving sourdough all around the world. Of course he was supposed to imply he was happy with his life and that he hoped you were too, but the cretin obviously got one look at you and decided he wanted a piece of that for himself.'

'But can you see what a dreadful thing it was to do?' Esme asked him. 'Charlie, what if Rory really had been snatched? What if Louis had turned nasty? Or Pog had left me?'

'Yes, yes, yes,' Charlie said. 'I have been torturing myself with the same possibilities. But that part of it is really not my fault. I mean, the slimy little bastard was supposed to disappear after the first lunch. I had no idea he was going to hoodwink you so badly, Esme. To hurt you all over again. Good Lord, that's the last thing I would ever want. You are precious to me. You are my oldest friend. I love you more than my new Rolex. Have you noticed it, Es? Twenty-four-carat gold. Anyway, if I ever see the lying, cheating, sneaky little toad again I will box him in the nose all over again, I promise you.'

'Well, if you are ever in Hounslow and feeling peckish,' Esme told him, 'don't hold back on my account.'

The waiter approached and Charlie looked at her, worry creasing his brow in a way she knew he would not appreciate. The damage had been done. And repaired. And with one smile they put their angst behind them and ordered vast quantities of food and another bottle of wine.

The truth was that Charlie was precious to Esme too. So, he would never understand what true love was, or what her idea of true love was, but then her idea of true love had completely changed. And she could not in all honesty stay angry with Charlie. The whole sorry mess had been her own fault.

She had stupidly told him she thought Louis was the key to her happiness, and in the bleakness of losing Granny Mac she had truly believed that to be the case. She had reached into her past and plucked out the most vivid, uncomplicated happiness she could find and dreamed of re-creating it. An impossible task, as it turned out. Not to mention a foolish one.

'The funny thing is,' she said sheepishly to Alice as they sat nursing their second cup of tea high in the Suffolk sky, 'despite all the drama, the upset I've caused, everything is better now.'

Better than it had been in two long, awful years. She knew now how much she loved Pog. She knew how much he loved her back and it was a thousand times more than Louis, than anyone else, ever could. Henry, finally trusting that she did not blame him, was a changed man, and while not exactly a delight to have about the place, not a curse, either. And Rory, well, Rory: her heart simply swelled with adoration. Something about relieving herself of the silent, secret ghost of Teddy had allowed her to love Rory in a way she had not thought possible before. And, free of the blame for taking his twin-ness away from him, she was able to see, as clear as day, that just like his father, Rory loved her back too. It was simply euphoric.

Pog, looking blissfully boyish, Alice thought, clattered into the kitchen, sniffing the air.

'Am I on time?' he asked as he kissed his wife and smiled at her friend.

'I swear,' said Esme, 'you are getting almost as good as I am.'

She moved over to the oven, put on her mitts and opened the door, letting the heat and strength of the sourdough aroma engulf her. Reverently, she lifted out the *pain au levain* and set it on the counter-top wooden rack she had for just that purpose.

The kitchen filled instantly with that moist, sweet, salty smell. Pog and Esme's eyes met above the *boule* and they smiled at each other. Their sadness aside, all seemed right with the world.

Even Alice licked her lips.

'What's that?' she asked, peering over Esme's shoulder.

Sliced into the loaf was not the E that Esme had so deftly carved all these years, but an impression of the house in which they now stood.

'It's Bread from the House in the Clouds,' Pog answered her, getting a jar of apricot jam from the pantry, a dish of butter from the fridge, and a bread board and bread knife from the kitchen drawers.

166

'You what?' Alice asked, sitting down again, as Esme brought the bread to the table.

'You tell her,' Esme said.

'Tell me what?'

'Tell you to make the most of Granny Mac's room while you can,' said Pog, handing the knife to Esme. 'Because in a month or two right where you were just sitting and gossiping will be a roaring oak-fired oven.'

Alice was confused. 'I don't follow,' she said.

'We're opening a bakery,' Esme said, 'right here at the bottom of the stack of Stacks. Bread from the House in the Clouds. What do you think?'

'I think I need a lie-down before Granny Mac's bed is chopped into a thousand pieces and fed into the furnace,' Alice answered

Esme laughed as she slathered a thick slice of her bread with home-made jam.

Alice chewed on her own unseemly chunk of sourdough. 'I thought your bread was just for you, Esme,' she said wickedly. 'Not for everyone. That you couldn't mass-produce it. That it's personal.'

Esme just smiled. 'Why, Alice,' she said. 'It's bread. It's the staff of bleeding life. People put butter and jam on it and eat it.'

'Seriously, Esme, you are going to do this for a job?'

'Yes, she is,' answered Pog. 'No one cares more about sourdough than Esme and artisan breadmakers are a dying breed these days, even in France, hey, Esme?'

'Hey, yourself,' Esme grinned back, her cup overrunning with love for him.

'You two!' Alice was disgusted. 'Get a motel! You've got a sad, sorry singleton in your midst, let's not forget.'

'I shall leave you to it, then,' Pog said. 'I'm sure there's a lot of girl talk still to be had. Have you told her about you-know-who?'

Alice looked confused. 'I thought you hadn't told him?' she said to Esme.

'I haven't.'

'Haven't told me what?' Pog wanted to know.

'Nothing, Pog. Something Granny Mac said. Some things Granny Mac said. I will tell you later.'

Pog disappeared down the stairs.

'What is going on here?' demanded Alice. 'Who is you-know-who?'

'Jemima Jones,' Esme announced, swallowing the last mouthful of her bread. 'I banged into Jemima Jones again.'

It had been the same day she'd lunched with Charlie, she told Alice. He'd had to get back to work and she had decided to walk to Portobello

Road and have a coffee at The Electric before heading for her train.

But no sooner had she sat down with her low-fat latte, than who should fly in the door but Jemima, her cream Armani coat flapping at her sides and her stilettos screeching across the floorboards.

'Vodka tonic, double, and be quick about it,' she slung at the barman as she collapsed in a chair at the table right next to Esme. She flung her tote bag on the chair next to her and scrabbled around in it, eventually pulling out a box of tissues and loudly blowing her nose.

Esme pressed herself back into her own chair and twisted slightly away from Jemima, in the hope she would disappear. She did not.

'Oh,' said Jemima Jones, looking up and noticing her. 'Esme.'

Esme nodded, dumbly.

'How's the book coming along?'

Esme opened her mouth to speak but nothing came out.

'If you're worried it's going to end up in my column,' Jemima said, 'don't be. They've dropped it. I've been given the boot. Fucking Primrose Beckwith-Stuyvesant. How was I supposed to know her uncle is apparently patron bloody saint of all newspaper bosses and godfather to half of News International.'

The barman delivered her drink, which she knocked back in almost one gulp. 'Same again,' she said, then put one bare pretty ankle on her knee and took off her shoe. 'Bloody corns are giving me hell,' she said, rubbing her toes. 'What kind of demented, homosexual woman-hater would design shoes like these, anyway?'

And to Esme's amazement and alarm, the gorgeous Jemima burst into loud, wet tears.

Esme and the barman stared at each other for a moment, then he quietly put Jemima's second drink down beside her and slithered away, leaving them alone together. Not knowing what else to do, Esme went and sat beside the weeping woman and cautiously gave her a rub on her bony little back. The coat felt beautiful.

'Gregory's leaving me,' sobbed Jemima. 'And this time, it's for good. I'm not "adventurous" enough for him, apparently, and he's found some eighteen-year-old Eastern European model-cum-waitress. GQ hasn't come out of his room since he found out—Christ only knows what he is doing in there with that sodding computer of his, porn I expect, he is such an odd boy—and Marie Claire is eating us out of house and home. A home we won't even have for much longer.'

Her mascara had done scary things to her flawless face. Tears swept, unfettered by wrinkles, down her smooth cheeks. 'It's all gone horribly wrong and I don't know what to do about it,' she wept.

'What about your television show?' Esme asked feebly.

'Those twitty nine-year-olds!' Jemima cried. 'They wanted me to bankroll it. Dropped me like a hot potato when they realised that wasn't going to happen. It's so unfair. The world is a horrible place.'

Esme kept rubbing.

Jemima stopped crying.

'I'm sorry,' she said, blowing her nose again. 'I really am sorry.'

'Don't mention it,' Esme said brightly. 'I'm constantly blubbing into my vodka tonics.'

'No,' said Jemima, sniffing. 'I'm sorry about stiffing you at *TV Now!*. You were always nice to me and it was a rotten way to pay you back.'

'Oh, that,' Esme said, as though she could barely remember it. 'That was nothing, really.'

'And I'm sorry for writing about you like that in my column.'

'Oh, was that me?' Esme asked, wetly.

Jemima cleared her throat. 'Someone at the *Sunday Times* told me about your little boy. I didn't know that's why you left London and put on the weight. I would never have said anything in that stupid bloody column if I had known about that. I'm a mother. I can't imagine how awful that must have been. I felt like a real shit, I can tell you.'

She burst into tears again. Put on the weight? Esme repeated in her mind, her fingers itching to give Jemima a pinch.

'My life is such a mess,' Jemima wept. 'I wish I lived in the country and wrote books about hair clips like you do.'

How long would that blessed lie come back to haunt her? Esme wondered. She looked at the sorry sight in front of her and marvelled at the way the world worked.

'Actually,' she said, deciding then and there to set the record straight. 'There is no book about hair clips, Jemima. Please, stop crying. Look, I'm sure everything's going to be all right. Do you think we should have a cup of tea?'

Upon hearing this part of the story, Alice lost her rag. 'You asked her if she wanted a cup of tea? You were nice to her? You bloody well *have* lost your marbles, Esme. Truly!'

Esme was prepared for this.

'She was a wreck, Alice. A total disaster area—it was terrible.' She picked up a tray she had prepared for Henry and Rory and started down the stairs, indicating for Alice to follow her. 'She's just another one of us, you know, trying to muddle through and make sense of it all without having a nervous breakdown or killing someone. She's not so different from you or me after all.'

She could feel her friend's eyes boring into her back. 'Oh God,' said Alice. 'There's more, isn't there?'

Esme nodded, as she negotiated the next flight of stairs. 'I think you will find that we are having little Cosmo to stay next weekend.'

'I give up,' Alice said behind her in disgust. 'I seriously give up.' But before she could say anything else, they were distracted by a loud and very nearly tuneless singing coming from somewhere below them.

As they approached the ground floor they came upon Rory, sitting on the front doorstep pulling on his Wellingtons, and rasping in a decidedly Celtic tone. 'If we want his body,' Alice echoed him, 'and we think he's sexy?'

She turned to look at her friend. 'It's the body of a small boy,' she said in astonishment.

'But the voice of an old Scottish woman?' suggested Esme. 'Now do you believe me?'

'Now,' Alice answered, 'I believe anything.'

SARAH-KATE LYNCH

I had just finished reading the manuscript of *By Bread Alone* when Sarah-Kate Lynch contacted me to say that she was coming to London from her home in Queenstown, New Zealand and would I like to meet for lunch. Immediately I said yes and we arranged to meet at The Orrery in Marylebone, London—well, having read *By Bread Alone*, where else could we meet? Like Esme in the novel I arrived half an hour early and decided to browse around the Conran shop, which is situated beneath the restaurant, but unlike Esme I quickly made sure that I did not have any suspect bubble gum on the seat of my trousers before trying out the Barcelona chair!

'It's an absolutely amazing shop, isn't it?' Sarah-Kate enthused, as we chose our bread in the restaurant—sadly, there was no sourdough in the bread basket—'I could spend hours in there.' As we sat chatting, Sarah-Kate told me how a number of ideas she had had in her head for some time made up the mixture for *By Bread Alone*. 'Grief, lost love and bread—they were my ingredients. I've always liked eating bread, but before starting this book I was far from an expert at baking it. Luckily for me, I met a baker in New Zealand who was a sourdough officianado, and he showed me the beauty of *pain au levain*. Then I was fortunate to be invited to the famous Poilâne bakery in Paris, where Felix the baker deserved a medal for putting

up with my schoolgirl French—he's probably still wondering what I meant when I said the flour is on the bicycle! The Poilâne bakery is in an ancient building which used to be an Abbey and for hundreds of years they have been baking bread in the basement. As I watched Felix mixing and knead ing, it was like being inside a loaf of bread. The smell was absolutely intoxicating. I could have moved in there for ever, it was just so gorgeous.'

Before exploring breadmaking, in her first novel, *Blessed Are the Cheesemakers*, Sarah-Kate explored the making of cheese. 'What's next?' I asked her. 'Champagne,' she replied, with a giggle. 'I live in Queenstown, which is a small lakeside town in the mountains of New Zealand's South Island, but one of the joys of being a writer is that you are by no means confined to your own neighbourhood. So I set my books in places where I want to go and hang out for a while. Hence, cheesemaking in West Cork, breadmaking in Paris, plus the wonderful eccentric village of Thorpeness in Suffolk, where the House in the Clouds actually exists. The book I'm writing at the moment, *Eating With the Angels*, which is about a restaurant critic, has taken me to New York and Venice. Then, next book, next stop: French champagne country in Epernay. It's a tough, tough life, being a writer!'

Jane Eastgate

Katie Fforde

Restoring Grace

Abandoned by her husband, Grace Ravenglass finds that her future in the house she loves is threatened by her family, lack of money and dry rot. Then, out of the blue, bubbly Ellie Summers rings her doorbell, and suddenly Grace has an ally and friend. Determined to help Grace find happiness again, Ellie sets about helping her to restore her home and her life—with far-reaching consequences for both of them . . .

Chapter One

IT'S A LOVELY HOUSE, thought Ellie. Perfect proportions. Probably Georgian, Queen Anne, something like that.

There were five sets of small-paned sash windows in the house and a couple of dormers in the roof. The front door had a fanlight above it and a neat path led up to the jasmine-covered porch. Looks just like a doll's house, she thought, and then laughed at herself: doll's houses were built to look like real houses, not the other way round.

The high walls that enclosed the garden were of fine grey stone and, peering through the gate, she saw carefully pruned fruit trees interspersed with something less formal, possibly roses, growing up them. A large patch of fragile, mauve crocuses broke up the green of the lawn and there were clumps of daffodils lining the path.

She put down her bag and inspected the gate. It looked sturdy enough and she put her foot in the gap between the posts, trusting it would take her weight, and hauled herself up for a better view.

Propped against a stone pillar, one of a pair that framed the gate, she could see the house in its entirety. It was what estate agents would call a gem. It looked empty, but there could easily be someone observing her from behind one of the windows that glinted so symmetrically back at her. Hoping fervently that there wasn't anybody looking, she jumped down. Then she remembered, and wondered whether, in the circumstances, she ought to have jumped.

Sighing, she fished her camera out of her bag and climbed back up to her vantage point. She took several shots, got back down to ground level and put the camera back in her bulging raffia bag. Then she took out her nose-stud, removed two of her pairs of earrings and tweaked at her clothes and hair. It was important to appear respectable; owners of Georgian rectories tended to be on the conventional side.

As she tucked a strand of scarlet hair under her bandanna, she realised she could be making herself look like a tepee-dwelling New Age traveller. However, she put her shoulders back, picked up her bag and opened the gate. This was the brave bit.

She hoped the owners of the house didn't have dogs. 'Not that I don't like dogs,' Ellie muttered, in case they did have dogs and they were listening. 'I just don't want to be bounced on.'

But no dogs came bounding up, and she made it to the front door unmuddied. She took a deep breath and pulled hard at the knob that protruded from the stone door jamb, hoping it was attached to something. It jangled encouragingly.

She didn't have to wait long. A young woman wearing several layers of jumpers, cardigans and scarves over her jeans, sheepskin boots and an anxious expression, answered it quite quickly. Almost certainly not the owner, Ellie decided, more likely the daughter of the house. Probably a bit older than she was herself—late twenties, early thirties— she had an ethereal quality, as if she had been out of the world for a while. Her hair was light brown, recently washed and looked difficult to manage. Her eyes were a sludgy green and a few freckles peppered her nose and cheekbones. Ellie liked freckles; she had them herself, and seeing them on this woman gave her confidence.

'Hello,' she said. 'I wonder if I can interest you in a picture of your house . . . your parents' house?'

The young woman shook her head, making her shiny hair even more disarrayed. 'No, it's my house.'

This was a bit of a surprise, but Ellie tried not to show it. 'Well, I've just taken some photographs of it and, if you're interested, I could paint a watercolour from them. See?' Ellie produced her album from the bag. In it were photographs of houses, and next to them, photographs of the pictures she had painted. Then, deftly, she produced an actual painting, mounted but not framed. 'And here's one I did earlier!' She laughed.

The young woman took the sample painting. 'It's lovely. The trouble is, I couldn't possibly afford—'

'I'm very reasonable. I could do you one for about fifty pounds.'

'That is reasonable,' the woman agreed. 'But the thing is . . .'

Ellie shifted her weight to her other foot. It would be fatal to rush this woman when she might be about to decide to have a painting, but on the other hand, her need to go to the loo, which had been faint but bearable up to now, was becoming more pressing.

'I'm sorry, I know it's an awful cheek, but would you mind terribly if I used your loo? Normally, I'd just hang on but I'm pregnant.' She blushed as she said it. She'd told almost no one, not even her parents, and it was shocking to hear the word out loud.

'Oh! How lovely! Of course! Do come in. The place is in a bit of a state, I'm afraid.' The young woman opened the door.

Ellie paused on the doorstep. 'I'm Ellie, Ellie Summers.' She took hold of the woman's hand. 'It seems sort of rude to use your loo when you don't know my name.'

The woman laughed and instantly became pretty. 'I'm Grace Ravenglass or Soudley.' She wrinkled her forehead. 'I'm recently divorced and I can't decide if I should go back to my own name.'

As they shook hands Ellie wondered what it was about this young woman that made her feel all right about mentioning her pregnancy. Possibly it was because she appeared slightly vulnerable too.

'Come in,' said Grace. 'I'll show you where to go.'

Grace hadn't opened her front door to anyone except builders for a while, but there was something about Ellie that she warmed to. It might be to do with her easy smile, bright clothes and even brighter hair escaping from under her scarf, but more likely it was because she was fairly near her own age and female.

She probably wouldn't buy a picture—she could never justify the expense—but she felt OK about ushering the young woman down the passage to the downstairs cloakroom, freshly cleaned for tonight.

She hovered in the kitchen nearby so she could hear when Ellie had finished and she could show her out. She rearranged the bottles on the table, scouring her memory for where she might find something else to sit on. Her few chairs were already in place round the table, but there were a couple of empty spaces. There were probably some more tea chests in the attic. They were a bit high, but comfortable enough if she put cushions on them. A fan heater was valiantly gusting into the icy air.

She heard the old-fashioned flush and was ready when Ellie emerged. 'It's a lovely house,' Ellie said eagerly. 'Even the cloakroom has got period features. I love that cistern! And the washbasin! Just like an old washstand, only china!' She bit her lip. 'Oh, sorry. I hope I didn't sound too like an estate agent.'

'It *is* a lovely house,' agreed Grace, pleased with Ellie's enthusiasm. If everyone reacted like that she need feel less worried about opening her house to strangers. 'If rather on the cold side.' On an impulse she added, 'Would you like a bit of a tour? I could do with the practice.'

'You're not opening the house to the public, are you?'

Grace laughed. 'Not exactly, but I have got lots of people I don't know from Adam coming this evening, and I haven't had anyone here for ages.' She smiled. 'And I wouldn't mind showing you round.'

'Well, if it would be useful, I'd *love* a tour.'

I must be mad, thought Grace as she led the way down the passage, inviting people in off the street to look round my freezing cold house. As they passed the kitchen, she said, 'Shall I put the kettle on? Would you like a cup of tea or coffee afterwards?'

'That would be great, if you're making one. When I was looking for a loo earlier, I couldn't find anything like a coffee shop for miles.'

'No, we are far away from everything here. How did you find me?'

'I drove past the other day, when I was delivering a picture and got lost. When I saw your house, I knew it would make a lovely painting.'

'I'm sure it would . . .' Grace became diffident again, and Ellie hurried on. 'No pressure, honestly. I do understand about being broke.' She paused, embarrassed by her frankness. 'You may not be broke, of course.' She shivered, inadvertently drawing attention to the cold.

'Broke about covers it. I'll put the kettle on.'

Well, then, this is the hall, obviously.' Grace stood in the square, pan-elled space from where a stone staircase led to a gallery. She had always liked the way the shadows of the window bars patterned the bare stone flags. 'And here's the drawing room,' she went on, when Ellie had had time to admire the perfect proportions, the fine panelling and the arched space under the stairs, which now contained boxes of wine and glasses.

The drawing room was also panelled, but was brighter, holding on to the last hour of February light. As well as the two floor-length sash win-dows, there were French doors looking onto the garden.

'What period is the house?' asked Ellie.

'It's been messed around with so much it's hard to tell, but my aunt always told me it was William and Mary. There's an inscription saying 1697 over an archway in the garden.'

'That's so old!' Ellie wandered round the room, absorbing its lovely proportions, wondering about its emptiness. 'This is a beautiful fire-place,' she said, admiring the delicate stone carving.

'And it draws really well too,' said Grace. 'We used to light it all the time, when we were together.' She hadn't had the heart to light the fire and sit in the big room by herself all winter, so she'd spent most of the evenings in bed, snuggled up with the radio, a pile of books and a goose-down duvet. 'Come on, I'll show you the dining room.'

They went back into the hall and down a passageway. Grace opened the door. 'This part of the house is much older than the front. Even when Edward—my husband—was here we didn't use this room much. It's too far away from the kitchen, really, and it gets forgotten.'

'If you didn't have the drawing room you'd love it,' said Ellie, thinking of the house where she lived in Bath, where the front door opened straight into the living room.

Grace blushed apologetically. 'Of course. I'm just so spoilt.' By way of apology she said, 'The curtains in here have been up for ever. I don't dare draw them in case they fall apart.'

After an inspection of the study, they moved upstairs. After a more cursory tour of that, Ellie said, as they came back downstairs, 'I don't want to be rude, but I can't help noticing that you haven't got very much furniture. You weren't burgled or anything, were you?'

The idea was horrifying. 'Oh, no, it wasn't stolen! It went of its own accord.' Grace chuckled. 'Not by itself, of course. It was accompanied by an adult. It was my husband's.'

'Oh.'

Grace, aware of the kettle on the gas, said, 'Let's go back to the kitchen before the kettle boils dry. It should be warmer in there now.'

Together they went into the large, rather bleak room. It had a high ceiling and stone flags on the floor.

'Now, is it tea or coffee?' asked Grace, but she'd lost Ellie's attention. She was standing in front of the huge, built-in dresser, on which a few unmatched but ancient-looking plates tried valiantly to fill the space.

'That's wonderful! It would take whole dinner services at a time! I suppose your husband couldn't take it?'

'Oh, no. He left it for me. He was very scrupulous.' Suddenly it seemed important to Grace that Ellie shouldn't think badly of Edward— she still loved him, after all. 'He didn't take anything that wasn't his, and he left me the bed and the duvet, which were his, too, really. Do sit down. So is it tea or coffee?'

'I'm off coffee at the moment,' said Ellie. 'But tea would be great.' She pulled out a chair. 'I don't usually get hospitality before I do the picture, although I sometimes do when I deliver.'

Grace laughed. 'I'm not sure if you'd quite describe this as hospitality, although it's the nearest thing I've been to it in a while.' There was something very cheering about having Ellie sitting at her kitchen table. She was so up front and, if she was a little outspoken, she wasn't critical.

Now Ellie said, 'I know it's cold, but why are those bottles wearing socks?'

'It's to hide the labels,' Grace explained, laughing again. 'I'm having a wine-tasting here tonight. We're testing supermarket wine basically, seeing which one we like best. I'll write up the results for a couple of local papers, then I'll be able to quote the article if another paper or magazine wants a wine correspondent.'

'Imagine being a wine correspondent. It sounds very high-powered. I don't know a thing about wine.'

'You don't have to unless it's your job. You just have to know if you like it. You could stay for the wine-tasting, if you like.' Grace hadn't known she was going to say that, but once she had, she realised it was because she quite wanted the moral support of someone she could relate to. That was the trouble with living in a large house away from other houses: it was hard to get to know your neighbours, especially if you were single.

'That's really kind of you,' said Ellie, 'but I'm not drinking at the moment. Because of being pregnant.' Then, to Grace's surprise, she began to cry. 'I'm so sorry. It's my hormones or something. It's to do with telling—people.'

'Have you told many people? Has it happened every time?' Grace wished she wasn't too shy to put her arms round Ellie.

Ellie sniffed. 'No. In fact, only my boyfriend . . . and now you.'

'Oh.' Grace felt tremendously flattered. 'Well, it's often easier to tell people things when you're unlikely to see them again. Like on trains.'

Ellie sniffed again and nodded.

'So you haven't told your parents, then?'

Ellie shook her head. 'It would be all right if I could say Rick and me were going to get married. But we're not.'

'I don't recommend marriage myself, having got divorced. You could just live together,' Grace suggested.

'We could, only Rick doesn't want a baby. He thinks . . .' She sniffed some more. 'He thinks I should—God, I can't even say it!'

'No, don't. I know what you mean. He thinks you shouldn't go on being pregnant.' Grace got up and found a box of tissues and put it in front of Ellie. 'I'll make the tea.'

'So, why did you get divorced?' asked Ellie a couple of minutes later, having taken a heartening sip. 'Did he find someone else, or did you?' Realising she'd let her curiosity get the better of her again, she bit her lip. 'Sorry! It's none of my business. I'm terribly nosy.'

'Well, on the understanding we're unlikely to see each other again—'

Grace frowned, suddenly sad at the thought that this cheerful-even-when-weeping person would soon go out of her life for ever—'I may as well tell you.'

'Why did you marry him? Not because of his furniture, presumably.'

Grace chuckled. 'He had some wonderful antiques . . . but I didn't know about his furniture when I fell in love with him.'

'So why did you?'

'He was—is—terribly attractive. He's older than me and I was very young when I met him. He was so witty and cultured, and for some reason he turned his attention to me. It was like the sun was shining on me alone. I couldn't resist him.'

'So how old is he now?'

'Forty-six. I'm thirty-one.'

'It is quite a large gap,' said Ellie cautiously.

'Yes, but I don't think that was the problem. Not really.'

'What was, then?'

Grace sighed. 'Well, the main thing was that I wanted a baby and he didn't. He's got a son and a daughter by his first wife. But, really, I wasn't up to his speed intellectually. He found someone else who was more on his level. I can't blame him, actually.'

'That's generous of you! Don't you want to scratch her eyes out?'

Grace shook her head. 'Not really. And in a way it was sort of a relief when he went, because the thing I had been dreading had actually happened. So I didn't need to dread it any more. I'm not saying I wasn't devastated'—she paused—'but I never believed he truly loved me—or if he did, that he would go on loving me. And I was right there,' she added ruefully. 'Although he has been very kind.'

She looked at Ellie, so calm and together in spite of being pregnant by a man who didn't want her to have the baby. 'Why am I telling you all this?'

'We're on a virtual train,' Ellie reminded her. 'We're never going to see each other again.' She paused. 'Did he give you the house?'

'Oh, no. I inherited it from my aunt.'

'So did he give you money when he left?'

'Yes. He gave me a very generous settlement, but although I've got enough left to keep me going for a few months, I've spent most of it.'

'I can't exactly see what on, from here,' Ellie smiled.

'Well, no,' Grace laughed. 'But if you went into the attic you would see that every joist and beam is new, and that every dodgy tile has been replaced by a reclaimed stone one. It cost a fortune. Then I bought a car with what was left after the roof.'

'That's awful. And he's left you with hardly any furniture?' Ellie was confused. 'Didn't your aunt have any furniture, either?'

'Oh, yes, she did. But it went to my older brother and sister. They got the furniture, I got the house, because she was my godmother as well as my aunt. They were livid.'

'Why?' Ellie was staggered.

'They felt the house should have been sold and the money divided between us. But it just so happened that Edward and I were newly engaged when she died, so living here made perfect sense. Besides, it's what my aunt wanted, or she'd have made her will differently.'

'So from his—your ex-husband's—point of view, marrying a woman who had a really great house was a good idea, if he had lots of lovely antiques that needed a home.'

She shook her head. 'No. He didn't marry me for my house, I'm quite sure of it.'

'So how long were you together?'

'We married two years after we met, when I was only twenty-two, and had five very happy—ecstatic really—years, one less happy, and one downright unhappy. It's taken nearly two years to get divorced.'

'He sounds a complete bastard.'

'He wasn't, really he wasn't. He was very fair to me.'

Ellie shrugged. 'I think it's very grown up of you to feel like that.'

'I'm not saying he didn't make me suffer, but he didn't do it on purpose. And the baby thing is understandable. After all, he had two perfectly good children already.'

'It is a bit ironic,' said Ellie, draining her mug. 'Here are you, wanting a baby, and here's me, pregnant, not wanting one.'

'I thought you did want one? I thought you said you couldn't . . . do anything about it.'

'That's slightly different. I didn't want a baby before I got pregnant. But now I am pregnant, I couldn't not have it.'

'And you don't think your parents will be supportive?'

'Well, yes, they will. But they'll tell me off terribly for not being more careful.' She gave a wry smile. 'I was on the pill, but I threw up. It must have been just at the wrong moment.'

'Or the right moment. From the baby's point of view. Would you like another cup of tea?'

'No, thank you, but another trip to the loo would be very welcome.'

Grace stayed in the kitchen while Ellie visited the cloakroom again, then went with her to her car and waved until she was out of sight. Back in the house, it suddenly felt larger, lonelier, and possibly even a bit colder, than it had done before.

As Ellie drove away from the house, beneath an evening sun colouring the sky, she thought about Grace and her story. It was kind of bizarre, her being alone in that big, freezing, empty house, her marriage over, preparing to have strangers in to taste wine.

On the other hand, her own existence was far from perfect: she and Rick, living together in a tiny cottage in Bath, less happily day by day.

She bit her lip to ward off the sadness she felt when she remembered how happy they had been when they first moved in together. It had been such fun finding the cottage to rent, and then making it a home.

Rick was an installation artist. He rented a corner of someone else's studio and spent most of his waking hours there. Not that there were so many of those, thought Ellie, irritated. Not getting up until midday was fine when you were a student, but when you were a working person, you had to put the hours in.

It was easier for Rick. He didn't have a day job, he devoted all his time to his art, and, at first, Ellie had thought this was perfectly right and proper. He'd been two years ahead of her at university, doing Fine Art, and had got a first. Of course his art was more important than hers.

Ellie had done Creative Art, but although she had sold several paintings even before she finished the course, she knew she wasn't an artist in the way Rick was. She'd been happy to work in a café during the day and a bar in the evenings so that he could concentrate on developing what everyone acknowledged was a special talent.

But now, eighteen months after moving in together, she'd started to resent his tunnel vision—even before she got pregnant and he threw a tantrum. At the time she had wept bitterly at his attitude.

'Now breathe, Ellie,' she instructed herself as she got into the town and started to negotiate her little car down the narrow lanes towards their cottage. 'Don't get into a state all over again. It's not good for the baby.'

Once outside, she parked the car and got out, then put her key into the front door, mentally preparing herself for the mess that awaited her. Opening the door, she paused to pick up the pile of letters on the mat. 'Hi, babes,' she called up the stairs as she stepped into the living room and put down her bag.

'In the bath!' Rick called back, and she went upstairs.

His long, elegant limbs could not be contained in the tub and he had draped them over the edges. Water threatened to spill every time he moved. A large sponge sat on his stomach, and patches of bubbles still lingered in the water. Part of Ellie thought how gorgeous he was, and remembered how passionate and excited he was about everything when they'd first met. The other part was aware that he would have used every drop of hot water but wouldn't have switched on the immersion heater, so that if she wanted a bath, she'd have to wait at least an hour.

'Good day?' she asked, noticing the towel she had washed and dried only the day before lying on the floor, already in a puddle.

'Crap day. Why don't you get in with me? Make me feel better?'

Ellie shook her head. She didn't want water all over the floor, she didn't want to have sex when she had to work later, and she needed to pee again.

'Did you do anything for tea?' she asked him.

'No time. When I finished at the studio I got straight in the bath. Needed to sort my head out.'

Ellie smiled, hoping he wouldn't spot that it was false, picked up the towel and draped it over the washbasin, and left the room. His fabulous body and irresistible smile had lost their charm somewhat these days.

Back in the kitchen, a small, often mildewed extension behind the living room, she filled the kettle so she could deal with the dishes. Considering he spent most of his time at the studio, and that he and his mate always went to the pub for lunch, it was amazing how much washing-up he managed to generate.

He'd obviously had a fry-up, including fried bread and baked beans, for breakfast, and added a lot of tomato ketchup. And in spite of pre-sumably having had his routine pie and chips and several pints at lunchtime, he'd had time and appetite to grab a handful of Bombay Mix and some crisps. The Bombay Mix packet had fallen over and tipped half of its contents onto the floor.

While she washed mugs and scraped ketchup and egg yolk off the plate with a nail, and her boyfriend luxuriated in hot water, Ellie thought she could do with a little of the latter herself. What would it be like to be a pampered mistress, fêted and adored, every whim indulged?

However, that would be slightly hard to arrange now that she was pregnant—soon she'd be too fat to attract anyone. She stopped her scrubbing for a moment. Perhaps she should just go for a fling, a quick, fabulous affaire, before her pregnancy showed? After all, it was often the beginning of a relationship that was most fun. Why not just have the wonderful, exhilarating passionate sex—and then call it quits?

The idea lifted her spirits and she turned her thoughts to Grace. How was she doing with her wine-tasting? By the time she'd finished the washing-up, she'd decided she would do the painting of the house anyway, and give it to Grace as a present. She'd seemed so forlorn that Ellie wanted to do something to cheer her up.

'So,' said Rick, when, clean and nearly dry, he presented himself downstairs and sat on the sofa. 'How did you get on? Flog any daubs of mansions to the bloated plutocrats?'

Ellie shook her head. Grace had not been a bloated plutocrat, even if some of her ancestors had been. 'No, but I took some photos of a really lovely house.'

'Get a commission?'

'No. The owner couldn't afford it.'

'I think it's a waste of time, Ellie, spending all that petrol money trying to sell your paintings. You'd be better off with a job.'

She realised that this was Rick 'taking an interest', and she wished he wouldn't bother. 'I have two jobs already, Rick, and they both involve standing. I'm not supposed to stand too much now I'm pregnant.'

Rick scowled. 'I thought we'd agreed you were going to do something about that.'

Ellie bit her lip. She didn't have the energy for a row, but how could he bring this all up again? All Rick's sensitivity seemed to go into his art; there wasn't any left for his relationship.

'You agreed. I didn't,' she said.

After Ellie had gone, Grace had continued with her preparations for the wine-tasting. It was a new project, based on her memory of tastings she'd gone to when she worked for a wine importer. She was quite successful with her articles—the local papers had been keen for more—but she had been writing about special wines, which most people couldn't afford. The wine-tasting project was an effort to get ordinary people involved in tasting wines that most people drank.

Each place had six glasses placed over a sheet marked with numbered circles, so people knew which glass applied to which numbered bottle. On a sheet of paper, she had drawn round the bottom of six glasses and then made photocopies at the local post office. While the man behind the counter had helped her when the machine broke down, she had discovered he was a wine buff; he and his wife were coming tonight.

Beside the glasses was a score sheet, with numbers and letters down the side and columns for comments on the smell and taste of each wine. There were also places for scores. At the bottom of the sheet was a list of the wines, their origins and their prices.

Grace was surprisingly nervous. It was, after all, only a very informal wine-tasting—it was even free. She hoped people might make a contribution for the wine, but would they want to drive out to the country and go into someone's house to taste supermarket plonk?

When the telephone rang, she assumed it was someone ringing up to cancel—probably on behalf of everyone—leaving her to drink all the wine by herself. She picked up the receiver.

It was her sister. 'Hi, Grace, how are you?'

'Oh, hi, Allegra. Nice to hear from you.' In some ways it was nice, it would pass some time and stop her being so nervous.

'I was wondering if you'd thought any more about selling the house?'

Typical Allegra, straight to the point. 'Well, obviously I've thought about it, since you suggested it, but I'm certainly not doing it.'

'It just doesn't make sense, you living there on your own.' Allegra was obviously convinced by the water-dripping-on-stone theory: if you went on at someone long enough, eventually they would agree.

'Edward left ages ago. Why should I sell now?'

'Because now you've had the roof fixed you'd get a proper price for it.'

If Allegra wasn't pulling her punches, then neither would Grace. 'You mean you'd get a larger chunk.'

'Don't be silly!' Allegra could be very sharp. 'Of course the money you spent on the roof would be taken off before the money was divided. It was your divorce settlement, after all. But you know that it was unfair of Aunt Lavinia to leave Luckenham House to you and not to all of us.'

'She left you and Nicholas most of the furniture! That was worth quite a bit.' Grace felt both bored and exasperated. It was not the first time they had had this conversation and she knew it wouldn't be the last.

'Nothing like the value of the house.'

'Well, she was my godmother.'

'Really, Grace, I wish you'd stop being so stubborn about this! Aunt Lavinia never paid much attention to you when you were a child, so why did she leave you her house? Obviously she was starting to go gaga, so it's only fair that you should do the decent thing and share the house.'

'Do say if you want to come and live here with me,' said Grace crossly. 'But I thought you were happy in Farnham with David and the boys.'

'Oh, don't be ridiculous!'

'Well, why bring it all up again now? I've had the house for almost nine years.'

'Yes, but when you had Edward it made a little more sense. And how can you live in a house without any furniture in it?'

'I've got a bit.' She looked round at the kitchen table, which she had bought from a junk shop. 'Tea chests are very versatile, and if my wine project takes off, I'll get lots of nice wooden crates. There was a girl I used to work with who built a whole kitchen out of wine crates.'

A sigh of irritation gusted down the telephone. 'Anyway, Nicholas asked me to ring you.'

'He could have rung me himself.' In spite of her indignation, Grace was quite glad that her brother had not done so; he was even more bossy than Allegra.

'He's very busy. He's got a very high-powered new job. Offices in Canary Wharf.'

'That sounds good,' Grace snapped. 'His ego will fit in nicely among the other skyscrapers.'

Accustomed to a much milder younger sister, Allegra was shocked. 'Grace! You never used to be so rude.'

'No, well, I've grown up, I suppose. Divorce does that to you.'

There was a silence. Grace could tell that Allegra was debating whether she should say that she always knew her younger sister's marriage was doomed to failure, or whether she could keep her mouth shut. Edward's antique furniture had meant that Allegra and Nicholas had been able to strip the house of everything that wasn't nailed down.

'I'm sorry, Grace. I suppose I am being a bit tactless, but I do think it would be better for you to sell the house. It must be worth a fortune.'

'Not necessarily. The property boom is over and I might well have deathwatch beetle.'

'You haven't, have you?' Allegra sounded seriously alarmed. 'You've just had the roof redone.'

'There's lots more to the house than the roof,' said Grace, disconcertingly pleased at having rattled Allegra.

'Well, have you had it checked out?'

Deathwatch beetle was obviously not to be made light of. 'Not yet.'

'You must! I insist on it. In fact, I'll do more than that, I'll send my friend's son along to do it . . .'

Grace held the telephone away from her ear. Her sister was getting very shrill.

'. . . he'll be very reasonable. In fact, I'll pay for it myself, then you can't possibly find any excuses for not having it done!'

'Er, no,' said Grace, acknowledging the truth of this.

'Let me know when would be convenient.'

'I'm here almost all the time, Legs.'

'I do wish you wouldn't call me that!'

'Sorry.'

Allegra sighed. 'No, well, it's a habit, I suppose. Bloody Nicholas started it. But, really, Grace, I am a bit worried about you. You really should get out more.'

'But not now, I've got a lot of strange people coming for wine-tasting in a minute, and I haven't put the bread out.'

Strangely, the telephone call from her sister had reinforced all Grace's thoughts and feelings about the house. She was determined not to sell it. She loved it; it was hers. Her brother and sister could go on envying her good fortune. After all, the furniture they had taken had been very valuable. They were both settled in successful careers, and had partners—a wealthy husband in Allegra's case and a glamorous female investment banker in Nicholas's.

On the other hand, the upkeep of such a house, even if she lived very simply, was a constant worry. She either needed a way of earning a living, which was sufficiently well paid that she could keep the house in good repair, or—and this was her present course of action—she could use the house itself to provide an income. Hence the wine-tasting which, to her horror, she noticed was due to start in less than an hour.

As she rushed upstairs to change, she reflected that although she'd only visited her Aunt Lavinia once, when she was about seventeen, her aunt—who was a great-aunt really—must have sensed how Grace had fallen in love with the place.

Digging into her ancient make-up bag, she breathed heavily on the mascara and hoped there was some left. As she scrubbed away with the dried-up wand she realised that was why she'd been left the house and not the furniture. She'd seen what there was beyond the obvious.

To her enormous relief, Mr and Mrs Rose from the shop-cum-post office were the first to arrive.

'I can't tell you how curious I've been to come to this house!' said Mrs Rose. 'My aunt used to clean here when I was a little girl and she used to tell me about all the wonderful things there were.'

Grace laughed. 'I'm afraid the wonderful things have all gone, but the house is still the same.' She steered the kindly couple to the most comfortable chairs. The latecomers could have the tea chests.

The next couple, the Cavendishes, used to live in London. They were young, well dressed and overtly rich, but Grace warmed to them.

'Hi! I'm Sara and this is Will,' said Sara. She was dressed in a scarlet suit and draped with a most heavenly black scarf. 'Will, darling, this is Grace; we chatted over the phone. Will's always spending a fortune on wine and I thought it was time I found out a bit about it. Oh, I know you!' she said to the Roses, who were sitting rather stiffly on their chairs. 'You run the post office!' Sara put her hand out so Mr Rose had to take it. 'I love your little shop! It's like a treasure box!'

Mr Rose softened visibly, responding with satisfaction to Sara's compliment about his pride and joy.

'May I sit on a tea chest?' asked Sara. 'Such fun!'

'You might ladder your tights!' said Grace, suddenly noticing the sheerness of Sara's legwear.

'Oh, don't worry about that,' cried Sara.

'My wife has no idea of economy,' said Will.

Sara grinned. 'You spend your money on wine and fast cars, and I spend mine on clothes. Who else is coming?'

'Um . . . one more couple. The'—Grace checked her list—'Hamilton-Laceys. And there's someone called Margaret Jeffreys and a friend of the wine-shop owner, a Mr Cormack.'

'First name?' asked Sara.

'Flynn,' said Grace.

'Oh, how heavenly! I love Irishmen, they're always so good at flirting!'

Will frowned affectionately at his wife. 'Darling, do pipe down a bit. Wait until you've got the wine as an excuse for being outrageous.'

Sara shrugged apologetically. 'Sorree! What did he sound like on the phone?' she asked Grace in a stage whisper.

'I didn't speak to him.' In fact, Grace suspected him of being sent by the wine merchant to check if she knew her stuff. Which was fair enough, she supposed, because, if she proved herself, he might send wine for her to taste.

The doorbell rang and Grace let in the other couple, who looked rather anxiously about them.

'Come into the kitchen,' said Grace, realising she'd forgotten their names again. Pointing them in the right direction, she took their coats and draped them over the banisters. They took their places and made token attempts at smiling.

There were still two more people to come. Grace had put out slices of bread and a jug of water as well as the wine bottles, and she noticed people picking at the bread to fill the hiatus.

'Well, I wonder if we should begin?' Grace ventured. 'It's after eight.'

But, at that moment, the doorbell jangled. Margaret Jeffreys and Flynn Cormack had arrived together.

'Sorry we're late,' said Margaret to Grace as she held the door open. 'We got lost. Flynn kindly offered me a lift because I said I knew the way, and then I turned left at the crossroads instead of right.'

Grace smiled. Margaret Jeffreys and Sara Cavendish would both take the edge off everyone's natural shyness. Flynn Cormack might well have been Irish, but he certainly didn't exude the bonhomie Sara had been expecting. In fact, he seemed distinctly irritable.

Margaret talked her way into the kitchen and when she got there looked brightly round the table. She waved hello as she realised she knew Sara and Will and recognised Mr and Mrs Rose.

Grace relaxed. If they felt comfortable with each other, they wouldn't feel inhibited about expressing their feelings. 'Well,' she began. 'As you know, we're here to discuss supermarket wines.' She poured a small amount of the first wine into her glass. 'If you circulate the bottle, and each pour yourselves a little, I'll give you a bit of spiel about this grape. Take a good hard sniff and tell me what you think.'

The spy caught her eye and regarded her with an intent look. Grace wondered if her ancient mascara had done something funny to her face.

Eventually, it was over. Almost everyone had gone home except the spy and Margaret Jeffreys. Margaret and Mrs Rose had had a guided tour of the drawing room and Margaret was still in there, having a cigarette.

The spy was helping Grace clear the table. 'Are you going to wash these up now?' He indicated the glasses.

'Not tonight, no,' said Grace. 'It's much better when it's sunny, don't you think? Washing up?'

'I have a dishwasher.'

Grace shrugged. How could you explain washing up to a man with a dishwasher?

'But if you have to do them by hand, I could help you,' he offered. 'I could dry, anyway. It would be quicker with two.'

Grace shook her head. 'No hot water,' she explained with a smile, glad to have a proper reason for refusing his offer, when really the reason she didn't want him to help was that she found his presence in her kitchen, where she was used to being alone, oddly unsettling. 'I forgot to put the immersion on. I'll do it in the morning.'

'Surely a house this size needs a better way of heating hot water than an immersion heater? It must be so expensive, for one thing.'

'Not really. There's only me.'

He frowned. 'That's strange, too.'

She bristled. 'What's strange? The fact that I live in this house all on my own?'

'No. The fact that you're single. You *are* single?'

Grace hovered between telling him it was none of his business and just answering the question. She decided a simple 'yes' would be quicker. 'Yes. But I like it that way.'

He nodded, as if in understanding, but then said, 'I was wondering if you might like to come out to dinner some time.'

Grace, her head still a kaleidoscope of names, wines and the state of the hot water, stopped. 'Why would I want to do that?' she asked.

For the first time the spy smiled, and Grace wished she could remember his name.

'Because you might get hungry, perhaps?'

Grace shook her head, on certain ground at last. Since her divorce, she hardly ever got hungry. And the thought of going out to dinner with a man whose name she couldn't remember was not appealing.

'I don't think so.' Then, aware she might have sounded abrupt, she added, 'But thank you very much for the invitation.'

The spy regarded her speculatively. He was about to say something else when Margaret appeared.

'Shall we go, darling? I've finished my fag. Lovely house,' she said to Grace.

Grace smiled. Margaret probably got hungry a lot. *She* could go out to dinner with the mysterious Irishman.

Chapter Two

ELLIE GOT HOME at half past midnight. She was supposed to work until three, but she'd asked to go early. She hadn't had to say why she was so exhausted; she'd just said she felt sick. Which she did.

Rick was out, probably still at the pub, which was famous for its lock-ins. His dirty dishes filled the sink, accompanied by cold, greasy water. The water was Rick's idea of help, and it did help in that the food wasn't welded quite so solidly onto the plate, but Ellie found putting her hand through the layer of orange grease to the plug almost unbearable. She did it, because in the morning she'd feel even sicker. Then, having started the process, and because she'd put the immersion heater on earlier for a bath she'd never quite made time for, she washed up.

She would have to leave. She suddenly realised this had ceased to be a thought too dreadful even to form into words in her head and become an acknowledged truth without her processing the notion at all.

What had changed between them, apart from the pregnancy? In some ways, nothing; he was still the student she had fallen in love with. He got up late, he left beer cans, fag ends and roaches all over the house. He wouldn't ever bother to wash up while there were still plates to eat off and he still wanted sex every night and every morning.

But he used to be loving. He used to buy her little presents: chocolates, flowers, a little heart-shaped cheese. He'd decorate her pillow with flowers, and once, when she'd gone to bed much earlier than he had, he'd written 'I Love You' in sweeties on the table.

Without all that, clearing up after him was just a chore, not a home-making, nurturing thing to do. And even before he'd first been shown the thin blue line on Ellie's pregnancy test, he'd become less affectionate and more slob-like. He'd always done exactly as he wanted, and now he was losing interest in Ellie as a person. Well, he'd find another loving young art student soon enough: she was getting out.

The following morning at about eleven, before Rick was up, and before she had a chance to change her mind, Ellie took a deep breath and telephoned her mother. She was a highly successful interior designer who had kept her career going more or less uninterrupted by Ellie's arrival. Her father worked in insurance and felt his contribution to child-rearing was not to interfere with the nanny, in any sense. They both loved Ellie, she knew that, but they seemed to love their careers more.

Ellie was their only child and she had always felt that her initial arrival in the world and her subsequent existence were baffling to them. To their credit, however, her parents had allowed her to follow her dreams of studying art, hadn't visited her at university and didn't comment on her friends as long as she kept them out of the sitting room.

'Hello, darling!' Her mother's voice greeted Ellie with a kind of mixture of surprise and pleasure Ellie had become used to.

'Hi, Mum. How are you? Did you get that suit you were talking about?' This was partly to remind her mother that they had in fact spoken recently; Ellie had rung up to tell her parents she was pregnant, but bottled out.

'Yes. Frightfully expensive, but so lovely.' She paused. 'So, what news?'

'I thought I might come and stay for a bit.' After she'd said it, she realised that at one time she would have said: 'come home for a bit'. Now it seemed more like paying a visit as a guest than going home as a daughter. Her bedroom had been redecorated and redesigned as a study for her father long since.

'That would be nice.' Her mother sounded flustered. 'Would you be staying for long? Only we're going away next weekend.'

Ellie sighed. 'I thought I might stay a few days, if that's all right. I'm thinking of looking for somewhere else to live.'

'Oh.' A pause. 'Are you and Rick all right?'

'We're both fine. We just may not stay together, that's all.'

'Oh, darling!' Ellie heard genuine sympathy and warmed to it. Perhaps it would be OK telling her mother about the baby. Perhaps her mother might discover all those mothering instincts that had been a bit lacking when Ellie was a baby herself.

She'd left a note for Rick. He would read it when he got up, and would probably be relieved that she wouldn't be there nagging him any more. He'd be annoyed about having to pay the rent on his own, but Ellie felt fairly sure he'd soon find someone else to look after him.

Having stuffed the few possessions she felt attached to into a series of carrier bags and bin-liners and put them into her car, she'd taken a deep breath and shut the front door on her home for the past eighteen months. Then she'd set off to the little market town in Gloucestershire where her parents lived.

Her parents' house was beautiful. It was modern, energy-efficient and elegant. It would, however, never be cosy, Ellie realised a few hours later, after a pointless day of driving around waiting for her mother to get home from work. As she parked her 2CV in the driveway next to her mother's little MGTF, she thought of the cottage in Bath she had left, for which the word 'cosy' was almost too expansive.

Her mother's eye for design was evident everywhere. The house had once appeared in a magazine in an article about the use of white paint, illustrating just how many shades of white there were.

Now, a scarlet amaryllis in a steel pot was the only colour evident, apart from her mother's suit, also scarlet. Even while they hugged, Ellie remembered how difficult it had been growing up in such a sterile space when she had been a teenager. It would be an impossible house for a baby. Fortunately the thought that she might bring up her baby in her parents' house had not dwelt for long in Ellie's imagination.

'Come in, darling. It's so good to see you! It's such a shame you have to leave that charming little cottage—'

'But it's Rick's name on the lease,' confirmed Ellie. 'And I could never get him to leave.'

'Drink, darling? Gin and tonic?'

The thought made Ellie feel violently sick. 'No, thanks. I'll make a cup of tea, if I may. I've brought some peppermint tea bags with me.'

'So, you're still a dippy-hippy?' Affectionate amusement, with just a hint of disappointment, was Val's most frequent response to her daughter.

Ellie laughed. ''Fraid so. Can I get you anything?'

'Oh, no. I'll wait until your father gets home and have a drink with him. He won't be long now. We're going out for dinner. There's a new place we've been longing for an excuse to try.' Her voice faded as she looked rather pointedly at Ellie's many earrings. 'I don't suppose . . .'

Ellie removed the excess and the stud in her nose without a word.

As Ellie made tea in the stainless-steel kitchen, she realised that her instincts for making a house into something special and beautiful were all inherited from her mother. It was just that their ideas of what consti- tuted beauty in the home were diametrically opposed. Ellie liked colour, hand-thrown pots and gingham curtains. Her mother liked matt black, metal and the wrought-iron chandelier that hung over the kitchen table.

'Do you want me to help you find somewhere to live?' Her mother followed her into the kitchen, a pristine dishcloth in her hand to wipe up the drips from the tea. 'If we found somewhere nice, Daddy and I could help you out a bit. Pay your first month's rent and the deposit.'

'That's really kind but I might find it difficult to keep paying the rent on anywhere remotely "nice".'

'But you've managed all this time. And you'd share, presumably. Goodness, you work long enough hours! You hardly have any time to do any painting.'

'I know. The thing is, Mum—'

'Oh! I think I hear your father!' Val rushed from the kitchen as fast as her pencil skirt would allow while Ellie reflected on the old saying that the children of lovers were orphans—and she was an only orphan.

After only a few days in her parents' immaculate dwelling, Ellie started to feel restless. She had rung her employers and belatedly, guiltily, handed in her notice. They had been satisfyingly sorry to lose her— though not as sorry as she was to lose the income, now that she was homeless as well as pregnant.

In the mornings, when she had the house to herself, she ate dry toast, drank peppermint tea and made sure she left no trace of her habitation. After she had tidied up behind herself, she painted. The idea that paint might land on some of the virgin whiteness of the sitting room terrified her. She was dicing with death painting in there, she knew, but the light in the kitchen was hopeless, and she did drape everything in newspaper before she started. It would all be worth it when Grace saw the picture.

One morning she decided to go back to the beautiful house she was painting and have another look at it. It took her just over an hour to get to the town nearest to the house, but she wasn't sure of her way from there. She found a parking spot and went on a hunt for a loo and some information, in that order. She was on her way down the High Street when she thought she saw Grace coming out of a shop further down the road. It was too far to shout, so Ellie sprinted. 'Grace? It is you! For a moment I thought I might have done something really embarrassing.'

It took Grace a minute to recognise Ellie, not because she'd changed, but because she was out of context. 'Oh, hello! What are you doing here?'

Ellie didn't want to say anything about the picture, in case it didn't turn out well, so she said, 'I just thought I'd have a look around. I'm staying with my parents and I'm getting a bit bored.'

'Well, why don't we have some coffee or something?'

'That would be nice, as long as I don't have to drink it.'

Grace smiled, cheered by this chance meeting. 'The pub has got a cosy snug and there won't be anyone there at this time of day. They'll let us have what we like.'

When they had settled themselves by the log fire in the pub, and were sipping mineral water, Grace turned to Ellie. 'So, how is it going with your parents?'

'I haven't told them I'm pregnant yet, if that's what you mean.' Ellie put down her glass, rubbed her hands and held them to the flames.

'Oh.' Grace regarded Ellie, wondering how she'd have told her parents if she'd got pregnant before she was married. It would have been very hard. She didn't blame Ellie for not having had the courage to do it.

'I'm staying for a few more days, so there's still time. In the meantime, I've decided to leave Rick and I've got to find somewhere else to live. The trouble is, Bath is terribly short of accommodation at the best of times, let alone accommodation I can afford. Although my parents have offered to help out,' she added, falsely bright—but not before Grace had glimpsed a look of extreme sadness.

It was ironic, Grace realised. Here was Ellie, pregnant when she didn't want to be, with no place to live in, and here was she, Grace, who had so wanted a baby, with too much space.

'I'm sure you'll find something,' said Grace. 'I mean, you're very resourceful and your paintings are lovely. I'm sure you'll have no trouble selling them, and you could carry on doing it when you've got the baby.'

Ellie nodded. 'Yes, I know. And there are other things I could do, too.'

'So it will be all right.' Grace put her hand on Ellie's wrist. She was not accustomed to this sort of closeness, but now it came very naturally. 'You're a great girl, Ellie.'

Ellie was touched. After Rick's casual attitude to the baby and her parents' fond indifference, it was nice to be with someone who had faith in her, and who cared.

'Thank you, Grace. You're a great girl, too.'

Grace laughed. 'More mineral water? The Ladies here is quite nice!'

Ellie drove home feeling much more positive. She would start ringing accommodation agencies: there must be somewhere where she could afford. She was resourceful, she knew, but it was nice that Grace spotted it and reinforced it. She was definitely going to finish the picture now, even if she hadn't had time to go and look at the house again.

One evening, a few days later, when Ellie had been there a little over a week, her mother said, 'Well, darling, it's been lovely having you, but don't you think it's about time you moved on?'

Ellie knew she couldn't stay any longer—didn't want to—but it was still a bit of a shock to hear her mother say it. 'Er . . . yes.'

'You've got somewhere to stay while you're flat-hunting?'

'Yeah!' There was sure to be a floor she could crash on somewhere.

'So you don't think we're throwing you out?'

'No, but, Mum . . . there's just—'

'And I know it's difficult to find anything in your price bracket, but we'll pay your deposit and your first month's rent for you, as I said.'

'That's really kind,' said Ellie. 'I'll let you know how I get on. I'll go tomorrow morning. Now, if you don't mind, I'll go to bed. I'm awfully tired, for some reason.'

In the morning, while her mother was plying her with orange juice, Ellie finally managed to say what she'd been trying to say for days.

'Mum, Dad, I don't want to worry you, but I think I should tell you I'm pregnant.'

There was only the tiniest pause. 'Oh, darling!' said her mother. 'You can't possibly have it here! I don't want to seem unwelcoming, but you can see how impossible it is!' Her mother's speech seemed to come out very well prepared.

'Did you know I was having a baby, Mum?'

Val glanced across at her husband. 'We guessed, because of you not eating anything normal, and we thought about what the best thing to do would be, and what we decided was to support you in every way we can, but not to tell you to come and live with us. We just couldn't cope.'

Ellie stared at her mother's flawless face. 'Oh. Well, at least that's honest.' It was only what she'd been expecting, but she was surprised at the sudden hurt that lanced through her.

'You do want to keep it?' asked her father.

'Of course she wants to keep it!' snapped her mother. 'Otherwise she'd have done something about it by now.'

'Mum's right, I do want to keep it.'

'And what about Rick? Is he going to take any responsibility for his child?' asked her father.

Ellie shook her head. 'No. He rang me the other day and he doesn't want it and would be a hopeless father anyway.' It had been a short, painful conversation that had underlined for Ellie the rightness of her decision to leave.

'It's not going to be easy, bringing up a child on your own,' said her mother. 'But I don't suppose there's time to find a suitable father for it now!' she added brightly.

'No,' said Ellie, 'although I dare say I could fit in a short fling.'

Her mother laughed anxiously. 'Silly girl!'

Ellie smiled. The idea had lots to recommend it.

'Well, I've written you a cheque,' said her father, impatient with all this frivolity. 'For five hundred pounds. It's all we can lay our hands on at the moment—things are a little slack at the firm.'

Val put out her hand and took hold of Ellie's. 'I hope you don't think we're dreadfully unsupportive, but I was a hopeless mother and don't suppose I'll be much better at being a grandmother. And you won't let it call me Granny, will you? It's so ageing!'

Ellie set off for Luckenham House with a cheque for £500 and a painting. She planned to deliver the painting, and then look up an old college friend who lived in the area. She was bound to have a bit of floor space.

When she arrived, there was a van parked outside the house with GOSCOMBE WOODWORM AND PEST CONSULTANTS written on it in very smart gold lettering. Heavens, was the house infested? Ellie felt instantly protective of Grace. She parked her 2CV behind the van, picked up her bag, and marched down the path.

The front door was open, allowing the biting wind to knife through the house. 'Hello? Anyone at home? Grace?'

Grace heard Ellie's friendly shout, abandoned the young man in a boiler suit who was rapping at the wainscoting in a way almost guaranteed to make a hole, and ran to the gallery. 'Hi! How nice to see you! Come in.'

'Shall I come up?' said Ellie.

'No,' said Grace, grateful for an excuse to exchange lovely, cheerful Ellie for the young man who sucked his teeth in such a depressing way. 'I'll come down. I've got to make some coffee, anyway.'

'Who is he?' asked Ellie when Grace joined her and they set off together for the kitchen.

Grace sighed. 'Oh, it's a man my sister sent. I should be pleased, really.'

'Why? If you don't want him here, why do you have to be grateful?'

Grace sighed again and put the kettle on. 'Because I'm so pathetic! I let myself be bullied by my sister and then grumble about it. Anyway, it's great to see you.' Grace sought for a way of asking Ellie why she was there without seeming rude. Her presence was so welcome.

'I brought you this,' said Ellie, producing a painting from her bag. 'I did it while I stayed at my parents'. It's a present,' she added hurriedly.

Grace took hold of it, incredibly touched and charmed by the vision of her house. 'It's lovely! But you can't just give it to me.'

Ellie shook her head. 'I knew you couldn't afford it when I painted it.'

'But you probably can't afford just to give it to me either.' Grace let herself admire her house, and the way Ellie had captured the warmth of the stone, the delicate violet of the crocuses and the bright yellow jasmine, which wasn't actually out yet.

'Well, I *am* giving it to you. How did the wine-tasting go? I was so wrapped up in my own troubles, I forgot to ask about it the other day.'

Grace, aware that Ellie was not going to be argued with about payment for the picture, said, 'Well, thank you very much. I love it. It's so kind. I must get it framed. And the wine-tasting—well, it was all right in the end, I suppose. It was really very informal. There was a couple who were obviously expecting something very different and a man—can't remember his name—who wrote lots on his sheet and didn't say much.' Grace frowned. 'I think he was a spy. He certainly knew his wine.'

'A spy! How do you know?'

'Well, he said nothing all evening, but stayed and helped clear up at the end, while his girlfriend had a cigarette in the drawing room. I didn't think I could make her go outside in the middle of winter.'

'But why is he a spy?' Ellie was obviously fascinated by the concept.

'I think he was sent by the man at the wine shop in town to see if I knew my stuff.' She frowned. 'It was funny at the end though. He asked me to have dinner with him.'

'And he came with a girlfriend?' Ellie was appropriately horrified.

'I said no, of course. But fancy asking me out when he was with another woman!' Grace frowned. That wasn't the reason she'd turned him down. 'Although, to be fair, he might not have really been *with* her. Actually, I just thought they'd shared transport until she came in and called him darling.'

'Maybe she calls everyone darling,' suggested Ellie. 'Would you have gone out with him if you hadn't thought he was attached?'

Grace was horrified. 'Oh, no. I couldn't possibly go on a date. It's far too soon after my divorce.' Though it wasn't really. It was just too soon for her. Meditatively, she stirred the mug of coffee she had just put two spoonfuls of sugar into. 'I'll just take this up.'

'I don't suppose you've got any biscuits, have you?' called Ellie as Grace left the room. 'I'm suddenly *starving*.'

Grace came back. 'I suppose the man'll want biscuits too.' She got down a cream enamel jar with 'Biscuits' written on it. 'Ginger nuts?'

Ellie nodded enthusiastically. 'Perfect.'

When Grace had reappeared, having taken the coffee and some of the biscuits to the young man, who seemed intent on dismantling her house, plank by plank, she joined Ellie at the table and sipped her own tea.

'So, how did you get into wine?' Ellie sighed apologetically. 'God, I'm sorry. I am so nosy! And rude! Demanding biscuits, asking all these questions. What must you be thinking?'

'I think a few biscuits are the least I owe you. After all, you've just given me a painting. And I don't mind about the questions. It's quite nice to be listened to, instead of lectured. Perhaps that's why I want to do wine tastings. The getting into thing was straightforward enough. I didn't want to do A levels.' Grace frowned at the memory of her parents' horror that one of their children should be so unacademic as to want to go and get a job rather than go to university. 'I got a job at a wine importer. I became quite interested in it and did the preliminary exams.'

'Are your parents still alive? Sorry, I'm one of those people who has to know everything.'

Grace laughed. 'They're still alive but they live in Portugal, surrounded by golf courses, other elderly people and about a million books. I was an afterthought, which is why my sister Allegra got to boss me about so much. They'd lost interest by the time I came along.'

'Did you meet your husband at the wine place?'

Grace nodded. 'He was a customer. My family were beginning to nag me to go in for improving my wine skills, try for a Master of Wine. But Edward liked me as I was.' Grace stopped. 'Have you told your parents that you're pregnant yet?'

Ellie nodded.

'Were they horrified?'

'Sort of, but they'd guessed.'

'So what did they say?'

'They said I couldn't bring the baby up with them, and they're quite right, I couldn't possibly. Their house is like a show home. No place for a baby.' Ellie smiled, but it didn't reach her eyes. 'They gave me a cheque, though. For a deposit and rent on another place.'

'Have you got anywhere in mind?'

'Yeah. There's a friend of mine from college who stayed in Bath. I'll be able to kip on her floor until I find something. I won't be able to afford to live anywhere on my own, so I'll have to find people to share with who don't mind babies.'

'I don't mind babies,' said Grace, aware she sounded wistful.

'Yes, but you're not looking for a flatmate.'

'I could be looking for a person to share the house if I thought anyone else would want to live out here in the sticks.'

'But it's lovely here! I'm sure you could find someone . . . Grace?'

Grace had a curious expression on her face. 'I was just thinking—I don't suppose for one minute you'd want to, but you could stay here until you found somewhere you could afford in Bath. I know it wouldn't be any good to you permanently, but . . . I have got a blow-up mattress.'

There was a silence while Ellie took in what Grace had suggested.

Then Grace rushed on. 'I realise it's not a very attractive proposition. Freezing cold, miles from anywhere, but there's plenty of space. And I would love having the baby here.'

'And I would love to live here! I don't want to live in Bath at all. It's just the work thing.'

'I've got an attic you could have as a studio.'

'And I've got a bit of money to tide me over.' Ellie suddenly frowned. 'Oh, I do hope it didn't look as if I was dropping hints. I would so love to live here. It's such a beautiful house, and we could have so much fun doing things to it. But only if you want to do things to it, I mean.' She suddenly felt rather awkward. After all, they hardly knew each other.

Grace smiled. 'The reason I haven't done much is because I don't know if I can afford to go on living in it.'

'But if you had a lodger—me, for instance—that's another way of making money out of it. Apart from the wine-tastings.'

'Oh, Ellie! It would be such fun! Facing all this alone is dreadfully daunting and it does get terribly lonely.' There was a huge banging noise from above. 'And the poltergeists are dreadfully noisy!'

Ellie smiled at this little joke. 'So what do you think would be a fair rent? It's hard to relate this house to anywhere I've stayed before.'

'I really don't want to charge you rent—'

'I won't stay if you don't. You need the money.'

Grace capitulated. 'No! You must stay. But not too much rent. We don't have many facilities! Though I might buy a television licence and rent a television.'

Ellie got up and hugged Grace. 'Thank you so much! Instead of being a homeless single parent, because of you I'll be living in a mansion.'

Grace hugged her back. Meeting her was the best thing that had happened to Grace for a very long time.

'What happened to all the beds that were here?' Ellie asked as they trooped upstairs. 'There must be at least five bedrooms. What would your brother and sister do with so many beds? They couldn't have been worth anything.'

'Well, no, they didn't take the beds,' Grace explained, trying not to feel embarrassed. 'They were all burnt when I first moved in. They were fairly old and smelly, with horsehair mattresses.'

'Oh,' said Ellie. She stopped on the landing. 'The futon that Rick and I used to sleep on is actually mine. When I'm feeling a bit stronger I'll go and get it. In fact, I bought most of the furniture. We could bring it here.' She paused. 'It's all tat, really. It won't fit in this house at all.'

'But it'll be better than nothing. I was going to have to trawl the junk shops for stuff, as and when.'

'At least they left you a bed.'

Grace chuckled. 'It's not as bad as all that. Edward left me our bed, the goose-down duvet and pillows and bed linen, the wardrobe and a chest of drawers.' Ellie noticed a shadow of sadness pass across Grace's face and saw her try to shake it off. 'It must be rather expensive, having to buy a new bed every time you get married. At least for Edward, who's on his third wife now.' She made a face designed to be comical, but didn't quite manage it.

'Serves him right,' said Ellie. 'Now, which is your room?'

'In here. You can have any of the others. But I suggest you use one in this section of the house. It's slightly less arctic than the rest of it.'

The young man in a boiler suit emerging from one of the rooms made them both jump.

'Right, Miss Ravenglass—' he began.

'It's Mrs, actually.'

The man looked down at his clipboard. 'I was asked to come by a Mrs Statherton-Crawley. She told me to speak to a Miss Ravenglass. She said I was to send the report to her, and just tell you when I've finished.' He frowned. 'Is that right? I mean, you live here?'

'I do, but that's fine. You do what Mrs Statherton-Crawley asked you.'

'You just sign here, then.'

When Grace had signed, she said, 'I'll come down and show you out.'

When she came upstairs again, Ellie had found the bedroom she liked best. It was double aspect with a fantastic view, and Ellie was kneeling on the built-in window seat admiring the distant hills.

'This is a nice room,' said Grace. 'Good choice.' She frowned. 'Pity about the wallpaper. Those roses must be about a foot across! They'll give you nightmares.'

'So why did you leave them here, if you feel like that about them?'

'After Edward left, I never got round to doing anything about it. But now you're here perhaps . . . would it be very difficult?'

'Of course not! Easy as pie to paint over that lot.'

'And it needn't cost a lot?'

'No! And redoing it could be such fun! If you could see what I did in the cottage—I hardly spent a thing, but it looked wonderful in the end.'

'Oh. You must be sad to have to leave it,' said Grace. 'I mean, however you feel about Rick, it was your home.'

'Oh, I'll get over Rick soon enough. Leaving the cottage did cause a pang or two, because we were happy there in the beginning. But Rick . . .' She sighed. 'He was just an interlude, I guess.'

'That's how I feel about this house. Edward and I were happy here, too. Unfortunately he was a bit more than an interlude.'

That flicker of unhappiness passed across Grace's face again and Ellie, determined to cheer her up, chirped, 'But we're both going to survive! We're strong, modern women!'

'Yes!' Grace tried to punch the air to demonstrate her positive spirit, but even the air seemed too much of an opponent just then.

'Hey!' Ellie didn't comment on Grace's pathetic little gesture, but an idea had suddenly come to her. 'I must tell you! It's just that I thought I'd like to have an affaire! Why don't you have one, too?'

Grace couldn't help laughing. 'Ellie! That's so silly! I couldn't possibly have an affaire!'

'Couldn't you? Not ever?'

'Well, possibly, in the future, but it's far too soon after Edward.'

'It's probably a bit soon after Rick, but I haven't time to wait!' Ellie explained. 'If I'm going to have a love life again, it's got to be soon and short, because, let's face it, no man is going to want me when I'm the size of a house.'

'What about after the baby is born? When is it due, by the way?'

'I'm not quite sure, early autumn, maybe.'

Ellie seemed embarrassed by her vagueness, so Grace didn't press her.

'You could have an affaire when you've got a baby. Lots of people do.'

'No, I'm just going to have a quick fling, and then give up men until the baby's older.' Ellie regarded Grace, who was being maddeningly inscrutable. 'I haven't shocked you, have I?'

'No. No, I'm not shocked. It wouldn't do for me, but I perfectly understand how you feel.' Grace looked at her watch. 'I tell you what, let's whiz into town and get what we need to redecorate. I've got to go anyway, to deliver my article about the wine-tasting.'

'Excuse me,' Ellie asked the man in the junk shop, who had been a bit taken aback by Grace and Ellie's appearance just as he was about to go home for the day. 'Is the paint in those tins likely to be usable?'

'Oh, yes, and at fifty pence a can, you can't go wrong.'

'If you can still get it out of the can,' said Ellie. 'But we'll take it.'

'Don't you want to see what colour it is?' asked Grace.

'It's a soft grey. You can see from where it's dripped over the edges of the tin. If it's nice we could do more than just my room with it. But we'd better get some white emulsion as well. You don't happen to have—?'

'No,' said the man. 'Hardware, over the road.'

Ellie turned to Grace. 'Could you go and get that? A nice big tin? I'll carry on here.'

Grace wasn't long on her errand but when she returned she was impressed by the accumulation of furniture and bric-a-brac that Ellie had assembled in her absence. 'Are you sure we can afford all that?'

'Oh, yes. He's done us a deal. Come on, let's go home.'

'I'm sure you shouldn't be painting when you're pregnant,' said Grace to Ellie the next day. 'Especially not standing on a chair.'

'I'm having a baby. It's a perfectly normal condition. If I didn't stand on the chair I wouldn't be able to reach. I like the colour, don't you?'

The paint wasn't quite the same as it had been on the side of the tin, it was a little darker and not quite so soft. 'Sort of. It's quite dark.'

'It'll dry lighter.'

'I should be doing it really. Edward always got people in to do painting, but I'd like to give it a try. I've missed out on a lot of perfectly normal activities, getting married so young. Can I have a go now?'

In the end, it wasn't until half past nine that night, when they were both exhausted but the decorating was starting to look as if the end might be in sight, that they finally collapsed in the kitchen. After a while, Ellie got up to cook and Grace got out one of the leftover bottles of wine. 'Is alcohol forbidden for pregnant women?'

Ellie turned round from the stove, where she was making scrambled eggs. 'I think a little is OK, but to be honest, I've gone off it.'

'But you don't mind . . .'

'Good God, no! I think you need a drink, something to help you relax. Do you want Marmite on your buttered toast? And do you like the eggs actually on the toast, or just beside it?'

Ellie went for Marmite, Grace for plain, and they ate in companionable silence before wending their way to bed. Later, Ellie regretted her choice, because she woke up in the night incredibly thirsty. She went to the bathroom and scooped up handfuls of water and then, her thirst quenched, she realised she was hungry again, too. She spent several freezing moments trying to talk her stomach out of this idea but eventually gave in to it. She was fairly sure there were still some ginger biscuits in the cream enamel jar.

When she reached the kitchen and opened the door, she was shocked to see a large shape apparently draped over the kitchen table. Some instinct stilled her hand on the light switch, and a second later she heard the sound of sobbing.

Grace looked up when she heard Ellie, gasped, and then sniffed loudly. 'Hi! Can I get you anything?'

'Grace, why are you crying down here in the dark? I'll put the light on.'

'No! Please don't. I'll get a candle.'

Once the candle was lit, Ellie realised that Grace had her duvet with her, which was why she'd looked such an odd shape.

'What's going on, Grace? What are you doing here?'

'I could ask you the same question! Oh, I didn't wake you, did I?'

'No. I was hungry and I came down for a biscuit. What's your excuse? It's freezing down here.'

'I know. That's why I brought my duvet.'

'But why are you here?' Ellie wondered when persistence became plain rudeness.

Grace sniffed again and found a tissue up her sleeve. 'I woke up and—and I felt like crying, so I came down here, so as not to wake you.'

'Oh, love!' Ellie came over to Grace's side of the table and sat down next to her, so she could put her arm round her. 'Is it Edward?'

Grace nodded.

'Do you want to talk about it? It might help.'

'There's nothing that you don't know, it's just it's been nearly two years and I'm so bored of being so unhappy! When will I get over him?'

'Well, does it go in phases, or is it constant?'

'Fits and starts, really. I seem to be getting on quite well, don't think about him for quite long periods of time and then, *woomph*, something reminds me of him and it all comes flooding back.'

'So what happened this time?'

'I don't know really. I think it's something to do with having had such a good time with you.'

'So do you think my being here will make things worse for you? If so, I could easily find somewhere else to live.'

'No! Please don't do that! I just think that having good times sort of points up how bleak I feel inside.'

'You won't be bleak inside for ever,' said Ellie. 'Let me cheer us both up. I'll make you some hot chocolate and toast. Would you like that?'

'Yes, I think I would.' She watched as Ellie rummaged in a cupboard for a saucepan. 'You're mothering me, Ellie.'

Ellie looked up apologetically, pan in hand. 'I know. It's an awful habit of mine.'

'No, it's a good habit. Convenient, if you're going to be a mother.'

Ellie chuckled. 'God, I suppose I am.'

The following morning, Grace's eyes were distinctly puffy and Ellie's back was aching. The blow-up mattress was designed for women who didn't have curves. They were sitting at the kitchen table eating a late breakfast when the doorbell jangled.

'Oh God, who can that be?' muttered Grace, jumping to her feet and scraping her hair back from her face.

On the doorstep was a man who Grace recognised perfectly well, although she still felt muddled about his name. It was the spy.

'Hello,' he said. 'I was here the other night. For the wine-tasting?'

'Oh, yes. Did you leave your coat or something?'

'No. I just wondered . . . it may not be appropriate, but I'm getting rid of an old Rayburn and I wondered if it might be of use to you.'

'Why would it be?' asked Grace.

'It would heat your kitchen, provide hot water, possibly run a few radiators. I'm offering it to you. For nothing,' he added.

'Oh, I don't think . . .' she began, embarrassed, wishing he wouldn't look at her with that sort of intenseness.

Ellie, who'd followed Grace to the door in case the mystery caller was a mad axe-murderer, realised Grace was going to send away an offer of warmth without even considering it. 'You definitely want it, Grace. Rayburns are great.'

'Oh. Well, perhaps you'd better come in.' Grace was aware she was being less than gracious and tried to smile. She stood back so the man she wrestled for a moment with his name—could get into the hall.

'Perhaps we should all go to the kitchen?' suggested Ellie.

'Good idea,' said the man. 'I can have a look at the chimney.'

'I don't think there is a chimney,' said Grace, almost hoping there wasn't. She hadn't had much sleep and was aware that her eyes were very puffy and swollen. The spy was too big and bulky and male: she didn't want him in her house when she was looking so awful.

'Of course there's a chimney!' said the spy irritably. 'They wouldn't have taken it out!'

'That's good,' said Ellie, wondering why Grace was being so offhand in the face of this very generous offer.

Grace led the way to the kitchen.

'It is a lovely house,' said the man. 'If a little fridge-like.'

'It's February,' snapped Grace. 'It's bound to be cold.'

'There's a draught through this house that would clean corn, and it's nothing to do with February,' he said. 'A Rayburn would help.'

To Grace's annoyance the site of the house's original range was obvious. She just hadn't really noticed it because it was behind the cooker and someone had put some pale green tiles over the brickwork.

'Perfect for a solid-fuel stove,' said the man. 'Do you mind if I pull out the cooker and have a look?'

Grace shrugged, and Ellie said, 'Not at all. Shall I put the kettle on?'

'That would be nice,' said the man, looking at Grace. She was aware she should have introduced him by now, but still hadn't decided which name came first. She had a fifty-fifty chance of getting it right. 'This is—Cormack Flynn.'

'Flynn Cormack,' he said.

'Flynn Cormack,' went on Grace, trying not to care that she'd got it wrong. 'This is Ellie Summers.'

'It's really kind of you to offer us . . . er, to offer Grace . . . a Rayburn,' said Ellie. 'How much will it cost?'

'It's a present,' said Flynn. 'I'm replacing it. It's going spare.'

'Fantastic! That's so kind!' said Ellie, delighted at the thought of a permanent heat source.

'So, if it's so fantastic, why don't you want it any more?' asked Grace who, in spite of trying, couldn't make herself behave in a normal way.

'Because I'm installing a gas-fired one,' he explained. 'But I imagine you have a good supply of wood, what with owning the spinney.'

'How do you know I own the spinney?' demanded Grace.

'It's in the curtilage of the property,' said Flynn, bringing his eyebrows together. 'Everyone locally knows that—'

'Shall I make some tea?' interrupted Ellie, afraid that Grace was not only going to look this gift horse in the mouth but send him away with a flea in his ear.

'It would probably be very expensive to put in,' said Grace cautiously.

'I'll organise it for you,' Flynn replied.

'I couldn't put you to the trouble. I don't know you—'

'For God's sake, woman! I am offering you something you need! Could you not just say thank you?'

Grace confronted him. He had the very slightest Irish accent, which was more to do with the order in which he used words than anything else. He was not as handsome as Edward, not anything like, but he had a certain energy that she found somehow challenging.

'Tea?' repeated Ellie.

'What a good idea,' said Grace, trying to live up to her name just a little.

'What room is above the kitchen?' asked Flynn.

Grace had to think. 'The bathroom, I think.'

'Excellent. Would you mind if I had a look? Presumably your hot-water tank is up there somewhere, too?'

'I'll show you,' said Grace.

'No, don't bother. I'll find it myself.'

'I'm a bit fed up with all these men poking about in my house,' said Grace, when Flynn was out of earshot, wanting to explain to Ellie why she'd been so unenthusiastic.

'But a Rayburn would make such a huge difference,' insisted Ellie. 'They produce gallons of hot water. It's a slightly different way of cooking, and of course you have to get used to dealing with the fuel—you mustn't put a great wet log on if you want to boil the kettle—but you get used to that too. Do you have a wood supply?'

'Actually, one of the old stables is full of it. A big tree came down when my aunt still lived here and there's still masses left, as she didn't bother with fires much. Oh!' She turned round, surprised, as Flynn reappeared far too soon. 'Was the bathroom in the right place?'

'Perfect. You could have a radiator in there and another couple along the hallway, or in the bedrooms.'

'That would be like central heating. My aunt didn't approve of it. Said it was bad for the furniture.'

Flynn raised a sceptical eyebrow. 'Doesn't seem to me that there is much furniture. And your aunt's dead, isn't she?'

'Yes!' Grace said defensively, aware that she sounded absurd. 'But that doesn't mean she can't haunt me from beyond the grave, if I do something to her house she doesn't like.'

'Don't talk bollocks,' he said firmly, and Grace was horrified to discover she found his robustness oddly attractive. She turned away to make the tea that Ellie had offered with such abandon.

'And it will be better for the baby if it's a bit warmer,' said Ellie.

'Oh!' said Flynn. 'Are you pregnant?'

Grace turned round. 'Are you talking to me? No, I'm not pregnant.'

'I am,' said Ellie, and realised she felt proud of her condition.

'Oh,' said Flynn again. 'It doesn't show.'

'It wouldn't,' said Ellie. 'It's approximately the size of a broad bean.'

Flynn grunted, probably to avoid saying 'oh' again.

'Here's the tea,' said Grace, putting mugs on the table. 'We're getting a little short of milk, I'm afraid.'

Flynn drank his tea rather fast, as if he hadn't really wanted it but good manners had compelled him to accept. Then he stood up. 'Well, I'll be off then. Would it be convenient for me to bring the Rayburn round later this week? I've got a builder who could help me with it.'

'Yes, that would be fine,' said Grace. 'Thank you.' She forced herself to get up so she could show him out, although she didn't want to be alone with him. Not because she was frightened he'd do anything: it was just the expression in the back of his eyes which she didn't understand but couldn't ignore.

'Well, I think he's gorgeous,' said Ellie, when Grace got back to the kitchen. 'Why were you so off with him?'

Grace sighed, feeling silly. 'I don't know really. I think it's partly because he asked me out, and then that woman, Margaret, came in and called him darling. Edward had his faults, but he didn't pick up women while I was actually there.'

Ellie made a dismissive gesture. 'You shouldn't worry about Margaret! Calling him darling doesn't mean a thing.'

'It does if I say it,' said Grace crisply. 'Now put the kettle on, and I'll wash the mugs.'

'When you've got a Rayburn you'll have plenty of hot water . . .'

'Oh, shut up!' Grace threw a tea towel at Ellie who, annoyingly, caught it.

Why don't we go to my house in Bath and get my stuff,' said Ellie later on, feeling the need to get up and do something.

'Do you feel up to it?' asked Grace.

'Yeah, I think I do. I think I'm a lot shallower than you are Grace. My broken hearts don't last nearly so long as yours do.' Ellie pushed Grace's arm affectionately. 'Come on, let's get some stuff. I'm really looking forward to having some of my things around.'

They were in the hall, about to go, when the doorbell rang.

'It can't be Flynn again,' said Grace, uncertain how she'd feel if it was, and opened the door.

Standing on the doorstep was a tall young woman wearing a rucksack. It was possible she had been on the doorstep, on the point of ringing, for some time: she looked very cold.

'Oh! Demi,' said Grace, who took a moment to recognise her step-daughter. Aware that she had been about to add, 'What are you doing here?' she stopped herself. Whatever she was doing there, she did not look happy. 'Come in. How did you get here?'

Demi was Edward's daughter. Grace didn't know her well, but they had always got on all right when she came for visits. She had grown quite a lot since Grace had last seen her and was very thin now. She had a look of an orphan foal which Grace found quite touching. But why on earth was she here?

'This is Ellie,' introduced Grace, when Demi and her rucksack were through the door. 'She lives with me now.'

'Hi,' said Ellie, realising that this news was not entirely welcome; Demi was regarding her defensively. 'Shall we move out of the hall? Would you like a cup of coffee, or something?'

'Don't mind,' murmured Demi, gazing at the floor.

'Well, let's dump your stuff here,' Grace said cautiously, wondering why Demi should have so much stuff with her. 'Are you OK?'

Demi sniffed. 'Can I crash here for a bit?' she asked nervously.

Grace forced a laugh. 'Um, well, there's just a bit of a problem because we haven't actually got any beds.'

'I don't mind sleeping on the floor.' Demi sounded so pathetic, Grace's heart lurched. But why wasn't she at home?

'I've got to pee,' said Ellie, sensing that Demi wanted Grace on her own. 'Why don't you guys go into the kitchen? You probably need to talk.'

Once there, Grace filled the kettle again. 'I'm practically waterlogged, so I won't join you,' she said to Demi. 'But it looks like you need a cup of something.'

'You haven't any vodka, have you?'

'No,' said Grace, hiding her shock at Edward's daughter asking for vodka in the middle of the day.

'It's just that life's been quite shit lately, and I don't want to cry,' Demi explained, looking intently at the table.

'It's probably better to cry than drink vodka at this time of day. In the long term, at least.'

'I'll have black coffee then, if that's all right,' she said, her rebelliousness fighting with years of conditioning.

Ellie came back from the loo and hovered in the doorway. 'Would you two like to be alone?'

'No,' said Grace, suspecting that whatever was up with Demi, she might need Ellie's help.

'I wasn't expecting anyone else to be here,' said Demi.

'Well, Ellie is here, and she's staying,' said Grace gently, but firmly. 'She's my friend, and I want her here.'

'But I have to stay too!' said Demi to Ellie. 'I'm Grace's stepdaughter!'

'I'm not sure you still are,' said Grace, 'now Edward and I are divorced.'

Demi put her arms on the table and banged her head down onto them. 'Oh, that's so crap!'

'Demi's a really cool name,' said Ellie, trying to cheer things up.

Demi raised her head. 'It's short for fucking Demeter.' She lowered her head again.

'Oh,' said Ellie.

'Her father and mother won't call her Demi,' said Grace. 'They think it's common.'

'Oh,' said Ellie again. 'I think Demi's really cool.' She looked at Grace. 'Apart from the bed problem, is there any reason why Demi couldn't visit?'

'No reason at all.' Grace smiled at Demi, aware of the dark circles round the girl's eyes, and wondering if Edward had seen her lately.

'I don't want to visit,' said Demi. 'I want to live with you.'

'Why?' asked Ellie while Grace sat down, looking distinctly shocked.

'Because . . . it's crap where I live.'

'Why, what is it?' Grace took hold of Demi's hands across the table. 'You can tell me.'

'I just don't want to live at home any more,' Demi said in a strangled voice, 'that's all. I want to live with you.'

'But, sweetheart, you can't!' said Grace. 'What would your parents say?'

'They wouldn't care.' Demi buried her head in her arms again.

'Yes, they would! They would go mad at the idea of their precious daughter living with me! And Edward, well, he wouldn't ever think of me as a fit person to have the care of his daughter.'

Demi raised her head. 'Yes, he would! Now they've both got partners, they've forgotten all about me.' She sniffed and wiped her nose on the back of her hand.

'I'm sure they haven't.' Grace got up and found Demi a bit of kitchen towel. 'I know children always blame themselves when their parents get divorced—' she began, dragging out the party line.

'I didn't blame myself!' said Demi firmly. 'I know perfectly well why Dad left Mum—she's a cow! But for a while she was at least a mother. Now she's in "lurve" she doesn't give a toss!'

'Well, what about Edward?' Grace continued. 'I know he thinks the world of you. Always has.'

'He may think the world of me, but that bitch he's shacked up with doesn't! You were cool, you never tried to come between me and him, but she won't ever let us be alone together, and when I asked if I could live with them she . . .'

'Went mental?' suggested Ellie.

'And the rest! So that's why I've come here.'

'Well, you did the right thing,' said Ellie firmly.

'What?' demanded Grace. 'She did the right thing, running away from home? Oh God, Demi, does anyone know where you are?'

'They won't have noticed I've gone, don't worry. They think I'm out with my friends. They always think I'm out with my friends, but they've no idea where I am really. I went and stayed with mates up in London for two days, and no one said a thing.'

'But that's quite cool, isn't it?' suggested Ellie. 'Not being nagged for a timetable of who and where and what all the time?'

Demi bit her lip. 'It should be, but when you know it's just like that because they haven't noticed you're not there, it's not.'

A spasm of anxiety shot through Grace. Supposing Demi was pregnant. 'You're not pregnant, are you?' The words came out as a whisper.

'No!' Demi was clearly just as horrified as Grace at the thought.

'OK. What we'll do is ring your mother and ask her if you can stay for a while.'

'Are you at college or something?' asked Ellie.

Grace had forgotten about that for a moment. 'Oh, hell, they'll never let you stay if it means you'll miss college. Your mocks must be any minute! Demi, you'll have to go back. A levels are important!'

'It doesn't matter,' said Demi. 'I haven't been to college for weeks, and no one's noticed. They're not likely to make a fuss now.'

'But they will find out,' said Ellie. 'Although at college they reckon that if you're over eighteen—'

'Demi's not over eighteen,' said Grace.

'But I look older,' said Demi. 'Everyone says so.'

'Looking older is not the same as being older!'

'I don't know about anyone else,' said Ellie soothingly, 'but I'm starving—because I *am* pregnant. Shall I make us all something to eat? Sandwiches, something like that?'

'That's a good idea,' said Grace. 'Do you need me to do anything?'

Ellie turned to Demi. 'I don't know if you know this, but if Grace was left to her own devices, she would never cook and hardly ever eat, which is why I've taken over the cooking. Self-defence.'

This got a grudging smile out of Demi. 'I am quite hungry. I didn't have breakfast.'

'Demi,' asked Grace tentatively, sure she didn't want to hear the answer, 'how did you get here?'

'I hitched.'

Grace groaned. 'You're to promise never to hitch on your own again.'

'OK,' agreed Demi. 'The bloke who drove me here gave me a terrible telling off. He said it was dangerous, too.'

Ellie suppressed a smile, and went over to the table by the fridge. She observed Demi and Grace talking quietly at the kitchen table. Grace seemed far too young to be a stepmother, but she could understand why Demi would choose to come and live with her.

Ellie took care with the sandwiches, mostly to give Demi and Grace more time to talk, but also because she was an expert at making meals that cost virtually nothing. She put a plate of sandwiches on the table between Grace and Demi.

'Oh, wow!' said Demi. 'Can I start?'

'So what have you guys agreed?' asked Ellie, biting into a ham and salad sandwich.

Grace sighed. 'After lunch we're going to ring Demi's mother and tell her Demi's here.'

'She won't care,' said Demi, her mouth full.

'Yes, she will! But if it's OK with her, and we can sort something out about college, she can stay here. Providing the parents agree.'

'Good,' said Ellie. 'So, who wants to come with me to get my furniture?'

'I do,' said Demi, who was looking a lot more cheerful now she was eating. 'This is going to be so cool.'

'It might not be,' warned Grace. 'Your mother may not allow you to stay with me.'

'I told you! She doesn't care! All she cares about is that new bloke of hers. It's so gross. They touch each other all the time—in front of me.'

'That is a bit gross,' said Ellie.

Grace said nothing. She was remembering how she and Edward couldn't keep their hands off each other when they were first in love. Demi would have found that gross, too.

'Right, let's ring her up, shall we? Will you call her?'

'Oh, OK.' Demi got out a mobile from a pocket and pressed a few keys. 'She's not in,' she said after a few moments.

'Leave a message,' said Grace firmly. 'Tell her it's very important that she rings you back as soon as possible. Now ring Edward.'

Demi tried to hand Grace the phone. 'You do it. I can't bear that cow of a wife of his.'

'Haven't you got his mobile number?' asked Grace.

'But I don't want to speak to him!' said Demi. After she had produced a ringing tone, she thrust the phone at Grace, who didn't want to speak to Edward either. There was a tense silence.

'Hello?' said Grace eventually. 'May I speak to Edward, it's Grace.'

Demi and Ellie watched as Grace pushed breadcrumbs into little piles, bracing herself, obviously waiting for Edward to be brought to the phone. 'Edward? It's me. I've got Demi here.'

There was a pause while Edward responded to this.

'She just arrived. She wants to stay for a bit.' Another pause. 'We've left a message for her to ring back, but she hasn't.' Then Grace sighed, and handed the phone to Demi. 'He wants to talk to you.'

'Dad!' Demi's voice had an edge of hysteria to it. 'I'm not going home! I hate it there! Mum hates me! Her bloke hates me! And as for those poxy children of his, why can't they stay with their own mother?'

Ellie and Grace both looked at their plates. Ellie started following Grace's example and drew a palm tree in crumbs. They both felt they were intruding.

'I don't care about fucking A levels!' Demi shouted. She was crying when she handed the phone back to Grace. 'He's such a bastard!'

'Listen, Edward,' Grace plunged in, not wanting to hear Edward's side of the story. 'Demi's quite upset about a lot of things. I know college is important, but she says she hasn't been going in anyway. Did you know she's been spending time in London with no one having a clue where she is?'

While Edward responded to this at length, Grace mouthed 'Sorry!' at Demi for betraying her secret, but indicated by more mouthing that she felt it would help Demi's case if Edward knew the whole story.

Eventually Grace just lowered the phone and pressed a button.

'Did you get cut off?' asked Demi.

'Well, we certainly weren't communicating,' said Grace.

'You mean you put the phone down on him?' asked Ellie. 'Respect!'

Grace was puzzled. 'I would never have done that when I was married to him, but I just suddenly thought, I don't have to be shouted at or told off any more.' She smiled at Demi. 'I'm really looking forward to you living here! Why don't we go and choose you a room?'

'Then we can go to my cottage'—Ellie found a lump in her throat and swallowed it away—'and see how much stuff we can get into my car.'

'We're going to steal furniture?' said Demi, obviously much cheered by the prospect.

'Not steal it,' said Ellie. 'Take it away. I paid for it.'

'We could go in my car,' said Grace. 'It's a bit bigger than yours—' She stopped speaking as the phone rang. 'That'll be your mother, Demi.'

'No, it won't. I left a message for her to ring my mobile.'

'And I just put the phone down on Edward.' Grace picked up the receiver, preparing to be thoroughly told off. Flynn's deep tones, with their subtle Irish accent, were strangely soothing.

'I was wondering if I could bring the Rayburn round this afternoon. I've got someone who can help me now, who may not be available later.'

Grace took a longing look at Ellie and Demi and realised she would not be able to join them. 'That would be fine.' She pulled herself together. 'I mean, thank you very much.'

When Ellie and Demi set off in Ellie's 2CV, having first put the back seat down, they both felt a sense of excitement.

'So tell me about us taking the furniture,' said Demi. 'Will your boyfriend be there?'

Ellie took advantage of a road junction to glance at her watch. 'I shouldn't think so, but you can't be sure.' She couldn't decide if she wanted to see Rick or not. 'The most important thing is to get the futon. We should be able to get that in the back of the car if we take the base apart. And there are some bits and pieces in the kitchen I'd quite like. My mum bought me a food processor for Christmas; I'm not leaving that behind.'

'But supposing he is there? Will there be trouble?'

Ellie could hear the mixture of anxiety and excitement in Demi's voice. 'Well, I hope it doesn't turn into a scene from *EastEnders*,' she said, trying to sound reassuring. 'I don't think Rick will mind my leaving him because he doesn't want the baby and he knows he can get someone else to cook and clean up for him. But he might be a bit pissed off about me taking the bed.'

'Right. I can't decide if I want him to be there or not.'

'Listen, if you're nervous, you can stay in the car.'

'No, no. I'll come in. I'm sure you shouldn't move furniture if you're pregnant.'

Rick's van was parked outside the house when they arrived and there was nowhere else near where Ellie could park.

'Bugger!' Ellie said, not sure if she was annoyed because Rick was there, or because she couldn't park outside. 'Now we'll have to carry the futon for miles.'

'But will there be a row?' demanded Demi.

'I don't know. Let's find somewhere to park and we can find out.'

'I suppose it's better if we can sneak up on him,' said Demi after Ellie had found a spot in the next street. 'And then, while he's not looking, we can drag the futon down the stairs and run off down the street with it.'

Ellie couldn't help laughing. 'You can't run with a futon, you know.

They're very solid. We'll have to get Rick to move the van so we can park outside. Come on, I've got my key.'

'Rick?' Ellie called as she opened the front door. 'Are you home?'

The most gorgeous man Demi had ever seen appeared at the door of what seemed to be the kitchen. 'Hi. Oh, hello,' he said to Demi, looking at her hard. 'Who are you?'

'Hi, Rick, this is Demi. We've come to get my things.'

'You got somewhere to live?'

'Yes. Now, do you mind if I take the futon? I paid for it and I need it.'

Rick scowled, an expression which diminished his good looks not one jot. Demi was finding it difficult to breathe. 'What am I going to sleep on?'

'I have no idea, but I'm sure you'll manage to scrounge a bed from somewhere.' Aware of the effect Rick was having on Demi, Ellie took her by the arm. 'Come on, Dems. Let's go and get it.'

Demi, more than a little reluctant to be dragged away, followed Ellie up the stairs to the bedroom. Ellie opened the wardrobe and produced some carrier bags. 'The bedside light is mine: I made it at college. I've already got most of my clothes and my portfolio so we can just fill the car up with furniture. Can you take that little table, and the vase.'

'What about the wardrobe?' said Demi.

'It won't fit in, or if it does, nothing else will,' said Ellie. 'I'll just go and ask Rick to move the van so I can park outside.'

'I'm coming with you.'

Rick was sitting in the kitchen smoking a joint.

'Could you move the van so I can park my car outside and load my stuff?' asked Ellie.

'I don't see why I should help you to move out,' said Rick, unhelpful, but not aggressive. 'After all, you're taking my bed.'

'My bed. And you may as well cooperate because if I'm out of the way, it'll be easier for you to move someone else in.'

Acknowledging this point, Rick carefully rested his roll-up on the side of an ashtray, got up, and felt in his pocket for his keys.

'You do it,' he said to Ellie, passing them to her.

'Come on, Demi,' said Ellie.

When they were in Rick's van, trying to find another space big enough for it, Demi said, 'Do you think it will take Rick long to get a new girlfriend?'

'About five minutes, if he hasn't done it already. Bastard!' Ellie shouted at a red Mercedes. 'This is my space! Don't even think about taking it. Thank you!' She smiled and waved as the man moved on.

Chapter Three

DISAPPOINTED THAT SHE WAS not able to be part of the raiding party, Grace washed up the mugs and plates from lunch while wondering what she could do to make the house more homely. She and Ellie had done a certain amount upstairs, but downstairs was still fairly austere.

It was starting to get dark; soon she would go round the house and put the lights on—her strategy for living alone had included putting lights on early, so she didn't have to go upstairs into the dark. She was about to do her rounds of the house when the telephone rang.

'I cannot believe you've been so irresponsible!' It was Demi's mother. So much for her phoning Demi's mobile.

Usually, Grace would do anything to avoid a conversation with Hermia; Edward's first wife terrified her. But today, for some reason, she felt brave enough to speak her mind. 'If you want to speak to Demi, why don't you try her on her mobile?'

'Her name is not Demi! It's Demeter! And you're to bring her home immediately.'

'She's not here.'

'What do you mean, she's not there? Where the hell is she?'

'She's gone with a friend to pick up some furniture. Anyway, how did you know she'd come here?'

'Edward told me. He expects me to come down to you and bring her home! I can't just drop everything for that stupid girl! I've got people coming for dinner.'

Grace was shocked, but stayed calm. 'Well, I suppose there's never a good time for your daughter to run away from home.' Demi's statement that her mother no longer had time for her was obviously true.

'What?' Hermia had obviously not put this interpretation on Demi's absence. 'Demeter has not run away from home! What are you talking about?'

Grace couldn't unsay her words, but now tried to be a bit more soothing. 'If she hasn't run away, why are you getting so worked up?' Too late, she realised she should have said 'upset'.

'I'm not worked up! Or if I am, it's with perfectly good reason. I grounded her the other day and she just went out anyway! I've stopped her allowance, of course, but what can you do?'

'Well, she's not here just now. Shall I ask her to ring you when she gets back?'

'No! You will *tell* her to ring me! And you'll make sure she gets on the first bus home in the morning.'

Annoyed as she was, Grace began to feel sorry for Hermia. There she was at the end of the phone, giving orders, with absolutely no ability to make sure they were carried out. 'I don't think I can do that.'

'Why on earth not?'

'For one thing, there are no buses at the weekend. She hitchhiked here. And for a second thing, I can't make her do anything she doesn't want to do. And thirdly, I'm very fond of Demi and think she *should* stay here for a bit.' She hadn't realised she was going to say that because, in principle, she felt children should live with their parents.

'Out of the question! She's to come home and finish her education. What a suggestion! Stay with you? I wouldn't trust you to look after a hamster! You're to tell that young woman, when she gets in,' went on Hermia, 'that she's to stop being so disobedient and come home!'

'Your daughter is your responsibility, not mine, you know,' said Grace gently. 'You and Edward have to sort it out between you. I'm very happy to have Demi here. I think she's a lovely girl, and with a little under-standing might even be persuaded to go back and do her A levels.' Then she put the phone down.

Grace decided it would be nice for Ellie and Demi if they came back to a house with lights shining from all the windows and not just the ones she usually put on. She went first to the drawing room and switched on the wall lights. Then she went into the dining room. From here she could see the spinney, its leafless trees silhouetted against a darkening sky edged with pink. She gazed at the view for a few moments, admiring the tracery of the branches against the backdrop, and then, because beauty always made her think of Edward, without thinking she reached out and pulled the curtain.

'Oh, bugger!' she said as it collapsed into a pool of tattered silk on the floor. 'Why did I do that?'

Then she gave a scream of shock. There was a figure, pale and spec-tral, behind where the curtain had been. It took her a heart-thumping moment to realise that she hadn't seen a ghost. The figure was a paint-ing, almost life-sized, on the panel of the shutter.

How could she not have known it was there? she asked herself as she crossed the room to the door, to turn on the light. To think it had been lurking behind the curtain all these years, and she'd never known. She felt quite guilty as she flicked the switch.

The only illumination in the dining room now came from a central bulb, covered by a heavy shade that conspired to keep all the light to itself. It didn't so much add light as emphasise how dark the room was. Grace decided to get a torch. There was one in a tea chest in the hall.

She had just found it when the doorbell rang. She jumped at the noise, her nerves already jangled, then took a breath and looked out of the window. It was Flynn. She opened the door reluctantly.

'Why is it I always get the impression that you're not pleased to see me?' he asked, with a slightly crooked grin.

'Possibly because I'm not.'

The fact that she'd answered so acerbically shocked Grace almost as much as thinking she'd seen a ghost. It was so out of character for her. She tried to smile, but it didn't feel very convincing.

It obviously didn't look convincing, either. 'I hope you're not planning to hit me on the head with that blunt instrument.' He indicated the torch. 'I have come to give you something, you know.'

He stood there as if expecting some sort of explanation. Well, she had no intention of telling him about the painting. 'I thought I saw something move on the stairs and it made me jump.'

'I see. The house isn't haunted or anything, is it?'

'No, of course not! And even if it were, I don't believe in ghosts.'

'That's all right, they won't appear to you then.' He paused. 'Is there somewhere we can put the Rayburn? An outhouse or something?'

'Yes, of course. There's a stable you could use. I'll show you.'

He put a hand on her arm. 'No, don't. We'll find it.'

She smiled, mildly relieved. 'Don't you want a hand?'

He shook his head. 'We have a special trolley and moving Rayburns is man's work.'

'Or strong women's work?'

He shook his head. 'No woman is that strong, and you certainly aren't.' He glanced down at her slender form.

'I'm thin, but I'm tough,' said Grace.

'No, you're not. Why don't you put the kettle on? Or do something else that'll make you feel useful and keep you out of our way?'

'That's not very polite!' Honestly, this man was beyond the pale.

'I'm sure the hot water will come in useful.' He was teasing her.

'That's hardly the point!'

'You're very argumentative,' he said, amused.

'No, I'm not!' Grace scowled at him, determined not to let him have the last word, and then realised what she'd said and tried not to laugh. She fled towards the kitchen, half wanting to hit him and half to indulge in her suppressed laughter.

For want of something better to do, Grace did indeed put the kettle on, and then inspected the wooden crate that was her wine rack. Maybe Flynn's mate might like a glass of wine when he came in. She pulled out a bottle, examined it for a few moments and then extracted the cork.

There was a knock at the back door and Grace went down the passage to open it, determined to be polite and sociable and not to let Flynn Cormack make her do or say anything out of character.

'This is Pete,' said Flynn. 'This is Grace, who doesn't live up to her name.'

Grace ignored this and directed her smile entirely towards Pete. Then she glared at Flynn. 'I boiled the kettle,' she said, 'as instructed. And there are some biscuits. But I wondered if Pete'—she smiled at him again, to point up the fact that she was not smiling at Flynn—'would like a glass of wine?'

'What about me?' asked Flynn indignantly.

'You're driving!'

'No, I'm not. Pete is. I'd love a glass of wine.'

'What about you, Pete?'

'I'm more of a tea man, myself. And I'd love a biscuit.'

She made the tea, and poured a glass of wine for herself and Flynn.

'Not exactly *chambré*, if I may say so,' he said, having held his glass up to the light and taken a sip.

'People don't realise that "room temperature" was the room temperature of the eighteenth century, not of the centrally heated house of today,' she said, aware she was sounding incredibly pompous.

'Ooh! Get you!' Flynn directed his glass towards her in a toast. He was looking at her in a way she found unnerving. There was nothing improper in it, but feeling his eyes upon her in that quizzical, speculative fashion was unsettling. To her enormous relief, the front doorbell's jangle indicated that the others were back. She rushed to open the door.

'How did you get on?' she asked.

'Really well! Come and help us!' said Demi, who seemed excited and looked particularly pretty. 'We've got loads of stuff!'

'Flynn's here. And Pete. They're in the kitchen.'

'Who's Pete?' asked Demi. Ellie had filled her in on Flynn.

'Friend of Flynn's, I think,' said Grace.

'I must say, I'm dying of thirst,' said Ellie, sensing that Grace wanted company in the kitchen. 'I could murder a cup of peppermint tea.'

'We *must* buy peppermint tea bags,' said Grace. 'In fact, now that Demi's come, we'll probably have to get lots of things. We must make a list so we can go shopping.' As they walked down the corridor to the kitchen, she added, 'Once we've got these men out of the way.'

Ellie, anxious lest Grace should banish the men before she'd taken advantage of them, said, 'Would you mind if I asked them to help with the futon?'

'Of course not. You shouldn't be carrying things if you're pregnant.'

'Great. I'll go and ask them,' said Ellie, going ahead into the kitchen.

'Hi, Flynn!' She turned to Pete. 'I'm Ellie,' she said. 'Would you two mind giving us a hand with some furniture? It's just that I'm pregnant and I shouldn't really lift things.'

'What is it you need shifting?' asked Flynn.

'A futon.'

'Should be able to manage that all right,' said Pete, rising to his feet.

When they arrived at the car, Grace found that Ellie and Demi had got lots of the smaller items out. They loaded themselves up with plastic bags and boxes and went inside the house and up the stairs.

'Where are you going to sleep?' Ellie asked Demi.

'I used to sleep in a little room by the bathroom. It's really pretty in a chintzy sort of way.'

They reached the landing and Demi led the way. The room revealed itself to have pretty Victorian wallpaper, possibly original, very much nicer than the ghastly overblown roses Ellie had covered with grey paint.

Ellie dumped her load of bags on the floor. 'I'm glad we got that small chest of drawers in. Would you like it in here?'

'Oh, that's really kind. I could use the top as a dressing table, for my make-up and stuff. But don't you want it?'

'I haven't got all that many clothes. I'll be fine with those boxes you were practically sitting on.'

'We got quite a lot in the car, really.' Demi frowned. 'Will Rick be all right without it? I don't know how you can leave him. He's so gorgeous.'

'Not that gorgeous to live with,' Ellie said wryly. 'And he didn't want me to keep the baby.'

'Oh,' said Demi, and Ellie realised she didn't quite understand.

'I think we'd grown apart, really,' she went on, 'but he was the best-looking bloke in college.' She shook herself, there was no benefit to reminiscing. 'Let's go and get the blow-up mattress from my room.'

'I don't think Grace likes Flynn,' said Demi as they carried the mattress along the passage.

'I don't know why not. He's a nice bloke.' Ellie sighed. 'She was very upset when your dad left her.'

'Being dumped is always crap,' said Demi, as if she knew from personal experience. 'And she was potty about him. You could see it.' They lowered the mattress onto the floor of her bedroom. 'She was always so nice to me,' Demi went on. 'His new wife is potty about him, too, but I don't think she realises I exist.'

'Oh dear. Doesn't she make an effort at all?'

Demi shook her head as they walked back to Ellie's room. 'Nope. And Mum only cares about her new bloke—that and having beauty treatments so she can keep him. He's a bit younger than she is.'

'Oh. My mum's very keen on therapies too,' said Ellie. 'I feel like an old sack tied up with string when I'm next to her.'

'My mum's like that too! She only ever speaks to me to tell me to do something to my skin, or to do my college work.'

They smiled at each other, a moment of mutual understanding, then turned as they heard a crash from the landing.

The futon was coming up the stairs on the shoulders of Pete and Flynn, and Grace trotted behind them, carrying an armful of bedding.

'Where do you want it?' asked Flynn.

'In here,' said Ellie. 'We've moved the blow-up mattress out.'

Flynn and Pete deposited the futon on the floor in Ellie's room and set off back to the car for the pieces of the base.

'I'd better come with you to help,' said Grace, sounding reluctant as she followed them.

'I don't know why she doesn't like him,' said Ellie *sotto voce* to Demi, when the two men had disappeared downstairs again.

Demi shrugged. 'He's not good-looking like Dad.'

'No, but he's OK-looking, in a rugged sort of way.'

Demi giggled. 'If Grace liked rugged men she would never have married my dad.'

'Oh. That might explain it.'

'Anyway, it's a bit soon, isn't it?'

'I don't know. After all, your dad's got someone new.' The more Ellie thought about it, the more she thought an affaire with someone like Flynn might be just what Grace needed.

'Now,' said Pete, when all the various bits of pine, fixings and Allen keys had been assembled on the bedroom floor. 'Do you want a hand putting this thing together?'

'Oh, no!' said Grace. 'It's been very kind of you to help, but we'll be fine now.'

Ellie shook her head and frowned at Grace. 'No, we won't! It was hard enough taking the damn thing apart! It would be brilliant if you'd help us get it set up.'

'Yeah,' said Demi. 'Ellie must be really tired. She'll need to sleep on it quite soon.'

Grace glanced at Demi, wondering at this sudden flash of consideration. 'I'll go and get some wine, then,' she said, feeling it would be better if she offered hospitality now, while everyone was doing something.

By the time she came back upstairs with the wine and glasses, the futon was nearly complete. Demi was wrestling with a duvet cover and Ellie was putting pillows into cases.

'They've been marvellous,' Ellie said as Grace appeared. 'Got it together in no time.'

'How kind,' said Grace. 'Would you like a glass of claret? My husband bought it in France a few years ago.'

'But he's not your husband any more,' said Ellie.

'No, but the wine's still wine,' said Grace, wondering why Ellie was being so pedantic.

'Dad's latest wife doesn't drink,' announced Demi.

'You make him sound like Bluebeard,' Grace protested.

Demi shrugged. 'Well, it is wife number three he's on now, you know.'

'Yes, but is that so many?' asked Ellie.

'Yes,' said Flynn. 'More than one is "so many".'

Grace looked at him. 'Which one are you on, then?'

'Oh, I'm Bluebeard too,' he said solemnly. 'My wife couldn't stand always living in a building site and walked out. I'm a property developer.'

Grace's shudder of distaste was nearly visible. Sensing it, Ellie said, 'But what about your present wife?'

'I haven't found her yet.'

'So you're not Bluebeard yet?' said Demi. 'Just gearing up to be?'

'Oh, for goodness' sake!' said Grace, hating this conversation for lots of reasons. 'Let's just have a drink.'

'Perhaps Ellie, or Demi, or whoever's bedroom we're in, might not like us drinking wine in it,' said Flynn.

'No, it's fine,' said Ellie.

'And you're pregnant! You don't want to drink alcohol!' Grace was grateful for an excuse to escape. 'I'll run and get you something soft.'

She was out of the room before anyone could speak, but was caught up with by Flynn in the kitchen.

'Actually, Pete and I really must be going. Thank you for the wine.'

'You didn't have time to drink it.' Now that he was actually going, she wanted him to stay. 'And I should be thanking you for helping Demi and Ellie with the bed and everything.'

'It was no trouble. And I would just like to say that I'm not the sort of property developer you thought I was when I said it.'

'I don't know—'

'I couldn't help seeing your expression. You thought I was the kind that puts up nesting boxes on greenfield sites. I don't. I buy houses, do them up and move on.'

'Oh . . . I didn't mean to be rude.'

'You weren't rude, you just winced.'

'The thing is, my family have suggested that I sell off part of my land, for building, but I won't.'

'You shouldn't. Besides, nowhere round here would ever get planning permission.'

She smiled. 'That's a relief!'

'I'll be off now. I'll ring you when we can come round and install the Rayburn. It will make a big difference to this kitchen, you know.'

'I'm sure it will. It's very kind—'

'No, it's not. It's surplus to my requirements.'

Then he walked out, leaving Grace rather confused.

As she went to join the others she noticed the dining-room light on and suddenly remembered. She ran up the stairs. 'Hey! You'll never guess what happened while you were out.'

'What?' Ellie and Demi had been patting pillows into place, and now they looked up at Grace.

'I thought I saw a ghost, but it turned out to be a painting!' said Grace. 'Come and look. Bring your glasses and the bottle. Oh, Ellie! I never got you anything.'

'Never mind that. Let's go and look at this painting.'

Demi, who'd drunk her wine rather fast, said, 'Ooh, this is so exciting!'

'It might not be,' said Grace. 'It might be just a daub. I was getting a torch to look at it better when Flynn arrived.' She collected the torch and then led the way to the dining room. 'It may not be anything, really, but I was just in here drawing the curtains—'

'I thought you said you never drew the curtains in here,' said Ellie. 'Because the material was too fragile.'

Grace made a face. 'We never used to, but I forgot and one of the curtains fell to pieces. Then I thought I saw a ghost.'

'Why?' asked Demi, thrilled and horrified.

'Because of that,' said Grace, shining the torch at the window shutter. The beam highlighted the painted figure.

'Wow,' said Ellie after a few moments. 'I can see why you thought it was a ghost. It looks really old.' She went closer. 'I think it's Eve.' She frowned. 'I can't quite see if the panel has been painted, or if it's on a board stuck on top.'

'Oh my God,' said Grace softly.

'What?' said Demi, obviously spooked.

'Nothing. It's just—'

'Come on, Grace!' said Ellie. 'You find what could be a wonderful painting and you're not jumping up and down with excitement. It could be really valuable!'

'That's the problem,' explained Grace. 'What will my bloody sister do when she finds out about it?'

'You mean she'll try and claim it as hers?'

Grace nodded. 'She could. She and Nicholas could do just that.'

'I'm really hungry,' said Demi, who had been staring at the painting and not really concentrating on what Ellie and Grace had been saying.

'Let's go and eat,' Ellie agreed, hungry herself and aware that Grace was distressed.

Grace stood by the light switch and waited until Ellie and a slightly tipsy Demi left the room. Then she switched off the light and shut the door, wondering what on earth she'd discovered. If it was as old and interesting as Ellie seemed to think, it could create all kinds of problems. Or, possibly, solutions.

'Well,' said Grace the next morning, watching Demi spread butter on a piece of toast she had previously cut into tiny squares. 'What first?'

Demi yawned. 'I might go back to bed for a bit.'

'I really want to have another look at the painting,' said Ellie.

There was a moment's silence. 'Oh, yes,' said Grace. 'The painting.'

'Our looking at it won't cause a problem, and the more we know the better. "Information is armour", or something.'

'You're right. Are you coming, Demi, or are you going back to bed?'

'Oh, no. I'll come if there's something good going on.'

'Come on then,' said Grace, but she lacked what Ellie felt was the appropriate enthusiasm.

In the dining room, Ellie carefully removed the remnants of curtain still hanging and bundled them up with the rest of the fabric. Then she allowed herself to look at the painting. 'She's awfully mouldy, poor thing! I wonder how long she's been hiding behind the curtains.'

Demi giggled. 'Perhaps she was playing sardines and no one came to look for her.'

'Look, there's a hole,' said Grace. 'I wonder what did that?'

'A mouse, possibly,' said Ellie. 'But look at the details! Those wonderful flowers and animals. Look at this little rabbit!' She was ecstatic. 'I think there's probably a matching painting on the other side. I don't think this lady has been alone all these years. I think she might be Eve. See? There's the serpent. I bet you Adam is behind that curtain.'

'I'll get a chair and take the other curtain down,' said Grace.

Ellie watched as Grace slowly detached the fabric. When it was all safely in Grace's arms, Ellie saw what she was hoping to see.

'It's covered in dust and grime,' she said, gently stroking it with her finger. 'But he's there. Look.'

Adam was even more salacious-looking than Eve. His member stood proud and upright, with not a fig leaf in sight. He was leering, there was no doubt about it, and a couple of extra nymphs—certainly not present in the traditional Bible story—cavorted behind him, their hands flirtatiously over their faces.

'I didn't realise old paintings had stuff like that in them,' said Demi.

'It's antique pornography,' declared Grace, safely down from her perch.

'If it's old, it's considered art,' said Ellie. 'These paintings must have been here for years. Did your great-aunt know about them?'

'If she did, she never said anything.'

'Have you got something we could dust them with? A really soft cloth? I'd like to have a better look.'

Wishing that she could say no, Grace sighed. 'I'll go and have a rummage in the rag bag.' She didn't move.

'What is it, Grace?' Ellie asked, concerned. 'You should be thrilled. These are beautiful paintings, possibly done by an important artist.'

Grace sighed deeply. 'Yes, but you don't understand. If they're valuable, my sister and brother will want some of their value.'

'I didn't think you were serious last night. Do you really mean they'd want you to take them down and sell them?' Ellie was outraged.

Grace nodded. 'Everything that wasn't nailed down, they inherited. I got the house, so obviously my inheritance was much more valuable than theirs was. They can't get past that. If they knew I had two valuable old paintings . . .'

'Well, there's no reason your brother and sister would find out about them, is there?' said Ellie. 'How often do they visit?'

Grace sighed again. 'Not all that often, but my sister is on my case at the moment. She thinks that now the roof's been repaired, I should sell the house. She can't believe I'm happy to live here on my own.'

'But you're not on your own,' said Demi. 'You've got us.'

'Yes,' said Grace, 'and that's not going to please her either.'

Ellie was beginning to feel frustrated by Grace's lack of enthusiasm. 'Let's get a cloth and get rid of some of this dust! We can sort out the stuff about your brother and sister later.'

Very gently, Ellie stroked the cloth downwards over Adam's delicately painted pectorals. 'I'm not sure I should be doing this.'

'Then don't. Let's go and do the washing-up,' suggested Grace.

'I think you should get an expert in.'

'I can't afford to do that,' Grace stated.

'It would cost loads,' agreed Demi, and yawned. 'Where's the telly, Grace?'

'There isn't one. Sorry.'

Ellie frowned. 'Why not? Don't you like telly?'

Grace shrugged. 'It made me feel lonely.'

Feeling that this question was now settled, Ellie changed the subject back to her most pressing concern. 'So, what shall we do about the paintings?'

'Nothing,' said Grace firmly.

'They will need to have *something* done to them,' said Ellie, 'just to stop them deteriorating further.'

'I'll get some new curtains for them to hide behind,' said Grace, opening the dining-room door in a way which suggested the others went through it. 'And I'll have a think. But there's no way I'd let a picture restorer in here. If they need attention, you'll have to do the job, Ellie.'

The following morning Grace abandoned Demi and Ellie to their own devices and went into town. She wanted to buy the local paper, which should have run her article by now.

She was also worrying. Demi's education could not be ignored for much longer, and the nearest market town lacked a sixth-form college. To cheer herself up, she called in at the wine shop.

The wine-shop man was pleased to see her. 'Grace! How nice to see you! I've had very good reports of how your wine-tasting went!'

Grace, feeling disadvantaged because she didn't know this man's first name, and had been unaware that he knew hers, said, 'Oh, so you did send a spy.' She thought of Flynn.

The man made a gesture which was only nearly apologetic. 'Well, Flynn's very knowledgeable and I had to check you out if I was going to tell other wine merchants about you.'

'Oh, are you going to do that? In that case, I'll forgive you for the spy!'

'Flynn was very impressed by *your* knowledge. Now, what are you going to do next time?' asked the wine merchant, whose name Grace realised she must discover in record time. 'What about English wines? I have contacts with a vineyard.'

'Why don't you give me your card?' Grace felt this was a masterstroke. 'Then I can get in touch if anyone wants an article on English wine.'

When the card was handed over, and Grace had glanced at it, she went on, 'I'm thinking of doing New World whites. Could you let me have a discount . . . Graham?'

'Tell you what, I'll supply the wine for nothing, as long as you give me a good plug.'

Grace wandered over to a shelf of New World reds. 'I could say how helpful you'd been, and what a marvellous range of wine you supply, but I absolutely cannot recommend your wines above other people's unless they really are better.'

Graham grinned. 'I'd better send you a really good selection then.' He came out from behind the counter and picked up a machine for sticking on prices. 'We're in a wealthy part of the world, Grace. Lots of the weekenders like a really decent bottle to offer their friends.'

'Yes, but they don't read the local paper!'

'They may not, but I've got a friend who writes articles on food for one of those glossies. He said their wine columnist had packed it in. Want me to put in a word for you?'

'Graham! That would be great! That's just what I need.'

While Grace was out, and Demi was rearranging her room, Ellie cleared up the breakfast things and then cleaned the cooker. Only when the kitchen was looking as pretty as possible, with a few fronds of forsythia, the yellow buds still completely closed, in a jug on the table, did she allow herself to go and look at the paintings again.

They were so beautiful in the morning light, but their condition was worrying. Grace might want them out of sight behind their tattered silk robes but even if they were never on show, they ought to be restored. Her words—'you'll have to do the job'—still lingered in Ellie's mind.

She shook her head. An amateur picture restorer could ruin something that had been beautiful for centuries. Her History of Art tutor's strictures about the 'almost criminal over-restoration' of the Sistine Chapel still rang in her ears. Remembering her tutor now gave her the thought that he might know of a picture restorer. Ellie made a decision. She would go back to her college and track down Mr McFadden.

Grace got back from town a couple of hours after Ellie had left. She went in through the back door and saw the note in the kitchen: *I've gone to Bath to track down my History of Art tutor. Oh, and your sister rang. Can you ring her back? It's urgent.*

Demi ambled in. She was wearing a dressing gown and her head was wrapped in a towel.

'Hi, Grace. I've just been putting some streaks in my hair.'

'Oh. Right.' Grace tried to appear positive. 'I look forward to seeing it when it's dry. Now I've got to ring my sister.'

'Oh, pooh,' said Demi sympathetically. 'I'll leave you to it.'

'Thanks,' said Grace with a laugh, and then pulled a chair near to the telephone and settled down for a long harangue.

'I'm sorry,' the university secretary explained. 'It's more than my job's worth to give out a tutor's home address to a student.'

'I'm not a student here any more. I left a while ago.'

'Even worse.' Then the woman softened. 'What do you want him for?'

'I need a picture restorer. I thought he might know of one.'

'Well, have you tried the Yellow Pages?' The woman produced a ragged copy. 'It's always worth a look.'

'You're a genius,' said Ellie. 'Why didn't I think of that!'

Once she had found the right section, Ellie jotted down the names and numbers of several picture restorers. When she had eventually found somewhere in the college that was both quiet and had good reception, she looked at the list. It was sort of embarrassing, ringing to pick the brains of someone who'd trained and practised for years, just so she could try her hand at what they did for a living.

And she couldn't even say why she was doing it, because Grace's insistence on secrecy forbade that. She would just have to think of something else. Seeing a group of students walk by and hearing a snatch of their conversation gave her the answer.

'Hello,' she said to the up-market-sounding person who answered the telephone at the first number. 'I'm an art student and I need to study a few basic techniques about picture restoration. Would it be—'

'We don't have time to talk to students. Sorry.'

When the next two numbers produced similarly negative results, Ellie changed her tack. 'Hi, I'm an art student looking for a work placement for two weeks. You don't have to pay me and I'll do anything.'

There was a long silence, then a sigh. 'Well, my storage space needs clearing out. Will you do that?'

'Yes, as long as I have the opportunity to get some idea of how to restore pictures.'

'Why? Are you thinking of going into the business?'

'It's an option,' said Ellie, who'd had lots of opportunity to think of the reply to this question. 'It's very difficult to earn a living in fine art.'

'Hmph. I don't think of what I do as second fiddle to pickling sheep.' God! The man did sound hostile! 'What I do is an art and a science.'

'I'm sure it is,' said Ellie. 'Which is why I want to study it.'

There was another grunt. 'Well, you'd better come over and I'll have a look at you. You'd better come now. I'm busy later.'

'Oh, good. Where are you?'

There followed a stressful few moments, during which Ellie had to write down the myriad directions he gave her, but at last she said, 'I'll be there in an hour, then.'

'*An hour?* It's only twenty minutes away, for God's sake!'

As she walked back to the car park, Ellie seriously considered abandoning the hostile picture restorer, but by the time she reached her 2CV she had decided she'd better pitch up, even if it was a waste of time.

She got there in thirty-five minutes, which she felt was pretty good, considering the complications of Bath's one-way system and the narrowness of the streets. Even more extraordinary was the fact she managed to find somewhere to park nearby.

She knocked on the door of one of Bath's huge Georgian houses, most of which were divided into flats. The man who opened the door was surprisingly clean. For some reason Ellie had thought he would look like an artist: streaked with paint. He was tall and thin with black hair streaked with grey, and he still appeared hostile. It might have taken Ellie thirty-five minutes to get there, but that hadn't been long enough for him to become welcoming and pleasant. 'You've come to do work experience?'

'No!' Ellie put her hand in his. She smiled, making sure she captured his attention with her eyes. 'I'm Ellie Summers. I'm offering my services to you as unpaid labour. Work experience is what you do at school.'

Her silent insistence that she was offering something no sane man would refuse made him smile. It was a very attractive smile.

He shook her hand. 'Randolph Frazier. Sorry, you look about seventeen. You'd better come in. Coffee?'

'I'd rather have tea.'

'Come through, then.'

The flat was a huge, loft-like space. Natural light flooded in through the tall windows and she realised that he must have knocked out every wall in the place, and had possibly extended into next door.

Ellie was accustomed to being in artists' studios: cluttered spaces, their floors, walls and doors covered in paint. The space she was led through to, where a small kitchen lurked under a window, was immaculately clean and tidy. A couple of easels stood with paintings on them.

'Wow,' said Ellie, drawn to one of the easels. It was a picture of a St Bernard dog. She went close up to it and peered at the beautifully painted fur, the softness and nobility of expression in the huge dog's eyes, the brightness of the brass ring in the collar. 'That's really lovely.'

'A touch sentimental for my personal taste,' said the man, who had presumably restored it. 'It was quite badly torn and some of the paint was flaking. The frame was in a bad condition too.'

Ellie peered closer. 'Where was the tear?'

'Can't you see?'

'No.'

'Try these.' He handed her a pair of magnifying glasses with lights in them. 'Right. Look over there.'

'I can just see something,' said Ellie after a few moments' staring.

She straightened up and handed back the glasses. He wasn't good-looking in the way that Rick was, but he had an arresting quality.

'So why do you want to get involved with picture restoration?' he asked, walking across to the kitchen.

'I got my creative art degree and want to use it, but I also want to earn money.'

'You don't need a fine art or even a creative art background to be a picture restorer. A degree in chemistry would be more useful.'

This was a rather dampening statement. 'Oh.'

'I mean,' Randolph Frazier went on, 'if you're going to do it remotely seriously you'd have to do a course at somewhere like Newcastle. It's for two years and they won't let you in without a science A level.'

'There aren't any shorter courses you could do without the A level?'

He didn't deign to answer this. 'If you're going to do it, do it properly. How do you like your tea?'

Ellie sighed. This whole idea was probably a complete waste of time, but perhaps if she could get him chatting over the tea mugs he might inadvertently give her a few hints. 'Just a drop of milk, no sugar, thank you. So how did you get into picture restoration, then?'

'I left school at sixteen and wanted to work in the summer holidays before going to college. I applied for a job—someone wanting just what I was, a completely untrained school-leaver—and got it. I wasn't allowed near a painting for months, but by that time I'd given up the notion of university and knew what I wanted to do with my life. But it's not something you can learn in five minutes, you know.'

Ellie looked into her mug to hide her disappointment. 'Well, of course,

I didn't think you could. How do you start on a painting? Dust it?'

His horror made her blush. 'Certainly not! Supposing there was some loose paint?'

Ellie blushed harder. There definitely was loose paint on those panels. 'You mean dusting it would damage it in some way?'

'Of course! You'd lose paint for ever.' He frowned. 'Why are you looking so guilty? You've gone bright red.'

'I'm not! I mean, I haven't!' If only she could tell him about the panels, but she supposed he was the very last person who should know. He was bound to tell some higher authority. 'I'm pregnant,' she added as a diversion. It seemed to work.

'Oh, I see. I suppose that does explain your somewhat shifty manner. Not married, I assume?'

'I don't know how you can possibly tell that!' she protested.

'You're not wearing a ring, and you wouldn't be doing this if you had a husband to help support you. Are you really an art student?'

The bloody man could obviously read her like a book! 'I graduated nearly four years ago, actually.'

His eyebrows went up. 'So you're older than you look. Well, you're welcome to work for me for nothing, for a fortnight.'

'But it won't really be just cleaning out your cellar, will it? What I'm really after is some sort of training. Like an apprenticeship.'

'Apprenticeships last approximately seven years. And there's something you're not telling me.'

Ellie sighed. 'There is. Unfortunately, I can't tell you.'

He stared at her for what seemed like for ever. Then he slowly nodded. 'Very well, then. You clean out my cellar and I'll tell you about what I do. It is a fascinating subject.'

He smiled again, just very slightly, and Ellie suppressed a sigh. He's far too old to think about having an affaire with, she told herself as she went down the steps to the pavement. Now concentrate!

While Ellie was hunting out someone to help her with the picture restoration, Grace was telephoning her sister.

'Oh,' said Allegra, 'I'm glad you've rung back. The thing is, I think I should come round and see you. I've got this report. From the man who came round and inspected the house. It's awfully bad news, I'm afraid.'

Grace was determined not to let Allegra hear her heart sink. 'Well, couldn't you just send me a copy of the report?'

'I don't trust you to read it at all!' Allegra went on. 'You know what you're like about that wretched house. You refuse to see its faults.'

'I don't think that's true. Did I tell you someone's given me a Rayburn? It should make a vast difference to the kitchen.'

A moment's silence while Allegra considered. 'I think that's a good idea. A range always adds a homely touch and some people might be put off if the house seems too chilly.'

'Sorry?'

'Grace, I know you're not going to like it, but when you read this report, and find out how much money it's going to take to put it all right, you'll realise you're going to have to sell. But don't worry,' Allegra added. 'There will be plenty of money for you to buy something really sweet with your share of what's left.'

Grace suppressed a sigh. 'Allegra, what makes you think I'm going to want to sell the house this time? I haven't before when you've asked me.'

'Because you won't be able to afford to pay for the dry-rot treatment.'

Dry rot. Those words did create a bit of a sense of doom. 'Oh. So how much is it?'

'I don't want to discuss it now. The thing is, you're never going to be able to raise the cash to have it done. So I can pay, and then you can pay me back when you've sold the house.'

'I could probably take out a loan. The house isn't mortgaged, after all.'

'If you do that, you'll be paying the loan back for the rest of your life!'

'But as I'll also be living in my house for the rest of my life, that won't matter,' said Grace sweetly.

'Don't be silly. I can come over now, or tomorrow night.'

Grace needed time to think. 'I've got to go and do something with Demi now.' She crossed her fingers in the hope that it would prevent Allegra asking her what.

It worked. Her question was more *who*. 'Demi? Your ex-stepdaughter?'

'Oh, didn't I mention it? Demi's come to live with me for a bit.'

'For God's sake, why? You can't look after a teenager on your own!'

'I'm not on my own. I've got Ellie to help me.'

'Who's Ellie?' Allegra's sharp tone made Grace wince.

'Oh, didn't I tell you about her? She's another lodger.'

'It sounds as if you're turning the place into a dosshouse!'

'Honestly, Allegra, why you should object to me having a couple of people to live with me—women, both of them—when you've been saying ever since Edward left that it is ridiculous me living here alone . . .'

'It's not the same! Having lodgers—'

'Demi is my stepdaughter—'

'Not any more.'

'—and Ellie is my friend. Now I do wish you'd keep your nose out of my business!' Allegra obviously had far too much time on her hands. 'Tell me how much the dry rot will cost and I'll pay!'

'Very well, then, thirty thousand pounds!'

'Oh my God,' breathed Grace, unable to feign indifference to mere money any more. 'How much? How can it possibly cost all that?'

Allegra's anger turned to sympathy. 'That's why I wanted to come and tell you in person. I knew it would be a shock.'

Grace gave in. 'I suppose you'd better come over then—come tomorrow evening, for supper at about eight.'

It was only after she'd put the phone down that she took in the fact that she'd invited her sister for a meal. What had she been thinking of?

When Ellie returned, she was bubbling with excitement. 'I've had such a good day! I went to Bath to try to get in touch with my old tutor—'

'Did you do it?' asked Demi, who was bored.

'No, but I did get in touch with this ace picture restorer.'

'You didn't tell him about the paintings?' asked Grace, who had not had a good day and was inclined to panic.

'No! I just got him to agree to have me on a work placement.'

'What does that mean?' asked Demi.

'Working for nothing,' Ellie said, sinking onto a chair.

'And you're doing it for my paintings. You're a star,' said Grace.

'Grace's sister is coming for supper tomorrow,' said Demi. 'I've met her. She's really scary.'

'Is she? Oh, Grace! Did she invite herself?'

'No, I invited her, but she'd said she had to see me. I didn't have much choice.'

'And what are you going to give her to eat?' Ellie asked, knowing Grace didn't really do cooking.

'I don't know. A joint, perhaps?'

Demi giggled. 'You're going to give your sister marijuana for dinner?'

Grace made a cross face at Demi. 'Which is easier, do you think? Beef, lamb or pork?'

'Quite honestly, they're all about the same and I don't recommend doing a joint,' said Ellie. 'Would you like me to cook the meal?'

'Oh, Ellie!' Grace hugged her. 'That would be brilliant!'

'But you'll have to go shopping tomorrow. I want to read some art books, so I don't look a complete idiot when I go back to the picture restorer's the day after tomorrow.'

'Of course! I'll have to buy some curtains, too,' she added, thinking aloud. 'Allegra's got the report that young man did on the house and she wants to discuss it. She might want to look round everywhere.'

'Then we'd better pin the old curtains up again,' said Ellie. 'She's bound to notice new ones. Especially if you buy them off the peg.'

'I was thinking of the charity shops or junk shops,' said Grace.

The tune of 'Jingle Bells' issuing from her shopping bag made Grace jump. Then she remembered that she'd borrowed Ellie's mobile and it was probably her, adding to the shopping list that Grace was now working her way through. She retrieved it. 'Hello?'

'Hello.'

It was Flynn. It was so strange hearing his voice in the supermarket that Grace felt herself blush.

'Demi gave me your mobile number. I've got a case of wine here for you, and she thought you might like to collect it on your way home.'

'Oh. Why have you got it?'

'It's from Graham in the wine shop. He sent it to the wrong address. Also, I wondered if I could come round and make a start on putting in the Rayburn soon. Possibly tonight? I'm going away and I want to get it done before I go.'

With part of her mind Grace was studying a packet of shiitake mushrooms, but the other part was wondering if having Flynn in the house would be a good distraction for Allegra.

'Um. I've got my sister coming for supper.'

'You have a sister, have you? Is she anything like you?'

'Not at all! She's very spiky and demanding.'

'Just like you, then.'

'I am not demanding,' said Grace, acknowledging that spiky did describe her when she was near Flynn.

'Well, then, shall I come over tonight or not? I won't be able to get it plumbed in, so it won't heat the hot water, but it would heat the kitchen and you could cook on it.'

Grace felt strangely flustered. 'My sister's coming at eight.'

'If it's all right with you, I'll come at six. I might well be out of the way by eight.' He laughed. 'We don't want your sister catching you with an Irishman in the kitchen.'

Because this was a fair estimate of how Allegra might react to Flynn, she said, 'No, no. I was just thinking it would be nice if you could stay for supper. Ellie's got a lovely meal planned.'

'Oh.'

'Well, make up your mind!' She didn't want to appear too keen. 'I'm in town now and if Ellie needs more ingredients, I'll have to get them!'

'You do have a way of making a man feel wanted.'

'I'm sorry! The supermarket isn't where I usually arrange my social life.'

'Social life, is it?' She could hear him smiling. 'I've been promoted.'

'For goodness' sake!' She felt herself blushing. 'Are you coming or not?'

'Thank you. Don't bother about calling in for the wine. I'll be there at six and I'll bring this case with me. Though it doesn't look as if there's anything drinkable in it. I'd better bring something decent myself.'

'I have plenty of wine, thank you!' said Grace and disconnected. What was it about that man? She was as meek as milk with every other human on the planet, but with Flynn Cormack she was a cow.

Grace's first thought when she turned back into the drive was that Ellie's little 2CV had been turned into two, much larger, newer cars. Then she realised that the inevitable visit from Hermia and Edward had finally happened and that Ellie was out. Grace hoped that Demi was with her.

Hermia and Edward were waiting beside their cars, their arms folded. When Grace had parked, she turned round to the back seat, ostensibly to gather up the carrier bags, in fact giving herself time to collect herself. She reminded herself that she was actually doing them both a huge favour. By the time she finally emerged from the car she was feeling positively belligerent.

'Hello, you two'—they would hate being lumped together like that—'have you been here long?'

'Fifteen minutes,' snapped Hermia. 'Where have you been?'

Tempted to answer 'the opera', Grace ignored this and carried her bags to the front door, dropped them, then fished in her bag for the key.

'Where's Demeter?' asked Edward, more pertinently.

'I'm not sure,' said Grace. 'I expect she's with Ellie—my friend—and they will have left a note. If you could just give me a hand with the bags?'

Reluctantly, Hermia and Edward helped Grace get the bags into the house and then followed her to the kitchen.

'Ah, yes. Here's the note,' said Grace, heartily relieved that there was one. '"Ellie and I have gone shopping for hair stuff, back soon",' she read.

Don't get back too soon, Demi, thought Grace, putting the perishables in the fridge, if you don't want your parents to see what you've done to your hair. She ignored the rest of the shopping—one advantage to having a cold house—and put the kettle on.

'I'm just going to make you comfortable in the drawing room,' she said. She had chivvied them as far as the hall when the doorbell rang. It was Ellie and Demi. As Grace opened the door, she wondered how much persuasion it had taken Ellie to get Demi out of the car; she must have freaked when she saw not just one parent's car, but two.

'Demeter!' shrieked Hermia. 'What have you done to your hair?'

'Hello, Mummy,' said Demi.

'Hello, darling,' said Edward, embracing his daughter.

'This is Ellie,' said Grace to Edward and Hermia. 'She's living here. Ellie, this is Edward and Hermia.'

'Hello,' said Ellie. 'Would you like me to go and make some coffee?' she said to Grace.

'That would be terribly kind,' said Grace, who seemed to Ellie to be coping quite well.

'I'll help!' said Demi.

Grace was about to forbid this when Ellie said, 'You'll need more chairs. Demi can help me bring them.'

'We don't want coffee!' snapped Hermia. 'I just want my daughter back!'

'Let's have coffee while we discuss it,' said Grace, opening the door of the drawing room, pleased to see how much early spring sunshine filled it, although it was still very cold.

'If you think I'm going to discuss my daughter with you'—Hermia almost spat out the words—'you are very much mistaken!'

'No need to be rude,' said Edward. 'Grace has made a very sensible suggestion.'

He always did stick up for me, thought Grace.

Hermia shivered loudly as they entered. Ignoring her, Grace said, 'I'll just go and tell Ellie there are biscuits among the shopping and then fetch something to sit on,' she said. 'Would either of you prefer tea?'

'No. Coffee, please,' snapped Hermia.

'Me too,' said Edward. 'Hermia, shall we go into the window embrasure? There's a wonderful view of the garden from there.'

'I daren't leave them in there alone for long,' said Grace in the kitchen. 'Come with me, Demi, and bring a chair.'

'No! Please, Grace! I'll bring the coffee and as many chairs as you want, but please don't make me go in there a minute before I have to!'

Looking at Demi's worried face, Grace took pity on her and returned to the drawing room alone, a chair in each hand, just in time to hear Hermia say, 'It's a heavenly house! Freezing bloody cold, of course. Wasted on her! A half-decent developer and it would be worth a fortune.'

Horribly reminded of her sister, Grace wondered if Hermia and Allegra knew each other, and remembered that they did, slightly.

'The coffee will be along in a moment. Do sit down.'

Edward held a chair for Hermia and tried to do the same for Grace, but she resisted.

'So how did you meet your friend Ellie?' said Edward.

'She's an artist. I met her through her work. She's perfectly respectable.'

Hermia snorted. 'Respectable or not, Demeter's got to come home. She has her education to think of.'

'I certainly agree with you there, but I think the trouble is, she feels a bit neglected,' said Grace boldly. 'You both have new partners and Demi feels you don't have time for her.' Seeing the door handle move, she said quickly, 'Please don't mention Demi's hair again. She knows she made a horrible mistake.'

Demi and Ellie came in. Demi, looking rather pale, was carrying a tea chest and Ellie mugs. While Demi turned the tea chest over so that it became a table, Grace muttered to Ellie, 'Only four mugs! Where's yours?'

'I'm going to unpack the shopping,' said Ellie. 'You don't need me, this is a family thing.'

'Quite right,' agreed Hermia. 'You don't need to be here either, Grace.'

'Yes, she does,' said Edward with the sort of authority not even Hermia would care to argue with. 'Demi! Where are you going?'

'To get a chair, Dad! If that's all right with you?' she said defensively.

'You're to come straight back,' he ordered, and Grace realised why she had never argued with him. He was very commanding.

'Right,' he said when Demi had joined the circle and was sitting looking down at her hands. 'Let's talk this over reasonably. Hermia, is it true you have no time for Demi?'

'She gets every spare penny and every spare moment—' Hermia began.

'Except there aren't any,' interjected Demi. 'You and Tod are always chewing each other's faces off.'

Grace winced. Hermia opened her mouth to protest. Edward raised a hand and no one said anything.

'Well, would you like to come and live with Caroline and me?'

Hermia gave a mirthless laugh. 'That bitch! She won't want a teenager cluttering up the place, making her feel old!'

'Hermia—' began Edward.

Grace felt obliged to mediate. 'I think, Edward, that Demi feels that you and Caroline haven't been together long and that Caroline wouldn't really appreciate having her there.'

Edward exhaled. 'It's true that Caroline does find Demeter difficult.' He frowned at his daughter.

'I can't think why. It's not as if she wasn't properly brought up,' said Hermia. 'Even if I did have to do it single-handed.'

'Possibly her role model wasn't all it might have been,' bit out Edward from between clenched teeth.

'For goodness' sake!' Grace exploded, really angry now. 'Will you two listen to yourselves? You're talking about Demi as if she wasn't here! You're supposed to be discussing what's best for her, but all you can do is score cheap points off each other!'

Demi, who had been sitting inspecting her nails, wincing slightly as each salvo was exchanged, sat up. 'Yeah! That's right, Grace. Thank you.'

At this moment, the door opened and Ellie came in with a tray. Grace realised she must have been waiting outside for a good moment to bring it in. Ellie put the tray down on the cloth-covered tea chest. She and Grace exchanged glances.

'Are you going to join us, Ellie?' asked Grace, a little desperately.

'I won't, if you don't mind.' She looked up at Edward and Hermia and explained, 'I'm pregnant and the smell of coffee makes me nauseous.'

Hermia yawned. 'So it's a home for unmarried mothers you're operating then,' she said, loud enough for Ellie to hear.

'Hermia!' Grace glared at her. 'We are here to think what's best to do for Demi!'

'Yes,' said Edward. 'It's your education I'm concerned about, Demeter,' he said, more kindly now. 'How will you continue it here?'

'She can't stay here,' stated Hermia.

'Well, she won't go back to you,' snapped Edward.

'Of course she will. Demeter dear, you've made your statement, now go and pack your things and wait for me in the car.'

'No! I'm not going back with either of you!' shouted Demi, and she ran from the room. Grace thought she was crying.

'Now look what you've done,' said Edward drily.

'What you've both done!' said Grace. 'What I suggest,' she went on, 'is that Demi stays here. I will undertake to get her to and from her sixth-form college, but it is quite a trek.'

There was a long silence as both parents realised that Grace had offered to take on the girl that they both found so difficult.

'That is a very generous offer,' said Edward. 'But are you in a position to get Demeter to and from college?'

'I don't see why on earth not,' snapped Hermia, less inclined to be grateful than her ex-husband. 'She's got a very nice car to do it in.'

'But I will need petrol money and money for Demi's keep.'

'Well, I can't afford to pay you anything! She's got a perfectly good home with me!' Hermia got up and wandered over to the fireplace.

Edward cleared his throat. 'Very well, Grace. I will make you an allowance to keep Demeter here on the understanding that she attends college every day and works for her exams.'

'I didn't realise you had funds to spare,' said Hermia. 'I thought Caroline was high maintenance.'

'Oh, she is,' said Edward. 'Which is why I'll be transferring the money I am currently paying to you for Demeter's keep, to Grace.'

I so wish I'd been there to see Mum's face when Dad said that!' said Demi, half an hour after Grace's unwelcome guests finally left.

'I wish you'd been there, too, but you bailed out on me and left me all alone with a virago,' said Grace a little grimly. 'Although I must say, it will make a difference to our finances, getting your keep from Edward.'

Demi frowned. 'What's a virago?'

'A woman who's really, really angry. Which hardly describes her, actually. She went completely . . .'

'Mental?' suggested Ellie.

'That's it. But Edward coped, as usual. He's very good with her.'

'It's all right for him,' said Demi. 'He doesn't have to live with her.'

'And nor do you, now, thanks to Grace,' said Ellie.

'I know.' She looked up at Grace and smiled awkwardly. 'Thank you so much, Grace, you're the best. Really.'

She looked very vulnerable, and Grace suddenly remembered how young she was. 'It's a pleasure, Demi. It's good to have you here. Now, come on, let's wash up the coffee things so that Ellie can start cooking.'

'Have I really got to go to college tomorrow?' asked Demi.

'I'm afraid so.'

'Then there's an essay I should be doing . . . Oh, shit!' Demi threw her hands in the air. 'I should have asked Mum if I could have my computer!'

Grace frowned. 'It might be better to let your father handle that one.'

Chapter Four

IN BETWEEN BANGING pork fillets into next week and taking the filling out of sausages and trying to read up as much about History of Art as she could in the loo, which seemed to be the only place she didn't have to be doing anything else, Ellie helped Grace in the dining room.

'If we put this plain gold silky curtain in that gap, we can drape the original curtain beside it, and the painting won't show,' said Grace optimistically, clambering onto one of the stouter kitchen chairs. 'Hand me the hammer, Dem. I think that's the best match, don't you, Ellie?'

'The curtain is fine, just don't bang nails into the panels! Can't you drag the original one along a bit?'

'I'll do my best.' Grace tugged at the tattered silk of the original curtain, which they had just put back in place. A few bangs, a bit of falling plaster, and the two paintings were more or less concealed again. Ellie rushed back to the kitchen, leaving Grace and Demi to finish.

'That should do it,' said Grace. 'But if I light the fire in the drawing room and make it cosy, Allegra won't be keen to come out into the cold.'

'I thought she was coming to discuss some report she had. She's bound to want to see the rest of the house.'

'Demi, your logic is faultless, your tact is not! I'm in denial here. Please don't make me come out of it.'

Demi laughed. 'You are funny, Grace. You never used to make me laugh before, when you were with Dad.'

'Didn't I? I'm not sure I mean to be funny now. Oh, well, Flynn will be here soon, spreading himself all over the kitchen, Dems. You'd better get started on that essay.'

Demi sighed. 'Oh, pooh! I wish I'd never told you about it. I can't do it at all without the computer.'

'Nonsense. You can make a plan, write notes and then type it up at college. I'll tell you what, if you make a good start, I'll ring Edward and ask him to tell your mother that you need your computer urgently. And your television. Deal?'

'Suppose so.'

Flynn arrived just as Grace had finished checking things in the drawing room. She opened the door to him and suddenly felt shy, remembering how sharp she'd been on the phone to him when he'd rung her at the supermarket. 'Hi.'

'Hi, yourself,' he replied, regarding her quizzically. 'You've lost your spikes.'

'No, I haven't!' she replied, smiling despite herself. 'Do you want to bring your stuff in this way? Or shall I unlock the back door?'

'The back door is traditionally the servants' entrance,' he replied.

'Oh, pooh,' said Grace, aware that living with Demi had influenced her language.

He leaned forward and brushed her cheek with his lips. 'Go on then, Lady Chatterley, unlock the back door.'

She blushed all the way to the kitchen, glad he wasn't there to see her.

'Hello, Allegra,' said Grace, kissing her sister on the cheek. She realised, rather to her surprise, that she was quite pleased to see her and only wished Allegra wasn't carrying a briefcase. 'Let me take your coat. No, I expect you'd like to keep it on.'

'It is only February,' said Allegra, returning the kiss.

'Well, come into the drawing room. I've lit the fire in there.'

In fact, Grace was quite proud of the drawing room. Ellie, with her artist's eye and talent for homemaking, had put branches of newly unfurling leaves in a bucket in the window embrasure. She had up-lit it with her bedside lamp and the branches cast shadows on the wall. The stone mantelpiece was lit with candles on odd saucers found in a box in the old tack room, and the most comfortable kitchen chairs, made inviting by well-plumped cushions, had been drawn up next to the fire.

Allegra allowed herself to be ushered into it. 'But, darling!' she cried. 'Where's all your furniture?'

'It was Edward's,' Grace replied a little stiffly. 'It was only right he should take it. And, as you keep reminding me, he made me a generous settlement; I had the roof fixed and bought a car, and have got enough left to keep me going for a while.'

Allegra put her briefcase down on the floor and sat as near to the fire as she could get without singeing herself. 'I had no idea,' she muttered. 'I suppose that time I came just after he'd gone, we sat in the kitchen.'

Thinking of the chaos in the kitchen now, Grace was relieved that Allegra wouldn't be near it until it was a little more organised.

'Let me get you a glass of wine, then you must meet Ellie, who's living with me, and Demi, of course. Oh, and Flynn,' she added.

'Who's Flynn?' demanded Allegra.

'Wine first, Legs, then you can meet everyone.'

Grace took a bottle of wine and a couple of glasses from the boxes under the stairs and then popped into the kitchen, which was warm and full of bustle and delicious cooking smells. 'You lot have got to come and meet my sister.'

'I can't leave the sauce just at the moment,' said Ellie, stirring madly.

'My essay! I do have to do it, you know!' said Demi.

'What's your excuse?' Grace demanded of Flynn, who was observing the scene with quiet amusement.

'I need to wash my hands and take off my boiler suit,' he said gravely.

'Oh, yes,' Grace acknowledged. 'But you're to come in as soon as you can. Demi, you can come now.' She was nearly out of the door before she turned and said, 'The Rayburn is going to be great, Flynn.'

'Oh God, I'm so nervous!' said Demi as they hurried across the hall.

'There's no need. She won't bully you. Now be a love and open the door . . . Allegra, you remember my stepdaughter, Demi, don't you?'

'Yes, we met at the wedding,' said Allegra, acknowledging Demi with a small smile.

Grace put the wine and glasses down on the tea chest. 'Have a glass of this. I think you'll like it.'

'May I have some wine?' asked Demi.

As Grace wanted Ellie and Flynn prised out of the kitchen, she said, 'Of course. Go and get a glass and find out what Ellie and Flynn are up to.'

'So who is Flynn?' asked Allegra when Demi had gone.

'He's a friend,' said Grace. 'What do you think of the wine?'

'Very nice,' said Allegra. 'Now let me tell you about this report. Oh—'

Ellie came into the drawing room, followed by Flynn. She was wearing an apron over her jeans and her hair was wrapped up in a bandanna. A brooch, consisting of a bunch of bananas, decorated her sweater, and there were matching bunches dangling from her ears.

'Allegra, this is Ellie Summers, who's agreed to live here for a bit.'

Ellie offered her hand. 'It's so kind of Grace to let me stay.'

Allegra gave a polite smile and waited for Flynn to be introduced. 'This is Flynn Cormack. My sister, Allegra Statherton-Crawley.'

'How do you do,' said Flynn, taking Allegra's barely offered hand.

Allegra's smile didn't move; she was confused as to Flynn's status. He wasn't wearing a suit, but he obviously wasn't a workman, either.

'Demi's just finishing her essay,' said Ellie. 'And keeping an eye on the potatoes. We don't want overcooked vegetables, do we?'

Ellie had brought more glasses with her and Flynn, to Grace's gratitude, poured more wine for Allegra and Grace and some elderflower pressé for Ellie. When he had poured himself a glass of wine, Allegra turned to him.

'So what is it you do, exactly?'

'Oh, you'll approve of him,' said Grace. 'He's a property developer.'

Allegra turned to her sister. 'Grace! Have you seen sense at last?'

'We're just friends,' said Flynn. 'We both have an interest in wine.'

'Pity. There are probably millions tied up in this property. There's a lot of land, you know,' said Allegra.

'I do know,' said Flynn. 'But you'd never get planning permission for anything out here.'

'So, Allegra,' asked Grace, grateful to Flynn for slipping in this useful information. 'Tell me about the report, then.'

'I'd rather wait until we're alone, Grace. In fact, I had no idea you intended to have a dinner party as such. I thought we were going to have a working supper.'

'It is a working supper,' said Grace. 'Flynn's been working.'

'And so have I,' said Ellie. 'Well, cooking anyway.'

'And there's nothing you can't say in front of my friends,' said Grace. She gave Flynn a quick, furtive smile and realised that for the first time she did think of him as a friend.

Ellie, glad of an excuse to retreat to the kitchen, got to her feet. 'Well, I must go and see to my sauce and set the table.'

'Don't go!' Grace pleaded.

'I have to. I can't trust Demi not to let the broccoli turn to mush.'

'I don't understand why that child isn't living with one of her parents,' said Allegra. 'And isn't her name Demeter?'

Grace regarded her sister. 'Tell me about the report, Allegra, please.' Allegra glanced at Flynn who immediately got to his feet. 'You don't have to go, really,' said Grace, feeling more abandoned by the moment.

'I do,' said Flynn. 'I still haven't cleared up all my tools. We don't want Ellie tripping over them.'

'Alone at last!' said Allegra. 'Now, as I told you, it'll cost thirty grand to fix the dry rot, and you told me you don't have that amount.'

Grace shook her head slowly.

'Then you'll have to sell. I'll lend you the money and you can pay me back when you sell. As well as giving me and Nick our share, of course.'

'Are you willing to sue me for what you describe as your share?' asked Grace softly.

Allegra nodded. 'Of course we would hate it to come to that, but Nick and I feel that it's perfectly possible that the courts would agree that the aunt was not in her sound mind when she made her will.'

Grace sighed. 'Have some more wine, Allegra,' she said. She felt infinitely tired and infinitely depressed.

'Well, this is very nice,' said Allegra, seated at the head of the table with Flynn on her right-hand side. 'Although as you know I was hoping to get an opportunity to talk to Grace on her own.'

'There's nothing private about dry rot,' said Grace.

'It is a terrible nuisance,' said Flynn. 'It can get everywhere.'

'Does the report say whereabouts in the house it is?' asked Grace.

'Of course! It's mostly upstairs, on the west side.'

'Oh,' said Grace after a moment and glanced at Ellie, confirming what Ellie had just worked out: that the dining room was on the west side.

'What would happen if you didn't do anything about it?' asked Ellie, knowing Grace couldn't ask but might want to know.

'It would spread,' said Flynn, 'and that would be a tragedy.'

'Just what I was saying to Grace,' said Allegra, swooping a piece of pork round her plate to catch the last of the creamy sauce.

'Would anyone like any more?' said Ellie. 'Or shall we move on to apple crumble. And cream,' she added.

'You cook awfully well for an art student,' said Allegra.

'I've graduated, actually,' said Ellie. 'But I learned to cook during my gap year, when I had a job in France as an au pair.'

'We tried to encourage Grace to do a cookery course when she refused to do A levels, but she would insist on doing that wine thing.' Allegra drained her glass. 'If you hadn't done that, you wouldn't have met Edward, which would have saved everyone a great deal of trouble.'

'Would anyone like some water, to clear the palate?' asked Flynn, proving to Ellie that he could be tactful as well as kind.

'Actually, I think that would be a good idea,' said Allegra.

It turned out that Allegra had booked herself into a hotel in the nearest town. Flynn offered to take her there, and as Ellie had been thinking that she would offer to do this, she mentally hugged him. When Grace nodded her head at the door, and Ellie took it that she'd been sent to bed, she was so grateful she could have cried. She was so tired it was all she could do to summon up the energy to brush her teeth.

Grace returned to the kitchen, determined that Ellie wouldn't find a single dirty glass or plate when she came down in the morning. She was waiting for the kettle to boil for the third time, when she heard the front doorbell give a single jangle. It was one o'clock in the morning and she was cautious, but not frightened to open it. It was Flynn.

'You haven't brought Allegra back?' she said anxiously as she saw his figure outlined by moonlight. 'Or did you forget something?'

'In a manner of speaking. May I come in for a moment?'

Grace stood back to let him into the house. 'Can I make you a cup of tea or anything?' she said when they reached the kitchen.

'That would be nice,' said Flynn. 'I realised that I hadn't had the opportunity to show you how to keep the Rayburn going. This silver wheel is the draught. When you come down in the morning, open that right up, or even open that door, and put on some dry sticks, dried orange peel, a bit of a cardboard box, stuff like that. When the fire is going really well, or the kettle's boiled, you can put on some bigger logs and turn the draught down a bit. OK?'

'Fine,' said Grace. 'I'm extremely grateful.'

'If you're really that grateful,' he said, smiling at her, 'there's a favour you could do for me. I need you to feed my cat.'

Grace frowned. 'You have a cat?'

'I do indeed. A Siamese. And, as I told you, I'm going away and there won't be anyone in the house to feed her. I was wondering if you'd do it.'

'Of course I'll do it. Can I come over later to see what I have to do? If you give me directions to your house—'

'Could you come over at lunchtime? Or will Allegra still be with you?'

'I don't know.' Grace was too tired to keep the desperation out of her voice. She wasn't looking forward to seeing Allegra again.

'I'm going at two, so perhaps I'd better give you instructions about the burglar alarm now.'

'What about keys?'

'I went home and got them.' He raised his eyebrows and almost smiled. 'I presumed on your good nature.'

She laughed. 'Rash, considering how my good nature seems to keep itself to itself when you're around.'

The tension between them eased, but not entirely. Grace couldn't quite relax with him. 'Tell me about your alarm system then, and what your cat eats.'

'I'd better write it down.'

Grace found a piece of paper and he wrote a long list of instructions on how to get into the house. The cat feeding bit was just a line at the end of what could have been the plan for a major military operation.

'Try to come to my house before two,' he said. 'It would be easier if I could actually show you what to do.'

'And your house is . . .?'

Flynn turned back to the piece of paper and drew a map on it for her. 'Now, don't lose this bit of paper. It's got instructions on how to get to my house and how to disable the alarm when you get there.'

'Not to mention which flavour of Kittikins your cat likes. Highly explosive information,' she teased.

'In the wrong hands, it could be,' he said, his voice not quite as serious as his expression.

When Grace finally shut the door behind him and pulled the bolt she was aware of a sense of loss. It must be because he was large and left an equally large space behind him.

Everyone got up far too early that morning, in spite of going to bed so late: they were all so worried about oversleeping. Grace had to get Demi to college, and Ellie had to get herself to Bath by ten o'clock.

Ellie set off in her car to Randolph Frazier's wondering how on earth she and Grace would find £30,000 before the house fell down or the pictures fell apart. Several moneymaking projects had been discussed at breakfast, and most of them dismissed.

'I could sell the car,' Grace had said. 'It would be a start.'

'I think you should concentrate on beefing up the wine-tastings, and having food with them,' Ellie had suggested. 'You could charge thirty or forty pounds a head. You'll get the wine for nothing.'

'You're hardly going to make thirty grand doing that,' said Demi. 'At least, not for years.'

'But it would be a regular income.'

'I've been thinking,' said Grace, 'that I could just sell the paintings as they are. Would they fetch thirty grand, do you think?'

Ellie gasped. 'Grace, they could be worth an absolute fortune! They've got to be restored and then valued, at least then you'll get a proper return for them.'

Grace sighed. 'But I need the money *now*!'

Ellie was desperate. 'We'll raise the thirty grand, I promise you, but we must—*you* must not sell the paintings until they're back to their full glory. Apply for a grant or something.'

'But if anyone got to hear about the paintings, and they were actually valuable, the grant would have to go on insurance. I'd have to have a burglar alarm, like Flynn.' She smiled at the recollection of his late-night visit. 'He called round last night after he'd driven Allegra to her hotel. Asked me if I could feed his cat for a bit.'

'Hasn't he got any friends he could ask?' said Demi.

'I *am* a friend,' said Grace.

'I think he just wants to keep in touch,' said Ellie teasingly.

Grace laughed at the notion; it was about as funny as the thought of the virtually empty Luckenham House having a security system.

'But going back to the grant thing, Grace, let me get some tips and wrinkles from this picture restorer. Those paintings are probably a national treasure or something.'

The fact that Ellie managed to find a parking space relatively nearby was a good omen, and the fact that Randolph Frazier had remembered to expect her was another. But, as he ushered her down into a cellar, which had obviously never been used for anything more artistic than storing bottles of chemicals and bits of timber, she realised that extracting the 'tips and wrinkles' might be harder than she had anticipated. She'd have to get him talking in her coffee break, if he let her have one.

'You're getting a lot of work out of me for nothing, Randolph,' Ellie said a couple of hours later, when she was filthy and tired, but the cellar was clear apart from about twenty black sacks of rubbish.

'Call me Ran,' he said, watching her as she cleaned herself up at the kitchen sink.

Ellie was tempted to call him something much less polite, but she needed him more than he needed her. She also needed lunch.

'Ran, then. I mean, I'm supposed to be getting work experience—in picture restoration,' she added hurriedly. 'But I could go out for sandwiches first, if you like.'

'Oh, yes, that would be a good idea. There's a little shop at the bottom of the hill. I'll have egg mayonnaise. Here's some money. I don't expect you to pay for your own lunch,' he added.

Grateful for small mercies, Ellie took the note he handed her.

When she got back she found him upstairs in the studio. There was a picture of a battle scene—men wearing antiquated military uniforms—on an easel and as she came in he licked the end of what looked like a kebab skewer and dipped it into a roll of cotton wool. Then he took up a wisp and rolled it round, producing what looked like a doll's-house-sized stick of candy floss.

'Homemade cotton bud,' he explained. Then he licked it again. 'Spit is always the first thing you try. It's got enzymes in it.'

He rubbed at a tiny corner of the painting, changing the cotton wool several times, inspecting what was on the cotton wool intently. 'We start on the weakest chemical we can get away with.'

'Couldn't you just reproduce the enzymes and save yourself all that spitting?'

He shook his head. 'I was working at a major picture gallery, years ago, when an American came over. He thought the same as you. Got a chemist to work out what was in spit, had it reproduced, and put a tiny bit in the corner of the painting. Before he went home he checked that it was working. In the morning, what was fixing the paint to the painting had completely disappeared.'

'My God!'

'Which is why I like spit and not a fake version of it. Do you want to put the kettle on? We'll eat lunch in the kitchen.'

'So,' Ellie said when they were both sitting on stools at the counter. 'When do I get some hands-on experience?'

'You don't. It's all highly technical, you can't let amateurs do it.'

'So why did you take me on, if you're not prepared to let me have some real work experience?' She bit into her ham and salad baguette.

He shrugged. 'You saw how badly the cellar needed clearing out. I'm going to turn it into a dark room.'

'Well, now I've done that for you, and you took me on for two weeks, so could we do something to do with pictures?'

Ran looked at her warily. 'You've got to be extremely careful. You shouldn't go near anything if you haven't got the right qualifications.'

'But getting them would be a huge commitment of time and money.'

He frowned. 'If you're not willing to commit your time, picture restoration is not for you. It's not something you can rush.'

'I see that, and I am a careful and patient person, normally. It's just—' she was very tempted to tell him, but hadn't she promised Grace she wouldn't?—'what with the baby and things, I need to sort my life out.'

He regarded her sceptically, as if he wasn't quite convinced. 'I can see that, but it's still not something you can just rush into on a whim.'

'Really, it's not a whim. I'd be interested to know, for example, how you'd deal with some very old wooden panels. Just as an example.'

He sighed, a much beleaguered man. 'OK. After lunch I'll show you a bit more.'

When they had both finished eating, Ran stood up and walked across to the studio. 'Come over here and I'll show you a few techniques. Why are you so interested in wooden panels? Have you got one you want to restore yourself? It's not amateur work, you know, unless it's just some bit of junk you picked up in a car-boot sale.'

Because she was still annoyed and very tired after clearing out the cellar, Ellie didn't give her brain quite long enough before she let her mouth engage. 'I did not buy them at a car-boot sale!' she snapped as she followed him into the studio.

'So there's more than one of them? You picked them up in a junk shop, then. Or did your dear old Auntie Ethel leave them to you?'

'No! In fact, they're not even mine.'

Ran frowned. 'Have a seat. Over there, out of the way.' He settled Ellie in a stylish but not very comfortable chair. Out of the window was a fantastic view of hills and meadows. She stared at it moodily, wondering if it was her hormones that were making her so irritable, or Ran.

'Tell me about these panels. They're probably rubbish, you know, not worth restoring.'

Ellie sighed. 'I think the owner probably wishes they were rubbish, except that she needs the money.'

'What are they of?'

Ellie frowned. 'What's the subject matter got to do with anything?'

'It'll give me some idea about them. I wish you'd stop prevaricating.'

Not sure if she knew what prevaricating was, Ellie decided that the truth was the least exhausting option. 'You've got to promise not to tell a living soul, but I think they're probably by someone really important. They've been hidden in an absolutely ancient house for ever and the painting is superb. But there's a mouse hole, plus some of the paint has flaked off and there might be dry rot any minute.'

'What do you mean, "any minute"?'

'There's dry rot in the room above and we think it might have got down into the paintings. Which is why this is all so urgent. My friend needs to get the dry rot in the house seen to, and probably the only way to raise the money is to sell the paintings. But they won't get anything like what they might be worth in their present condition.'

'What's the subject matter?'

'Adam and Eve in the Garden of Eden, I think. But they're quite— explicit. No fig leaves. Adam . . . well, he has . . .' Her voice trailed off.

'Spit it out, woman. Do you mean he has an erection?'

'Yes.' Ellie found herself blushing.

'I'd really have to see them to make any sort of judgment. They do sound interesting though, if they're as old as you think they are.'

Ellie considered. How would Grace feel if Ellie took this man to see the paintings, the paintings that were supposed to be a deadly secret? Not good. 'I don't think that's possible,' she said cautiously.

'Well, there's nothing I can do to help then, is there?'

'I could tell you about them.'

'My dear girl,' he said in a way that Ellie found both patronising and alarmingly erotic, 'you could tell me about every flower and baby animal and I still wouldn't have a clue as to their age, their condition or anything that would help me to help you restore them. That was why you came here, wasn't it? To learn from me so you could restore them yourself?'

He made it seem like stealing. 'I'm sorry. It's Grace, my friend, she doesn't want anyone to know about the panels. Even if she was willing to have them properly restored she couldn't afford to pay for the work— not until after she'd sold them, anyway.'

Ran was silent for a moment. 'If they are really interesting I'd be willing to do them on those terms. But I do have to see the bloody things.'

Ellie thought hard. 'There is a way. Grace is a wine expert and she's going to do wine-tastings, with food, as a way of earning money. You could come to one and I could slip you in to see the paintings.'

'What, between the claret and the Sancerre?'

'Something like that. It's not ideal, I know, but if she'd already met you, she might feel better about you seeing the paintings.'

'She sounds highly neurotic.'

'She's not. She's just had a tough time lately. Her husband left her and took all his furniture, and she was living in a very old, very large, very lovely house, all on her own, when I met her. Now there's me and her ex-stepdaughter living there as well.'

'You've obviously taken her under your wing. Maternal type, are you?'

'I'd better be. Now, if I get onto Grace to organise a wine-tasting quite quickly, will you come?'

'I suppose so. But if these paintings are rubbish, I will be extremely cross and extract a hideous revenge from you.'

These unpromising words had a disturbing effect on Ellie's stomach. 'What would that be? Cleaning out your cellars for the rest of my life?'

'I've only got one cellar and you've cleaned that out already. I'll think of something else.'

Ellie looked at the floor, aware that she was blushing, and hoped that he wouldn't notice. 'Well, let me know.' She looked up. 'I may be giving you the best commission of your entire life.'

'In which case you'll want a reward?'

Ellie nodded, a smile which refused to be suppressed twitching at the corner of her mouth. 'I'll think of something.'

She already knew what she wanted. A lovely, uncomplicated, entirely physical affaire; no falling in love, no heartbreak, no pain on either side. And Ran would be ideal. Pity he didn't seem to fancy her at all.

Then she considered for a minute. If she got him to Luckenham House, and she was properly dressed and made up, he might not be so resistant to her charms.

Allegra insisted on showing the dry rot to Grace. Not, she explained, out of sadism, but so Grace would thoroughly understand the extent and urgency of the problem. At the top of the stairs Allegra referred to her notes. 'It's mostly in the west bedroom. Along here, isn't it?'

Before she knew it, Grace had followed Allegra into the room that Edward had used as his study. 'Ah, here it is,' said Allegra. The wood-treatment man had taken away the skirting board and revealed a substance with the look of grubby cotton wool branching across the wall like coral. 'And here's the fruiting body he mentioned,' she went on. Together they surveyed the rust-coloured fungus. 'It's very bad,' Allegra emphasised. 'He says so here in the report. It's spread a long way.'

'I can see it has,' said Grace, thinking of the paintings underneath. 'Does it spread rapidly?'

'It can do. What's the room underneath here?'

'The dining room,' said Grace. 'But I'm sure it hasn't got that far, or I would have noticed.'

'And I expect the report would have mentioned it if it had. This stuff does smell, doesn't it?' She wrinkled her nose disapprovingly.

Her sister at last out of her house, Grace picked up the phone to ring Edward about Demi's computer. While she was waiting to be connected she realised she had dialled his number without a trace of nervousness, something she had never achieved when they were married.

'I really think she should have a few of her own things, especially her computer,' Grace said firmly, after the preliminaries.

'Oh?'

'She didn't know she was going to college today until yesterday, but she put in a lot of time and effort making an essay plan last night. I read through what she'd done and was very impressed.'

'Hmph. I wonder when her mother last read any of her college work through,' Edward muttered. 'I'll bring the stuff over at the weekend. It might take me until then to prise the things out of Hermia.'

Grace swallowed. 'And the money, Edward? I can't afford—'

'Of course. I'm sorry. I'll sort it out today.'

When Grace reached Flynn's house it was two thirty, and there was no car in the drive; she'd missed him.

The house was bigger than Luckenham House and probably a couple of centuries younger. There was a circular drive in front and from the outside the house looked immaculate. She examined the bunch of keys in her hand and went through the order in her head. The scary bit would be when she had to rush into the house and unset the alarm before it went off. She had about three minutes.

The three locks in the front door worked well but as she was rushing through the hall in the general direction of the kitchen to find the alarm, it burst into hideous song before she could get to it. Her brain fighting for calmness through the cacophony, she punched out the numbers.

Grace was not the sort of person who, given someone's keys and a cat to feed, would then go round the house, or help herself to the drinks cabinet, but after the shock of the alarm a glass of water seemed essential.

The kitchen was like something out of a magazine. It had shiny stone worktops, dozens of cupboards, and a stone floor that felt suspiciously warm beneath her feet. He probably had underfloor heating.

Then she found a note. *Dear Grace, I'm sorry I couldn't be here to welcome you, but I hope you find everything OK. Perhaps when I get back I could feed you in payment for you feeding my cat? Best, Flynn. PS It's not crucial what time you feed her. There are always dry biscuits down so she won't starve. She likes her sachets freshly opened or the floor cooks the food.*

After a glass of water, she set about finding the cat food and the cat.

She was just wondering whether finding the cat would involve a search of the whole house, when a loud yowl from behind her made her jump more guiltily than any burglar.

'Oh, there you are,' she said. 'Now all I have to do is find your stash of food and give you some. OK?'

The cat rubbed herself against Grace's legs, implying no one had spoken to her or fed her for days.

Grace regarded her sceptically while scratching her under her chin, then she left the luxurious kitchen and found the pantry.

'This is a fabulous house,' she told the cat as she squeezed jelly-covered chunks of meat into a dish marked CAT. 'Allegra would love it.'

It was only after she had completed the ceremony of the alarm and the keys and had driven away, leaving the cat twitching the tip of her tail, that she acknowledged that she quite liked it too.

Chapter Five

'WE MUST GET ON and organise the wine-tasting,' said Ellie when she got back from Bath, allowing Grace to make beans on toast for supper.

'What's the huge hurry?' Grace shared the beans between three pieces of toast. 'I want to get Graham to come and bring his magazine friend. I don't suppose I could arrange that without a bit of notice.'

'I think we should do a dummy run to see how it goes, and then ask the posh people.'

'I wouldn't quite describe Graham as posh.'

Ellie suppressed her irritation, annoyed that she couldn't tell Grace why they needed to do something immediately. As far as Ellie was concerned, as long as Ran Frazier came, no one else mattered.

'I've got an idea!' she said. 'If we made a poster tonight, I could take it down to Bath tomorrow. It's not too far for people to come.'

'You're very keen about this, Ellie. Considering all the cooking you'll have to do,' said Grace, looking suspicious.

'But it'll be fun!'

'Dem,' said Grace. 'Can you come and eat, now? And will you want more toast?'

'And I really want to know how you got on at college,' said Ellie.

'It was OK,' said Demi, coming to the table. 'And I saw Rick at lunchtime. We had a chat. He was riding his motorbike. Very cool!'

Ellie laughed. 'It is very cool on the back of it, I can tell you. So, Grace, do you know what wines you'll have?' Ellie tugged the conversation back to what was uppermost in her mind. 'Or shall we set a date first?'

'I haven't really thought about it,' said Grace. 'I've hardly had a minute to myself what with running round after Flynn's cat.'

'I wish we could have an animal,' said Demi. 'We've got lots of room.'

'I'll think about it,' said Grace. 'An animal would make the house more homely.'

'So would furniture,' said Ellie. 'Did you say you had a table we could put people round?'

'You'd think after a day of clearing out cellars you wouldn't want to think about inviting umpteen people for a six course dinner,' said Grace.

'It was only one cellar, and we can't afford to hang around.'

'Well, can we at least wait until Edward's money comes through? I spoke to him about your computer and things today, Dem.'

'I tell you what,' said Ellie. 'I'll pay for all the food for the first one, and you can pay me back later. After all, if we charge enough, we'll get the money back straight away.'

'No, I can't let you do that. I have got some money, after all.' Grace crinkled her forehead. 'What would be a reasonable amount to ask people to pay?'

'Well,' said Ellie, 'my parents go out to restaurants for meals and they spend sixty quid easily, and you're offering "education".' She emphasised the word. 'People love that.'

'But I'm not offering them food cooked by a professional chef! With health and safety regulations, in fact, the whole idea is probably illegal.'

Ellie was not going to be defeated by a few rules. 'I know! We won't charge people, we'll invite them and, at the end of the evening, suggest that if they enjoyed themselves, they might like to recommend it to their friends or come again. And ask them if they'd mind making a contribution—next time—the first time being free.'

'OK,' said Grace, feeling bulldozed. 'Who shall we have?'

'Let's set a date first. Next week?' asked Ellie, determined to get the day nailed down good and hard.

'Isn't that a bit soon? Who will be able to come at such short notice?'

Ellie realised she should have asked when Ran was available. 'All right, the week after, then.' She decided that if the date they agreed on didn't suit Ran, she would find an excuse to change it.

'Are you going to ask Flynn?' said Demi.

'Yes, have Flynn, definitely,' said Ellie.

'Yeah. He's cool,' agreed Demi.

'He is?' Grace was surprised at this.

'For an older man. He's definitely attractive.'

'I'm not sure how long he's away for,' Grace stalled.

'Oh, well, never mind,' said Ellie. 'Perhaps I could invite the picture restorer? Ran? He's interested in wine.' Aware that she was blushing, Ellie started gathering plates.

'Is he attractive, too?' asked Demi.

'Definitely. Sexy, anyway.'

'Isn't it the same thing?' asked Grace, feeling terribly naive.

Demi shook her head. 'Not necessarily. Quite ugly men can be sexy. And quite good-looking ones.' Demi lowered her head, alerting Ellie to the fact that there was someone in Demi's life she liked.

'So two weeks today, then?' said Ellie, aware that they had begun to get distracted. 'I want to start thinking up menus. You tell me what sort of food you want, Grace, and I'll plan it.'

Grace thought for a moment. 'Shouldn't we wait until you've finished your work placement; you'll be far too tired to cook. Won't that be around the end of your fortnight?'

'No, please! I really want to—' Ellie stopped for a breath. 'I just really want us to start making some money.'

Grace sighed resignedly, and decided not to comment on the fact that so far, the wine and food idea looked like costing money rather than earning it.

Demi's mobile phone, which was lying on the kitchen table, growled, squirmed and then burst into song. She picked it up, checked the name and said, 'Oh, shit! Mum! Do I have to answer it?'

'Yes!' said the others in unison.

Demi sighed, got up from the table and wandered over so she could lean on the Rayburn. 'Hi, Mum,' she said sweetly.

Ellie was feeling a bit guilty as she set off for Bath the next day. Ran didn't need her, didn't want her hanging around, and once she had delivered the invitation for a date a fortnight hence, she would really have no business being there.

But there was Grace; as far as she was concerned, Ellie was learning all she could about picture restoration. And there was Ran. How did one go about seducing a man who appeared not to fancy one at all? She'd have to be subtle. She put on an old, tight-fitting cardigan, which she wore with a bright silk scarf round her neck. And, so as not to clash with the scarf, the previous evening she had dyed her hair to the nearest colour akin to brown as she could, given that it had been red before. Ellie hoped that appearing to be more conventional might be the key to opening his eyes to her as a woman.

Later, when she was squashing her 2CV into a space slightly smaller than her futon, she wondered about her chances. Ran would be lovely to have an affaire with, and she was just not ready to settle for housework instead of sex.

Housework definitely came first, though, as it turned out. When Ran opened the door to her, he said, 'So, you're back, are you? Well, I've got a nice little job sorting cupboards for you.'

'And I've got a nice invitation to a very interesting evening with wine and food for you.' She smiled. No response. 'You'll love it.'

'I thought the point was that I was going to get to see the paintings during it, not indulge myself in bacchanalian delights.' He smiled, just enough to tweak Ellie's libido, although she knew he wasn't doing it on purpose. 'Come and sort cupboards.'

Ellie sighed. It was probably the best offer she was likely to get.

At lunchtime, when she gave Ran his coffee and sandwiches, she laid everything out in a way that involved quite a lot of bending over, revealing enough cleavage to tell him that she had one, in case he'd overlooked it. He gave her no hint that he'd noticed. She sighed, and bit into her cheese and pickle.

'You know, there's really no point in you coming here each day if I'm going to look at the panels for you,' said Ran.

Ellie was ready for this. 'But I've told Grace I'm doing it. If I don't come, she'll wonder why. You don't mind me coming, do you? I mean, there are things I can do for you . . .' She smiled in a way that would have had the punters at her old bar job buying her drinks and asking for her mobile number and offering to walk her to her car.

He smiled back, but there was no suggestion in it, no hint that he was responding to her in the way that she wanted.

Demi was not happy. Hermia had told her that a white van would be arriving at Luckenham House the next day full of Demi's bed, her bedding, in fact everything that currently filled her bedroom, including her computer and her television.

'But that's good, isn't it?' said Ellie.

'Yes,' said Demi, 'sort of! But she's going to turn my room into a gym!'

'Must have been a big room,' said Ellie.

'She's going to put in all sorts of equipment so she and her bloke can sweat it out together. It's disgusting!' She looked both furious and on the verge of tears.

'What is? Keeping fit? Surely not,' said Ellie, trying to lighten things.

'No, the thought of her and him . . . you know. Doing stuff. Yuck!'

Grace looked at Demi, feeling it was possible it wasn't so much the thought of her mother 'doing stuff' as the fact that her mother had eradicated her daughter's presence from her house.

'We must decorate you a room, get it just how you like it,' Grace said reassuringly. 'Put all your things in it, and then you won't feel you've been replaced by a cross-trainer-stepper combination.'

'Thanks, Grace,' Demi said in a very small voice. 'Is there any hot water? I really feel like having a bath.'

'Poor love,' said Ellie when she and Grace were alone. 'It was bad enough my mother turning my room into a study when I went to university, but at least she hadn't replaced my dad with a younger model.'

When Ellie rang the bell to Ran's house the following morning she felt excited by the thought of seeing him again.

He opened the door. 'Good morning. How are you today?' he asked.

'I'm fine. Could I just . . .?' She indicated the bathroom.

'Oh, yes. Frequency of micturition.'

Ellie halted in horror. 'What?'

'It's a symptom of pregnancy. Means you go to the loo a lot.'

'For God's sake!' said Ellie, running. 'As if I didn't know that!'

How did he know that constant peeing was a symptom of pregnancy? Did he have children of his own? Perhaps he was married! There were definitely some important questions to be asked before she embarked on her seduction.

'Sorry about that,' she said as she joined Ran in the kitchen. 'But you didn't seem surprised I needed to go. Does that mean you're a father yourself?' Then she wondered if she'd been a bit blunt.

He shook his head, unfazed. 'Nieces and nephews, but my sisters didn't spare me a single symptom from the moment they got pregnant. Would you like me to relate how long they were each in labour for?'

'No, thank you!' Ellie was horrified at the notion, but enormously relieved that his knowledge was not even secondhand. 'What would you like me to do today?'

'I thought I ought to show you what I do.'

'Brilliant! I am really interested in picture conservation, so if I could actually do something—'

'I meant, I'd like to show you some work I've already done. There's an antiques fair not far from here, and there's a picture for sale in it that I restored. I'd quite like to see it. I thought we'd go along.'

'Lovely!'

'Come on then. Have you got your coat?'

'I'm wearing it.' She indicated her gilet, which was lined with fake fur and very warm.

'Sorry. I didn't recognise that thing as a coat.'

Ellie stood aside while he opened the front door. What was wrong with her gilet? She opened her mouth to ask him, but shut it again.

He unlocked a sturdy-looking Volvo estate and opened the passenger door for her. 'Heave yourself in.'

'I do not need to heave myself!' she declared indignantly. 'My pregnancy hardly shows!'

'It doesn't show at all. I was just preparing you for what's ahead.'

'Thank you, but please don't bother,' she said primly.

The sun was shining and the air sparkled as they climbed up out of the town into the countryside. Spring was just beginning to assert herself, decorating the trees with green fuzz. They drove through south Gloucestershire to where a stately home had become a very smart girls' school. Elegant horses, wrapped up well against the cold, grazed in the fields that surrounded a long drive leading to a Victorian house.

Ran turned the car into a field designated for parking. As they walked towards the entrance to the house, Ellie admired the pillars, the pediments and general air of prosperity the building proclaimed.

'It's rather splendid,' she said.

'I think that sums it up adequately,' said Ran. Then he regarded her through slightly narrowed eyes. 'I don't suppose I could get you in for half-price, could I?' he continued as they tagged on to the end of a queue of several dozen people. 'You don't look more than sixteen.'

Ellie was incensed. 'If you're too tight to pay the proper, full price for a pregnant woman, I'll buy my own ticket! I expect you could get a reduced rate, though, for being a senior citizen,' she added sweetly.

'The cheek of it! I'm not a day over thirty-five, I'll have you know!'

'Sorree!' Ellie said blithely. Then she sighed. How would she ever seduce him if he treated her like a child and she treated him like an old-age pensioner?

Once inside the antiques fair, Ran led her through several rooms, past furniture, ancient garden tools and ornaments to where there was a stand selling paintings. There, in the middle, was a portrait of a young woman. Ran and the proprietor greeted each other.

'Ted, how are you?' said Ran. 'I've brought an apprentice along with me, so she can see the work of a master.'

The man laughed. 'You're good, Ran, but maybe not that good.'

'Come on, you know you wouldn't use me if I wasn't. This is Ellie . . . what's your other name?'

'Summers,' said Ellie, suddenly shy.

'This is Ted Matthews, who makes his living fleecing innocent victims of their pension money.'

'My paintings are as good as a pension. Pure investment, and at least you get to look at them while they increase in value.'

Ellie moved away from the men, fascinated by the figure in the painting. She couldn't decide how old the girl was, such was her composure. She could have been nineteen, made old for her years by her responsibilities. Or she could have been in her mid-twenties, Ellie's age. She had clear brown eyes and was dressed in a simple pale grey gown. The ruffle of one elbow was held back with a string of four pearls which could have been real, they were so glowing and opalescent.

'She's wonderful!' she said, genuinely impressed as Ran came up and stood behind her shoulder. 'What did you do to her?'

'There was a tear right across it. Can you see the mark?'

'No. Not a thing.'

'You need a magnifying glass,' said Ted. 'Ran thinks he's the best conservator around, and to be honest, he's not far wrong. Should be, the prices he charges.' He turned his attention to Ellie. 'So, Ellie, wasn't it? What do you do?'

'I'm a creative arts graduate and I'm interested in studying picture conservation. As the training's long and hard, I thought I'd better gain some experience first, to make sure it is really what I wanted to do.'

She stopped for breath and smiled, pleased with how all that came out, but she was relieved when a woman with a determined expression came up to the stand, getting Ellie out of any further interrogation.

'I know a nice pub where we could have lunch,' Ran said. 'We'll have to sit in the garden though.'

'Why? It's freezing!'

'I'm not sure you'll pass as being over eighteen.'

Ellie grimaced. 'It's all right. You're allowed into pubs when you're sixteen if you're with a parent.'

He growled and she grinned, pleased to have got the last word.

The pub had a log fire, and because it was still quite early, they were able to get seats next to it. 'This is lovely,' said Ellie, looking at the menu that Ran had handed to her.

'What do you feel like eating? Have you developed any strange tastes?'

'Not really, I just get very hungry.'

'That's nice. I get fed up with women who are on diets and can't eat anything except steak without the chips or salad without the dressing.'

'Well, I'll have the steak and the chips and the salad and the dressing.' She smiled at him and he smiled back. God, he was attractive, she thought. 'Excuse me, I'll just—'

'—go to the Ladies. Tell me what you want to drink first?'

'Mineral water. Fizzy, please,' she said, and left.

She was back in her seat when Ran returned with the drinks.

'So, tell me about this wine-tasting with dinner I'm being dragged to?' he said, sitting down again.

Ellie bit back her natural indignation at his attitude; it would do her no good. 'Well, it should be very pleasant. You'll get good food, good wine and possibly good company.' Without knowing who else was going, she couldn't promise he'd find someone interesting to talk to. 'And at some point during the evening you'll excuse yourself, come into the kitchen'—where I will be looking particularly sexy, she added silently—'and I will take you to see the panels.'

'Having concealed my magnifying glasses about my person?'

'Exactly. It's going to be easy! Ah, here's the food. I'm starving.'

'So you're not nauseous any more?' he asked as the waitress set down plates heaped with food on the little table in front of them.

'Oh, yes, sometimes. But in between times, I could eat a horse.'

'Pity it wasn't on the menu. I would have liked to have seen that.'

Chapter Six

'OK, WE'VE GOT TO DO it now,' said Ellie as she and Grace sat together in the kitchen a fortnight later. They had been enjoying a late, leisurely breakfast after Grace had delivered Demi to the bus that went all the way to her college.

'It does save time, not having to take Demi to the door,' said Grace, putting the last square of toast and marmalade into her mouth.

'Yes, and to be honest we need the time. There's the drawing room to be decorated. If we tackle it now we can make it really beautiful.'

'It's already beautiful,' said Grace, trying not to mind that Flynn hadn't responded to her invitation, in fact hadn't spoken to her at all since his return, although she'd driven to his house to feed his cat every day for a fortnight. She'd seen his car outside his house yesterday morning. but hadn't gone in to say hello.

'In a minimalist sort of way, it is,' agreed Ellie, so as not to hurt Grace's feelings. 'But apart from anything else, we need a table.'

Grace sighed and accepted that the room would have to be faced. Now the day was upon them, she found herself edgy. 'OK. Let's go into the stables and find the ping-pong table. It may not have all its legs.'

Chairs scraped on the stone floor as they got up. 'It's such a shame that Graham and his magazine friend couldn't come,' said Grace. 'Even when we changed the date for this Friday night. All this work would seem more worthwhile if they were going to be there.'

'This is a dummy run,' Ellie reminded her, not for the first time, aware that if Ran agreed that the panels were valuable, Grace's financial problems would be over.

'And I can't talk you into eating with us? I could do with the support.'

'Really, it would be so much easier for me if I was in the kitchen, cooking the next course, taking away plates.' Sneaking off to the dining room with Ran, she added silently.

'I suppose so. But shouldn't you be there for—what's his name? Ran?'

'No. He's only coming for the free food and wine. He's not interested in me. As a person,' she added hurriedly. Since their day out at the antiques fair, Ellie's plans to seduce him were no further on, but tonight would be a turning point. When she whisked in and out of the room with plates, she was going to be wearing a very little black dress and he would notice her as a woman if she had to tip boiling soup in his lap!

'It's a pity Demi ducked out of helping and arranged to spend the night with a friend,' said Grace, carrying their breakfast plates to the sink. 'But it's nice that she's settled in so well back at college, and has met new people and stuff. It can't have been easy for her.'

'You don't sound as happy as you ought to be about it,' said Ellie.

'I'm not. There was something about the way she asked me, something a bit shifty about it. It didn't seem like Demi, somehow.'

'You could ring the mother of the girl she's staying with and check?'

'I could—possibly should—but Demi would never trust me again if she thought I didn't trust her.'

'True.'

'I'm sure she's fine,' said Grace. 'Let's go and tackle the spiders.'

'Oh, is that why you've been so reluctant to go into the stables! Scared of spiders, huh!'

Apart from the spiders, of which there were a great number, the stables contained some very useful bits and pieces.

'Do you mind about Flynn not coming?' asked Ellie, dragging out an old carpet by a corner and disturbing a spider as big as a mouse.

'I suppose I do, really,' said Grace, watching the spider warily. 'I mean, he's so not my type, but there is something rather . . .' She paused, looking for the word.

'Nice?' suggested Ellie, who had spotted the ping-pong table and was trying to work out how to get to it.

'No. I don't think that's quite what he is. He's just totally unlike Edward.'

'I think if we get this lot out first, we should be able to get to the table,' Ellie said, deciding against commenting on the man who had left Grace with this pile of junk while he swanned off with his antiques.

Preferring not to ask Flynn to lend her china, as she hadn't seen him since his return, Grace had gone to the local junk shop. There she had managed to buy a couple of incomplete dinner services as well as some chairs, some occasional tables and some serving dishes. Grace had spent the afternoon washing china, while Ellie cooked what she could in advance.

At five minutes to eight, the two women hovered in the drawing room, now converted into a dining room, tweaking cutlery, realigning napkins and checking that the candles were all burning evenly.

'It does look lovely,' said Grace.

They had lit the fire and about fifty candles so the room was warm.

'It's amazing what you can do with enough space and enough candles,' said Ellie now, extremely satisfied with the result. 'The trouble is, my mother says, that most people have far too much clutter.'

'Well, there I am in with a head start,' said Grace wryly. 'No furniture cuts down on clutter really well.'

They had just managed to convince each other that no one was going to come, and they could have a private party of their own, when the doorbell jangled.

'I hope it's that young couple who came last time. The Cavendishes. They were great,' said Grace.

'Well, answer the door, then. You can't sell evenings of food and wine to people if you don't let them in. Just let me get away first.'

Grace sighed. 'I'm not really cut out for this, you know.' Then she went to the door.

It wasn't the young couple, it was Flynn. He came in and hugged Grace

261

roughly. An odd combination of relief and excitement rushed through her. 'I'm sorry I haven't been in touch. Family crisis. Can I still come?'

Grace thought of the ten individual tarts that Ellie was probably putting in the oven now, the ten individual soufflé dishes, greased and collared, waiting for their mixture, the ten perfectly arranged plates of salad.

'I'll have to ask Ellie. And I'd need to set you a place.' Resentment and nerves at her first reaction tugged at her, making her ungenerous.

'I'll ask Ellie,' said Flynn and strode off to the kitchen.

Ellie, Grace knew, would say it was fine and that it was no trouble to make another tartlet, or rustle up another soufflé. As she went back into the drawing room, she was aware that somehow the evening loomed less heavily over her now that Flynn was here. She smiled.

'**N**ow, if you've all finished marking, I'm going to ask you to pass round the next bottle quite quickly as the next course is a cheese soufflé and we'll want to get stuck in as soon as it arrives.'

Grace happened to catch Flynn's eye and his smile was a mixture of approval and congratulation. She permitted herself to smile back. The evening was going well. Ran was proving a success with the female members of the party: he didn't say much, but he did look stunning in his dinner jacket.

The food had all been superb so far, and one guest had been particularly complimentary about a South African Sauvignon, which he said had chocolate aromas and was 'drinkability itself'. Grace was still basking in this compliment when Ellie came in, plates with individual soufflés balanced up her arms, her mobile phone clamped in her armpit.

'It's Rick,' she muttered urgently from the corner of her mouth. 'He's ringing from Demi's phone. Apparently she's ill or something!'

Grace's heart stuttered as she took the phone and got up from the table so she could speak. Why on earth was Rick ringing about Demi?

'Is that Grace?' demanded a slurred voice. 'I've got Demi. She's a bit wasted. She wanted me to ring you.' Grace had to take a couple of deep breaths to steady herself. Rick sounded fairly wasted himself and questions were flying around in her head like moths.

'OK,' she said, her calm voice belying her rising panic. 'I'm coming to get her. Where are you?'

'At home,' said Rick.

'You're at the cottage in Bath, yes?'

'Yeah.' The phone apparently slipped from Rick's hand, because Grace could hear background noise and then a clunk.

For a moment, all the moisture left Grace's mouth and apparently transferred itself to the palms of her hands. She forced herself to remain calm. Ellie had already left the room. Grace returned to the table.

She cleared her throat. What on earth could she say? Keeping it simple and truthful seemed the best way. 'I'm awfully sorry, everyone, my stepdaughter's been taken ill and I have to go to her. But please do carry on—Ellie will look after you. Flynn, perhaps you could take charge for me?'

'You need someone with you,' Flynn said.

'Yes, you do,' said Mr Rose, who ran the village shop and post office. 'If you've got an emergency, you have to see to it. We'll be fine. I'll make sure everyone writes down what they think about the wine.'

'If you're sure—'

'Just do what he says, love,' said Mrs Rose. 'Now off you go.'

Mrs Rose was so motherly that Grace succumbed to the temptation to give her a hug goodbye before she left the room, followed by Flynn.

'Is it Demi?' he asked when they were outside.

'Yes. I don't know what can have happened.'

'So where is she?'

'That's the weird thing. She's with Rick, Ellie's ex. How did she get to his house? I'm so confused.'

By this time they were in the kitchen. Grace handed Ellie her phone. 'I didn't know Demi knew Rick that well. Did you?'

'I suppose I did know she fancied him. And she did mention meeting him, but I thought it was just casually. Don't you remember, she told us about seeing him in the street, on his bike? I'm so sorry. I feel so responsible!'

'It's not your fault. Don't be silly! But can you give me directions to the house? How long will it take us to get there?'

'Grace,' said Flynn. 'Why don't you get some things organised for Demi, just in case . . . I'll help Ellie get the next lot of soufflés in and then get directions.'

'Oh. Yes, of course. I should get some things. Oh, Demi. I do hope you're all right.'

By the time she got downstairs Flynn was waiting in the hall, jingling his car keys. 'I think I know where we're going.'

Grace was struggling into a cardigan when the drawing-room door opened and Ran appeared. 'I'll help Ellie. Could you direct me to the kitchen?'

'Oh! That's so kind. She will need someone to give her a hand. It's just down that passage and then right. Do you see?'

'Fine. Yes, I do. Good luck.'

'I've come to help,' said Ran from the doorway of the kitchen. 'What would you like me to do?'

Ellie, who was taking a tray out of the oven, put it on top of the Rayburn before turning towards him. He was looking incredibly attractive, she thought. He was wearing a dinner jacket with the shirt undone at the neck and his bow tie loose. 'I can't decide,' she said. 'Should we grab the opportunity to look at the paintings? Will they be all right in there on their own for a bit?'

'I wouldn't leave them too long. There's a woman whose name I forget with a delightful cleavage and, while I don't want to seem conceited, I think she has her eye on me.'

Ellie was quite sure the woman had her eye on him. In fact, she'd noticed it earlier.

'OK. I'll get you to help me take in the next course, and then I'll show you where the panels are.' Ellie loaded him up with beautifully arranged plates of salmon, dill, quails' eggs, stuffed cherry tomatoes and a dribble of balsamic vinegar dressing, then she frowned. 'I can't help feeling it's my fault in some way. If Demi hadn't come with me to fetch my stuff, she wouldn't have met Rick. And she told me about seeing him on his motorbike. That wouldn't have helped matters.'

'Is Rick particularly desirable, then?'

'Greek god, definitely,' said Ellie frankly, looking up into Ran's eyes and deciding that she'd grown out of Greek gods and was now into men with crinkles at the corners of their eyes. She looked down at the plates he was holding, hoping that her blushes would look like heat from the kitchen, which was now considerable. 'OK, let's get these in.'

'By the way, have you got a claw hammer handy?' Ran asked, just as Ellie was opening the door to the drawing room with her elbow. 'I might need to take the panels off.'

'*What?* Take them off? Will you have to?'

'Yes, I probably will. I'll need to see both sides.'

'Oh, well. Perhaps it's too late to worry about what Grace will say. There's a hammer in the kitchen. I'll get it for you.' She gave the door a push with her hip and entered, smiling. 'Here we are, everyone! Mr Rose, did you volunteer to be in charge?'

'Yes, and it'll be no trouble,' said Mr Rose. 'The bottles are numbered quite clearly.'

'And the food is lovely,' added Mrs Rose, with a smile.

'Good,' said Ellie. 'I'll get back to the kitchen then. Ran?'

Ran, who had been exchanging 'I'm sorry, I wish I could but I'm being dragged away' looks with the owner of the cleavage, followed Ellie out of the room. She walked ahead rather briskly, cursing her high heels. 'I'll get you the hammer,' she said, still crisp.

'No need to get snappy,' he said down the back of her neck. 'I'm only flirting to be kind.'

'I thought you didn't do "kind",' said Ellie, rummaging in a drawer, wishing she didn't sound jealous.

'Oh, but I do. Which is why I'm here now.'

She turned and handed him the hammer. 'I'll get you a torch, too. Then I'll take you to the dining room.'

Flynn drove awfully fast, even faster than Edward. 'I'm sure you don't need to drive quite so quickly,' Grace said, holding her seat belt.

'Sorry.' He slowed down. 'I've done so much driving lately and always with less time than the journey takes.'

Partly to take her mind off Demi, Grace said, 'Any particular reason?'

He nodded. 'My ex-mother-in-law is in a home and has been ill. My ex-wife isn't in the country, and the rest of the family are so . . .' He paused, his lips pursed. '. . . useless.'

'Well, I hope your ex-wife is grateful to you for looking after her mother.' She was wondering if Edward would have done such a thing for her mother. She decided probably not and sighed.

Her sigh must have been audible because Flynn said, 'Are you worrying about Demi? I shouldn't think it's as bad as you're imagining.'

'I know it's not really my fault, but I can't help blaming myself. I should have rung the mother of the girl she said she was staying with, but I didn't want Demi to think I didn't trust her. And I shouldn't have trusted her! God! Children are such a worry, and Demi isn't even mine.'

'Would you like to have children of your own?'

'Oh, yes,' she answered, before she could consider whether it was a question Flynn should have asked her. 'Definitely. It was the main reason Edward and I broke up.' She hesitated slightly. 'That and the fact that he found someone else.'

'Those problems combined would probably be beyond the scope of most agony aunts,' said Flynn seriously.

'Are you laughing? My marriage broke up and you think it's funny?' Grace didn't quite know how to react.

'I'm not really laughing,' said Flynn, who was, 'but there is a certain irony in it. You see, I've just spent the last fortnight looking after my ex-mother-in-law, you're making a mercy dash for your ex-stepdaughter, and our marriages both broke up for the same reasons.'

'Oh?'

'Mm. Annette was very into her career. I wanted a family but there was never a good time. I even offered to be the main carer. I wasn't asking her to give up her career. But she had found someone else, too.'

'Are you bitter about it?'

'Not any more. The sad thing for me was my house. I always did up houses, sold them and moved on. But the house I'm in now is the one I planned for the family I'm never going to have.'

'That's something else we've got in common,' said Grace. 'Beautiful houses, no babies to put in them.'

Flynn laughed. 'Well, it looks as if you'll have Ellie's baby to keep you going until you have babies of your own. And you have got Ellie and Demi to keep you company.'

'Yes,' she said on a sigh. 'I just hope Demi's all right.'

Ran joined Ellie in the kitchen while she was boiling kettles for coffee.

'Well?' she demanded, piling gold foil-covered mints onto saucers.

'I've put them in the car. I can't do anything about them in situ, and the condition is really worrying. I cut out the shutters in the end.'

'My God!' For a moment she thought of the devastation but then dismissed this as trivial. 'But are the panels any good?' She was practically jumping up and down with frustration.

After what seemed to Ellie to be about ten years, he smiled. 'Oh, yes. They're very good. But I need to have a proper look, in daylight.'

'I'll tell you what, though, we'd never have managed it if it weren't for Demi getting into trouble.' Her exhilaration faded. 'I wonder why they haven't rung?'

'I'm sure they will the moment they've got something to say,' said Ran, taking the coffee tray from Ellie and heading for the door. 'Just try to put it out of your mind.'

In the drawing room, Mr Rose handed Ellie the completed forms. 'All present and correct, I think.'

'Thank you so much for taking charge, Mr Rose. Without you the entire evening would have been a complete waste! And I'm sure Grace will want to confer with you when she comes to write her article.'

'She's welcome. I just hope her stepdaughter is all right,' he said. 'It's been a grand evening. Grace should do it again. And charge next time.'

When everyone had gone home, Ran followed Ellie into the kitchen.

'Ellie—' he began, and then, life being what it is, her phone rang.

It was Grace. She sounded very tired but not completely distraught. After some discussion about Demi she added, 'I don't think we're going to get home tonight. Will you be all right on your own?'

'I think so,' said Ellie, who suddenly felt that she wouldn't. 'As long as Demi's all right. I've been so worried.'

'She will be,' said Grace. 'I'm just plucking up the courage to ring Edward or her mother.' Grace paused. 'There must be loads of clearing up, but please leave it for me.'

'No, it's fine. I'd rather do it. You know me. See you tomorrow. And love to Demi when she's conscious.'

'Was that Grace saying she wouldn't be home tonight?' said Ran.

'Yes. Shall we go and put out the candles in the drawing room?'

'Will you be all right?' He followed her down the corridor. Ellie didn't reply as they crossed the shadowy hall to the drawing room, where there was light and signs of life. The candles still flickered and, although the table was full of dirty glasses and plates, it still had an air of festivity— the air of a party, over now, but with the ghost of it still present, 'The room does look lovely, doesn't it?' said Ellie.

'You know the French refer to still life as *nature morte*. There has been life; now it's gone, but its spirit remains.'

'You've got very philosophical all of a sudden,' said Ellie, blowing out candles, understanding and agreeing with him completely.

'Would you like to come back with me and stay the night?'

'What?'

'As my guest, rather than leave you here on your own. I have a spare room with a futon in it.'

Ellie would have liked time to think, but Ran was looking at her, waiting for an answer. 'I don't know. I mean, I'm sure I'll be fine.'

'I know you're a very capable young woman, but I think you might be a bit lonely, spending the night here on your own.'

'Well, I'm glad you think I'm capable. I thought you thought I was a child hardly out of school.'

He narrowed his eyes at her. It made him impossibly sexy. 'Go and get your things and come and spend the night with me—on the futon in the spare room,' he growled, in case she hadn't got the message.

'I'll have to take my car. I need to be back really early in the morning.' Ellie felt short of breath and dithery.

'I'll drive you back. I'll want to be up early too.'

'What will Grace think if she comes back and I'm not here?'

'It's unlikely, but you could leave her a note. Now I wish you'd stop making difficulties about doing something you know you're going to do!'

'OK. I'll go and get my stuff.'

'And change out of that dress. It's very distracting.'

Ellie smiled broadly. 'Is it? Oh good.'

Chapter Seven

GRACE SHIFTED Demi's position a little; her arm felt as if it would drop off through lack of blood. She looked at the clock. The hands seemed to be going backwards. They'd been here three hours. Flynn had gone off in search of coffee. Grace closed her eyes and tried to doze, but it was hard with Demi slumped on top of her.

It had been such a shock, finding her like that. They'd been lucky that the front door was ajar or they could have knocked all night before anyone heard them. Only the kitchen seemed to have any lights on, and it was there that they found Demi. She was sitting on a chair, staring into space, blood pouring down her face. A young man, presumably Rick, was beside her, dabbing at the wound with a filthy tea towel.

'What's happened!' Grace shrieked at him in panic. 'You never said anything about her being injured, when you rang Ellie!'

Rick made a supreme effort to keep upright and to enunciate clearly. His eyes were in a condition that told even Grace that he was high on something. 'She wasn't. Injured. When I rang. She fell downstairs after.'

'It looks quite a bad cut,' said Flynn. 'I think it needs stitches. We'd better get her to A and E.'

'Demi?' she shouted into her face, almost pleading with her to wake up and not be dead. 'Can you hear me? It's Grace. Demi?' She patted her cheeks until at last Demi turned towards her and blinked.

'Grace?'

'Yes.' Relief that Demi could talk and recognise her made Grace feel a lot calmer. She turned to Rick. 'What has she had?'

'Only some dope. And alcohol, of course.'

'How strong was the dope?' asked Flynn.

Other people, aware their space was being invaded by people who were very uncool, shifted away slightly. 'It was skunk,' said someone who seemed to be working his way through an entire packet of biscuits.

'And what alcohol?' Grace asked the man who had known about the dope.

'Mate, I have no idea!' He held up his packet of Rich Teas in a gesture of surrender. 'I don't do alcohol.'

'Oh, let's just get her out of here,' said Grace. 'It's no good asking this lot anything.'

'Shame,' said Flynn. 'The hospital is likely to ask us a whole lot of questions we don't know the answers to.'

The woman behind the desk in A & E looked very tired. Glancing at the clock on the wall, Grace noticed it had gone eleven. 'I've come with Demi Ravenglass. She's over there,' said Grace.

'Drunk, is she?' asked the clerk.

'Yes. And I think she's taken some drugs.'

'Are you her mother?'

'No! I'm her stepmother—her friend.'

'OK. Give me the details, then.'

Above the desk was an electronic sign, which presumably altered as patients came and went. WAITING TIME THREE HOURS.

'Have we really got to wait three hours?' asked Grace, when she'd supplied the woman with all the information she could.

'You're lucky. The night is young. You got in before the rush. There's a coffee machine down the hall. Next?'

The 'next' was half a dozen very large young men escorting their friend who seemed to have walked into something tougher than he was.

Grace felt dreadfully vulnerable among all these noisy people who all, without exception, seemed to be drunk. How would she have managed without Flynn? She resolved to thank him at the first opportunity.

Flynn came back with something in a plastic cup. 'It's called Hot Chocolate, though it might be Chicken Soup. But it's hot and liquid.'

Grace rearranged her oversized baby and took the cup. It was chocolate and very soothing.

The nurse and the doctor, perhaps predictably, were not very patient with Demi. The doctor decreed that her wound didn't need stitches, just a clean-up and some Steri-strips to hold it together.

The nurse, who was tired, made it quite clear how she felt about people who got out of their heads on drink and drugs and then fell over.

'How should I look after her when I get her home?' asked Grace.

'She'll be all right as long as she doesn't choke on her own vomit. Treat the hangover in the morning. If the cut doesn't heal take her to her own GP to see the practice nurse.'

Flynn and Grace walked slowly one each side of Demi and got her out of the hospital. Then Grace and Demi waited in the freezing air while Flynn fetched the car. The cold woke Demi up a bit.

'Oh, Grace, I'm so sorry! You won't tell my parents, will you?'

'I won't tell them yet, Dem, but I may have to later.' Grace frowned, wondering how she should deal with this.

'I think I'm going to be sick!'

Before Grace could plan how to get her back inside to the lavatory, Demi deposited a large quantity of red wine and some unidentifiable food items onto the grass verge, just by where they were standing.

Grace sighed. 'I suppose that's a good thing. Better an empty house than a bad tenant, as my father used to say.'

'I think I'm going to die,' said Demi.

'Then I'll definitely have to tell your parents, both of them. What sort of music do you want at your funeral?'

'Don't joke, Grace! It's not funny!' Demi was near tears.

'I know it's not funny!' Grace glanced at Demi, wondering if now was the time for a lecture, and decided not. She'd suffered enough.

To her enormous credit, when Flynn appeared with the car and opened the back door, Demi said, 'I am so sorry, Flynn. I've made a complete idiot of myself.'

Flynn smiled. 'Get in. And don't vomit on the upholstery. There's a rug there to cover yourself with. Grace, you'd better have my coat.'

It was like a warm embrace round her shoulders and smelt faintly of Flynn's aftershave. 'Won't you be cold?' she asked him.

'No. There's a very good heater. Now you get in the back with Demi.'

Both women slept, sharing the rug, in the dark warmth of the back of the car. When Grace woke up, she realised they were nearly back.

'You must be shattered,' she said.

'I expect you are, too.'

'But I've just had a nap and I haven't driven however many miles it is. And you were probably driving before this.'

'I probably was.'

'I can't thank you enough, really I can't.' Her rush of gratitude made it hard for her to speak. 'I could never have coped with all this alone.'

'I know. That's why I came with you.'

There was no sign of Ellie when they got through the front door and into the hall. The light was on, but that was all.

'I expect Ellie's gone to bed,' said Grace. 'You go up too, Demi.'

She waited until Demi had gone upstairs, then she turned to Flynn.

'I don't know what to say.'

'How about: "Would you like a cup of coffee or tea, or something, Flynn." Or a sandwich? I'm starving.'

Grace laughed. 'There are bound to be some leftovers in the kitchen. Come on. Let's see.'

What they saw was Ellie's note. *Didn't want to be on my own in the house. Sorry! Pathetic, I know. But I've gone to stay in Ran's house.* Grace could picture her, chewing the pen, trying to write something which wouldn't give Grace—or Ran—the wrong impression. *I'll be back early in the morning. Lots of love, Ellie.*

There were only puddings left, so Grace found bacon, eggs and tomatoes and made Flynn breakfast.

'Where's yours?' demanded Flynn.

'I hardly ever have breakfast, and not at four in the morning.'

Flynn didn't reply. He loaded his fork with a sample of everything on his plate, then he turned it towards her. 'Open wide.'

'No, honestly. I'm fine. You eat it.'

'Pretend you're a baby bird. Open your mouth.'

Giggling, Grace obeyed him. He placed the forkful carefully in her mouth. 'There.'

She ate it, still laughing. It was delicious. He loaded up another forkful and she ate that, too. There was something silly and sweet and tender about sitting opposite each other, him feeding her.

After three mouthfuls she really had had enough and his plate was emptying. 'That's enough, really it is. But it was nice.'

'Yes, it was,' said Flynn. He was looking into her eyes and didn't seem to be talking about food.

'I'd better make some tea,' said Grace, thinking she should break the invisible thread between them.

He put his hand on hers to stop her moving. Then, his hand still there, he got up, came round the end of the table and drew her to her feet.

His arms round her were so strong they made her feel weightless. Her eyes closed in spite of her efforts to resist the swimmy feeling, the dizziness, the sensation of being in his arms gave her. His kiss tasted of bacon and made her feel like heaven.

Either it went on for a very long time, or she lost all sense of time. When he finally released her mouth, but not, thank goodness, her body, she felt boneless, brainless and insanely happy.

She forced herself back to reality. It's only a kiss. Nothing to get fussed about. People kiss each other all the time, it doesn't mean a thing.

As if sensing her doubts he pushed his hand into her hair and looked intently at her. She could almost feel his eyes on her face, taking in each freckle, the line of her mouth, the mole on her cheekbone. She lowered her lids, embarrassed by the intensity of his expression.

'Come on,' he said and, keeping his arm round her, he walked her out of the kitchen, along the passage, into the hall and up the stairs.

'What are you doing?' she laughed, knowing perfectly well what he was doing.

'I'm taking you to bed,' he said, opening the door to Ellie's bedroom and rejecting it. Another few paces and he found her bedroom, recognising it by its simplicity.

'Are you coming with me?' she whispered as he hesitated on the threshold. She knew he wouldn't cross it unless she invited him.

'Only if you want me to.'

Grace sighed. 'I know I'll regret this in the morning, but, yes, I do.'

'It is the morning. And I don't want any regrets. I don't want a single unhappy thought about me crossing your mind. Do this with your brain fully engaged. Think about this, Grace.'

'Oh, shut up,' she whispered, taking his hand and leading him into her bedroom.

Ellie turned onto her back to get more comfortable on Ran's futon. It was in his spare room, and initially she'd slept, but the hardness of the mattress had woken her. Now she lay and thought about the humiliations of the evening.

Once inside the house, Ran had been quite host-like. He'd offered Ellie a hot drink, which she'd accepted. Not because she yearned for cocoa, but because she wanted to watch him make it, and make him watch her watching him. This was the moment, she'd decided. It was now or never. If she couldn't make him have an affaire with her now, she'd never make it. She wiggled on her stool, put her head on one side and gave a little lopsided smile.

'How much sugar would you like in your cocoa?' he asked. He was in the process of mixing cocoa into a paste with cold milk. Unfortunately he didn't turn round, so he didn't see the smile or the wiggle.

'Two, I think,' she said hastily. 'I usually have drinking chocolate.'

He went back to his stirring. How seductive was that? 'I usually have drinking chocolate!' Who could resist? Irritated with herself, Ellie decided to postpone her plans until the cocoa was actually in her hands.

At last he handed her a mug of cocoa. 'Would you like a biscuit?'

'No, thank you.' Then she wondered if that had been a mistake. After all, if he was intent on going straight to bed, being forced to stay up while she ate a digestive would give her some valuable extra time. 'Actually,' she said, cooingly, 'can I change my mind?'

He gave her a sort of long look. 'If you take your cocoa and your biscuit to bed with you, you can have the whole packet, but I'm not in the mood to play games.'

'What do you mean?' Her velvet tones developed an edge of acid. 'I asked for a biscuit, not a Scrabble tournament!'

'You know what I mean, Ellie. You're trying to seduce me. And, while I think you're a lovely, bright, sexy girl, I am not going to take advantage of your wild hormones and let you do something you may regret.'

'What do you mean?' she said again. 'My wild hormones? What's that all about?'

'You're pregnant.'

'Not in my head! It doesn't affect my brain! I am not out of my mind!' She was furious. 'I know perfectly well what I'm doing!'

'That is as may be, but you'd better content yourself with cocoa and biscuits because I'm not interested in casual sex with a very young woman who may not be emotionally stable.'

Ellie only just stopped herself throwing the cocoa at him. She slid off the stool and the hot liquid slopped over the edge of the mug onto her jeans. She squeaked.

'I don't think you realise the risk you're running with this sort of behaviour. Other men might take advantage of you.'

'I—I am not emotionally unstable!' she spluttered, incensed at his suggestion that she would throw herself at just anyone. 'I'm pregnant! The two things do not necessarily go together!'

'Go to bed, Ellie. You'll feel very relieved in the morning that nothing happened.'

Ellie had flounced out, indignation having to do instead of dignity.

Now, awake in the early hours, she considered her situation. Was Ran right? Would relief be her strongest emotion in the morning? She felt like crying. It had all gone so horribly wrong. She punched her pillow, turned onto her side and tried to think about something other than Ran. It was impossible. Oh God! She hadn't fallen in love with him, had she?

It was only after a huge effort of concentration that she managed to wonder about Demi, Grace and Flynn.

Grace woke, but didn't open her eyes, aware that she was naked and that there was someone else in her bed. For a nanosecond she was confused. Was it Edward? Then she realised it couldn't possibly be Edward, not only because he'd left her, over two years ago now, but because there was a hand on her shoulder, and she and Edward had always slept in bed together without touching.

Flynn. It wasn't that Grace's heart sank, exactly, but the feeling of 'What have I done?' flooded over her. She knew she ought to get up and check on Demi, but that would involve opening her eyes, and opening her eyes would force her to deal with the situation.

Why had she invited him into her bedroom? Was she just grateful to him for being her rock when she needed someone to rely on?

She allowed her mind to shift from the philosophical to the physical and realised she was content. She had had sex. And what sex! With this realisation, she discovered why she had invited Flynn into her bed. She had wanted him, and for very good reason.

Flynn stirred, turned over, and pinned her to the bed with his arm just as she'd been contemplating slipping out. She shifted a little, testing to see if she could creep out from under without him noticing.

'Where are you running off to?' he murmured huskily.

'I'm not running! I want to check on Demi, that's all.'

He kissed her. 'I'll check on Demi. You stay here. I have plans.'

She closed her eyes as he got out of bed and she heard him pulling on his trousers. She didn't want to see him naked, it might confuse her. She stretched and gave her pillow a thump. Right now it was very pleasant to lie in rumpled cotton sheets and close her eyes.

Flynn came back. 'She's fine. She's had a drink of water, and has gone back to sleep. She's dreadfully embarrassed about what happened.'

'So am I.'

'Well, it was hardly your fault.' He slid off his trousers and got back into bed with a bounce.

'I didn't mean that.'

He turned and propped himself up on his elbow. He seemed very tanned and very sexy and she realised she hadn't really seen him last night, and he hadn't really seen her. In a fit of belated modesty, she checked that the duvet covered her breasts.

He noticed her gesture. 'You're embarrassed about what happened between us?'

She nodded.

'Why?'

'Because! Because . . . I don't know you very well.'

'Did it seem wrong?' He looked into her eyes intently and spoke softly.

'Not at the time, no.'

'But now it does?'

Grace bit her lip. 'Not wrong, just unexpected. Too soon, possibly.'

'You're not sure you wanted to make love yet?'

She shook her head, still confused. 'At all! If you'd asked me say, yesterday morning, if I had any intention of sleeping with you, I would have laughed.'

'Oh?' He sounded offended.

'Not because there's anything wrong with you! But because I was just someone who fed your cat.'

His eyebrow went up a millimetre and his voice was soft and husky. 'You were never just someone who fed my cat.'

Grace swallowed. He'd just made cat-feeding seem incredibly sexy. 'Well, good.'

'You've been in my mind constantly, almost from the moment we met. Why do you think I asked you to feed the damn cat in the first place?'

'I don't know! So it wouldn't starve to death?'

'No. My cleaning lady is always happy to feed her. I did it to get close to you. It was for the same reason I gave you the Rayburn.' He frowned slightly 'Although there were humanitarian reasons for that as well.'

'But why?'

'Are you really so unself-aware? You're a very attractive woman and I—like very attractive women.'

'Margaret's a very attractive woman.'

'She is, but in a different way.'

'Sara Cavendish thinks you're attractive, too.'

'Are we going to waste our entire morning in bed together discussing women who think I'm attractive? Because I should warn you, there are lots of them you don't know about, and if I have to tell you about them'—he kissed her, and brushed her hair back from her face—'we could be here for hours.'

'You're so vain,' she breathed, as his fingers moved from her shoulder to her breast. Then she sighed deeply, and he pulled away the duvet.

'And you're so beautiful.'

She should have argued, but he started kissing her and she forgot.

Grace finally got down into the kitchen at ten thirty. There had been no point in going down earlier, Flynn had insisted, because there would have been no hot water to do the washing-up, as it was past nine before Grace remembered to put the immersion heater on.

'If I can't get the Rayburn plumbed in myself,' said Flynn, 'I'll get a friend to do it. This situation is ridiculous.' They had both had rather small, chilly, separate baths.

'We can boil kettles. What would you like for breakfast? I'm afraid the bacon is all gone, but there are still some eggs. And leftover puddings.'

'Do you want bacon? I could get some, and the Saturday papers?'

Grace smiled. 'You could go if you want, but I'd better stay here for Demi. I don't want her waking up and finding the house empty.'

'Better a stale loaf where love is, than orange juice and croissants and hatred therewith,' said Flynn, hunting in the bread bin.

'What are you talking about?' Grace was clearing the end of the table of their previous breakfast.

'Just misquoting one of my favourite bits out of the Bible.'

'So what's the quote?'

'"Better is a dinner of herbs where love is, than a stalled ox and hatred therewith."'

Grace blushed at the word 'love', so unsure was she of her own feelings. She wiped the table and found two clean plates and mugs, no mean feat in the circumstances, wondering how she felt about Flynn, who was now washing up glasses. Did she love him? Now was definitely not the time to start philosophising. Flynn needed feeding.

After they had enjoyed a companionably inelegant breakfast of toast and marmalade, Flynn took the plates over to the side.

'Are you going to tell Demi's parents?'

Grace bit her lip and shook her head. 'I haven't decided! I know I should, but I don't know what's to be gained if I do.' She screwed the lid back on the marmalade jar. 'Her mother will go mad and Edward . . . well, Edward might be very angry.' She smiled. 'Not one I'd put Demi through without very good reason. What do you think?'

'It's not my business. I'm not a father myself, you're not a mother . . . What is it?'

Grace had suddenly felt slightly sick. 'I've just thought—'

'What? Tell me, woman!'

'We had unprotected sex,' she whispered, hugely embarrassed to talk about what they'd done now they were both dressed and in the kitchen.

'Is that what it was? I thought we were making love.'

Flynn's expression had an edge to it, as if he were hurt in some way, and yet he would surely accept they had been very irresponsible. 'We were—we were doing both.' Grace was still blushing ferociously.

'OK, so what's the worst that can happen because of it? You could get pregnant. How bad is that?'

'I do want a baby, more than anything, but not—not as a single parent! I'm not brave like Ellie. I couldn't cope with everything on my own.'

'And why do you think you'd have to? Why do you assume that I'd run off and never speak to you again if I made you pregnant?'

'I don't know! Perhaps you wouldn't. I'm all confused. I just don't understand how I got myself into this situation.' She smiled ruefully, trying to lighten the atmosphere. 'It's totally out of character for me.'

He came up to her and put his arms round her. 'So you let yourself get carried away. Is that such a sin?' He ruffled her hair and stroked her neck in a soothing way. He smelt nice, his arms were strong and his voice was low and comforting. And very sexy. She struggled gently.

'Let's not worry about any of that now,' she said briskly. 'I need to get the rest of the stuff out of the drawing room.'

Reluctantly, he allowed her to free herself. 'Tell me: in a house this size, why did you choose to have the meal in the drawing room? There must be a dining room, for goodness' sake.'

'There is. We didn't use it because it hasn't been used for a while and we tidied up the drawing room for Allegra—as you might remember.'

'I'd love to see the dining room. I've always been curious about this house.'

'And you've never had a tour? You should have said. Come and see the dining room.'

She took his hand and led him out of the kitchen to the dining room, then opened the door and drew him inside. The curtains that she and Ellie had hung up so carefully had all fallen onto the floor . . .

'Oh my God,' she said. The spaces where the shutters and the panels had been were vacant. She felt sick and felt herself sway slightly.

'What?'

'The paintings. The paintings are gone! They must have been stolen!'

'What paintings?'

She put her hands up to her face, as if she needed to hold on to herself so she wouldn't collapse. 'There were some painted panels, here, on the shutters. They've gone!'

'Well, who else but you knew about them?'

'Ellie does.'

'Would there be any reason for Ellie to do anything to them?'

'She was going to restore them so that I can sell them to pay for the dry rot, which is thirty thousand pounds' worth, I should tell you!'

'It is expensive stuff.'

Now her hands were in her hair, clutching at it. 'And how am I going to pay for it if someone's run off with the bloody paintings?'

'If no one knew about them, it is terribly unlikely they've been stolen. It will be something to do with Ellie. What did she say in her note?'

'Nothing about stealing the paintings!' Grace wailed, running from the room so she could look at the note again. 'She just says she's spending the night at Ran's house,' she confirmed a few minutes later, when she had gone through the rubbish and found the note.

'Then she'll be back soon. It's nearly twelve, all we have to do is wait for her to come back and then ask her. Meanwhile, why don't you ring her on her mobile?'

'Of course! Where's the bloody phone?'

Chapter Eight

ELLIE HAD INTENDED to get up early and be in the kitchen, making break-fast, before she encountered Ran. Instead, he was already there, grind-ing beans, making coffee, which was unfortunate because the smell of coffee made Ellie so sick she had to leave the room again.

When she came back, she said, 'Morning! No coffee for me, please,' and tried to be her usual breezy self, as if he had not practically told her she was a tart the night before.

'Sorry. I forgot. What would you like?'

He looked, if such a thing were possible, even more sexy. His cheek-bones were enhanced by his stubble, and his hair, all ruffled and 'just got out of bed', begged to be smoothed by sensitive fingers. Bastard! thought Ellie. He might have put a shirt on. For although the little kitchen was not all that warm, Ran had chosen to make breakfast wear-ing nothing but a pair of torn jeans.

'Tea. I'll make it!' Ellie cursed herself for sounding like a Girl Guide. If she hadn't felt so miserable, she would probably have had a last crack at seducing him. 'Would you like me to cook you something?' she asked, when she had found a mug and a tea bag. 'I'm a very good cook.'

'I know,' said Ran, regarding her over his coffee mug. 'I ate your food last night.'

'I'm glad you liked it.' Ellie wrung out a dishcloth, which smelt slightly, and wiped the work surface. What am I doing? she asked her-self. Trying to housekeep my way into his heart?

If she couldn't drag him into bed, she wanted to get back to Luckenham House. She didn't want Grace facing the mess alone and, more importantly, didn't want her wandering into the dining room and finding the paintings gone. She also wanted to be out of this awkward situation as quickly as possible.

Ran, to his credit, seemed to realise this. 'I expect you're in a hurry to go,' he said. 'I'll just finish this coffee, have a quick shower, and drive you back.'

'It's terribly kind of you—' she began.

He got up from the table and she turned to face him. She was still clutching the cloth. 'I thought we'd established I don't do kind. I expect you to pay me back.'

'But I haven't got any—'

'Shush. I've been thinking. Were you serious when you said you were interested in picture conservation?'

'Yes! I told you—'

'Then you can be my apprentice. You can make yourself useful, watch what I do, and eventually, I might let you do a little scraping off glue from the backs of paintings. Under strict supervision of course.'

A flicker of optimism, the size of a birthday candle, lit itself in her heart.

'But I thought you didn't want me!' She put down the cloth and wiped her hands on her jeans.

'Oh, I do want you,' he said softly, 'but possibly not in the way you want me.'

Ellie lowered her eyes, which was unfortunate because her gaze landed on the zip of his jeans, which was not what she needed just now when she was trying to hold herself together. She was dumped, she knew that; he'd made it perfectly clear. But she would see him again, and even if she ended up as his cleaning lady, that would be better than not seeing him.

He lifted her face so she had to look at him, his hand tender on her cheek. 'I want you to come over a couple of mornings a week, do what I need doing, and study what I'm doing. I will pay you the going rate.'

'Oh, no! I'll do it for the pictures. You're restoring them.'

'Sweetheart, you could redecorate this house from top to bottom, and clean it with your toothbrush, and you couldn't pay me for restoring the paintings. I'm doing that because they are very beautiful and very precious.' He paused. 'And Grace might be able to pay me if she sells them.'

'So why do you want me . . . to come and be your apprentice?' she asked.

'Not many people understand how something that can seem mind-numbingly boring is in fact incredibly important. I need someone who is painstaking and careful and pays enormous attention to detail. I've needed someone for some time but haven't got anyone because there aren't many people I can stand being around while I'm working.'

'Oh.'

'Yes, that is a compliment, sort of. Now go and get your stuff sorted out. I won't be long.' Then he leaned forward and kissed her nose.

She stood in the kitchen, immobile from every sort of emotional agony. Here is a man, she fumed silently, whom I have practically told in words of one syllable that I will go to bed and have mad passionate sex with, and he kisses my nose! As if I'm a kitten or something!'

Indignant as she was, she couldn't help feeling warmed by his gesture.
'You're a fool, Ellie Summers,' she told herself as she stuffed her things into her bag. But the bubble of hope wouldn't be suppressed.

It was only when they were nearly at Luckenham House that Ellie thought it would be nice to ring Grace and tell her she was arriving, so she turned on her mobile phone. 'Six messages,' she said. 'Oh, they're from Grace.' Listening to the messages, she learned that Grace had spent part of the night at the hospital with Demi, and that she was frantic with worry about the missing panels.

'Beside herself' didn't really describe Grace when she opened the door to Ellie. Flynn was in the background, and Ellie had time to wonder why and how long he'd been there before she realised how Grace was feeling.

'The paintings! They've been stolen!' she wailed.

'Let them get through the door,' murmured Flynn. 'We can't have this scene on the doorstep. There isn't room.'

'And the paintings haven't been stolen,' said Ran. 'I've got them.'

'What?' Grace turned to him. 'Who are you?'

Shortage of sleep and the conviction that her only asset had been taken from her, had affected Grace's memory.

'I'm Randolph Frazier. I'm a picture conservator. I'm going to restore the paintings for you. Let's go into the kitchen. We can discuss what's happened or what should happen in there.'

'It's OK,' said Ellie. 'Really it is. I'm sorry about the paintings, but Ran insisted they shouldn't stay here another night.'

'They were deteriorating rapidly,' he said from behind Grace's head as they trooped to the kitchen.

Ellie went to make hot drinks, as the situation seemed to demand the ritual. Flynn sat Grace down at the table. Ran sat next to her.

'I realise it must have been a dreadful shock to find the paintings gone,' he said. 'But I felt I had to get them out of here as soon as possible. They've already got dry rot in the top and it spreads rapidly.'

'Tell me about it,' said Grace, putting her elbows on the table and hiding behind her hands. 'Thirty thousand pounds is what I'm going to have to pay to have it put right. It's as much as a house.'

'No,' said Flynn, 'but it's quite a good car.'

Grace opened her eyes and regarded him. He seemed to be being flippant again.

'Anyway,' said Flynn. 'Much as I would like to discuss fine art, now that your pictures have turned up safely I have got to go.' He leaned over the table, ruffled the back of Grace's head and kissed her cheek. 'I'll give you a ring later, my love.' He raised his hand to the others. 'See you!' Then he left the kitchen.

Grace knew she was blushing. She could feel it, and even if she couldn't, she could tell by the way the other two were looking at her. She took a breath. 'The paintings . . .' she said at random, with no idea what she was going to say about them.

Fortunately for Grace, Demi appeared. She looked as ruffled and sleepy as a toddler picked up out of a cot. 'What's going on?' she said.

As Grace had a very confused expression, Ellie took over. 'Demi! What happened to you? Are you all right? Your face!'

'I cut it when I fell over,' said Demi.

'Yes,' said Grace, pulling herself together. 'How are you this morning? Have you got a headache?'

'A bit.' Demi frowned at Ran, confused. 'Sorry, should I know you?'

'No,' said Ran firmly. 'I am not generally considered someone that young women in oversized T-shirts should know.'

'Don't tease her, Ran!' said Ellie, jealous of this flirtatious remark. 'Let me make you something, Dem.'

'There's no bacon,' said Grace. 'But there are some eggs.'

'There is bacon,' said Ellie. 'I got some a couple of days ago.'

'Flynn and I ate it,' said Grace, trying not to blush all over again.

'Oh.' Ellie continued to rummage in the refrigerator. 'We've got lots of milk, you could have cereal.'

'Mrs Ravenglass . . .' began Ran, not wanting to be party to a conversation about Coco Pops.

'Grace, please,' said Grace.

'The paintings. I think I should tell you, I consider them to be very fine. I'm not an expert about value, of course, but they should definitely go to an auction house or something to be properly valued.'

'Was it really necessary to take them away?' asked Grace. 'It was a bit of a shock to see them missing like that.' She frowned; she'd suffered so many shocks in such a short time she seemed to have lost her ability to form proper sentences.

'It must have been, and I'm terribly sorry, but I could do very little with them *in situ*. Until the dry rot's fixed, you shouldn't put them back.'

'I'm going to have to sell them anyway, I think.'

'It seems a shame. They've obviously been in the house a very long time, and were possibly painted here. This is where they should stay.'

'But I need money to pay for the dry rot,' said Grace.

'And the insurance would be astronomical,' agreed Ran. 'What sort of security system do you have here?'

'Minimalist?' suggested Demi, who, after a few spoons of sugar-coated puffed rice, seemed to have perked up quite a lot.

'Which isn't a problem if the paintings aren't in the house,' said Ellie, wondering about Ran's own locks and bolts.

'The thing is, I can't pay you,' said Grace, 'until I sell the paintings.'

'I'd do them for nothing—' began Ran.

'I'm going to be his apprentice,' announced Ellie.

'So I'm perfectly happy to wait for a bit for any money,' Ran continued. 'Now, if you're quite happy for me to have the paintings and to do what I can to restore them, I'll go.'

Grace was finding it hard to think straight. 'As you've already got them, and I know nothing about picture restoration, I suppose I am happy. But I don't know very much about you, either.'

'I could give you some references, if it would make you happier. I have worked for some major museums and stately homes.'

Grace's earlier doubts faded to nothing. 'I don't need references. I trust you.'

'That's good,' said Ran. 'Without being too modest, I am the best.' He smiled, and Grace realised why Ellie had chosen this man to have a last fling with: he was gorgeous.

Ellie got up. 'I'll see you out.'

'There's no need. I'll give you a ring to make arrangements about you coming over.'

Then he was gone. The three women who lived in Luckenham House watched the space he had left by the door for a few seconds, each drawing breath to question the others about what had happened to all of them since they were last together, but before any of them could say a word they heard voices and footsteps coming along the corridor.

'Oh, shit!' breathed Demi as the kitchen door opened. 'It's Mum!'

Grace would have said the same, only it wasn't Demi's mother who would have inspired such an expletive, but the additional presence of her own sister, Allegra.

'We more or less met on the doorstep and that man let us in,' said Allegra disapprovingly.

'Demeter!' said Hermia. 'What has happened to your face?'

Grace dragged her last atom of good manners up from somewhere and got to her feet. 'How nice to see you both. Coffee? Tea?'

'I'll make it!' said Ellie quickly, forcing Grace to sit down again, deprived of her escape route.

Flynn found Grace later that afternoon at the far end of the garden, pulling at dead brambles with the fierce determination of one intent on demolishing Sleeping Beauty's magic forest armed only with a pair of blunt secateurs. 'I tried to phone you, but I couldn't get an answer.'

'Sorry. I just had to get out of the house for a bit.'

'Darling! What's wrong?'

'Nothing.' Grace felt herself blush at his endearment and tugged at a particularly stubborn bramble. She tore her gardening glove and then her palm. 'Oh, shit,' she muttered, aware that she was very near tears.

'Are you hurt?' Flynn moved forward to look, but she snatched her hand away.

'I'm fine! No need to fuss!'

'Then let's go in. I want to talk, and unlike you, I'm not dressed for the Arctic. We can light a fire and I'll make you tea.'

'I've drunk so much tea I'm awash with it,' Grace grumbled.

'I'll find something stronger then. Ellie's in the kitchen making Demi some scrambled eggs. They sent me out to get you in.'

Her hand was hurting and her nose was beginning to run. The thought of a fire, friendly people and alcohol was very tempting.

'OK.' Being near him made Grace feel calmer, and she was proud of herself for not flinging herself into his arms when he first asked her what was wrong. She didn't want to put him into a position where he might feel obliged to invite them all to stay at his house. She didn't want him thinking he had to look after her just because they'd slept together.

'So why were you gardening on a cold winter's afternoon?' he asked conversationally as they walked in together.

'Well, these things pile up if you don't get round to them.'

'Most people do these things in daylight.'

She allowed her mouth to twitch. It *was* a strange time of day to be pulling up brambles. 'I've been busy. This was my only opportunity.'

He smiled back. 'Right. But Demi's obviously fine now.'

'Yes, thank goodness. Did they tell you her mother turned up? She'd had a call from Rick, too. I didn't mean to lie to her, but when the time came I found I just couldn't drop Demi in it. It was terribly irresponsible.'

'I don't think anyone could accuse you of being that, Grace.' He paused and looked down at her. 'A little odd in some ways, possibly, but not irresponsible.'

'What do you mean?' she said indignantly. 'I'm not remotely odd!'

'It may be news to you, but usually when people have spent a very pleasant night in bed together, they're a bit more friendly when they see each other again.'

Grace stopped and turned to him, overcome with remorse. 'Oh, Flynn, I'm sorry! Was I being unfriendly?'

'A little chilly. What's the problem?'

'Oh, nothing much. Did Ellie and Demi tell you that my sister arrived at the same time as Demi's mother?'

'I think they did.'

'Well, she always manages to rattle me. That's all.'

'Are you sure? She didn't bring you bad news?'

For a moment she considered denying it, but decided it wouldn't work. 'Just boring stuff about the dry rot. They're coming to do it on Monday, and you know how tiresome it is having people in the house.'

He regarded her intently. 'I do indeed. And I also know that they probably want you out of the house while they do it. It's easier for them if they can just take all the plaster off and get on with it.'

'Hmm.' Grace opened the gate that led to the path to the back door.

'So would you all like to come and stay with me?'

'Oh, no! There's no need for that! In fact, I'm not at all sure it's necessary for us to move out at all!'

He paused, stopping her with a hand on her arm. 'Grace, what's the matter? Why aren't you telling me anything? Was it something I did? Or are you just regretting going to bed with me?'

In many ways she was. She could have happily gone to stay with him, accepting the help of a neighbour. Making love to him had made things more complicated. She moved to avoid his question, but he stood in front of her and took her face in his hands. 'Well?'

Grace looked up at him, into his kind brown eyes with the curly eyelashes. She let her gaze slide over his firm, curved mouth and strong chin, and wondered why she hadn't realised how attractive he was when they first met. 'I loved making love to you,' she said, 'I loved everything we did together. But life has suddenly become rather complicated.'

'It's been complicated ever since we met,' he said. 'What's different?'

She didn't want to tell him. She didn't want his sympathy, she didn't want him to sweep her into his arms and hold her while she sobbed out her troubles.

'Come on, Grace.' He gave her a little shake. 'Spit it out.'

'It's nothing. Just a money thing.'

'And you can't tell me?'

'No! I can't! Don't you see? If we were just friends, perhaps I could have told you, but now . . . now you'll feel obliged to help me and I don't want to be helped! I want to sort things out for myself. I was too dependent on Edward, and it was so hard getting myself back together again after he left. I feel as if I've climbed a long, high hill, and I'm tee-tering at the top. If I'm not careful, I'll fall back all the way I've come.'

'Carrying on your analogy to its logical conclusion, if you take a step forward, you'll fall down just as far. It's going to be uncomfortable, tee-tering on that peak, unable to move.'

She smiled at him. 'It does sound rather precarious.'

'And lonely.'

She sighed very deeply. 'But I'm used to that.'

'There's no need for you to be used to it now. You've got Ellie, and Demi and—' He paused only for the tiniest second. 'Me.'

'I know. But Ellie won't live here for ever. Demi will probably go back home eventually, and if not, she'll go to university   '

'And me? I know we haven't known each other that long, but surely you don't need to assume that I'm going to wander off in the future?'

'Don't I? You said it yourself, we hardly know each other. I have no idea what you're likely to do! I certainly shouldn't have slept with you!'

'I thought you said you loved it!'

'I did! But we don't know how we feel about each other really, and you shouldn't go to bed with people just because you want to!'

'Why not? We're both single.'

'Just look at the trouble it's caused!'

He sighed. 'The only trouble it's caused is in your mind, Grace. Now let's go in. You're getting cold.'

Ellie could tell straight away that things weren't quite right between Flynn and Grace.

'Hi, guys. Scrambled egg? We've just about got enough eggs.'

'Actually, we've decided to go out for dinner, if you two won't miss us too much,' said Flynn.

'No, we haven't!' said Grace. 'You didn't even ask me!'

'I wouldn't have got an answer if I had. Now go and get the brambles out of your hair and hurry up. You don't need to change.'

Ellie and Demi didn't mean to wait up for Grace, but Demi, having been asleep all day, wasn't tired, and there'd been a film they wanted to watch on telly. Ellie had slept through it all, but woke up with the closing credits.

The sound of a key in the front door made her sit up. 'That's Grace! Let's go and see how her evening went.'

It was hard to tell in the very dim light of the hall, but Grace appeared to be blushing. 'Oh, hello. I hope you didn't wait up for me.'

'No,' said Demi. 'We were watching a film, or at least I was. Ellie snored her way through it.'

'I don't snore!'

'No, not really. So, how did you get on?'

Grace sighed for a moment, deeply happy, and determined to hold on to the feeling before her worries started to batter away at it. 'We had a lovely meal.'

'And?' demanded Demi.

'And—well, he persuaded me that we should all go and stay with him while the dry rot is fixed. But we're having our own bedrooms.'

'You're not sharing with Flynn?' said Demi. 'Why not? He's so cool!'

'Well, yes, he is. But I don't think—I mean . . . Anyway, it's none of your business, and I'm really tired.'

Ellie went to her own room feeling lonely, and envious of Grace for having Flynn so obviously devoted to her. Not that she begrudged Grace her happiness, but she so wanted some for herself. And then a thought occurred to her. Why shouldn't she stay with Ran while Grace and Demi stayed with Flynn? It would make perfect sense, or at least, it would by the time she'd framed her argument. Ran had telephoned to ask her to come over the next day. She smiled as she put toothpaste on her brush. She still had a chance of a fling, even if it was a bit flimsy.

The next morning, Ran let her in almost as soon as she rang the bell. 'I'll give you a key,' he said. 'So you can come and go as you need to.'

'Thank you,' said Ellie, feeling this was progress.

'After all,' he went on, spoiling the effect of his previous statement, 'I may not always be in when you come.'

'No. Actually . . .' She bit her lip as he stared at her. 'I was wondering . . . the thing is . . . I need somewhere to stay for a few days. Luckenham House is being treated for dry rot and we've all got to move out. Also,' she went on when he didn't answer, 'I haven't seen a doctor or anyone since I discovered I was pregnant because I'm signed on in Bath. It would give me an opportunity to go to her.'

'Where are the others going?'

'Grace is going to stay with Flynn.' She didn't mention Demi.

'So you want to stay here?' His expression was inscrutable.

'If that's all right. Of course, I don't have to, it's just . . . my parents live miles away, and—'

'Well, I suppose that's OK,' he interrupted her, looking at her rather sternly. 'When do you want to come?'

'They're starting next Monday.'

'So you could just bring your stuff when you come?'

'Yes, I could.' Somehow, everything had worked out all right. Perhaps it was a good omen.

In the studio, the panels were lying on their backs on an old sheet.

'I haven't done anything to them yet. I wanted to think how best to proceed. They could be priceless, although there isn't a signature, unfortunately,' he went on. 'There were a couple of initials, but one has been virtually eaten away.'

'Where is it? Perhaps I could make it out.'

He showed her the place. There was a clear letter R and the second letter looked a bit like a C.

'Would it add to their value if we knew who did them?'

'Hugely. And if we could also find some provenance, how they came to be in the house, stuff like that, it would help enormously.'

'So how are you going to find out all that?'

'I'm not. You are.' He said it very coolly, as if it were perfectly simple.

'I am? But I don't know anything about things like that.'

'I'll point you in the right direction, but you'll have to do the spade-work. It'll be good training for you.'

'So where will I have to go?'

'The Witt Library. It's part of the Courtauld Institute, in Somerset House. You'll have to go through all the artists with first names beginning with R, and see if anything fits with what we know.'

'But we know nothing!'

He shook his head. 'We've got a rough date—within a century or two—we have a locale, and we have a subject.'

'But I don't feel remotely qualified to do anything like that! I'm an artist, not a historian!'

'Look, do you want to do the best for these panels or don't you? I don't have time to do the research—I'm working on the panels for nothing, when I've got my own clients stacking up. I can't take days off in London to do research.'

'No, sorry. I wasn't thinking . . .' She lowered her eyes contritely.

'Well, then, start! And then get the Hoover out. Oh, and make an appointment with your doctor.'

'Yes, sir,' said Ellie, trying not to laugh.

By the time Ellie got back to Luckenham House that night she had not only cleaned Ran's house and had her first go at scraping off glue with a scalpel, but she had a sheaf of notes about the panels. She was very glad that Grace was in the kitchen so she could spill out her enthusiasm. 'I've had the most amazing day!' she said. 'Ran is fascinating.'

Grace smiled as she put the kettle on. 'I know that, you've made your feelings quite clear.'

'I don't mean like that! I mean as a conservator!'

'I thought he was a picture restorer.'

Ellie shook her head. 'What Ran does is much more about conserving what's there, making it stable, so it doesn't deteriorate any further. He does do restoration, but they don't like to be called picture restorers.'

'Those sound like words from the master!'

'You'd better believe it! He's so gorgeous when he's strict!' She looked up at Grace. 'By the way,' she added. 'I've arranged to stay with Ran while the dry rot is being done. Is that all right?'

'Oh! Yes, of course it is. I'll have Demi as a chaperone.'

'Do you need a chaperone?'

'No!' Grace sounded startled. 'No, of course I don't. I just . . .'

'What?' demanded Ellie, unable to be tactful any longer. 'What's going on with you and Flynn?'

'Nothing. We're just . . .'

'What? He's a lovely man, Grace, and there aren't many like him!'

Grace looked confused. 'I just don't want to rush things. And if I was staying with him, in his house, on my own, I'd feel I was pushing him into something. Anyway, it'll be fine. Demi will be there with me.'

'I see,' said Ellie, deciding that Demi wouldn't. Perhaps she'd benefit from a little spell with her mother while Luckenham House was full of toxic chemicals. Grace needed pushing, and if she wouldn't be pushed with Demi there, Demi would not be there. After she had had the facts explained to her, Ellie was sure Demi would go back to her mother's, if not happily, at least with resignation.

The following Monday morning, they assembled in the hall of Luckenham House.

'Right, Demi. That's the bag you want for tonight?'

Demi nodded. She and Ellie hadn't actually told Grace that Demi was going to stay with her mother yet. They didn't want to panic her.

'OK. We'd better get in the car. I'll come back after dropping you at the bus, let the men in, and then move out.'

It was only when they were nearly at the bus-stop that Demi said casually, 'Oh, by the way, Grace. I thought I'd spend a couple of nights at Mum's. She's picking me up after college.'

'What? Demi! Why didn't you tell me? Anyway, I thought your room had been turned into a gym!'

'She's got a spare room, and I thought I should go and check in with her, just for a little while. So she can see that I'm doing my college work.'

'Demi—'

'It's all right, Grace. Mum really is collecting me. You can phone her if you like. I rang her the other day. Ellie suggested it. She said if I volunteered to go home for a couple of nights, Mum would worry less.'

A twinkle of light flickered in Grace's brain. Ellie suggested it, did she? 'You and Ellie aren't throwing me together with Flynn, are you?'

Demi managed a look of pure innocence. 'Grace! Now would we do a thing like that?'

'Yes! Now hurry. There's the bus.'

Grace drove back towards the centre of town slowly and thoughtfully. 'Sometimes I wish I lived in Victorian times,' she muttered, scanning the rows of cars in the car park, looking for a space. 'There'd be none of this nonsense then! We'd just live with the dry rot. Ah! A space!'

Her first errand was at the bank, where she had arranged to get her jewellery out of the vault. She then had an appointment with a jeweller, who was going to value and then sell it for her. She thought it might be worth about £5,000.

Then her plan ran out, and she didn't have another one. How was she going to raise the rest in a week?

Two hours later she drove back to her house, where she found the woodwork-treatment men already there, getting stuff out of their van. They had protective clothing and masks with them. Flynn's friend, Pete, was also there.

'Flynn asked me to come along and plumb in the Rayburn while all this lot's going on,' he said.

'That was nice of him,' said Grace, wondering how she could possibly pay for Pete on top of everything else.

She tried to smile as the foreman approached her, but it was the vain attempt of someone trying to appear pleased as the dentist asks them to open wide, drill in hand.

Grace sat in the car for a few moments, psyching herself up to knock on Flynn's door. She would have stayed there longer, only he came out of the house and round to her side of the car. Feeling that he might physically wrench her from it, she got out of her own accord.

'Hello, Flynn,' she said, overcome with shyness.

'Hello, you. How lovely to see you!' He wrapped his arms round her and hugged her tightly. 'Come in.'

There was something extremely nice about being welcomed in this way, Grace acknowledged as she picked up her handbag and her post while Flynn got her bag out of the boot.

'But I mustn't get used to it,' she said aloud.

'What's that?' Flynn called from the doorstep.

'This personal service,' called Grace. 'I mustn't get used to it.' It was a convincing sounding lie and she smiled.

'I don't see why you shouldn't,' said Flynn as Grace joined him on the doorstep. He ushered her into the kitchen. 'Someone to carry your bags for you, from time to time, would be no bad thing. Now, coffee?'

'Yes, please. I saw Pete, by the way. He said you'd sent him to plumb in the Rayburn. You must let me have a bill when he's finished.'

'It's a present.'

'No,' she said firmly. 'It can't be. I can pay him myself. You gave me the Rayburn in the first place, and made it cook. You don't need to plumb it in for me. Not literally, of course.' She laughed.

'I could have done it myself. I've done similar jobs many times,' he said, pouring coffee beans into a grinder. 'Electrics, plumbing, building, joinery, I've done it all in my time.'

'You're a useful man.'

'Yes, I am.' He regarded her intently, as if there was a subtext he was willing her to understand.

'Shame you don't do dry-rot treatment.'

'I have done that, but not on the scale that you've got it in Luckenham House.' He ground the beans and Grace sat down.

'I suppose so.'

'But, of course, it is fantastically expensive,' he went on. 'I'd be very happy to lend you—give you, in fact, but I know you wouldn't accept that—the money for the dry rot. I know you don't want to borrow it from your sister.'

'And how do you know I haven't got the money in my current account?' Grace tried to hide her confusion behind false indignation.

'Because you wouldn't be having wine-tasting evenings, sitting on tea chests, if you had. Do you want milk?'

'Black with sugar, please.' A cup of strong coffee might be just what she needed to help her cope with Flynn.

'I've got to pop out for a short time,' he said, sipping his coffee. 'Why don't I show you where I've put you, let you sort yourself out, and then take you out for lunch? There's a new restaurant I want to try. It's a bit of a drive, but it should be worth it.'

'You're spoiling me. If we go out I insist on paying. It's my turn.'

He put his hand on her cheek and kissed her. 'No,' he said firmly. 'Now, come upstairs. Let me show you the guest suite.'

The guest suite was gorgeous. It consisted of a bedroom containing a double bed the size of a patio and a bathroom with a walk-in shower and freestanding bath. There was a dressing room next to it, with a little balloon-backed chair in the corner.

'This is delightful! Did you choose all the colours and materials?'

He shook his head. 'I employed a very talented, very expensive, interior designer. She did a good job.'

'She certainly did,' said Grace. 'She has excellent taste.'

'So have I. And I do appreciate the good things in life.'

This time he put his arms round her and kissed her long and hard.

In Bath, Ellie had been to see her doctor. She had phoned the surgery that morning, and the receptionist had been able to give her a last-minute cancellation.

'How did you get on?' asked Ran as Ellie hauled bags of shopping into the house. He took the bags from her as she did so.

'Fine, I'm well. I'm going to have a scan, and I've bought some lovely steak for supper. It was on offer,' she added.

'Good. I'm certain you should eat red meat when you're pregnant. And I'm glad you're well, because I want you to go to London tomorrow, to do a little research.'

Ellie cooked steak, sauté potatoes and wilted spinach. It was, she was forced to confess, extremely good. She had taken immense pains with it, as it was their first supper together, and she was privately very smug about the outcome.

'I haven't eaten a steak as good as this since I was last in France,' said Ran, spearing a piece of meat which was perfectly pink in the middle and slightly charred on the outside.

Ellie blushed and awarded herself a point. 'I learned to cook steak while I was an au pair in France. And I suppose that's when I learned to like food, really. I'm glad you approve. Have some potatoes.'

Ran picked up the dish and shovelled half of them onto his plate. 'You must make sure you take the money for all this out of the petty cash box.'

'No! This is on me, to thank you for having me. My parents gave me some money when I told them I was pregnant.' Quite why Ellie felt obliged to tell him this, she didn't know. Maybe so he'd know she wasn't entirely dependent on his largesse.

'Why? Did they want you to have an abortion?' He frowned.

'Oh, no. At least, they didn't say so. They just didn't want to offer to have me at home. My mother can't face the thought of being a grand-mother just yet and the thought of a baby, or worse a toddler, in that house, was enough to give all of us nightmares.'

'Oh. So Grace took you in?'

'It wasn't quite like that. She wanted the company. It's been very lonely for her since her husband left.'

'It must have been, in that great big house all on her own.'

There was a pause as they both got on with their steaks, then Ran broke the companionable silence. 'So how long do you think you'll go on living with Grace?'

Ellie frowned. 'I don't know. As long as she'll have me, I suppose. She was very keen on the idea of me having the baby there. She wanted children, it was one of the reasons she and her husband broke up—she wanted them and he didn't. He already had Demi and there's a son, too.'

'He must have been quite a lot older than Grace, then.'

'Oh, he was.'

'How old are you, Ellie?'

'Twenty-five. Why?'

'I'm thirty-five. Ten years is quite a large gap.'

'So it is,' said Ellie. 'Just as well I'm not planning to marry you then, isn't it?' Then she blushed the colour of the piece of steak on her fork. A moment later, she forced herself to meet Ran's gaze and realised that he was explaining why he wouldn't let her seduce him. 'On the other hand,' she went on, willing herself to stop but somehow unable to, 'lots of people don't get married. They just have a relationship.'

Ran sighed. 'Ellie, I should tell you, although you may well have guessed, that I have had quite a lot of relationships, long-term and short-term, mostly the latter, and they have always been with sophisticated women, either older or the same age as me. I like you a great deal, but you are far too young and sweet to be part of that string of women.'

'Sweet!' She dropped her knife and fork on her plate. 'Sweet! If you really wanted to insult me, you couldn't have done better than that!'

'Sorry. Insulting you really wasn't my intention.'

'Well, it was the effect! I may be young, but I've had my own failed relationship, you may remember. I'm quite capable of deciding for myself if I want a relationship.'

'So am I, and I don't, in this particular instance.' He spoke very gently, and that somehow gave Ellie confidence.

'Fair enough.' She regarded him, not shy any more, but challenging. 'That's your choice. Don't blame me if you live to regret it.'

He returned her look and they confronted each other, the sexual tension between them almost palpable. Ellie knew he wouldn't give in and sweep her off to bed, but more importantly for her, she knew that he wanted to, very much.

Over lunch, Grace had lost her awkwardness with Flynn. By the time he had fed her, bought her several large drinks, and made her laugh so much she wondered if she could ever be serious again, she no longer had any anxieties about their sleeping arrangements; she would let things run their course. If they ended up in bed together, they did, and if they didn't, well, that was all right too.

'Would you like some tea?' asked Flynn as they got back through the front door.

'I'll make it. Do let me. You've looked after me so well all day, it's the least I can do.' She turned and smiled as they entered the kitchen. 'Well, actually, it's probably the most I can do.'

'I don't know how you can know so much about wine and not care about food.'

'Oh, I do care,' she insisted. 'I just can't cook. Edward always did it and he was such a foodie—' she broke off. 'I was scared to try, I suppose, in case it went wrong.' She smiled, trying to get him off the subject. 'I'll make the tea. Go away and leave me to it.'

While she was in the kitchen, Flynn's cat appeared and rubbed itself against her legs, asking for food. She found the cat biscuits and put some in a bowl and watched as she crunched into them. 'Perhaps I'll get a cat,' she said aloud, and then filled the kettle.

She carried the tray into the sitting room, which was beautiful. It had elm boards on the floor with a few very worn old rugs. The furniture was a mixture of antique and modern and the room felt elegant and yet still comfortable, somewhere to relax.

'Biscuits?' asked Flynn, who had been lying on one of the pair of sofas with his feet up and had swung them down as she entered the room.

'You can't want biscuits. You ate a huge lunch. Besides, I've no idea where they are.'

'I'll get them. You sit down and pour the tea.' He rose, but stayed for a moment, looking at her as she sank into the feather cushions and silk velvet. He came back with a packet of the sort of biscuits her sister Allegra would serve: organic, with royal connections. Grace noticed that he was also carrying her post, which she had left in the kitchen.

'What's this?' he asked, handing her a flier with her handwriting all over it.

'Oh, just some doodling.'

'It doesn't look like doodling to me, Grace.' He sat down on the sofa next to her and made her look at it. 'It looks like calculations for borrowing money from loan sharks. Please tell me that you're not thinking of borrowing money from these people.'

Grace snatched the paper away from him. 'Flynn, who are you to say who I can borrow money from or not?'

Flynn snatched the paper back. 'I'm someone who cares about you and I will not let you be fleeced by these sharks.'

'How dare you! It's none of your business! It would be my loan! My responsibility! How many times have I got to tell you?'

'You can tell me until you're blue in the face, but you're not borrowing money from loan sharks! Not while there's breath in my body to prevent you!'

'Flynn—'

'I love you, Grace! And it's why I'm not going to let you do this bloody stupid thing. If you need money you can borrow it from me.'

'No! Don't you understand? I can't borrow money from you. It wouldn't be right. It would be like selling a car to a friend. It could ruin the relationship.'

He made a sound between a grunt and a chuckle. 'At least you acknowledge we have a relationship.'

'No, I don't! That sounds awful!'

'Only to you, Grace. To me it sounds just fine.'

'Well, it may do, but I'm not borrowing money from you.'

'Borrow it from your sister, then.'

'I'm not borrowing it from her, either. I don't want her knowing about the paintings any more than I want the bank knowing.'

'They'll all find out eventually.'

'But not before they absolutely have to.'

'Then I'm your only option. You can't or won't borrow it from normal lenders, or your family, so it's me or go without.' He chewed his lower lip for a few moments and she noted how white and even his teeth were. 'I'll tell you what,' he said. 'I'll lend you the money, but I'll charge you interest. That way you can't possibly feel obliged to me because I'd be earning money from you.'

'OK,' she said slowly. 'That sounds good. But it'll be the same rate of interest I would have paid the loan sharks.'

'You're a tough woman, Grace.'

Grace suddenly smiled. 'I know! It's good, isn't it?'

He came towards her and drew her to her feet. 'I do love you. I know you don't love me, or if you do, you don't recognise it, but that's OK. I just want you to know there's no ulterior motive in anything I do for you. I don't want or need anything back—or at least . . .'

'What about passion?' whispered Grace, putting her arms round him. 'Can we do things because of passion?'

'I think that would be fine,' he whispered back. 'Come on.' He put his arm round her to usher her out of the room when the phone rang. He paused. 'I'll ignore it. They'll ring back.'

'I think you should answer it,' said Grace. 'It might be important.'

He reached for the phone, laughing into her eyes. 'If it's a double-glazing salesman, I'll be very annoyed. Hello? Demi? Grace, it's for you.'

Grace came back into the room and took hold of the telephone, prepared for disaster.

'Demi? Are you all right?'

'I'm fine,' said Demi in a small voice, 'but I think I should tell you . . .'

'What? What's happened? What's the problem?'

'There may not be one,' she hedged. 'But Mum knows about the paintings. I'm afraid I told her, by mistake. It just slipped out.'

Grace licked her lips and swallowed. There was no point in being cross. It wouldn't change anything.

'I'm terribly sorry,' said Demi. 'She was asking about the house and everything and the dry rot and I said we had to get the paintings out because of it. She said, "What paintings?"'

'Well, she would, but never mind. She might not tell anyone else.'

There was a silence which indicated that Demi did not agree with this statement.

'So who will she tell?'

'Your sister.'

'Oh,' said Grace after a moment. 'Are you absolutely sure? I mean, they don't know each other that well—'

'I've only just managed to get the phone—Rick's still got my mobile. Mummy and Allegra were talking for hours.'

'Do you know what Allegra said?'

'Not exactly, but going on how Mum was, I imagine she was livid.'

'Why? It's not my fault I found valuable paintings in my house!'

'But you didn't tell her about them. She thinks that's deceitful.'

'Figures, I suppose.' Grace sighed deeply.

'But she doesn't know where Flynn lives,' went on Demi, sounding pleased with herself. 'I refused to give them his address.'

'Oh, well done, Dem! That was good. How did you manage it?'

'It wasn't that hard,' Demi mumbled. 'I didn't know it.'

'Oh. But I suppose Allegra now knows the telephone number?'

'Yup. I'm so sorry, Grace! I'd better go now. Mummy will kill me if she finds out I've warned you.'

'Don't worry, I'm sure it will all be all right,' said Grace, with an assurance she didn't feel.

'So that's it,' she went on when she had replaced the receiver. 'That's the cat well and truly out of the bag.'

'And is the cat on her way round to scratch your eyes out?' asked Flynn.

Grace laughed in spite of herself. 'No, not yet. We're spared that because Demi didn't know your address. Poor little thing. She was riddled with guilt. But what should I do about Allegra?'

'Do you have to do anything?'

'Eventually I will. I'm only safe for a few days, while I'm here. After that, she can attack at any time.' She smiled, trying to make light of what was, in fact, making her feel sick with anxiety.

Flynn moved round behind her and put his arms round her. 'Come on, let's sit down in comfort and talk about this. I'm sure it's not as bad as it seems. We can sort something out together.'

Ensconced in one of Flynn's comfortable sofas again, with a glass of very nice wine in her hand, Grace did feel a bit better.

'The thing is this,' she explained to Flynn. 'Allegra and Nicholas are quite likely to say that the pictures are theirs, because they're not fixtures and fittings. If they'd been painted on the shutters, they'd have been part of the house. As it is, they're not.'

'I think the fact that they were nailed down means that they are.'

'You would think that because you want the paintings to belong to me—but Allegra and Nicholas might think differently.'

'I'm sure they're not going to be that unreasonable.'

'People are always unreasonable where money is concerned.'

'True.'

Grace curled her feet under her and closed her eyes for a moment.

Flynn regarded her for what felt like a long time. 'I tell you what, darling. I'm going to take one of your worries away from you.'

'You've already done that, by offering to lend me the money.'

'Another one. I'm not going to try to lure you into bed with me until this whole picture thing is sorted out. Unless you decide you want to sleep with me, we'll sleep apart.' He hesitated. 'Am I right in thinking you were worrying about that, too?'

She looked up at him and nodded, surprised and touched by his perceptiveness. 'I would find having . . . a relationship . . . distracting, while everything else in my life is confused.'

'Then that's fine. I would hate you to be distracted.'

It was only after he'd said this that Grace wondered if a little distraction might be a very good thing, and maybe a night of unrestrained passion was what she needed. Still, she could hardly ask for it now.

'Now, you go up and have a long, hot bath,' Flynn said. 'And when you come down I'll make you something nice on toast.'

She sighed, annoyed with herself for turning down the chance of more than 'something nice on toast'.

Chapter Nine

It took Ellie a little thought to work out which bit of the Courtauld Institute she wanted, but eventually she found the right door and asked for the Witt Library. Ran had told her it was the most comprehensive library of all the artists on the planet, practically, and it was where they would find their artist. The first room she entered was lined with shelves on which sat file after green file.

'Can I help you?' A respectable, middle-aged woman, of the kind likely to be put off by a nose stud and several earrings, spoke to Ellie.

Ellie cleared her throat. 'I'm trying to research an artist . . .'

'Who?'

'That's the thing . . . I only have his initials. And only the first one is quite clear.'

The woman didn't snort derisively, or laugh, but nodded, as if situations like this were not all that unusual. 'English?'

Ellie nodded. 'Most probably.'

'And you know his dates, roughly?'

'Very roughly.'

'Well, over there you'll find an index of all the artists we have records for. If you plough through them, you should find artists with the right initials, and then you can narrow it down by date. But then you'd have to be able to recognise their work to make sure it's the right artist.'

'That's all right. I think I can do that.' In her bag she had some Polaroids that Ran had taken, should her memory fail her.

The woman smiled. 'Good luck.'

The index boxes reminded Ellie of the school library system, before it had gone onto computer. She loved their old-fashioned woodenness. Very happy now, she dumped her bag at her feet and began to go through each card in the 'C' section, looking for artists with the initial 'R'.

There were a couple of matches that weren't the right date, but at last she got a good match of the right period, and went to hunt out the file. There were several files: he was obviously a prolific painter, but was Richard Coatbridge also the painter of the panels?

When Ellie opened the files, and saw the photographs of what he'd painted, she realised that the subject matter was totally different to the panels. This artist painted portraits, landscapes, tasteful subjects— nothing like the rioting foliage, the profusion of animals and the erotic figures of the panels. But possibly they were something he'd painted on a whim; not commissioned, but just for his pleasure and amusement.

She went outside and telephoned Ran. 'I've found this artist, right initials, right period. His name is Richard Coatbridge, but he's done nothing remotely like the panels.'

'Check all the other artists of the right period with the same initials, but don't panic. They could still be by him. I wonder if Grace has any written provenance.'

'Considering she didn't know the panels existed till recently, it seems unlikely she'd know if she had any provenance. And there's very little stuff in that house, considering how big it is.'

'What about the attics?'

'I don't know about them.'

'Go back and see if you can find another artist. If you can't, make a note of the whereabouts of this guy Coatbridge's most prominent works. I could tell a lot by looking at his other stuff.'

Back went Ellie to her quiet, green-lined space and continued her research. It didn't matter personally to her if the panels were old and valuable or not, but it mattered to Grace that they were precious. She needed them to be by a painter of some repute, and although Ellie checked all the other possibilities, none of them gave her the breath of hope that her first artist had.

One of his paintings was in the National Portrait Gallery. A little look at her *A to Z* told Ellie she could walk there easily. She put back the files, said thank you to the woman in charge and left the building. She phoned Ran as she walked.

'There's something by him at the National Portrait Gallery,' she told him. 'I'm going there now to see if I can decide if it's him or not.'

'Are you sure you'll be able to tell?'

'Well, are you offering to come to London and look?'

'Don't get all worked up. I'm sure you'll manage just fine.'

'You're so patronising sometimes, Ran,' she said, and disconnected. But she was smiling.

Seeing an actual painting, in its full, enormous, glowing glory, made Ellie gasp. The subject was a great man leaning up against the horse his wife was sitting on, sidesaddle. They were under an enormous tree, and there was an equally magnificent mansion in the background. The wife was looking down at her husband, who was looking into the middle distance. The horse was objecting to the dog, which looked up at it, unsure whether to bark or run away.

Unfortunately, this stately masterpiece was so unlike Grace's panels that Ellie felt it was unlikely to be by the same artist. She glanced at her watch: it was time to go for her train. But something drew her back to the painting. She could not stop looking at it. The colours were all as light and vivid as a colour slide; she felt she could climb into it and walk through the trees, scattering the birds and animals as she did so.

Then she spotted it: a tiny rabbit, so small it was hardly noticeable among the painted grasses. But she recognised it! She definitely recognised it! There was one very similar on the panels. And once she'd spotted the rabbit, she realised there were birds which, if not identical, were very similar to those that frolicked by the feet of Adam and Eve.

She got the Polaroids out of her bag to check, but, frustratingly, the detail was nowhere near good enough to be of any help. She looked back to the painting before her. This was their artist, she was sure.

She rushed back out into the bustle of London and telephoned Ran again. 'It's him, I'm sure it is! The panels must be worth a fortune!'

'Calm down,' he murmured, but she could hear a definite note of excitement beneath his caution. 'Don't get too worked up. You may be doomed to disappointment.' He was maddeningly sensible.

'Would you like to come up here and tell me I'm wrong?' she raged. 'If you won't take my word for it, that's what you'll have to do! There's an identical rabbit!'

'It is hard to tell one rabbit from another you know. They're all brown with white tails.' He was teasing her now. 'You need to get onto Grace to see if there's the remotest possibility she's got any papers. Richard Coatbridge is a famous artist. If she's to get full value for the paintings, we need to be a hundred and ten per cent sure it is him.'

She sighed deeply, disappointed that he didn't share her optimism. 'OK. But I'm coming home now. I'm exhausted.'

On the tube journey to the station Ellie lost some of her enthusiasm. Supposing she'd just thought the rabbits were the same because she wanted them to be? Perhaps she'd transferred what she saw in the portrait into her memory of the panels, because she wanted them to be by the same artist? By the time she slumped into her seat on the train at

Paddington, she had lost all hope, and was not at all pleased when the ticket inspector told her that her cheap ticket was not valid on that train. Fortunately, he didn't make too much fuss, just made her pay the excess.

It's an omen! she thought. Having the wrong ticket is an omen. They're not by him, after all!

Her mobile phone battery lasted just long enough for her to tell Ran which train she was on, which was a good omen. As the train pulled into Bath, she asked herself why it was so important to her that it was Richard Coatbridge who had painted those panels. She put it down to omens again.

'I think being pregnant has made me terribly superstitious,' she said to Ran, kissing him on the cheek and ignoring the fact that this greeting came as a surprise to him. 'I was wondering why I care who the artist is—they'll be valuable, whatever. But somehow I do care. If the baby's a boy, I'm going to call it Richard.'

'It's terribly unlikely it is him, you know. I mean, he's very famous, or he wouldn't have work in the National Portrait Gallery.'

'But I'm completely certain it is him. I can feel it in my water.'

'I'm afraid that doesn't mean a thing either.' He unlocked the car and she got in.

'Ooh,' Ellie said suddenly, just before Ran switched on the ignition. 'I think the baby moved!' She stared at him in wonderment, trying to connect the fluttering in her stomach with all that had gone before that moment; she was not just pregnant, she was having a baby.

Ran didn't speak, he just returned her solemn gaze. Then he lightly kissed her slightly open mouth.

Grace answered the telephone nervously, expecting it to be her sister. She had spent all yesterday on tenterhooks, but Allegra, astonishingly, had not rung. Flynn had gone out somewhere and she was tempted just to let it ring. On the other hand, if it was her sister, about to give her hell, she was a grown-up, she could cope.

It was a pleasure to hear Ellie's enthusiastic voice.

'I think I've found him! Our artist! I went to London yesterday and did research. It's Richard Coatbridge!'

'Um . . .'

'I hadn't heard of him either, but according to Ran he's famous! Those panels could be worth millions! If they are, it means you can pay for the dry rot and give loads to your sister and brother. But . . .' Ellie paused for dramatic effect, and Grace felt her rising spirits descend a notch.

'There's always a but.'

'Have you got provenance for the panels? I mean, are there any old letters or papers or anything that might refer to them?' Ellie hurried on, 'Could there be any papers, of any kind, in your attic?'

'I don't think so. I had the roof done and I don't remember finding a treasure chest up there.'

'Anyway, we're going to have a look.'

Ellie arranged to see Grace in just over an hour.

Grace wrote Flynn a note: *I am going home to search in the attic for valuable papers I know are not there, but Ellie thinks might be.*

Then came the hard bit. If she wrote 'Love, Grace', would Flynn read anything into it? She put 'Love, Grace' anyway. It didn't matter if he read anything into it, she was beginning to think it was possibly true.

The two women met outside Luckenham House. 'I'm sure there's nothing up here, because I cleared it all out when I had the roof repaired,' said Grace, as they climbed the stairs to the attic.

'So did you throw everything away?' asked Ellie.

'It was mostly rubbish. I put a couple of boxes in one of the stables.'

Ellie hesitated. 'Anything we might find will be in one of the stables?'

Grace nodded. 'The one with the table-tennis table, remember?'

'Spiders?'

'That's the one. It's the driest.'

'Let's go down and look there then.'

'But, Ellie, it's cold and I really don't think we're going to find anything.'

'Maybe,' said Ellie, leading the way back downstairs, 'but we can take the boxes into the kitchen, and look through them in the warm.'

'Except it's not warm. The Rayburn isn't lit. Although it is plumbed in,' she added. 'Flynn had it done for me. Isn't that kind?'

Ellie shook her head in despair. 'And you're still doubtful that he has feelings for you?'

Grace blushed, remembering their recent argument when he'd made his feelings quite clear. 'No.'

Ellie paused, her hand on the door. 'So are you and he . . . you know?'

'An item?'

'I meant sleeping together, but the item thing will do.'

Grace stopped. 'I rather blew the other bit. He said he's not going to come near me until my life is in order and I'm not stressed.'

'But that's very considerate! He's lovely, Grace, really he is!'

'I know! But I want to go to bed with him now, not wait until this is all sorted out!'

Ellie giggled. 'Come on. Let's face the spiders.'

Eventually they found the two boxes Grace was fairly sure she had put in the stable, but then Ellie spotted something else.

'Look! That box is wooden and says 'Ulster Apples' on it. Did you put it there?'

'No, I don't think so. That must have been here before.'

'It looks like it's got some old files in it. Let's take that inside as well.'

They retreated to the house, carrying their separate burdens.

'You go first,' said Grace, indicating the Ulster Apples box that she had dumped on the kitchen table.

Ellie got out the first manilla file. The corners had been eaten by something. 'Have you any idea what these papers are?'

'Nope. Let's see.'

They were love letters, probably dating from the war, all bound up with blue ribbons. 'Oh, it's so sad!' said Grace as she looked at them. 'They're to my aunt! Her lover must have been killed!'

In another file they found an awful lot of ancient household bills, which were fascinating, but, Ellie insisted, not relevant and therefore not to be pored over. There were also some dress patterns and a sheet of paper that told you how to make knickers out of parachute silk. They searched through every file.

'Oh. That's a bit disappointing,' said Ellie.

'Sorry.' Grace felt disappointed for Ellie, but hadn't been expecting anything else. 'Do you mind if I just have a look through this stuff?' she said, referring to the pile of bills they hadn't bothered with.

'No, go ahead. Shall I help you? Quicker if we both do it.'

At first they amused themselves by trying to decipher the disintegrating scraps of paper that described items of haberdashery—ribbons and trimmings—but soon they just gave each one a quick glance. Near the bottom of the box Ellie found some letters, tucked into the same bundle as a bill for rebuilding the stable wall, and another, very ancient bill for repairing the panelling in the dining room. It caught Ellie's attention because, unlike the others, it didn't have 'paid' written on it.

'Grace,' she said, holding a scrap of paper. 'Could this be anything?'

Carefully, Grace took the paper. It was brittle and yellow with age and covered in elegant, sloping writing that was almost illegible. 'I don't know. Let's take it to the drawing room and look at it under a lamp.'

Both women flew down the passage and across the hall.

Grace switched on one of the table lamps and put the paper under the light. 'I need a magnifying glass.'

'Haven't you got one? This is so frustrating!'

'Flynn has. There's one on his desk. Let's go.'

Flynn's drive was full of cars, or so it seemed.

'Flynn's back, and he's got guests,' said Grace, nudging her car into a space next to the wall. 'I wonder who?'

'Perhaps I shouldn't come in,' said Ellie, suddenly aware of her clothes, 'I'm filthy.'

Grace looked down at her own long skirt and matching sweater and cardigan, which had looked quite smart when she'd put them on that morning. 'I'm covered in cobwebs too,' she said. 'Never mind. We can sneak in and go into the study. They may not see us, whoever they are.'

'They', or at least one of them, was hanging about in the hall, waiting for Grace and Ellie. It was Demi.

'Oh, hi, Dems!' said Ellie, holding the envelope with the scrap of paper to her as they hugged.

'Is your mother here?' asked Grace, when she too had kissed Demi.

Demi nodded. 'In there. With Flynn.'

'I'll go and say hello,' said Grace with a sinking feeling that good manners should take precedence over her desire to inspect the paper. Flynn had probably been entertaining Hermia for hours, waiting for her return.

Her hand had depressed the handle before she heard Demi say, 'Your sister's there, too!'

'Oh God,' muttered Grace, and carried on into the room. 'Come with me, Ellie!'

Ellie slid the envelope with the paper under her jumper, and then prepared to follow Grace.

There were three people in the room, and they all looked round as Grace and Ellie entered. Flynn seemed relaxed but his expression warned Grace that she was in for trouble. Allegra was wearing an expression of exasperation which was very familiar. And Demi's mother, Hermia, was looking at her with a strange combination of respect and resentment.

'Hello, everyone,' said Grace, wondering how Allegra and Hermia had discovered where Flynn lived from just a telephone number.

'Darling, you're horribly dirty,' said Flynn, making this seem like a good thing to be. He walked across the room to kiss Grace's cheek. 'Hi, Ellie.'

'We've been to Luckenham House,' said Ellie. 'Checking on the men doing the dry-rot treatment.'

'Yes . . .' How to explain the dirt? Grace thought frantically. 'I thought I'd left something important in one of the old stables.' Grace hoped no one could see she was blushing.

Ellie, seeing Grace's reaction, tried frantically to cover for her. 'We were looking for an old bill,' she said.

'Where's Demi disappeared to?' asked Grace, looking round desperately.

303

'I expect she's playing on my computer,' said Flynn. 'Would you two like a drink? We're trying some Madeira. I think you might like it. Hermia's brought Demi back to us.'

'She wouldn't stay with me,' said Hermia. 'She's been in a terrible strop. Said she couldn't cope without her computer and got all moody.'

'And I'm sure you know why I'm here,' said Allegra crisply. 'I've been talking to Hermia. Grace, you've been lying to me.'

'No, I haven't! What on earth are you talking about?' Grace's indignation was more from guilt than anything.

'Sit down, both of you,' said Flynn calmly. 'Ellie, can I get you something soft?'

'No, an ordinary chair will be fine.' All the tension had made Ellie flippant.

'I meant to drink!' said Flynn, probably grateful for the light relief. 'I'm not sure what I've got, but there will be something.'

'I'll come with you and choose,' said Ellie. 'Then I want to see what Demi is up to.'

Knowing Flynn would be back as soon as he could, Grace faced the two women who now confronted her.

'Why didn't you tell me about these panels?' demanded Allegra. 'Really, it almost borders on deceit.'

'No, it doesn't! We found some old painted panels, which might be worth something or nothing, and I didn't tell you! For goodness' sake, do you tell me every time you find something you didn't know you had?'

'It's not the same, and you know it,' snapped Allegra. 'By rights, those pictures belong to me and Nicholas.'

'No, they don't!' said Grace. 'Or if they do, so do all the doors and windows and skirting boards! The paintings were nailed down!'

'*Were* nailed down? So where are they now?'

To Grace's enormous relief, Flynn and Ellie came back into the room, with a reluctant-looking Demi. 'I'm having them restored.'

'So how are you going to pay for that?' demanded Allegra.

'Allegra! I'm surprised at you, asking me to discuss my personal finances in front of . . . non-family members,' she managed eventually.

'Whatever the relationships,' said Allegra, 'we're all adults. I'm sure we can be frank with each other.'

'Let's all have another drink,' said Flynn.

Ellie glanced at her watch. It was one o'clock. She was starving and she desperately wanted to look at the paper which crackled occasionally from its place under her jumper. 'I really should be getting back—'

'No!' Grace jumped to her feet. 'I promised you lunch! Flynn?' She met his eyes across the room and blushed again. 'Is it all right if I get Ellie something to eat? She's pregnant—'

'I think we know that.' Hermia yawned.

'—which means she has to eat regularly.' Grace took Ellie by the arm and almost dragged her from the room. Once in the kitchen they flopped down at the table.

'My God!' Grace was shaking with rage and frustration. 'I don't believe it! My sister is the limit. She'll claim those pictures if she can.'

'She can't. They were nailed down. Now, come on, we need a magnifying glass. Could you go and get one out of the study?'

Grace shook her head. 'Not with them in there. Will Ran have a magnifying glass, do you think?'

'Of course. He's got special glasses with lights in them. You have to have that if you're conserving paintings,' she added, pleased with her new knowledge.

'Then you take it to him,' said Grace, glad to pass the responsibility to someone else. 'Get him to read it. And ring me immediately. I have to know if they are by this Richard Coat-thingy.'

Ellie was affronted. 'I know they are, Grace. I told you about the rabbit.'

'No, you didn't.' Grace was confused. 'What rabbit?'

'Oh.' Ellie dismissed this oversight. 'It's one in a painting by Coatbridge in the National Portrait Gallery. It's a dead ringer for a rabbit in the panels. I told Ran about it, but he's not convinced I could tell one rabbit from another. It's why he's insisting on some sort of proof.'

'Which that bit of paper may not provide.'

'It might. But you're right, it might not.'

'And in a way it would be a good thing if they're not all that valuable,' said Grace, trying to look on the bright side. 'I mean, think of the trouble if they really are by . . .'

'Richard Coatbridge,' helped Ellie.

'Richard Coatbridge!' came a voice from the door that could have reached the back of the stalls, no problem. 'Did you say Richard Coatbridge?' Allegra marched into the kitchen.

'It's terribly unlikely,' said Grace.

'Yes, Ran—the picture restorer—doesn't think they are for a minute,' said Ellie. 'And now I've got to go.' She looked longingly at the biscuit tin and then opened it and helped herself to a couple of biscuits.

Grace shot to her feet. 'Fine! You go. And ring me, if there's any news. About the baby.' she added desperately.

'I'm having a scan,' said Ellie helpfully.

'I'll come to the hospital with you,' said Grace. 'Is it now?' It was rather grasping at straws, but she didn't want to be left with her sister.

'No!' Ellie frowned and shook her head as if Grace had gone completely mad. 'But I'll tell you as soon as I know when it is, I promise.'

Grace exhaled as her window of opportunity for escape closed. 'OK. Good. I'll see you out.'

Flynn arrived in the kitchen, possibly in pursuit of Allegra.

'Ellie's just going,' said Grace.

'Oh,' said Flynn.

'Yes. Is it all right if I take these?' Ellie indicated the biscuits.

Flynn seemed confused. 'Yes, yes, of course. But do you have to rush off? I was going to suggest we all went out for lunch.'

'Ellie's got things to do,' said Grace.

'Right,' said Flynn. 'But, Allegra, you can come out to lunch with us? And Hermia?' By leaving the kitchen himself, he lured everyone else out.

'Yes. Yes, I think I could.' Allegra smiled, oddly girlish in the presence of Flynn's charm.

Demi, who had come into the hall, looked pained, as if invited to go on a cross-country run in the middle of winter. 'Can I stay here? You've got some really good games.'

'Of course,' said Flynn.

'Perhaps you should ask your mother,' said Allegra.

'Do what you like. There's no pleasure in taking sulky young women out for meals,' snapped Hermia.

Grace sighed, wondering whether if she put on a really good pout, she could ally herself with Demi and not go either.

Ran took the paper carefully. 'Why is it warm?'

'It's been up my jumper. I was hiding it from Grace's sister. What does it say?' Ellie had been jumping from foot to foot, beside herself.

'Obviously, most of it is missing . . . but what there is left says: *called away*, then there's a splodge, but there's quite a clear bit . . . *not to embarrass your servants, I have concealed two panels behind the curtains. I will collect them on my next visit* . . . Then it goes on about the weather and something about paying for something.'

'But is there a signature?'

'Not on this scrap of paper, there isn't. Are you sure you've got it all?'

'Yes. We were very thorough. We were quite pleased to get that bit.' Ellie felt deflated. All that work, all that searching, the reward of actually finding something, and now the 'something' wasn't enough.

'It's still useful. What we need is someone to tell us whether Richard Coatbridge was known to visit Luckenham House.'

'He says "on my next visit".'

'The person who painted the panels did. It's checking who that is.'

'But surely an expert could tell if the panels were by Richard Coatbridge?'

'Experts have been known to make mistakes, but yes, I'm sure an expert could.'

'And you can't be our expert?'

'No.'

Ellie felt very tired. 'More research? Finding the expert we need?'

'I'm afraid so.' He looked at her. 'Have you had lunch?'

'I've had biscuits. With bits of ginger in them. Very nice.'

'But not lunch. Let's go and eat.'

'I must ring Grace first.'

'Ring her mobile while we're waiting to be served.'

'Grace hasn't got a mobile. And they were going out to eat, too, and won't be back for hours. I know, I'll ring Flynn's mobile.'

Grace took Flynn's mobile into the Ladies to talk to Ellie. It was too cold to stand outside the pub.

'So there's nothing on it that says who did the panels?'

'No, I'm afraid not. But it does mention hiding the panels behind the curtains, and coming to collect them next time he visited.'

'So it definitely links whoever wrote that letter with the panels?'

'Yes. Ran thinks we need a Richard Coatbridge expert.'

'And how do you find one of them? Oh, hello, Hermia,' said Grace. 'Ellie, I must go. I'll ring you when we get back home.'

'Was that about your friend's scan?' asked Hermia, obviously sure that it wasn't.

'No.' Grace swallowed.

'Grace, I really do think you're behaving badly over this painting. You got far more from your aunt than your brother and sister, and Edward left you very well provided for.'

'Hermia, this is none of your business and, anyway, I refuse to discuss it in the Ladies' lavatory!' Grace stalked out.

But Allegra herself would be harder to deal with. Back at the table, she looked ready for battle. All through the meal Flynn and Grace had managed to keep the conversation away from the subject of the paintings, but now, with Allegra and Hermia deeply into the coffee, Grace knew she would have to talk about them.

She took a sip of the prophylactic brandy that Flynn had ordered her in case things got really sticky.

'Well,' demanded Allegra. 'Are you going to come clean?'

'Allegra! I have not been deceiving you!'

'Haven't you? Then how come I had to hear about the paintings from Hermia because Demeter told her? I think we should have a family meeting. Get Nicholas down to decide who owns these paintings.'

'Oh, Grace owns them,' said Flynn firmly. 'There's absolutely no doubt about that. I used to be a solicitor, and I know that for a fact. They were nailed down, you see.'

'Oh,' said Allegra after a moment's consideration. 'But she has been devious, Flynn. I'm sorry to say it, but she has.'

Grace took another sip of the brandy. 'Very well, Allegra,' she said quietly. 'I'll tell you everything we've discovered to date. OK? I found the panels, but had no clue about them, which is why I asked Ellie to ask her friend who is a picture conservator—'

'A what?'

'Restorer . . . to give his opinion. He had to take them away to look at them properly, and to stop them being attacked by the dry rot.'

'I thought they were nailed down,' said Allegra.

'They were.'

'So how did he get them out?' asked Hermia. 'If they're movable, they belong to Allegra.'

'I don't know how he got them out,' said Grace. 'I wasn't there. I imagine he used some sort of tool . . . Of course, if they do turn out to be valuable—'

'Well, why can't we find out?' demanded Allegra.

'We've done some research but we're still not certain who painted them. We think they might be by Richard Coatbridge.'

'Goodness!' said Hermia, impressed.

'We've only got initials. And Ellie is convinced that a rabbit she saw in a painting in London is almost identical to one in the panels.'

'Oh,' said Allegra, not impressed.

'So we need a Richard Coatbridge expert, who knows his movements, and who can recognise his handwriting. We've got a scrap of paper. We found it in the stables.'

Allegra looked at her watch and took charge. 'Right. I'll see to that. Give me the telephone number of this picture restorer. I'll get decent slides and a copy of the letter. Leave this to me! We're going to get the proper amount for those panels, or I shall die in the attempt.'

While Hermia and Allegra went to the Ladies, probably to discuss Grace and Flynn, Grace said, 'At least she said "we", so perhaps she is including me.'

Flynn chuckled.

'And were you really a solicitor? I didn't know that.'

'No, I made that up. But I'm sure it's true about you owning the paintings. Part of the fabric of the house.' Then he kissed the top of her head.

'But I'm going to sell them, so they can't be part of the fabric of the house.' Then she sighed as he put his hand on her knee.

'Don't worry, the house won't fall down without them.'

 ## Chapter Ten

LATER THAT AFTERNOON, Ran received a telephone call from Allegra. The moment she realised who it was, Ellie went and made herself useful in the kitchen by knocking up a batch of cheese straws, having read somewhere that they were the fast track to a man's heart. She felt embarrassed that it was indirectly because of her that Ran had to deal with such an annoying woman. Fortunately, he came into the kitchen a little later appearing his usual calm, cynical self.

'I'm so sorry about that,' said Ellie, rolling pastry. 'She's a nightmare.'

'She had some very good ideas and is prepared to go to quite a lot of trouble to find out all she can about the panels,' said Ran.

'Only so they'll be worth more!' Ellie refused to give Allegra credit for anything. 'I'm sure she's trying to claim them as hers.'

'She said not. That Flynn had told her they definitely belong to Grace, because they were nailed down.'

'Pity it didn't occur to Grace to nail down some of the furniture, although I'm not sure exactly how you'd do that. Can you pass me the big knife?'

'You're always cooking. If I lived with you permanently I'd get as fat as a pig.'

Ellie concentrated on scoring straight lines in the cheese pastry. Was he telling her, yet again, to give up hope with regard to him? Just as well he didn't realise that she'd surrendered her free will with regard to him ages ago. 'I don't think so,' she said. 'You're a thin type.'

'And I'm unlikely to live with you permanently.'

Now he was definitely telling her something, but not anything she didn't know—in her head, at least. She looked up. 'So is she going to come here and look at the panels? If so, I'll arrange to be out.'

'I'm going to send her slides and a copy of the letter, such as it is. I've given her a few names that might be helpful, then she's going to find out who the expert on Coatbridge is, and he'll come and look at them.'

'Or she. It could be a woman, you know.' Ran had sexist tendencies that had to be suppressed.

'Or she,' he agreed without argument. 'What are you going to do with those strips of pastry?'

'You'll see. The telephone's ringing.'

She had the cheese straws in the oven by the time he came back to say the phone call was for her.

It was the hospital. 'They've had a cancellation,' said Ellie as she came back into the kitchen after taking the call. 'They can do my scan tomorrow. Isn't that good?' she added to disguise the fact that she felt a bit scared. 'I must ring Grace.'

'Why?'

'Because she's going to come with me. For support, you know. So I don't feel so much like a single mother.'

Ran frowned. 'Are you OK about being a single mother?'

Ellie shrugged. 'I think so. There's no point in being anything different, is there?'

'But you still want support?'

'Yes.' She frowned. 'Does that make me seem very pathetic?'

'Of course not. Ring Grace. And when will those things be edible?'

'When the pinger goes. Can you take them out of the oven for me?'

Grace was excited about the thought of Ellie's scan being so soon.

'I've been lucky,' said Ellie. 'Can you be here for eleven?'

'Of course. It'll give me time to take Demi to the bus, and then I've got to nip home to see the dry-rot people off and then I'll come down.'

'I'm quite annoyed with Demi for coming back,' said Ellie cautiously. 'I told her why she should go and stay with her mother.'

'And she did go, but we've had a long chat and it really is miserable for her there. She tried to stick it out but she just couldn't.'

'You're too soft for your own good,' said Ellie.

'So are you,' countered Grace.

That evening Grace and Flynn ate supper at the kitchen table. Demi had taken a tray up to her room so she could watch a video, although Grace suspected it was an excuse to leave her and Flynn alone together. Grace had cooked spaghetti and tomato sauce.

'It looks very appetising,' Flynn said, bracingly. 'Good thing I ate a lot of lunch.'

Grace looked at him. 'Thank you for that vote of confidence in my culinary skills.'

'A pleasure,' he said calmly, looking into her eyes in a way that made Grace look away.

'Ellie rang,' she said brightly, trying to change the mood. 'Her scan's tomorrow. I'm going to go to it with her. Just for moral support.'

Flynn smiled, his eyes crinkling at the corners so that his curly eyelashes mingled, but somehow managed not to tangle. Grace wondered why she hadn't noticed the way they did this before.

'That'll be interesting. Will you have something to eat afterwards?'

'I expect so. I'll take Demi to the bus, then pop over to Luckenham House, and then go down to Bath.' She paused. 'When the men have gone I can move back in.'

There was a moment of something: it could have been hurt; and then Flynn said, 'You don't have to. You could stay here. You're no trouble to have to stay. You clear up after yourself, the cat likes you, and you even cook.' He indicated the pasta and tomato sauce and made a perfect coil of spaghetti. 'After all, if I've got Demi here, you might as well be, too.'

'I would take Demi with me! That's one of the reasons I should go, Demi coming back.' She laughed. 'Honestly, we can't both stay here for ever.'

He was quite serious. 'But you can both stay as long as you like— until Luckenham House is properly habitable, anyway.'

'It'll be properly habitable tomorrow,' Grace insisted gently. 'The moment the men have gone.'

'I don't mean by your standards of habitability'—he made a dismissive gesture—'but by the rest of the world's. Central heating, furniture, perhaps the odd carpet?'

'Carpets?' Grace was shocked. 'On my beautiful wide elm boards?'

'The odd rug, then. But, seriously, wouldn't it be much easier to decorate, to set it to rights, if it was empty?'

'As you've so often pointed out, it is empty—enough to make slapping on a couple of coats of emulsion easy, anyway.'

'Is that all you want to do to it?'

Grace considered. 'Well, no. Since staying here I've realised that a few home comforts are, well, comfortable, but I've never had any money—'

'You might soon be going to have quite a lot of money.'

'I doubt it. Once I've paid for the dry rot and given Allegra and Nicholas a cut—'

'You're going to do that?'

'Yes. As long as those panels earn me enough to pay my debts and my siblings, I can manage without underfloor heating in the kitchen.'

'Hmm. Not sure that I can.'

'What do you mean?'

'Nothing. I was just thinking that if I was going to live there, I'd need a bit more background warmth.'

Grace nodded. 'I know what you mean. I might put a wood-burner in the hall, if I can find a chimney.'

Flynn sighed. 'You're not very good at taking hints, are you?'

'Aren't I? What are you talking about? You don't want to live in Luckenham House! You've made this house perfect and you love it. You're not going to want to up sticks and live in my draughty old barn even if . . .'

He only let her flounder for a moment before he said, 'Shall we change the subject?'

'Oh, please let's!' She smiled and thought again how easy he was to be with, even when things were difficult.

Luckenham House looked wonderful in the bright spring sunshine. The garden was just stirring into life with early primroses spangling the banks with yellow stars. I know why I want to live here, said Grace to herself. It's a beautiful house.

The men seemed satisfied with what they'd done, and proudly showed Grace where they had made good the walls. When she had seen them safely off in their van, she went into the kitchen to see the newly plumbed-in Rayburn. But something was wrong. It took her a moment to work out what, and then she realised: there was a puddle of water on the floor, yards away from the sink.

She looked up and she knew, without any experience or technical know-how, that the ceiling would come down at any moment unless she did something. If she wanted the ceiling to stay up she had to let the water out. She found a broom, stood on a chair, and very gingerly prodded the swelling. Water and what seemed like half a ton of plaster poured onto the kitchen floor, drenching her.

It took her a few moments to stop spluttering and gasping. 'That was a mistake,' she noted aloud. 'Perhaps I'd better go and see why all that water was there. Or should I go and change first?'

Then she remembered Ellie. Could she abandon the house for the sake of her friend? Of course she could. She would ring Ellie and tell her that she might be a little bit late.

'Ellie? It's me. I'm at the house.' She was starting to shiver. 'There's a bit of a problem. But don't worry!' she hurried on. 'I'm still coming. I've just got to change my clothes and may have to find a plumber first.'

'What's happened? It sounds dreadful!'

'Well, I came into the kitchen to find a puddle on the floor and a big balloon of plaster hanging from the ceiling. I poked it with a broom and it all came down.'

'Oh dear. You probably shouldn't have done that. I don't think you should leave the house in that condition.'

Grace laughed. 'It's not pregnant, you are.'

'No,' Ellie agreed. 'But unlike the kitchen ceiling, my waters haven't broken, which sounds like what's happened. Look, don't worry, Grace, it's only a scan,' said Ellie. 'I'll be fine on my own.'

'Are you sure?'

'Positive. It's no big deal. You can come with me next time I have one.'

Eventually, Ellie convinced Grace that her presence wasn't necessary. Ran came in as she was finishing the conversation.

'That was Grace. The kitchen ceiling's come down and soaked her to the skin. I've told her not to come. I'll be fine on my own, and she's got to sort out plumbers and things.' She concentrated very hard on making her voice matter-of-fact, hiding her disappointment and anxiety.

'Right.' Ran's voice was just as bland. 'That's OK. I'll come with you.'

'Sorry?'

'I'll come with you for the scan. For support.'

She was horribly embarrassed, and cross with herself for not hiding her anxiety better. 'But, Ran—'

'To stop you feeling so much like a single parent? Remember?'

Why had she ever told him all that? It was all coming back to haunt her. 'Really, it's not necessary,' she said firmly. 'I can go by myself.'

'Unless you'd prefer a woman, of course.'

Ellie suddenly wanted to cry. It was her hormones, of course. Ran was only being kind, offering to fill in for Grace, but her heart had leapt, even hearing him make the offer. And did she want him there? She closed her eyes. Yes, she decided, she always wanted Ran with her.

'It's really not necessary,' she repeated, hoping he'd ignore her.

'That's decided then. Tell me when we need to be there.'

'Thank you—' she began, but he cut her off.

'Oh, shut up.' He smiled, just slightly, and very lopsidedly, but it made Ellie sigh.

Why did she like him so much? He was bossy, very bossy. Old—well, ten years older than her—and look what had happened to Grace when she married an older man! He broke her heart! Not that that was an option for her, of course. Ran was the man who'd turned down the offer

of a fling; he would probably never get married, just glide from sophisticated woman to sophisticated woman, with no upset, no unpleasant
scenes and, probably, no babies. No wonder he didn't want her. But he
was kind to her, very kind.

Relieved of scan duty by Ellie, Grace contemplated her situation. She
was beginning to get extremely cold. She had clothes upstairs, but not
many as most of her things were at Flynn's. Besides, she couldn't find
where she should turn the water off. And Flynn would know of a
plumber who wouldn't rip her off. She decided to go home.

The thought alone shocked her. She'd thought of Flynn's house as
home! She paused in turning her car round. No, it wasn't the house that
was home, it was Flynn.

He happened to be in the hall when she opened the front door. The
moment he had taken in what she looked like, he laughed.

'It's not funny! I'm soaked to the skin and freezing to death!'

'It is funny. You've got plaster all over you. What happened?'

'It's all your fault!' said Grace. 'Or Pete's.'

'What is? Shall we continue this conversation in the bathroom?'

She allowed herself to be led upstairs while she related her grievances. 'I went into the kitchen to see the Rayburn—which was alight—
and noticed a puddle on the floor. It was coming from the ceiling!'

'What was? Come into my bathroom, it's bigger.'

'The water! There was a huge bulge in the ceiling, dripping.'

'And you poked it with a broom? Here, I'll turn on the taps. And you
might like some bubbles or something.'

'How did you guess about the broom? Anyway, it all came down on
top of me.'

'That's awful.' He was unbuttoning her cardigan and pulling off her
jumper, murmuring, as if he were grooming a horse.

'And I didn't know where to turn the water off, so it's still dripping
onto the kitchen floor.'

'That's so dreadful.' He lifted her feet so she could step out of her skirt.

'Just as well it's got good honest tiles on it, and no poncey underfloor
heating!'

'That is a good thing.' He eased off her shoes, one by one.

'I'll have to get the ceiling replastered now.'

'Mm. You will.' He slid her tights and pants easily down over her hips.

Without noticing how it happened, Grace found herself naked, in his
arms. 'It'll be an awful job painting it,' she said, trying for insouciance.

'It will,' he agreed politely. 'Now, would you like bubbles or bath oil?'

'Flynn, why do you have these things in your bathroom? Is there something you haven't told me?'

'Well, yes. I bought them specially, in the hope I might lure you in here someday soon. So which do you want?'

'Bubbles, please.'

'OK.' He poured in a generous amount and then dipped his hand into the bath and agitated the water. 'Is that too hot for you?'

She sighed and allowed him to hand her into the bath. 'That's lovely. Don't you think you should give me some privacy?'

'No, actually. I think I should get you something to drink.'

She slid down into the water and felt its blissful warmth work its magic on her chilly limbs. 'A drink would be too decadent. It's only about ten.'

'Eleven, actually. Darling, I'm just going to pop downstairs and make a phone call, put my life on hold. I'll be right back.'

'OK.' She slid further down the bath, revelling in the heat of the water, aware that it was much bigger than the bath in the spare room. She closed her eyes, thinking that she mustn't be tempted to doze off.

'Hey, don't go to sleep.' She opened her eyes again and saw Flynn, naked, holding a bottle and two glasses.

'What's this?' She tried to sit up and protest, but couldn't quite manage it. He had joined her in the bath and handed her a glass of champagne before she'd thought out what to say. By then, there seemed no point in protesting. She took a sip. 'Oh, that's nice. What are we celebrating?'

'Oh, I don't know. What would you like to celebrate?'

'Well, my kitchen ceiling is on the floor, making my house unlivable in.'

'I'll drink to that!'

'That's not fair. It's my kitchen. I'll have to redecorate it.'

'I'll drink to that, too.'

'And my house! I can't stay in it!'

'No. You'll have to go on staying with me. Have some more champagne.'

She took another sip. 'Are you trying to get me drunk?'

'Not drunk, just relaxed.'

'I am relaxed.'

'Good.' He took her glass away. 'Then close your eyes.'

Up to her neck in warm water, Grace shut her eyes as bidden. She knew she couldn't slip under the water now Flynn was there to prevent it, his warm limbs entangled with hers. It was nice, and quite sexy.

Flynn took hold of one of Grace's feet. 'Hey! What are you doing? That tickles!'

'I'm kissing your toes,' he said, and then kissed each one. 'It's the only part of you I can reach just now.'

'Oh,' she said. 'No one's ever kissed my toes before. Oh,' she said again as he took one into his mouth. 'That's very— Oh, my goodness . . .'

'I think we'd better get out,' he said a few moments later. 'I'd hate to drown you.'

It was an easy transition as the floor was thickly carpeted and there were lots of very large towels to hand. Flynn was, Grace decided when her brain was connected again, a very imaginative lover.

The champagne was less cold now, but still delicious. 'Did you plan this?' asked Grace.

'Plan what? Making love to you on my bathroom floor? Plan is putting it a bit strong, but fantasise, definitely.'

She giggled. 'Strange!'

'Not at all. I've thought about making love to you in every room in this house. Except the larder. Oh, and the downstairs cloakroom.'

'Honestly! Do you think about nothing else?'

'Only enough to get by. I'm very much in love with you.'

Grace pulled a corner of towel over her and buried her face in her champagne for a moment. 'It's probably just a sexual attraction.'

'Don't knock it! Besides, it isn't. I fell in love with you when making love to you was about as likely and as comfortable as making love to a thorn bush.'

'I wasn't that prickly, surely.'

'No, but you had a protective hedge about you which would have defied leprechauns. Invisible to everyone but me, naturally.'

'Naturally.'

'So . . .' He paused. 'I know I'm risking getting an answer I don't like, but . . . how do you feel about me?'

She closed her eyes and thought about it. She wanted to tell him exactly, and accurately, how she felt. It had taken her some time to work out in her head. She didn't want to make a mistake translating it into words. 'I'm not always very good at expressing myself, but when I was all soaking wet and miserable in the kitchen, I wanted to come home. Then I realised that what I meant was, home is where you are.'

'Oh. Right. I think that qualifies as a satisfactory answer.' They didn't speak again for some time.

'So if you think I should sell Luckenham House,' she said later, when she'd sat up and finished her champagne, 'I will.'

He tucked a strand of hair behind her ear and made himself more comfortable on the muddle of towels. 'No. No, I'd never ask you to do that. It's a lovely house and it's yours. You—we—should live there.'

'But you want to live here! It's so much more comfortable here.'

He nodded. 'Yes, it is, but we don't want to keep up separate establishments do we?' He became thoughtful. 'Although that would be fourteen locations for making love. At least.'

Grace ignored this frivolity. 'But you've put your heart and soul into this house.'

'I've put my heart and soul somewhere else now.'

'What do you mean?'

'You know what I mean. Or you should. They're with you. Where you want to be, where you are, is where I want to be. Besides,' he went on briskly, 'Luckenham House is beautiful, well worth doing up.'

'I know, I just don't know if I'll have the money.'

'If I sell this house we'll have shedloads of the stuff.'

Grace raised herself on one elbow and studied him earnestly. 'I've fought very hard to be independent and while I love you and trust you totally, I have to keep something for me. If you paid to have Luckenham House done up, I know it would be beautiful, but it wouldn't be all mine. I'll want your advice every step of the way, colour schemes, everything—' she indicated the opulent, comfortable bathroom where they were having this intimate conversation— 'although I did think that no one had carpet in their bathrooms any more and had tiles instead.'

'It rather depends on what you want to do in your bathroom,' he said.

Grace giggled but wouldn't be distracted. 'I just need to be the one to pay for my house to be done up. I hope you understand.'

He sighed. 'No. I do understand. I only hope those bloody panels turn out to be worth something. Come on, let's get up.'

'We should. I've got to organise a plumber.'

'So you have.' But he led her into the bedroom, and they didn't get round to organising a plumber until it was nearly time to collect Demi.

Ellie was shown into a room containing a low examination table and a lot of equipment she preferred not to see.

'Here goes,' she said.

'And I'm right behind you,' said Ran.

'Just hop onto the table. It's not high,' said the woman. 'I'm Suzanne, by the way.'

Ellie smiled, trying to look relaxed.

'Now, just pull up your jumper and pull your trousers down under your bump.' Ellie's eyes met Ran's. He smiled reassuringly. She gave a little sigh. She wouldn't have guessed that Ran had 'reassuring' in his repertoire of smiles, but he did it very well.

Suzanne spread jelly over Ellie's stomach. 'Now, I'm going to pass this instrument backwards and forwards over your tummy, and you can see what your baby's up to on those screens.'

Ellie tried to make out a baby from the wavy, black and white picture which looked like a badly tuned television. Suzanne moved her instrument forwards and backwards, until suddenly she stopped.

'Hang on,' she said, after peering into the screen for a few seconds. 'I'm just going to get someone else.'

Sweat broke out all over Ellie's body. She suddenly felt so frightened she couldn't move or speak as she registered the implications of what the nurse had just said: her baby might have something wrong with it. Why else would she need a second opinion? Ellie fought to stay calm. She raised her eyes and caught Ran looking down at her. He took hold of her hand and squeezed it. Ellie closed her eyes and started breathing deeply, repeating silently, like a mantra, It'll be fine, it'll be fine.

Ran didn't speak either. He just held her hand so tightly it hurt. Ellie opened her eyes to remonstrate but saw that he'd gone deathly pale. He must be squeamish about hospitals, she thought, which makes it extra kind of him to come with me.

Suzanne came back with an older woman. 'Now, let's see what's going on here!' the woman said briskly, and took Suzanne's instrument.

'No, no. It's all fine.' Ellie relaxed, and only then realised how scared she had been. 'It's just a shadow. There's nothing wrong with the baby's heart,' the woman said. 'In fact there's nothing wrong with any of him.'

'Is it a boy?' asked Ellie, eager to know.

'Oh, sorry. No. I mean, I don't know. I just said "he" for convenience; you can't tell reliably at this stage. You'll have to wait a bit longer for that information, I'm afraid.' She smiled at Ran. 'Don't buy the train set just yet.'

'I don't think we mind what sort of baby it is,' he said. 'As long as it's healthy. Isn't that right, Ellie?'

Ellie nodded. She couldn't speak and she didn't think she could move. She was glad to stay where she was while the scan was finished and the pictures taken, so she could sort out her emotions a little.

At last, Ellie was allowed off the couch so she could totter to the loo. When she came out, Ran was holding a grainy picture of what was obviously a baby.

'Do you need to sit down or anything? You don't look terribly well.' He put his hand on Ellie's shoulder.

'I'm fine.' She tried to think of something flippant to say, but couldn't. 'I just want to go.'

'Come on, then.' He put his arm round her shoulder and walked her to the door.

Once in the car, Ellie felt better. There wasn't anything wrong with the baby, and they had pictures to prove it. Now she should thank Ran for being so supportive.

'Ran.' She wanted to put her hand on his sleeve but felt suddenly shy. 'I just want to say . . .' She faltered.

'What is it?' He was very gentle and it made her even more shy. She needed him to be acerbic and sarcastic, then she'd be fine.

'Nothing. I just wanted to say, thanks for being there.'

He didn't answer immediately, then he said, 'That's OK. You needed someone around to look after you.'

Ran made Ellie lie down on the sofa when they got back. 'But I've got to ring Grace,' she protested as he covered her with a rug.

'I'll do it. I think you should rest.'

Ellie sighed and closed her eyes. Surely there would be an opportunity later to redirect Ran's caring for her as a pregnant woman into something a little less Madonna-like.

'I spoke to Flynn,' said Ran, just as Ellie had dropped off. 'He says Luckenham House won't be habitable for at least a week. In fact, he's going to try to keep Grace with him until the house is done up.'

'Oh. That's a bit of a surprise. I mean, I can't imagine Grace staying with Flynn until Luckenham House is decorated unless—' She cleared her throat, embarrassed. 'Well, you know, she and Flynn are—close.'

'Well, close or not, you're not going to want to be there by yourself, and even if you did, I wouldn't be happy about it.'

This snippet made Ellie very happy, but she didn't let on. 'Well, I won't be there by myself. Demi will be there too.'

'I wouldn't consider Demi, who I am sure is a lovely girl, a fit person to keep an eye on you while you're pregnant.'

'Wouldn't you?' It was music to her ears. 'But I don't need anyone to keep an eye—'

'Anyway, Demi's staying with Flynn and Grace.'

'Oh. Then I'd better go to my parents. Or there's the friend I was going to stay with before I went to stay with Grace,' she added, more enthusiastically.

'No. You'd better stay here. It's more convenient for doctors' appointments and things, anyway.' He looked away. 'Honestly, Ellie, I only realised today how fragile a pregnancy can be. You can't expect to just carry on as normal. You need someone to look after you.'

'I'd better go to my parents, then,' said Ellie, sad, but firm.

'Why? I got the impression you didn't want to do that.'

She didn't, but there didn't seem to be much choice. 'I know, but I ought to see them, and it would only be for a short time.'

Ran sat down on the end of the sofa and looked at Ellie.

'It would be much more convenient for you to stay here.'

For a moment Ellie was tempted, but then something pulled her back down to earth. Yes, it was a lovely thought, but she already liked Ran far more than was good for her, when he clearly had no intention of thinking of her as anything more than a friend. She took a deep breath.

'No. Sorry, but you don't understand. I can't stay with you, Ran.'

'Why not?'

'Because it's too hard for me.' She saw his confusion and forced herself to continue. 'Being here with you. I want something that you don't, and I thought I could hack it, but I can't. Thank you so much for everything, but I have to go.'

Ran looked stunned. 'But I don't want you to leave.'

'You've been incredibly kind—'

'I'm not being kind!' he said irritably. 'I just don't want you to leave!'

Ellie stared at him, hoping for some indication of what he really meant. 'I don't understand,' she breathed eventually.

Ran exhaled deeply. 'Nor did I, until you had the scan.'

'What?' Ellie was more confused than ever.

'I didn't realise, until that woman had to go and get someone else, how much I cared that you were all right. It was such a shock, all of it, but the biggest shock was that I was terrified that something would happen to you. Ellie, I couldn't bear to lose you.'

'There was never any question about there being anything wrong with *me*—'

'I know, but it didn't feel like it at the time. You were so calm—'

'I didn't feel calm.'

'—you were being so adult, and it made me realise how mature you are in some ways.' He gave a rueful smile. 'Quite old enough to be a mother.'

'Just as well!'

'So if you're old enough for that, I suppose you're not too young for me. Or at least, you don't think so, do you?'

It took a few moments for his words to sink in properly. When they did, she got up from the sofa and shook off the rug. 'Certainly not.' She put her arms round Ran's neck and then, when she felt she had hugged him long enough, she kissed him. A proper, adult, x-rated kiss he could not possibly misunderstand.

'Are you sure you want me to stay?' Ellie asked a few minutes later.

'I'm quite sure,' he said definitely and kissed her again in a way that left her in no doubt that he'd stopped thinking of her as a child.

'I expect it's just because I can cook,' Ellie commented later with a contented little sigh.

'Oh, no,' he contradicted her. 'You're good, but not that good.' And he kissed away her indignant protest.

Ellie smiled, blissfully happy. 'I'll tell you one thing, this feels right,' she said, snuggling up to him and kissing him again.

Grace rang Ellie at lunchtime the next day. She sounded dreamy and giggly and thoroughly silly. 'Don't tell me,' said Ellie. 'You've done it!'

'I'm certainly not going to tell you anything. Yes.'

'Oh, Grace! I'm so pleased! It's so lovely! Are you going to get married?'

'We haven't discussed marriage yet.'

'No, nor have we, but I think maybe—'

'Ellie? What's this? Are you talking about you and Ran?'

Ellie sighed deeply and nodded before remembering Grace couldn't see her. 'When we went for the scan. Did Flynn tell you he came with me?'

'Tell me!'

'Well, in the middle of it the woman who was doing it stopped, and had to get someone else to check everything was all right. Those moments while she was out of the room were about the worst in my entire life, but then afterwards Ran was really different. And finally, when I told him I was going to move out, he said he wanted me to stay, and . . . well . . . you can imagine the rest!'

'That's so wonderful! We could have a double wedding!' Grace was practically squeaking with excitement.

'I wouldn't start planning the double wedding yet. I think Ran and I have got a way to go before we start discussing marriage!'

'No, OK,' Grace agreed. 'But the reason I rang is Allegra wants to have a meeting of all the relevant parties, at Luckenham House, next week. Tuesday. Is that OK for you?'

'What do you mean "relevant parties"?'

'Everyone involved with the panels. She says she's got hot news and wants an audience to hear it. Can you and Ran come?'

'I'll have to ask him, but I expect so. Is the Richard Coatbridge expert going to be there?'

'I don't think so, though she did find one. She's terribly excited.'

'Should Ran bring the panels?'

'Has he finished them?'

'No. He's had to fit them round other work.'

'Then they may as well stay where they are, in safety.'

Chapter Eleven

WHEN RAN AND ELLIE drove up to Luckenham House four days later, they saw by the cars in front that Grace, Flynn and Allegra were there already. There was another car, long and expensive-looking, as well.

'That probably belongs to Nicholas, Grace's brother,' said Ellie. 'I hope they don't try to bully Grace.'

'They won't have a chance with Flynn there.'

The front door was unlocked and Ellie and Ran went in unannounced. They could hear voices from the dining room and followed them. Grace was standing by the window looking flushed and extremely pretty. Flynn was standing by a tea chest covered with a cloth, on which stood a couple of bottles of champagne and several glasses.

Allegra, in a black jacket with a hound's-tooth skirt, stood by the fireplace with a man Ellie didn't know. She assumed he was Grace's brother Nicholas. Next to him was a tall, slim, elegant woman.

Demi was the first to see Ellie and Ran and came up to greet them. Then Grace noticed they had arrived and danced across the room. 'Allegra is being terribly coy about what she's discovered, but Flynn and I thought we ought to celebrate anyway. After all'—she gave Ellie a meaningful look—'lots of good things have happened lately.'

Ellie smiled in agreement; an awful lot of good things had happened to her lately, too.

The doorbell jangled and Grace went to answer it. 'Oh,' she said. 'It's you, Edward. And Hermia.' Grace waited for her emotions to come rushing in to swamp her, but nothing happened.

'We didn't come together,' snapped Hermia.

'But why did you come at all? Not that you're not always welcome,' she added, opening the door, wondering what they would say when they saw that their daughter wasn't at college, and not really caring.

'I came to look after your interests, Grace,' said Edward. 'You're such a child in these matters.'

'What matters?'

'Money matters. Hermia told me about the panels.'

'Is everybody here?' asked Allegra, after greetings between parents and daughter had been exchanged, and murmured admonishments for bunking off college administered.

'I'll just make sure everyone knows each other,' said Grace. 'Edward, come and meet Flynn.' She made the introductions warily.

'So are you and Flynn together?' said Edward with a mixture of concern and amusement.

'We are,' said Flynn firmly.

Edward nodded. 'I thought Grace was looking more lovely than ever.'

Grace looked away so she couldn't see Flynn's reaction to Edward's statement. 'Edward, you know Nicholas, of course. And that's his girlfriend, Erica.' Erica nodded at Edward across the room.

'Right, can you all stop talking, please,' said Allegra firmly. 'As most of you know, it is thought that the panels are by Richard Coatbridge. And, fantastic as it may seem, it appears they are indeed by him!' Allegra smiled as if she were personally responsible for this.

'It's not fantastic,' said Ellie indignantly. 'I knew they were!'

Allegra glared in Ellie's direction. 'Apparently it was known that he spent time in this part of the world as he had a sister in Devon and he used to break his journey here, often for several weeks, and—'

'So what are they worth, Legs?'

Allegra gave her brother a withering look. 'My expert wouldn't say. He said it wasn't his business. He could only verify that it was ninety per cent likely the panels are by Richard Coatbridge.'

'All this for nothing?' said Erica.

'No!' snapped Allegra. 'I went to Sotheby's and asked them.'

'And what did they say?' asked Edward.

'They said they couldn't possibly judge without actually seeing the panels, but looking at the slides, and having documentary evidence—'

'That scrap of paper?' asked Grace, surprised.

'They would probably fetch around the two million mark. If more than one person was really interested, it could go through the roof.'

There was a silence; at last Allegra had the attention that she wanted. Grace was feeling sick and Ellie supremely smug.

'The publicity will be enormous. Something like this, hidden for centuries,' murmured Edward.

'No,' said Grace loudly and firmly. 'I don't want any publicity. I'm not having the place swarming with press and photographers.'

'I'd be there to support you,' said Flynn.

'I know, but I'm still not having it. Can you imagine it? The place full of people, the phone ringing all the time; it would be ghastly.'

'Perhaps now would be the time to tell people, darling,' said Flynn and then addressed the room. 'We're going to get married. If Grace doesn't want to sell the panels she doesn't have to. I'll pay for the dry rot.'

'You never said anything about getting married!' Allegra was furious.

'No, you didn't,' said Grace, turning to Flynn, her face a mixture of surprise and delight.

'I don't suppose we could open the champagne, could we?' said Erica. 'I've been staring at it for ages, and I am dying for a drink.'

'OK,' said Flynn, putting a cloth round a bottle and adjusting glasses. 'Just as long as we're definitely celebrating.'

'It seems to me there's loads to celebrate,' said Erica eager to get to the champagne.

'I wish you'd all concentrate!' said Allegra. 'Some valuable old masters have been discovered, and Grace is refusing all publicity!'

'And yet she does want to sell them,' agreed Nicholas.

'There must be another way,' said Ellie, handing round glasses.

'There is,' said Ran.

'What?' demanded everyone.

'Sell them to a private buyer.'

'But how can you find a private buyer if Grace doesn't want anyone to know they exist?' demanded Allegra.

'Sorry to interrupt, everyone,' said Flynn. 'But could we just have a small toast to our engagement? I know it's not important in the present scheme of things, but I wouldn't like the moment to go unmarked.'

'Oh, for goodness' sake,' hissed Allegra.

Grace caught sight of Ran putting his arm round Ellie and wondered if they had an announcement too, but decided it was too soon.

Allegra, fed up with sentiment, raised her glass. 'OK, to the happy couple! Hooray! Congratulations, all that stuff. Now! Can we please get back to the point!'

'Which is?' asked Edward.

'How are we—'

'Is Grace,' corrected Flynn firmly.

'—going to go about selling the panels, even to a private buyer, if she doesn't want anyone to know they exist!' Allegra took a big gulp of champagne, obviously relieved to have finished her sentence at last.

'What you all seem to be overlooking,' said Ran calmly, 'is the fact that I am a picture conservator.'

'Oh, what's that?' asked Erica.

'He restores pictures,' muttered Nicholas.

'But what's that got to do with anything?' said Allegra.

'I'm in contact with private collectors all the time,' Ran said. 'I've been making a few enquiries, and I happen to know a private collector who would be very happy to buy these panels. But I should warn you, Grace, that you won't get anything like as much as if you had a big auction. I think he'd pay the basic two million, but he won't go much above that.'

Grace suddenly felt faint. 'That would be more than enough for my needs,' she said weakly, after a few moments.

'Ring him up!' demanded Allegra. 'And put us all out of our misery!'

'Are you sure he'll pay two million?' said Grace, as Ran fished out his mobile phone and began to search through the phone book.

'He said he'd pay what a major auction house thought was the lowest they'd get. He'll also pay for the restoration. Now, if you'd all be quiet for a moment . . .'

'Ooh,' Demi squeaked, 'It's like *Location, Location, Location*.'

'I think I'll take this outside,' said Ran.

Although many were tempted, no one dared follow him. Flynn refilled everyone's glasses, including Demi's, until he got to Ellie. 'Oh, Ellie, we forgot all about you. I'll get you something soft.'

'I'll get it! I want to see the kitchen.'

'You don't,' said Grace. 'It's such a mess. But it's going to be gorgeous! We've got such plans. If only Ran's collector—'

'Ah, here he is!' said Flynn.

'Right,' Ran announced, entering the room. 'It's as I said, he's prepared to offer you two million for the panels, private sale, no publicity.'

'He's getting a bargain,' muttered Allegra.

'I think that's fantastic!' said Grace. 'Can you tell him I'm very happy to accept his offer? Thank you so much for organising all that, Ran.'

'A pleasure,' said Ran going to stand by Ellie.

'So what are you going to do with all that money?' asked Edward.

Grace took a sip of champagne. 'I've thought about this already. I'm going to divide it into four parts. One part, I'm going to keep for myself, to pay for the dry rot, and do up this house. Another part I'm going to give to Ellie, to help . . .' she hesitated for an instant, wondering if she dared make any assumptions about Ellie and Ran, but decided not although they seemed welded together just then '. . . her with her new life, and the baby and everything. And the other two quarters I'm going to give to Allegra and Nicholas, in case they feel they were treated unfairly by my aunt's will.'

There was a silence. Allegra blushed and even Nicholas looked abashed.

'That's awfully good of you, sis,' said Nicholas, 'but are you sure you don't want to get even more money for them? They're obviously worth a real fortune.'

Grace frowned at her brother. 'Two million is a real fortune, and I'm quite happy with it.'

'I was only thinking,' her brother persisted, 'now you've got a man to sort things out for you—'

Grace interrupted. 'Listen, everyone, I've made my decision and I'm sticking by it. I don't need a man to sort things out for me. I love my man'—she gave him a look which confirmed this more than adequately—'but I can look after myself.'

'And there's no need for you to give me money—' started Ellie, but Grace cut her off.

'I'm not going to discuss it any more!' she said firmly. 'Is that clear?'

The room fell silent. It seemed it was indeed clear.

'Well, I don't know about the panels,' said Ellie, 'but it seems to me that Grace is definitely restored.'

'Yes, I am!' Grace confirmed. 'And now could I please have some more champagne?'

KATIE FFORDE

I met Katie Fforde in the rooftop restaurant at the National Portrait Gallery, with its stunning, panoramic view across Trafalgar Square to Big Ben and the London Eye. I knew that she'd been to the gallery when doing research for *Restoring Grace*, and as we settled ourselves with a glass of wine she said gleefully: 'I've got a story to tell you about that. I was visiting a local antique dealer with my husband when he spotted a painting that he really liked. It was of a woman in period dress and she had an amazingly serene face. I was so surprised, because Desmond just isn't interested in acquiring things—and so I really wanted to buy it for him. But we decided to go away and think about it. When I phoned the auction house the following week, and put in an offer, I got it! We didn't know much about the painting, other than that it had come from a country house sale somewhere near Stroud, where we live. So I decided to come up to the Portrait Gallery to do some investigations—then, of course, the whole thing had to appear in *Restoring Grace*!'

Picture restoration was something else Katie was keen to explore, and here again it was her husband who set her on the right path. 'He suggested that I should look in the Yellow Pages to find a picture restorer. And I found this really lovely girl, who lived very near us. She showed me what she did and then took me to see another picture restorer who had even more equipment.' Katie says she's currently 'heavily into auctions', and has even worked as a porter in a family-run auction house in nearby Cirencester. 'I wasn't

carting heavy furniture around, it was more keeping an eye on things to make sure nothing was taken before the sales. It was great fun. I loved it.'

It's hard to believe that there's anything Katie Fforde doesn't enjoy or feel enthusiastic about. She seems to exude energy and happiness, especially when talking about her writing or her family. Her three grown-up children have moved away from home now, but she is still very close to them. 'And I do love teenagers,' she says, perhaps a little wistfully. 'They're so sparky and challenging. I've been to India on school trips, for three weeks at a time, and when you're looking after children who aren't your own you really get to know how they tick. I think if you treat them on the level and keep the dialogue going, you get a much better response.'

Teenagers and friendship between women have featured strongly in all Katie Fforde's novels, and I wondered whether female friendship was important to her in her own life. 'Oh, terribly. I love men, and I have a wonderful relationship with my husband, but I really need that other kind of friendship and fun that you have with women friends.'

Katie is currently finishing her eleventh novel and I asked her whether, as an author, there was one thing she couldn't do without. 'My computer, though my first book was written on a manual typewriter, so I could go back to that if I had to. Don't ask me to write with a pencil though!'

Anne Jenkins

SARAH DUNCAN

Adultery for Beginners

When the Freeman family return to live in
England after eighteen years abroad, Neil
settles down immediately but Isabel feels
restless. With the children at school all day,
Isabel decides to look for a job, and within
days hears of someone in desperate need of
part-time office help. But as she starts to
work closely with Patrick Sherwin, she finds
herself disturbingly attracted to him. Her
head keeps telling her to think of Neil and
the children . . . but how often does the head
rule the heart?

One

DAMN, ISABEL THOUGHT, feeling a cooling trickle of stickiness on her inner thighs. Neil lay heavily on top of her, as if the effort had given him heart failure. The huffing and puffing seemed to have expelled all the air from him. Perhaps he wasn't breathing. The tissues were out of reach, supposing there were any left in the box. Damn, damn, damn, she thought. I only changed the sheets yesterday. He stirred slightly and nuzzled her neck. Not dead then. She gave him a little push.

'You're heavy.'

'Sorry.' Neil rolled off her. He heaved himself out of bed and shambled off to the shower room. Isabel lay flat under the duvet, listening to the water cascading next door and Neil singing. The sheets were clammy under her. Too late to do anything about it now. According to the papers, she thought, this is my sexual prime. Men peak at eighteen, women at thirty-six. Thirty-six. It seemed awfully old.

Neil came back in. He was a big man, broad about the shoulders, with a smattering of freckles, already fading now they were no longer exposed to strong sunlight. She noticed that his skin, usually taut with good health, had a slackness about it. Two months of desk work, two months of pale sunshine. It had been a terrible summer. All those years abroad she'd slept in a loose cotton T-shirt but returning to a damp English summer required something warmer. Thinking of the winter to come she had been tempted by head-to-toe winceyette but settled for a long nightdress. Pretty, but not exactly sexy. Neil didn't seem to care.

'Perhaps there'll be a brilliant job for me in the paper today,' Isabel said brightly. 'The trouble is, they'll want experience or qualifications. Neither of which I have.' Neil wasn't listening, preoccupied with testing socks for holes. They looked like glove puppets on his hands.

'I want a job,' she said in a squeaky voice, moving her fingers as if they were in the socks and talking. Neil looked at her, his face blank. She let her hands flop back onto the bed. 'Don't put them back in the drawer if they've got holes. I'll get you some more today.'

Neil found a satisfactory pair and sat on the bed to put them on.

'You don't have to work, you know,' he said. 'We can manage.'

'Only because we let out my father's house. It's not just the money.' She squinted at the ceiling. 'I want something more, I suppose.'

'More.' He rolled his eyes. 'Like what? What could you do?'

He doesn't mean it to sound like that, she thought. What could she do? She'd been rejected for the few jobs she'd applied for, hadn't even made the interview. 'Something in an office. Filing?'

'Darling, it's easy to see it's years since you've been in an office. No one does filing any more; it's all on computer. Never mind.' He patted her feet. 'If you want to do filing, you can always help me.'

'It's not that I want to do filing, it's just, I want . . .' Nebulous sentences buzzed in her head. I want to do something, I want to be different, I want to be . . . I want . . . I want . . . Instead she said, 'But doing a job wouldn't stop me from helping you. I could take over all the household stuff. Pay the bills, keep track of the statements, that sort of thing.'

'If we relied on you the phone would keep on being cut off.' He paused with his trousers half on. 'Do you remember when you lived in that flat and the electricity got stopped, and you had to chat up the man to come round and reconnect it because people were coming to supper?' His voice was amused, indulgent. Isabel felt mortified.

'But that was years ago. And it only happened once.'

He shrugged and turned away. 'We went abroad after that.'

Isabel twisted a dark strand of hair. 'You said you wanted help.' Even to her, her voice sounded childish, sulky against Neil's briskness.

'No, it's sweet of you to offer, but better not.'

Isabel traced the pattern of the duvet cover with her index finger. Neil was choosing a shirt, one she'd erratically ironed the day before while listening to Woman's Hour, daydreaming of being interviewed by Jenni Murray as a woman with something worth saying.

Neil hummed as he did up the buttons. His moustache hid his upper lip, making a secret of his mouth. He held up two ties against his shirt and looked at her, eyebrows raised in a question. He did this every morning. Isabel felt exhausted, limbs turned to lead.

'The one on the left,' she said, without looking. 'Why don't you shave your moustache off?'

He looked surprised. 'Why?' he said.

'I don't know. For a change? Something different?'

'Kissing a man without a moustache is like eating a boiled egg without salt.' He kissed her forehead. 'I'd better be off. D'you want me to bring you up a cup of tea?' He checked his watch. What would he do if I said yes, she wondered. But that wouldn't be playing the game.

'No, thanks. I'll get up in a minute. You don't want to miss the train.'

'See you later.'

'Usual time?'

'The usual.'

Isabel lay in the bed, quite still. How odd to have established a 'usual time' so quickly. A move of 2,000 miles, a new country, and yet within a few months they had acquired patterns to hitch their lives to. But England wasn't a new country. It was *their* country—their home. So why did she feel out of place? Stranded in some no-man's-land between the cosseted expat life and the demands of the strange new England. A home that had become harsh and modern in her eighteen-year absence.

She turned to look at her bedside clock. Five minutes till she had to get up. What was it that magazine articles were always saying? Get up five minutes earlier every day and exercise, write a poem or practise deep breathing to release stress. Breathing seemed the easiest option. She inhaled deeply, breathing in through her nose, feeling her rib cage expand, holding it—two, three, four—and then releasing it through her mouth in a gentle whoosh. There. One thing she could do.

Then she remembered. There was a coffee morning for new parents at the school that morning. A chance to meet other mums, the notice had said. Isabel bit her lip. She shouldn't be nervous, but knew she would be. They can't eat me, she told herself, standing up. With her remaining extra two minutes and thirty-seven seconds she'd wash her hair in honour of all those new mums she was going to meet.

Isabel slammed her foot down onto the brake to avoid the car in front, forgot she wasn't driving her old automatic, and stalled. She was part of a line of cars on the road to the school; it was as if every parent in Milbridge had decided that 8.46 a.m. was the ideal time to drop the children off for the first day of school.

'Eyes peeled for a parking space,' she told the children, who made no response. Michael was reading his fishing encyclopedia and Katie was tracing faces on the side window. Isabel shook her hair out in front of the heater, regretting her impulse decision to wash it. It would never dry in time. The wretched coffee morning for new parents was straight after the school drop.

She managed to find a parking space and hurried the children into the playground. St Joseph's was a small private school on the edge of Milbridge. Isabel knew it was going to be hard for Michael and Katie to adjust and hoped the smaller classes would lessen the culture shock.

The entrance hall was full of women talking at the tops of their voices, greeting each other, waving, talking about holidays. One woman was lifting her skirt to show a group of others a spectacular set of bruises on her thigh. Isabel could hear them roaring with laughter as the woman described how her horse had kicked her. Holding the children firmly by the hand she wove her way through to the classrooms. She dropped Michael off first; he was the elder and seemed more confident. She lingered in Katie's classroom, anxious about leaving her, only leaving when she realised that she was the last mother in the class.

Isabel followed the coffee-morning signs and found herself in a gym. Confident voices echoed round the room, mingling with the clatter of cups. She hesitated at the door. There wasn't a man in sight, she noticed, only mothers, and they all seemed to know each other. Some were dressed casually, others in suits as if for work. Isabel felt dressed too brightly, the colours bold and garish in the soft September light. She made a mental note to wear something beige next time.

Isabel looked around to find someone to speak to and noticed another woman on her own, standing stiffly and holding a coffee cup as if she might drop it unless vigilant. She had an angular face and an impressive set of teeth. But her expression looked how Isabel felt, so she took a deep breath, then went up to her, hoping that her hair didn't look too peculiar.

'Hello,' she said. 'Are you new here too?'

The woman nodded and smiled slightly. 'Year Two. Millicent.'

'Katie,' Isabel said. 'Year One. And Michael, he's in Year Four.'

'My son, Rufus, is in Year Four. Not here though. At another school.'

Isabel waited to see if she was going to say any more, but the woman just stared at her. Isabel ran her hand over her hair, hoping to smother any excessive vitality. 'We've only just moved here,' she tried.

'From London? So have we. Is your husband commuting?'

'No. I mean, yes. Sorry, I'm not being clear. We didn't move from London, but yes, he is commuting.'

'Where did you come from?'

'All over the place: Syria, Saudi, Thailand. My husband works for a big engineering company, so we've gone wherever we've been posted.'

There was another pause. Isabel realised that the woman was even more nervous than she was. 'Where did you live in London?'

'Twickenham.'

'I went to school near there,' Isabel said.

'Not Richmond House?'

'Were you there too?'

'I was. Gosh, what a coincidence.' The woman's cheeks were flushed and she seemed less nervous at having made the connection. Isabel also felt better.

'Wasn't it a dump?' Isabel asked.

'Awful. When were you there? I left in seventy-nine.'

'Eighty-two, so I doubt you'd remember me. I was Isabel Cooper originally, Freeman now.'

'Helen Delapole then, Weedon-Smith now.' Helen shrugged her bony shoulders. 'What a small world it is.'

Isabel was about to ask Helen where her family had lived, when a cup of murky brown liquid was thrust into her hand. 'Coffee?' a voice said. She turned and saw an imposing woman wearing a pink sweater decorated with a herd of sheep, of the sort that Isabel remembered people wearing when she'd left England eighteen years before.

'Thanks,' Isabel said, managing to slop half into her saucer.

'I'm Mary Wright, Chairman of the PTA. And you are?'

'Isabel Freeman,' Isabel said, resisting the urge to step back a pace or two. The herd of sheep were neatly arranged in fluffy white lines on the sweatshirt looking off towards Mary's right armpit, drawing attention to Mary's expansive chest. One had an odd expression and was facing the wrong way from the rest of the flock, just how Isabel felt. She dragged her eyes away. 'I'm new here.'

'Of course you are; I'd know you otherwise.' Mary turned to Helen who obediently supplied her name. 'And where do you live?'

'In Battleford,' Helen said, stammering slightly. 'We've just moved in.'

'Ah, you must be the new people in the Hurstbournes' old house.' Vigorous nodding. 'An accountant, I believe Vicky said.' Mary asked more questions. Helen racked up lots of points: accountant-in-the-City husband, the Old Manor, double-barrelled surname, pony.

'My Clemmie's in the same year as your daughter. You must bring her along to the pony club,' Mary said graciously, then added, 'I run it.' Surprise, surprise, thought Isabel. Then it was her turn.

She could see that her real life would score *nul points* on Mary's system, so instead she said, 'We live in the Old Palace, my children are called

Raphael and Hermione, and my husband is an international trouble-shooter, the engineering version of Red Adair.'

'Really?' Helen's eyes were wide.

Isabel laughed. 'No, not really. We live in a brand new house, Neil's just an ordinary engineer and the children are called Michael and Katie. But the international bit is true. We've lived in nine different countries since we married.'

'How interesting,' said Mary, who looked as if she hadn't appreciated Isabel's pretend life. 'Well. Nice to meet you, and you must come to all the PTA events. Now, I should circulate, but before I go, I must make sure you're labelled,' Mary said. With what? thought Isabel, feeling labelled already with 'Not to be taken seriously'. Mary was scanning the chattering mass of women.

'Ah, there she is. Justine!' she called, waving.

A woman squeezed through the crowd. Her blonde bob looked as perfect as her clothes, which managed to be both smart and casual at the same time. Isabel felt dishevelled and garishly bright, like a moulting parakeet confronted by a peregrine falcon.

'Justine, none of these people have labels,' Mary said.

'Never mind. You carry on and I'll make sure they get labelled.' There was nothing in Justine's attitude or voice to suggest that she was saying anything untoward but Mary gave her a suspicious look.

'I must circulate,' she repeated and went back into the crowd, the women parting like the Red Sea in front of her.

Justine gave a pussycat smile. 'Mary's put four children through this school, which may explain why she acts as if she runs it. The thing to remember is that it's not just you she's patronising, she does it to everyone equally.' She pulled a roll of labels from her bag. 'If you could just put your name and your children's year onto these and stick them on. Then you can find the other mothers in your children's years, and go up and introduce yourselves.' Justine tore off two labels and handed them out. 'Have you both got a pen?'

Helen started writing out her label while Isabel rummaged in the bottom of her bag. 'I think so,' she muttered.

'Never mind. I've got one.'

Isabel straightened up. 'Isabel Freeman,' she said as Justine wrote it down. 'I've got Michael, Year Four, and Katie in Year One.'

'Year One,' repeated Justine. 'I've got a daughter in Year One. Rachel. In Mrs Baker's class.'

'So is Katie.'

'Brilliant; they've been completely swamped with boys. Rachel will be thrilled another girl's joined them. Perhaps you and your daughter would like to come and have tea with us after school one day.'

'That'd be lovely.'

Justine handed Isabel a business card. 'My number's at the bottom.'

'How smart.' Isabel peered at the card. 'Is this you?'

Justine nodded.

'Wardrobe, Colour and Image Consultant,' Isabel read out. No wonder Justine looked so immaculate. 'It must be odd being on show all the time,' she blurted out, and then blushed. 'I mean, I expect you feel you always have to be an advertisement for your business.'

Justine cocked her head to one side. 'Yes, but once you know what you should be wearing, then everything looks right.'

'It obviously works for you,' Isabel said, knowing that she would never look as smart as Justine. Her hair was all wrong for a start. 'We lived abroad until the summer and I can't get used to the weather here. I'm either freezing, or boiling because I've put too much stuff on.'

'It's not just colours. I can organise your wardrobe and help with what you should be buying,' Justine said.

Isabel hesitated. The idea of someone rummaging through her things appalled her, however much she might need it. It seemed too exposing.

Justine touched Isabel's arm lightly. 'Don't worry, I'm not going to do a hard sell on you.'

'I've always meant to have it done,' Helen said.

Justine gave her a card. 'Give me a ring if you want to know more.'

'I will. I could do with a clear-out. I've still got loads of work clothes from before I had children.'

'Do you still work?' Isabel asked, wanting to change the subject.

Helen pulled a face. 'Lord no, the children are quite enough for me.'

'What about you?' Justine asked Isabel.

'It's almost impossible for expat wives to work; you move around too much and in a lot of the countries we've been in, women aren't allowed to work. But now we've settled back in the UK I'm looking for a job.'

'What sort?'

'I don't know. I've only done a bit of TEFL before.'

'Teffle?'

'Teaching English as a Foreign Language. I rang round the local language schools but they all wanted the new qualifications—my old TEFL certificate doesn't count. The alternative would be to get experience through casual work, but that would be next summer and I want something now. So I'm not sure what I'm looking for.'

'Can you type?' Isabel nodded and Justine continued, 'I do know someone who's looking for somebody to work in his office, part-time. He offered it to me, but to be honest, now I'm single again, I have to work full-time.'

'Part-time sounds wonderful.'

'I don't think it's very exciting, just basic office stuff.'

'No, that would be fine.' Isabel didn't care what the job was.

'If you give me your phone number, I'll find out if the job is still going, and if it is, get him to give you a ring.' She handed Isabel one of the PTA labels.

Isabel started to write down her phone number, then had to check it with her address book. 'It's silly, but I still can't remember it by heart.' She thought that didn't sound very organised, so she added quickly, 'I don't usually have a problem remembering things.'

'Don't worry, he's the world's most disorganised person. Anyone would seem a paragon of efficiency next to him.' Justine gave her a long look, as if considering. 'In fact, I'm probably not doing you a favour,' she said. Isabel wanted to ask her what she meant but was distracted by Mary's voice calling from the far side of the hall.

'Justine! Labels needed here, please.'

Justine wrinkled her nose. 'I must go and avert disaster. Mustn't have anyone unlabelled, you know.'

Isabel watched her squeeze her way through the crowd, then turned to Helen. 'I suppose that's networking,' Isabel said, wanting to sing. 'It probably won't get me anywhere but . . .'

'You never know.' They said it together and Isabel's heart lifted. Perhaps she'd found a friend.

Isabel got back from the town centre and slowly unloaded her shopping. Having stored the food, she thought she would eat something as it was lunchtime. What she really wanted was a peanut-butter sandwich, with squishy white bread, but she got out a low-calorie instant soup instead. She scanned through the post while waiting for the kettle to boil. Neil sorted it before going to work and usually took out his letters for reading on the train. Isabel got left with catalogues and junk mail. She poured the hot water on the powdered soup. It looked thin. It tasted thin. Would it make her thin? Wistfully she thought of peanut-butter sandwiches. Still, as she'd been so good, just having the soup, she could let herself have one biscuit.

She selected one of Katie's red felt pens and sat down with the local paper. Pen in one hand, biscuit in the other, she turned to the recruitment section. Hundreds of jobs, it promised. Packers, salespersons, fork-lift truck drivers. Nurses, welders, executive this and that. Trainers, FE lecturers, waste-disposal operatives. So many jobs, none of which she could do. She reached for another biscuit and realised she had eaten half a packet of chocolate-chip cookies. Far worse than a peanut-butter sandwich. Oh well, at least they had been two packets for the price of one so she hadn't wasted money. She'd start her diet properly tomorrow.

The phone rang and she went to answer it, tripping on a stray chunk of Lego and falling, wrenching her ankle. 'Ow. Hello?'

A man's voice asked, 'Is that Isabel?'

'Yes, speaking.'

'You sound in pain.'

'I fell over.'

'I see.' The deep voice paused. 'My name's Patrick Sherwin. I hear you're looking for a job?'

'Yes.' Isabel grimaced. She must sound like a complete disaster area. Think 'good telephone manner'. She took a deep breath. 'That was quick. I only spoke to Justine this morning.'

'She moves fast.' Isabel thought his voice was wonderful, as rich as handcream. 'I need someone to come and help out with my business. Nothing too alarming, keeping the paperwork in order and up-to-date, answering the phone. That sort of thing. Are you interested?'

'Absolutely.'

'Why don't you come round to my office and we could chat. Would tomorrow be possible? I'm flying to Rome late that evening, so . . .'

'No, no, tomorrow's fine,' she said.

'Good. I'm at number forty-five, Downton Road. I'll see you there at, say, twelve thirty.'

'That's fine,' she repeated. She put the phone down and hugged herself. A job interview. She'd got a job interview.

Isabel could hardly wait until Neil came through the front door. The minute she heard his key in the lock she rushed up.

'Guess what? I've got a job interview.'

'Well done. What's the job?'

Isabel rubbed her nose. 'Just general office admin stuff, I think.'

Neil stretched. 'Sounds good. I'm just going to pop upstairs and change, and then you can tell me all about it.'

'I've got supper waiting for you.'

'Great. I'll be down in a second.' Isabel watched his feet trudging upwards. Not so long ago he would have taken them two at a time. She went into the kitchen and took the fish pie out of the oven, then sat down and waited till Neil came down.

'So, what does the business do?'

Isabel doled some fish pie onto Neil's plate, trying to think.

'Um. I'm not sure. Help yourself to salad.'

'Thanks. What's the business called?'

'Not sure.' She mumbled deliberately.

Neil looked puzzled. 'What did it say in the ad? Show me.'

'It wasn't from an ad.' Isabel felt her excitement seep away like water in sand. 'Someone said that they knew someone who wanted someone and, well, he rang up and asked me to come for an interview.'

'So who rang up?'

'His name's Patrick—' Sherman? Sherden? 'Patrick Sherwin, I think. He's a friend of a woman I met at the new parents' coffee morning.'

'And do you know her name?'

'Oh, yes. Justine. She's got a daughter in Katie's class.'

'It all sounds a bit dodgy to me. Where is this interview?'

'Forty-five Downton Road.'

'Where's that?'

At least she knew the answer to that one, having looked it up. 'Close to the centre. It's the bit that has loads of those Georgian artisans' cottages, painted in pastel colours. Terribly pretty.' Neil had dismissed them when they were househunting as being too small and too expensive.

Neil grunted. 'Is it an office address?'

'He said it was.'

'Doesn't sound like it.' She had to admit he was right; it didn't sound like an office address. She watched his face, trying to gauge his mood. Perhaps she could divert him.

'Guess what, I met someone from my old school at the coffee morning. It's a small world, isn't it? Her name's Helen, and her husband's called George Something-Smith. He commutes to London on the same train as you. They live just outside Milbridge and she's asked us all over to Sunday lunch next weekend . . .' Her voice trailed off.

Neil pushed his plate back and sucked his moustache. 'I can't say I like it, Bel. This job.' He looked at her like a kindly headmaster (firm but fair) about to admonish a small boy. 'You don't know what the business is, what it's called, the name of the man who rang, or what you're going to be asked to do. Darling, this man could be anyone.'

'He sounded all right on the phone.' He'd sounded gorgeous, in fact, but she didn't think Neil would be impressed with that.

'Isabel.' He leaned back in his chair and raised his eyes to the ceiling. He looked so pompous and sure of himself, Isabel felt like she could hit him. And she'd cooked him treacle tart. She took it out of the oven and started cutting it up, stabbing at the pastry. Unfair, unfair.

'Are you saying I can't go?'

'I'm only concerned for your safety.' He calmly picked up his spoon, then paused. 'Aren't you eating any?'

'I'm on a diet.' She folded her arms and watched him eat. Her jaw ached from clenching her teeth. It was unfair. She'd been so excited and now Neil was ruining everything.

'You just don't want me to work, do you?' she blurted out.

'That's nothing to do with it. I'm concerned—' but she cut him off.

'You make it sound so reasonable. It's just so I look in the wrong, but I'm not. You don't want me to go out. All you want me to do is look after you and the children. Washing and cooking and cleaning for ever.'

'Don't be ridiculous.' He sounded almost bored as he stood up.

'And don't go off. This is important, I want to talk about it.'

'Perhaps when you've calmed down.'

'I am calm,' Isabel shouted.

'Thank you for supper.' He pushed his chair in and smiled at a spot just above her head, a tight smile that left his face untouched and his eyes shielded. 'I'm going to watch the news.'

'I'm more important than the news,' she cried, but he was gone. I am more important, she thought. I am. She cleared the plates into the dishwasher then, slowly and deliberately, she cut herself a large slice of treacle tart and drowned it in cream.

Two

THE NEXT DAY Isabel couldn't decide what to wear. A job interview meant a suit, which she didn't have, so it would have to be a skirt. Although it hadn't sounded like a formal sort of set-up. She shied away from thinking about Neil's questions. She opened the wardrobe and started to rifle through the tightly packed clothes, ticking them off in her mind. Too tight, too short, too old-fashioned. Her hand paused on her favourite dress, white splashed with pink hibiscus. Too bright. Too girlie. No, the only possibility was a long, straight, dark navy skirt.

She sucked her tummy in as she pulled the zip up and looked in the mirror, arching round to check the rear view. It would work but she didn't have the right sort of high heels. Why should it matter what she looked like anyway? Her abilities were what counted, surely? She looked at her reflection, pushing her hair away from her face and wishing that just once it would lie sleekly like Justine's. Why would someone employ me? she thought. What can I do? How do I sell myself?

I've got O levels and A levels and a TEFL certificate. I've taught children in schools where the nearest clean water was two miles away. I can whistle and hum at the same time. I can drive a Jeep up sand dunes and I'm better than Neil at wadi bashing. I've read the whole of *War and Peace*, even the boring bits, and I find Anthony Trollope funny. I love nineteenth-century literature and baroque music.

None of which seemed to be relevant attributes for a woman looking for an office job. But I want to be useful, she thought. I want to do something beyond sitting around drinking coffee and playing the occasional game of tennis. She would wear the skirt with flat shoes if need be, she decided, but if she got a move on there might be time to pop into town and hunt for a new outfit. After all, it was about time she treated herself to something other than doughnuts.

'Great shoes,' Mr Sherwin said, raising one eyebrow.

'Thanks,' Isabel said, slightly flustered, both that he'd noticed and also commented. She had meant to buy something sensible, not plum-purple suede with three-inch high heels and a finger's-width band of snakeskin across the extravagantly pointed toes. For a second in the shop she'd rebelled against being sensible.

'Let's find you a place to sit.' He looked around him. Every surface of the room appeared to be covered with papers. He bundled some of them to the side, uncovering part of a faded chintz sofa.

Isabel sat down and tensed as the sofa springs threatened to give way.

'The office is upstairs, but that's even more chaotic. I'm just going to get myself a chair,' he said as he left the room. Isabel could hardly imagine anywhere more chaotic than the paper-strewn living room she was in.

Patrick came back in with a kitchen chair. 'As you can see, I desperately need someone who can sort out my paperwork. I meant to have a go at the weekend, which is why there's lots of stuff down here but . . .' he shrugged, palms up. 'Paperwork's not my thing,' he added. Isabel could see that. She wasn't sure if paperwork was her thing either.

'What is it that you do?' she asked. Neil hadn't actually said she wasn't to go, but she knew he didn't approve. The least she could do was ask his questions.

'I set up computer systems for people, supply software, hardware, whatever's needed. You don't happen to speak Italian, do you?'

'No,' Isabel said, thinking she'd blown it.

'No matter,' he said. 'It would have been a bonus. I have clients in Italy as well as here, that's all.'

Isabel wondered if he was Italian himself. He was dark skinned with dark brown hair, but it was his gestures that seemed Italian, and the obviously expensive clothes. His accent was impeccably English.

He leaned back in his chair. 'Tell me about yourself, what you've done workwise. That sort of thing.'

Isabel clutched the handles of her bag. It was quite hard to make nothing sound impressive. 'I haven't been working recently, not formally at least. My husband's job has meant that we've had to travel around, often to countries where women aren't allowed to work. We came back to the UK this summer, which is why I'm interested in this job. You said you wanted someone part-time?'

'You have children?'

Isabel nodded. 'Katie's six and Michael's eight. They're both at school.'

'Does that mean you can't do a full day?'

'Well, yes, really.' She bit her lip. 'The school does have an after-school club, but I'd rather not use it, at least, not in their first term.'

'So when would you want to go?'

'Three?'

'I see. And in the morning?'

'After the school run. I could be here before nine if you wanted.'

'Mmm. I'm not famous for being an early riser.' Patrick looked at her as if considering.

Isabel inwardly cringed. 'What exactly were you looking for?'

'Someone who can manage all this,' he said, waving a hand. 'Also, answer the phone and deal with clients if I'm out and generally act as a PA. I want someone who's prepared to be flexible about what they do and not expire in horror if I ask them to take cheques to the bank or pick up my dry-cleaning.' His eyes dropped to her feet as if in doubt that anyone who would wear such shoes could do anything as mundane as going to the dry-cleaners.

'I wouldn't have a problem with doing that,' Isabel said, tucking her feet under her, trying to make the shoes less obvious.

'I work mainly on computer—' he paused. 'I take it you can use one?' She nodded and he carried on. 'I use standard office software—Sage, Word, Excel and so on. Are you familiar with them?'

'We've got all of them on the computer at home,' Isabel said, omitting to say that it was Neil's computer and that she'd hardly ever used it.

'And the Net?'

'Oh, yes,' Isabel said, relieved that she could offer some evidence of her skills. 'I'm an expat. The Net's the easiest way to keep in touch with friends when they're scattered all over the world.'

'Good.' Patrick scratched his nose. 'What work have you done before?'

'Before I married I worked at the BBC as a researcher.' No need to tell him that it was two months' unpaid work experience one summer. 'And I've taught English abroad, both privately and in schools.'

'So no office experience to speak of, in fact,' Mr Sherwin said.

Isabel stared at the floor. All those years and nothing to show for it except a fast-fading suntan and a competent backhand. What had she been doing with her life? 'No, but I have spent many years running a household, often in quite difficult circumstances. From what you've said, you need someone with organisational abilities rather than specific office skills.' She put what she hoped was a confident, efficient expression on her face but inside she felt close to tears.

'I wouldn't want more than fifteen hours' work a week. That's five hours on three days,' he said. 'Mid-week would suit me best.'

'You mean, Tuesday, Wednesday, Thursday? That would suit me too.' She could hardly breathe with excitement.

'Look, why don't you start next week and we'll see how we get on. Call it a trial period, no strings on either side.'

'That sounds fine.' She beamed at him. She felt wonderful. A job meant purpose, and validation and wages and . . . Oh! She had completely forgotten about the money. She swallowed.

'Um, can I ask about wages?'

'Ah. I thought three pounds fifty an hour.'

Her ego deflated rapidly. 'That's outrageous. I mean, that's less than cleaning ladies.'

He shrugged, unperturbed.

'Five pounds,' she said, breathless at negotiating.

'You've no experience, no qualifications. You could say that I'm offering you on-the-job training.'

'That's taking advantage. Supermarkets pay more than that.'

'Then take a job in a supermarket.' He leaned back, completely relaxed.

'Four pounds.'

'Three pounds seventy-five,' he countered, smiling at her. The smile irritated her.

'Four pounds,' she repeated, determined not to give in. She didn't want him to think she was a pushover. 'It'd make the maths easier.'

He laughed, and stood up. 'Let it not be said that I'm taking advantage of inexperience. Four pounds an hour it is. Deal?' He held out his hand.

Isabel stood up too. She'd forgotten about the plum high-heels, and the factory-smooth soles slid on the rug under her feet. She nearly stumbled, grabbing at his hand to steady herself. His grip was warm and firm. 'Deal,' she said.

I've got a job, I've got a job. She could see herself telling Neil, imagining his delighted surprise. 'Good for you,' he'd say. 'Well done.' She pictured the living room without the layer of paper, the office tidy, everything filed away alphabetically with herself at the centre, a Miss Moneypenny figure with striped shirt neatly tucked into a slim waistband. Her daydream stopped suddenly as she realised that she'd forgotten to ask Mr Sherwin the name of his company. Neil wouldn't be impressed.

Neil wasn't.

'I don't understand why you didn't ask,' he kept saying. 'What's the big secret?'

'I didn't think to ask,' Isabel said, feeling stupid and wishing she hadn't told him, had kept it quiet. Neil had been in such a bad mood when he'd got back from work that she'd avoided telling him about the interview. On Saturday afternoon they had driven into town to buy a sofa. Sitting in the passenger seat, she'd been lulled into thinking that he'd have forgotten his objections. But no such luck. Neil couldn't leave the subject alone.

'Look, I'll find out on Tuesday. What about this one?' Isabel sat on a sofa at random. 'It's very comfortable.'

'I think it's hideous,' Neil said, the corners of his moustache drooping.

'We wouldn't have to have the same cover. Try it for comfort.' She patted the sofa beside her. Neil sat down, and leaned back.

'Aren't you pleased I've got a job?' she tried.

'Of course I am, darling.' Neil sat up with a sigh. 'It just seems very dodgy to me. It's in this man's house, you don't know the name of the company, there's no job description—'

'I know what I'm supposed to be doing. Personal assistant things. Filing. Sorting. Organising. That sort of thing. Nothing I can't do.'

Neil rubbed the back of his head with his hand and stood up. 'It's not a question of what you can or can't do. It's a question of safety.'

Isabel stood up too. 'You didn't want me to go to the interview because of safety but it was fine. Not everybody is a mad axe murderer.'

'But he could have been.' He set off down the aisle. Isabel watched him peering at the sales tags and then letting them drop with a sniff.

Isabel marched up to him and pulled at his sleeve to get his attention. 'Why are you being so bloody unpleasant?' she hissed.

Neil looked past her left ear. 'I'm sorry. I don't mean to be unpleasant,' he said in the reasonable voice that always drove her mad. 'I'm concerned that you're being naive.'

'Neil, I'm a grown woman. I've spent all these years trailing after you, going from one country to the next, and that's been fine. I've accepted that there are certain constraints living in a different culture.' She bit her lip, concentrating on sounding as reasonable as Neil. 'But we're not there now, and I'm not going to live as if I'm in purdah. This is my home.'

'I'm only concerned for you.'

'You don't need to be.'

There was a short silence. 'I don't like these square ones,' Neil said, touching the arm of the nearest sofa with his fingertips. 'I'd rather get something with cushions.'

'You mean more traditional.'

He shrugged, then moved along towards the children on the far side of the shop. They'd found a garden swing seat and were rocking backwards and forwards. For once they weren't squabbling.

Why are we always arguing? Isabel thought. Since we've been back it's been one thing after another. Neil used to be my closest friend, but now we're always fighting. Perhaps we shouldn't have come back.

She trailed after Neil, who had settled on a large sofa with scrolled arms. She sat on the other side, very conscious of the space between them. 'D'you like this one?' she said finally.

'It's not bad,' he said. 'It's a nice colour too.'

It was a dreary in-between brown, not cream, not chocolate, but a nothing colour. 'You can choose whatever colour you like,' Isabel said.

'I like this one.'

'Don't you think it's a bit, well, dull? I mean, we could have something like this.' She pulled out the book of fabric swatches and handed it to him, open at a vibrant terracotta. He took it as if the swatch might surge up and swamp him, like being attacked by a vat of tomato soup.

'I know this is a silly job,' she said. 'It's not what I want to be doing for the rest of my life, or even for more than six months. But it's a start, and I have to start from the bottom.'

'Why do you have to start at all?' he said, thumbing through the swatches.

'Neil, we've been through this so many times. I want to work, I want to be useful. The children are at school all day, so what else am I supposed to do with my time?'

'It didn't matter in Syria.'

'The children were younger then. And it was different. I had to shop every day, and make everybody's lunch, and there weren't opportunities to do anything else. It's not like that here. And everything's so expensive here, we could do with the money.'

'It's hard to imagine what they'd look like from such a little piece,' he said, frowning at the swatches. 'I think the one it's got on is the best.'

Isabel said nothing as she looked at the sofa. Sludge would be the most apt description. She took the book of swatches from him and flicked wistfully through the squares of jewel-bright colours sapphire, emerald and ruby. Still, she supposed that sludge would go with almost any other colour. 'So you'd like this one?'

'Yeah, why not?' He paused. 'Look, I accept you want to work. I don't see why it has to be this job.'

'Because I've not been offered anything else,' Isabel wailed in exasperation. 'I can't pick and choose. I've no experience, no qualifications. I probably couldn't even get a job selling sofas.'

'You can sell me a sofa any day. Come here and give me a kiss.' So that was the end of the discussion. Isabel thought about pushing harder for a different colour, but as he had relented about her working she shuffled along the seat to him. He put his arm round her. 'That's better. Now, c'mon, let's grab the kids and go and pay. By the way, how much are you getting for this job?'

'Four pounds an hour.'

'You're kidding. That's less than the minimum wage, you know.'

'I didn't,' Isabel said. 'I didn't know there was a minimum wage.'

'Oh, Isabel. What shall I do with you?' Neil stared at her. 'You really are hopeless.'

How was I supposed to know there's a minimum wage? There wasn't one when I last lived here, she thought, as the children charged over and bounced on the sofa Neil had chosen. At least I got the job. Mr Sherwin didn't think I was hopeless. The idea that he might have thought her a mug skittered across her mind. After all, he had originally offered her three pounds fifty an hour. But then, remembering the chaos, she thought it more likely that Mr Sherwin hadn't heard of the minimum wage either. And I don't care anyway, she told herself. It doesn't matter how much I get, it's the experience that counts.

She followed Neil and the children to the sales desk, where Neil negotiated a price reduction for the sofa in the showroom. The sales assistant's probably relieved to get rid of such a boring colour, Isabel thought, and then felt disloyal.

'We could deliver on a Wednesday, Thursday or Friday,' the sales assistant said.

'It'll have to be a Friday,' Isabel said, feeling immensely proud. 'I work on Wednesdays and Thursdays.' It was wonderful to be able to say that. Neil snorted into his moustache but said nothing to her as he got out his wallet and paid for the sofa. Perhaps she could think of the colour as being baby donkey. She could team it with speedwell blue.

Isabel rang the doorbell. Nothing. She knocked, a sharp series of raps. Still nothing. She took two paces back and stared up at the windows. The curtains were drawn and she wondered if Mr Sherwin lived there as well as using the house as an office. Perhaps he was still in bed. She walked to the gate, wondering what to do next. Then she realised that a man was strolling down the street, a pint of milk dangling from his hand, and in the next second recognised him. Mr Sherwin stopped, pulled out a mobile phone and started talking into it. He was still talking when he registered Isabel. With his free hand he brushed the palm of his hand against his forehead, universal sign of forgetfulness—or stupidity—and grinned at her, still chatting into the phone. He walked past her to the house and unlocked the door, then beckoned her in. The room looked even worse than it had done the previous week. She hesitated then sat down carefully on the sofa, watching him stride around the room talking, as if oblivious to her presence.

After a few minutes he said, 'Look, I must go. Ciao.' He turned the phone off and looked at Isabel, who was inwardly seething. He could obviously have stopped talking any time he wanted.

'Isabel. Is it Tuesday already? I'd quite forgotten about you. Never mind, it's good you're here. I'm up to my eyeballs at the moment.' He gestured vaguely at the room. 'What would be great is, if you could tidy all these into some sort of order, and then make us a couple of coffees— the kitchen's through there—and then I can run through what I want you to do today. I've got a few calls to make, but I'll do them in the garden. You can bring the coffee out there. Got to make the most of the sunshine, right?' And with that he left the room, already dialling.

Isabel stood blinking in the empty room. Well, that's put me in my place, she thought. How Neil would laugh at this. She started to collect up all the printed matter ready to sort into piles—newspapers, brochures, letters. She wasn't sure how else to sort them, not knowing what they were about. As she went through them she registered certain names and made new piles for them. Invoices, bills—an alarming amount of red reminders—glossy advertisements for computers, bits torn from newspapers. Some were written in what she recognised as being Italian. Bank statements, reports, cuttings from the *Financial Times*. Official-looking letters from Customs and Excise and Companies House. By the end she had lined up the material into eight rough piles along the top of the old oak dresser and not a paper lay on the floor. And she now knew the business was called Patrick Sherwin Associates.

She followed where he had gone and found herself in the kitchen. There were dirty plates and mugs in the sink, and foil dishes indicated that Mr Sherwin had been eating a lot of takeaways over the weekend. She filled up the kettle with water and switched it on. While she waited for the water to boil she did the washing-up and chucked the takeaway containers into the bin, hoping that she wasn't setting a precedent. It was bad enough clearing up after two children and a husband without adding an employer as well.

Having finished, she looked around for something else to do. The kitchen now looked functional but impersonal so she went back out to the front garden and picked some of the nerines that were sunning themselves at the base of the house wall. The fragile pink flowers were unscented but beautiful as she put them in a jam jar on the kitchen table. She started to explore the cupboards. Mr Sherwin appeared to have only real coffee, not instant, so she made a cafetière-full. She added two mugs to the tray along with the cafetière and milk, and went out to the back garden, screwing her eyes up against the sunshine.

Mr Sherwin was seated at one end of a garden table, still talking into his phone. As soon as he saw Isabel he finished off his conversation.

'Thanks, that's just what I needed.' He smiled up at her. 'What I'd like you to do today is answer the house phone and take messages, and start sorting the office out. It's the room upstairs, at the back.' His mobile started to ring, and he reached for it. 'When you've finished your coffee, can you find out about flights to Milan on Friday? Returning Sunday—from Heathrow, if possible—use the Net to get the best deal. The computer's in the office.' He looked at the phone display. 'Christ, it's that fool Andrew again.' He pressed the answer button and, with a big smile, said, 'Andrew! What can I do for you?'

Isabel sat for a minute, then took her coffee inside. She decided to do the flight booking while he was yabbering on his mobile so he wouldn't see her first attempt at booking something over the Internet. She rinsed out her mug, then went upstairs to discover the office.

The office was the back room, not the one with the closed curtains. More papers were stacked on the floor or spilled off the edges of the bookcase. Computer monitors and keyboards were stacked haphazardly in the corner. In the middle of the room was a desk, and on the desk was a computer. She eyed it nervously. Although she'd told Mr Sherwin that she knew what she was doing, she'd only used the Internet for email before. Neil had given her a computer lesson at the weekend. It had reminded her of him teaching her to drive, endlessly patient with her mistakes. A good teacher. Time for work, she thought.

The first priority was the flights. She quickly ran through the different airlines and came up with a selection of times and prices that she wrote down in her neatest writing. Rome the weekend before, Milan this. It seemed very glamorous.

Flight information sorted, she turned her attention to the room. There was an old filing cabinet in the corner, almost empty. She wrote labels for the front of the drawers: Clients and Accounts were the first two drawers. The magazines, newspaper articles and advertisements could all become Information in the third drawer. And everything else could go into the bottom drawer marked Stuff. That settled, she began to work through the piles of paper, dividing them into the categories.

Underneath some computer magazines she found a scarlet clipboard, complete with pen. She made a list of what she had to do. As she looked at the clipboard with a sense of achievement, the phone rang. She found it on the floor underneath the table.

'Good morning, Patrick Sherwin Associates,' she said in the sort of voice she imagined an efficient personal assistant would use. 'Can I help you?' She inwardly prayed they wouldn't ask any awkward questions. Which could have been almost anything. But luckily the caller simply wanted to speak to Mr Sherwin.

Isabel opened the window. 'Mr Sherwin, Mr Sherwin,' she called down into the garden, waving her hand. 'Telephone.'

'I'll take it downstairs,' he called back up to her. 'Who is it?'

Isabel grimaced. 'Sorry.'

He shook his head. 'No matter.' Isabel felt dim for not asking. He was squinting up at her, eyes closed against the sunlight. 'You don't have to call me Mr Sherwin.' He went into the house. Isabel turned back to the phone. 'He's just coming,' she said, forgetting to put on her ultra-efficient voice. She then waited until she heard the click as he picked up the downstairs phone. Then she put the phone down, thinking about calling Mr Sherwin Patrick. It seemed almost disrespectful to call an employer by their first name. Or was that old-fashioned? But then, he doesn't call me Mrs Freeman, she thought. Neil would probably think he ought to. But then Neil thinks I ought to be at home washing his socks or something. Instead, here I am—at work. And it feels good.

'You'd have been very impressed by your old mother,' Isabel said to the children as they ate spaghetti, spattering tomato sauce over the table. 'I even did the bit with the credit card when Mr Sherwin had chosen the flight he wanted.' She'd got used to calling him Patrick over the day, but felt reticent about using his first name to the children. 'Mr Sherwin is half-Italian. And he's very untidy, much worse than me.'

'Do you tell him off?' Michael asked.

'Of course not. He's my employer. C'mon you two, eat up. There's chocolate cake for afters.'

'Mmm.' Katie started to eat properly.

Only bought cake, not homemade, because she didn't have time to make her own. The first pangs of working-mother guilt gave her an illicit thrill. No longer merely someone else's adjunct, but a working woman too busy for trivia, rushing from one meeting to the next. A life filled to the brim with purpose.

She sang to herself as she cleared up the tea things, and the good mood continued all the way through Neil's return home. He asked a few questions about her day, which she answered as neutrally as possible, not wanting to trigger any unpleasantness. She hoped that if she kept it low key, Neil would accept her working for Patrick. She'd sent a few emails to her friends about the new job, but she wanted to talk to someone about it.

She fished out Justine's business card from her handbag, now dog-eared and creased, unlike the immaculate Justine.

'I just wanted to say thank you. I've started working for Patrick Sherwin.'

'I heard.' Justine sounded amused.

From him? Isabel wondered what he had said about her. She paused, uncertain of what to say next.

'I don't want to rush you, but I was just on my way out,' Justine said.

'I wondered if you and Rachel would like to come round for tea after school one day next week?' Isabel blurted out.

'That sounds good.' They fixed a date for the following week.

'Look, I must dash,' Justine said. 'I'll see you next week. I expect you want me to dish the dirt about Patrick,' she added.

'No, no, of course not,' Isabel responded, but couldn't stop herself from asking, 'Is there any dirt?'

Justine laughed. 'Gotta go. You'll just have to wait.'

Later, Isabel undressed for bed as Neil sat in bed reading some company report. She wondered if he would notice if she grew a thick coat of body hair all over or developed a third breast. She pulled her nightdress over her head and hopped into bed. After a minute she snuggled up to him, letting her mind drift back over the day. It had been tiring. But she'd enjoyed bringing order out of chaos. She screwed up her eyes against the light from Neil's bedside lamp, willing for sleep to come quickly. In the half-darkness she could hear him turn the pages of his report. Strange how such a little noise could fill the room. After a while he laid down the report with a sigh and turned his light off.

A whisper of breath.

'Isabel?' A hand sneaking towards her, groping its way up past her nightdress. The hand pawed an inert breast. A cold, thick hand with stubby fingers. She closed her eyes, not that Neil could see in the dark.

He pressed against her and asked, 'Is this . . . ?'

Pointless to say no. She always said yes, because yes was easier than no. No meant discussion, fumbled attempts to arouse her that she found deeply embarrassing. No nearly always meant giving in later. She got more sleep with yes and, most of the time, sleep mattered more

She hooked her leg over his hips to draw him towards her. Needing no further encouragement he plunged in, losing himself to the physical sensation, a dance that both of them knew, smooth and practised over the years. Practised to the point when it had ceased to have any meaning. Once, of course, it had been the most wonderful thing ever, but eighteen years and two children later, sex had dwindled into a routine activity. She didn't think she was unusual.

Sex with Neil was like a hobby, like playing golf. Neil was still keen and Isabel, supportive wife that she was, joined him. Sometimes it engaged her, held her interest, other times she merely strolled around the course with him, breathing deeply, applauding Neil's good shots, and vaguely hoping that the exercise at least was doing her good. It was nothing to be either unhappy or happy about—just another facet of married life.

But that evening there was something else, a lurking question: is this it? There should be, ought to be, something more. Acceptance was not the same as contentment. No matter how Neil pumped away, she felt empty. An unexpected hot tear slid out from under her tightly closed eyelids and suddenly she wanted nothing more than to be alone.

Knowing it would hurry him up she dug her nails into his arms, breathed more heavily, muttered, 'Go on. Now.' Encouraged by those sparse tokens of passion he reached the eighteenth hole and collapsed down onto her. He kissed her, then rolled off and settled himself down for sleep. Curling up into a foetal position, she realised that she couldn't remember when he'd last bothered to ask if it was all right for her.

Three

WHEN HELEN HAD INVITED the whole family over to Sunday lunch, Isabel had been thrilled at the invitation, their first since coming back to the UK. Now, standing outside Helen's large Victorian house in the countryside outside Milbridge, she was not so sure. She hardly knew Helen, and had never met her husband, George. Neil rang the bell, an ornate piece of cast-iron work that pulled out on a chain.

Silence.

'Perhaps I've got the wrong week.' But no, there were footsteps inside, and Helen opened the front door, her cheeks flushed. Then it was introductions, children being sent off to the playroom, and drinks for the adults—mean dribbles of gin and vast slurps of tonic. George and Neil recognised each other from the station platform and Helen exclaimed about yet another coincidence.

'Hardly,' snorted George. His eyes were pale blue and surprisingly large in his red face, like a Hanoverian portrait. 'Everybody takes the seven twenty.' His voice was contemptuous and Helen seemed to shrink.

'What a lovely house,' Isabel said quickly, although she thought the house depressing.

'We were so lucky to find it,' Helen said, brightening. She launched into a long story of estate agents and probate. 'It took nearly a year.' They talked about houses and house prices, then moved on to soft furnishings. Isabel wasn't sure if it was her attention, or the fact that George and Neil were deep in some masculine bonding session of their own that seemed to be based on the best way of travelling from Hull to Bristol, but Helen became positively girlish. She was in the middle of describing some magic netting (available by mail order) that stopped rugs from creeping on solid floors, her teeth gleaming with enthusiasm, when Rufus and Michael came in, on the scrounge for food. Helen flapped her hands while Rufus helped himself to handfuls of crisps.

'Mu-um, when's lunch? I'm starving.'

Helen got up, suddenly anxious. 'I'd almost forgotten about lunch.'

In ten minutes they were all sitting round a large polished table in a formal dining room while George hacked a large joint of beef, making a sterling attempt at impersonating a Victorian paterfamilias. Isabel looked across at Neil, wanting to share her amusement, but he was talking to Helen. Helen was nodding, but with an abstracted air as if counting spoons. Isabel could imagine the litany in her head—pepper, salt, mustard, gravy, horseradish sauce—and realised with a stab of sympathy that Helen was not going to relax until all the food had been eaten and the children were running about in the garden or watching a video. It was as if she felt that her whole value as a woman was measured by her ability to produce a Sunday roast.

'This is wonderful, Helen,' Isabel said. 'Such a treat. We haven't had a meal like this for ages, have we Neil?'

'No, more's the pity,' Neil said, tucking in with gusto. Isabel felt guilty. She ought to be preparing this sort of meal for Neil.

'In hot countries you often don't want to eat big meals, do you?' Helen said with her soft voice, smiling sympathetically across the table at Isabel. 'Just salads and pasta and things.'

Isabel smiled back and opened her mouth to speak, when George butted in.

'Got to have decent food. Sunday wouldn't be Sunday otherwise.'

Isabel tried to think of witty things that, while not actively offensive to her host, would show him up for being a pompous twit. But the phrase that would allow her to be both exquisitely polite and downright rude at the same time escaped her, so she made no reply.

As Isabel had predicted, Helen didn't relax until the last apple crumble plate was ensconced in the dishwasher and the coffee was on the table. Rufus slid off his chair with a sidelong look at his father, busy expounding on the follies of the euro. Michael hesitated, looking across to Isabel. 'Is it OK for the children to get down?' she whispered to Helen, who nodded. 'Run along and play, darlings.'

George brought out brandy and two glasses, which irritated her. Not that she wanted a brandy, but she felt he should have asked. George was persuading Neil to join the golf club, and for some reason Isabel thought of Patrick. She'd hardly thought of him all weekend but now she had, she could imagine him all too clearly—relaxed, his deep voice mocking George's pretensions. She frowned. She should have been pleased that Neil was getting on so well with George, but instead she felt slightly disturbed. Both men were now leaning back, George's red checked shirt straining across his stomach. He lit a small cigar.

'So,' he said between puffs. 'How did you two meet up?'

'At a party,' Isabel shrugged. 'Same as most people.'

'Come on, darling. Hardly like most people.' Neil was beaming at her, brandy glass in his big hand. She smiled tightly at him, hoping that would be an end to it.

'Aha. There's a story here, I can tell,' George said, cheeks shining like a raddled cherub.

'It was a very hot summer night, a mini-heatwave in fact, and—'

'Neil, they don't want to know. It's too long a story,' she said.

George thumped the table. 'Come on, spit it out.'

'Neil, I really don't think—' Isabel started, but Neil cut her off.

'It's a good story. Don't be silly.' He waved his hand dismissively at her. 'Anyway, this party. A joint eighteenth and twenty-first, I think.'

'Lin's eighteenth and Peter's twenty-first,' Isabel said, trying hard to think of a way out of this conversation. 'Lin was at Richmond House too,' she said to Helen. 'Did you come across her—Lin Hetherington?'

But whether Helen could remember Lin or not, Neil was determined to carry on. 'Whatever. Really good do. But it was boiling in the marquee. So, some bright spark jumped into the swimming pool—fully dressed—and soon everybody was going in. Including Isabel.'

'Neil, you didn't save Isabel from drowning, did you?' Helen sounded impressed.

'Better than that,' Neil said with satisfaction. 'Now, I'd spotted Isabel earlier. Obviously she was the prettiest girl there, but she was also dressed differently from the other girls in this long, floaty thing.'

'It was a second-hand dress I'd bought from Portobello Road market.' She could remember the dress clearly. Fine navy crêpe, the sort of thing worn by Hollywood actresses in the forties. A collector's item now; then it was a cheap way of dressing. And the style suited her, emphasising her small waist (those were the days) while skimming over her generous hips. 'I loved that dress,' she said, more to herself than to the others.

'So, what happened?' prompted Helen.

'Isabel got out and went into the marquee. She starts dancing, right? But each time she moves, this dress tears a little.'

'Tears?' Helen looked at Isabel, eyebrows raised.

'I think it must have been the chlorine in the swimming pool. The fabric just couldn't cope.' It was like candy floss, the damp fibres pulling apart. She could remember so clearly, looking down and seeing—. She tried to send telepathic messages to Neil. She hoped her face was smilingly casual, with an underlying hint of steel that Neil would pick up. 'Please, Neil, stop there.'

'But this is the good bit,' Neil said, untouched by telepathy, unmoved by her embarrassment. 'She wasn't wearing anything underneath.'

Isabel wanted to curl up and die. They were all looking at her, Helen wide-eyed, Neil pleased with the effect his story was having, and as for George, his eyes had been designed for boggling.

'It was a very hot night,' was all she could think to say.

'I should say,' said George. He didn't actually nudge Neil in the ribs and say 'Phwoar', it just felt to Isabel as if he did. She tugged at her cardigan, barricading herself against George's prying eyes that were fixed on her chest. And suddenly she felt eighteen again, exposed, distressed, with people laughing and pointing. She had crossed her arms over her breasts, feeling the back give way, and walked to the side, moving slowly to minimise the damage and the humiliation, laughter echoing in her brain, and then there was a man holding out a dinner jacket. 'Take this,' he'd said and wrapped it round her shoulders.

'But that's so romantic,' Helen exclaimed, her eyes shining, as she smiled at Isabel. Isabel shrugged, sliding a look across at Neil, one-time saviour, now humiliator. How could you? she asked him wordlessly, but his eyes weren't focused on her.

George's eyes glittered. 'I hope she was properly grateful.'

'I think so,' Neil said smugly. He even winked at George as if to convey all sorts of sexual adventures, whereas Isabel knew that the evening had ended with him driving her back to the flat she shared in Fulham, then a few kisses over the transmission of his Ford Mondeo.

For some reason an image of Patrick came into her head. Would he have rescued her, or would he have been part of the laughing crowd like George? A rescuer, she thought. She could see him slipping his jacket over her shoulders, but then he would have happily taken advantage of her gratitude and ravished her behind the marquee. She gave herself a little shake. What an extraordinary thing to think, she told herself.

Katie came into the dining room and sidled up to her.

'What is it?' Isabel said, relieved at the distraction.

'I want to go to the loo,' Katie whispered, her breath hot.

'Can't you ask Millie?' Isabel whispered back.

'I want you.' Katie's face was screwed up in embarrassment.

Isabel excused herself to Helen, grateful for the reason to escape, and went with Katie into the hall. She realised that the loo door had no lock, which was why Katie was anxious. Isabel stood outside, guarding Katie against unwanted intrusion, not that the boys were anywhere to be seen or heard. This seemed to her what motherhood was about. The little things. Tiny noses gently wiped. Cool hands placed lovingly on hot foreheads. Toast soldiers buttered with the crusts cut off just so. Love bound by a thousand daily intimacies, a thousand daily acts of service.

They left late in the afternoon, George promising Neil to nominate him for membership of the golf club. Isabel was cross with Neil on the way home for what she saw as his betrayal, but he was unrepentant.

'I've told that story to loads of people,' he said yawning.

'And I've never liked it,' she snapped back.

It wasn't strictly true. But a story told to friends was quite different to hearing one's past revealed under the gaze of George's bulging eyes. Would she have minded Neil telling Patrick? She wondered what Justine would say about Patrick when she came to tea.

'I like this house,' Justine said looking around Isabel's kitchen, the bell of her hair swishing round like a girl in an ad.

'I don't,' Isabel said, then realised how odd that must sound. 'I mean, we've been living in modern houses for such a long time, and I suppose I dreamt that when I got my own house it would be more traditional. And I thought we'd live in the country rather than a town.'

'A cottage with roses round the door?' Justine sounded amused, her eyes sparkling with gentle mockery. Isabel couldn't decide if she liked her, but she enjoyed Justine's acerbity after Helen's cosy conformity.

'Something like that.' Isabel sipped her tea. 'I don't know, I spent all my childhood traipsing around from one house to another, and I always promised myself that my own children would be settled in one place.'

'Was your father in the army?' Justine asked.

Isabel drank the rest of her tea, hoping that Justine would think she hadn't heard the question, then carried on talking. 'If we'd stayed abroad our next posting would have been either Nigeria or Eindhoven, neither of which appealed. And I wanted to come back to the UK anyway, so Neil applied to go into management at Head Office. We looked at anywhere close to a station that ended up at Waterloo. So here we are.'

'Well, it seems very nice to me. Very spacious.'

'Magnolia everywhere works wonders.' Isabel looked around the kitchen, her own personality asserted over the blandness by the addition of copper pots from Morocco and a string of scarlet chilli peppers like an archaic coral necklace. 'We're lucky, we had a house in London that we let out while we were abroad, so it meant it wasn't such a shock when we came back.'

'Do you still have it? It must be worth a fortune,' Justine said.

'I don't know about that,' Isabel said, embarrassed. 'I suppose I ought to start getting the children's tea ready. Does Rachel like pasta?' Justine nodded and Isabel fussed in the kitchen area, putting water on. 'Do you know Patrick Sherwin well?' she asked, as nonchalantly as she could.

'Oh, Patrick,' Justine said. 'I've known him for about eight years.'

'Quite a long time.'

'It seems like for ever. Goodness, we were both married when we met.'

'So he has been married,' Isabel said, feeling guilty about talking about Patrick but unable to resist. 'But he's divorced now, isn't he?'

Justine let out a snort of laughter. 'Don't you know?'

Isabel prodded the spaghetti down into the saucepan. 'I wouldn't expect him to talk about something personal like that,' she said, feeling she was sounding prissy.

Justine stared up at the ceiling. 'I don't think Patrick or Caro were suited from the start. She was very much part of the hunting and shooting set round here. Still is, in fact. After their divorce she married some man with two thousand acres towards Petersfield. It's funny how the rich always seem to marry the rich, isn't it?'

Isabel blinked. 'I don't know. Do they? Perhaps that's how they get to be rich.'

'How they stay rich anyway. One thing you'll learn is that there are an awful lot of people with money round here.'

'So Caro's rich?'

'Rolling in it,' Justine said. 'You'd have thought with all that money she could afford to dress decently.' She sounded as if the way Caro dressed was a personal affront. Then Isabel realised that it might be.

'Did you do your wardrobe thing with Caro?'

'Sure, she had the full wardrobe consultancy, colours, clear-out, the works. Not that it did her much good. Or me come to that,' She added like an afterthought. Isabel wondered what she meant but Justine looked cross so she didn't like to pry.

'Tell you what, the pasta's nearly ready. Why don't you call the children down?' Isabel quickly laid the table with three places, drained the pasta and made a sauce by adding a knob of butter, some cream and a mixture of quickly grated Gruyère and cheddar.

Justine was very complimentary about Isabel's cooking skills, gushing about how clever she was. Isabel was uncertain how to react, since it was obvious the dish was simple, so Justine's praise seemed excessive. She was now standing and looking along the mantelpiece at the clutter of postcards, finger paintings, dusty treasures and 'to do' lists.

'Is that Neil?' she asked, pointing to a photograph of a man standing, hands on hips, relaxed, confident, while behind him the sky was streaked with the beginnings of sunset, turning a range of jagged mountains gold.

'Mmm. That's the Arabian peninsula, the Empty Quarter. I've always liked that photograph,' Isabel said. 'We'd only just got married, and Neil had given me a camera.'

'He looks young.'

'Neil was twenty-six and I was just nineteen.'

'Nineteen!' Justine's eyes were alert with speculation.

Isabel pulled a face. Yet again she'd have to make it clear that she and Neil didn't have to get married because she was pregnant. 'Neil was just about to start a two-year contract in Saudi and I couldn't go with him unless we were married. And then, under their law, I became his property and so they paid for my airfare and provided us with suitable accommodation for marrieds. Otherwise Neil would have had to stay in a ghastly sort of hostel place.' She shrugged. 'And there wasn't much to keep me in the UK, so we got married, went off to the desert and lived happily ever after.' Occasionally—usually after a row—she wondered what would have happened if they hadn't had to get married so quickly. Recently the thought had become more insistent.

Katie and Michael, having finished, pushed their chairs back and ran from the kitchen, but Rachel lingered. 'Please may I be excused from the table, Mrs Freeman?' she said.

'Of course, if you've had enough to eat. Go and find the others. What lovely manners,' she said to Justine, while Rachel ran after Katie.

Justine smiled, gratified, and started to clear up.

'No, no, leave it. I'll do it later. More tea?' Isabel asked, thinking wistfully of the sitting room and a conversation that didn't involve children and domesticity. A conversation about other things. Like Patrick Sherwin. But Justine had taken over, clearing things away. They had just finished when Neil came into the kitchen.

'You're home early,' Isabel said as he kissed her cheek.

'I caught the four twenty.' He turned to Justine and held out his hand. 'Hello. Neil Freeman.'

She took his hand. 'Justine Torens.'

'Justine's daughter is in the same class as Katie,' Isabel chipped in, hoping that Neil would go upstairs or into his study and shut the door. But he didn't. He stood there drinking tea and chatting to Justine and showing no sign of disappearing.

Finally Justine ended it. 'I really must be going,' she said, picking up her bag. 'I've completely outstayed my welcome.'

'Not at all,' Neil and Isabel said together, Isabel mechanically and Neil with a beaming smile as if he meant it. 'Have a drink,' he added.

'That's so kind but, no, thank you. I must be on my way.' She went into the hall and called up to Rachel, who came clattering down the stairs, followed by Katie. 'Thank you so much for having us, we've really enjoyed ourselves, haven't we, Rachel?'

As Justine passed through the doorway she paused. 'I was going to tell you all about Patrick, wasn't I?'

Isabel nodded, conscious of Neil hovering in the hall behind her.

'There's not much to tell. I mean, he doesn't keep his skeletons hidden in his cupboard. If anything, Patrick's skeletons are thoroughly out and probably drinking with him down at the Mason's Arms.' She shot a glance past Isabel towards the hall and whispered, 'You know what they say about him, don't you? They say he's very good in bed.'

Good in bed. Isabel sorted the post into letters, junk mail, bills. Good in bed. The words seemed engraved on her brain. Who were the 'they' who said it? And how did Justine know? Had she and Patrick . . .? Isabel thought about it as she made coffee for Patrick in the cafetière. She knew Justine was divorced, but little else about her.

The phone rang. 'Patrick Sherwin Associates,' she answered. Good in bed, she thought. 'I'll just see if he's in.' She hollered upstairs. Patrick came clattering down the stairs and took the phone from her. 'Yup?' he said. Isabel tried not to listen to his conversation as she handed him his coffee. He smiled as he took it from her and she felt herself blush. Good in bed. The phrase nagged like a football chant in her head.

She went back into the kitchen and made tea for herself. What was it that made a man good in bed? Perhaps it was experience that made the difference. But the man might just be repeating the same moves, over and over. She frowned. It couldn't be size—well, not just on its own. And as for inventiveness, there seemed something off-puttingly mechanistic about ticking off the various positions. Up a bit, left a bit, bull'seye! She sipped her hot tea. How irritating of Neil to pitch up when Justine was going to tell her something interesting.

'Why must I work with imbeciles,' Patrick shouted as he came in, making her jump. 'It's enough to drive you mad.' He opened a cupboard door then slammed it shut. 'Where's my coffee?'

'Where you left it,' she said, watching him with trepidation. His anger seemed to fill the room.

'Well, get it,' he said, throwing up his hands as if exasperated beyond endurance by her obtuseness. Obediently she went into the living room and collected his cup, only thinking of saying 'Get it yourself' as she turned to take it back. I mustn't be a doormat, she thought. But she went back into the kitchen and put the cup on the table.

Patrick didn't appear to register her return. He was too busy pacing up and down, cursing clients for their infinite stupidity.

'And then they have the nerve to tell me—me!' he stabbed his chest with a finger for emphasis, 'that the system doesn't work.'

Isabel shrugged her shoulders and tried what she hoped was a calming smile. 'Never mind. I'm sure you'll be able to sort it out.'

He turned on her, his eyes blazing. 'Never mind? What the hell does that mean? Of course I fucking mind, you stupid woman. I'm going out.' He swept past her, the swing of his shoulders expressing pent-up energy so strongly that she involuntarily took a step back. Patrick slammed the front door. The sound reverberated through the house.

Isabel stood rigid. She'd never seen someone so angry, so physically angry, close up before. Should she go? Or was that being hysterical? Neil would be horrified if he knew what Patrick had called her, she thought. It was outrageous to call her stupid, let alone with such passion. Neil would want her to go.

Good in bed.

It would be cowardly to go, she told herself. And she didn't want to go back to the weekly trudge through the Situations Vacant and the humiliation of being ineligible even for an interview. She would stay for the moment and see what happened.

She was upstairs in the office, trying to sort out which invoices had been paid and which hadn't, when she heard footsteps downstairs.

'Isabel?'

'Mmm?' she said, not turning round, apparently intent on her work.

'I'm sorry. I shouldn't have lost my temper like that.' His deep voice was contrite. She could feel his eyes on her and perhaps he sensed her mood because he came and stood next to her.

'It doesn't mean anything. My Italian blood coming out, maybe. My mother is a great one for flying teacups. I hope this won't stop you working for me.' He paused. His voice sounded hesitant and she realised that he was not used to apologising. It made her feel powerful. He lightly touched her arm. 'Isabel?'

She looked up at him and for a mad second thought, He's going to kiss me. But he didn't.

'Let me take you out to lunch at the pub, to make up for being so foul.' She could feel the blood rush to her face.

'Thank you for the offer, but I'm going to eat my sandwiches for lunch. I think that's best.'

'You haven't forgiven me.'

'No, really. Actually, I hadn't given it a moment's thought till now.' She smiled what she hoped was a particularly bland smile at him. The efficient and very respectable Mrs Freeman. 'Now. There seems to be a batch of invoices missing. From about 4550 onwards. Any idea where they are?'

'You could try in that box.' He pointed to an old photographic paper box, flat and shiny yellow, perched on top of a pile of computer monitors. She started to search for the missing invoices, hoping that her body language would indicate that she was busy, although all her senses were alert to Patrick, who left the room after a few minutes.

She sighed and carried on looking through the box. She found old business cards, an Indian takeaway menu, a photograph. She picked it up. Patrick smiled lazily at her, his arm casually draped over a slim brown girl with silver-blonde hair in a white bikini. His ex-wife? Or some other girlfriend? They were on a yacht and the sky behind them was an intense cobalt blue. There was nothing written on the back, no indication of when it had been taken. She slipped the photograph under the takeaway menu and tried not to think of Patrick looking impossibly glamorous. And good in bed.

She worked upstairs for the rest of the morning, having located the missing invoices, scrunched behind the radiator. When she looked out of the window she could see Patrick pacing up and down the garden. I was right not to go out to lunch with him, she thought. It was important to keep the lines drawn, not to cross them. But she liked working for Patrick. The last two weeks had been absorbing and purposeful. She liked sorting all his stuff out, typing his letters, answering the phone in her special efficient voice; she liked it when Patrick went out for a meeting and she had the house to herself; she liked it when Patrick was in, and the way he talked to her while she worked. Sometimes he would lean across her to change a word or two as she typed, close enough for her to feel the heat from his body. She liked that too.

'Right. No excuses. You're coming to the pub with me.'

Isabel jumped. Patrick had come in and was handing her her coat.

'But my sandwiches—'

'No buts. It's company policy.'

'What is?'

'No one's allowed to say "but". And employers who shout at employees have to take them out to lunch in compensation.' He lowered his voice as they went down the stairs. 'Stops all sorts of harassment lawsuits.' He opened the front door. 'After you.'

Isabel giggled, hesitated for a second, then stepped outside.

The Mason's Arms was at the end of the road. Isabel had passed it often, but never been inside.

'What do you want to drink?' Patrick said.

'Something soft. A bitter lemon please.'

'Have a proper drink.'

'I'm not used to drinking at lunchtime.'

'I insist.'

'A glass of white wine then.'

He went to the bar while she looked around, feeling guilty at being in the dark, traditional interior when it was a gloriously sunny day outside, perhaps the last sunny day of the year. It felt wickedly decadent, like going to an afternoon showing at the cinema in high summer.

'Let's grab somewhere while we can,' Patrick said, handing her a glass of wine and indicating a table by the fire. They sat down, Patrick totally relaxed. Isabel perched on the edge of her seat. She shot a glance towards him. Not good-looking, with a crooked nose, perhaps broken in a rugby match, and hooded eyes. She had often wondered what it meant to have 'come-to-bed eyes', and now she thought she knew.

'It's getting quite full so I think we'd better order food now. Have you thought about what you want to eat?'

'Ploughman's please,' she said, being the only food she could think of.

She watched him weave his way through the other drinkers to the bar, tall enough to have to stoop under the beams. She wondered how old he was. Forty? Forty-two? The pub was filling up with people—she remembered Justine saying that Patrick's skeletons were more likely to be drinking with him in the Mason's Arms. Patrick was a regular, judging by the number of people who nodded to him.

He came back with another round of drinks. She fumbled with her purse, but he stopped her.

'My treat.' He settled back in his seat. 'Do you know Justine well?'

'I only met her, what, three weeks ago.' She blinked in the smoky atmosphere, surprised at how her life had changed. 'And you? Do you know her well?' Good in bed, she thought.

'Justine and I go back a few years.' His voice was still deep, still relaxed, but there was a finality about it. 'Tell me about working at the BBC. I know a few people who work there.'

'It was ages ago.' She took a swig of wine, feeling the cool oiliness around her mouth. 'Before I married.'

'And did you stop working the second you got married?'

'The sort of places Neil was posted, it was difficult for me to do anything.' She fiddled with a beer mat, thinking back. 'At the time it seemed logical. Neil was going abroad on a two-year contract, and I could only go with him if we were married. And I wanted to travel, so . . .'

'It sounds a very convenient arrangement.' His voice was dry. She didn't want him to get the wrong idea.

'We were madly in love, of course.'

'Of course.' His eyes were half-closed, but she caught a glint of reflected firelight. 'And now?'

Isabel ran a finger round the rim of her wineglass. 'Well, of course. That goes without saying,' she said, conscious of a stiffness in her voice. 'Look, is that our food?' Patrick turned and beckoned the waitress to their table. She put down the ploughman's lunch in front of Isabel and a pie with chips in front of Patrick.

'And another round of drinks on my tab,' he added to the waitress.

'Oh, no, I mustn't,' Isabel said. 'I've got the school run later.'

'That won't be for ages. And you're not doing anything else this afternoon, are you?'

'Working for you?'

'And this is what I want you to do. You did say at your interview you were prepared to be flexible.' Was he teasing her? Isabel looked at Patrick, but he was busy digging into the steaming pie.

'That smells good,' Isabel said.

'Guinness and beef. They make them here. Try some.' He speared a chunk of steak onto his fork and held it out to her. Isabel hesitated, then opened her mouth. It was delicious. Their eyes met and Isabel blushed. I shouldn't have done that, she thought. A boundary had been crossed. She reached out for her glass of wine, spilling a little on the table.

'Sorry.'

'A beautiful woman should never apologise,' he said. 'Help yourself if you want more.' He indicated his plate.

'No, I'm fine,' she said. Had he called her a beautiful woman? She hugged the idea inside. It was a long time since anyone had said anything about the way she looked. She stole a glance at Patrick and tried to think of something to say that would steer her back to safety. 'Have you lived here long?'

'About eight years. My wife wanted to move out of London, find somewhere for her horse. It was costing a fortune at livery in London.'

'So you moved to the country?'

'Yes. Biggest mistake I ever made.' He leaned back in his chair.

'Why, don't you like the countryside?'

'I don't dislike the country. Not real country at any rate. I dislike what this sort of commuter-belt country does to people. The men go off to work during the week, while the women stay at home and have babies and run houses. Or they become horsey, and sublimate all the energy they should be putting into their sex lives into some wretched quadruped. Or worse, both husband and wife take up horses and start hunting. And that's the end.' He rolled his eyes.

Isabel wasn't sure what to say. 'You're anti-hunting then?'

''Course. I don't give a stuff for foxes, and nor would anyone else if they looked like rats, but hunting people are the pits, puffed up on snobbery and self-importance.'

'Your wife didn't hunt, I take it?'

'Yes, she did. She was mad keen on it. Still is, she's always fiddling about with a martingale or polishing her snaffles.'

'Didn't that make life difficult?'

''Course not.' He grinned at her. 'We got divorced.'

Isabel felt very stupid. 'I'm sorry.'

'Don't be. Best thing for us. Except it left me in this dump instead of in London.' He stretched. 'Mmm, that was just what I needed. D'you want something else? Stay and have a brandy. Or a coffee.' She hesitated. She'd had three large glasses of wine and felt distinctly woozy.

'Perhaps a coffee would be a good idea . . .'

He ordered two coffees and two brandies despite her protests. When they came they looked suspiciously like doubles. 'If you don't drink it, I will,' he said airily. He raised his brandy glass towards her, and out of politeness she touched it with her own. It was years since she had drunk spirits and even the little sip she took caught the back of her throat.

'I'm always impressed by people who manage to stay married,' Patrick went on. 'And are happy, of course. It's not impressive to stay married and be miserable.'

'It might be. All marriages have rough patches.'

'That's a euphemism for cowardice. Being too frightened to get out of the cage.'

'No, it's not cowardice,' she said, stumbling over the words in her eagerness to defend. 'It's about being a family, staying together whatever.'

'For better or worse? Sounds too much like that poem—"And always kept a hold on nurse for fear of finding something worse".'

'That's not my experience,' she said.

'Then I congratulate you on being one of the lucky ones.'

There was a short, uncomfortable silence. I'm not used to drinking in the day, she thought. I shouldn't be here.

'Perhaps I am cynical about marriage.' Patrick leaned forwards and she realised that his eyes weren't brown, as she'd thought, but a dark green. 'You see, my wife left me.'

'I am sorry.' Her heart went out to him, and she touched his hand lightly to show sympathy, then drank some more brandy.

'Yes, she left me,' he said almost to himself, his voice soft and low. 'Left me for that bloody horse.'

Isabel let out a shriek of laughter, which she stifled with her hand firmly over her mouth. 'I'm sorry,' she said when she could.

'Not very funny when it happens to you,' he said, but his eyes were twinkling at her. Isabel tried to be serious.

'That's dreadful,' she managed, before having to put her hand over her mouth again to stop giggling.

'Glad you find it so funny.' He added lugubriously, 'And it was a bloody mare too.'

I've drunk too much, Isabel thought, eyes watering with laughter. But I haven't laughed like this for ages. Patrick started to talk about Milbridge and the business, but her brain wouldn't concentrate, it kept skimming over the surface.

'I'm really enjoying working for you,' she said.

'Despite my terrible temper?'

She nodded happily.

'Well, I suppose we'd better get some work done.' He drained his brandy. 'Although it's practically going-home time for you.'

'Oh, no!' Isabel leapt to her feet. 'I should have gone ages ago.'

'You've plenty of time. I'm glad you haven't been put off working for me.' He nodded at her, then strolled to the bar to settle the bill.

Isabel blinked as she went outside, hit by fresh air and eye-achingly bright sunlight.

'Are you OK?' He was frowning at her.

'I'm fine.' Isabel squinted up at him. 'I don't think I should drive, though. But I can walk to the school and then we'll take the bus.'

'Sure?'

'Absolutely,' she said carefully, so as not to slur the word. She was conscious that Patrick had his hand on her elbow and was gently steering her down the pavement. 'I'm fine, really.' She caught her toe on a cracked paving stone and stumbled. Patrick caught her.

'Sorry,' she said, out of breath. 'Thank you for saving me.' She smiled up at him, and realised that he was bending towards her. He's going to kiss me, she thought just before his mouth met hers.

She didn't think to protest, to push him off. Her head buzzed; she felt the blood rush to her cheeks. His hand was warm and rough as he held her head firmly, the other round her back, holding her to him. He tasted of brandy and coffee. She was so surprised she let him kiss her for several seconds before her brain kicked in and she opened her eyes. But before she could react, he released her.

'I shouldn't have done that.' He let his hands drop from her arms. 'What can I say? I can't keep on apologising to you.'

Isabel stared at him. Her brain seemed to have seized up and the only thing she was able to register was the taste of him on her mouth.

'Look, treat it as a moment of madness. See if you can forget it happened.' He looked at her uncertainly. 'D'you think you could?'

Isabel nodded, then added, 'Could I do what?'

'Forget it happened.'

'Oh.' She straightened her back and slung her bag over her shoulder. 'It's fine, you don't need to say anything more. Well, I'd better be on my way.' She held out her hand. 'Thank you for lunch.'

He shook her hand formally. 'You're welcome.'

'Well. See you tomorrow morning.'

She walked carefully up the street, trying to keep in a straightish line.

Isabel kept on losing things in the kitchen later that evening. The wooden spoon in particular seemed to have a life of its own, vanishing and then reappearing in unlikely places. It was tiring having to search for things all the time, especially when you kept on forgetting what it was you were looking for. She tried to have the house reasonably tidy and supper waiting for when Neil came back, but today they'd had to wait ages for a bus and nothing was ready.

What was she going to tell Neil?

Neil, Patrick took me to lunch and then kissed me outside the pub.

Neil, would you believe it? Patrick kissed me today, but we've decided to pretend it never happened.

Neil, my boss kissed me outside a pub and I did nothing to stop him and now I can't get him out of my mind.

She couldn't remember when she had last been kissed like that. If she had ever been kissed like that. She and Neil must have, at some point, surely? But kissing Neil had been like coming home, a safe haven, not the start of a dangerous voyage. Not that this was going to be the start of anything. She replayed the moment, the feel of his mouth pressing down on hers, his arm about her. Her eyes closed, her lips parted.

Bad move. She snapped her eyes open and shut her mouth firmly, heard the television churning in the sitting room and thought of Neil sitting immobile in front of it in his special leather armchair. Poor Neil, he was shattered after a hard day working, while she . . .

She filled a pan with water and put it on to boil. Think horror. Think disgust. She played the scene again in her head, this time concentrating on her feelings of outrage. How dare he? The trouble was, she kept sliding back to the unexpectedness of it, the delicious sensation of melting that flowed through her body. I should have slapped his face. It was all so sudden, she told herself. You couldn't have done anything about it. Better not to have made a scene.

I should say I've decided the job isn't what I wanted, and forget the whole incident. She stirred the chicken thoughtfully. On the other hand, I could carry on and pretend the kiss never happened. And if it happens again? No, I'd make it clear that it must never happen again. I'd have to tell him. She could picture Patrick's amused smile . . . she'd have to pretend to be someone else when she told him. Someone bossy. Like that Mary woman at the new parents' coffee morning. He'd do what Mary wanted, she was sure.

The rice water was starting to boil, bubbles pricking the surface. She started counting in handfuls of rice. Three per person. Was that four or five that had gone in? She shook the pan and peered in. She wasn't very good at judging quantity. She added another handful for luck. Patrick's hands were long and elegant, tanned with short fingernails. One had wrapped around her, holding her close to him, while the other had tilted her head towards him, his skin firm and warm—

Stop that. She clamped a lid onto the rice pan. Lay the table. Knives. Forks. Spoons. There wasn't anything for pudding. Put the spoons back, lay out side plates and knives for cheese and biscuits. Napkins. She rummaged in one of the drawers and found a couple of paper napkins, slightly crumpled. As she smoothed out the creases she had an image of Patrick spreading his napkin over his knee, his fingers strong but delicate. What if she had responded? What if his hand had slipped down into her shirt? She shivered. It was impossible. She couldn't carry on working for him. It would be tantamount to agreeing to . . . what? She resolutely threw him out of her mind. Concentrate on supper.

She checked the rice. There seemed rather a lot. Carefully she drained and arranged it round the edges of the dish, and started to spoon the chicken in, making a small but mountainous island in the middle of a lumpy white ocean.

'So how did you spend your day?' Neil, gin and tonic in one hand, leaned against the doorjamb of the kitchen.

'Oops.' A bit of chicken shot off onto the floor.

'Perhaps we should get a dog. A Westie maybe.'

Neil's parents had an ancient Westie with accusing black eyes and a matted coat, yellowed with age to a pee-stained shade of white. She turned round to face Neil. 'A dog would need walking every day.'

'It'd be company for you.'

'But I'm busy. Working.' I ought to chuck in the job, she thought. I ought to tell Neil what happened.

Neil sat down and smiled at her. 'Are we going to eat? I'm starving.'

'Help yourself. I made too much rice. Neil, about this job . . .'

'You could never make too much for me. I've always liked rice.' He was spooning great forkfuls in, rice grains catching in his moustache.

'This job . . .'

'You're finding it too much.'

'I didn't say that.'

'I expect you're finding it a bit dull. Why don't you chuck it in and find something a bit more interesting?'

'It's not dull,' she said, images of Patrick whizzing through her head.

Neil smiled indulgently. 'Ah, the novelty value hasn't yet worn off.'

She didn't know what to say to that. She didn't think the novelty value of Patrick kissing her would ever wear off.

'If you don't want to carry on, that's fine by me,' he said.

'You don't want me to work, do you?'

'Let's not start this up again,' he said in his kind-but-firm headmaster voice. 'That was delicious. Is there anything for pudding?'

'Cheese and biscuits.' She indicated with her head.

'If you don't mind, I'll take them through. There's a programme I want to watch.'

She sat quite still as he chose some biscuits and cheese, and left. A few seconds later the television kicked into life. She stayed sitting, watching the rice form cold sticky lumps. Is it me, or is it him?

She got up and cleared the dishes. Kitchen tidy, she went upstairs and got ready for bed. She turned the light off and lay straight under the duvet, feeling the cool cotton settle around her. Downstairs the television went off and the staircase creaked as Neil came up. He undressed quickly in the darkness and got into bed beside her. She stiffened, waiting.

'I've got a headache,' she said as soon as he touched her.

The hand paused, then carried on. 'You just need to relax.'

Isabel screwed her eyes tight. Yes was easier than no.

'No,' she said, pushing him away. 'I have a headache.' It was true.

'Darling, you'll feel better—'

'I won't. I'm tired, I have a headache and I want to go to sleep.'

'But—'

'No!'

A pause. Then, 'All right, keep your hair on.' Neil heaved himself over so his back was towards her. In the darkness she could sense his hurt, but also his sulkiness. She knew he expected her to give in, to stroke his back and apologise. Two weeks ago she would have.

Instead she buried her head under the pillow.

Four

ISABEL RAPPED on Patrick's front door the next morning. Over the last two weeks she'd learned that the doorbell didn't work consistently and that Patrick was sometimes still asleep when she arrived. She wished she could stop thinking about Patrick kissing her. I shouldn't be here, she thought, not moving.

'Isabel!' She looked up. Patrick was leaning out of the window above, his shoulders naked. 'You caught me in the shower. Catch!' He threw the keys down to her, then disappeared back into the house.

Isabel looked at the keys in her hand. I'm a grown-up; I can handle this, she told herself. 'I'm here to work,' she muttered as she let herself into the house. She could hear Patrick moving about upstairs as she picked up the post from the floor and started to sort through it.

Patrick clattered down the stairs. 'Good morning, good morning. Sorry about that. Hang on to the keys, by the way. Save dragging me out of the shower another time.' He stretched out his arms. 'I should have given you a set before. Mmm, time for coffee, I think.'

Isabel followed him into the kitchen. 'You're in a good mood.'

'Am I?' He spooned coffee into the cafetière. 'Just a good night's sleep.'

Obviously, he hadn't lain awake half the night worrying about the kiss. Isabel watched him as he made his coffee, quietly humming.

'Anything interesting in the post today?'

'You look.' Isabel shoved the post at him and stomped upstairs to the office, not caring if she'd been rude. It's too much, she thought. She turned on the computer and waited for it to boot up. I could be doing all sorts of things. Not faffing around here with stupid Patrick Sherwin.

'Here.' A mug of tea was placed on the desk beside her.

'Thanks,' she muttered, not looking at him.

He cleared his throat. 'Um, is there a problem?'

She looked up at him then, struck by the glaring truth of the situation. He had completely forgotten the kiss.

'No, no, there's no problem. Really. Thanks for the tea.'

'Any time.' He went, shutting the office door behind him.

As soon as he had gone, she dropped her head into her hands. What a fool I've been. She blushed, thinking how she had imagined telling Patrick how she had decided to ignore his disgraceful behaviour and that it was never going to happen again. Then Patrick would say something like 'But how can I help myself?' And then he would come close and . . . Most of the time she managed to stop herself at that point. The one thing she hadn't imagined would be that he would have forgotten. Well, she would forget it too. She smiled wryly to herself, aware of the scratchy lace of her best bra under her striped shirt. No one need know how silly she had been. Or might have been. Her bra straps felt tight, constraining her breasts into rounded hemispheres. She had dreamt of Patrick touching them, hands warm and insistent. She felt as if she had been close to the edge of a dark place, somewhere very strange where a different Isabel had beckoned. But somehow she had managed to pull away, to come back to herself. And to Neil, of course.

Yes, to Neil, whom she'd shouted at last night. I'll make it up to him, she thought. I'll try to be a better wife, try to be more interested in what he's doing. I can forget the kiss. After all, what did it mean? Nothing. Thank God I didn't make a complete fool of myself.

She entered the accounts programme and started to prepare customer statements, which took up most of the morning. Impatient for the computer to finish, she pressed the Shut Down button, realised her mistake, tried to go back into the programme to close it down properly. The computer refused to respond to anything she did. She pressed the Escape button several times but nothing happened. 'Drat.' In frustration she thumped the computer and immediately regretted it as the wretched machine gave a high-pitched whine.

'Patrick,' she called. 'The computer's gone wrong.'

'What's the matter?' he said as he came upstairs.

'I don't know. It's gone all funny.'

'Let's have a look.'

He leaned over the desk, one hand casually on the back of her chair, his shoulder just touching hers, watching the screen as he used the mouse. His mouth was nearly level with hers. She raised her eyes to his, but he was watching the screen.

'There.' He stood up. 'Not sure what the problem was, but it seems OK now. If there are any more problems, just call me.'

'I will.' She stared ahead at the screen. Was it her imagination or was the mouse still warm from his hand?

At lunch she went downstairs and ate one of her sandwiches in the kitchen, although she didn't feel very hungry. While she ate she could hear Patrick outside in the garden, talking on the phone. The flowers she'd picked on her first day, two weeks before, were still on the table, going mouldy. She threw them away, then replaced them with the last of the nerines from the front garden and a few sprigs of rosemary. Rosemary for remembrance, she thought, and immediately remembered the kiss. Forget it, she told herself as she went back upstairs.

But she couldn't settle down to work. The room was too stuffy. Down in the garden she could see Patrick, leaning back in his chair, legs crossed and feet up on the table, loafers off. He wriggled his toes in the autumn sunshine, oblivious to her watching him.

The air was dense, as if all the oxygen had run out and the world was holding its breath. The light seemed golden, making the brick houses of the town glow a fiery red. Lowering over the town was a bank of dense black-purple clouds. She went into the garden.

'I think there's a storm coming. Do you want me to give you a hand with bringing in your papers?'

Patrick looked up, annoyance crossing his face. 'It'll pass.' He went back to scrawling notes in green ink over the report he was reading.

Isabel shrugged and went back into the house. She decided to make some tea. As she filled the kettle the sky darkened and the light took on a greenish hue. Looking out through the kitchen window she was pleased to see Patrick look up, then leap out of his seat, his shirt showing a few dark splodges where fat raindrops had fallen.

'God!' He started to gather the papers on the table together, then bellowed, 'Isabel, where the hell are you?'

Serves you right, she thought. I'm not a stupid woman after all. She counted to twenty, then went out to help him, ducking her head involuntarily as a crash of thunder sounded. As if that were a cue, the rain started in earnest. They grabbed armfuls of paper and ran with them into the house. Patrick shook his head, spattering raindrops like a dog.

'This is such miserable country to live in,' he said, staring out of the window at sheets of rain. 'I've left my shoes outside.'

'Too late now. They'll already be ruined.' Isabel turned to look at him and at the same moment he met her gaze and held it. She was caught, suspended in time. Her breathing changed, becoming light and shallow. She touched his shirt, feeling the warmth of his chest beneath.

Very slowly he traced his forefinger along the line of her jaw then down her neck. Instinctively she raised her head slightly, leaving her throat vulnerable and open. He paused at her collarbone, then took his hand away, and she ached for its return. As if in slow motion she reached out for him, slipping her hand to curl around the back of his neck.

He frowned, pulling away slightly. 'Isabel?' His voice was uncertain.

In answer she pulled him down to her, feeling his mouth on hers, searching, tingling. She pushed herself against him shamelessly, as if she could be absorbed into his body, delighting at feeling him hard. She had never wanted anything as much as for him to touch her and she tugged at her shirt, not caring what he might think of her boldness, just wanting him. He undid the buttons so her shirt hung open, then bent his head and traced the exposed swell of her breast with his tongue, so her skin goosebumped all over with the teasing.

She fumbled with the catch of his trousers, any remaining inhibitions lost in the urgency of her need. He pushed her knickers down, then he lifted her onto the table, spread her legs and slipped into her so easily that she realised she had been waiting for this since he had kissed her. No, before that, since Justine had said that he was good in bed. And here he was. She clamped her legs around his back, tightening her grip as the pleasure surged over her body in shades of pink and red. Someone was moaning, please, please, please, and with each please he went faster and deeper until the red turned to gold and great shuddering waves swept over her.

Isabel kept her eyes shut, aware of Patrick moving beside her. She had crossed an invisible line, the line that divided the faithful from the faithless. She would never be Neil's faithful wife again.

Something tickled her stomach. She opened her eyes.

Patrick was watching her, his face about a foot away from hers, his hand lazily stroking her stomach. His olive-green eyes were flecked with brown streaks turning to warm gold. He kissed her softly then pulled back. His eyes looked more hooded than ever but she thought he looked hugely pleased with himself.

'Well,' he said, tracing circles round her navel. 'That was a surprise.'

'For me too,' she said, then felt herself blush, awash with guilt, happiness, uncertainty. All at once she felt like crying.

'It wasn't that bad, surely.'

'No, it was wonderful. I just feel—' But expressing her feelings was impossible. She realised that he had dressed, trousers in place, shirt buttoned. Overwhelmed by embarrassment she sat up, pulling her skirt down and tugging her shirt across her chest. Her bra seemed to have got twisted under one armpit and she struggled to pull it into place.

'Allow me.' Patrick, his face serious, straightened her out and did up the buttons. She hung her head, too shy to meet his gaze.

'You're very quiet.' His tone was conversational.

'Mmm.' She tried to find the words. 'I've never done this before.'

Patrick raised an eyebrow and she shook her head. 'I've always been . . .' Even saying the word 'faithful' seemed inappropriate. 'I always thought that if I was to . . . well, that it would be more drawn out, that there would be time to think. Snatched meetings, getting to know each other. And lots of agonising and worry.'

'Yeah, well, I don't go in for much worrying and agonising. It seems a waste of time to me.' Patrick went over to the window. 'Still pissing down,' he said, almost to himself. 'Why don't I live somewhere sunny?'

Isabel hugged herself. She didn't like to say that she'd also thought that an affair would involve cuddling afterwards.

Patrick looked at her. 'So. What do you want to do?'

'Oh.' With an effort she pulled her mind back into the harsh real world. 'I know what I ought to do.'

'Let me guess. Walk out of here and pretend it never happened?'

Isabel nodded, eyes lowered. Patrick was leaning against the kitchen units, as if talking about nothing important at all.

'If that's what you want to do, that's fine by me.'

Isabel felt devastated. 'Is that what you want?' she said.

'We're not talking about what I want,' he said. 'Who I screw is nobody's business but my own. I have no commitments, no ties. The only person who gets hurt is me.' He paused and she glanced up at him.

'Still, I'd like to know what you want.'

'I can't make your decision for you.' His eyes held hers. 'An affair would complicate both our lives, but yours far more than mine. So it must be your decision.' His voice softened. 'But I would be sorry to see you go.'

'Really?' she said, feeling less depressed.

His lips twitched. 'My filing's never been so well organised.'

I know what I ought to do, she thought, so why am I hesitating?

'I'm not offering you anything,' Patrick said quickly. 'No romance, no commitment. And I'm famously unreliable,' he added almost as if it was something to be proud of.

Famously good in bed . . . she shivered all over at the thought.

'I've been married eighteen years. Half my life.' She felt confused, having this weird conversation. Did Patrick want her, or not? It was a good thing the coil she'd had fitted after Katie's birth meant she didn't have to worry about pregnancy. But nowadays there were other things to worry about.

'I hope you don't mind me asking, well, I'm not sure how to ask, but . . . well, we didn't use anything. I know I'm OK, I mean, I've been in a monogamous relationship for eighteen years.'

'How do you know your husband hasn't—'

'Neil? Oh, no, never. He wouldn't.' Patrick raised his eyebrows.

'Hmm. I'll take your word for it. As for me, I'm clear.' He smiled. 'I'm usually extremely careful. Unless the unexpected arises. And you, Mrs Freeman, were very unexpected.'

An image ran through her mind, herself spread-eagled over the table, arms flung out wide in abandon. She realised she'd made her decision long before, without knowing about it, when she had touched him during the rainstorm. The line had been crossed then. Now she turned and touched him again, hesitating, unused to taking the initiative, excited to be making the first move.

He stood close to her, his hands stroking the hollows of her collar-bones. She let her head fall back, letting the sensation flow through her. Feeling very daring she undid his top trouser button.

He put his hand on hers to stop her. 'Sure? No regrets. No falling in love. No tears when we part?'

'No.'

'Two adults enjoying each other with no strings on either side?'

'Yes.' He released her hand, then slid his own up her thigh. It was almost painful when he touched her. 'Oh, yes, yes please.'

And this time it was better. Slower, deeper, longer. They went upstairs to the bedroom, where Patrick carefully removed the rest of Isabel's clothes. She had always thought that the embarrassment of exposing her body would be enough to stop her having an affair, yet here she was allowing Patrick to cover her with kisses. He made her feel that her body, for all its flaws, was beautiful. Encouraged by his appreciation, she relaxed and, without shame, opened herself to him in a way that she had always been slightly embarrassed to do with Neil.

And afterwards he held her close as her mind drifted, half asleep. 'Which do you prefer,' he said, running a lazy hand over her body, 'fast and furious on the kitchen table or slow and sensual in bed?'

'Both. I want both.'

'Exhausting. You'd better pass me the water; there should be a glass on the floor on your side.'

Isabel rolled over and looked on the floor. She saw Patrick's water glass and alarm clock. She was an hour late for the school pick-up.

'Help! The children!' Isabel jerked upright. 'No, it's all right; Michael's late tonight and Katie's at a friend's house.' It felt strange, to have forgotten them, the same sickening jolt in the stomach as when you think there's an extra step on the stairs only there isn't one, but magnified by so many times it hurt to think of it. How could she have forgotten the children for one second? She swung her legs over the side of the bed.

'I trust Madam found the service satisfactory?'

'Oh, yes.' She remembered Patrick saying 'No falling in love' and kissed him, to stop herself from saying anything more. She took a deep breath. 'I ought to be going.'

'Off into the real world.' He smiled, then patted her behind. 'Go on, scoot. No guilt trips though, promise?'

'Promise.' She eased herself off the bed. Patrick stopped her.

'Isabel.' She looked at him and saw him suddenly look uncertain and vulnerable. 'Will you come again tomorrow?'

'Oh, yes,' she said shyly. 'I do hope so.'

Isabel was convinced that one of the other mothers would notice something different about her, but they appeared oblivious. As she waited for Michael to finish Cubs, it seemed extraordinary that no one should notice. The heat given off by her body alone should have been enough to generate a few raised eyebrows. And the smell. She must reek of sex. It was wicked, but, oh, it was wonderful.

Michael came out, grumpy about some argument over badges. Isabel nodded and made soothing noises without listening as she drove to Helen's to collect Katie. Back home she quickly made Michael a sandwich, then charged upstairs into a hot shower. She had just finished dressing when she heard Neil's cheery 'Hello' downstairs.

'Just coming,' she called back. Neil's footsteps on the stairs. She bundled her clothes into the dirty linen bin, just in case some lingering scent of Patrick remained on them, then checked her face in the mirror. Was this how she normally looked? Eyes bright, cheeks flushed. She had to be normal. Neil came into the bedroom.

'Sorry, didn't mean to disturb you. I was just going to change.' He looked at her curiously, as if surprised to see her upstairs.

'No, you carry on. I've finished here. I forgot to wash my hair yesterday,' she added. 'I thought I'd do it now so it'd be dry by bedtime.'

'No need to explain.'

No, she didn't have to explain. Be normal. 'How was work? Busy?'

'Same as usual.' He shrugged. 'Meetings and more meetings. Office politics.' He got out of his jacket. 'What about you?'

'What about me?' Isabel froze in the middle of reaching for the jacket.

'Your job.'

'Oh.' She picked the jacket up and put it on a coat hanger, like a good wife. 'It's just me and Patrick so there's not much opportunity for office politics. We'd have to have factions of one and gossip to ourselves in corners,' She paused. Perhaps it wasn't a good idea to stress that it was just her and Patrick in the house. 'Of course, Patrick is out a lot. Most of the time. In fact, almost all the time. Seeing clients, that sort of thing.'

'So how are you finding it?' Neil's face was politely enquiring, rather than challenging. He hardly appeared interested, and she relaxed.

'Fine. A bit boring in fact. I just answer the phone and do the filing.'

'Doesn't sound very stretching.'

Isabel brushed imaginary fluff off the jacket, trying not to think of being stretched out across Patrick's bed. She felt herself go scarlet.

'When's supper?' Neil asked, now dressed in old cord trousers.

'I don't know. Soon. About an hour.' How could he not have noticed her face, flaming with desire and longing? She hoped her voice at least sounded casual. 'You can have some pâté on toast if you can't wait.'

'That'd be nice.' He yawned and stretched. 'That's better. I think I'll go and watch the news.'

'Send Katie up for her bath, would you?'

He nodded and left the room. Isabel sank onto the bed, her legs threatening to give way for the second time that day, this time the reaction to deceit. Although she hadn't needed to lie to Neil; he hadn't noticed anything different about her. Which was strange as she felt gloriously, rampantly different. Patrick. Fourteen hours until she saw him again. Would it be as good tomorrow? She smiled to herself. He was quite right. She didn't feel guilty. She felt great.

Five

HELEN AND ISABEL arrived at the church for Harvest Festival at the same time so it was natural for them to sit together. Isabel was pleased, as she still didn't know many of the other mothers. Helen, on the other hand, seemed to know lots of people. Isabel commented on that.

'It's the PTA committee,' Helen said. 'I've met loads of people through it. You should join. They're always on the lookout for new blood.'

'We were always having coffee mornings when we were abroad. I'm not sure I can take many more.'

'It's not just coffee mornings,' Helen laughed. 'And all the meetings are in the evening. Not everyone's a lady of leisure, you know.'

'Nor am I any more.'

'Of course, you're working now. How's that going?'

'Fine.' Five weeks of work, three weeks of them as Patrick's lover. It seemed incredible to Isabel. She was brought back to the present by Justine slipping into the pew next to her.

'May I join you?'

'Of course,' Isabel said, moving up.

'I was telling Isabel how she ought to join the PTA committee,' Helen said. 'She thought it was too much on top of her job.'

Justine gave her a sidelong glance. 'Is working for Patrick that tiring?'

Isabel stiffened inside. Had Justine guessed? Had Patrick said anything? She made herself smile. 'Not tiring, but time-consuming.'

Helen persisted, talking about what the committee did and pressing Isabel to join. Isabel was touched that it mattered to her. In a sudden flash of insight she wondered if George was always nice to Helen. Helen was rearranging one of her hair combs, and her sleeve fell back from her wrist. Was it Isabel's imagination, or was there a shadow of a bruise?

'If you want me to come onto the committee, I will,' Isabel said. 'But can I join just like that? Wouldn't I have to be elected?'

'Being elected implies that there are lots of people who are just dying to join,' Justine said. 'I can't see Mary, but she'll be about somewhere. Probably organising the vicar. We'll catch her at the end of the service.'

After the service Helen found Mary, who was wearing a tweed hat complete with jaunty pheasant feather, and explained that Isabel had volunteered to join the PTA committee. Mary was pleased, then set off to accost the headmistress, leaving Isabel feeling that she had just had a close encounter with a steamroller.

'Don't worry, you'll get used to it.' Justine walked beside Isabel as they made their way out of the churchyard. 'I meant to ask you earlier, but have you lost weight? You look terrific.'

'Thanks. I have lost some.'

'What's your secret?'

Isabel blushed, thinking sex, sex and more sex. 'I've taken up swimming,' she said. Not for the first time, Isabel wondered exactly what Patrick and Justine's relationship was. He said they were friends and, when she pressed him, that Isabel shouldn't pry. 'You wouldn't like it if I talked about you, would you?' he'd asked. Which was unanswerable.

'I must dash,' she said. 'I promised Patrick I'd be back.'

'The next committee meeting is on Monday,' Justine called as Isabel escaped to the security of her car.

Isabel swam steadily, eating up the lengths and letting her mind roam. She hadn't lied entirely to Justine; swimming at lunchtime was her cover for the frequent afternoon showers and hairwashing needed to wash the scent of sex away. If caught with wet hair she just said 'I've been swimming', and two days out of the five it was true. At first she had been puffed after a few lengths, but to her surprise she had quickly got fit enough to swim for half an hour nonstop. She swam serenely, enjoying the feeling of her muscles working while her mind wandered.

Sometimes she replayed scenes with Patrick, or excuses with Neil, lies that she had got away with. Other times her mental cinema scrolled up images from a possible future, a future as different as possible to her present: perhaps a modern apartment in London, somewhere trendy like Notting Hill. Or there was the Italian fantasy; dark glasses and cappuccinos in the Piazza Navona. Patrick lounged elegantly in these settings, but she kept slipping out of the frame.

In the changing rooms Isabel soaped her body, feeling the new firmness, the definition around her waist where once there had been flab. It had only taken a few sessions before she had started noticing the difference. She washed herself thoroughly, scrubbing away the chlorine, just as on Tuesdays, Wednesdays and Thursdays she scrubbed away the scent of Patrick and sex in a bath at his house. The smell of guilt is soap and water, she thought. Cleanliness is next to adultery.

And Neil. She had wondered how she would feel, but in the end felt nothing. It was easy to deceive someone when they trusted you absolutely. But was it really trust that Neil felt—or arrogance? He trusted her because he thought she would be incapable of deceit, because that required mental agility and confidence. Stuff the morals, he thought that she lacked the nerve. That he was enough and she would never feel the desire to go elsewhere. Then she thought how unfair that was. After all, she assumed that he was faithful to her. Would *she* notice the signs?

There was the distinct possibility that she took Neil for granted in exactly the same way that she felt he took her for granted. Before Patrick she had felt that she was invisible to him. Did he feel that about her? But she had tried to talk to him. She could think of all too many occasions when he had snubbed her approaches, treating her like a loved but wayward child who really shouldn't bother the adults. And now she was convinced that she was invisible to him. Otherwise, surely he would have recognised her mistakes, the lies, the slips of the tongue?

She was brought back to the present by one of the women swimmers saying a cheerful goodbye to her.

'Bye,' she said quickly. 'See you Friday.' A whole new week lay ahead, and three blissful days of Patrick. But she'd got the rest of Monday to get through first. Her heart sank, remembering that tonight she had agreed to go to the PTA meeting.

After swimming she walked into town. She thought about buying some new clothes—the ones she had were getting loose around her middle—but decided to wait and see if she would drop down another dress size. One of the advantages of an affair, she thought. The sun was bright, lemon-sharp, but the wind was cool on her wet head and she felt cold. She ought to get inside.

Isabel turned into the bookshop and started to browse. Books were laid out enticingly on tables, covers as glossy as sweets. And entirely non-fattening. She sighed. Adulteresses in fiction ended badly, like poor Anna Karenina, losing her children and dying under a train. Isabel put down the book she was holding and moved to the children's section where she chose a book for each of the children.

She paid and left the shop. In the street she looked up and down. Left to collect the car and go back home, right to walk into the heart of town. She shifted from foot to foot, trying to decide. Left looked unenticing, right looked—was that Patrick? She peered. At the end of the street, a tall dark man was talking to a woman with shimmering blonde hair. Justine? Isabel couldn't tell at this distance. The man threw his head back and laughed and Isabel became almost certain it was Patrick. Then he kissed the woman. It was brief, the social kiss of casual acquaintances, but something about it—the placing of his hand on her upper arm maybe—made Isabel freeze. They parted and the woman turned and was swallowed up by shoppers. The man came towards Isabel; it was indeed Patrick.

She waited for him, questions buzzing in her head like a hive of angry bees. I mustn't ask him, she thought. I promised I wouldn't make demands on him. He seemed oblivious to her until about twenty feet away, then his face lit up. 'Isabel,' he said. 'How nice to see you.'

'What are you doing here?' she blurted out.

'I do live here, remember.' He leaned forwards and kissed her cheek.

'You smell of garlic and booze,' she said, trying to sound playful.

'Been out to lunch.'

She couldn't stop herself from asking, 'With a client?'

'Mmm.' He reached and took the bookshop bag from her. 'Now, what have you been buying? A present for me?'

'No, for the children.' She took the bag back from him, as if by handling the books Patrick would spill out into her domestic life. He hadn't answered the question about the client.

'Your hair's wet,' he said, fingering a strand.

'Who were you with?' There. She'd said it.

'You ought to dry it. I don't want you off work because you're sick.' He smiled at her, his hair ruffling with the breeze, his eyelids heavy.

'Was it Justine?'

He paused, looking up at the sky as if deciding what to say. Or what lie to tell. Isabel bit her lip. He looked at her, his face serious.

'I told you at the start. No commitments. No falling in love.'

She tried to laugh lightly. 'I'm just curious.'

'I see.'

'Please?' She registered that she sounded neither cool nor sophisticated, but she didn't care.

'You know I don't discuss people, and especially not one woman with another. You really ought to get that hair dried, you know.'

She stared at him. Would he suggest going back to his house? Her heart beat faster, and she realised it didn't matter if he had been out with another woman, been out with Justine. She wanted him, badly.

'Patrick,' she said, touching his hand, feeling his skin warm and alive.

He moved his hand away, brushing back his hair. 'This is a small town, darling,' he said quietly. 'Let's be discreet. I'll see you tomorrow.'

She watched him saunter up the street, turning up his jacket collar against the wind. He didn't look back.

'Sorry I'm late,' Isabel mouthed at Mary, squeezing into the last empty place in the school library. Mary glanced towards her, obviously annoyed, then majestically turned away and listened to the woman on her left. Isabel looked round the table. Again, like the coffee morning, it was all female. Of the twelve women there she recognised only a couple, apart from Helen and Justine. She looked at Justine. Had it been her with Patrick? As if aware of Isabel's gaze, Justine looked up and smiled at Isabel, her pussycat smile brimming with secrets. Flustered, Isabel looked down at her agenda. Item number three was school uniform and a woman she didn't recognise was getting very agitated about the service at the school shop.

Mentally Isabel switched off, although keeping an alert, listening look on her face. Most of the rest of the committee were fidgeting, playing with pencils. School uniform was obviously a regular item. Justine sat still, her manicured hands resting lightly on the table in front of her. I mustn't be jealous, Isabel thought. I don't own Patrick, and anyway, Justine knew him before I did. What if they did have lunch together?

Mary, obviously sensing the restless mood of the women present, decided to hurry things along. 'Now, next on the agenda is the bonfire party. Rebecca, perhaps you'd tell us how things are going?'

Isabel gathered that the committee brought hot dogs, baked potatoes and mulled wine—made to Mary's special recipe—and sold them along with sweets, fizzy drinks and sparklers. She volunteered to be a roving sparkler seller, a job that she hoped meant she would be able to keep an eye on how the children were coping with the noise. In Syria the rattle of gunfire had been an everyday occurrence, sometimes for a wedding, sometimes more sinister. Perhaps the children wouldn't remember the sound of guns, or if they remembered, wouldn't associate them with fireworks. She wanted to be near them at the bonfire party, just in case.

She listened to the discussion, which had moved on to how they were going to ensure that the sausages were cooked through, without leaving them hanging around in a lukewarm state for hours, given that they couldn't use any of the cooking facilities at the school. It seemed extra-ordinary that something so simple could require so much organisation. Isabel closed her eyes, scrolling through images of Patrick: Patrick on the phone, Patrick searching for some vital bit of paper and getting crosser by the second, Patrick saying 'Come to bed'.

'Wake up!' Her neighbour elbowed her in the ribs. 'It's you.'

'Sorry.' There was a small ripple of amusement.

Mary did not look amused. 'As I was saying, we'd like to welcome Isabel Freeman, who is a new mother and I'm sure she will be an asset to the committee.'

Isabel felt that she was going to be anything but an asset.

The meeting dragged on for what seemed like ages. Isabel got home after ten to find Katie in the middle of a complicated game involving all her stuffed animals and Michael still in the bath. Quickly she hustled them into their respective beds, inwardly seething at Neil. 'They kept saying they wanted you,' he said as if that explained Michael's ever-lasting bath, the unwashed dishes downstairs, and Katie's unread bed-time stories. He had managed to get himself to bed, she noticed sourly, and was halfway through a gold-embossed thriller.

She loaded the dishwasher and tidied up downstairs, then came back up and got ready for bed. As she slipped under the duvet Neil looked up from his book. 'By the way, my parents rang.'

'Are they well?' she asked, polite as ever about Neil's parents, safe in Scotland. Far enough away for her not to have to think about them.

'Fine. I've invited them down for the weekend.'

'No, you haven't?' It was an appalling thought. 'When are they coming?'

'Two weeks' time.'

'Two weeks.' She mentally ran through their diary. 'I don't think we're doing anything. I suppose I'd better ring Moira up and confirm.'

'No need, I've already said it's OK.'

'But I might have arranged something else.'

'Have you?'

'It's the first weekend of half term. We could easily have been doing something—going away, even.'

'But we're not.'

'No, but don't you see . . . You should have asked me.'

'You weren't here. You were off at your PTA meeting.' He went back to his book, making what sounded like a little grunt of satisfaction.

'I can't win, can I?' She closed her eyes. Everything seemed so difficult with Neil at the moment. All conversations ended up in antagonism. Underneath the irritation, was there love? She couldn't imagine her life without Neil being in it, but that could be habit.

'I'm sorry I was sharp,' she said. 'Just tired, I suppose.'

'Perhaps you should give up work,' he said. His voice sounded neutral but she thought she could detect a spike of something else, like guacamole laced with chilli. 'By the way,' he said, 'speaking about work, I know you said you weren't earning much but the accountant needs to know. Give me your payslips and I'll pass them on to him.'

'I don't get payslips.'

'What then, cash stuffed down your bra?' He sounded amused and for a second she hated him.

'No, of course not.' She hunched the duvet over her shoulder. At the end of the first week she had asked about her wages. Patrick had looked surprised, and said they were having a four-week trial period. He'd pay her at the end, and if both wanted to continue the arrangement, at the end of every month thereafter. It had sounded reasonable. The afternoon of the storm had come before the four weeks were up. Since then, Patrick had not offered her any money, and she hadn't liked to ask. Neil made an irritated 'tsk' noise.

'I've told you before that it's important to keep proper records. It doesn't take much to go over the tax threshold. We'll have to do a certain amount of juggling.'

'We?'

'Gordon and me. Our accountant, yes? We've been minimising my tax bill through using your allowances as a non-earner. You know that. Now you're making some money, however little, we'll have to look again. And there's National Insurance to consider.' He smiled at her, as if metaphorically patting her little head. 'But you don't have to worry about it. Just make sure he gives you a proper payslip.'

'I don't think I can.'

'If you like, I'll give him a ring and sort it out for you.'

'No!'

'All right, don't bite my head off.'

'You're not to phone.' Her nerve ends jangled at the thought. 'I promise I'll ask, just please don't phone. Please.'

'He wants a payslip.' Isabel looked at Patrick stretched out on the bed stark naked, eyes closed, as unselfconscious as a cat. Patrick opened one eye and squinted at her.

'What are you rambling on about, darling?' he said on a yawn.

'Neil. He wants me to have a payslip to give to his accountant.'

Patrick considered this for a moment then shut his eye. 'Prat.'

'Patrick!'

'Man's a complete arse.'

'He's my husband.'

'I rest my case.' Patrick rolled over and twitched the sheet away from her. 'Look at you. *La bellezza.*' He ran his hand over her outline. 'You must let me photograph you one afternoon.'

Isabel reached for the sheet again; too hard to concentrate on holding your tummy in and talk at the same time.

'Seriously, what am I going to do?'

'Ignore him. Let me teach you Italian. This is your *pancia*, your *ance*, your lovely *coscia* and down here, down here is your *figa*. C'mon, relax.'

'I can't,' said Isabel, sitting up and swinging her legs over the side of the bed. She started to get dressed.

'For a mistress you're being very boring.' Patrick flopped back.

Isabel paused from doing her new jeans up. 'Is that what I am?'

Patrick shrugged. 'What else? Employee, if you prefer. What's wrong with mistress anyway?'

'It's just—' Isabel paused, trying to work out in her own mind what she felt. All these labels defining her with reference to someone else. Wife, mother. Now mistress.

The phone started to ring and she crossed the landing into the office. 'Patrick Sherwin Associates . . . yes, I'll just see if he's available.' She held the phone to her chest. 'It's Andrew. Are you available?'

'No. Damn, I should speak to him. Tell him I'm coming.' Patrick started to pull his trousers on. 'Make me a coffee, would you, hon?'

'He's just coming,' Isabel told the long-suffering Andrew, then put the phone down on the table and went downstairs to the kitchen.

384

Only three weeks, she thought, staring out of the window and waiting for the kettle to boil. Three weeks ago I was standing here watching Patrick get wet in the rainstorm. And now I'm his mistress. Such a loaded word. She pushed the cafetière plunger down hard, too hard. The cafetière broke and scalding coffee spurted out, splattering across her top and jeans. 'Shit!' She grabbed a tea towel and scrubbed at her front, leaving hot, dark coffee splodges. Her jeans were burning her legs. She took off her sweatshirt and saw that the coffee had gone right through to her white shirt. Bugger. Now what?

'Problems?' Patrick was leaning against the door, half dressed.

'I've stupidly managed to get coffee all over me.'

'Bad luck.' He didn't sound very sympathetic and she felt put out.

'But I've got nothing else to wear.'

'Just how I like you,' Patrick leered at her, then relented. 'Grab one of my sweaters from upstairs.'

Isabel went back up to the bedroom and stripped off. There were red marks on her legs where the coffee had scalded. She rummaged through Patrick's clothes, choosing the largest sweater she could find. She rubbed her cheek against her shoulder, inhaling his smell. He's selfish and he doesn't love me, she thought. He might even be seeing someone else. As a mistress I have no rights, no claims. I can't even ask. This relationship is about sex, and that's all. Falling in love is out of the question.

She came back down to the kitchen and bundled her coffee-stained clothes into the washing machine.

'Why don't you chuck some of my stuff in while you're at it?' Patrick said, slipping his arm about her waist and planting an affectionate kiss behind her ear. She twisted round to face him.

'No, your dirty washing is your own. Don't sulk.' She kissed the palm of his hand, thinking, is this really just sex? 'Wives get the dirty socks, mistresses don't. Even I know that's the deal.'

'I see . . . And what do you think mistresses should get? Apart from payslips, of course.'

'It's not me that wants a payslip, it's Neil. And his bloody accountant. Actually, you haven't given me any pay.'

'How much do you want?'

'What I've earned, of course.'

'Ah. Now that's an interesting issue.' He was very close to her. 'Are you charging me for services rendered, or am I charging you?' He reached into his back pocket, brought out his wallet and shook it out, coins spilling onto the floor, notes fluttering down. 'Every penny I possess I give to you. All I have.'

She put her arms round his neck. 'Everything?'

'Of course. Will everything be enough for Madam?'

'Mmm, s'pose so. In some ways the money's not really important, but in other ways it is. Coming to you was, in a very small way, a chance to do something with my life. Keep myself, rather than be kept.'

'Money's the most important thing there is.'

'More than love?'

'Oh, yes. If it's a choice between love or money, money will win every time.'

'That's not true.'

'Look around you. Look at all these empty marriages.'

'They didn't all marry for money.'

'But they stay because of it. Don't you?' he asked very softly.

Isabel paused. 'If I say I stay for things like security and stability and company, you'll say that's just the same as money, won't you?' She clasped her hands in front of her, trying to disentangle her thoughts. 'I do love Neil. Perhaps not in the same way I once did, but . . . we've shared so much. That matters. And then there are the children.'

'The clinching argument.'

'At the end of the day, yes. Don't sneer; just because you're not interested, it doesn't mean that other people aren't. I'd never leave my children, they want to be with both me and Neil, and so we stay together.'

'So romantic.' He looked back at her, as if in contempt.

'What about us? Is that any more romantic? Sex without love? Without a future?' She spoke more bitterly than she had meant and the atmosphere became as brittle as icicles.

'I'm going to do some work,' Patrick said. 'As for your husband's payslip, as far as I'm concerned you're self-employed and therefore you can sort out your own tax and National Insurance. Just invoice me for the hours you've done.' He touched her shoulder lightly and said more kindly, 'I'll show you how to lay it out later.' He hesitated. 'Isabel, don't forget what I said. No falling in love.'

After he'd left the kitchen Isabel pressed her hands to her face. I don't love him, she told herself. I don't. I can't. I mustn't.

The money was still scattered over the floor and she bent down to pick it up—£85.76, and sixty-five euros. Even if she said she spent half the day in bed with Patrick it wasn't enough to cover all the hours she had worked. I have earned this money, she thought. So why do I feel like a prostitute if I take it?

There was a knock at the door and she got up, her bones aching as if she had flu. Patrick's sweater came halfway down her thighs, making her decent enough not to give anyone a thrill. More knocking.

'Coming,' she called and opened the door, expecting to see a delivery-man with a box of computer peripherals to be signed for. What she saw was Mary Wright, her eyebrows shooting upwards.

'Isabel, good morning. May I come in?'

Isabel nodded, speechless. Of all the people she expected to see, Mary was as likely as Nelson Mandela. What was she doing there?

Mary came into the house and wrinkled her nose. 'Do I smell coffee?'

'Yes, in the kitchen . . . ' Mary started to move through into the kitchen and Isabel trotted after her, very conscious of her bare legs and naked feet padding on the cold floor. 'But you'll have to have tea. I smashed the cafetière and got coffee everywhere, which is why ' Her voice trailed away. Mary didn't seem to be listening.

'What did you make of the meeting last night?'

'Um. Very interesting.' Isabel tried to think of something to say. 'The bonfire party sounds fun.'

'Yes, people seem to enjoy it. Anyway, I just thought I'd pop in to make sure everything was fine.'

Isabel stared at her. Why was she there? What business was it of hers to check if everything was fine? And what did she mean by that anyway?

Mary gave Isabel a quick up-and-down, sniffed, then carried on. 'I haven't seen Patrick for ages. You know what men are like; they're use-less about staying in touch.' Isabel wasn't sure what to say.

'Oh, look, my clothes have finished washing.' She hoicked them out of the machine, and shook them out. 'I'll just hang them up. Help your-self to tea.' She pulled the airer out of the cupboard and escaped to the living room, calling to Patrick up the stairs.

He stuck his head over the landing. 'Who is it?'

'Mary Wright.'

'Mary? Good.' He clattered down the stairs.

'What's she doing here?' Isabel hissed at him as he passed by, but he didn't seem to register the question.

'Good to see you,' she could hear him say as she draped her damp clothes over the airer in front of the fire. 'And how's Richard?'

Her ears strained to catch Mary's response, but she couldn't distin-guish the words. What could Patrick and Mary be talking about? When she felt she couldn't arrange her clothes any longer she dithered between working and blatantly hanging over the banisters to eavesdrop. The decision was made for her by the phone ringing.

She hesitated in the kitchen doorway. 'Sorry to disturb you, but it's Andrew on the phone again.'

'I'll have to take this call,' Patrick said to Mary. 'Can you hang on for five minutes? Isabel will look after you.'

He left the room. Mary looked at Isabel in the same way that her formidable headmistress had done at school.

Isabel tried for a beaming, welcoming, 'I'm not bothered' smile, but had a horrible feeling her lips had formed a sort of 'I'm as guilty as sin and please don't tell me off' simper. 'More tea?'

'No, thanks.' Mary hesitated and lowered her voice. 'Patrick told me he'd got someone in to work for him. He didn't say it was you, however. I hope you know what you're doing.'

'I don't know what you mean,' Isabel said, heart pounding.

'I don't know you very well, but I know you have a husband and children.' Mary carried on, inexorable. 'I am very fond of Patrick but he is, how shall I put it? Unreliable.'

Isabel felt her face flush scarlet. 'Patrick is my employer,' she said, gripping the edge of the table. 'That's all there is to it.'

'I dare say,' Mary said. 'When I think what poor Caro had to put up with . . . I feel partly responsible. It was my idea that they move to Milbridge in the first place. Then there was all the trouble with Justine.'

'Justine?'

'Didn't you know? Caro found them in bed together—in her bed, what's more. It was the last straw and she chucked Patrick out.'

'I didn't know about . . . not for sure.' Isabel held her hand to her mouth, seeing Patrick and Justine together.

'Not that Justine stayed with Patrick for long—if I were gossiping I'd say she discovered that the money was Caro's and not Patrick's. Justine's a clever girl, but greedy. Always one eye on the chequebook, though I think she'd settle now for a good provider,' Mary added.

'And Patrick?' Isabel asked, despite herself.

'You're not the first and you won't be the last. I'd hate to see another marriage break up because of him.'

'I work for Patrick, and that's all,' Isabel said, trying to keep calm. 'There is no question of anybody's marriage breaking up. He means nothing to me.' She could feel her lower lip quiver.

Mary looked at her, an appraising sort of look. 'Just be careful.'

Isabel felt her spirit shrivel up. Lying to Neil was one thing, lying to Mary another. 'I don't know what business it is of yours, anyway. What right have you got to come here and say these things?'

'There's no need to get upset. It's common knowledge. You should know what you're getting into.'

'Know? I don't want to know this . . . this gossip. Gossip and jumping to conclusions. Just because I spilt coffee over myself and had to wash my clothes, you've decided I'm having an affair with Patrick.'

Mary paused. 'I am only warning you. Patrick has made a lot of women very unhappy. It's up to you if you're one of them.'

'You hardly know me. Why should you care?'

'I don't, particularly. But I do care for Patrick.'

'You're jealous, aren't you?'

Mary snorted. 'Hardly.'

'You must be, or why else would you be saying this?'

'Hasn't he said?' To Isabel's surprise, Mary suddenly laughed. 'Well, I can see it might look a bit peculiar to you, as you don't know.'

'Know what?'

Mary smiled. 'Why, that Patrick's my brother.'

Six

'WHY DIDN'T YOU TELL ME that Mary was your sister?'

Patrick shrugged. 'No reason. It never came up.'

They were sitting opposite each other at the kitchen table the following day. Isabel had left the money, unable to bring herself to take it, and now it was gone. She knew she wouldn't ask for it again. After Mary's visit, Patrick had disappeared to deal with the importunate Andrew, so this was the first opportunity Isabel had had to ask him. Patrick appeared nonchalant, but Isabel knew him well enough now to detect the tension lines pulling at the corners of his eyes. The more tense he got, the more controlled his movements. Then, finally, the eruption.

Now he sat sipping coffee, his lids drooping, hiding his eyes from her. Isabel put her head in her hands. 'It was so embarrassing.'

'So what? She won't say anything. She's already ticked me off and given me the usual lecture about being irresponsible.'

'Is what she said true? About you and Justine?'

The tension lines tightened. 'It depends what she said.'

'That Caro discovered you in bed with Justine.'

Patrick stood up and looked out of the window. 'Caro wanted to come out to the country,' he said at last. 'She wanted somewhere to stable her horse. I didn't want to leave London, but Caro's father gave her the money to buy a farmhouse with a bit of land. Her family's well-off,' he added. 'Anyway, we moved down complete with quadruped. She took up hunting and left me to different sorts of country pursuits.'

'With Justine.'

'Sometimes.' He smiled, as if at a private joke. 'Not exclusively. There are quite a lot of bored married women out there.'

'You mean, like me,' Isabel said flatly.

'No. Not like you.' He frowned. 'I don't know. Perhaps. If the cap fits . . .' He smiled charmingly as if to take the sting from his words.

Isabel felt sick. He had told her to expect nothing from him, but now she realised what nothing might be.

'I don't understand how you can do it. I mean, sleeping around like that, saying it means nothing. You were married.'

'Look who's talking.' He spoke clearly and Isabel hung her head. 'You're doing now exactly what I was doing.' There was a slight pause before he continued. 'I told Caro that I couldn't promise to be faithful to her. She knew that, right from the start. Same as you did.'

'And you think that lets you off the hook?' Isabel said slowly.

Patrick shrugged. 'If Caro didn't mind, I don't see why you should. After all, you have Neil. I'm the one who's sharing you, and you expect me to put up with it. He gets all your loyalty, your commitment, all your—' He pulled himself up sharply and Isabel wondered if he had been going to say 'love'. He drummed his fingers on the kitchen work-top, then turned on her. 'I ask nothing from you. Nothing,' he said.

'But it doesn't have to be like that,' she said, her own voice trembling, as she got up and stood by him. She reached out for his arm. 'Patrick?'

He flung her arm away from him. 'Yes, it does,' he shouted, his face dark. He stalked out, slamming the door behind him.

Isabel mooched around the house waiting for Patrick to come back. She watched the wall clock. In ten minutes I'll go to the pub and see if he's there, she thought. When ten minutes were up she waited another five. When the second tranche of five minutes was up she went down-stairs to get her coat. At the foot of the stairs she paused, hearing a noise. A key in the lock, then Patrick came in. They stared at each other. Then they moved closer, like magnets being drawn to each other and Patrick was kissing her and saying 'I'm sorry'. She felt miserable and happy and confused because all that mattered was that he had come back.

'I—' she started to say, but he put his hand over her mouth as soon as he heard the start of the word 'love'.

'Don't say it,' he murmured. 'Don't say it. Come to bed.'

'Is it your father or your mother who's Italian?' Isabel said, snuggling under Patrick's arm.

'My mother.' He sighed. 'My father had three children by his first marriage. Then his wife died leaving him with Anna, June and Mary. My mother came over from Italy to help look after them. He had that tweedy English gentleman sort of charm and I suppose my mother thought it exotic. Anyway, they had me. But after a bit my mama discovered that he wasn't exotic, in fact he was just like any other Nigel or Henry you might meet at the golf club. And then there were the girls.' He raised his eyebrows. 'If you think Mary is bossy, you should meet Anna and June. It can't have been easy.'

'So what happened?'

'My mother ran off with a Tunisian airline pilot.'

'Did you go too?'

'No. She left us all.' Patrick sat up. 'I ought to get some work done. Lord knows why I'm telling you all this, you're probably bored to tears.'

'No, I'm not. How old were you?'

'Mmm? About seven.'

Isabel kissed his shoulder. 'Poor boy.'

'Yeah, well, that's the way it goes. Besides, I wasn't really badly off, I had three splendid surrogate mothers in my sisters. I went to live in Rome with my mother in my teens, after I was chucked out of school. I was persona non grata at home, as you can imagine, and Dad had remarried and got a new family, so he wasn't really interested anyway.'

He spoke lightly, but Isabel could sense the hurt behind the words. She could imagine him as a small dark boy, bewildered at his mother's departure, then a sulky teenager rejected by his father.

'What about you?' Patrick surprised her by saying. 'You've had the Sherwin tale of woe, now you tell me something about your family.'

'Um. Well, I'm an only child and my father was a businessman. Sometimes things would go well with the business, and sometimes they wouldn't. We moved around a lot, depending on the money, everything from a caravan to an Elizabethan mansion, ending up in a terraced house in East Sheen. I've still got that. My mother was always waiting for the bailiffs to turn up. I promised myself that I would give my own children a proper home and that we'd stay there. Not that I've managed that very well so far: Michael's already lived in four different countries. But here we are.'

'Your father sounds quite a character.'

'He was. He looked a bit like Errol Flynn, but without the muscles. He always smoked a cigar, even when he was broke.' Isabel smiled, remembering him talking expansively, cigar in hand. 'He would have loved mobile phones,' she said, looking at Patrick. 'You'd have got on.'

'Did he get on with Neil?'

'He encouraged Neil. With hindsight, I think he thought Neil was responsible and would look after me. You see, my mother had died a few years earlier, and he knew he was ill, although he didn't tell me. He died three months after we married. I was stuck in Saudi with Neil. So he died alone.' She pressed her lips together.

Patrick stroked her hair. 'Poor little girl,' he said gently.

Isabel rubbed her cheek against his chest. 'Makes two of us then.'

She was thinking about Patrick and that exchange as Neil drove them over to Helen and George's house for dinner on Saturday night. Wednesday had been the best yet, with Patrick tender and considerate. Loving, she would have said of anyone else, but that word was banned. The next day he'd been irritable, as if she'd come too close, and he had to put up the barriers again. She sighed. If she'd learned anything in the six weeks she'd known him, four as his lover, it was that he was unpredictable and edgy about any emotions.

George and Helen's driveway was blocked by two cars so Neil parked their car hard against the verge. 'I bet you anything that Helen will get the women to withdraw after dinner while George dishes up the port,' Isabel said as they walked up the flagstone path.

'You don't like port anyway.'

'But I want to be offered the choice. And I bet he's stingy with the booze. Let's hope Helen's made something alcoholic for pudding.'

'Sherry trifle,' Neil suggested.

'Tiramisu.'

'Syllabub.'

'Um . . . um . . . um . . . I know, rum truffles.'

'Nearly got you there.' He gave her a gentle push.

Isabel stuck out her tongue at him. 'Know-it-all.'

'You're just jealous,' he said, giving her shoulder a squeeze.

'You're in a good mood,' she said, suddenly realising that it was ages since they had gone out together. Perhaps if we did things together more often, just us, there would be more life in our marriage, she thought. Neil rang the doorbell.

'Isabel! Neil, good to see you. Come on in and have a drink.' George led them into the drawing room and indicated the other guests. 'Now, who do you know?'

Four faces turned towards her. Mary Wright's was as welcoming as a slab from Stonehenge and Justine was looking as bland as if rain had washed all expression away. The two men were unknown to Isabel.

'My husband, Richard,' Mary said, social graces presumably beating private misgivings, introducing a portly man.

'And this is Quentin Anderson,' Justine added. Isabel shook his hand, which was disturbingly soft and cool. His face was plump and slightly pink as if his razor had newly scraped his skin. Perhaps he's rich, Isabel thought, and was ashamed of her meanness.

Isabel introduced Mary to Neil. 'And you remember Justine, don't you?'

'Of course,' he said, rather stiffly. Isabel was surprised; she'd thought he'd quite liked Justine when they'd met.

'So, you're working for Mary's little brother,' Richard Wright said. 'Quite a handful, I'd have thought.' Isabel prayed Neil hadn't heard.

'I really couldn't say. I just do the paperwork and answer the phone.'

'Pretty young thing like you, thought he'd have difficulty keeping himself to himself, if you know what I mean.' He leaned closer, so Isabel got a good view of the network of spidery red veins that webbed his face. 'Terrible reputation the boy's got.' Richard shook his head. 'Terrible one for the ladies. But I expect you can handle yourself.' His eyes twinkled at her in a way that should have been avuncular, but which Isabel found sinister. Had Mary said anything?

'If you'll excuse me, I must go and say hello to Helen,' she managed to say before escaping into the hall, ignoring Neil's questioning turn of the head. Pull yourself together, she thought. It's only natural that people ask about Patrick. She moved to the kitchen to find Helen.

'Hello, I came to see if I could help.'

Helen looked up, her fair hair flopping over pink cheeks. 'You couldn't give me a hand to take these starters out of the oven?'

'Sure.' Isabel looked around and found a pair of oven gloves. 'They smell delicious.' She pulled out a tray of scallop shells piped with mashed potato, some of them burnt around the edges.

'I wish I'd never started them,' Helen said vehemently. 'They're fiddly, take ages and they don't look anything like the photograph.'

Isabel immediately felt better. 'Never mind,' she said consolingly. 'I'm sure they'll taste wonderful.' It was so reassuring to know that other women weren't perfect cooks.

'I wanted to have a kitchen supper, just simple food and friends,' Helen was muttering to a bowl of whipping cream. 'But, oh no, George wants to make it dinner. Well, it's all right for him. He doesn't have to do any of the work.'

'Let me give you a hand.'

'That's sweet of you, but it's more or less under control.' Helen looked around the kitchen rather wildly.

Isabel realised that Helen was waiting for her to go so she could scrape off the burnt bits. She wanted to tell her that it didn't matter, that it was mad to expect anyone to produce restaurant-quality food at home. But she thought that if she said it, it implied that all Helen's efforts had been worthless.

'Are you sure there's nothing I can do?'

'Absolutely,' Helen said. 'Go and grab a drink.'

Isabel left the kitchen and slowly went back into the hall. Poor Helen, she thought. The doorbell rang just as she crossed the hall. She called out, 'I'll get it.' One less thing for Helen to worry about, she thought. She opened the big front door.

Patrick stood there, with his arm around a woman with short blonde hair who looked familiar. With a start Isabel recognised her. The woman on the yacht, in the photograph she'd found in the office.

'Patrick!' She was so surprised to see him, her legs felt as if her knees had just taken a trip to the Bahamas. 'What are you doing here?'

'What do you think? Gate-crashing, of course. Are you going to let us in or just stand there?' She could tell from the way his head was tilted back that he hadn't expected to see her, and was on the defensive. His arm was no longer round the woman-from-the-photograph's shoulder.

Isabel realised she was hanging onto the door like a crutch. She let go and stepped back to let him and his companion through. 'Would you like me to take your coat?' she said, aware that she sounded too formal.

'Thank you.' The woman slipped her coat off and handed it to Isabel, who chucked it over the banisters. She was dressed in a simple shift dress, low-cut with slim spaghetti straps that crossed over her beautifully tanned back. Isabel, who had been feeling quite sleek and attractive, immediately felt fat and frumpy.

'What a lovely dress.'

'Thank you.' The woman smiled politely showing even, white teeth. She wasn't as young as Isabel had first thought, nearer to thirty maybe.

'This is Victoria,' Patrick said. 'And this is Isabel, who works for me.'

Isabel's ego plummeted. 'Come into the drawing room and get a drink.' She walked forwards, trying to act nonchalantly. She'd always known that, logically, she was bound to run into Patrick at some point. It was just that, somehow, she didn't expect it to happen. What went on in Patrick's house was so far removed from her daily life, it was like some private fantasy world. And now there was Victoria. She wondered when the photograph had been taken, and she realised it could have been taken that summer. Possibly just before Isabel started working for him. The thought made her feel sick and cold.

'Are you all right?' Neil was at her side. 'You seem a bit . . .'

'What? No, no, I'm fine. Really. How's your drink?'

Neil shrugged, then looked down at his glass. 'It's all right.'

'You're doing better than me. I haven't managed one at all yet. Do you want me to drive?'

'No, no, darling. It's my turn. You have a good time.'

She went up to where George was fussing with ice cubes and tonic water. 'Could I have a drink please, George?'

'Isabel, I'm sorry, did you get missed out?' He made her a drink, measuring the gin carefully, and handed it to her. She went to the armchair furthest from Patrick and Victoria and plonked herself down. Over the edge of her glass she studied the room. Neil and Richard stood in front of the fire, hogging the heat. Mary, feet firmly planted on the ground, was talking to Quentin. He, poor man, was leaning backwards as if to escape contact, but Mary's gravitational pull was stronger than his desire to escape her orbit. Justine was talking animatedly to Victoria and Patrick. Victoria kept touching Patrick.

Isabel hoicked out a bit of ice cube from her glass and popped it in her mouth. Wake up and feel the ice water, she thought.

'Have you forgiven me for being here?' Patrick was standing before her, his crotch level with her eyes.

'I was startled. You didn't say you'd be here.'

Patrick touched her arm. 'Isabel—'

'I expect she's just an old friend.'

'She is.'

'And as you have pointed out to me on many occasions, there is nothing between us beyond what goes on in the office.'

'I'm sorry.' He ran his hand through his hair. 'If I'd known you'd be here I would have said something. I didn't expect—'

'Obviously.' She glared at him. He looked down at her, his lips twitched and involuntarily she almost smiled back at him. But he was aware of the internal smile, and smiled broadly himself.

'Oh, Isabel, what shall I do with you?'

He made her sound like unwanted baggage, she thought. She felt confused at her emotions—anger, jealousy, love swirling round together like primeval soup—but knew that she must control them. No one must know how she felt. She stood up from her chair.

'Hadn't you better introduce me properly to your girlfriend?' she said.
'If you wish.'

They crossed the room together, Isabel careful not to let her hips sway and bump into him accidentally, and joined Justine and Victoria. 'I'm so pleased to meet you at last,' Isabel said to Victoria. 'Patrick has a lovely photograph of you in his office.'

'Patrick, I'd no idea. That's so sweet of you,' Victoria said, wrinkling her nose and blowing him a kiss. Old friend, my arse, thought Isabel.

'Now, Patrick, I can't let your ego get even bigger by having three adoring ladies surrounding you,' Justine said gaily. 'I'm off to seduce your husband, Isabel.'

'Be my guest,' Isabel answered, equally gaily.

'Now, which is your husband?' Victoria asked.

'The one talking to Richard. You know Richard, I expect.'

'Gosh, yes. I adore Mary and Richard, don't I, darling?' Victoria slipped her hand around Patrick's arm, clearly staking her claim. Patrick looked harassed, Isabel realised with amusement, slightly surprised that she could feel amused in the situation. Poor Victoria, if she's only half aware of Patrick's activities she probably feels every woman she meets must be either a past, current or future mistress of his.

Helen saved her by coming in and announcing that dinner was ready. They all trooped through to the candlelit dining room. Helen had even gone as far as to put copperplate place-name cards round the table. Isabel found her place, sandwiched between George and Quentin, who seemed to have wilted after Mary's monologue. Directly opposite her was Mary, with Patrick on her right and Justine to his right.

'These are delicious, Helen,' Justine said, leaning forwards so she could smile sincerely at her. Helen looked flustered but pleased.

'I'm afraid they got a bit burnt.'

'Oh, no, it's wonderful to have something hot to start with, especially now the evenings are drawing in.'

There was an echoing chorus of congratulations. Isabel asked Quentin what he did.

'I'm a dermatologist. That's skin problems. Eczema and so on,' he explained. 'The skin's the largest excretory organ of the body, you know.'

'Really?' Isabel said, looking at her scallops and trying not to think about excretory organs. 'Fascinating.'

Encouraged, Quentin started to talk about dermabrasion, the new PUVA light treatments available and Chinese herbal medicine. It must have been murder for him to have to listen to Mary's monologue. Isabel nodded and interjected a suitable word every now and again, watching

Mary and Patrick across the other side of the table. Mary was talking, and judging by the look on Patrick's face she was telling him off. He prodded a bit of scallop around his plate, then looked up and saw her watching him. His face went from miserable to happy in one second and, despite herself, Isabel's heart contracted with longing for him. Mary sensed his change and turned her head as swiftly as a striking hawk. Isabel felt herself blush and turned back to Quentin.

'What an interesting area of medicine,' she said faintly. 'I had no idea.' She saw Helen pick up her plate and clutched at the chance of escape. 'Can I help you take things through?'

'No, no, sit down,' Helen responded. Isabel slumped back in her seat. She felt confused. She knew what Patrick would say. You have a husband, what's wrong with me having a girlfriend? She didn't like being deceived herself, but she was deceiving Neil. Wasn't this what she deserved? And what about Victoria? Funnily enough, she felt as uncomfortable about deceiving her as she did Neil. Oh Patrick, she thought. Life was so much easier before you kissed me.

He was now having a conversation with Neil and Richard, something about a mutual acquaintance and a deal involving preference options. Patrick was animated, while Neil seemed slightly withdrawn.

'You've got to admit he sailed pretty close to the wind,' Neil said.

'All perfectly legal,' Patrick shrugged. 'And think of the profit margin. After all, if God didn't want them to get fleeced, he wouldn't have made them sheep.' He leaned back in his chair and grinned across at Neil, his face brimming with mischief.

'They said that after Lloyds, and I don't think many people found it funny then either,' Neil said quietly.

'Hear, hear,' Justine said, and Patrick flashed her a look of annoyance. Isabel felt annoyed too. It should have been her backing Neil.

'Lloyd's is still a sore point round here, Patrick, old boy. As you well know,' Richard said heavily. 'We shouldn't talk business anyway.' He swivelled his attention to Neil. 'I understand you have children at St Joseph's too. How are they finding it? Settling in all right?'

'Yes, thanks to Rachel,' Neil said, to Isabel's surprise. She wasn't aware that Neil had known anything about Justine's daughter. Katie must have told him. He added, 'Those girls seem to have hit it off.'

'How nice for her,' Victoria said. 'School can be hellish without a friend.'

'Send 'em all off when they're seven, if not earlier,' Patrick said.

'You don't really mean that,' Victoria frowned.

'Sure, why not? Get rid of the ankle-biters until they're old enough to appreciate a good Burgundy and have a decent conversation.'

Justine smiled very sweetly at him. 'Perhaps you say that because you don't have any children.'

'Don't intend to either.'

Isabel was aware of Victoria fiddling with the cutlery.

'Bet you will.' Justine was leaning back in her chair, challenging him.

'No, I'm far too selfish.' He shifted in his seat as if bored. 'Hey, Isabel,' he called across the table. 'Why don't you get Justine to do her colour thing on you?'

Isabel froze, caught in the spotlight of attention. Patrick's eyes held hers as they had done once, years ago it seemed, during the thunderstorm. 'Sorry?' she said, horribly conscious of Neil down the table.

'Justine does a colour thing—what's it called?' He turned to Justine.

'Beautiful You,' she said quietly, but her face was alert, eyes darting between Isabel and Patrick.

'You're kidding.' He laughed then swung back to Isabel. 'Why don't you let Justine turn you into a Beautiful You?'

'I don't know,' she said, trying to sound casual. She felt that everybody was listening to them.

'You really ought to,' gushed Helen suddenly. 'It's wonderful. We had a session, didn't we, Mary, with Rebecca too—you know, from the PTA—just the three of us and it was such fun, wasn't it?'

'Yes, I'd certainly recommend it.'

'Thank you, Mary,' said Justine. 'I'm glad you enjoyed it.'

'Why don't you have it done, Isabel?' Patrick interrupted. 'I'll pay.'

Isabel felt that all eyes swivelled to her. 'No. Thank you,' she said, hoping that she seemed at least vaguely natural despite the stiffness in her voice.

'In lieu of wages, if you prefer.' He was laughing at her, daring her to respond. 'It might even be tax deductible.'

'I hardly think that's necessary.' Neil's voice was firm as he cut across. 'I'm sure Isabel can make whatever arrangements suit her.'

Patrick shrugged, sitting back in his chair. 'If she doesn't want to . . .'

No, I don't want someone rummaging through my wardrobe, Isabel shrieked inside her head, but she could see that Justine was staring down at her plate, shoulders hunched in embarrassment.

'I'd love to do it, Justine. I've always meant to. Let me give you a ring and we'll make a date,' she said quickly. Justine perked up. Great, thought Isabel. What have I let myself in for? I could murder Patrick. She didn't care if she looked like an alcoholic, she needed a drink. 'George, some more wine, please.'

George removed his gaze from her cleavage and looked as wide-eyed as Bambi in a panic. 'I'll have to open another bottle.'

'Great. Carry on. Wield the corkscrew.'

She realised Patrick was looking at her, his face unreadable. What did he want from her, blowing alternately hot and cold like an erratic April day? He held her gaze for a moment then turned his attention to Justine. Isabel watched him smiling and being his most charming. She became aware that Quentin was also watching Justine and Patrick.

'D'you know him well?' he asked.

Isabel knew immediately who he meant. 'He's my boss. Sometimes I think I hardly know him at all.'

Quentin leaned towards her and spoke conspiratorially. 'I've heard a rumour Justine's seeing someone here in Milbridge.'

'I thought you were—' Isabel was startled into saying.

'Oh no. I'm Justine's fallback position, you could say. Justine told me that there's been nothing between her and Patrick for years,' Quentin continued. 'But you don't suppose . . .'

'No,' she said. 'I don't suppose anything where Patrick is concerned.'

She hardly managed to eat any of her *poussin provençale*, pushing chunks of courgette around the plate. As Helen cleared the plates away Isabel excused herself and slipped out to the loo. She ran cold water over her wrists and wiped the back of her neck with her cold hands. Patrick was pushing her boundaries, seeing how much she could or would take, but she didn't know why.

He was waiting in the hall for her when she came out of the loo.

'Why are you doing this?' she said, keeping her voice low.

'What?' he said, his voice caressing her. 'What am I doing?'

'You know. The colour thing. And Victoria. No, don't touch me.'

'Don't? That's not what you usually say. Normally it's please, please, please, Patrick.' He imitated her voice, his eyes hard.

She tried to go past him, but he stopped her. 'Why so stand-offish, sweetheart? You're normally much more accommodating.'

'My husband is in the next room. Along with your girlfriend.'

'Are you jealous?'

'No,' she said, not looking at him.

'But I have to share you, so it's only fair that you have to share me, don't you think?' He kissed the top of her head. 'You smell delicious,' he murmured. 'I want you.' He put his hand under her elbow as if to steer her to some corner but she resisted.

'No, I must go back. Someone will notice we're gone.'

'Back to your hubby,' he sneered. 'No wonder you're like a bitch on heat, the man's a patronising bore. You'd be better off with me.'

'Don't you dare talk about Neil,' she hissed at him. 'He's worth a hundred of you.'

'I love it when you get angry.' He was close, she could smell his scent, feel the warmth of his body, the danger of being with him. His eyes held hers and she felt she was falling, falling. 'Bitch,' he whispered before kissing her. '*Carissima*.' His hand was on her breast and she could feel him against her. She felt as limp as a puppet, where sex was the puppet master and Patrick pulled the strings. She wrapped her arms round his neck and kissed him back, almost lost to the moment.

Almost. With the tiny corner of her brain not curling up under Patrick's caresses she registered a noise, a voice. George. She tore herself away and scuttered down the hall. She met George at the door.

'Excuse me,' she said, slipping past him. She quietly sat down next to Quentin, hoping no one had noticed her absence.

Patrick didn't come back into the dining room, which flustered Helen as she doled out profiteroles.

'D'you think he's all right?' she said. 'Perhaps I should . . .'

'Please don't worry,' Mary said. 'My brother's manners are atrocious and I apologise on his behalf.'

'If you'll excuse me,' Victoria said, standing up and leaving the room.

The next ten minutes were hard for Isabel. Quentin tried having a conversation with her, but she found she kept on thinking of Patrick and then realising Quentin was waiting for her to reply. 'Sorry,' she kept saying. 'Sorry.'

She lost her bet with Neil. Helen didn't expect the ladies to remove themselves from the dining room, leaving the men to port and cigars. Instead she served coffee in the drawing room.

Justine came to sit next to Isabel. 'So, what do you think's going on with Patrick?' she said, tucking her slim legs neatly underneath her.

Isabel's heart flipped. 'Who knows?'

'Bit of a surprise him turning up with Victoria. I thought that was over ages ago. Poor girl, she's been dangling after him for years, and every now and then he deigns to notice.' Justine shrugged her elegant shoulders. 'He really does treat women badly.'

All at once Isabel felt angry with Justine. 'Speaking from personal experience?' she said as lightly as she could.

'No,' Justine purred sweetly. 'I don't believe in letting men treat me badly. Especially not men like Patrick.'

'What do you mean?'

Justine paused. 'You can divide people up into cats and dogs. Dogs are loyal and dependent and trustworthy and look at you with big doggy eyes. Cats are independent and think for themselves. They can bestow affection, but they usually demand it.'

'So?' said Isabel, trying to work out if she was a cat or a dog. Dogs sounded better people, but cats were more glamorous.

'So cat people can be happy with other cats but they're happiest with the uncritical attention of a dog. And dogs can be happy with other dogs, but they're happiest with a cat to worship. Patrick and I are both cats, so we're better off with dogs.' She drew out the word and Isabel wondered if she meant to be insulting.

'You don't really want me to do your colours, do you?' Justine said, disconcerting Isabel with the abrupt change of subject. 'I got the impression that you weren't too keen.'

'Well, it was a bit embarrassing, but it's probably a good idea. My wardrobe is stuffed with things I don't wear.' She picked up her bag and fished out her diary. 'What about the Friday after half term?'

'That's the bonfire party night. I'll be busy setting up.'

'Help, I'd forgotten. I'd better write that in. The Friday after, then—the morning would be best for me, I think.'

'That's fine by me. I look forward to it.'

As Isabel replaced the diary in her bag there was a clatter and Victoria came back in, her face glowing. Patrick behind her looked almost sleepy, sleek and well fed, the look he had after—

Isabel took a sharp intake of breath. Patrick looked across at her, and very deliberately smiled.

Seven

ISABEL LET HERSELF into Patrick's house on the Tuesday after the dinner party. Patrick was dressed and sitting on the sofa.

'Good morning,' she said. 'You're up early.'

He stood up. 'I was waiting for you,' he said.

'We need to talk,' she said. She hesitated, then started to take her coat off, turning her back on him. 'About Victoria.'

'She's irrelevant,' he said.

She spun round. 'And what about me?' All the emotion that she'd been feeling flooded her mind, anger melting the cold indifference. She hit him, her fists pounding into his chest. 'Am I irrelevant too?'

He grabbed her wrists and kissed her though she struggled against him, and suddenly she was kissing him back, and they were snatching at each other's clothes, desperate for each other, and then he was inside her and her back was pounding against the cold flagstone floor.

Afterwards she lay on the floor, feeling too feeble to move. She turned her head towards Patrick lying beside her. 'What do I mean to you?' she whispered.

He kissed her neck, her hair. His voice was muffled but she heard him clearly. 'Everything,' he said. 'You mean everything.'

'And Victoria?'

Patrick sat up. 'What about her?' he said, and started to get dressed.

'You're sleeping with her.'

'So what? You sleep with your husband, don't you?'

'We haven't for ages,' Isabel said, starting to get dressed herself.

'Oh, sure,' Patrick said, stalking off to the kitchen.

'No, really,' Isabel said, wriggling into her skirt, following him.

Patrick seemed on a mission to slam all the kitchen cupboard doors while taking out the new cafetière and a single mug.

'I don't know why you're so cross,' Isabel said. 'If anything, it's me who should be cross. Doing it under my nose like that.'

'I asked you first: you wouldn't, she would.' Crash. 'I think the word is prick tease.'

Isabel was shocked by his crudeness. 'That's a horrible thing to say.'

He fiddled with the signet ring on his little finger, then sighed. When he spoke his voice was quieter, more measured. 'You were waving your husband under my nose. How do you think I felt?'

'I don't know. I don't know how you feel.'

He stared out of the window, his mood unfathomable.

'I'm going to start working upstairs. There's a lot to do,' she said. Just as she was through the kitchen door he called her name.

'Yes?' she said from the living room, longing for him to come to her.

'Do you love me?'

Isabel stared at the ceiling to try to keep the brimming tears from overflowing. How can he even ask me this? she wondered. She didn't know how she felt. 'No falling in love. That's what you said.'

'So I did.'

Isabel waited for him to say more, or to come out from the kitchen, but there was nothing but silence. After a while she went up to the office. This is it, she thought. This is the beginning of the end.

Patrick was irritable for the rest of the day, shouting at her for losing some vital telephone number, shouting again when she told him she wouldn't be in next week because of half term. The next day he was out most of the time with a client. At least, that was what he said. He kissed her gently before leaving, but a kiss could mean anything. Or nothing. She started to think about money. She hated the idea of discussing it with Patrick, especially in his mood, but she couldn't work for nothing.

On Thursday morning first thing, before she had time to lose heart, she laid the envelope containing her invoice in front of Patrick, who was working at the kitchen table.

He looked up at her, and reached out an arm to pull her towards him. 'What's this?' he said, with a smile in his voice as he ripped open the envelope and pulled out the invoice. His expression changed. 'What's this?' he repeated, in quite a different tone.

'An invoice for the work I've done,' she said, faltering. 'You said that's what I was to do,' she added. She'd only invoiced him for half the hours she had been at the office, on the grounds that they might have been making love for the other half. It didn't come to very much.

Someone rapped at the door. 'I'll get it,' she said. A deliveryman stood outside, almost hidden behind an enormous bouquet of flowers.

'There you go, love,' he said, pushing the flowers into Isabel's hands.

There must have been at least a hundred flowers in the bouquet. Isabel had to cradle it, almost overwhelmed by the scent from the lilies and freesias—freesias, at the end of October. Isabel looked for the card with trembling fingers. '*Mi perdone, carissima*' it read.

Patrick. She looked up from the flowers. He was leaning against the kitchen door, watching her.

'They're amazing. Thank you.'

'The timing was interesting.' His voice was cold, his face withdrawn. He had the invoice in his hand.

'Patrick, I can't work for nothing.' She hugged the preposterous flowers to her. 'We agreed this is what we'd do.'

'I'll write you a cheque,' he said, turned abruptly and went back into the kitchen. She hesitated, then followed him in.

'There you are.' He held out a cheque to her. She disengaged a hand from the flowers and took the cheque.

'Thank you.'

He sat down at the table and started to read as if she wasn't there.

'Patrick.' She touched his shoulder. 'What does the card mean?'

'Nothing.' He shook her hand away. 'Absolutely nothing.'

On Friday morning cleaning the house in anticipation of the in-laws worked off some of Isabel's spare energy. She scrubbed at floors, dusted tops of curtains and wiped fingermarks off woodwork. Windows were washed, toys put in graded ranks. She paid particular care to the guest bedroom, putting out new geranium-scented soap. There were so many flowers in Patrick's bouquet that each room could have a bunch. She'd have to tell Neil that she'd bought them in honour of his parents' visit, although he was unlikely to notice. More likely his mother would comment on the unnecessary extravagance.

Her lower back was still sore from Tuesday, the desperate coupling on the sitting-room floor. At the beginning of the affair she'd been excited by the roughness; common sense and rationality overcome by a more urgent force. Lust, she supposed. But at the dinner party everything had changed, become complicated and dark. Poor Victoria. She'd looked so happy, her face lit up. Isabel wondered if that was how she'd looked after the first time with Patrick, and was amazed yet again that Neil hadn't noticed. She felt dishonest, sordid even. Oh, Patrick. Was he thinking of her, as she was of him? *Mi perdone* meant 'forgive me'. She couldn't work out what he meant. Forgiveness for what he had done, or for what he was going to do?

She plumped up the pillows on the guest bed, shaking them out and thumping them so they looked temptingly soft. Why were mothers-in-law quite so irritating? Everyone she knew was driven mad by their mother-in-law. Perhaps it was the forced intimacy with strangers. Or perhaps it was the power issue, suppressed for the sake of family harmony; like dogs, sniffing, circling, growling, but unwilling to fight outright.

Why do I feel the need to compete with her? she thought. The tidying, the cleaning, the Stepford wife stuff? It's so dishonest. Suddenly she laughed. Imagine what she'd say if I announced that I was being unfaithful? 'Whore, slut, always knew my Neil was too good for the likes of her.' And she'd probably be right.

Neil stuck his head round the kitchen door just after Isabel brought the children back from school. She was trying to feed them without making any mess in the kitchen, an enterprise that was successfully tightening all her nerve endings.

'Hello, everybody. Any chance of some tea?' he said. 'I'm knackered.'

She made him a cup while he listened patiently to Katie explaining about some dreadful act of injustice at school. She desperately wanted him to look after the children so she could have a bath. Her skin felt covered by a thin film of dirt that she longed to soak away. She put the mug of tea down in front of him.

'Look, would you mind if I had a five-minute lie down before I help?' he said.

'Is everything all right?'

'I'm fine, just a bit tired that's all.'

What's the point of coming back early if all you do is go to bed? she wanted to scream at him. But she suppressed her irritation. When all was said and done, her tiredness came from having an affair that was disintegrating whereas poor Neil was having to spend three hours a day commuting as well as often having to stay late at the office.

'It's fine,' she said, gently touching his shoulder. 'I've got everything ready. Go and relax.' He looked relieved, kissed her cheek then went. Isabel could hear his feet treading heavily up the stairs to their bedroom. So much for helping. Never mind. Just so long as they didn't come early.

Whatever time they arrived it would have been too soon. But Isabel hadn't reckoned on their appearance before seven. At five thirty-five she registered the sound of a car engine outside, but ignored it, assuming it must be the neighbours. She carried on mopping the kitchen floor, when a loud rap startled her. She clutched the mop in surprise as the face of her mother-in-law loomed through the kitchen window.

'Cooee,' Moira said, her Exocet eyes pinpointing immediately the bit Isabel had missed. 'Sorry, I didn't mean to make you jump.'

Liar, thought Isabel, whose heart was pounding as if she had seen Frankenstein's monster. Still, two can play at that game. She put her perfect daughter-in-law face on. 'Moira. How wonderful to see you. And so early, too.' She opened the kitchen door. 'Where's Ian?'

'Getting the luggage out of the car.' Moira ran one pearlised pink fingertip over the window sill, and sighed happily at the sight of dust.

Isabel tried casually to tidy the mop and bucket away, a difficult task as it was full of soapy water. 'I didn't hear the front doorbell.'

'Och, I didn't want to bother you with that. Shouldn't you empty the water out before putting that away?'

'I will later.' Only two minutes and Isabel could feel her cheeks aching with the effort of keeping a welcoming expression on her face. 'I'll go and help Ian with your things.'

Neil's father was ponderously taking luggage out of the boot of the car, hampered by his walking stick and the dog, Buster. Isabel rushed to help take out a matching pair of suitcases and a carrier bag that clinked as she put it down. Please, Isabel prayed as she embraced Ian, not more whisky. She led the way upstairs to the guest bedroom.

'I expect you'd like to wash and relax for a little,' she said hopefully. 'Come down and have a drink when you're ready.' She escaped without waiting for their reply. She carried on down the landing and gently opened the door to her bedroom.

'Neil? Your parents have arrived.'

He was lying on the bed fully clothed, snoring slightly. Isabel eased his shoes off, then covered him with the bedspread. She ran downstairs to the sitting room where the children were watching television, the toys Isabel had so carefully tidied earlier spread out all over the carpet.

'Quick, quick, pick everything up,' she hissed. 'Granny and Grandpa are here.' She nipped into the downstairs cloakroom and quickly brushed her hair. She wanted to wash her face but heard the sound of heavy feet on the stairs so contented herself with moistening a bit of loo paper and wiping the dust streaks off before going into the sitting room.

'What can I get you to drink?' She smiled at them, using her best hostess smile, and surreptitiously tried to push one of Katie's plastic ponies out of sight behind the sofa with her foot. The children had half cleared up and then scarpered.

'We've brought you a little gift,' rumbled her father-in-law, holding out the carrier bag.

'Whisky! How super.' I'll be saying jolly hockeysticks in a minute, Isabel thought in desperation. 'Is that what you'd like?'

'Well, now, that would be an idea,' he said, as if he didn't have a whisky and soda at six o'clock every evening without fail. Isabel poured him a drink from the bottle she'd opened the last visit but three. She'd given up wondering if they would ever notice that neither she nor Neil drank whisky.

'Moira?' She noticed Neil's mother scan the drinks tray. I mustn't be paranoid, she told herself. She couldn't possibly be deliberately choosing something that was not there. She was.

'A gin and tonic, please. If it's no bother.'

'None at all,' Isabel answered just as sweetly. 'I put the gin and tonic water in the fridge to keep them cool.' One up to me, she thought, as she went to fetch them.

'When does Neil get in?' Moira's expression was sour.

'He's here already, but went upstairs to lie down.'

'Is he ill?' Moira looked concerned.

'No, just a bit tired I think.'

'The poor boy. And to think I'm sitting here drinking.' She glared at Isabel and stalked out of the room. Isabel shrugged apologetically at Ian, trying to think of a conversational starter.

'The traffic wasn't bad on the way here then? You made good time.'

It wasn't much, but Ian was off, front runner in the traffic relay stakes, describing the route they had chosen and the bad driving encountered on the road. The rot had set in during the sixties, apparently, which opened up whole new conversational avenues: homosexuals, hippies, asylum seekers, all of whom deserved to be shot. Fortunately, the children created a diversion by coming in. Ian embraced them stiffly, tweed suit rough and unyielding. Katie lolled against his armchair, her shrill voice explaining exactly how chocolate Labradors were bred while her grandfather pressed against the seatback in unconscious alarm. He found Michael easier, his passions for fishing and racing cars safer topics for masculine conversation than Katie's twitterings on dog breeding.

'I'll just go and see about dinner,' Isabel mumbled and escaped to the kitchen where she tripped over the forgotten mop and bucket. Dirty water splashed over the clean floor. She slopped at the grey tide, sloshing water back into the bucket with angry jerks, a latter-day Cinderella. But no ball in prospect, no Prince Charming, no Fairy Godmother.

She turned the oven on ready for their meal. Smoked salmon roulade, then pheasants in apple and cream sauce and *pommes dauphinoises*, followed by lemon tart. Too much cream, too much stodge, but just right for drowning bad feelings in calories and carbohydrates.

She took the pheasants out of the fridge, draped them with streaky bacon, drizzled them with oil, chucked a few onions into the roasting dish and shoved it in the oven. While she was beating the salmon mousse for the roulade, Moira came in, shoes clacking like tongues.

'Is Neil up yet?'

'He's poorly.' Moira's mouth compressed.

'Really?' Isabel blinked. 'I thought he was just tired.'

'The boy's exhausted,' Moira said. She obviously felt it was all Isabel's fault. 'And going down with flu.'

'Poor Neil,' Isabel murmured, concentrating on spreading mousse over the roulade base. His mother sniffed loudly.

'I'm going to make him a hot toddy.'

'Oh. Help yourself. Just ask if you need anything.'

She finished the roulade, then started to get the children ready for bed. Once Katie was in the bath, Isabel slipped in to see Neil, still lying on the bed with the curtains drawn. Isabel noticed that the hot toddy was undrunk on the bedside cupboard. He was awake.

'Your mother thinks you're dying.'

'I am.' He flopped his head back and rolled his eyes.

'Are you really ill?'

'No. She just likes to fuss. A bit under the weather, maybe.' He rubbed one eye and yawned. 'It's been a tiring week. Office politics.'

'I'm sorry.' She realised how little she knew about his work at the moment. 'Do you want to talk about it?'

'Do you want to listen?' The question hung in the air between them.

'Of course,' she said finally. 'I always want to listen.'

'You seem rather preoccupied at the moment.'

'Sorry. I don't mean to be.'

'No.' He smiled and took her hand. 'Never mind.'

Isabel felt like crying. There seemed a huge chasm between them, impossible to cross. So many things to say, which could not be said. 'I've had a lover, but I think we're breaking up,' she wanted to tell him, and have him comfort her. 'I'm confused, I don't know what to do. It was exciting at first, but now it's something else. I'm so unhappy.' And Neil would cuddle her and say 'There, there, never mind, I still love you'.

But that wasn't going to happen, was it? However tolerant Neil might be, he was hardly likely to tolerate that. So many deceits, pressing down like stones, the only possible release being confession. But why should Neil share the burden of her guilt?

'I'm sorry,' she repeated, shaking her head.

The evening was a disaster. Michael and Katie, oblivious to their grand-parents' belief that children should be seen and not heard, refused to stay in bed. Michael at least was bribable, negotiating successfully for five pounds in exchange for staying in bed. Katie kept on appearing at the door wanting a drink, a biscuit, a story. Wanting a good smack, according to Moira.

'When Neil and Heather were little—' she started, but Isabel had ush-ered Katie out. Pointless to even think of getting into a conversation about the rights and wrongs of smacking. Bad wife, now bad mother. It seemed pointless having Ian and Moira there: they moaned on the phone that they were longing to see their grandchildren but, once there, they either ignored or criticised them and, by default, Isabel.

On Saturday the children were up bright and early despite the lack of sleep. They ran out of energy in the afternoon, halfway round a nearby stately home that Moira wanted to visit. Katie clung to Isabel's arm, weighing her down like a floppy anchor, while Michael became diso-bedient and surly, scuffing his shoes on the gravel drive. They squab-bled over who was going to walk Buster around the grounds and their crossness transmitted down the lead to the dog, who became crotchety, finally nipping Katie on the ankle.

Sunday morning, and yet another meal. Neil was downstairs cooking bacon and eggs, judging by the aroma permeating the whole house, when she heard his voice. 'Bel? Can you get the phone?'

'Sure,' she called back, going to pick up the hall phone. 'Hello?'

'Isabel,' said a familiar deep voice. Patrick.

'What do you want?' she muttered.

'To see you.'

'Why?'

'To say sorry. I behaved like a complete shit on Thursday.'

'Yes, you did,' she whispered, turning round to face the wall.

'Can you get away? Please, just for a few minutes. I've got something I want to talk to you about.'

'I don't know . . .' She twisted the cable round between her fingers.

'Meet me at the Italian café in half an hour.'

Neil's voice. 'Who is it?'

'No one,' she called back to him. 'OK, in half an hour,' she whispered to Patrick, and put the phone down.

She went into the kitchen. Neil was in an apron, pushing bacon round a frying pan while Ian and Moira read the Sunday papers.

'Who was that?' Neil said.

'Someone selling double-glazing,' Isabel said, sidling up to stand next to him. 'I've forgotten to get anything for pudding,' she said in an undertone. 'I'm just going to pop out to the supermarket, OK?'

'I thought you'd done apple crumble.'

'It went wrong,' she whispered, hoping he wouldn't think to look in the fridge. 'And I haven't got enough apples to make another.'

'What's the problem, Neil?' Moira said.

'Nothing,' he said, automatically covering for her. 'Isabel just needs to go out for a bit.' He tilted his head at her, telling her to go. Feeling horribly guilty, Isabel escaped from the house.

It had started to rain by the time she had parked. Patrick was sitting with an espresso inside the Italian café opposite the bookshop. He looked up and smiled at her. 'Can I get you a coffee? No,' he stopped himself, 'you'll want a tea. You see, I do notice.' He went up to the counter and ordered. 'Would you like something to eat? A *palmieri*? Or a *bombalone*—that's an Italian sort of doughnut; they're very good.'

'No thanks,' Isabel took off her mac and draped it over the back of her chair. Patrick brought over her tea and she had a moment of déjà vu. Of course, she remembered, Patrick bringing over the drinks that first time in the pub, when he'd kissed her. That had been the beginning of everything. It came to her then that this might be the end of everything, that this might be what he wanted to talk to her about.

What had he said? 'No regrets, no falling in love, no tears when we part.' Well, she could manage the last part. She sat up straight.

Patrick settled next to her. 'There's a *pasticceria* round the corner from Santa Maria del Popolo in Rome that makes marvellous *bombalone*. I used to go with my mother, the first year I was with her.'

'I can't stay long,' she said.

'No.' He reached out and took her hand, his thumb stroking hers. They sat in silence, while the staff greeted other customers. The man sitting on the next table turned the pages of the weekend papers in a flurry of newsprint. He seemed vaguely familiar to Isabel, but he disappeared from her mind as she stared at Patrick's hand holding hers.

'When I was a child, it always seemed to be raining, just like this,' he said, looking at the window where the condensation had made rivulets down the inside. 'I hate the English weather. Here we are, end of October, it's pissing down, and there's probably another six months of it to come.' He sipped his coffee. 'I'm thinking of moving back to Italy.'

Isabel was so surprised she could have fallen off her chair. 'When?'

'I don't know. Soon, possibly. It depends.'

'On Victoria?'

'Partly.' His voice was so soft Isabel had to lean forwards to hear him. 'I was so angry with you at that stupid dinner party. I still am angry.'

'Why? What did I do?'

'Nothing. Everything. You were beautiful and desirable and married to someone else. It's funny, but I've never minded before, never felt bothered by sharing. That side of it is usually dead anyway within the first few years of marriage.' He looked at her directly. 'But you seemed to be very much a couple.'

'You know that . . . . We've already talked about this,' she said.

Patrick drained his coffee cup and spoke briskly. 'I could stay here and marry Victoria. She's good-looking, rich and for some strange reason, keen to marry me. She thinks that she can change me.'

'And can she?'

'No.' It was a bald statement, spoken so flatly that Isabel knew it was true. He paused, cleared his throat. 'Someone else could though.'

He paused and she wondered if he meant her. But after the dinner party that seemed unlikely.

'Anyway, she wants to move to the Midlands, which is where her family come from. I want to give up the business: it's not making any money and I hate dealing with clients. Victoria will support me while I look around for something else to do. Rather a modern arrangement, don't you think?' His voice was harsh.

'And the alternative?' Isabel whispered.

'The alternative is to move to Rome. My mother's current husband wants to start exporting into the US; he could use an English-speaking partner. I could try it out, see if I liked it.'

'It sounds a bit uncertain.'

'Life's more fun without a safety net.' He grinned at her, his eyes teasing. Then he shrugged. 'But I have a flat in Rome. I could move there, sell up here and live off the capital for a while. What do you think?'

'Me?'

'Yes, you. What do you think?'

'I think,' Isabel said slowly. 'I think I'd hate to be Victoria.'

'D'you think she'd be unhappy? Mmm. Possibly.'

'You really are a shit sometimes. Don't you think of anyone else's feelings?' She felt on the edge of tears. 'Look, I must go. I've got to get back.'

'Don't go yet.'

'Why not?'

'I haven't said . . . I haven't told you . . . I don't find this sort of thing easy, Isabel. Talking about things. I've been very happy these last weeks with you. Happier than I can remember.' His hand shook as he picked up his coffee cup. 'I'm good at taking. Take and you don't get hurt.' He smiled at her and her heart melted. 'It's asking that's hard.'

She clasped her hands in front of her to stop herself from touching him. 'What do you want to ask me?'

'I want you to leave Neil. I want you to leave Neil and come to Rome with me.' He sat very still. 'Will you? Will you come with me?'

Eight

ISABEL AND NEIL stood waving goodbye to Moira and Ian. Neil had one arm around Isabel as they stood in the doorway of their suburban house, with their two children in front of them. The perfect family. Except instead of stormy skies and sodden leaves in the street, the mother was seeing blue skies and grapevines.

'Well, that's that,' Neil said. 'I think they enjoyed themselves.'

Isabel was jolted back to raining reality. 'Do you think so? All your mother does is complain.'

'She likes complaining,' he said. 'Gives her something to think about apart from Dad's health.' They went inside and Neil offered to give Isabel a hand clearing up.

The detritus of Sunday lunch was stacked in the kitchen. Isabel started to fill the dishwasher. She worked quickly, wanting to get upstairs and be on her own. What was she to do about Patrick? Rome sounded exciting, but terribly hand-to-mouth. If she took the children it would mean giving them the same sort of childhood she'd had. Neil stripped the remaining meat off the roast chicken and put it in a dish.

'I find them difficult too, you know,' he said. 'It's not just you.'

Isabel looked up, amazed. She had never heard Neil utter a word of criticism about his parents before. 'But they're always saying how wonderful you are.'

'All those digs about the business.' He covered the dish with foil.

'Your father's business? I didn't think you had anything to do with it.'

'Exactly. But I was supposed to take it over. Fourth generation and all that. Got to keep it in the family. So when I said no . . . The irony is that Heather would have jumped at the chance, but it didn't cross the old man's mind to ask his daughter. So he sold up instead.'

Isabel frowned. 'I don't remember this. When was it?'

'When you were expecting Michael. They'd assumed we'd come home when we had children.'

'You didn't tell me.' Isabel couldn't believe that he would have kept such a thing secret.

'I was worried you might want to come back.'

'It's like you've got a secret life.'

'Don't be ridiculous.' He shoved the dish in the fridge and slammed the door shut. 'I'm not sure coming back was a good idea,' he said abruptly. 'Life's more complicated here.'

And how, thought Isabel. Then she became wary. Did he know something about Patrick? 'In what way?' she said as casually as possible.

'Things. People. We seemed happier abroad. Things were settled.'

'Perhaps too settled.'

'Maybe.' Neil looked at the floor.

'I know you don't like me working—' she started to say, picking her words carefully, but Neil cut across her.

'Someone said something about that man the other day. They said he has a dreadful reputation.'

'Which man?' She knew what he was going to say before he said it.

'Your boss. Patrick Sherwin.'

'Oh, him,' Isabel said as if she knew thousands of men with dreadful reputations. To her surprise she was completely calm and in control of herself. 'Yes, I've heard that too. Who was it who said it to you?'

'It doesn't matter; it was just in passing. I'm sorry, I shouldn't have said anything.' He looked so guilty that she felt sorry for him.

'I don't mind, really. He does have a dreadful reputation.' I bet it was George, she thought. It's the sort of thing he'd do. 'Patrick's going out with Victoria. You met her, remember? At Helen and George's.'

'I know.'

'There you are then.' She looked around the tidy kitchen. 'That's about it here. I've got a slight headache; I think I'm going to have a lie down.' She left the kitchen and went upstairs, adrenaline starting to pump into her system. She fell onto the bed. It was true she had a headache, her brain bulged with information: Neil with secrets, Neil asking about Patrick, Patrick asking her to go to Rome with him.

Rome. She'd had fantasies about going off to Italy with Patrick, but she had never really thought he would ask her. Did he love her? Last week she would have said not. But now? She remembered him that morning, his hand trembling as he asked her to go with him.

She stretched out, feeling her toes spread out, her fingers extend. Her body felt strong, tight around the middle, muscles firm from swimming. She closed her eyes thinking of the moment, that first time, when she had wrapped her legs round him and pulled him in deeper. It had been good. No, more than that. Wonderful. The physical side of her affair with Patrick would be hard to give up if she stayed behind. But if she went with him, the physical side might dwindle, as it had with Neil. And if it did, what was left? I hardly know Patrick, she thought. All we have in common is sex. She shut her eyes remembering his face, lined with anxiety, as he asked her to go to Rome. It had cost him a lot to ask. Perhaps he did love her.

And then there was Neil. Steady, reliable Neil who had kept a secret from her for nearly ten years. A bubble of resentment floated into her brain, jostling for space with all the other thoughts and emotions.

She sat on the edge of the bed. If she went now she could catch one of the swimming-pool lane sessions.

The pool was not busy. As she swam she turned the arguments over in her mind. You're safe. Neil doesn't know. Finish it now and it'll be as if it had never happened. I can't give him up, she wanted to cry. But was it Patrick or the sex that she couldn't give up? Perhaps she could find what she wanted in Neil. Take the initiative, show him what she liked. If I stay with Neil I know what I'll be doing every day from here to the grave. Then make more of a life for yourself outside the house. Forget

Patrick. I can't forget him, a small voice wailed in her head. I want him. But what about the children? You can't leave the children. They can come with me. It'll be fun. A new country, yes, but a European one. A new father, one who says he doesn't want children, a man of whom you know nothing except for the way he makes you feel.

She swam until the last possible moment. Everybody else had gone; for a few minutes she had the pool to herself. The only sounds were the gentle slap, slap of water on the tiled sides. She rolled onto her back and floated, arms and legs outstretched, mind clear of all thought.

Over half term Isabel arranged to walk with Helen and the children in the arboretum. The leaves made a scarlet and orange carpet of the ground. 'They'll be too old for this, soon,' Isabel said suddenly, watching Michael sprint and catch his sister, then dart off again in a swoosh of fallen leaves.

'Oh, no, don't say that,' Helen said. 'I hate the way children have to grow up so quickly nowadays.'

Isabel stood up. 'Shall we make a move? It gets dark so early now, and I'm freezing. Let's have tea at my house.'

They called to the children and started to make their way to the car park. Isabel kicked at the leaves with each step, making little puffs and flurries of action. If it weren't half term, she would have been in the house with Patrick. All week she had been thinking about life with Neil and Patrick. Rome was impossible, of course. She couldn't leave Neil. Or could she? Swish, swish, went the leaves on the path.

Helen was agitating over whether Rufus would pass Common Entrance. Isabel hardly listened, but watched Michael dashing about, twisting and turning to escape outstretched arms. He ran towards her, clasped his arms around her and leaned into her, head on her chest. Isabel hugged him, awash with maternal feelings. And then he was off with a shout. 'Race you round the lake!' and the two boys hared off, splitting up and running in different directions on the encircling path.

'Boys! I don't know where they get all that energy from,' Helen said.

'We feed them too much, I expect,' Isabel murmured absently. She wanted to be left alone with her thoughts, trying to work out what to do. It was confusing being different people, reconciling the woman she was with Patrick to the mother she was to her children. By sleeping with Patrick she had added another dimension to her life. An exciting, dangerous dimension for sure, but her life was the same. Perhaps the time had come to move on, do something mad.

What would she do in Rome? It would probably be easy to find work

as a TEFL teacher. She could teach privately and help Patrick with whatever he was doing. The trouble was that all this sounded ordinary, and
she had no experience of Patrick and ordinary. They had never shared a
takeaway in front of a video. Could Patrick change a tyre or mend a
fuse? Perhaps Patrick didn't do 'ordinary'. Once she had given up the
safety net of Neil, there would be no going back.

So, a very different life in yet another new country, and possibly—no,
probably—insecure financially. A life like her childhood. It hadn't been
ideal, but then whose childhood was? A stable and secure home for my
children, she had promised herself then. But it was silly to let yourself
be swayed by a childish vow.

'I couldn't leave the children,' she'd said in the café and Patrick had
said she could bring them. Patrick, the man who had made it very clear
that he didn't want children, had no interest in children. Had he hesitated before saying they could come too? It was hard to remember, she
was so agitated at the time. But why would he want to take on another
man's children? Come to that, would Neil let her take the children
away? She couldn't leave them. She thought about Patrick's mother.
She'd left her little boy. Could Isabel do the same? She stamped her feet,
but the fallen leaves muffled the noise. Katie and Millie trotted ahead of
her on the path.

'There's the bonfire party coming up. And soon it'll be Christmas,'
Helen offered.

'Christmas!' The thought appalled her. Life was being doled out in a
series of school holidays and events: Christmas, Easter, half term. She
felt like Katie's hamster, running for its life on a tiny treadmill that was
getting smaller every year. Was this the price of a stable childhood?

She screwed her eyes up, and when she opened them she saw Rufus
loitering ahead, at the point where the path that circled the lake joined
with the path to the car park. 'Where's Michael?' she called to him.

Rufus shrugged. 'Dunno.'

'What do you mean, "Dunno"?' She walked faster, past the girls, and
up to the boy. 'Where is he?'

'He raced me round the lake,' he said, pointing to the far side. Isabel
strained to conjure up Michael's figure, but couldn't see it. The path
looped into a small shrubbery. Drat, Isabel thought. 'Sorry, Helen. I
expect he's hiding in the shrubbery waiting to jump out at us. I'll go
round and get him.' She set off briskly thinking, if I call him, he'll only
sit tight, so I'll let him jump out at me.

The shrubbery was very still. Isabel walked through, expecting at any
moment to be leapt on with bloodcurdling yells. But the rhododendrons

and laurels remained undisturbed. She turned and walked back, calling out this time. The walk became a run as panic grew in her.

'Found him?' Helen's face was anxious.

Isabel shook her head, not wanting to say the word no.

'Maybe he's gone to the cars?'

Isabel half walked, half ran up the path to the car park. No sign of him there. She ran back to the others.

'Not there.'

Helen patted her arm. 'Don't worry. He'll be around, somewhere.'

They walked back, calling his name. '*Michael! Michael!*' The sound reverberated around the trees, bouncing off the surface of the lake.

'He can swim OK?' Helen said softly.

'Like a frog.' Isabel looked at the reeds around the edge, reeds that even a competent swimmer could get entangled with. But the lake wasn't deep, everybody knew that. 'A child can drown in a few inches of water' popped into her head.

'He must be hiding,' Helen said firmly. 'There's nowhere else he could have gone. Don't worry.' She put her arm round Isabel's shoulders and gave her a quick hug. 'We'll find him.' She bent down to Rufus.

'Rufus, when you were running round the lake, did you see anyone? Or hear a car? It's really important.'

'Maybe a car.' Isabel's heart froze. Rufus screwed up his face with effort, trying to squeeze out something helpful.

'I didn't hear a car when we were walking.' Helen hesitated, then turned to Isabel. 'Did you?'

'No.' I was too wrapped up in my own stupid thoughts to be paying attention to what Michael was doing. She could feel panic rising in her throat and put her hand over her mouth to keep it in. This can't be happening, this isn't happening. Please, don't let this happen.

'You go and check the car park again. I'll go back to where we were sitting.' She meant to walk calmly, but her feet broke into a run. The light was closing in and the shrubbery looked menacing. She ran on into the clearing, reached the bench where they had sat. Michael wasn't there. She started to run back, heart thumping. She saw herself talking to the police, then pleading for Michael's safe return. Another missing child, another headline. How long had it been since he had disappeared? Ten minutes? Fifteen? This isn't happening. Past the lake, the surface a dark glass reflecting the looming trees behind, back to the hedge where the others huddled in a small group.

'Any luck?'

Isabel shook her head, out of breath, gulping down the cold air. She hugged herself, clutched at her sides as if trying to stop herself fraying as the world disintegrated around her.

'We need to get help,' Helen said. 'I don't have a mobile. Do you?'

Isabel shook her head again. 'No. Perhaps we can call from the village.' She said it reluctantly. Stay where you last saw your mother and she will come and find you, that's what they always said to children. But she had to leave. She felt in her pocket for her car keys when—

'Yah!' Michael leapt out from behind the tree trunk and jumped at her back. She spun round, clutching her heart.

'Oh! Michael!' The shock of seeing him, the relief, made her knees buckle. He danced in front of her, delighted with himself.

'I got you, I got you!'

Isabel's arm swung back and clouted him across the side of his head. 'Don't you ever do that to me again,' she shouted. 'Don't you dare.' Then she grabbed him to her and hugged him, ashamed of her violence. 'I'm sorry, I'm sorry,' she murmured. 'I was so worried. I thought . . . I thought . . .' His body was compact, so precious, the only thing that mattered. She started to cry, sobbing into his anorak. Crying because he was with her, in her arms and safe, and crying because, in losing Michael, she had found the answer to Patrick's question.

Isabel spooned the cake mixture into two tins, smoothed the surface and put them in the oven. She cleared the utensils away, running a finger round the mixing bowl to take the last smears of mixture. Uncooked cake tasted nicer than cooked cake, she thought, but you couldn't eat as much. Still, millions of calories with every lick. She'd weighed herself that morning and discovered that she'd lost nearly a stone. It must be the swimming—swimming and sex.

It's funny, she thought, but the more I have to do, the less I need to eat. It occurred to her that she wouldn't have a job any more. Not that working for Patrick could count as a proper job, as she hadn't been paid. His cheque, written in anger, was still folded in her purse. I should get a proper job, a real one. Or maybe I should do a degree. History? English Literature? She loved reading, devouring classic novels as a child then rediscovering them as an adult.

She put the kitchen scales away. She considered the balance: Patrick, sex and excitement on one side, Neil, Michael and Katie on the other. In her heart she knew that there wasn't any contest, but she toyed with the idea of shifting the weights around to make the decision more clear-cut. The children couldn't go onto Patrick's side, but could sex and excitement go onto Neil's side?

'I wondered where you were.' Neil stuck his head round the door.

'Making cake.'

'I'll look forward to that. You haven't made cakes for ages.' He leaned against the edge of the table, looking genuinely pleased at the prospect.

'I felt like trying again.' Isabel filled the kettle with water, more to give herself something to do than from any overwhelming desire to make tea. Her overwhelming desire was for something quite different. It had been over a week since she'd been at Patrick's house. Could she show Neil what she wanted? She looked sideways at him. The children were still watching the video they'd hired as the solution to entertainment on a wet Saturday afternoon.

'Fed up with the ants?' she said.

'I expect you need a really wide screen to see the animation properly. Still, it's keeping the children happy.'

She went past him to get milk from the fridge, lightly brushing against him on purpose. She wasn't sure if he had noticed. He seemed very masculine. Very different to Patrick's smoothness.

'Neil, the catch of my necklace seems to be caught in my hair. Can you look?' She turned her back to him, lifting her hair up and exposing the nape of her neck. She felt slightly guilty, as if she was betraying Patrick. But excited too, and her breath quickened.

'Seems fine.'

'Are you sure?' She leaned back slightly so their bodies were close.

'Yes.' His voice was more alert. She twisted around and kissed him, rubbing her aching body against his. She licked the base of his throat, salty to the tip of her tongue. A real person, known yet strange. The strangeness was exciting. They kissed, more urgently, losing awareness of their surroundings, concentrating on being together, now.

'Touch me,' she murmured. His hand was tentative so she pushed herself harder at him. 'Like this.' She reached down and felt him hard, wanting her, heard him sigh as she clasped him firmly. He pulled away.

'Upstairs.'

Hand in hand they sneaked up the stairs and into their bedroom. They fell onto the bed, clothes scattered around the floor, hands touching, stroking, probing, mouths joined, sharing breathing, gasping. He slipped his fingers inside, and she yelped with surprise and pleasure, for it was unusual for Neil to touch her like that. Wordlessly he slipped into her and she opened for him, and for a moment they were still, caught on the moment, the rightness of what was happening. Then he started to move. She shifted her position in the bed, as Patrick had taught her, bringing him deeper, making him move faster and faster, as she lost all sense of self, of time, just alive to the sensations that were juddering over her, making her cry out as if in pain, awash with love.

They lay, their faces inches apart, arms round each other, skin glowing. Eyes fixed on each other, clear blue examining brown depths, searching and finding answers to unspoken questions. Gradually the world reasserted itself, outside noises returning, a child's voice calling. Reluctantly, they returned to the mundane life of getting dressed. But not without giggles as they remembered what they had done.

Isabel took her cake from the oven, a little too brown, but not much. At teatime they sat round the table, mother, father, munching children, boy, girl, lovers. Now and again Neil and Isabel's eyes would meet, sharing secret smiles. What's so funny? the children kept asking, and Neil and Isabel would smile again and say happily, nothing. It's nothing.

Isabel posted the video through the letterbox of the video store, hearing it drop onto the mat with a clunk. Now it had gone she had to face up to her decision. Yesterday it had seemed clear. Her place was with Neil. But now she had to tell Patrick of her decision. She wished he would vanish into thin air so she could pretend it had never happened. But he was all too real. She had seen this happen to women getting divorced. Having ditched their irritating husbands they breathed a sigh of relief, thinking that they could move on and leave the wreckage behind them. But ex-husbands were not like flotsam and jetsam, floating away on the tides, they had their own agendas, their own grievances. Grievances to be vociferously aired until civilised behaviour degenerated into bitterness.

But we have no shared history to squabble over, she argued, trying to convince herself that there was no reason to fear Patrick's reaction. He has Victoria and we're grown-up. She'd never felt particularly grown-up. It was Neil who'd been the grown-up, she realised, letting her remain a child. She didn't think Patrick was very grown-up either. He'd said 'no tears when we part', but she knew he fully expected that it would be him who would be doing the dumping, not her.

Earlier, before anyone was up, she'd written him a letter. Should she drive to the house now and knock on the door? Or slip it silently through the letterbox? She bit the side of her thumbnail. What to do? She felt stupid, standing in the street umming and ahhing, so she got in the car, and stuck the key in the ignition.

It would help if she knew whether he would be in or not, she thought. If she knew he was out, she could knock on the door and then, when he didn't respond, drop the letter off and drive away fast with a clear conscience. Clear-ish, anyway. But if he was in . . . He might be angry. Worse, he might take no notice of her, and stop her talking with a 'Don't be stupid, woman', then screw her. And if he did, she wasn't sure that she could withstand his confidence.

No, she didn't want to see him alone inside the house. But it seemed so awful to write, a coward's way out. Don't be silly, she told herself. The reason it seems bad is that it gives the other person no chance to respond. And that's what you want, isn't it? No comeback. She glanced at her watch. He often went away at weekends, she knew. Perhaps he was with Victoria. Even if he were at the house, he probably wouldn't be up yet. She slid the car into gear and drove off.

The house looked deserted, curtains closed at the upstairs windows. She parked and looked around but couldn't see his car. She stepped up the path, tapped the front door softly. Nothing. Either asleep, or not there. She slipped back to the car and read her letter through.

Sunday morning

Dear Patrick,

I've been thinking really hard over half term and have decided that I can't come with you to Rome. I can't leave the children, and I can't take them with me. So I must stay here and make the best of things. I expect you'll be angry, but hope you can forgive me. You told me from the start, no regrets, and we both knew it was never going to last. I've had a wonderful time but I can't risk the children's happiness. It's too high a price to pay for my own.

Love, Isabel

She found a pen gathering dust in the footwell and crossed out the sentence about it being too high a price to pay for her own happiness. If she made the break it had to be final. Patrick mustn't know how difficult it was for her to leave him. She read the letter again and as she did so, she remembered her father saying, be careful what you put in writing.

She tore the letter up. Scrabbling around the car she found a piece of paper. She paused, then started to write.

Sunday morning

Dear Patrick

I came over to tell you in person, but you're not in so I'm writing this letter. Please forgive the grotty paper and biro. I have decided that, due to family commitments, I can no longer work for you. I'm sorry to leave you in the lurch, but I'm sure you'll find someone else soon.

I'm giving no notice in lieu of wages.

With best wishes, Isabel Freeman

It would have to do. At the door she hesitated for a second. Was this right? What she wanted? She pushed the note through quickly. There. It was gone. Too late to change her mind. As she got back in the car she felt light-headed. It was good to have made the decision.

Nine

THE EUPHORIA of Sunday morning had vanished by Monday morning. She spent the day in a state of anxiety, fearing for Patrick's phone call. In town, she walked nervously along the pavement, expecting to see him emerge and accost her. Sick with nerves, she loitered in the bookshop, watching out of the shop window to see if he went into the Italian café opposite. She realised the man at the till was watching her, presumably because he thought she looked shifty. Flustered, she bought a book called *Rekindling the Passion: Rediscovering the Joys of Marital Sex*, blushing slightly as the man at the till gave her a sideways look.

On Tuesday, when she should have been at work, she started writing the Christmas round robin they sent every year to friends. She struggled for a while with anodyne phrases before giving up. Instead, she read the book she had bought and tried rekindling the passion, or rather, tried kindling with Neil the passion she'd had with Patrick. Neil now seemed wary of her advances, almost embarrassed, as if that Saturday afternoon had been an aberration. He did what he usually did and seemed thrown when she tried whispering suggestions or showing him what she liked. After her second attempt she gave up and they each retreated to their own side of the bed.

She thought of Patrick a lot. He would be angry when he got the letter. She kept thinking about him being angry, anger turning to passion.

By Friday she had got used to feeling sick when the phone rang, and fed up with agonising about whether to pick it up. It rang again and she realised she was bored with jangling nerves. She picked it up.

'Yup? Oh, Mary. Hi.' She listened to Mary reminding her about the bonfire party. She had to admit, she had forgotten completely.

'I hear you're not working for Patrick any more.'

'No.' Her hand gripped the phone, as she thought back to Mary coming round to Patrick's house. 'It just didn't work out.' There was a slight pause.

'Well. See you tonight,' was all Mary said. 'Don't be late.'

'We mustn't be late,' Isabel said, bundling the children into layers of coats and sweaters. She nipped back into the kitchen to collect her car keys and checked Katie's note was still there for Neil.

Dear Daddy we have gone to the bonfire party. Here is a tikket for you if you get home in time.
    Love Katie. XXXXXXXXXXXXX

The children, excited about being out in the dark, chattered in high-pitched voices as she drove. The children's excitement was infectious, and Isabel felt it too, even though the weather was threatening rain.

Isabel's wasn't the only car in the car park but she was one of the first. She presented herself at the classroom they used as HQ on Bonfire Night. 'I'm here. Where are the sparklers?'

Justine detached herself from a group fussing over the heated trolleys.

'In this box. And the matches are here. Mary's got all the float money.' Isabel crammed as many packets of sparklers and matches as she could into her basket and went outside. The children had joined Rufus, Millie and Rachel and several others and were running about, bodies criss-crossing the dark lawn. She called Katie and Michael to her.

'They'll be lighting the bonfire soon. And then the fireworks will be in half an hour. Be careful. Here's some money for hot dogs and sweets. Rufus's mother is dishing up; she'll help you. Please watch out for Katie, Michael. I'll be wandering around outside but if you miss me, go into the classroom where the food is.'

She gave them a packet of sparklers each and lit the first. They streaked off up the lawn towards the top field, sparks of light emitting from their sparklers so they resembled boisterous Tinkerbells.

Car headlights started to flash up the track to the car park. Isabel sold sparklers to children and parents; children wrote their names in sparkler fire; parents talked loudly, fuelled by mulled wine, while their children ran wild. The bonfire blazed. The first firework went up, a large rocket that exploded into a chrysanthemum head of green petals, and everybody oohed.

Isabel sold the last of her sparklers to the crowd in the top field, and, standing alone in the cold night air, felt torn between watching the rest of the fireworks display or continuing her duty by trudging all the way down to the school building to collect fresh supplies.

Reluctantly she started to walk down. The darkness pressed in on her, making her stumble, and the money she had taken nearly fell out of the basket. As she passed the cedar of Lebanon, part of the trunk detached itself and turned into a figure, making her jump.

'God, you gave me a shock,' she said, hand on heart.

'I didn't mean to make you jump.' A rocket exploded and flooded Patrick's face with lurid green light. 'Mary told me you'd be here.' His voice was steady, but in the brief flash of light she saw that his face was set in deep lines. Then all was darkness again.

'What do you want?' She could hear the fear in her voice.

'Why, you, of course. What else would I want here?' He took a step towards her and involuntarily she stepped back. There are hundreds of people all around me, she thought. There's no danger.

'You can't have me.' She said, trying to make her voice cool. 'I'm not available.'

'Aren't you?' he said, his voice almost purring as he came closer.

'No. Not any more. I told you, in my letter.'

'Ah, yes, that charming document.' He was close now. She'd always loved his voice. 'Do you know, I don't believe you.'

'What do you mean?' Run, her mind screamed at her. Run.

'I think you are available.' He removed the basket from her hands and his hands cupped her face. She tried to keep her body stiff and unyielding as he kissed her, keeping her lips clamped shut. But she could feel herself responding. He steered her back to the tree and leaned against her, pinning her down with his weight, while one hand undid her coat and fumbled with her clothes, yanking her underwear down.

'No,' she said, twisting away from him. 'I don't want . . .'

'But you do.'

'Oh God, no.' Involuntarily her back arched, body trained to respond to him. Her breathing was heavy and she turned her head, battling inwardly with the reactions his fingers were bringing. 'Please . . .' she said, and she didn't know if she meant please, no or please, yes.

He was undoing his zip. She had to stop. Had to. 'No,' she moaned.

'But you want me to.' His voice buzzed close to her ear. 'They won't be finished for another ten minutes. No one will catch you.' He settled himself between her legs, hands on her hips, ready to take her. If I do this now I am lost, she thought, and in reaction cried out.

'No. I said no.' She jerked herself away from him.

He grabbed at her, missed and swore. Seizing her chance she ran for the school, feet stumbling, hobbled by her clothes. The classroom lights were on and she could see the committee chatting. She headed for the side of the building, which was in total darkness. She ducked behind a bay window and crouched down. If he found her she would not be able to break away from him again. She felt her body was imprinted with Patrick, like the after-image left by the sparklers. Her breathing slowly returned to normal. Voices started talking nearby, getting louder, and she guessed that the display had ended. If Patrick had been looking for her he must have given up.

She stood up slowly, adjusted her clothes. Her skirt was rucked up, tights torn. They would be hidden under her coat. Isabel retraced her way, back to the party, and realised that Mary was drawing the raffle.

'Mum, Mum, where've you been?' Michael came zooming out of the crowd, followed closely by Katie. 'Where are our tickets?'

'Oh. In my pocket, I think. Hang on.' He jiggled up and down while she felt in her coat pockets. Isabel felt very stupid and slow, as if her hands were disconnected from her brain. 'There.' She took out several strips of blue paper, which he snatched from her hand.

'Blue, thirty-six. They've had that.' Michael grabbed her wrist and pulled. 'Come on.' He pushed through the crowd heading for Mary, Isabel following meekly. 'Sorry,' she kept saying as she bashed into people. Her legs didn't seem to work properly. 'Sorry.'

Michael marched straight up to Mary. 'Excuse me,' he said politely. 'But my mum's got blue, thirty-six.'

Mary turned with a smile. 'Blue, thirty-six? Yes, it did win something. It'll have been set aside for you, in there.' She indicated the classroom.

Michael's face lit up and he rushed off to see.

'Thank you, Mary,' Isabel said. She took Katie's hand and they went through to the classroom. Michael was standing by a small table laden with boxes and bottles of whisky, and beside him was a man. A man with a basket on his arm. Isabel stopped dead on the doorstep.

Katie pushed past her. 'What is it? What have we won?'

Isabel followed her with reluctant steps.

'Here it is!' Michael's voice was triumphant. He waved a small wooden box around. 'Look, Mum.' He turned to her. 'What is it?'

Patrick looked at her, his face tinged with triumph. Isabel walked up to Michael and took the box, turning it over.

'Cigarillos,' she answered. 'They're little cigars.'

'Very useful.' Patrick's voice was sardonic.

'I'm sure they will be. Come along, children.'

'So these are your children?'

'Yes.' She took Katie's hand. 'Come on, Michael.'

'I should have guessed they were yours.' Patrick crouched down so he was Katie's height. 'Pretty,' he said. 'Like her mother.' He stood up. He was very close to her.

'Michael, come now,' Isabel called, failing to keep anger from her voice. Michael reluctantly came to her, clutching his box of cigarillos.

'May I see?' Patrick held out his hand, and Michael handed them to him. 'Do you know who I am?' Michael shook his head. 'Your mother works for me. My name's Patrick, and you are?'

'Michael.' They shook hands, Michael's hand looking small and trusting in Patrick's.

'Michael, we're going. Now.' Isabel set off, dragging Katie with her, praying that Michael would follow. She walked fast up the path that led to the car park. She heard footsteps and panting behind, and then Michael was with her.

'Last one to the car is a big fat twit,' he shouted, and he and Katie took off into the darkness. They were leaning against the car when Isabel arrived. She unlocked it and they scrambled in. She was about to get in herself, when she heard Patrick's voice.

'You forgot this.' He was holding out the basket.

'Stop following me.' She shut the door so the children couldn't hear.

'You might say thank you.'

'What for?'

'Why, returning this of course.'

'I wouldn't have lost it if it hadn't been for you.' She took the basket and started to get in, but he stretched his arm across the door.

'You shouldn't have run away from me.'

'You practically raped me,' she whispered angrily.

He laughed. 'You want me as much as I want you.'

'Go away. Just go away.' She pushed past his arm and got into the car. Her hands were trembling and it took two attempts to get the key into the ignition and accelerate away from the school.

Neil was at home when they got back.

'Had a good time?' he called from in front of the television.

The children ran in to greet him while Isabel hung back. The phone rang and she answered it without thinking.

'I must see you.' Patrick said.

'No. Leave me alone.' But she didn't hang up.

'Don't be so melodramatic. I just think we should talk.'

'There's nothing to talk about.'

'You know there is. It's not fair to leave me like this. I asked you to come to me, offered you everything I have, and you sent me that letter. I think you owe me some explanation. Let's meet up for lunch and talk.'

'I go swimming at lunchtimes.'

'Not every day, surely? We could go to the pub if you like.' His voice continued, seductive and low. 'I never took you out to lunch properly when we were together. Let me do it now. You owe me that much.'

'I owe you nothing after tonight.' She made her voice harsh.

'I'm sorry. I thought you wanted to as much as I did.'

He paused, and she knew she ought to say, no, you're mistaken. But the words wouldn't come.

'The house seems empty without you,' he said. 'I miss you.'

I miss you too, she thought. Despite everything, despite her decision.

'Let's be friends. Let's not end badly, not like tonight.'

'All right.' Her voice was little more than a whisper. 'But not the pub.'

'No, that's fine. What about that new place in town? Bentham's. Tomorrow? At twelve thirty?'

She swallowed. 'Just to say goodbye properly. Nothing more.'

Isabel drove past Bentham's, looking for a parking space. She passed Patrick's car and felt a stab of recognition. A few cars on there was a space and she reversed into it. She checked her make-up in the mirror. Her eyes were bright, cheeks flushed like a woman going to meet her lover. She examined herself more closely. Low-cut cardigan, no shirt underneath so it clung to her breasts, worn with a wrap-around skirt. Dressed for action. She closed her eyes. Who was she kidding? This wasn't to say goodbye, this was to start up all over again. She had even arranged for the children to go to Helen's house for tea that evening so she could dawdle over lunch. Dawdle all the way to bed.

I've made my decision, and it's the right one, she thought. I must stick to it. I can't leave the children, and the children need to stay here, so I have to stay here. Going to Rome with Patrick is impossible. But it's what you want, her internal voice answered. To be with him, starting out again, the excitement.

I am addicted to him, she thought. And he was waiting for her. She had only to get out of the car and go to him. The alternative was cold turkey. Hard, but not impossible. I have to get away, she thought. She started the car and shot off, heart pumping. A sign to the station caught her eye and she turned into the road and parked.

'When's the next train?'

'Where to?'

'Anywhere.' The ticket man looked at her as if she was mad.

'The Intercity to London should be here in five minutes.'

'Fine. A cheap day return please.'

426

Isabel aimlessly trawled down Knightsbridge looking in shop windows. There was so much stuff. She stood looking at a red bias-cut dress, head on one side. Now she had lost some weight and had firmed up it might look good. It was certainly different from everything else she had.

She went into the shop and tried the dress on. She looked sexy in the dress but what was the point when you can't have sex with the man you lust after? It was so unfair. She loved Neil, but it was . . . safe. She wanted more.

She sat down on a little stool, the red dress swirling round her. Her hair frizzed out in a halo around her face. All that swimming's doing it no good, whatever it's doing to my body. Perhaps I should cut it all off.

'You all right?' An assistant stuck her head round the curtain. 'That looks good.'

'Yes.' Isabel sighed again. 'But when would I wear it?' What was the point of looking sexy, feeling sexy, when your husband didn't care?

'Pity.' The assistant withdrew with a shrug and a rattle of curtain rings.

Isabel slowly took off the dress and left the shop. She turned the corner into Sloane Street, thinking she'd walk down to Peter Jones. Her shaggy-haired reflection marched alongside her, past a hairdresser's. On impulse she turned in.

'Have you got a free appointment? Now?'

The receptionist looked surprised. 'I'll check the book. Let's see.' She ran a perfectly manicured finger over the appointments book. 'I suppose Karl could do you a cut and blow-dry in about twenty minutes.'

'OK,' Isabel nodded, hoping her nerve would last. 'I'll wait here.' She was halfway through *House & Garden* when Karl collected her.

'And what can I do for you?' he asked, combing through her hair.

'I want it all off.'

'All of it?' He looked so horrified that Isabel backtracked.

'Well, perhaps not all. But most of it. I feel it's dragging me down.'

He started to play with her hair. 'Well, we could take the weight off here and here and . . .'

Isabel bounced up Sloane Street towards the tube station, watching her reflection bounce along with her, tossing its head and running its fingers through a mass of short curls. She felt as though a huge weight was off her shoulders, literally. She was light-headed and light-hearted, young, free and sexy.

At the entrance to the tube she hesitated and checked her watch. She had a few minutes to spare. She ran down to the shop.

'The red dress I tried on,' she panted. 'I'm going to take it.'

'Pretty Mummy!'

'Your hair. It looks amazing. Where did you go?'

Both Katie and Helen had been approving. Isabel had been a little nervous of Neil's reaction; after all, he had once said he would divorce her if she ever cut her hair, but he seemed to like it, walking round her, making appreciative noises.

'Just you wait until you see my new dress,' she promised. She chucked a ready-made meal from the freezer into the oven, then got the children to bed. She slipped on the red dress and sashayed over to Neil. She swung her leg over so she straddled him, hoicking the swirling skirt up over her thighs. Neil ran his hands up under her dress.

'What a sexy girl you are.' They kissed. It was like Saturday afternoon again. Perhaps this was the answer, not wait until they were in bed, laid out side by side like medieval effigies on a tomb, but catch him unawares, before his Protestant angst could react. The phone started ringing, and she pulled away from him.

'Let it ring. If it's important they'll call back,' Neil mumbled.

Isabel paused. The ringing tones were urgent. She knew it was Patrick. 'It's probably a wrong number,' she said.

'But I love this,' Isabel said, holding the dress up to her and hugging it.

'Is it your size?' Justine said.

'No.'

'Your colour?'

'I suppose not. Oh, all right, no.' Isabel pulled a face.

'Have you worn it in the last two years?'

'No.'

'Five years?'

'No.'

'Ten years?'

'Help. No. Can't I keep it just because I like it?'

'No.'

'Gosh, you're hard. I'm going to have nothing left.'

Justine sat down on the bed and leaned back on her elbows. 'Don't worry. You'll have less, but what you have will suit you and you'll wear it all the time. All I'm doing is getting rid of the clutter that drags you down and stops you seeing what you really do have.'

Isabel looked at the piles of clothes, some for charity, some destined for the dress agency. She flicked through the clothes left in the wardrobe. It was embarrassing how many clothes she had that had only been worn once, or sometimes not at all.

428

'You're not working for Patrick any more, I hear.' Justine's voice cut across her thoughts.

'No, that's right.' Isabel was glad Justine couldn't see her face. 'It was too much hassle and as I don't really need the money . . .' Her voice trailed away. What money? She had finally put Patrick's cheque into her bank account, where it had promptly bounced. She wished she'd torn it up instead.

'Is that your doorbell?' Justine said, her head turning.

Isabel frowned. 'Probably someone collecting for the RSPCA or something. Hang on, I'll be back in a second.' And she skipped down the stairs. First her hair had gone, now all those old clothes. Excess baggage, she thought. Got to get rid of it all. She opened the front door.

'Oh.'

Patrick stood in front of her. She had been so deliberately not thinking about him that to see him in the flesh was shocking. He looked equally surprised. 'What have you done to your hair?'

Without thinking she touched it. 'Cut it.'

'You look different.' He frowned. 'Older.'

'Thanks.' You look older too, she thought. His face was strained and for the first time she noticed lines of white in his hair.

'I didn't mean it like that. More sophisticated. It suits you.'

'What do you want?' She could feel her heart thumping.

'I don't want to discuss it in the street. Ask me in.'

'No. Go away.'

'That's not very friendly, is it?' He smiled at her as if she was welcoming him in. She caught the scent of stale alcohol. 'Don't you want to hear what I've got to say?'

'No. There's nothing to talk about,' she managed. 'Go away.'

'Make me.' His voice teased, but his eyes were hard. She suddenly thought of Justine upstairs, Justine possibly listening.

'We can't talk here,' she said quickly, trying to conjure up a way to be rid of him as soon as possible. 'Somewhere else. Wherever you like, I promise I'll be there.'

'I'm afraid it has to be here, right now. I don't want you standing me up again.'

Isabel bit her lip. She checked the front door was on the latch then stepped outside, closing the door behind her. 'Say what you have to say, right here, then bugger off.'

'So. On the doorstep it is.' His attitude changed from playful to businesslike. He pulled out of his jacket pocket a manila envelope. 'Now, what do you want?' he continued. 'You want your nice house, your nice children and your nice husband. It's all a little dull of course, so you also want a bit of excitement. A lover. But then your lover asks you to come away with him, and you discover that you're not really brave enough. Or, you don't love him enough.' He paused, but she wouldn't meet his eyes. 'But I think you do love him. I think that if he hadn't asked you to leave your husband you'd have been happy to carry on. Isn't that so?'

She looked at the path, refusing to answer him.

'Isabel. Forget Rome. If I stay here, will you come back to me?'

'I can't.'

'I'll ditch Victoria.'

'It doesn't work like that, Patrick,' she cried. 'I don't love you.'

He flinched. 'You're lying.'

She wanted to tell him about promising a stable home for the children, how she'd felt when Michael disappeared. She wanted to tell him how Neil had provided the safe haven she had needed. How all these things were intrinsic to her sense of self. But it was impossible.

'It's too late. I can't go back.'

'I see.' He licked his lips as if nervous. 'So, you think you can't have the lover and continue to have the nice house et cetera.'

'That's not what it's about.'

'No? I think you're wrong there, but we'll come to that later. Now, what does Neil want? Well, he wants the nice house scenario too, and he likes the idea of having his wife all to himself. Yes, the last thing he wants is to know he's having to share her with someone else.' He looked at her, his expression serious. 'Trust me, I'm a man, I know this. I don't want to share you either.'

Isabel's mouth felt dry. 'And what do you want?'

'Let me tell you what I don't want. I don't want to be stood up, I don't want to be dumped by a pathetic note, I don't want to be pissed around, I don't want to be treated as if I don't matter, as if I have no feelings.' His voice rose until he was almost shouting at her. 'I don't want any of this shit you've been giving me.' His face was contorted with rage.

Isabel pressed herself into the door. All she could think of to say was I'm sorry, which she didn't think would go down very well.

'So, what do you want?' Her eyes challenged his.

He took a few steps away from her, breathing heavily, gaining control over himself. Suddenly Isabel was really frightened. 'What I want is for you to come back to me, of course. If you are honest with yourself, it's what you want. All this,' he gestured at the house, 'however nice and cosy it is, is never going to be enough for you. You need more. If you had been happy you'd never have come to me at the start.'

'It is enough,' she cried. 'And there are other things.'

'Like what?'

'I could get a proper job. Or do a degree.'

Patrick snorted. He fingered the flap on the envelope. 'Don't lie to yourself; if it's not me it'll be someone else, sooner or later.'

'It won't.' He looked at her, one eyebrow raised in disbelief. 'I *am* happy, this is enough for me. I love Neil and I don't want anything more. I'm not coming back.'

'We'll see.'

'Is that it?' She couldn't believe that he was going to leave it at that and, strangely, felt almost disappointed.

'I had hoped that it wouldn't come to this.' With one hand he lifted her chin so she had to look him square in the face. 'I would never, never hurt you. You know that, don't you? But I can't let you destroy what we have. Here's the deal.' He pushed the envelope into her frozen fingers, then leaned close and whispered. 'Do you remember that little session we had with the camera, one rainy afternoon? That day when you loved me properly?' She could remember clearly, how she had felt gloriously sensual, and then giggling at the photographs with Patrick under the duvet before making love, excited by her audacity. 'I'm leaving a set of photographs here to remind you and I've got another set for me, which I really don't want to send to your husband. But if need be . . . You have a choice. Either your husband knows by, let's say, next Tuesday evening, or you're round at my place on Tuesday morning, just as before. Don't look so worried, darling. I'm making it easy for you. You get what you really want and you needn't feel guilty about it. Just blame it all on beastly Patrick.'

'You can't expect me to come back because you're blackmailing me?'

He stopped as if it hadn't occurred to him before to call it blackmail, and looked shamefaced, like Michael when he'd done something wrong. 'I don't want you to leave me,' he said after a pause.

'Isabel?' It was Justine's voice from inside the house. 'Hello?'

'I'll be with you in a minute,' Isabel called through the door. She turned back to Patrick. 'Tell me you won't do this.'

'Not if you come back to me.'

'Please go.' She pushed the front door open with a shaking hand.

'You'll be back,' she heard him say as she shut the door behind her.

'Isabel? Are you OK?' Justine was leaning over the landing banisters.

'Yes, fine,' Isabel said on autopilot. 'I'll be with you in a minute.'

She took the envelope through into the kitchen and took a quick look at the first photograph. Her legs gave way and she sat down abruptly.

SARAH DUNCAN

Justine peered round the door. Isabel shoved the photographs back into the envelope. 'Are you all right?' Justine's face was anxious.

'No. No, I'm not.' Isabel's lower lip quivered. 'I'm sorry. It's just—I've had a bit of a shock.' She buried the envelope in the rubbish bin, then turned round, hand over her mouth.

'Sit down.' Justine came and sat next to her, putting her hand on Isabel's shoulder. 'What's the matter? Was it someone at the door?'

'Yes.' Isabel opened her mouth, gave a hiccupping sort of gasp, and then began sobbing. She couldn't help herself, she cried and shook, the shock devastating her nervous system.

'Would you like to tell me about it? Would that help, mmm?'

'He says . . . he says . . . He says he's going to tell Neil unless . . .'

'Tell Neil what?' Justine's voice was soft but insistent.

'I've been having an affair with Patrick,' Isabel cried, 'but it's over and he says he's going to tell Neil unless I go back to him and I don't know what to do.'

'I see.' Justine's face seemed rigid. 'When did it start?'

'Beginning of term,' Isabel began, 'but I finished it over half term.'

'Do you love him?'

'Neil? Of course.'

'No. Patrick.'

'I don't know. It was so exciting, I couldn't think.' She remembered all at once exactly how well Justine knew Patrick. She wanted to ask Justine how it had ended, once Caro had found them, how Patrick had reacted. Instead she said simply, 'Do you think he'll tell?'

'Even if he does, Neil might not believe him.'

Isabel went scarlet. 'He's got evidence. Photographs.'

'Oh, Isabel. No. How could you?' Justine's face was a mixture of horror and glee. 'What a stupid thing to do.'

'I know.' Isabel put her head in her hands. 'I don't know what to do.'

Justine stood up and walked round the kitchen. At last she said, 'I think you should tell Neil.'

'I can't.' Isabel shook her head. 'He'd never forgive me.'

'What about going back to Patrick?'

'Never.'

'Then the only option left is to call his bluff and hope he won't tell.' Justine's voice sounded distant. Isabel snuffled, trying to stop crying. After all, she hardly knew Justine. 'I'm sorry. All this stuff. It's so embarrassing. I haven't even offered you a coffee or a tea.'

'No, thanks, I'm fine.' Justine looked at her watch. 'I ought to be getting back. We've finished with the wardrobe sorting.'

432

'Oh, yes, that,' Isabel said vaguely.

'Could I have a cheque now? I know it's a bad time but . . .'

'Of course.' Isabel looked around her. 'I must have left my bag in the hall. I'll just go and get it.' At the door she stopped. 'Justine. You will—' she paused. 'You will be discreet, won't you?'

'Of course,' Justine said. 'Don't worry.'

Isabel spent the rest of the day going through the options. She thought about ringing Patrick up and pleading with him, but decided against it. She knew what would happen; he would suggest she came round to discuss it. Which was impossible. The children, sensing her preoccupation, became demanding. They fought all the way home from school, bickering at best, thumping each other at worst.

Back at home she wandered aimlessly round the kitchen, burning the first batch of fish fingers, while the children squabbled over the television remote control. She longed for Neil to come home, yet dreaded his appearance. If she told him, would he be kind and understanding? Or stern and unforgiving? It occurred to her that she had never seen him really angry. The thought made her feel sick.

How would she feel if he told her he had a mistress? She tried it out, but she simply couldn't imagine Neil doing such a thing. Would that be how he would feel about her? She hadn't felt like a faithless wife before, because in her mind the sexual side had been paramount with Patrick; the rest of her had continued to be a dutiful wife and mother. More so, in fact, as the affair had given her more energy and direction.

She sighed. She didn't think that that argument was going to appeal to Neil. The loss of trust would hit him badly, as it would do her if she had been in his position.

The children had their baths, then went to bed. Isabel read them their bedtime stories, all the time her mind churning over whether she should tell Neil. It dawned on her that Neil might forgive the affair—a moment of madness, ended almost before it had started—but he would never forgive the photographs. Because the Isabel they showed was an Isabel he had never seen. She blushed to think of them. They had shocked her. She could remember posing, feeling free and empowered, the old uncertain Isabel left behind. She could weep at her naivety.

Neil came back late, grumbling about the trains, and stomped off upstairs to change. She heard him shouting and rushed up.

'What the hell is this?' He pointed to the mounds of clothes.

'Sorry, Justine came over and did her colours and wardrobe thingy. I had forgotten all about it.' It seemed like years ago. 'You go down and have a drink. Supper'll be ready in about ten minutes.' She started to shovel clothes into bin liners—charity, jumble, second-hand shop. This morning I felt as if I was getting rid of my old life, like a butterfly emerging from a chrysalis, she thought. And now, just half a day later, here I am, trying desperately to think of a way to save it.

The weekend passed. Isabel did the things she usually did: cook, clear, tidy up, chauffeur Katie to her ballet class and sit on the canal next to Michael fishing, the dreary water suiting her mood.

On Monday morning she knew she had to decide, and soon. Perhaps it would be better to go back to Patrick and wait for him to get bored with her. She couldn't imagine wanting to have sex with someone who didn't want you. But then Patrick didn't believe that she didn't want him. He thought that he was helping her to make the decision she really wanted to make, but was prevented by conventional morals from doing so. Or so he said. Did she want him? She had, but not now. How could she want a man who would blackmail her?

She swam up and down the pool at lunchtime, trying to work Patrick out. Funny, wilful, spoilt? Yes. Spiteful? Possibly. But would he go through with it? By length thirty-three she had convinced herself that he wouldn't do anything.

She was very sweet to Neil that evening, aware that it was possibly the last one when he still believed in her. On Tuesday morning she drove the children into school as usual. At the exit to the school drive she stopped. Left to Patrick, right to home. She hesitated. The woman behind her tooted her horn and Isabel decided which way to turn.

Ten

ISABEL SAT IN THE KITCHEN waiting for Neil to come home. When the woman behind had sounded her horn she had let her subconscious mind make the decision and the car had swung to the right, towards home. Around midday she heard a car pull up, then footsteps. Hands hammered on the door. She could hear Patrick shouting.

'Let me in. Let me in.'

She let him shout, while she stared at bland kitchen units. I think I'll paint them, she thought, paint them in cheerful colours that make me smile. She felt drained, beyond anger, beyond hatred, curiously detached. She didn't care what the neighbours thought. Eventually she got up and went to the front door.

'Why aren't you at work?' Some of the aggression had gone now she had opened the door and he sounded plaintive, a small boy who has been thwarted. She used the voice she used sometimes with Michael and Katie: ultra-reasonable but firm.

'I'm not coming.'

'I'll ruin you.'

'Oh, Patrick. Why won't you let me go? You don't love me.'

He turned his face away from her. 'Why did you leave?'

'You told me not to fall in love with you,' she said softly. 'I can't separate out bits of myself, and you don't want the children.'

'And if—?'

'It's too late for that,' she said quickly.

'I want you back.'

'Goodbye, Patrick.' She started to close the door, but he stopped her.

'Isabel, you will come back.' She shook her head and closed the door. She heard him shouting at her. Then he drove off, his tyres squealing. She sat still in the kitchen while the silence closed in around her again.

She was still sitting when she realised that it was time to collect the children. On autopilot she drove to the school, thinking about Patrick and Neil, about what might happen. She had called Patrick's bluff, and now she felt sick, sick at heart, sick with worry.

When Katie came out she hugged her tight, as if she wanted to absorb her back into her body. Someone tugged her arm, and she looked down. She saw, almost as if at the end of a microscope, another child. She found it hard to focus, then realised it was Rachel, Justine's daughter.

'Please, Mrs Freeman, could Katie come to tea at my house today?' Isabel looked past her and saw Justine. She remembered herself confessing, and the blush rose.

'How did you get on?' Justine whispered. 'What did you decide?'

'I'm sorry?' Isabel stammered.

'About Patrick? Did you go back?'

'Please, Mummy, I want to go to Rachel's house.'

'What did you do? Did you tell Neil?' Justine seemed excited.

Isabel was horrified at her eagerness. Faces loomed up at her, everyone was looking at her. She felt naked, exposed, and twisted round looking for escape. But Rachel held her arm. She shook her off.

'No,' she gasped. 'Katie can't come to tea. We've got to get home.' She registered the child's face crumpling, Justine's becoming angry. Isabel turned and ran, not caring who saw her, Katie held tightly by the hand. Safe inside the car, Isabel asked Katie to go back and collect Michael.

'Why should I? It's not fair, why do I—'

'Just do it,' Isabel shouted at her and then felt terrible as Katie burst into tears.

Isabel rang later to apologise to Justine and Rachel. Justine sounded polite but distant. Isabel wished with all her heart that she had confessed to someone else. Even better, kept it to herself.

Wednesday improved, Thursday got better. She didn't hear anything from Patrick, and neither, presumably, had Neil. She allowed herself to relax a little. On Friday, life was almost back to normal. Neil off first thing, school run, another trip to the supermarket. She got back to see Neil's car parked outside the house. It was unusual for him to forget something, although it did happen. She let herself in, laden with bags.

'Neil?' No reply. 'Neil?' she called again. It felt peculiar to be in an empty house when you thought it wasn't empty. Instinct drew her to their bedroom.

'Neil?' He was lying on the bed fully dressed, eyes closed, hands resting on his chest. He didn't answer so she leaned over the bed and reached out for his hand. 'Are you all right, darling? I saw the car.'

In answer he handed her the envelope he had been holding to his chest. Redundancy, was her immediate reaction.

'Look inside.' His voice was croaky. She pulled out the contents of the envelope. It only needed an inch for her to see what they were. Her legs gave way and she sat down abruptly on the bed.

'Don't be shy, let's have them out.' Neil took the envelope from her and sprinkled the contents on the space separating them. 'After all, you weren't shy then. At first I thought someone had sent me dirty pictures by mistake. I almost didn't bother to look and see who it was. A little note came with them. "Your wife is having an affair."' His voice was controlled. Too controlled.

'I'm sorry,' Isabel whispered. The photographs lay between them, as effective as a mile-high wall. She saw herself, legs and arms splayed out in abandonment. Mouth willing, fingers nimble. 'It's over. The affair, I mean. It didn't last very long, only a few weeks. I realised I'd made a mistake. Neil, I know you're angry, but you must listen to me, please.'

'Why? Why should I want to listen to anything you say ever again?'

'Because I'm your wife. I love you.'

He recoiled from her outstretched hand and went to stand by the window. She followed him.

'Neil, please. I'm so, so, sorry.'

'Go away.'

'Please. I love you.' She touched his shoulder and he spun round, his anger flaring.

'Get out, you whore. Go on, get out. Don't come near me again.'

'But Neil—'

'How do you think it feels? To see your wife like that. Your wife, whom you trusted. Did you think of me at all while you were prancing around, of the children? You were the one who insisted on coming to live here and look what happens.'

'That's not fair.'

'Fair?' His voice rose alarmingly. 'Was it fair when you spread your legs for him, you bitch? Look at them.' He grabbed her hair and forced her down on the bed.

Her nose was squashed against her open-mouthed image; his fingers were laced in her hair, his weight pressed down on her. 'You're hurting me,' she managed, her voice a thin squeak. He pressed down harder. Her mouth filled with bedspread, tongue smothered by cloth, blocking her airways. She gasped for breath, arms waving feebly. Then he released her, and she slid down off the bed, hand to her chest, sucking the air in. He sat on the armchair, shoulders hunched.

'I want to kill you,' he said, his voice thick with defeat.

She slumped against the side of the bed. Her face crumpled with the effort of repressing her sobbing. Why had Patrick done it? The only thing he gained was revenge. She had come so close to loving him, and for what? For it to end like this, her and Neil crying together, alone in an empty house. She shuffled round and put her hand on his knee.

Finally he spoke. 'Who was the man?'

'Patrick.'

'So when I was warned about him . . . they were telling the truth?'

'Yes.'

She could see this came as a shock, as if he hadn't been able to believe it was true, despite the photographs. He had needed her to tell him.

'Will you go to him?'

'No!' She was horrified. 'I told you, it's over. I finished it ages ago, at half term. That's why he's sent the photographs to you.'

'I see. I hadn't taken that in.' He sighed. 'It doesn't change anything. The photographs exist, whether you are still . . . still with him or not.' He rubbed his hands, feeling the knuckle joints as if they were sore with arthritis. 'I can't bear to be with you. I want you to go.'

'What do you mean?'

'Leave. Go. At first I thought that I would go. That's what usually happens. The husband moves out. Whatever she's done, the wife gets everything, the house, the children. Then I thought, why should I go? It's not me who's wrecked this marriage. So it has to be you.'

'But why does anyone have to go? Can't we talk about it?'

'What is there to say? You disgust me. I want you to go. Now.'

Isabel stared at him. 'But what about the children?'

'I rang my mother before you got back. She's willing to help for the time being, until I can make other arrangements. Take what you like and go. The lawyers can argue about it later.'

His eyes had filled with tears and a nerve jumped in his jaw. Isabel realised he was very close to breaking down and she felt overwhelmed with guilt that she should have brought him to this.

'I haven't got anywhere else to go. The children, you, this house. You're everything.' She felt the tears start again.

'You should have thought of that before.' His voice was hard.

'Neil, please. Think of the children.'

He looked at her then, his eyes as stony as pebbles. 'I have thought of the children, which is more than you seem to have. Why should they have to suffer because of your . . . your . . . antics?' He spat the word out. 'If you go now there's a chance the scandal will die down.'

'But there needn't be any scandal. No one knows; they couldn't.' She guiltily thought of Justine. Thank God she had thrown the photographs away and not shown her.

'I opened the envelope on the train. I didn't realise at first it was you. I was sitting with the others, George, Richard, the usual crowd.'

Isabel looked at Neil with horror. 'Oh no. Oh please, no.'

'Unfortunately, oh yes. They saw. We were laughing and joking, guessing what the person who was supposed to get them might have got instead, when one by one they went quiet. Then someone—Richard, I think—said I should put the photos away. I hadn't looked at them. Not properly. It's not my sort of thing. I just looked enough to see that they weren't for me—or so I thought.' The lines in his face were etched deep, thrown into relief by the grey light coming from the window. 'I got off at the next station. They're good chaps, but they won't keep this quiet. They'll go home and tell their wives, and the wives'll tell just one really good friend, and so on.'

She bowed her head, already feeling the weight of the gossip lying on top of Neil's pain.

'It'll be hell, of course, but people will rally round. Keep an eye on the children, help out, that sort of thing. If you're not here.'

'I see.' People they knew locally would rush to help Neil, the innocent victim, and the gossip would die down sooner if there wasn't an object to vilify. Her not being around would make it easier for the children. But she couldn't leave them. Couldn't.

'I can't . . .'

'This isn't about you. It's about what's best for the children.'

'No,' she said, pressing her fists into her eyes. But it wouldn't have to be for long, just until the gossip had died down a bit, a week at the most. I must do what's right for them, she thought desperately. She tried to calm down. If I stay, it'll be like this all weekend, fighting, crying, recriminations. And they shouldn't see us like this. She thought of Neil pressing her face down into the bed. If Michael saw that, would he rush to rescue her? And then what? She had to protect the children from the ugly consequences of her affair. Finally she spoke. 'I'll pack some things.'

He pulled down a weekend bag from on top of the wardrobe and Isabel started to pack at random. I can't believe I'm doing this, ran through her brain incessantly. She caught sight of the envelope lying on the bed.

'What are you going to do with that?'

'I hadn't thought.'

'I'd like them destroyed.'

In answer he rummaged in the drawer of his bedside cabinet and found a dusty book of matches. He lit a corner of the envelope. It burnt with a glowing golden flame, turning lurid green as the fire flickered over the photographic paper. Neil dropped the blazing envelope into the metal waste paper basket, and they watched in silence as it burned brightly then subsided into smouldering charcoal and ashes.

They walked down the stairs. Isabel had the feeling she was wading through treacle. 'What are you going to say?'

'That you had to go away suddenly. I hadn't thought.'

'It's only for a few days, I'll be back soon. You will tell them that? You will tell them that I love them?' She hugged herself, trying to keep the sobs inside. 'Please, Neil, let me stay.' She couldn't go. It was impossible. Her chest ached, her brain was spinning. Impossible.

'No.' He stopped. 'I am trying hard to be civilised. If you stay I will . . .' His voice trailed off while he regained control. 'I can't bear to see you. Every time I look at you I see . . .' He shut his eyes as if shutting out pain. Isabel couldn't bear to look at him. She took a deep breath, then picked up her bag and opened the front door.

'Isabel?' She turned back. 'The photographs. Is that what you . . . I mean, do you like . . . I'm sorry, I shouldn't ask.'

'It's all right. It was different. Exciting. Fun. Eighteen years is a long time. You know.' She shrugged. 'I didn't love him. I never loved him.'

Neil didn't say anything so she walked stiffly on shaking legs to her car. She caught Neil watching her. Please, she said to him with her eyes. Please. But he turned his head and refused to look at her. He looked old and shrunken, the family resemblance between him and his father very strong. He went back into the house and shut the door. Isabel started the engine and drove off.

She drove aimlessly, circling the lanes around Milbridge until the third near miss made her realise that she wasn't safe on the roads. She was near the escarpment of the Downs so she headed up the next track that led to the summit. She pulled the car over, and then got out. Stumbling, she made her way to the brow. There was a clump of trees and she settled down with her back against the largest of them, ignoring the cold wind that drove its way through her coat, her sweater.

The valley was stretched out before her, shrouded in twilight. Milbridge itself was a cluster of lights, gold and silver, creating an aura of dark orange in the darkening sky. In one of those houses Katie and Michael were eating their tea, and asking where she was. She hoped they were, anyway.

She sat there a long time, letting the chill creep in. The valley became dark, lit only by the twinkly lights that showed where people lived. On the ground there were rustlings in the leaves and an owl swooped by on silent wings. She realised that she was cold, really cold.

Thinking vaguely that she should find a B&B, she staggered down the escarpment, slipping in the mud and getting caught by brambles. She opened the door to the driver's seat. As she stood there she changed her mind, closed the door and clambered into the back. Anything was preferable to going back into the harsh real world, even a night in a freezing car. There was an old blanket that the children used on frosty mornings. She wrapped herself in it, finding some comfort in the traces of their presence, arms folded across her stomach, trying to hold in the pain. Perhaps if she lay perfectly still nothing would hurt her again.

But the loss of the children was like a dull ache that filled her mind, blocking out any other thoughts and even awareness of the cold, despite her shivering. She could picture them now: Michael, leaping among the windswept leaves; Katie, serious and intent, star-fish hands unfurling to show some small treasure. If someone said to her, 'You may have the children back, but you must lose your right arm,' she would instantly hold it out. Nothing mattered except them.

440

She thought of Michael, lost in the woods. She had thought then that she would die if he had been lost, yet here she was without him, and it was entirely her fault. She should have been faithful, and if not that, then at least more careful. Oh, Patrick, why? If only he had not carried out his threat, she would be safely at home with Neil and the children. Would Neil know that Michael liked seven kisses before being tucked into bed, that Katie couldn't sleep unless the bathroom light and not the landing light was left on?

She scrunched her face up, every molecule in her body yearning to hold them. But they were gone.

Isabel woke to someone thumping on the car window. She squinted at two faces peering in at her through windows covered with condensation, one face black and white and hairy, the other red and blue and fluffy. Was she hallucinating? She wiped the window with her sleeve and the faces transformed into a border collie and a woman in a woolly hat. The woman was mouthing something to her. Isabel pulled herself into a sitting position and gingerly opened the car door.

'I thought you were a suicide.'

'No.' God, she was cold. 'Not dead yet.'

'You do get them up here. They put bricks on the accelerators so the car goes until the petrol runs out.'

'I'll know another time.'

The woman looked horrified. 'I didn't mean . . .'

'It's all right; neither did I.'

Isabel leaned back against the seat, eyes closed.

'Do you need help?'

'I'm fine. Just fine.' She kept her eyes shut.

'I'll be on my way then.' Isabel made no response. 'Well.' A deep intake of breath. 'It's a beautiful day. Come on, Tan.'

Isabel listened to them go, then other sounds began to impinge. Birdsong in short snatches; rustling in the hedgerow; a fieldfare searching for hawberries. She opened her eyes and saw a spider had made a web between the car and the wing mirror. It glistened with ash-white dew strung like beads along the silvery threads, the sunlight passing through the dew, prisms converting the light into sparkling rainbows. Slowly, with her joints feeling as rusty as the Tin Man's, she pushed the door open and stood up, her lungs aching as she breathed in the sharp, thin air. The sky was high, a clear pale blue floating over ploughed fields, earth rich as chocolate, and the escarpment of the Downs, sweeping across the horizon. The dog walker had been right. It was a beautiful day.

So what was she doing up on the Downs when her children were waiting for her? Neil wouldn't know the routine, getting Katie to her ballet class, Michael to football practice. She was part of the fabric of their lives; Neil couldn't throw her out or banish her to the furthest corners of the kingdom like a king in a fairy story. Anna Karenina had no option but to kill herself because she was created by a nineteenth-century man. She had to pay the price for her adultery regardless. But Isabel didn't.

Suddenly it struck her how easily she had accepted Neil's demand that she leave. Throughout their life together she had always deferred to his decisions. She might make requests and state her opinions, but in the end it was Neil who would decide, Neil who would weigh the evidence and pronounce his verdict. No more, she thought, staring out at the wide valley sprawling below her. No more. It's time to go home.

The children were pleased to see her, holding her tightly as she knelt to greet them.

'Daddy said he didn't know when you'd be coming back,' Katie said.

'Did he?' Isabel said lightly, her eyes meeting Neil's as he stood in the hall open-mouthed. 'Silly Daddy. He must have misunderstood me. Now, run and get your ballet things.' She eased Katie away. 'Quick, or we'll be late. Michael, hurry up and get dressed. Your kit should be ready for you by the back door.'

Michael looked confused. 'But Dad said Granny was coming to look after us.'

'Don't you worry about that. You just get dressed as quickly as you can.' She went up the stairs after him, quickly washed her face and changed. Newly spruced up, she went back into the hall where Neil was still waiting, hands on hips, mouth tight under his moustache.

Checking the children were out of earshot she faced him. 'I'm not going. I'm sorry for what's happened, but I can't just walk away and let you pretend I don't exist.'

'I don't want you here.'

'I am here, and I intend to stay. I'm not going to be separated from my children.' She heard Katie skipping down the stairs and spoke in a more normal voice. 'We'll be out for the morning and back at lunchtime. We'll talk this evening.'

'My mother's coming.'

'I didn't marry your mother, I married you. You deal with her.' She managed to get the children out of the house and off to their respective classes, all the time her heart thumping. As she dropped Katie off at ballet there were a few sidelong glances, conversations that stopped suddenly, but none of the other mothers said anything except Justine. 'I'm surprised to see you here,' she said.

'Oh, really? Why?' Isabel said, as casually as she could.

Justine flushed slightly. 'I heard—' She stopped as Isabel looked up.

'You shouldn't believe everything you hear,' Isabel said. She flashed a smile at Justine. 'Must dash,' she said, and ran to the car and the waiting Michael.

She dropped him off at football practice. Where would we be without the weather? Isabel thought, having called 'What a beautiful morning' with a forced cheeriness to several parents. She tried not to register who had raised their eyebrows or who had been startled. Her luck held and she found a parking space immediately in the town centre.

She wondered what to do next. She had been surprised at how easy it was to breeze back into the house and tell Neil she wasn't going, to take control of the situation. What would happen next was less predictable, depending on Neil's reaction. Guilt overwhelmed her for a moment. But remorse wouldn't help her now. She needed to know her legal position. Any lawyer could tell her but she wanted to know now, before seeing Neil again. She went to the library and quickly looked through their legal section, but the books she wanted were out on loan.

So she went to the bookshop, trying to creep in without attracting any attention in case Patrick was sitting in the Italian café opposite. There wasn't a book on matrimonial or even family law, so she picked up a book on divorce. She flicked through, looking at the chapter titles. Mediation and reconciliation. Blame. Guilt. Adultery. The book had it all. She decided to buy it, but had to wait to be served.

'You're busy today,' she said when she got to the end of the line.

'Christmas,' the man said. 'Busiest time of the year. Next four weeks we'll be heaving. If you know someone who wants a job . . .' He tapped the top of the counter.

Isabel took her change and looked where he was pointing. A notice taped to the counter read:

Temporary sales assistant required from now until Christmas.
Apply to the manager.

'Me,' she said, to her own surprise as much as his. 'I need a job.'

'Seriously?' He handed her a plastic bag containing the book.

'Yes.' She realised that she was serious, that she did need a job.

'Look,' the man said, scratching his head. 'Come in on Monday morning, first thing. It won't be so busy then.'

'That'll be great. Monday morning, then. Thanks.'

She drove off to pick up first Katie, then Michael. Moira's car was in the drive when they got back.

'Granny's here,' she said to the children. 'Katie, darling, go and change. You too, Michael. And put your track suit in the dirty-linen bin, not under the bed, this time,' she called after him as he scampered upstairs, closely followed by Katie.

Moira was in the hall. She turned, hands on hips.

'Good journey down?' Isabel said cheerily.

'Yes, thank you,' Moira replied tersely. 'Though rather unexpected.'

'Couldn't agree more,' Isabel said. 'Very unexpected.' She looked Moira straight in the eye, challenging her to say more. But to her surprise, Moira hesitated, then looked away. Her hair was messy and Isabel could see a bare patch on her skin where she had failed to blend in her foundation. The exposed skin looked waxy white, deadened by age. In comparison Isabel felt young and strong, and she was ashamed.

'Moira. You've driven a long way. Why don't you go and sit down and I'll bring you a coffee.'

'Will it be real or the instant?' Moira said, straightening up into her usual belligerent posture. But her messy hair and slapdash make-up spoilt the invincible effect. She looked more like a tired old turkey hen, scrawny-necked and flightless, but defending her chicks to the last.

'Instant. Take it or leave it, it's all I have.' She spoke quietly but firmly, too tired herself to play games of one-upmanship.

Moira looked uncertain, as if puzzled by an Isabel who didn't respond. Perhaps that's the secret, Isabel thought. All these years I've been striving to be the good daughter-in-law, when the careless one would have served better. She wondered what Neil had told his mother. Even if he'd left the details out she must be aware that something had happened. So pointless to quarrel over trivia when there were real battles to be fought.

She smiled and said gently, 'You look tired. Go on, sit down. I'll bring the coffee to you.' Isabel went into the kitchen. Neil wasn't there, and she wondered where he had gone. On the side was a large pie, all the way from Moira's freezer, she guessed. An image of Moira diligently stocking her freezer with family-sized pies, slaving on an eternal domestic treadmill even though her children had grown up and left twenty years ago, came to Isabel's mind.

She went back into the sitting room. 'Here's your coffee,' she said. 'Do you know where Neil is?'

'He said he had to go out and make some arrangements.'

Arrangements. It sounded a horribly cold word. Isabel sat down beside Moira. 'I don't know what Neil's said to you but—'

'Enough.' Moira sipped her coffee, mouth pursed.

Isabel counted to three, then ten. 'Neil's very angry with me,' she said. 'And he has every right to be. But he can't just chuck away all those years together because of one mistake.'

'Some mistake.'

'Yes,' Isabel said simply and the two women sat in silence.

Moira broke the silence first. 'I suppose you think I'm on Neil's side.' Isabel thought of Michael. 'Of course.'

'I may love my son, but that doesn't blind me to his faults.' Moira sniffed. 'Not that he says much to me. He always was a secretive little boy. Keeps it all bottled up. I can see that might be hard to live with. Not that I'm condoning your actions,' Moira continued briskly. 'A fine way to carry on. But I can see you're a good mother, even if we don't see eye to eye. And we don't go in for divorce in our family.' She made it sound as if divorce was on a par with putting ketchup on the table.

Isabel opened her mouth in surprise. Moira, whom she had assumed would be a fearsome enemy, might turn out to be an ally.

But where was Neil? He hadn't come back for lunch.

They played Monopoly in the afternoon. Moira amassed a fortune quickly, built an empire and beadily collected her rent. Isabel kept on being sent to jail. Neil came back at teatime, his presence indicated by a resounding crash of the front door and heavy footsteps up the stairs. Isabel followed and found him packing.

'What are you doing?' she said.

'If you won't go, I must,' he said, stripping shirts off their hangers.

'Where are you going?' He didn't answer. 'Neil, we need to talk.'

He looked at her then. 'You might want to talk, but I don't.'

'You can't just walk out.'

'Watch me.'

'What about your mother? She's driven all this way.'

He shrugged. 'You've come back; you deal with her. If I stay, it could be construed that I condone what you've done.'

'What? Have you been speaking to a lawyer?' He turned his back on her and zipped up the case. 'Where are you going?'

'It doesn't matter.'

'But what if there was an emergency? How would I reach you?'

He paused, then took out his diary, scribbled on a page, tore it out and tossed the scrap to her. 'My mobile phone number.'

Isabel stared at the number, confused. 'I didn't know you had a mobile phone.'

'The company gave me one.' He picked the case up and left the room. Isabel ran after him.

'Stop being so melodramatic,' she hissed. 'People have affairs all the time and it does break up some marriages. But it doesn't have to. Going won't make the past vanish. All it'll do is make it hard for the children.'

'I've made arrangements,' he said abruptly without looking at her.

'Un-make them.' She watched his face intently as he paused, as if weighing up his options.

'I can't.'

'You mean you won't. Not even for your children,' she said, unable to keep the anger from her voice.

He turned on her and pushed her against the wall. 'Stop using the children as a weapon, you selfish cow,' he spat. 'You're the one who's wrecked everything. I did everything for you and you've thrown it away. And now you're making me leave. I despise you.' Neil picked up the case. Isabel watched him go down the stairs, then turn as the children came into the hall.

'Where are you going?' Michael said.

'I'm going to stay with a friend for a while,' Neil said easily, despite having been hurling abuse at her a few moments before.

'Can I come?' Katie asked.

'We'll see.' He bent and kissed Moira's powdery cheek. 'Sorry, Ma.'

'I should think so,' Moira said tartly, but she clung onto his arm. 'I hope you've thought about what you're doing, Neil.'

'Of course.' He picked Katie up and buried a kiss in her neck. 'I'll see you soon.' He tousled Michael's hair. 'Bye.'

He didn't look at Isabel as he left.

Isabel, Moira, Michael and Katie stood in the doorway and watched him drive away. 'He is coming back, isn't he?' Michael said, his voice uncertain.

'Och, of course,' Moira said, giving him a hug. 'D'you know, when your daddy was a wee boy he packed his case and walked out. He was off to Australia, he said, to see if they were all standing upside-down.'

Katie removed her finger from her mouth. 'Did he get there?'

'He was back by teatime. Now, I expect it's time for your baths.'

Moira stayed until Sunday afternoon and although Isabel had flashes of exasperation they were less extreme than before. Neither Isabel nor Moira mentioned Neil, as if chary of admitting his absence. With the children they both maintained the idea that he had gone on a nebulous business trip. Deprived of Ian and Neil, Moira fussed over Michael, who was torn between embarrassment and pleasure. Katie, meanwhile, clung to Isabel. She followed her round the house, one finger firmly in her mouth, a babyish gesture that Isabel thought she had abandoned.

Isabel didn't think about the bookshop until she was putting out the children's coats, bags and PE kits for Monday and came across her bag with the book on divorce. She had said she was interested in working there as an automatic response, but now she was unsure. On Sunday evening, however, she read the divorce book, making notes as she went. One thing was quite clear: however it was divided, Neil's income was not enough to support two households in the way they had been living. Working was no longer an optional extra.

So much else had happened over the weekend that the photographs had almost slipped from her mind. Not so the other parents at the school. On Monday morning, there were whispers and snickers of laughter as she passed by. She gripped Katie's heavy PE bag tightly and tried to look as if she couldn't hear, her eyes fixed on a point just above people's heads. Don't let them know you mind, she told herself. Don't let them see you care.

Isabel hung Katie's bag up in the cloakroom, then headed for her car, attempting to make an unobtrusive escape through the entrance hall. She tried not to look at anyone directly, to avoid the sliding glances and raised eyebrows. Then, in front of her stood one unavoidable figure.

'Isabel, the very person.' Mary's voice dominated the hall and Isabel was conscious of a hush of anticipation. To her surprise, Mary linked arms and walked with her, talking loudly. 'I was sending out the invitations to our Christmas party and I couldn't find your address. So stupid of me to mislay it. I do hope you and Neil will be able to attend.'

Isabel could see that Mary's friendliness to her was silencing the whisperers. She was grateful, but she was also angry at the fact she needed rescuing. They reached Isabel's car, Mary having talked all the while.

Isabel unlinked her arm. 'Thank you for the invitation but I doubt we'll be able to come. You were quite right about Patrick breaking up marriages. He has been very successful at breaking up mine.'

Mary lowered her voice. 'I've heard. That toad George Weedon-Smith was full of it, Richard said. Yakking on for hours at the golf club.'

Isabel felt sick. 'No wonder everybody seems to know.'

'Never mind. It'll be a nine-day wonder, you'll see. People will forget.'

'Neil won't.'

Mary patted her arm. 'My dear, in my experience, what men say in the heat of the moment and what they actually do are quite different.'

'Oh, but that was exactly where I went wrong,' Isabel said, her voice shaking with suppressed fury. 'Patrick said he'd use the photographs and I didn't think he would.'

'Patrick has behaved very badly, but he says he didn't send them.'

Isabel flung open the car door. 'Then he's a liar as well as a shit,' she said, 'because who else could it have been?'

Her hands were still trembling as she knocked on the bookshop door and she had to take deep breaths to try to steady herself. The door had a closed sign on it, but there were lights on inside. The man she'd seen on Saturday appeared and let her into the warmth.

'I've just made tea. D'you want some?'

'Please,' Isabel said. Behind the counter was a stairway that led down to a narrow corridor, made even narrower by stacks of books. She'd expected the office to be untidy and shabby, but to her surprise it was functional and modern, with a stunning glass-and-steel desk.

'Sit down,' he said, indicating the black leather armchair opposite the desk. 'I realise I don't know your name.'

'Isabel,' she said. 'Isabel Freeman.'

'Adam Rockcliffe. I'm the owner.' She was surprised; he seemed too young to own a bookshop. He must be about her own age. She'd imagined bookshop owners would be older.

Adam handed her a clipboard. 'Now, while I get you some tea, perhaps you can fill in this form.' He left the room.

Isabel's heart sank as she tried to fill in the form. Adam Rockcliffe came back in with a mug of tea. Silently she handed the clipboard back.

'You've not filled in much,' he commented.

Isabel felt anger rise in her, anger at everything and everybody. 'You've not asked the right questions,' she said, standing up. 'I've done lots of things but none of them fit your boxes. The last job I had went wrong. I can't give you a P45 or a proper reference. So what am I to do? Lie?' Her body was shaking but she carried on. 'And you might as well know, because everybody else seems to, that my lover wanted me to leave my husband and go with him to Rome, but I wouldn't, so he blackmailed me, and my husband first of all threw me out but I wouldn't go so now he's left me, and all I wanted was a job where I could earn some money and support myself, and I don't think that's much to ask, is it?'

She stopped, horrified that she could have blurted all that out.

Adam blinked, but that was the only sign that anything untoward had happened. 'Seems reasonable,' he said mildly.

'I'm sorry,' Isabel said, picking up her bag. 'I've wasted your time.'

'No, don't go. Please, sit down.'

Isabel perched on the edge of the chair and stared at the floor in embarrassment.

'Look, I have two full-time assistants and a Saturday girl. Maria's had a threatened miscarriage and has been told to take things easy, so she's not here, and Angela's father had a stroke on Friday so she's had to go back home. My Saturday girl would come in, but she's still at school. It's the busiest time of the year for me and, frankly, I'm desperate. I don't care how many boxes you can tick so long as you're willing to work.'

'I need the money,' Isabel said.

At that he looked sharply at her, but merely said, 'I pay twenty per cent above the minimum wage, which isn't great, but better than most shops. Hours are nine thirty to five thirty, although I'll probably stay open later a few nights closer to Christmas. Can you do Saturdays?'

Isabel shook her head, reeling from the quickfire information.

'Pity. Well, do you want the job?'

'Yes,' she said impulsively.

'Then you're hired. Could you start today?'

'What, now? I suppose I could, though I'd have to go at three.' She could book the children into the after-school club for the rest of term, but it would be unfair to sign them up without warning.

Adam quickly showed her round the shop, and then gave her a crash course in using the till. His instructions were clear and logical.

The first customer came in ten minutes after opening and from then on she was busy all day, muddling change, checking customer orders, taking deliveries down to the stockroom and unpacking them. She found the day exhausting and was thankful to be finishing early. She collected the children from school and drove home. She made the children supper, supervised their baths and dozed off while reading to Katie.

The next two days were worse, the physical tiredness dragging at her body. The shop was busier too, which meant more pressure, but it was a blessing to be so tired that she couldn't think.

By the end of the week her body had started to adapt to the rhythm of the job and she'd found a pair of shoes that didn't pinch. She had thought that the work would be boring, but there were few opportunities for standing around. When not working at the till there were piles of books to be straightened and queries to be answered. Overall she realised she enjoyed working there. The bookshop had a warm, comfortable glow to it and was a safe haven from the darkness outside.

Neil had rung each evening to speak to the children. She'd discovered that he had moved out of his friend's house and into a B&B.

'You can come back here,' she'd whispered.

'Don't let's go there,' he'd said, and asked to speak to the children. Later she thought that that was a very un-Neil-like thing to say and wondered where he'd picked the expression up from.

On Friday, as she was going, Adam put a brown envelope into her hand. 'What's this?' she asked, and he gave her a surprised look.

'Wages, of course. If there's any way you can work the next two Saturdays let me know. Even a couple of hours would help.'

'I'll let you know,' she said, holding the envelope. Once outside the shop she carefully tore across the top. A small wad of notes with a larger piece of folded paper. She took it out and unfolded it. A payslip with her name on it. She thought of Neil demanding she get a payslip from Patrick. She hadn't thought of Patrick for days. He occupied an angry, sore place in her mind that she didn't want to explore in case it exploded in a deluge of accusations.

She looked up and saw Adam looking at her through the window. She smiled and gave a little wave. Perhaps one day she'd know him well enough to tell him why a humble payslip could make her both laugh and cry at the same time.

Eleven

MICHAEL AND KATIE AGREED: it had to be buttercup yellow. 'Don't you think it's a bit bright?' Isabel asked, blinking. The night before she had drunk a bottle of wine and stumbled to bed deciding that she couldn't live with a magnolia kitchen any longer. The small square of egg-yolk brilliance was enough to give anyone a headache, even without a crashing hangover, but Isabel still bought the paint. She paid in cash—her cash—and then took the children for a pizza as a treat.

When they got back to the house the air smelt different and she realised that Neil had been there. She ran upstairs and, yes, he'd taken a suit and some weekend clothes. It seemed tragic that he felt it was preferable to sneak like a thief into his own house rather than meet her. And she wondered how he could bear not to see the children.

The kitchen was so bland that the yellow paint was like an all-out assault, Isabel thought as she rollered dramatic arcs of colour over the walls. Michael got bored quickly and drifted off to play on the computer, but Katie diligently worked away in her corner, spattered with yellow freckles, and letting the paint drip over her hand.

Isabel did the second coat of paint early on Sunday morning. The kitchen was aggressively yellow, a challenge to depressives everywhere. Later that day, Isabel moved her possessions back in: the string of Mexican chillies, the Moroccan pots. She paused at the photograph of Neil in the Empty Quarter. He looked so young. She touched his face and the image of Neil carried on smiling confidently, frozen in time.

Back to work on Monday. Saturday had been a good day, Adam said, and Isabel spent much of the morning putting out replacement stock.

'Don't you worry about the big chains taking away your business?' she asked.

Adam shook his head. 'Milbridge is too small for a big chain. It's just a question of playing with the numbers, guessing what will sell at what price.' He glanced round the shop. 'Speaking of which, as it's quiet now, I'm going to do the orders. Give me a shout if you need help.'

He clattered down the stairs to his office, leaving Isabel behind the counter. A young mother with a baby in a pushchair came and bought a cloth picturebook. As she handed the book over the shop bell rang and she looked up to see a familiar shape coming through the low door.

'Hello, Isabel,' he said. 'As you won't come to me, I have come to you.' Patrick's voice was as deep and smooth as ever, but controlled.

Isabel swallowed. 'I suppose Mary told you I was working here.'

'No, Justine. Mary isn't speaking to me at the moment.' He gave a rueful grin. 'Or rather, she has said so much to me that we're both exhausted. Apparently it's all my fault.'

'And isn't it?' Her own voice sounded metallic.

'C'mon, we're both adults. You knew what you were getting into.'

Isabel turned her head and stared up at the ceiling. Yes, she'd known at the start: he'd made his limits for a relationship clear. But he was the one who had tried to blackmail her. She hadn't known about that.

He was leaning forwards now. 'Poor baby, you've had a rough ride.' His finger traced the line of her jaw, touched her lips. 'My offer still stands.'

'I must have been mad to get involved with you,' she said slowly. 'Have you any idea of the damage we've done?'

He had, at least, the grace to look a little shamefaced. 'You knew the risks. Nobody made you have an affair.'

'So it's all my fault. Is it my fault for making you blackmail me? I should have thought more about what I was doing. Not just let myself get swept up into it.'

'But it was fun, though,' Patrick said and their eyes met.

'Expensive fun.'

'Then come with me. You don't have to stay here.'

Isabel tried to stay calm. 'I can't just run away, I still have responsibilities, and you are the last man in the world I would run away with. Whatever I may have felt for you has been wiped out.' She stopped to try to control her breathing. If she let him make her feel angry it meant he could still control her feelings. 'When you sent the photographs to Neil you knew what was likely to happen, and you did it anyway, without thought for anyone except yourself.'

Patrick straightened up. 'I didn't send the photographs.'

'Oh, sure.'

'It wasn't me.' His face was a sullen red.

'Go away, Patrick. Just go. I really don't want to see you any more.'

'No.' He grabbed her arm. 'I didn't send them.'

'Let me go.' She pulled at his hand but he was too strong. In desperation she bent her head and bit his wrist as hard as she could.

Immediately he released her. 'You bitch,' he spat.

'What's going on?' Adam's voice behind her.

Isabel turned, unable to speak. He put a reassuring hand on her shoulder and looked across at Patrick. 'Well?' he said.

Patrick swept his hair back, his eyes narrowed as he looked from Adam to Isabel. 'My, my,' he drawled, 'you are a fast worker, aren't you?'

Isabel gasped. 'How dare you?' Adam moved in front of her.

'I'm afraid I have to ask you to leave the shop,' he said to Patrick, his voice neutral. 'You're upsetting my staff.'

'And if I don't?'

'Look,' Adam said, 'I'm running a business here. If I have to call the police to remove you I will. So why don't you just go?'

They stared at each other: Patrick more thick set than Adam, his body tense; Adam tall and lean, apparently unruffled.

'It's over, Patrick,' Isabel said.

He looked at her, his face red with anger. Then he turned and barged out, knocking over a pile of books and slamming the door behind him.

Isabel realised she was trembling. 'I'm sorry, Adam,' she said. 'I had no idea he'd come here.'

Adam raised his eyebrows. 'Monday mornings are certainly interesting when you're around. I suppose next time it'll be your husband.'

Isabel felt herself go scarlet. 'I'm sorry,' she said.

'Think no more about it. Go downstairs and recover, if you want, and I'll hold the fort up here.'

Isabel slipped downstairs. She felt light-headed, as if by confronting Patrick she had released all her anxieties. She rubbed her arm where he had gripped her. She had bitten him! She gave a little giggle, amazed at herself. She wondered why he was so persistent. And his refusal to take any blame was strange, as no one else could have been responsible for sending the photographs.

'Isabel?' Adam's voice from upstairs. 'Could you please bring me up the figures on my desk?' She took them to him, along with a mug of tea. 'Thanks. OK?' His grey eyes were warm with concern.

She nodded. 'Yes. I'll take over if you want to carry on with these.'

'I don't need a computer for everything.' She watched him run a pencil down a column of numbers and add them up so quickly she could hardly follow.

'Wow. Are you really doing the maths that quickly?'

'Sure. Sign of a misspent youth.'

'Are you sure they're right?'

'Test them if you like. There should be a calculator about somewhere.'

She searched and found the calculator.

'OK, we'll do that column.'

'On your marks, get set, go!' Isabel punched in the numbers as fast as she could, but she was still slower than Adam. 'That's incredible. You ought to be able to do something with that.'

'Like what?'

'I don't know. Become an accountant?'

Adam laughed, his eyes creasing at the corners. 'No, thanks.'

'Seriously, you ought to be able to do something more than—' She stopped, embarrassed at what she had just said.

'More than running a provincial bookshop?'

She nodded. 'I didn't mean to be rude.'

'I know. Don't worry. I used to be a futures trader in the City, playing with numbers. I always said I'd stick it for five years then get out with my stash, but when the time came I thought I'd do just another year. And then another. You get hooked on it, then it burns you out.'

'You're so good at maths, it's like magic,' she said. 'Couldn't you do something else with it?'

'Before I worked as a trader I was a Cambridge academic.' He grinned at her surprise. 'Pure mathematics is even worse than the City for burn-out. Most people have done their best work by the age of twenty-four. Cambridge in the eighties and nineties was full of headhunters after people like me—maths PhDs at a loose end.'

'Why?'

'Speed. At the end of the day, trading is about speed, and the quicker you can do the calculations, the more money you make.'

'Do you miss it?'

'Most of the time, no. I play around a bit on the markets for fun, there's a poker game that meets once a month, and the shop keeps me sane.'

Poker. Another Adam that sat strangely with the diffident bookshop owner. But she realised it made sense, the ability to calculate, the calm reserve. She looked at him shyly. 'Lots of people would find working in a shop would drive them mad.'

'But a bookshop like this is different. It's fascinating, like taking part in people's lives, you can tell what's happening to them by what they buy.' He glanced at her. 'I knew who you were, for instance.'

'Me? What did you know?'

'I knew you bought a lot of children's books, so I guessed you have children, and also fiction. There were some other books as well.' He looked sheepish.

Isabel mentally went back over what she had bought, and remembered the divorce book. 'Mmm. I can see how books might be revealing.' She wondered what Adam read himself.

Adam fiddled with his pencil. 'It isn't the first time I've seen you and the man who came in today. A few Sundays ago, I was in the Italian café.'

Isabel thought back. Of course, the man with the newspaper on the next table who'd seemed familiar. 'Were you listening to us?'

Adam shrugged and smiled. 'Sorry. It was the most riveting conversation I've ever overheard. I take it you didn't go.'

'No.' Everybody seemed to know what she was doing before she did.

'Milbridge is a small town,' Adam said gently.

The kitchen still seemed too bright, but at least it was cheerful to come home to. Once the children were in bed she rang Neil's mobile. There was a lot of background noise, people talking, glasses chinking, and she wondered if he was at a party, but he sounded depressed and tired.

'I miss the children,' he said.

'They miss you. I understand if you don't want to see me, but that doesn't mean you can't see the children.'

He said something she didn't catch.

'I can't hear you properly. Let's meet up and talk. Please?' Silence apart from the background noise. 'Neil?'

'I have to go,' he said, and cut her off.

She put the phone down and went into the sitting room. Whatever she'd felt for Patrick was dead now, blown out like a violent storm. She didn't know how Neil felt. You can't make someone love you, just because you've decided it would be better for the children, she thought. And was there any point in staying married if love wasn't there? But then, what is love, in the context of a marriage? Liking someone an awful lot, feeling comfortable with them, knowing them. It didn't seem enough. Not an all-powerful, all-conquering emotion that moved mountains and shook the earth.

But I didn't love Patrick, she thought. There were times when she had thought she did, at the beginning. But never more than the children. Perhaps that was why he became so angry. Perhaps he thought she should have abandoned her children for her lover, as his mother had done. If it hadn't been for the photographs, she would have stayed with Neil, sighing wistfully at the memories of her mad affair when she was feeling bored. She frowned. Patrick had said that if the marriage had been happy she would never have had an affair. Was that true? If it hadn't been for the photographs, perhaps she would have taken another lover, become a serial adulteress.

I love the children, she thought, but that didn't stop me jeopardising their happiness, wilfully disrupting their home.

The phone rang. It was Neil, this time with a silent background.

'I'd like to have the children this weekend,' he said abruptly.

'The whole weekend?' Isabel stammered, horrified at the thought of them going. 'What will you do?'

'Take them to my sister's. Heather would love to see them.'

They arranged that he would pick the children up on Friday evening and return late on Sunday afternoon. Isabel put the phone down feeling as if someone had removed her insides and wrapped them round a rusty skewer. She had never been without the children for as long as a whole weekend. She decided she'd work in the shop on Saturday and on Sunday would paint the sitting room a clear high-summer blue.

The weekend seemed to stretch into infinity. Friday evening she spent clearing the sitting room and trying not to feel as if her heart had been ripped out by the children's joy at seeing their father and their gleeful departure with him. Neil had stayed in the car. Saturday was chaotic. It felt as if the whole of Milbridge filled the shop. On Saturday evening she had started to paint the sitting room, finishing well after midnight. The next morning she did the second coat, although her arms were aching.

Neil stayed in the car when he dropped the children off. She ushered them into the house then ran out in the rain to speak to him.

'Come in,' she said, rain dripping down her neck. 'We need to talk.'

'Not yet,' he said and drove off, spraying puddle water in dirty arcs.

'When?' she yelled as the car was swallowed up by the darkness.

At work on Monday they were setting out new stock when Adam said, 'What are you going to do with yourself?'

'What d'you mean?'

'Angela will be coming back after New Year, but I don't think Maria will. There'd be a job going here, if you wanted it.'

'I haven't thought about what happens next. Making it to Christmas seems hard enough.' She spoke without thinking, her voice bleak.

'Perhaps you should think about it,' he said gently.

'I've sort of been waiting for Neil to decide . . .'

'It's your life,' Adam said, 'but if it was me, I'd want to make some of my own decisions. It might be that bookselling is your ideal job. On the other hand something else might be.'

Isabel could have spat with irritation. 'I've been through that. I don't have any experience, I don't have any qualifications and I'm too old.'

'You can get experience, and you can get qualifications. It's a question of deciding what you want to do and then going out and doing it.'

'If it was so easy, everybody'd be doing it.'

Adam laughed. 'Everybody is doing it, Isabel. Something like one in five students is a mature student. People are changing careers all the time. There are loads of books for women returners. Do some research. Or don't: it's your life. If you want a job here, you can have it.'

'I'll think about it.'

'Good. Now, I want to clear part of Fiction away and make a larger cookery display.' And they moved books around for the rest of the morning until Adam was satisfied he'd maximised the space according to his calculations of profitability per square foot. Isabel loved the way he took his calculations so seriously, the way he'd stand weighing two books in his hands as if gauging their relative chances of success with the readers of Milbridge. Once he caught her looking at him.

'What's so funny?' he said, grinning at her.

'Nothing,' she said, giggling at being caught out.

'You think I'm mad, don't you?'

'Mmm. But in the nicest possible way.'

Isabel went to the library during her lunch hour and looked through their careers section. She started to discuss ideas with Adam, hesitantly at first and then with more confidence.

'Adam,' she'd start. 'What do you think of horticulture?'

'Depends,' he'd answer. 'I can't see you in dungarees on a municipal lawn mower, but something like landscape design would be good.'

'Except I know nothing about plants. Well, not English ones anyway.'

'Exotic gardens are fashionable right now.'

'Why are you always so positive?'

'Natural optimism?'

'What about a lion tamer?'

'Working with animals. Plenty of travel opportunities. Snazzy outfit.'

'But if dogs have stinky breath, imagine a lion's breath.'

'Yeah, but you'd get a whip.' He raised his eyebrows and she giggled.

'Seriously, what do you think I should do?'

'Seriously, I think you have to decide for yourself.'

'It's all right for you, you had a career, and are free to do what you like whereas I haven't, and I'm not.'

'Not what?'

'Free. I have children and a husband—I think.' She sighed. It would help if she knew what Neil was intending, if he was coming back.

'It doesn't have to be all or nothing, you know. The choice isn't between working an eighty-hour week or drooping at home.' Adam straightened up suddenly, his tall frame unfolding like a laundry airer. 'Customers.'

'If I became a student,' she said to Adam later, 'I wouldn't have to worry about the school holidays. And when I graduated the children would be older, so it wouldn't be so much of a problem and I'd be able to get a better job.'

'Sounds good. What subject?'

'Before I met Neil I wanted to read English.'

'So why not now?'

'It'd be a bit self-indulgent. I ought to do something more vocational.'

'Do something you enjoy. You can always specialise later. Why don't you phone up for some prospectuses? Use the phone in my office.'

The first call was nerve-racking, but nobody asked any awkward questions and she became blasé about making the calls. She was just about to ring the fifth and last college when Adam stuck his head round the door. 'You've got a visitor.'

Isabel followed him up to the shop floor, wondering who it could be.

'Helen.' The last time she'd seen Helen was on the other side of the school playground. She was sure that Helen had seen her, but had avoided eye contact. Isabel crossed her arms.

'Hello, Isabel. Mary said you were working here.' Helen rubbed her hands together. She looked so nervous that Isabel softened.

'Are you well?'

'Yes,' Helen said, but she didn't look it. There were dark shadows under her eyes and her nails were raw. She took a deep breath. 'I came to invite you and Katie to tea. If you'll come.'

Isabel was astounded. 'What about George?'

Helen's face flushed. 'It's my house too,' she said, her air of defiance worthy of Joan of Arc about to go to the stake rather than a woman arranging for a little girl and her mother to come to tea. But Isabel knew how much the invitation meant.

Isabel smiled. 'Katie would love to come for tea. And so would I.' She would, too. She felt so sorry for Helen. It must be awful being married to George, who Isabel knew to be a bully, and had wondered if he was something worse. She thought about what she wanted to say, and chose her words carefully. 'You know, these last few weeks, they've probably been the worst in my life. But although it's been bad, I think things are going to work out. Neil and me, we were stuck. And however painful it's been, I'm not stuck any more. Do you understand what I'm saying?'

Helen flushed, and nodded. 'But I'm not brave, like you.'

'Oh, Helen, I've not been brave.' Isabel gently put one hand on her arm. 'Look, there are people, organisations, that can help. If you want.'

Helen blew her nose. 'It's not that easy,' she said.

'I know.' Isabel gave her a hug. 'But when you're ready, ask.'

On Friday evening, Isabel opened a bottle of Rioja to celebrate another week of work, spread the prospectuses out and read through them. And the more she read, the more the idea of going back to college to read English appealed. She looked at the grades required; most of the prospectuses said that entry requirements could be waived for mature students. Then there was the money. She'd need enough to maintain herself and the children, and to pay tuition fees. She wondered how much her father's house was worth.

As she went upstairs to bed she thought about how peaceful her evening had been. She felt guilty, but it was pleasant just to be on her own, despite the difficulties. The weekend lay before her. She'd booked a visit to a local wildlife park that did Father Christmas specials— Michael was too old, but he wouldn't miss out on a 'free' present and Katie still believed. Then they'd go into Fordingbury and go Christmas shopping, with cakes at a café for tea. On Sunday morning she was going to paint Katie's room.

I can do what I please, she thought. If I want to read English I can, and I can use my own money, I don't have to consult Neil. And once I get a degree, I can become a teacher and be with the children in the holidays. She started to drift off to sleep, mulling over her plans. She'd enjoyed teaching. On the edge of sleep she heard a noise. She listened. There it was again, as if someone was cautiously opening the front door. And then a shuffle of footsteps. Somebody was definitely downstairs. The room was very dark, shadows menacing. She listened carefully. Silence. Then a creak. Someone was climbing the stairs. She slid out of the bed as quietly as she could and slipped her dressing-gown on, all the while desperately thinking of what she could use as a weapon. She remembered the bookends, carved wooden elephants on a soapstone base. Perfect: heavy enough, but not too heavy for her to hold.

She gripped an elephant tightly and crept towards the door. She always kept the door open in case the children called out for her. The footsteps were coming closer. Her heart was thumping, blood was whooshing in her ears. Taking a deep breath ready to yell, she raised the elephant and switched the landing light on.

Neil stood in front of her, breathing heavily. 'I'm back,' he said.

Twelve

'BLIMEY,' NEIL SAID on entering the kitchen the next morning. 'A bit strong.'

'D'you like it?'

He looked round, his face as gloomy as the room was bright. 'It's only paint, I suppose. You could always go over it with something.'

'Have you seen the sitting room yet?'

'Oh no, what have you done there?'

'It's blue. Come and see.' Isabel held out her hand to him but he didn't take it, although he stood up and followed her. 'Well?'

'Yup. It's blue.'

'Don't you like it?'

'No, not very much.'

Isabel watched him as he rocked back on his heels, hands on hips like a farmer surveying the damage to his crops after a rainstorm. The night before, she had lain awake for hours in bed, listening to Neil's snoring. He'd come back, but seemed distinctly uncommunicative. Isabel glanced at the clock. If they didn't get on they'd miss their slot at the wildlife park.

'Neil? I'd made a few plans for the day.'

'I've got things to sort out here.' He sounded distinctly huffy.

'No, you misunderstand me. I meant, do you want to come too? We're only going to the wildlife park to see Father Christmas, and then I thought we'd go shopping in Fordingbury.'

'You've got it all organised, you carry on.'

The wildlife park was bleak, the wind whipping in off the Downs. She'd been right. Michael was too old, and so was Katie. She sat on Father Christmas's knee, eyeing his white beard warily.

'So what do you want for Christmas, Katie?'

'For my Daddy to stay at home and not go away any more,' she said in a clear voice. Isabel felt the words like a stabbing pain in her heart.

Father Christmas looked uncomfortable. 'Well, that's a hard thing to fit down a chimney. Is there anything else you'd like?'

'A puppy,' Katie said firmly. Isabel shook her head and Father Christmas moved on to Michael.

Michael looked terminally embarrassed, although he was quick to supply a list of what he wanted for Christmas: a twenty-foot pole rod, a keep net and a priest, which made Father Christmas blink in surprise.

'You use it for knocking fish out. Like a cosh,' Michael said, demonstrating with gusto. Father Christmas gave them each a present—a tea set for Katie and a jigsaw of a steam engine for Michael—and beckoned the next family on with relief.

'Why didn't Dad come?' Michael asked, but Isabel hadn't got an answer for him.

The children made a huge fuss of Neil when they got home, insisting that he read stories and put them to bed. Isabel worked quietly in the kitchen preparing supper, opening a bottle of Rioja to let it breathe. They sat opposite each other, Isabel trying to get a conversation going while Neil gave monosyllabic answers. She wasn't sure what he wanted. Perhaps he was expecting her to beg his forgiveness, or perhaps they would fall back into being together without ever discussing what had happened. But it couldn't be swept under a bland carpet of politeness.

Finally she couldn't bear it any more. 'Neil, what's going on? Are you back, or what? I don't know if I'm about to be divorced or reconciled.'

'Do you want a divorce?'

'Do you?'

'I don't know what to say. Or what you want me to say,' Neil said. 'I want to be here, for the children. I want to keep the family together. But you—' He stopped and poured himself some more wine. 'Every time I look at you I see those photographs.' His hands shook when he raised the glass to his mouth. 'Sometimes I wish you were dead.'

She hung her head, as if baring her neck for the executioner's axe. 'I know I deserve every horrid thing you can say about me. I had finished with him. It was over.'

'I don't know, Isabel. I don't know if I could ever trust you again.'

'But you have to. If we're going to live together again.'

'How do I know it won't happen again?'

'You don't know. You can't. People don't come with guarantees. All I can say is that I won't risk the children's future again.'

'So for the children's sake, I'm to forgive and forget?'

'If you can.'

'I don't know if that's possible.' Neil drained his glass. 'I don't want to divorce,' he said abruptly. 'We don't do divorce in my family.'

'So your mother told me,' Isabel said. She wondered if this was going to be the deciding factor in her marriage continuing. Not because Neil forgave her, or loved her, but because the Freemans didn't 'do' divorce. It seemed a mean little reason, as if all ills could be solved by never referring to them; letting them dwindle into a miserable compromise.

Neil went upstairs to bed. Isabel tidied up in the kitchen, uncertain of what she was to do. In the end she, too, went upstairs. She undressed in the dark and slid into the cold bed. She curled up facing away from Neil and closed her eyes for sleep.

She was dreaming about being buried under flowers, rosemary tangling with nerines and winter jasmine. The weight on top of her was pressing down like stones, crushing the breath out of her. She woke, confused, but the weight was still there. Neil was on top of her, pushing into her. Still half asleep, she cried out.

'Shut up,' Neil muttered.

She was going to protest, push him off, then she remembered Katie wishing for her Daddy to stay for ever, and she let her hands fall back and clamped her lips together.

She knew why he was doing this: he was reclaiming her as his own after Patrick. Pushed up the bed, her head thumped against the headboard, she put her hand up to try to cushion the blows. Push, push, push. Her lower body burned with a dry, searing ache. But she made no effort to hurry him up, just lay passively accepting the pain, hoping it would be over soon. And it was. A sudden crescendo, then Neil rolled off and she was left to try to go back to sleep.

The weekend ground on. The children frisked around a monosyllabic Neil who settled down amid the Sunday papers and the Grand Prix on the television as if he had never been away. Isabel piled Katie's things into the centre of her room and slowly painted it lilac. It'll match the shadows under my eyes, she thought.

Monday morning was grey. Neil left for work, leaving behind the post, Isabel noticed. Most of it was for her. Two more prospectuses, Christmas cards from Saudi and Malaysia and a white envelope. She opened it: an invitation, Mrs Richard Wright. At Home. Isabel had to think for a second who it was from. It was ironic that someone so full of personality as Mary could be subsumed by her husband's name. She flipped it over. On the back Mary had written in neat, round writing: 'People have short memories. Do come, with or without.' Your husband, Isabel supposed. It was kind of Mary to invite her.

By coincidence, she bumped into Mary at the school. She reiterated the invitation verbally, then: 'My dear, Patrick is devastated. He says—'

'Neil came back this weekend,' Isabel cut in quickly.

Mary paused, then said, 'I see.'

'It's going to be difficult,' Isabel said carefully, 'but I think we're going to make a go of it.'

'Ah.' For a second Mary looked disappointed, then gave a little shake as if putting the mantle of PTA Chairman back on. 'Good for you. A very sensible decision.' She patted Isabel's arm.

I don't feel as if I've made any decisions, Isabel wanted to wail, sensible or otherwise. It's all happening to me and I don't get any choices.

'You know you can call me and talk about it,' Mary said very gently. 'I would understand.' Isabel looked sharply at her. Did Mary mean that she'd had an affair? 'All marriages have their rocky patches,' she said. 'It comes with the territory. So ring me if you want to. And come to my party. It'll do you good.'

'I don't think—'

'Patrick won't be there. He's gone to Italy.'

She didn't want to ask, but had to. 'Alone?'

Mary shot her a look. 'Victoria's gone to London,' she said. 'I think she realised that Patrick was emotionally involved elsewhere. As much as Patrick can be emotionally involved.'

'I'm sorry,' Isabel said, but she wasn't sure if she was sorry for Victoria or Patrick. Or herself.

'Never mind, it wasn't your fault. Now, I must go. Look after yourself.' And she bustled off.

Isabel went to work. Like most Monday mornings the shop was

quiet. She trudged back and forth between the stockroom and the shop floor, restocking the shelves, thinking about Patrick, about Neil, about choices and sensible decisions, sick with unhappiness. But I've got what I wanted, she thought. A stable home for my children, complete with father. I've even got a job. It'll just take time to settle back to normal.

Business picked up in the shop over the afternoon. In between customers Adam asked if she had filled in the college application forms.

'Not yet. Neil's back,' she said. Adam didn't answer immediately.

'You must be pleased,' he said finally, sounding formal and distant.

'Yes, I am. Of course.' She felt close to tears.

'I'm pleased for you.'

'Thanks.'

'Isabel? What's all this stuff doing, cluttering up the place?' Neil was scratchy with irritation. He was picking up the stack of prospectuses.

'They're mine,' Isabel said. 'I was thinking of going to college.'

'What for?'

'For me. Because I want to do something with my life.'

'So who will look after the children while you're off being a student?'

'There are three universities within an hour's drive of here, plus the FE college at Fordingbury. It won't make any difference to the children. They're at school all day and I'll have the same holidays as them.'

'What about money? You don't get grants any more, you know.'

'I know. I'm going to sell my parents' house.'

'But we use the rental money for the school fees.'

'I know, but it's worth a lot of money. There's enough to fund me going to university as well as paying the children's school fees.'

'We agreed it would go on education.' Neil's face was mulish.

No, Isabel thought of saying. You decided and I agreed. But instead she said lightly, 'Why not my education?'

'So, what will you do with your education?'

'Teach.' She searched his face, trying to gauge his response.

He leaned back in his chair.

'I suppose there's no harm in trying.'

She waited to see if he was going to say anything more.

'What's for supper?' he said.

It was fortunate that Neil had stopped searching through the mail before he left for work, because a few days later Isabel received a plump letter with a Rome postmark. She tucked it into her bag without opening it, knowing who it was from, wondering what he had to say. The shop was busy so she had to wait until her morning break. She escaped into the stockroom and closed the door. She took the letter from her bag and opened it.

Inside was another envelope, containing three film negative strips, a postcard of the Colosseum with an address on the other side, and a small package wrapped in kitchen paper. She sat with it in her hand, thinking of the beginning, the first kiss. She had felt so excited, expectant, electric with life and its possibilities. And now?

The door opened and Adam came in. 'Everything OK?'

In answer Isabel held out her hand. Patrick's signet ring glistened in her palm. 'I don't seem able to break free,' she said. It should have felt strange saying something so personal to her employer, but it felt natural to confide in him. Adam leaned against the door, his face serious.

'Do you want to?'

'Yes. And no.' She fingered the ring. 'If I let go, I feel as if I'm closing the door on everything that's alive.'

'Do you love him?'

She shook her head.

'And Neil?'

'I don't know. I've been with him for ever, my whole adult life. Everything that I am, that I have, is bound up with him. I can't imagine life without him. Is that love? It's not violins and rockets, we just trundle along in our little world, every year settling deeper into the ruts.'

'It doesn't sound like love to me.' His face was sad, and she wondered about his past. The shop doorbell rang and he moved to go. 'I must go back. Come up when you can.' At the door he turned back to her. 'Don't forget that there are always alternatives.' He looked as if he was going to say something else, but the bell rang again. He smiled at her and shrugged. 'I have to go.'

She thought about what Adam had said. Perhaps her choice was not between Patrick and Neil, but between staying in a rut and moving on. Moving on didn't have to mean moving to Patrick, or leaving Neil. She could move on through developing herself. In that way she could maintain the stable home for her children that she so wanted for them. Talking about becoming a student hadn't seemed real before, but now she realised that it was more important than that.

When she got home she waited until Neil had gone up to bed. The blue of the sitting-room walls was nearly as blue as the sky behind the Colosseum. She wrote the address on an envelope, then tore the postcard into pieces and put them on the fire, along with the strips of negative. Finally she put the ring into the envelope and sealed it. It was over.

Neil rang Mary's doorbell. As it sounded, Isabel felt panic rise inside her. She wanted to run, be anywhere else. Neil must have sensed her panic because he put one arm round her waist so that when the door opened they were coupled together.

'Isabel, my dear, so pleased you could come.' Mary sailed majestically towards them. 'And Neil too, how nice. Now come and meet some people.' She briskly introduced them to a small group. 'Neil and Isabel Freeman, back in this country after years of expat life.'

With Mary's introduction the conversation ran the usual path: which countries, what did you do out there, how long for? Neil did most of the talking; Isabel concentrated on the conversation, nodding and smiling. Canapés, champagne. She began to relax. None of the people seemed to know of her, or if they did, they hid it under an impenetrable layer of sociability. Mary had written that people had short memories, but to forget something as shocking as the photographs would imply the attention span of a flea. Isabel wondered what the reactions would have been like if Neil hadn't been there. After all, if Neil forgave her, then no one else had anything to say about it. This is easy, she thought, relaxed on her third glass of champagne. Even if they know, no one is going to refer to Patrick. She turned and bumped into a man standing behind her.

'Oops, sorry,' she said. The man turned and stared at her.

'Well, well, if it isn't Isabel,' George said. He put his hands on her shoulders and kissed her, his palms moist with sweat, his breath hot on her cheek. One hand brushed—accidentally?—against her breast. He was standing too close, looming over her, but she couldn't move away.

'I hardly recognised you with your clothes on,' he drawled, his eyes lingering on her body.

'Excuse me.' Isabel tried to push away from him, but George moved to stop her.

'Why so unfriendly?' he said, placing a fat hand on her bottom. 'We all know you're not exactly exclusive.'

He didn't bother to keep his voice down, and Isabel sensed a few heads turning. She caught the glint in his eye. He's enjoying this, she thought. But I don't have to be bullied by George.

'I think you need to cool off, George,' she murmured, and very deliberately poured her glass of champagne over the front of his trousers. Ignoring his splutters she tried again to escape through the crowd, and succeeded in reaching the door where Neil was talking to Mary.

Neil raised his eyebrows. 'You look flushed.'

Isabel nodded. 'It's awfully hot in there.' She heard a noise behind her and turned. 'Oh dear, it looks like George has had a little accident.' Her voice carried further than she meant to, so several heads also turned to see George pushing his way towards them, his trousers dripping wet, scarlet in the face, his eyes bulging. He opened his mouth to speak, but was prevented by Mary cutting in.

'Now, come with me and we'll sort you out, there's a good chap,' she said, sweeping him away from Isabel and Neil.

Richard joined them. 'What was all that about?'

'George has got a little problem,' Isabel whispered. 'You know. But don't tell anyone,' she added, thinking that the golf-club gossip machine might as well work to her benefit as her detriment.

'Really? Goodness. Poor fellow,' Richard said. 'I must circulate, but I'm so pleased you were able to come. Both of you.' He smiled at Isabel, and she blushed at his kindness and, thinking back to George's face as he realised that she was actually going to pour champagne over him, smiled back. Not the world's wittiest riposte, but it'd do.

'What's so funny?' Neil asked. 'You really shouldn't laugh at poor old George.'

'Poor old George, my foot.' Isabel glanced at Neil. Perhaps all this had started when Neil had told the story of the dissolving party dress to George. She remembered the way he'd leered at her then.

'I'm going to go to the loo,' she said. In the hall one of the waitresses directed her upstairs to what was obviously Mary and Richard's room. When she came out of the bathroom a woman was standing examining the objects on top of a chest of drawers.

'Justine.'

As she turned round and saw Isabel, she looked so guilty, so dismayed, that for a second Isabel wondered if she'd caught Justine helping herself to something of Mary's. But Justine's smooth, confident expression reasserted itself.

'I haven't seen you for ages,' Isabel said. It occurred to her that both of the women she had initially made friends with had been absent while she'd dealt with the fallout from her affair. Only Mary had been supportive. Perhaps it was that thought that made her comment, 'Neil's back, you know.'

Justine sat on the bed. 'I know.' Her face was hard. 'So Neil has forgiven you. Lucky you. Why didn't you go with Patrick?'

'How could I?' Isabel said.

'He seemed smitten.'

Isabel tried to keep her voice light. 'I expect it was the novelty factor of being refused.'

'Maybe.' Justine stood up. 'I'm sure Neil's told you his version of events, but I want to make it clear I didn't mean you any harm. We'll be meeting up at school, at social events like this, so it's best to be civilised. Or at least, civil.' She examined her nails. 'Mary's obviously decided to support you, and who am I to go against Mary? Especially as I don't have a loving husband to support me. And there was I thinking you were bored to tears with each other.'

'We're not,' Isabel said automatically, completely adrift.

'Obviously. Or boredom's better than risk. That's what Neil chose, but somehow I didn't expect you to. Still. Don't let's go there.'

Isabel started in recognition. She could remember Neil using the expression, and thinking how strange it was. The world seemed to have changed angle, like a distorting mirror at a fairground. She could hear what Justine was implying, she just couldn't understand it. Then she thought of Patrick in the shop insisting that he hadn't sent the photographs. She had assumed he was lying because there wasn't anyone else with knowledge, opportunity and motive. Or so she had thought. Her body felt as wobbly as if she'd just got off a rollercoaster.

'How did you get them? From Patrick?'

'Patrick? No, why would he give them to me? It was your set.'

There was a bitter taste in Isabel's mouth. 'When?'

'When I did your wardrobe. I was curious, so I retrieved them from your bin. Then I thought they might be useful.'

'Why did you do it?'

'Well, obviously because—' Justine stopped, her eyes narrowing. 'I should have guessed . . . He hasn't said anything, has he?'

'Who? Patrick?'

'No. Not Patrick.' Justine looked almost amused.

Isabel tried to think who else Justine could be referring to. It couldn't be . . . Isabel caught her arm. She wanted to shake some answers out of Justine. 'Who are you talking about?'

Justine looked down at Isabel's hand on her arm, and Isabel dropped her hand. 'Thank you,' Justine said.

'Please, Justine,' Isabel said. 'Please.'

Justine looked at her with cold eyes, then smiled her pussycat smile. 'Why don't you ask Neil?' she said. 'Try asking your husband.'

Isabel waited until Neil had parked the car outside the house. 'I spoke to Justine this evening,' she said, breaking the silence.

Neil shifted in his seat. 'Do we have to talk about this now? It's late.'

'I think it's important. Justine said she sent you the photographs. When I asked why, she said I should ask you.'

Neil leaned back in his seat, head on the headrest. His face in profile seemed relaxed. Unsurprised. The cold entered Isabel's marrow.

'You knew. You knew it was her. I don't understand what's going on.'

Neil turned to her, his face lit up by the street light. 'There's nothing going on,' he said, bland as a vat of magnolia paint. 'But there was.'

'I was flattered by the attention,' Neil said, leaning against the sink. 'What more can I say? I don't want to go into detail, any more than I expect you want to hear it.'

Isabel, elbows on the kitchen table, put her face in her hands and rested it there. Her head felt it might explode with information and questions and anguish and the blood thumping at her temples. Neil and Justine. Neil and Justine.

'When did it start?'

'Not long after you went to work for that man.'

'So at that dinner party . . .' She could remember thinking that Neil had been unfriendly to Justine, and being surprised. 'I feel I've been very stupid,' she murmured. 'So stupid.'

'You had other things on your mind.' She looked up at him. Neil rubbed the back of his neck. 'It's late. Let's call it quits. Both of us have had flings. Both of us have ended them.'

'But why?' Isabel said.

'I don't think you realise how difficult moving here's been for me. The move from being hands on, your own boss more or less, to working in an office, all the politics and manoeuvring. You weren't interested.'

'And she was?'

'Yes. Oh yes, Justine would be the perfect corporate wife, knowing who to suck up to, who mattered, playing the political game.'

Isabel felt guilty. She knew she'd taken little interest in Neil's work. But Justine had. Neil and Justine. 'How could you?' she cried out. 'I trusted you.'

'And I trusted you. I trusted you even though Justine had warned me about that man.' He shrugged. 'I'm not going to feel guilty about this. These things happen.'

'So we just forgive each other and say everything's OK.'

'What else is there?'

'You've made me feel like dirt these last weeks, made me crawl, when all the time you were . . . It's so hypocritical.'

'And what about you? Did you think of the children? At least I left no evidence.'

'So it's OK so long as you don't get caught?'

'No. But my God, it makes it less painful.' He wiped his hand across his face. 'Water under the bridge now. That's how it's got to be.'

She didn't, couldn't, answer him although she seethed inside with a jumbled mass of emotions. She felt like screaming and howling out her fury, but they were obviously going to be civilised and grown-up.

Neil yawned. 'I'm going to bed.' He touched her hair. 'I'm sorry,' he said awkwardly. 'Perhaps I should have told you before. But I thought you were better off for not knowing.'

'It's funny,' she said to Adam on her last day at the shop. 'People are always trying to protect me from the truth, which makes it twice as painful when I find out.'

'Honesty is the best policy, or so they say,' Adam said, raising an eyebrow at her. 'What's brought this on?'

'Oh, Neil's been telling me some things.' And we're pretending they haven't happened, she thought, her head aching.

Adam looked sideways at her, but he didn't ask any more. It was one of the things that she liked about the shop, working with Adam who never pried, never pushed her into saying things.

Instead he said, 'Have you decided if you're coming back? Maria's let me know she's giving up work for the moment. We're closed until New Year, then Angela's coming back. I'll need someone else.'

'What are you doing for Christmas, Adam?' she said suddenly. She had a vision of him sitting alone in the flat above the shop.

'Big family gathering. My mother likes to go the whole hog so it's very traditional, extended family, lots of friends, food, that sort of thing.'

'It sounds wonderful,' Isabel said. Certainly better than Moira and Ian, Heather and her husband, and competitive mince-pie making, which was what her Christmas was going to be. 'I never had that sort of Christmas, being an only child.'

She served a desperate-looking man with a stack of books, obviously his last-minute Christmas shopping. When she'd finished she said, 'I always wanted to give my children a traditional family Christmas, in their own home with lots of friends as well as family. I thought that maybe we'd do it this year, but things haven't worked out like that.'

'I don't have children, so perhaps I shouldn't say this,' Adam said slowly, 'but I think you have to be careful about giving children the things you wanted as a child, rather than what they actually want.'

He moved away to help a customer. Isabel thought about what he'd said. Surely all children wanted a stable home, with parents who loved them? The shop filled with customers rushing to buy books, and they were busy until half an hour before closing, when the crowds thinned, leaving only a few browsers.

'You still haven't answered my question,' Adam said. 'Are you coming back? And if so, when?'

'I'm sorry,' Isabel said. 'I should have told you before. Yes, I'd love to come back in the new year, once term starts again.'

'Great,' Adam said. He looked delighted.

'I didn't realise it meant so much to you,' she said, embarrassed.

'I usually take several weeks off in February to go abroad. I couldn't if it was just Angela on her own.'

Which left Isabel feeling curiously deflated.

Adam finally ushered out the last customers. Isabel put on her coat and scarf and gathered up her bag. 'Here.' He handed her a brown envelope. 'Wages. Happy Christmas,' he said.

'And to you.' She fiddled with the strap of her bag. 'And thank you. I'm glad it's not going to be goodbye.'

'Me too.' He frowned. 'You won't forget about applying to university, will you? It would be a shame to miss the deadline.'

'It's waited nearly twenty years; it'll wait another year.'

'That's what I used to say on the trading floor,' he said. 'I'll get out next year. I stayed too long and it broke me.' He touched a strand of her hair. 'Don't let it happen to you.'

As far as Isabel could see, Michael and Katie had a good Christmas at their grandparents, although Isabel thought none of the adults enjoyed themselves. Isabel found Heather prickly at the best of times; Moira grumbled about Ian's health; Ian grumbled about indigestion; Heather's husband spent a lot of time staring out of the window; Neil shut down completely, emerging from the latest paperback only at mealtimes or to watch an action adventure film on the television.

Isabel spent much of her time wrapped in layers of coats while she supervised Michael and Katie playing with Buster in the garden. In a rash moment she found herself promising to consider getting a puppy.

'A puppy would be fun for the children,' she said to Neil.

'And what happens to it if we go abroad?'

'But we're not going abroad again, are we?' she said.

Neil stroked his moustache. 'It might be for the best,' he said. 'A new start for us, where no one knows our history.' Isabel blushed. 'And I'd rather be back in the field. This commuting . . .' He shook his head.

'But we've settled back in the UK. We can't move again.' Isabel was surprised at how horrified she felt.

Neil shrugged. 'I don't think the children mind that much about moving from house to house, to be honest.'

'What about my job? And going to college?'

'A poxy little job in a bookshop?' Neil laughed. 'I hardly think that matters. And as for going to college, if you really want to, you can always get a degree through the Open University.'

Isabel clenched her fists in an effort to control her temper at his patronising attitude. 'Have you applied for a posting?'

'I've put out feelers,' was all he would say.

Isabel sat on the soggy bench in the garden, sightlessly watching the children play with Buster. Whatever Neil said or did, she couldn't, wouldn't, give up her dreams so easily a second time.

When they got back home from Scotland, before she did anything else, even before putting a load of clothes in the washing machine, she dug out the university application forms and filled them in.

She didn't tell Neil she'd sent the forms off.

On New Year's Eve Neil opened a bottle of champagne and Isabel cooked a special meal, but their hearts weren't in it and the bottle was left half-full. They went to bed well before midnight. Sex ensued, a furtive coupling in the dark, mercifully quick. Start the new year with a bang, thought Isabel, lying awake on her side of the bed.

The only bright spot was starting work again. Angela was back, a woman in her mid-fifties, Isabel guessed, with neatly permed hair and doleful eyes.

Adam went a few weeks later: first to Prague, then to stay with friends in Switzerland. He said he'd be gone for at least four weeks. It was strange being in the bookshop without him. Angela loved talking about Adam and was full of information about his past. It was curiously irresistible to learn that he'd been married briefly to someone in the City and had had a few relationships in Milbridge, although he'd steadfastly resisted the advances of Angela's niece, the one with forty-six piercings, including three 'down there' as Angela referred to it.

Isabel was turned down outright by two of the universities she'd applied to, but the third, the former FE college in Fordingbury, asked her to come for an interview, bringing essay samples.

'Essays!' Isabel wailed. 'I haven't done an essay for years.'

'If only Adam was here,' Angela said. 'He'd know what to do.'

'Well, he's not,' Isabel said, more sharply then she'd intended. How on earth was she going to find some essay samples? She could hardly resurrect her old A level schoolbooks. She couldn't run to Adam for help and she wouldn't ask Neil. She thought for a few minutes, then laughed. 'I'm so stupid,' she said. 'Here I am standing in the middle of a bookshop. There must be at least one book on essay guidelines.'

That evening, after the children had been settled down, supper had been cooked and eaten, and the dishwasher stacked, she started to have a go at writing an essay on Carol Ann Duffy at the kitchen table. It was ages since she had tried to do anything like that, and she wasn't convinced she had been any good at it when she was doing her A levels. But this time, she seemed to understand better.

Neil came in and sat down at the other side of the table.

'What are you doing?'

'Writing an essay,' she said. 'I've got an interview.'

'What for?'

'I told you. A place at college.'

'I didn't think you were serious.'

She took a deep breath. 'Well, I am.'

'That's a pity. I've been offered a posting to Ghana.'

'Ghana?' Isabel said. 'We're not going to Ghana.'

'Why not?' Neil said. 'It's stable, reasonably safe, and there's a good-sized expat community.'

'Because we've just moved here. What about schools?'

'There's an international school in Accra.' He scratched his ear.

'You know as well as I do that most of the boys will be sent to boarding school back home. There'd probably be only one or two boys in Michael's year and I don't want that for him.'

'No reason why he shouldn't board.'

'Board? Are you joking?' Isabel shook her head, horrified at the idea. 'And what about my course? I might be starting a degree in September.'

'You can postpone it.' He spoke as if it was of no importance and the accumulated anger of the past few months swept over her.

'No,' she said. 'No. I'm not postponing it. I've postponed enough. I'm not your property, trailing after you round the world. And nor are the children. It's unfair to expect them suddenly to up sticks when for the first time they've got their own rooms in their own house.'

'And you expect me to sacrifice myself simply for the children to have their own bedrooms? I hate commuting and I don't intend to carry on. I'm going to Ghana.'

Isabel looked at him. He was sticking his neck out in an aggressive manner and he resembled his father, laying down the rules, believing his loud voice would convince. She thought of Moira, freezing meals that no one wanted to eat, taking out frustration in petty vendettas. And she thought of the children, of Michael being sent away to board, of Katie being moved away from her friends yet again, brought up in a home of wintry politeness.

'Well? Are you coming with me or not?'

She was quite calm when she spoke. 'Not.'

Thirteen

ISABEL AND NEIL maintained a pretence of togetherness. They were civilly distant with each other, never touching, careful not to impinge on each other's space. The distance between them made Isabel realise how far they had grown apart. Or how far she had grown away from him.

They didn't discuss divorce. It was not unusual among expat couples for the wife and children to stay behind when the husband was posted to somewhere the wife considered unsuitable. But it was also known that marriages often didn't survive the separation.

The interview came closer. Isabel read as much as she could and got Angela to ask her test questions. When Isabel answered, Angela would be very impressed, but Isabel had no idea whether what she was doing or saying was right. One day, as they chatted, the shop door opened.

'Adam!'

He stood in the doorway, browner and leaner. 'I heard there was an emergency. An interview?'

'What?' Isabel turned to Angela who flapped her hands.

'I only sent a postcard saying you'd got an interview and had to write essays and everything for it, and how we didn't know what to do.'

'Oh, Angela,' Isabel said, torn between annoyance and being touched that Angela had cared enough to bother. 'You shouldn't have.'

Angela bustled off to make him a cup of tea while Adam took his things into the flat upstairs. When he came back down Isabel said, her face scarlet with embarrassment, 'I hope you haven't really come back because of a stupid interview.'

'I felt like coming back early.' Adam shook his head. 'To be honest, I was bored. I just wanted to be back here.' He looked at her sideways. 'Pathetic, or what?'

'Don't be silly. No one who knows you could ever think you're pathetic.' She traced a figure of eight on the counter with her fingertip. 'I'm glad you're here,' she said.

Angela spent the next few days clucking over Adam, bringing him cakes and doughnuts to fatten him up. Isabel kept her distance, feeling suddenly shy. She decided against letting him look at her essay attempts or coach her, although Adam had gently offered to help.

'You see, I want to know I can do it myself, without someone else helping me. Pulling the strings. It sounds stupid but—'

'It's not stupid. Don't worry, you'll be fine.' He paused. 'I expect your husband's been helping you.'

'No.'

'Oh?'

'Neil's going to Ghana in the next few weeks,' she said.

'And you?'

'I'm not going.'

'That sounds a major decision.'

'Oh, no,' Isabel said. 'There's been no decision. It's just happened, and neither of us cares enough to stop it. Do you know, I've felt so much sadness and unhappiness over the last few months that it's as if it's all been washed out of me. Now we are separating I feel, well, nothing. It's odd.'

Adam pushed up the sleeves of his sweater. Isabel could see that the cuffs of his shirt underneath were just starting to fray. 'Are you actually separating?' he said, not looking at her.

'Yes. We haven't said as much, but this is the end, and we both know it. Not that we've discussed divorce. Neil's family don't "do" divorce.'

'Doesn't that leave you in limbo?'

'I don't mind. It's a halfway house, still safe, but I'm able to look outside and see what's going on.'

'You mean, like a bird that carries on hopping round the bottom of the cage even though the door has been opened.'

'You make it sound dreadful.'

'It's like after a shipwreck. You can see the shore, but you're worried about striking out on your own so you're still clinging onto the wreckage. You know the wreckage isn't going to help you, in fact, you're doomed if you stay, but pushing off and leaving it is scary.' He sighed. 'I can only speak from my experience. When I was trading, I knew it was killing me, but I couldn't give up the lifestyle, the buzz, all that money. And each day I got more and more scared, and because I was scared I clung on all the tighter. And the shore got further and further away.'

'What happened?'

'I was pushed, in the end. No wonder, I was a wreck myself.'

'Did you sink?'

Adam looked away from her, his grey eyes unfocused as if seeing something other than the bookshelves. When he spoke his voice was low. 'Yes, for a little while. I did sink. And that was hard.' He turned to her and smiled. 'But you're stronger than I was then. You'll be fine. Look at what you've achieved. You've got a job, a home, plans.'

'I've also wrecked my marriage and become notorious in the process.'

Adam laughed. 'At least you've been doing things and not sitting at home weeping, waiting for something to happen.'

She could see that Adam was right, that she was clinging onto the wreckage, but it was hard to push away.

Her interview was late the next morning. Angela gave her a lucky rabbit's foot that had belonged to a great aunt before she'd been squashed by a collapsing wall on her way to bingo. Isabel's lips twitched as she met Adam's eyes.

'I can't guarantee this will be as lucky, but I hope you like it.' He held out a small tissue-wrapped package. Inside was a delicate silver bangle.

'It's beautiful.' She slipped it on her wrist. 'Thank you.'

The interview wasn't as terrifying as she'd thought it would be. One of the two interviewers, a young woman, seemed more nervous than Isabel was. The other was a man of about her own age who spoke very slowly. Isabel told them about what she'd read recently, her favourite authors, why she wanted to read English.

'I made the wrong choice when I was nineteen,' she said, twisting Adam's silver bangle round her wrist. 'This is what I want to do.'

Neil's taxi came late, so his departure was awkward. The children drifted off to watch Sunday-morning television leaving Isabel and Neil loitering in the hall, uncertain what to say. All those years when she'd believed him to be her best friend, Isabel thought, the one person she'd thought she could talk to about anything. And now there was nothing.

The taxi beeped outside. The children rushed in to hug and kiss their father goodbye. They stood in the doorway and watched him carry his bags to the taxi. Neil opened the taxi door and paused for a moment, his head lifted as if he could already scent the warm Ghanaian air, and for a second she recognised the young man she'd married, the man in the photograph that Justine had admired. Then he got in and closed the door.

On impulse, Isabel ran out to the taxi and banged on his window.

'Neil,' she said, not knowing what she was going to say until she said it, but when she'd said it the last piece of the jigsaw fell into place. He wound the window down. 'Neil, was Justine the first?'

Neil turned away from her, but not before she read the guilt in his eyes. 'Goodbye, Isabel.'

Isabel was unpacking books in the stockroom.

Why, why, why? Why hadn't she known?

Because I'm stupid, because I trusted him, because he had the opportunity. Because, because, because.

I'm not very good at adultery, she thought. And as clearly as if he was beside her she heard Patrick saying 'Practice makes perfect'. She could picture him saying it too, patting the bed beside him. But I don't want sex without love, all the time fighting against caring, she said to him in her head. I don't want to have or be a bit on the side where nothing mattered and no one got hurt and everyone behaved like adults.

Was that what Neil wanted? She ripped open a box of travel books, remembering all the nights when Neil had lain on top of her, squashing the life out of her, and she had let him because it was easier to say yes than have an argument. Why had she let him? Why hadn't she realised? She snatched up a roll of packing tape and hurled it across the stockroom, just missing Adam who was opening the door.

Luckily he had good reflexes and ducked in time. 'Are you all right?'

'No, I'm not all right,' she screamed at him. 'I'm fucking furious. You're all shits and bastards and I hate you.'

Adam touched her shoulder. 'Isabel?' he said tentatively. 'Don't cry.'

His voice was so warm, so comforting that without thinking Isabel turned to him and he held her while she sobbed into his chest.

'The worst thing is, I keep on thinking who else was there? Did it happen at every posting? I can't trust anybody ever again.'

'Shh.' Adam stroked her hair. 'Of course you can.'

'Sorry about that,' she said, gulping down the last lingering sobs. 'I'm a bit of a mess right now.'

'Would you like me to ask Angela to come down and be with you?'

'No.' She grimaced. 'I must be the world's worst employee. Always in tears, abusing the boss—'

'Throwing things at him.' Adam picked up the roll of packing tape.

'I didn't mean to throw it at you, you just came in at the wrong moment. And I can't believe what I called you, when you've been nothing but nice to me.'

'Yeah, well, good staff are hard to find.'

The envelope was laid out on the counter top, with Isabel, Angela and Adam looking at it.

'You silly girl. I don't know how you can bear to wait.' Angela reached out for the envelope. 'Would you like me to look first?'

'No,' Isabel snatched it away from her. 'Going to university was a stupid idea anyway,' she said. 'I'd be much better off doing something else.' There was only a flimsy bit of paper inside. She read it, hand over her mouth.

'Go on, Isabel. What does it say?' Isabel shook her head at Angela, unable to speak.

Adam took the slip of paper from her trembling fingers. 'It's an unconditional offer. It means they want her very much.' He hesitated, then stooped and kissed Isabel on the cheek. 'Congratulations.'

I'm going to go to university, Isabel thought. I don't believe it. She didn't stop smiling for the rest of the morning.

'I can't wait to tell the children,' she said. 'Even though I know they won't understand, I want to share it with them. What are you looking for?' Adam was rummaging through one of the drawers.

'Nothing.' He hesitated. 'I wondered if you wanted to go out for a drink. To celebrate.'

'Oh, Adam, that'd be lovely. But we couldn't all go at once, not unless you shut the shop.'

Adam fidgeted with his cuffs. No wonder they're frayed, Isabel thought. 'I meant after work.'

'But I have to pick up the children and Angela has to get back.'

Adam pulled at a long thread. 'I meant after after work,' he mumbled to the till. 'And I didn't mean with Angela.'

'Oh,' Isabel said, her heart thumping. 'You mean a drink drink.'

'Or dinner,' Adam said, engrossed in the till. 'If you'd like.'

Isabel thought about it. Dinner meant high heels and baby sitters and white linen napkins and bottles of wine in a wine cooler. Would she like dinner? She looked at Adam.

'Dinner would be lovely. Thank you. Oh—'

'What's the matter?'

'I'm not sure I should. You see, I promised myself that I'd never go out with my employer again.' She could feel herself going red.

'Mmm. I have to admit I did set a company rule when I started that I would never go out with an employee. To be honest, I haven't had any desire to break it. Until now.' He looked at her, and she felt herself flushing again. How strange this was, after all those years. But nice. She smiled as her heart started racing again. Oh yes, it was nice.

'Well. It was just an idea.' He turned to go and Isabel suddenly felt if she didn't seize the moment it would never come again.

'No, Adam, wait.' Isabel found a bit of paper and quickly scribbled on it. She handed it to Adam. 'My notice. I'm going off to be a student.'

'Not for a while, surely?'

'October.' She looked at him sideways. 'But I'm sort of not your employee now, am I?'

'I suppose not,' Adam said, a grin spreading across his face. 'So, Isabel Freeman, would you like to come out to dinner with me?'

'I'd love to,' she said, beaming. 'I'd love to.'

The shop doorbell rang and Angela came in from her lunch hour. 'Did anything exciting happen while I was out?'

Adam, busy tidying up the credit-card slips, looked sideways at Isabel. 'Maybe,' he said casually. 'What do you think, Isabel?'

Isabel pretended to be sorting through the order forms, although the words were dancing in front of her eyes and making no sense at all.

'Definitely,' she said, smiling to herself. 'A definite maybe.'

SARAH DUNCAN

'Are you a Patrick person or an Adam person?' Sarah Duncan asked me, referring to two of her characters in *Adultery for Beginners*. 'Adam,' I answered. 'How about you?' 'Oh, Patrick, most definitely,' she replied, laughing. 'I know Adam is the sort of person I *should* go for, but I'm fairly certain that of the two I would run off with Patrick. But then, I would never have married Neil in the first place!'

Having lived with her characters for more than a year while writing the novel, it's no wonder that Sarah feels so connected to them. Added to which, characterisation and role-playing was all part of her early training as an actress. 'When I left university, it dawned on me that acting was a job where you didn't have to get up early in the morning, and you got to wear fabulous clothes and prance around not doing much work. So, from the very beginning, my attitude was not the most positive. But I acted for three years and was successful, even playing one of Rodney's girlfriends in television's best sitcom, *Only Fools and Horses*.'

It was also around this time that the joy of acting began to pall for Sarah. 'Acting is one of those jobs that is like a ladder. You start out bright-eyed and bushy-tailed, moving up one step at a time, always in competition and always unsure if you look right for a particular part. You are never in control and I'm far too bossy to accept that. I wanted more control.'

Having decided to quit acting, Sarah began to write nonfiction books, one of which was about drama training in the UK, which she would subsequently update every two years. 'But I always assumed that I was going to be a fiction writer. I knew I was going to write a novel at some point in my life.' When she started writing *Adultery for Beginners*, Sarah knew from the outset that this was going to be a story about a woman who had an affair, ended the affair, and then was blackmailed by her lover. 'These were the three things that I had in my mind and everything else developed from that. I also had the idea of a friend who would betray you. You know how it is, you often tell something to a relative stranger, then think afterwards, "Oh my God. I shouldn't have done that." In my fiction writing, I want to explore the moral dilemmas that face women in everyday life.'

Sarah is married and lives in Bath with her husband and their two teenage children. Like Isabel, her heroine in the novel, she only enjoys cooking when she is entertaining friends. 'But I am very lucky,' she told me. 'My husband's family is Basque in origin and in the Basque country, they have cooking clubs for men only. Women are not allowed! It's traditional for the men to cook, so my father-in-law cooks and so does my husband. Leaving me free to do what I love most—writing.'

Jane Eastgate

601-026-1